TEN REALMS: BOOK 5

The Fifth Realm

MICHAEL CHATFIELD

Cover Art by Jan Becerikli Garrido
Jacket Design by Caitlin Greer
Interior Layout & Design by Caitlin Greer

Paperback ISBN: 978-1-989377-86-4

1 Alva's Military

"We owe you an apology," Erik started.

Glosil looked between him and Rugrat, not sure how to react.

"We upset the chain of command during the defense of Vuzgal. We gave you the position as the leader of the Alva military because we trusted your judgement. We micromanaged the fighting and we shouldn't have. We have only been trained to lead small sections and squads. It is why the rank system and the units are broken."

Rugrat cleared his throat. "So, we are going to take a step back. We want you to take complete control of the military. We will be there to assist and in times of war we may give you commands, but on the battlefield you will command us."

"We have our strengths and our weaknesses; our strength is the information that we brought over from Earth. Your strength is how you can work with the military, bring them together into a cohesive unit and see the whole picture. While we were worrying about the front lines, you were the one organizing trains to take resources to the rear and bringing up new ammunition. You took the ideas from Rugrat and modified them, creating a total defense. You turned objectives into reality and we'll need you to do that again." Erik looked at Glosil, who felt emotional.

He had refrained from saying anything, but it had felt as if he had turned more into their secretary than the leader of the military.

"So, grab a seat. First thing we need to do is work together to organize just what the military is going to look like. We're going to need to expand in order to cover both Alva and Vuzgal's defensive needs. And we need to do it before someone looks to attack us." Erik pulled out a piece of paper and put it on the table.

"Someone would be willing to piss off the large associations to take Vuzgal?" Glosil asked in a serious voice.

"It is possible, if the associations aren't attacked directly; they have agreed to help out in some ways, but they can probably find a loophole to cover their asses," Rugrat said.

"They are powerful people. We need to have backing in order to talk to them on the same level." Glosil nodded and took the piece of paper. "This is your plan for units?" Glosil reviewed it.

"Correct. Well, our basic idea," Erik said.

"Do you have any suggestions for leadership?"

"Review how people did in the fight for Vuzgal? Based off that and training scores, select those for higher ranking positions and create a pool of people who can be slotted into leadership later on," Rugrat asked.

"It's a good idea, but it doesn't make up for the lack of time as a leader," Glosil said, testing his boundaries a little.

"Maybe make a school that looks to train them in their new roles?" Erik asked.

"Who would run it, though?" Rugrat asked.

"Blaze?" Glosil interjected before continuing. "He led a unit of over three hundred people. He isn't part of the military anymore, but if he was able to pass on what he knew to others? He might have a better idea of how to train up leaders as well."

"Sounds like a good idea," Erik agreed.

Glosil felt relieved as he looked at the plans again. "We have engineer squads in these plans. Will they be recruited from the crafting school or through the military?"

"What do you think?" Erik asked.

Glosil held his chin, his brows pressed together for a few seconds before he started talking aloud as he worked through his own thoughts.

"If we were to get them from the school, then we would be able to get a lot of people who could make the necessary items. Though, if we need them in close combat, breaking down the walls and not supporting from the rear, we will need to train them up still. I don't think that it would be fair for us to help out people who haven't gone through any training—what if they fail out? If we send people from the military to earn an education, well, they get it for free and with their training, they can easily adapt what they've learned into lessons and effective tools to enhance our combat strength. Look at Alchemy and explosives. Han Wu didn't know anything about them but now he has gone and got an education in Alchemy and has taught others how to make explosives, ammunition and more, enhancing our current fighting ability."

Glosil was looking at just one aspect but he couldn't help but feel excited. He had a road map with their plan, but he needed to bring it to life and turn it into reality.

"What if they want to leave after all of their education and training?" Erik asked.

"That is their decision. The military is not for everyone. If we force them to stay, then it will not help the unit they're in—it will only harm it." Glosil looked to the two men, trying to discover their thoughts.

"Couldn't have said it better myself," Rugrat said. "Though we'll still support them. Even if they're not in the military, they're still our brothers and sisters."

"Another area we need to focus on, something that was highlighted in Vuzgal, is supply," Erik said.

Glosil and Rugrat nodded with grim expressions.

"We were having to limit how much we were firing as we kept on running out of mortars. As it is, we have kind of separated out military crafting from the rest of Alva but it is limited."

"I believe we will need to create a rear support team to supply Alva soldiers with gear, upgrades, and consumables," Glosil said.

"Veterans could assist, and we could hire civilians. If they're not in combat roles, we don't need to waste a soldier on it," Erik reminded them.

Glosil nodded. Having to use the special teams to move the carts of supplies back and forth irked him.

"I think we should also revise what the military's role is. We have the police to deal with civilian-related issues. Does the military watch the gates and the totem? Are they patrolling, or are they only fighting and training? If we can make clearer lines of what they should or should not be doing, it can allow them to focus on their tasks."

Erik and Rugrat both grinned as they looked at Glosil.

"Did I say something wrong?"

"Nope, instead you said everything right. Okay, so what will the overall structure of the military be?" Erik asked.

"I've been thinking on that a bit," Rugrat said, the other two waited for him to continue. "The forces stationed in Vuzgal, should be called the Vuzgal Defense Force, the VDF for short. Broken into the training legions and the operational units. Any of the forces that are in Alva will be the Alvan Defense Force, or ADF, again broken into training and those operational. This serves two purposes; it makes the different areas have their own assigned forces and command structure. If we are cut off from one another we will be able to operate on our own. The VDF will focus on Defense, their operational units scouting the area around Vuzgal, supporting the police and keeping Vuzgal safe. The Alvan Defense force is to defend Alva, yes, but they are also the active branch of the military. Say that there is an external threat then the Alva force will be able to deploy immediately to actively engage the threat. A quick reacting force that is ready to be activated at any given time. This gives us a greater flexibility, we will no longer have to defend passively, we can defend and strike at the same time," Rugrat said.

"Not just sitting back anymore, but able to reach out with our own strength, I like it," Glosil said.

"Better than anything I thought of," Erik admitted.

Yui and Domonos were waiting in the briefing room with Niemm and Roska when Glosil entered the room. They snapped up to attention as Roska pulled off a salute at the highest ranked and most senior officer in the room.

Glosil returned the salute. "As you were." He stepped to the front and looked at the other officers; they were the core leadership of the entire Alva military.

"Okay, so today we are deciding the future of the Alva military." He pulled out a piece of chalk and moved to the board.

"There will be front line forces, defensive forces, and rear supporting forces. The front line and defensive forces will be trained military, while the rear supporting forces will be mostly crafters with military oversight. The rear supporting forces will be there to supply us with weapons, food, ammunition, all of the supplies that we need to fight and the gear that is issued to us. It will also be their role to create innovative upgrades to all of our gear. There will be departments for: clothing, armor, weapons, ammunition—including explosives—food, medical supplies, mounted support, and miscellaneous. Miscellaneous is anything that isn't involved in those other departments—cover our asses." Glosil raised his eyebrows as he saw the others grin.

He smiled to himself and moved to the board and raised the chalk.

"Our forces will be reorganized in the following manner! A fire team will be created from four privates and one corporal, for a total of five people. A rifle squad will have three fire teams led by a sergeant. Three rifle squads and one scout squad, a squad that has undergone the sharpshooter and scout course, will form a rifle platoon, commanded by a second lieutenant, who will have a platoon sergeant as his second-in-command and a supporting staff sergeant. A rifle platoon will have a total of sixty-seven people."

Glosil circled the different units and the growing diagram on the board. "Following?"

There was a general nodding of heads as Glosil wrote down two names, and tapped on them once he was done. "Then there is the artillery platoon and the support platoon.

"The artillery platoons will have two mortar squads—same strength as a rifle squad again—two mage squads and one close protection or supply squad. They will be led by two staff sergeants and a second lieutenant, for a total of eighty-two members.

"Support platoons will have two medic squads, two engineer squads, and one close protection squad, with again a second lieutenant and two staff sergeants leading, again with eighty-two members.

"A combat company will be led by a captain, with a first lieutenant and a senior staff sergeant acting as his second-in-command. There will be three rifle platoons, one artillery, and one support platoon to a company.

"That is three hundred and sixty-eight people."

Glosil turned to the officers and tapped on the board with his chalk. "This will be the basis of the Alva military. One will serve in the rifle platoon, then be trained to become scouts, then moved into the artillery platoon to study as a mortar gunner or a destructive mage. Once they have served their time there, on to the support, where they will become corporals and have to complete training to become full-fledged medics, then engineers. Once they have completed their time there, they will be trained with the close protection details to utilize all of their skills. Once they complete a year, then they will hold the rank of sergeant or they will train to become officers through the officer school. Then, a year afterward, they can choose to apply to the special teams."

"Damn," Yui said. The word filled the silence.

"They're going to be some highly trained soldiers," Roska said. "What are we going to do to start? How do we fill the ranks up?"

"Well, we're going to start by forming the support elements, then we build up our first rifle platoon according to this plan. For the other positions, well, that's what we're here for." Glosil put the chalk down and looked at them. "Ideas?"

"So, we need to figure out a training routine to take people from being soldiers all the way to members of the special teams?" Domonos asked.

"I thought I was the slow one," Yui chided.

Domonos rolled his eyes at his brother, easing the tension in the air.

"Well, the training routine that Rugrat put forward for the scouts is easy to implement, an eight-week intensive course. We can pull the best performers to create a training staff," Niemm said.

"We'll need to rotate them every so often. How does training fit into this?" Yui asked.

"Asked as if you know you're going to be teaching the support course," Glosil said with a smile.

Yui shrugged.

"There are three overall branches. The fighting forces will be the ones operating in the field, or they will be doing light training. Brush up on their skills. To begin, there will be a platoon always active. Later there might be a company, or even more than one. Anyway, the forces will be only active as front line forces for three months of the year. They will spend three months as defensive forces, and another six on training. Active defensive is patrolling, checking the walls, and reacting to us getting attacked. Training is working in Vuzgal, in the field, and in Alva to increase their qualifications and progress."

"So we'll need a minimum of four platoons to make that happen. What about the people of Vuzgal? Are we just going to make them people of Alva as soon as they join?" Roska asked.

"They will need to complete initial training before they become a scout. When they become a scout, they will have to make an oath binding them to Alva. The scout training will be held outside of Alva."

"So for training, I guess I'll have to pull out the best people from my platoon to train others. What about mages? And what do engineers do?"

"The mages..." Glosil held an open hand at Roska, who groaned and sat back in her chair, making him smile.

"We just doing normal mages, or mages using formations?" she asked.

"Both, preferably. Might be best to have two different courses?" Glosil raised his voice and looked at them all. "I'm just giving an overview. For the courses, and training, we're going to have to work on it as we go along."

"I'll need to talk to some of the mages and formation masters from the academy and Egbert's Librarians." Roska said.

"Done, all the resources of Alva are at our disposal," Glosil said.

"What about medics?" Yui asked. The Medics position in the army was undeniable, they could save people's lives and get them fighting again. Glosil planned to grow their numbers rapidly.

"Medics will be an interesting course. People will go to Vermire or Vuzgal for the practical portion, with the theoretical part being taught in either Alva or Vuzgal's academies. In combat, the healers will be dispersed in small groups to work under the officers and help out the wounded. Same with the engineers. They are there to make a path for us, or defenses. When the army is at rest, they'll repair equipment. They will be attending the academies to learn about formations, weapons, armor, magics, and spells to remove obstacles or create them. They will be our resident crafters on the move. The CPDs, or close protection details, will be trained by the special teams. Niemm, you'll be heading this up. Advanced training in fighting techniques, magical or physical, and supplemental training in all other areas. They need to be ready to take on any role at any moment. Think of them as a reserve force for the special teams."

Glosil saw Niemm nod as he turned his attention to the others.

"Sounds like we will have our work cut out for us," Domonos said.

"We're going to need to pull in more people through Vuzgal if we want to reach company strength anytime soon. Though, if it takes a year for us to clear them for more advanced training, it's going to be tougher," Roska said.

"We could hire more people through Vermire. Look for just people willing to fight and with a family. I don't want to sound like an ass, but things are really good in Alva, and if they know they're fighting for their families, it will be better," Domonos said.

"Where do the skeletons fit in all of this?" Niemm asked.

"The skeletons will form special platoons, bolster the defensive company's strength," Glosil said.

"Are we doing anything to assist new recruits with cultivation?" Yui asked.

"Yes and no. We will get them up to a certain level in basic training to be a soldier. To increase their power past that point, that will be on them.

We will increase their cultivation further for everyone who reaches CPD level, but we will take the cost from their wages," Glosil said.

"Do we have a timeline?" Niemm asked.

"I want to have a company set up sooner rather than later. Though I can accept that we will have rifle companies instead of combat companies for the first year. The sooner we start, the better. In a few months, I want to be able to pull our Alva forces away from training and focus on clearing the lower floors of Alva Dungeon. That will give our people more room to use and should make Body Cultivation easier. The sooner we clear it out, the sooner we can start getting benefits from it."

Glosil looked up as Yui and Domonos filed into the room, followed by Roska.

"Niemm is making sure that Erik and Rugrat don't get into trouble." Roska smiled.

Glosil snorted lightly and waved for them to grab a seat. All of them looked tired. "How are things going?"

"Training up the regular troops isn't that bad. We have about a fifty percent fallout rate. There are a lot of people who think because they have high levels that they're going to be given the position. A lot of the nobles and the richer merchant family members who are using this to get position within Vuzgal have left. For the recruits from Alva, there is only ten percent that are falling out," Domonos said.

"How is the training, itself, going?"

"We're halfway through the three-month basic course and they're starting to shape up. The people from the other realms haven't fought much, so they're pretty green. People from the Fourth Realm have an advantage. Those who stay in are more attentive and absorb everything that might increase their chances of surviving and killing the enemy."

"From your messages, you think that we will be able to have a rifle company in another six weeks?"

"I think so." Domonos sighed. "We're training a lot of people at the same time. I think—I think that we should look again at pulling in the people of Vermire to our military."

"Oh?" Glosil held his chin.

Yui seemed to know what Domonos was going to say and Roska raised an eyebrow.

"We've got a lot of new people. We have just over one hundred people in the military right now. A combat company will hold three, nearly four hundred. We will have a *third* of the spots—okay, so that is ninety-eight leadership positions by my math: corporals, sergeants, officers, and so on. That is our entire strength as the leadership. Not everyone is suited for leadership positions. We won't have eyes and ears in the lower ranks. Sure, we'll have some new Alvans, but not many. From what I have picked up, it is kind of an open secret with the forces in Vermire that Lord Aditya answers to someone else. We can use Vermire as a place to train people up, then draw them into the military, like we have with the Adventurer's Guild. They have fighting experience, they are loyal, and they have been tested before they even enter the military."

"Hmm." *He has a fair point. Vermire is practically ours. Though they have their own operations they're carrying out. We can support and train them before they fight, and it can increase their chances of carrying out their operations.*

"Have you heard of the developments in Vermire?"

The others shook their heads in the negative except for Roska.

"Vermire is working with the other trading outposts around the Beast Mountain Range to set up a location in the middle of it. This would serve to consolidate their strength and create routes throughout the area. It would then become a hub of people trying to increase their strength, buying and selling supplies that are hard to find in the First Realm. It would also serve to make Vermire the overlord in the area. The alliance with the others will pave the way to dissolve the other outposts and take command of them. It will be a slow progression, but with our backing it won't be impossible," Roska said.

"With control over the outposts, it will be easier for us to know all of the activities of the different nations around the Beast Mountain Range. This will help to keep Alva secure and give access to more people who are willing to join Alva. We might have made it into the Fourth Realm and established our strength here, but we can't forget our roots. If Vuzgal falls, Alva must not ever."

Glosil looked into their eyes and saw unwavering loyalty. These were people who would die for their duty. Death was cheap in the Ten Realms, but they would use theirs to fight for the honor of Alva till the bitter end.

2 Mobilizing Alva

Elise took off her scarf. Fine dust fell from it as she shook her hair. Even with the scarf, it hadn't been able to block out all of the sand.

Ismail waited until she was done, then bowed.

"How are we looking, Ismail?" She waved for him to return to standing.

"The mine's output has increased by thirty percent with the new technologies you've implemented. The workers are also much happier with the health and safety. It has cost a little more but the miners are working harder than ever. Though there has been a problem with the jewelers and smiths." Ismail indicated for her to take a seat in front of a pot of sweet tea he had prepared.

"Other trading houses have been poaching them?" She moved to the couch.

"Yes, Master." Ismail bowed. "This one has been inept in his job. I accept any punishment you give me!"

"Did you collect the repatriation money?" Elise waved away his words as she sat down.

Ismail quickly served her sweet tea as he talked. "I did."

"Good. We can use that to entice more Novice jewelers and smiths,"

Elise said as he finished pouring the tea.

"Are you not angry?" Ismail asked, shocked as he poured his own glass.

"Annoyed, yes. Angry, no. If anything, those other traders have done us a favor, clearing out the muck that weren't loyal and interested in only benefits. If people wish to poach from us and our people want to leave, let them. I only want people loyal to our company." Elise took the teacup from the table and held it up.

Ismail quickly grabbed his own cup and raised it. "But if we only have Novices, how will we be able to refine the ores, separate out the jewels, and make jewelry?"

Elise smiled mysteriously over her tea. "Well, I have a solution to that." She touched her tea to his before taking a sip. He mirrored her actions as she turned her head to the side.

"Come in!"

The door opened and two women walked in. One was covered in muscle, her entire body toned. She wore rough clothes that were stained black from working in hot or smoky conditions while the other wore a fine dress that had intricate designs sewn into it with rare metal threads and jewels.

"Ismail, this is Reina and Brenda. Brenda is a low Journeyman smith and Reina is a high level Apprentice formation master, but she enjoys working with jewelry instead of runes and formations," Elise said.

Ismail's hands quivered as he looked at these two women who were studying him. *What is Master Elise's background to be able to invite such powerful people to this backward mine?*

"They will be paid directly by you, and they will be able to buy materials at a ten percent discount for their own projects. They will teach our jewelers and smiths. I hope that in the future we are not just making a few trinkets, but are able to make weapons and armor as well as jewelry pieces that can attract the people of the Second Realm over," Elise said.

Her words were simple, as if it were only natural that what she said would come to fruition.

Indeed, with these Experts, raising our own people is easy. We can use the funds from those who are poached to increase our ability to hire more miners, more people who want to be jewelers and smiths. Those who remain and bind themselves to our Red Permission Trading Company will be able to become much more than just apprentices. They might even become Journeyman-level crafters!

Ismail bowed deeper than before. Now he understood why she had not gone into a rage. Indeed, it was better to have people who were loyal to the trading house instead of tying those who didn't want to be there to their business.

"This one was blind." Ismail bowed to her deeply.

"Don't worry. There will be many more things that you can see in the future if you stay with the trading company," Elise said with that same smile filled with hidden meanings.

She finished off her tea and stood. "Look after them. And you two, don't raise too much trouble," she said, warning the duo.

They nodded with smiles.

A light appeared on Elise's wrist. She looked down at her communication device and listened for a few seconds. Her expression turned serious.

"I have another meeting I have to attend." She nodded to them all in the room and pulled her scarf back on.

Blaze looked at the men and women sitting in the room. They lounged over the desks or the chairs; the whole room looked more like a bar than a classroom.

All of them wore different armors and weapons that suited their fighting styles. There were ranged, melee, and stealth types mixed in with the mages and beast tamers.

They all had different fighting styles but each was a powerful fighter in their own right.

Blaze took a deep breath and opened the door into the classroom. The talking and discussion went silent as people saw Blaze.

"Guild leader!" a few yelled, getting to their feet. They were all members of the Adventurer's Guild and everyone knew Blaze's appearance. He had trained many of them and he could be seen all around the headquarters. Even if they came from the branch guilds and hadn't encountered him directly, they now eyed him in interest, remembering the stories they had heard about the guildmaster.

"Please sit." Blaze stepped in front of the room.

People moved to their seats quickly.

They come from all kinds of backgrounds across the realms, but they were all recommended to join Alva. The guilds and different groups created by Alva were all built to not only increase our influence but bring more people back to Alva and bring in fresh blood.

Everyone settled down as he cleared his throat.

"You have all been picked for special training. I cannot tell you the specifics of this training but it could very well change your lives and open up paths for your future that you might have thought closed. But you will need to swear an oath binding you from telling anyone else about your experiences. In fact, you will need to give an oath after this even if you choose not to join this special training. It will not be life-threatening but it pertains to some of the deepest secrets of the guild," Blaze said.

His words shocked everyone in the room. Some looked apprehensive but the majority leaned forward, looks of excitement on their faces at the new challenge that lay in front of them.

"You were picked for your perseverance, your determination, and your loyalty. That is all that I can ask of you. Loyalty to your oaths, determination to push forward no matter the obstacles, and the perseverance to continue on the path that you take." Blaze watched them all swell with pride as he let everything sink in. "Now, I ask, which of you would like to be part of this secret training?"

A mage stood up at the front, quickly followed by others. Soon, no one was sitting. All of them had accepted. They had different expressions on their faces but they chose to take a leap of faith with their future.

Sixty-three new Alva Dungeon members. Blaze couldn't help but smile as he raised his hand.

"Now, please repeat this oath after me."

3 Across the Realms

The atmosphere inside the briefing room was relaxed as Erik, Glosil, Rugrat, Egbert, Niemm, Roska, and Domonos studied the map that was in the middle of the table. It was a map of the second floor, the Metal floor.

"From the information that I was able to gather with the activated formations, the creatures in the second floor have been whittled down greatly with our use of the battlefield dungeon, though with their lower numbers, it seems that the boss of the level has been able to remove his challengers and control the floor completely," Egbert said.

"The boss is the Metal-attribute beaver that lives on top of the mountain, right?" Niemm asked.

"That is correct. There is a lake of lightning that has been created at the top of the mountain, in a sort of basin. It lives there, using the power of the floor and the lightning to increase its strength. Not even the battlefield dungeon would be able to pull it in for us to fight it," Egbert said.

Everyone's expression was solemn.

"How many of the levels have we cleared out by challenging the battlefield dungeon?" Rugrat asked and then turned to Erik and Glosil. "And do we know what will happen if we take over a level?"

"We can still only control a small percentage of the formations on the Metal floor, so we can only make educated guesses at this point. I would say about forty percent of the floor beasts have been killed so far," Glosil said.

"Only forty?" Niemm said.

"When in the battlefield dungeon, there are also beasts from the other floors included. Forty percent is much higher than I thought we would achieve at this point," Egbert said honestly as the others fell silent.

There are still four more floors after the Metal floor. Glosil cleared his throat.

"Look, I'll be perfectly blunt with you all. Taking the Metal floor is not just about taking the floor. It is about completing a promise that we made to the Alvan people. Many of them aren't able to go to Vuzgal to see what we did there. We promised to protect them and to make their home safe. If we can take the Metal floor, we show them directly the strength we've gained; they can see why we increased the military's strength," Erik said.

"I suggest that we continue to have Yui's platoon working in Vuzgal to deal with training there. When not training to clear the lower floors, Domonos, your platoon will be training those wishing to join the military from Alva and assisting in creating the training program for the medic, engineer, and mage squads. Niemm and Roska will assist and work on creating the training regime for the close protection details.

"Niemm, your special team will be split into two to protect Erik and Rugrat."

Erik and Rugrat started to make noise but waited for Glosil to explain himself.

"You are the heads of Alva and Vuzgal. You are personally strong, yes, but are you strong enough to take on people who are level sixty? We have had to fight those people before. Now that you are bigger targets than ever, you need protection. When moving between cities, one of the special teams will be with you at all times."

Erik and Rugrat stopped what they were going to say and agreed reluctantly.

"Good. Now, for the Metal floor, what we need to do is first we need to go and establish a beachhead. There needs to be a position that allows us to bring in supplies and reinforcements. It will also provide an escape route, if necessary. We need to train going through that teleport pad. Then we create a camp on the other side. With that camp, we can organize combat operations that will advance into the floor. We will go from objective to objective, capturing command formations. Unless there is a change in situation and we can find a way to speed up the process without taking unnecessary casualties. Once we have the command formations repaired, we will use them to exert control over the floor, and move to the main formation that controls the entire floor.

"Once we secure that, we have the floor. We have ideas of the strength on the floor as we have heard from Egbert but otherwise, we are going in there blind, so we're going to drill again and again until everyone can do this in their sleep." Glosil looked around the room.

"Won't be fun trying to sell that to the troops," Domonos said.

"Well, blame it on me then, but get them to do it," Glosil said. "Now, before I go over the plan, does anyone have any questions?" Glosil scanned the room.

"Okay, well then, let's figure out how we're going to take this floor back and show the people of Alva just how strong their military is," Glosil said.

Elan Silaz was covered in sweat as he jumped to the side, just avoiding a tentacle that had shot past him. *A boxing octopus? Of all the creatures, an octopus that uses melee attacks?*

The danger his mind alerted him to was stronger than the ridiculousness of the situation he found himself in as an octopus bobbed its large head out of the way. Yuli's ice spears missed as it lashed out with a hidden tentacle and struck at Tian Cui, who had to use a spell combined with a special technique to avoid the attack.

Setsuko fired her heavy repeater while running. A tentacle covered in mana was thrown backward, unable to escape the arrows that seemed to predict its actions.

Storbon dodged under one attack. He let out a yell and his body glowed with a golden energy. As Storbon threw his spear, a golden spear superimposed itself upon Storbon's spear, the two becoming one as a golden energy danced around it. A tentacle rose to block it but the spear's speed had increased too fast for the boxing octopus to stop it.

The spear hit the octopus. It staggered and Yuli took the opportunity, casting a control spell to restrain the injured octopus. Setsuko and Yawen, who had been looking for a weakness, pounced; their repeaters glowed as they buffed the weapons and their projectiles.

Tian Cui slashed a nearby tentacle. Red curses spread from her blade into the octopus as everyone piled on their attacks.

The octopus didn't have time to react as the attacks landed, claiming its life as it fell into the water. A tombstone appeared above it.

Elan was still crouched, looking at it all in shock.

Instead of celebrating, they all checked their weapons and armor, reloading what they had as Storbon retrieved his spear and inspected it.

Elan got up, looking at them all. *Monsters, monsters in human skin! How did they train to be able to work so flawlessly together?*

"Mister Silaz, did your level increase?" Storbon asked.

Elan smiled dryly and checked his notifications. "I'm now level thirty-one."

"Good, that's two more levels. We should be able to level you up in another two or three beasts now we're into the high thirty monsters," Storbon said.

"Why do I feel that you're not even trying hard?" Elan muttered.

"Well, it would be boring to finish them off so quickly and it's good for us to train our different skills by handicapping ourselves," Tian Cui said.

Elan nearly jumped out of his skin. He didn't realize she was so close.

"Really?" Elan had been joking, but as he looked at the sheepish smiles and shrugs from the rest of the group, he could only shake his head.

Hiao Xen sat up in bed, holding a light stone in his hand, just letting out a little bit of light so that he could read the report in his hand.

"You work more now than you did with the Blue Lotus," Nuo Xen, his wife, complained. The light caught her eyes as she looked up at him with a pouting expression on her face.

Hiao Xen stored the light stone away quickly. "I didn't mean to wake you."

"Is something worrying you?" She sat up and moved his arm around so she was nestled up against him. She yawned as she closed her eyes.

Hiao Xen smiled happily.

She poked him in the side, making him twitch and focus on her words. "Aren't all of the sects trying to set up places to recruit crafters from?"

"Yes, though I can't help but feel uneasy," Hiao Xen said.

"It will sort itself out," she said sleepily.

"It looks like that on the outside, but inside it means a lot of work to make sure that nothing goes wrong. Even against the Expert-level crafters, we were able to make it out okay." Hiao Xen relaxed slightly and then let out a tired laugh.

"Something else wrong?" She opened her eyes to check his expression.

"No, just thinking about it all. We have people buying up land from all across Vuzgal. I took the advice of Erik and have started to auction off land, piece by piece. The prices people are willing to pay is incredible. There are no less than ten Expert-level crafters in the city, hosted by the different associations. The crafting sector is being quickly built up. The first tier-three building has been completed and the other buildings are not far behind. I am not sure where Erik got the blueprints from.

"There are new buildings going up every day. We've already sold off all of the materials that we have remaining. The Alchemist Association has taken over running the admittance of people to the different dungeons in order to protect their growing lands.

"The associations have had to rebuild their facilities and it seems that they're competing with how big they can make them. The Sky Reaching Restaurants have all been doing a quick business, with the Wayside Inns hosting hundreds, if not thousands, of people who wish to visit the city. Vuzgal is booming. It—it, well…"

"It feels like something will go catastrophically wrong? It feels like if you let go of the reins even a bit, then it could all come crashing down?" Nuo Xen asked.

Hiao Xen let out a laugh and kissed her head as she'd been able to put his worries into words in just seconds. "Since when were you able to read minds?"

"Since I married you," she said with a happy smile. "Don't worry. You have built everything up to this point. Now it is time to see if it truly works. Erik and Rugrat placed their trust in you. They wouldn't leave you in the city alone if they didn't."

"It would be easier if I knew where they were," Hiao Xen said dryly.

"Everyone has their secrets, but they trust you for this position, the leader of Vuzgal. Now even the elders of the Blue Lotus in the Fourth Realm have to treat you with respect," she said.

Hiao Xen nodded.

"Now, go to sleep. Otherwise, you won't be able to do anything tomorrow!"

4 Rise of the Rifle Platoons

Yui looked out over the balcony over the training square below, seeing men and women wearing simple gray clothes jogging from one class to another. There was a corporal and a sergeant with each group looking over them. Making sure that they didn't mess up.

Even as they marched, they were learning, changing their movements so that they moved in time with the person ahead of them. If they didn't and they stepped on the other person's boot, then they would both be down on the ground and slow down the group.

"Taking joy in watching others' pain, sir?" Sergeant Sun Li saluted.

Yui smiled and saluted back. "Well, I hear that it really motivates them if I look over and frown a few times."

"Ah, yes, the secret art of frowning motivation," Sun Li said, as if his outlook on the world had been changed.

Yui rolled his eyes. "What are you coming and looking for me for?"

"Just wanted to bring you up to date on the latest group to go through scout training," Sun Li said.

"Walk with me. I have to go to the quartermaster's to check how things are going with uniforms, armor, and the like," Yui said.

"Will they have weapons and armor ready for everyone?" Sun Li asked.

Yui activated a formation that would keep anyone from listening to them. "I don't think on this training rotation. They should have their armor and their basic clothing, but they'll be using repeaters. Veteran units and scouts are first priority, though I have heard that production has increased, so it shouldn't be long until we have some more weapons for people."

"What about grenade launchers and the mortars?"

"Mortar round production is increasing as well. The number of grenade launchers produced is still low. To increase the speed and reliability, for now, until the crafters increase in skill, we will be only making launchers with one changeable formation socket. Though, the people in the formation workshop have been working hard to make different versions that will give us an edge in fighting." Yui stretched.

"Yeah, those things are badass," Sun Li said.

Yui looked over.

"Highly effective weapons of awesome explosiveness?" Sun Li raised his shoulders, in question.

"Looks like we might be making a professional military with no professionals in it," Yui said.

Sun Li just laughed.

"So, what were you saying about the scouts?"

"So the scout section has been broken down and they are training the other vets. Once they have completed training, they will be ranked as corporals, and get that sweet bump in pay. Once we have completed that training, we will focus on the recruits," Sun Li reported.

"How long until we have all of our people trained and we can train the recruits?"

"Take another week for Second Rifle Squad to become a scout squad. Then two more weeks and First Rifle Squad will finish their scout training as well. Give us all of our people back to train up shiny new recruits," Sun Li said.

"Okay, I got some information from Erik on the medic squads. They need to attend a weeklong course at the academy, then they will get hands-on experience in Vermire for a month. They will be qualified as medics. He's looking to set up a hospital here in Vuzgal so we won't need to send people far to heal others."

"The engineers, mages, and close protection?"

"Modified training, with assistance from academy teachers. Work in workshops first, get our basics down, then training in the field. Mages, there will be a new training course. Mages will be trained in close quarters combat as well as ranged combat at the barracks by the strongest in the army. Close protection is being organized by the special teams," Yui said. "Pass it on to the other sergeants so I don't have to."

"Leave it with me, sir," Sun Li promised with a grin.

"We might not be in the operation to clear the Metal floor but our job is no less important. We need to stabilize Vuzgal and grow our military as fast as possible to make sure that no one has plans to attack us from behind." Yui watched Sun Li closely.

Sun Li stood taller, looking more determined. "Yes, sir." There wasn't any hint of playfulness in his eyes.

"We also have to teach everyone how to use mortars in the not-so-distant future, so make sure that Sergeant Hall and his people keep their skills up to date."

"Will there be a switch up in companies and moving people around with the new people?" Sun Li asked.

"For now we'll remain in our companies, though if there are positions for advancement then anyone can apply for them. It might come with changing companies. We're all one military at the end of the day. Which reminds me, make sure that your squad is ready to move at all times. If something happens down below or here, we'll need your people to react first. I want to have trained soldiers on our walls as soon as damn possible."

"Agreed, though the first batch of recruits should be finished in five more weeks," Sun Li said.

"We've sped up the program. Should be able to fit into two months—going to have to make it up in the scout program. We have two hundred and twenty-five training here in Vuzgal, with the same amount training down in Alva. We'll have around five hundred people in our ranks, hopefully more if we don't have that many dropouts and failures. Dragon Company will have the advantage with people from Alva, so we're going to have a lot of people changing companies to get the fresh blood in and move people up the rank and training ladder. Captain Glosil has a plan."

"Five hundred soldiers? Well, damn, we had only a hundred a few weeks ago," Sun Li said.

"Quality over quantity, though," Yui repeated.

"Don't I know it. None of them will be making it past me unless I'd trust them to watch my ass."

Elise looked at the warehouses of Alva. They were secured and locked up. The people working there had all taken restrictive oaths; nearly all of them were from the academy. There were classes going through with their teachers, using this as an opportunity to expand their horizons.

The lower-grade students would separate out the loot, with the higher-level students or graduates getting it afterward to appraise the item, or if they didn't know what it was, pass it to others for them to figure out what the item was.

"So this is the system that you came up with," Delilah said as she stood with Elise.

"Yes, but it's a mess. We have thousands of items and hundreds of people to sort it all out. There's a lot of items that they have never seen. I've got Egbert down here a few times to look at things. He is like a damn book with the amount of items he knows. Somehow he keeps on getting away from me."

"Like master, like minion?" Delilah asked.

Elise had to shake her head as she let out a half laugh. "Yeah, it might be hard to get him to come down here but Erik and Rugrat have supernatural abilities in avoiding tasks they don't want to do."

The two of them sighed, thinking of their overlords.

"So, what are you thinking for these items?"

"I'm thinking that I would like to be a full trader instead of the person just representing them. But then I remember the stipend that I get for this, and know that my trading company is among them, and I don't want to be lynched by the other traders."

"In smaller words?"

"We hit one hell of a jackpot. We have cultivation resources, we have jewels from across the realms, there are texts and books that could fill the old library three times over. I have no idea what are in them. Thankfully, that was one thing I was able to pass on to Egbert, who has his librarians looking through them. Did you hear that they're going to be the teachers for the mage units?"

"The librarians? They haven't been in combat, or at least much combat," Delilah said incredulously.

"They might not have been fighting, but with all of their research and the knowledge they have, they've been studying magic most days. Most of them are also spell scroll scribes. Makes sense when you think about it."

"Yeah, but, just kind of hard picturing a warlock librarian, right? Am I wrong?"

"I'm just the lady who ran the only real store in a village."

"When you put it that way..." Delilah trailed off. "Well, I will leave you to it. Remember that the best aids should be recorded down and saved. Rugrat and Erik have plans for them."

"I think everyone would have a use for it," Elise said dryly as they shared a smile and waved good-bye, heading back to their other duties.

Glosil stood in his combats with the rest of the group that had come down from Vuzgal or been pulled from their duties in Alva on special orders. Others who were free had also come to see what the citizens of Alva had done.

In a corner of the park, there were some trees and shrubs. Outside, there was a placard with the Alva Army's emblem. It had been newly created.

It showed the Vuzgal castle with its pillar on top. If one was to look closely and were from Alva, they would notice that the pillar was actually modeled after the dungeon headquarters building. A light reached into the heavens, with two swords crossing in front.

Following the trails, one would first find a stone wall that was polished to a mirror finish. On it were the names of those who had fallen in the defense of Alva Village.

There was another tablet telling the story of Alva, from village to dungeon, and the history of the military.

One could only feel pride listening to what they had done.

Then there was the final tablet. On it there were names, thirteen of them. A picture was carved into the stone.

When someone stood in front of the mural, a formation would detect which name they were looking at and a voice would read off the citation of how they died, what they were doing, which unit they belonged to, and how old they were. At the end, a person would appear: a friend, a fellow member of their unit, a family member. The person who stood on that square would listen to them talk about the deceased. When they stepped away, they would no longer be just a name on a wall.

Glosil coughed and cleared his throat. To him, those names had never been names on a wall; they had been the sergeant who looked after his people. The private who put his shirt on backward when running to line up.

It wasn't a big ceremony. There were no grand speeches; people just wandered into the garden, slowly, in ones or twos. Many came out with tears in their eyes.

He didn't miss the looks they turned his way.

Glosil saw all of them standing a bit taller, here for their friends; some of them were the recordings for the ones lost.

People came over and talked to them.

In most armies, they look down on the people, seeing them as weaker because of their lower levels. Even when they're five times or ten times higher in levels, they respect the people and the people respect them. Not due to their strength, but for their sacrifice.

Glosil turned his head, feeling eyes on him. He looked up to see two men leaving the garden. *Is that—?*

Glosil caught Erik's eye and Erik nodded to Glosil. Rugrat, beside him, greeted Glosil the same way as they headed off.

This is about the lost and about Alva. With us there, we don't want to distract or take away from it. Glosil remembered Erik's words.

He gritted his teeth.

They're commanders worth fighting for, dying for.

5 Move on the Metal Floor

Everyone checked their gear. Rugrat pulled on Erik's straps and had him jump up and down.

"Good," Rugrat said, seeing that nothing was going to fall out of Erik's gear as they were fighting in the Metal floor.

"Thanks," Erik said as the rest of the army were doing the same.

George moved around, pawing at the armor over his body. He didn't like wearing it so close to his fur, and looked at Rugrat with unhappy eyes.

"Who is a good boy?" Rugrat pat George and scratched through some of the armored plates.

George looked appeased with the praise. As Rugrat pulled out a big steak and waved it in front of George's face, he snapped at it. Rugrat pulled it back before he could get it. George gave him an accusatory look as Rugrat looked unhappily at him.

"Sit!" Rugrat said.

George planted his ass on the ground. His tail moved lazily from side to side, unable to hide his excitement completely.

Rugrat held the steak as Gilga looked over and made a screeching noise at Erik, who was checking his saddle and her armor.

"You just got food," Erik complained.

Gilga let out another screech and Erik let out a groan.

"Sit!" he said.

Gilga, the century-old beast, sat down eagerly, making the floor shake. She had her tongue hanging out of her mouth, not looking too different from George's expression.

Rugrat tossed the steak to George; he snapped it out of the air and chewed on it, quickly devouring it.

Erik tossed up the piece of meat for Gilga; she shot forward, grabbing it and tilting her neck back, looking at him with big eyes.

"I'll give you another once we're done," Erik said.

She let out a noise of complaint, trying to barter with him as Rugrat patted George, leaving the two of them to their discussion.

George had grown rapidly with consuming powerful monster cores in the Fourth Realm. His understanding of words had also gone through a change. Although he couldn't talk himself, only yowl and whine in half-formed wolf words, Rugrat could understand him through the bond that they shared.

Gilga also did the same.

"For having a high quality bloodline, they don't act it," Erik said.

Gilga stood and shook her large body.

George yowled at her. He had grown but he was still smaller.

Gilga looked down on him, making him let out more annoyed noises.

"Could you get Gilga to not rub it in so much?" Rugrat asked.

George licked his front paws, staring at her. She let out a snort and turned, her tail hitting the wolf and sending him flying.

He landed and yowled at her, annoyed at being thrown around.

"Beasts do as beasts want to." Erik shrugged but there was a grin on his face.

"With her powerful back legs, she looks more T-rex than anything," Rugrat muttered to Erik.

Gilga gave him a look, as if trying to understand whether he were saying something bad or not.

George pawed the ground and snarled, unhappy about being ignored.

Gilga snorted and looked away, ignoring them all.

"Were you able to find anything that might purify their bloodline more in the Fourth Realm?" Rugrat asked.

"There are a number of concoctions that would be good, but I will need time to understand them and make them. Most of the concoctions from the Third Realm are not out of reach now and they can help them increase their strength," Erik said.

"Mount up!" Glosil called from the front.

Everyone finished their last checks and got onto their mounts.

Erik and Rugrat mounted up and moved to the front of the formation.

"While Fred said that they have powerful bloodlines, even he didn't know what kind of bloodline it was," Rugrat said.

"Well, when have we ever been given the information?" Erik laughed.

Rugrat sighed and shook his head, but there was a light in his eyes. Forging their own path—it was exciting; it was a new path…a new way. *We've been able to come pretty far with just following our own path,* Rugrat thought as they moved to the front where Glosil waited.

Glosil got a signal from the sergeant to the rear. "We're good to go," he said.

"All right," Erik said.

"Ready when you are, Captain," Rugrat said.

Glosil stood up in his stirrups so everyone could see him. "When we head into the Metal floor, it is our goal to get to the top of the metal mountain as soon as possible. It looks like there are a great number of beasts around the teleportation formation. So we will have to charge forward and through them. Stick together. If you get separated, link back up. If you are wounded, trust your mount to bring you back to the formation. Cover one another.

"Once we reach the mountain, Dragon Company will establish a defensive position. The special teams will continue with First Sergeant Rodriguez and Major West. They will head to the top of the mountain to challenge the boss of the level. Once the boss is defeated, the special teams will clear the rest of the mountain. Dragon Company will head up to the summit of the mountain and establish a camp there. We will hold our position as the attached formation masters work to restore control over the formations located on the metal mountain.

"Then we will stabilize our forces and come up with a plan to clear the rest of the Metal floor! When we come back, we will have regained control over the second floor of the Alva Dungeon!"

There were slight cheers and smiles on the soldiers' faces.

Rugrat could read their thoughts.

Now we will show the people of Alva just how strong we are.

Their hearts beat with pride as they sat up higher.

Glosil looked to Erik, who nodded.

"Alva Army moving out! Open the gates." Glosil's orders covered the barracks.

The gates opened ahead of them. There were people already outside of the gates, civilians seeing them off on their journey.

They looked at the rows of the Alva Army all wearing their armor, their panther mounts armed and armored with heavy repeaters mounted to their backs.

Egbert floated into the air, looking like a skeleton shaman as his bones glowed with runes that were imprinted into his very bones.

"Well, this should be different," Egbert said as they rode out of the barracks.

The people of Alva broke into cheers as they passed.

The soldiers wanted to smile and wave but kept their stony expressions as they marched forward, not even looking away as they followed on after their commanders, row upon row.

Egbert turned around and started to fly backward, completely at ease, breaking the seriousness of the commanders as he started to read a romance book he had recently acquired from the various traders who had come back from their travels.

"What do you think about the other formation masters, the one in charge of them is Ida right?" Rugrat asked in a low voice.

"Yeah Ida's in charge of their little group. I think that they're skittish as hell. Thankfully they're riding Alva Army trained panthers and they're protected by Special Team Two," Glosil muttered back.

"Should we have Egbert keep an eye on them?"

"Yeah, that might not be a bad idea," Glosil agreed.

"Okay," Egbert agreed. A flaming eye floated out of his skull and drifted up above the formation and then circled Ida and the formation masters, who sat up even straighter than before.

"Well, looks like if they weren't nervous before, they are now," Rugrat said.

"Egbert—" Erik started.

"What?!" Egbert, lying on his back, put down his book, his one eye looking at Erik furiously, cutting quite the sight as he drifted backward until he was right next to Erik.

"Uh, nothing." Erik shook his head.

"Wasting the time of your elders—you should be ashamed," Egbert said.

"Says the skeleton who is reading lord romance books while floating in the middle of a military formation," Rugrat said.

"I don't tell you how you're supposed to spend your Sundays," Egbert said back as he found where he was reading.

Glosil coughed rather hard, but wisely didn't say anything.

They picked up their speed and went through the growing Alva Dungeon. People stood on either side of the street, watching them pass by, including those who hadn't seen them before, being new members of Alva. A sign of a group's strength was their military. The stronger the military was, the safer the people were from attacks. No power wanted to lose their fighting force for nothing.

"Such powerful auras—I nearly fainted from their strength and they're just marching by," one woman said, holding her chest.

"They are much stronger than even the lord's own order of knights at the city we used to live in," the man beside her said.

"You came from the Second Realm. Aren't they stronger than the people there?" someone asked a woman with scars and an axe on her hip.

The woman coughed slightly. She was one of the people Blaze had sent from the Adventurer's Guild to Alva. "Yes, they are much stronger."

"Why don't you join them? You look like someone who fights?" the person asked.

"I applied but I need to go through some increases in my cultivation before I can," the woman said awkwardly in a low voice.

"Ah, no worries. If you pass the logic tests and an oath to try your best in the tests to join the army, then you can get help from the medical staff," the Alvan said with comforting words.

"I didn't pass the logic test," the woman said in a low voice.

"What?" The man then coughed a bit, looking embarrassed. "Well, there are plenty of classes you can take that will allow you to pass the test," he said, trying to comfort her.

The group passed through the center of Alva, headed past the dungeon core, where the council members stood in the headquarters level, looking down on the army passing by.

"Eyes—left!" Glosil called.

Erik, Rugrat, and Glosil snapped their fists to their chests, saluting the council leaders, who all looked on as the members of the army all looked over to the left in one motion.

They passed and turned toward the formation.

"Eyes front!" Glosil called out.

Everyone dropped their salute and looked forward once more.

"All right, get ready," Erik said.

Erik and Rugrat picked up the pace and Egbert even turned around and faced forward, storing the book away into some storage bone.

"Load!" Glosil called out.

Everyone pulled on their charging handles for their heavy repeaters, chambering the first bolt. The riders lowered themselves. They were like unsheathed swords as they all looked out. They were arranged two abreast, with each of them aiming outward, splitting up their flanks so that they covered everything to their front, left, and right.

The teleportation formation started to glow with power as Egbert started to increase the power. A faint mist appeared around the formation as the different runes in the lines and shapes that made up the formation started to come to life.

There was nothing more they could do as they charged forward. Adrenaline flowed through their veins as they marched right after one another. The formation powered up as Erik and Rugrat reached the other side of the formation. They left behind the first floor and appeared in the Metal floor. George and Gilga had been building up power in their bodies and they shot out of the formation.

The beasts on the Metal floor had been alerted by the formation that was activating on their side. They looked up as Gilga let out a blast of Water magic and George let out his Fire magic.

Twin pillars crushed everything in their path.

Rugrat fired with twin repeater arrows. Mana condensed around him like a halo and his body glowed with power.

Erik's body grew as he let out mana blasts with his fists, hurling back the beasts that were closest. The ten-meter-long beasts were tossed to the side as if they were nothing more than cardboard cutouts, blasted out of the path.

The Alva Army were right behind, their repeaters firing as they pierced through the beasts in their path, lying in wait.

The formation flashed again as another section of the army appeared right behind the first group. They had run through the formation so they were in motion already by the time they were on the other side. They had separated out the formation, leaving gaps in between so that they could teleport one group right behind the others and not cut anyone into pieces.

Egbert was a master with the teleportation formation and had organized it.

He now glowed and rose up above the formation. From his hands, purple blasts shot out, hitting the creatures all around the formation.

The beasts seemed to lose their minds, backing away from the Alva Army and the formation, as they tried to get the flames off them. Then the flames seemed to enter their bodies, infecting them with madness.

They turned on one another, allies turning enemies. Several were killed, only to have their wounds covered in purple flames as they changed, becoming undead.

"Last man!" Lieutenant Chen called as he and Domonos made it through the formation.

They broke through the beasts camped around the formation, but now the beasts were chasing after them. Egbert floated above, hurling attacks down on them as the Alva Army used the mana barriers that they had got from the Blood Demon sect army, deflecting magical attacks from behind.

"Follow!" Rugrat yelled as he altered their path. With his magical vision and connection with metal from working as a smith, he was able to see through the landscape that seemed to be made from Metal mana, being bathed in it for centuries.

He felt the power of George as they crossed the ground. Like arrows from a bow, they moved straight and true, a powerful force that nothing could stop. They were their own force of nature. A feeling of power rushed through their veins as higher level creatures appeared.

Rugrat pulled out his rifle as a large rhino covered in lightning crested a rise and bellowed.

Three repeaters tracked onto the rhino, cutting it down. It slumped on the rise but several other rhinos appeared, rushing up the hill. Rugrat fired, killing one, and reloaded. The repeaters kept firing and picking out targets, all of them working together to break down the enemy. This was a trained military; they proactively picked out their targets and then positioned themselves to get maximum effectiveness of their weapon system.

They didn't need to talk, understanding one another simply by watching their tracers as they adjusted and altered. It was much like video games, how only a few gestures and watching what the others were doing would allow one to adapt to their play style so that they would do what was best for the team overall.

Rugrat focused on leading the group as they ran on. People were hit with attacks and wounded here and there, but nothing life-threatening. Most of them were able to use healing concoctions to recover while they were on the run.

"Egbert, how are we looking?" Rugrat asked on the command channel as he altered the path of the convoy. He wanted to know what the situation was on the mountain, to pick the easiest route up the mountain. Otherwise, they might take a route that they climbed up halfway before they had to descend again and try another route.

"Well, I think everything on the Metal floor knows that we're here. I can't see a clear path up the mountain right now. We'll have to circle around."

Glosil started to talk to his soldiers as Rugrat checked the map that they had on the floor and what he was seeing through his magical vision.

"Okay," Rugrat said to himself, making a mental map through the lower ground that would afford them cover and not expose them to too many beasts at once.

The ground started to shake as Rugrat felt a magical reaction from below the ground.

"Beasts!" Rugrat yelled out. "Break up and move for the sides!" He and Erik moved to the side of the valley. The formation split as a massive creature appeared. Its sides glowed red, with molten metal falling off it.

Gilga shot out a focused stream of water that cut through the worm's molten metal, revealing bands of metal beneath.

"Shit! They're metal worms!" Erik called out.

"Come on!" Rugrat complained, remembering the worm that they had faced in the second realm when they were searching for dungeon cores.

The worms grew stronger the more metal that they consumed; then that metal was turned into bands of natural armor around their bodies.

Rugrat urged George on as he jumped into the sky. Egbert rushed past him with a purple blade, meeting a worm that was rising up right in front of Ida and the group of formation masters.

The purple blade cut through the worm, splitting it into two. Sizzling waves of heat and molten metal covered the ground around him as he leapt into the sky.

Rugrat held his M20, waiting for the perfect target. He turned and fired three grenades. They curved through the air as a worm opened its mouth. They fell into the worm's mouth and exploded in its gut. The armor contained the shockwaves, so the damage killed the giant worm. Rugrat picked out another worm.

The worms seemed to get smarter as another collapsed on the ground; they reversed their direction and sunk back into the ground.

"We got separated but we're on our way back." Roska sounded pissed. Clearly it was not her plan to separate from the rest of the army.

Rugrat looked over as she led Ida and the formation masters back. It seemed that the worms had panicked the formation masters as their reins were now held by grim-looking members of Special Team Two.

Rugrat descended to the ground on George.

"I think I see a path up to the top of the mountain," Egbert reported.

He guided Rugrat, who led the reformed group back toward the mountain and the path up it.

"Looks like there is some company on the mountain coming down," Egbert said in a grim voice. "We've got Metal rams coming down!"

"That does not sound good," Erik muttered to Rugrat.

The Metal rams were just as they were described: pissed-off looking rams that had a bad day and a head of metal horns. They were much larger than the Earth variety, only about four meters long.

"Just what is the deal with this Metal beaver?" Rugrat hissed as the rams moved forward lazily.

"Glosil!" Erik called.

Glosil moved up to him.

"I want the platoon to advance side by side, moving section by section, fire and movement. Have the command element and the civvies with Special Team Two behind and Special Team One in the rear covering our asses," Erik said.

"Yes, sir!" Glosil quickly passed out orders as Alva Army quickly moved into their new positions.

Sections one and three fired on the rams, holding their position as two and four fired and bounded forward and then slowed down in their new position.

"Covering!" they yelled out as their targeting became more accurate. The rams were being cut down, in a panic now as they were smart enough to know that the bolts fired at them were deadly.

The rams fired back blasts of lightning between their horns, but they were trying to find cover and their accuracy was horrible, only getting lucky hits here and there.

Rugrat nodded as he moved with the command element and Special Team Two, pressuring the rams with effective and superior weapons fire. The rams, seeing the Alva Army advancing as if there were nothing in the world that could stop them, finally lost their arrogance, not even able to close with the enemy. They turned and fled.

"Scan and watch your arcs!" Glosil ordered as they continued to move forward, making sure to be in visual contact with one another, ready to react to threats.

"Move into arrowhead formation. Third platoon will be the leading section," Glosil said as they moved like an arrow with people on both sides. Special Team One was in the rear, making up the base of the arrow; the command group was in the middle with the formation masters under the careful watch of Special Team Two. There weren't any of their usual antics as they revealed the deadly soldiers that lay underneath their jokes.

There wasn't anything else on their way forward. The Metal floor seemed to have realized there was a new predator on the floor.

"The beasts are gathering together. It looks like they want to build up their forces again before making another attack," Egbert warned. With his spells, he was able to see over the dungeon with his vantage point in the sky.

"How are we looking on the mountain?" Erik asked.

"The mana density there is much higher, so it is hard to see through and the creatures there have been there for a long time, so they blend into it," Egbert said regretfully.

"We can only continue with our plan," Erik said.

They got to the base of the mountain. The path leading upward wound through trees and plants that were heavily Metal attribute, thriving in this Metal floor.

Domonos organized the platoon, quickly pulling out different parts of a fort and placing them down. The mages used spells to fuse them to the ground, erecting a fort in just minutes.

The ground started to shake as Rugrat, who had found a ledge on the mountain, looked up at the metal dust that rose as a group of beasts charged down.

His eyes turned solemn as he pulled out his grenade launcher once again. *Level thirty-sevens.*

The creatures were blown back by the blast. The defense around the camp was like an iron wall; the defenders didn't let anything through, handling the charging beasts with professional ease.

The Alva Army might be stronger on average, but even higher levels didn't mean that they were invincible and most of them were dismounted, making the base.

"I can deal with them but it will take mana," Egbert said.

Rugrat was trying to find a good angle, but rocks jut out all over the place, making it hard to get a good line of sight on the charging beasts.

"Go for it," Erik said.

Egbert cracked his fingers and his robes fluttered in the wind. His robes and bones glowed with a deep-blue light that had flickers of purple embers.

Spell formations appeared above the beasts as ice blocks hit the ground, covering it in ice. The beasts lost their footing and started to scramble, trying to recover.

Egbert landed on the ground and spell circles appeared on either side of him. Blue spears of mana shot out, tearing through the leading beasts, and exploded. The beasts charged forward, but under the destruction of Egbert's attacks, their front line was pushed backward. His attacks tore through their lines.

Rugrat, for the first time, was able to see the power that Egbert commanded. *If there was even more power in the dungeon, then wouldn't he have power close to that of a demigod?*

Currents of power revolved around Egbert, making him look as though he were a well of mana itself.

More spells were cast in the sky, hitting the charging beasts from above and in front.

Dust obscured the battlefield as mana explosions of blue and the occasional attacks from the beasts colored the mountain.

Suddenly, it ended. Egbert and the rest surveyed the mountain to look for any more threats.

"Captain, hold the camp. Be ready to head to the formation if needed!"

"Yes, sir," Glosil yelled back over the roars of the beasts coming from across the Metal floor and charging the mountain.

A roar answered them from the top of the mountain. The entire mountain shook as lightning rained down randomly, striking the mountain and breaking off massive metal chunks that fell below.

"Special teams on me!" Erik called out.

The formation masters would be left at the camp as Special Team One led the way, Rugrat and Erik in the center, with Special Team Two in the rear.

Their panthers let out roars as they charged forward. Roska and Lucinda buffed them with spells.

They wove up the mountain's trails and Egbert floated with them.

They reached an open area. Egbert looked for new routes forward as they slowed their pace.

"Watch out!" he yelled.

From three of the mountain paths, massive elks made of silver charged out, with racks of polished and sharpened metal on their heads lowered as they charged.

One of the elks was killed by the repeaters, explosives, and spells. Another slammed into Special Team One, tearing through the group as they tossed their head, sending them flying, their condition unknown.

Erik mentally kicked himself. They had been all grouped together as they moved and it made the perfect target for the elks' charge.

Rugrat jumped off George, who rushed forward. The elk turned and lifted its head proudly, only to see the firewolf appear with red eyes and flames dancing around him.

It didn't have time to lower its head as George leapt forward. His claws dug into the massive elk and his jaw closed on the elk's neck.

It might be made of metal but George was one of their strongest members and he was made from fire. His body showed blue flames as the ground underneath him melted and the elk cried out, stumbling and trying to fight back. Its attempts to survive became weaker and weaker.

Erik looked over to the last elk. It had missed its target for some reason. Storbon's spear turned into several copies, each of them striking the elk's leg, making it stagger. Tian Cui threw darts, and Niemm's rifle cracked, hitting the elk in the eye, causing a tombstone to appear.

Erik switched back to George. He shook his head as the blue sparks across his body faded. Erik could tell he was much weaker now, but the elk showed a tombstone above its neck now.

Erik looked over to Gong Jin, who was organizing the wounded. Simms, Xi, and Imani had all been hit.

As soon as the elk was killed, Gong Jin had people go over to collect the different wounded and had Lucinda work with their mounts to heal them or settle their nerves.

Gilga knew his thoughts and in two jumps, Erik was next to Simms. He was coughing badly.

Eric pulled out a needle and jabbed it into Simms's side. He injected all of the healing concoction into his side and his breathing became easier.

"All right, Simms, how you feeling?" Erik dropped to the ground, checking on him.

"Hit some rocks with my side, head's all fucked." Simms blinked and tried to clear his mind. He let out a pained hiss as the healing concoction went to work.

Erik checked him over. "Good work on the self-aid. You've got a couple of cracked ribs and a collapsed lung, not the best situation," Erik said. "This will hurt."

He forced Simms's ribs together as he cried out and then used Heal Bone spell, fusing them together. The healing concoction would do the rest and his lung would be okay.

Erik scanned Simms's head at the same time.

"Okay, looks like we need to work on the helmets a bit more. The extra weight fucked your neck up, but don't worry—I can deal with that." Erik didn't mention how it also looked as though he had a concussion. With the power of Focused Heal, he could repair that damage as if it never existed.

He looked up over to the other wounded. Deni had Imani and Yang Zan was working with Xi. A bloody spiked metal tree had been hacked down as he dealt with the several puncture wounds.

With the healing spells and concoctions, now it was as easy to diagnose what the condition of a person was as it was to render critical healing and leave the rest to concoctions.

"Yang Zan, Deni, you good?" Erik yelled.

"Good!" they yelled back, not turning from their patients.

Rugrat had formed everyone up, ready to move. Rugrat jogged over as Gilga surveyed the area.

"Leave a half section with Yang Zan to watch them and take them to the camp," Erik said.

"I can fight," Simms said.

"You need time to heal those ribs." Erik put more force into his words.

Simms looked as if he wanted to argue but he lowered his head. Erik was his commanding officer and the one who had trained him. He might be annoyed but he wouldn't go against his orders. "Sir," he said in a curt voice.

"I'll see to it," Rugrat said.

Erik got Simms stabilized and dealt with the head trauma so that there wouldn't be any problems later on. "Go and report to Gong Jin."

"Sir." Simms headed off at a jog and Erik mounted back up.

Deni had Imani up and limping. She had taken the elk's antlers to the leg and her mount had been directly killed.

She was put into Yang Zan's care and Gong Jin remained with them.

The five of them would head back to camp as soon as Xi was good to move.

Roska moved to Erik. "Ready to move," she reported.

"Egbert, lead on. Everyone, make sure to keep your spacing, three panthers in between you and the person in front of you!" Erik yelled.

Storbon led the way, with Egbert guiding them from above. He had scouted ahead as they were stabilizing the wounded.

They broke their mounted defense and headed up the mountain once again.

Erik got a message from Glosil. "Report," Erik said.

"We are under contact. Beasts are testing our strengths and weaknesses. Looks like they'll attack in force soon enough—" He was interrupted from a roar on top of the mountain.

"Shit, it looks like that stirred them up. We've got more coming in. Get those mortars firing!" Glosil yelled.

"Can you hold?" Erik asked.

"We should be good. On a one-to-one basis, we're stronger but they have got numbers on their side," Glosil said in a low voice.

"Do what you can, but we don't need a final stand. We're sending down a half section to you. Three wounded but mobile, with a medic and Gong Jin in command."

Erik wasn't concerned. Although they were pressured, it wasn't as if they didn't have an avenue to retreat. They still had untapped strength; if they went all-out, they could force their way back to the teleportation array.

"Understood," Glosil said.

Erik heard the mortars firing at the base of the mountain. "Report in if anything changes."

"Yes, sir." Glosil closed the sound transmission.

Egbert and Storbon, with the leading forces of Special Team One, cut down any resistance and creatures that appeared on the mountain, springing out of the Metal grasses and forests.

They didn't have drawn-out engagements as they passed quickly and reached the summit not long after.

The mountain wasn't pointed; instead, it had a bowl-like shape. The basin was filled with what looked like brilliant blue water, but one couldn't see the bottom and it gave off light. In its depths, one could see white sparks.

Lightning fell from the heavens, striking the water, but instead of it exploding like normal water would, the water only glowed brighter.

"The water is condensed lightning," Roska said. With her words, a chill passed through the group.

"Look there—is that a dam?" Niemm asked.

Everyone looked into the center of the pool. There was a large dam that had to be fifty meters in diameter in the middle of the lightning waters.

The waters seethed as a massive beaver over ten meters long appeared. He let out a low squeaking noise as he slapped the water with his long tail. The lightning water was disturbed, throwing bolts of lightning around, and the wave that headed toward the group discharged lightning.

"Find cover!" Erik yelled. They ran to the sides, and the lightning wave rushed forward.

They moved to the side as the water made it over the basin. Lightning arced between the trees, the vegetation, and the ground.

Gilga gave out a screech and chittered. The beaver's head snapped over and looked at her before snapping off a few more squeaks.

Three heads appeared in the water and the largest squeaked. The large beaver out of the water squeaked back at them in a panic and backed up, eyeing all of the Alva Army.

"It's defending its home," Erik muttered. Through his connection, he could feel that Gilga wasn't preparing to fight; instead, she was relaxing and he was able to get a basic understanding of what she meant.

"They don't want to fight? Do they mean us harm?" Erik asked.

She shook her head in the negative twice.

"You can understand one another?" Erik asked.

She nodded in the positive.

The beavers in the water were together. The larger one had given up arguing with the second largest. The two others looked at the special teams in curiosity.

"Get him to stop the fighting in the floor. We don't want to fight if we don't have to. Just want to take command of the floor," Erik said.

Gilga talked back at the beaver. It took some time before the second largest beaver spoke up. The largest one looked as if he were pouting but didn't do anything to interrupt.

Erik got a transmission from Glosil.

"The animals are backing off here," Glosil said.

"Looks like this has turned into a negotiation," Erik said. "I'll keep you updated."

Erik cut the transmission while Gilga and the other beaver talked.

Egbert landed next to him. "When we built this floor, the lightning was supposed to go through a formation, set up like a river through the entire floor. It looks like the beaver made dams across the floor. The dams, made from the trees and plants of the floor, spread the power more and improved the floor. They lived in the center of the lightning water and created that lodge." Egbert pointed to what Erik had called a dam.

"They're a keystone species, you know. With them, a lot of disasters are averted or decrease in lethality. They just consume plants—they're not meat eaters. With their lodges, it's hard to kill them. Here in waters made of lightning, their strength increased passively. Look at the plants in and around the water."

Erik looked at the plants. He had been focused on the beaver before but now that he changed his focus, he could see that these plants were much stronger than the plants in the lower parts of the mountain.

"Even though the floor has been cut off for decades, it has flourished," Egbert said as Erik looked around. The metal-looking plants were strange. It was hard to pick them out against the broken rocks and the metals of the floor, but as he looked around, he could see that there were forests of the plants. There were other pools of dimmer-looking lightning water here and there. It was easy to look over it all and think it barren because the Metal-attribute items were just so foreign to Erik. Seeing the blacks, silvers, blues, and golds of the floor, he thought of it like some shiny but desolate land.

"I was looking at it as if it were Earth, with forests of green and browns," Erik muttered.

It took another hour or two. Gilga lay down and talked to the beaver. The older beaver still looked alert, and the other two were fixing up different dams that they had created.

Gilga broke away from talking to the beaver on the bank, and walked to Erik.

"So?" Erik asked.

Erik felt emotions and images through his body, piecing things together.

"And for the rest of us?" Rugrat asked.

"Beavers been here for a while. Got closed off, stayed on the mountain, populated. They were the strongest; they control the floor. With their dams, they hid in the lightning, grew stronger with that and the materials they ate. Got stirred up by us and the fighting. They hid in their dams and let the others fight us.

"They're the leaders of this place. Remember short people—uh, guess that is the gnomes. They liked having them ruling. They want to go to a place of water. There are more like them?" Erik was confused; he looked at Gilga, who agreed with his words.

"They must be beavers from the Water floor. They must have used the pathways from below and ended up here for some reason," Egbert said.

"So what do you think about all of this?" Rugrat asked.

"I think it would be a great idea to keep them around. Dams are pretty useful! Though we'll need them to move their lodge so that we can access the formations that are underneath it."

Erik relayed this to Gilga, who went back to the beaver, communicating with tail slaps, yowls, and chitters between the two of them. Gilga looked back over her shoulder.

"Seems we have an agreement," Erik said.

A few more heads popped out of the water, looking at the humans with interest and then looking back to one another—a big beaver family reunion.

"Most of the creatures on the other floor were actually allowed to roam freely. They weren't a problem to the floors—the problems were with the species that were aggressive," Egbert said.

"So if we can get control over the aggressive species or get the beavers to control them until we can tame them, then what?" Erik asked.

"Once we have the main command formation, then all of the beasts in its range will come under our control. It was made with their ancestral blood. Be real hard for them to break that bond. If we treat them okay, then they won't have a reason to try to break it, either. They make it much easier to regulate the floors and advance quicker. Look at how developed this place has become in the time that they have been stuck in here. The Metal-attribute mana wasn't even ten percent as strong as this," Egbert said.

"We're going to have to clean out these impurities. We can last around two months on these floors now, but at our lower levels, our mana systems would have been filled with impurities and we would be in serious trouble after a few hours," Rugrat said.

"If we can increase people's Body Cultivation, they can come down to these floors without problems," Erik said.

"Have to remember, it's not always our duty to help them increase their strength. If they want it, they should work toward it."

"Yeah, that's true." Erik turned his gaze to the dam and then up at the ceiling. "Long-term gains—we'll get a burst of energy at first and then power slowly over time. We've got more than enough power right now. With this floor being under our control, we're gaining much more than we're losing," Erik said aloud, looking out over the massive floor.

The living floor where the academy was and where everyone from Alva lived was the smallest floor.

"The gnomes didn't think small," Erik said.

"Of course not! Though, it was a bit of an accident. They were trying to escape from someone else and then were swept down a cave into what is now the Water floor. They built upward, building each floor.

"Did you know, in the beginning, they would transport the dungeon core between the different levels? Ingenious, really, creating several dungeons layered on top of one another, turning them on and off at different times, managing them all with the dungeon core. Then finally the dungeon core, with the use of formations, was able to command all of the different floors. From being chased escapees, they created a nation, built families, and had a peaceful life, cut off from the rest of the realms." Egbert's voice was soft as his memories moved to a place that only he knew.

"But now you and Rugrat are creating a new nation. Who knows where it will go." Egbert infused his words with enthusiasm, drowning out the sad melancholy from the past.

The past is written but the future isn't. Erik felt the weight of responsibility on his shoulders.

"All right, well, if we can get her and her husband's agreement and an oath with the beavers, we can start to develop the Metal floor," Erik said to Gilga.

She turned to the beaver, talking. Then she made herself as big as possible, preening and showing off.

"What's she doing?" Egbert asked.

"If I was a betting man, I'd say she's showing off how well she has done with an oath to Erik. Beasts want to show off that they have the best of things." Rugrat laughed and patted George.

"How do you know?"

"'Cause George is all upset at how much she's bragging." Rugrat chuckled and Erik joined in.

6 Council Meeting

Erik and Rugrat spent their time working on projects that they had put off. Erik was in the Alchemy department, using the Expert-level facilities as he worked to create a stronger Age Rejuvenation potion and looked over information on pills and concoctions that would assist one in increasing their Body and Mana Gathering Cultivation.

"There are many aids that can help, but really one needs an environment attuned to the different attribute mana." Erik let out a heavy sigh and rubbed his strained eyes, the pages of the book giving him a headache.

"Really, the best situation would be to wait for the floors to be clear. Then, like how I did with the Earth tempering stage of Body Cultivation, I go to the floors, take supporting concoctions, and then temper my body with the different forces of the Ten Realms."

He became quiet. "The one problem—well, not really a problem, but something to consider—is that now with firearms, increasing my Body Cultivation isn't that high of a priority. The benefits are great, yes, but if I'm at range, then spells to increase the power of the rounds or to increase my accuracy would be more useful. I'd need a trainer in order to properly learn how to fight hand-to-hand."

He rubbed his face. More than anything, he didn't want to waste his efforts. If he increased the power of his body and then didn't use it, it was useless. He could use magic for his healing spells anyway.

A part of Erik just wanted to fight hand-to-hand, so that even if he didn't have a weapon he would be a fierce opponent.

Rugrat was in the military workshop district, a section of Alva Dungeon's farmland that had been reclaimed to create the compound that made munitions, weapons, armor, and other supplies. It was one of the first things that Glosil had done—consolidating all of the different workshops together and increasing production. With the growth of the military, just with training they would need an increase in supplies. They would also need to build up their reserves of consumables that would be used in a conflict.

Rugrat was touring the facilities. He stopped as Taran guided him through.

"Something wrong?" Taran asked.

"That? What is that?" Rugrat saw someone putting a block of metal into a spinning machine and Rugrat's stomach dropped.

"That's a spinning tool. We realized if we used something similar to your centrifuge to spin the metal, then we could round it out easier into a barrel. We have another machine that spins and cuts the inside of the barrel, adding rifling," Taran said.

"Dammit." Rugrat groaned.

"What is it?"

"You did good—I messed up. We have machines like that on Earth, called a lathe, and then I guess that the other thing would be similar to a drill. Wow, that was dumb of me. I made it for him, just thinking about separating out blood and solutions, didn't think of the smithing applications. What other things did I miss? Band saw? Router? Damn, maybe even a simple drill? Dammit! Shit! Dammit!" Rugrat walked over to a workbench and started listing down names and then doing drawings.

Taran looked at the others in the room before he backed away from Rugrat slowly and then walked away, whistling.

Jia Feng walked into the dungeon headquarters. Delilah was already there, working on some other paperwork.

"You're in early," Jia Feng said.

"Yeah, I had some things to catch up on. When I have spare time, I have been working with Erik on Alchemy. It all kind of piles up. You know, with everything happening across the realms, then in Alva and now in Vuzgal. Going to need a whole lot more administrators." Delilah sighed and then turned back to her work.

Jia Feng smiled and moved to her chair as she pulled out her own reports from the different departments. She had organized her own notes, filled with her own questions and theirs. She looked at the changes that had happened to the academy since their last meeting. The changes since Erik and Rugrat had left.

The next to arrive was Elise and Blaze. Both of them looked tired as they walked in.

"So good to see you," Jia Feng said. Delilah got up as well and greeted them.

"The time changes can be rough. Nice having the totem right in the dungeon now, though," Elise said.

"Makes it easier to get a few home-cooked meals." Blaze smiled at Jia Feng.

She let out a laugh. "What would the Adventurer's Guild think if they knew their valiant leader was sneaking off in order to get pastries?"

"I think they'd try to fight me for one if they knew how good they were." Blaze laughed.

"Well, seems lively in here," Egbert said as he entered the room.

"Have you sorted those books out yet?" Delilah asked.

"Yes, I sorted out all of my personal collection! Alphabetized by character's name and by author name!"

"I meant the ones from Vuzgal." Delilah sighed.

"Good to see that some things never change." Blaze moved to his seat.

"Do you know what kind of items we have from Vuzgal already?"

"So you just happened to forget what the inside of a machine shop looks like?"

"What? I got your centrifuge thingy done!"

"Taran is definitely making it to Master Smith before you!"

"It's Expert next, not Master!"

"You know what I mean."

"Morning," Erik said as he and Rugrat appeared at the top of the stairs and entered the room.

The duo looked tired but they had that look in their eyes. It didn't matter how tired they were; there was still work to be done and not enough time in the day to get it all done.

Jia Feng shook her head at them all and pulled out some food, setting it on the side. "If I know you all, then none of you have eaten anything yet and most of you barely slept!" She moved out of the way of the vultures—uh, council leaders.

They moved en masse for the cart, filling up on food and drink, eating as they got to the table.

Glosil was the last in. He looked around, moving to the cart and downing coffee, taking a second cup and then piling a plate with food before moving to the table.

"Having fun with training?" Blaze grinned.

"Ah, good, you're here. I need someone to take over training the officers. Here is the information." Glosil stuffed a sandwich in his face and dropped a report onto the table in front of Blaze.

"I'm not in the military now!"

"That's nice." Glosil smiled and went back to his seat.

"How am I supposed to train leaders?"

"You're the most qualified. We've got some information on it, but you'll have to build as you go." Erik cleared his throat. "This meeting is to get to see how everything is going, what you need, what can you supply, then overview of changes. Then we'll open up a connection to the Metal floor.

"First we'll talk on Vuzgal, the changes and such there. Then Egbert, Jia, Glosil, Blaze, Elise, and Delilah." Erik scanned the room as people continued to eat.

"Okay, so we got one city, various gems, miscellaneous items, weapons and armor, tools for different crafting professions, as well as raw materials. Anything monetary—mana stones, copper, silver, and gold—has been turned over to the treasury or will be soon, which should mean more loans available for people. The other items will need to be checked. We would like to enlist the help of the academy for this. Then we can pull out any items that are useful for the academy—tools, special weapons, and so on.

"The lower-grade weapons will be sold in auction to the traders of Alva. These trades will happen two months apart so that they can clear the first group of items out, sell them and have funds to buy more. Some will be sold by our stores and auction house that is being built in Vuzgal. Same goes for the gems. Some will be retained to be used by the formation department," Erik said.

"We were able to save a number of spell scrolls that we can use in further operations carried out by the military. All materials that can be used by the military have been turned over to them. Still, we were able to find a number of tools and kits such as this." Rugrat pulled out a set of formation inscription equipment, cooking equipment, and woodworking equipment.

Jia Feng's eyes lit up, looking at the equipment.

"We were able to get some of this appraised. These kits will be retained by the academy, but overall, their effects increase one's ability to create a complete item. They increase the speed that one can work as well. For now, these kits should be lent out to those who are performing the best within their different departments.

"There are also formations and clothing we were able to loot. Though our biggest wins are the manuals and books that Egbert is looking through. With these materials, the tools, and the books, Alva's standard should be at least the mid Journeyman level. It is our hope that in the coming days we can grow our own Experts. It is time that we recruited more people. We have plenty of tasks and jobs. Vuzgal has only increased this need."

"What are your plans for the city? Is it focused on crafting, on mercantile dungeons?" Delilah asked.

"All of the above?" Rugrat asked.

Delilah's eye twitched before she talked through her teeth. "For all of our sanities, please pick one thing to focus on at a time."

Jia Feng couldn't help but smile at the boys' awkward expressions.

"Okay, well, first, we need to build up the military, but then we're going to be clearing the lower floors, so we need to work around that. We need to have a force to control Vuzgal. Which means that we restrict how much land we sell. We build up our defenses, which won't take long. While that is happening, the dungeons will naturally develop on their own and the Alchemist Association will basically take over the running of that so people don't mess up their gardens. What about the traders? Can we start taking a chunk of the market?" Erik asked.

Elise had a pained look on her face. It was a great opportunity, but just beyond reach.

"Not yet." She coughed and took a drink from her coffee. "So we have a lot of traders, but most of them already have their trading routes. I have looked into some of the information on the Fourth Realm. Trading is not so *kind* as it is in the lower realms. Traders are likely to kill one another so that they can get an advantage, or steal the other's goods. We would be opening our traders up to that. We don't have people we can trust with protecting them. So most traders will need to move through the totems. That is a lot of cash to move from place to place and they will need massive loans in order to make a return. So, in the short-term it is not quite possible.

"That said, we can do things kind of behind the scenes: Open an auction house, sell items from the academy there. Open up stores that can sell off excess goods at cheap prices and purchase raw materials. Open markets and trading areas—imposing a light tax will be good for conducting business. These places will need to be regulated. Our system here in Alva is simple but effective and we can use it as a sample and scale it up to what we need in the Fourth Realm.

"I have looked at the terrain. To the west, it is still a battlefield, so there is not much trade to be had there. The east and the Chaotic lands should have plenty of people looking to trade. If we can clear the road to the north, we can possibly get people through there if we keep our tolls at the totem low. We don't want to reduce our prices too much or when we increase them, people will be displeased. If we can bring the people and the traders, then the associations are going to increase the quality of the products they sell. As long as there is demand, they'll try to take advantage."

"So regulate the market, build stores, and build an auction house. Will that piss off the Blue Lotus, though?" Erik asked.

"It shouldn't. In fact, they might like it. There are a lot of useless goods that people bring to them. With another auction house, the Blue Lotus will get to show off how they are a step above. Might be an idea to talk to them and make sure you don't step on toes there." Elise shrugged.

"How long do you think that it will be before we have Alva-based traders in the city?" Rugrat asked.

"Months." Elise shook her head. "It might be easier to make ties with merchants in the Fourth Realm. The amount of wealth that these traders have access to is high. Also, our traders have established their own trade routes—to suddenly leave for the Fourth Realm? They'll want to, don't get me wrong, but they'll want to finish what they've already built. Be easier to bring in merchant administrators and run it from above, and the Alva traders can enter the marketplace when they're ready instead of rushing in and failing."

"Okay." Erik and Rugrat nodded.

I never thought that deep into traders, just thought of them as selling our goods, but they have to build up a network of people who they work with. It takes a lot of time and work in order for them to succeed. Jia Feng thought to herself.

"Okay, so we'll need some help setting that up. We can get Hiao Xen, who is someone from the Blue Lotus we met in the Second Realm, to set up most of it, but best if we have some of our people review it and make sure we don't miss anything. Then, I guess our plans are to move into crafting more," Rugrat said.

"Well, more being that it would be the main objective we have," Erik added.

Jia Feng raised her hand.

"Jia Feng?" Rugrat stated.

"I have heard that you plan to make Expert-grade facilities in Vuzgal? Will students from the academy have access to these?"

"Well, actually there's a lot involved," Erik said. Rugrat indicated for him to go on. "Okay, so we know one of our biggest weaknesses is not having that many Expert-level crafters, which means we have a lot of crafters at the high Journeyman level but they have an issue with becoming Expert-level crafters as they don't have guidance. Tan Xue has become an Expert but she has trouble as well."

"Yes." Jia Feng frowned. When Tan Xue explained it to her, it made sense but it was also complicated. "She says that being an Expert is like finding the beginning of one's path?" Jia Feng found all focus was on her as she fell into her teacher mode.

"So in the Journeyman level, people gain access to their skill book. This allows them to assimilate and remember information quickly. Now, that acts as a basis for people to expand their knowledge. When advancing into Expert, it looks like people don't just use that information that they gather. They figure out a truth from it…a theory. This theory is backed by the information that they have gathered, and by pursuing this theory and applying it to their crafting, one is able to create higher level items.

"Though there are right and wrong theories. Our people have been compiling different theories, proving and disproving them, testing them out. But there has to be others who have tried out these theories or have a higher level of understanding of the craft who could come along and tell us which theories are wrong and why. They can tell us what theories do work and we can build upon and expand from those. Instead of just throwing out theories into the dark and seeing if they work or not, we have a larger foundation to build upon."

"Okay, so if we were able to learn of Expert-level theories, then we could advance the strength of crafters?" Rugrat said.

"Yes, and no." Jia Feng had a complicated expression. "While we can figure out which theories are right or not through testing, knowing which theories are correct and applying that knowledge are two different things. I can tell you the recipe for a cake, but it doesn't mean that you'll make it the same way as someone else with the exact same recipe, or that it will be the same quality. There is a difference of applying the recipe as well as knowledge, tools, ingredients. This is part of why knowledge propagates slowly through the Ten Realms and that most of the information is passed from teacher to student. When the teacher dies and doesn't have a student, then that information is wiped out."

"Our aim with Vuzgal for crafting has several points: To use the dungeon to attract Expert-level crafters. To build up the academy there to draw in students as well as teachers and support the academy here. Draw in crafters who want to build items. With the Crafting trial attached to the main Vuzgal

Dungeon, we can observe their actions, create recordings, understand what the participating crafters are doing and learn from it. The academy will have Expert-level training facilities, high-level ingredients, tools, and resources. Then we will have external crafting workshops that we own so that crafters, even if they are unable to go to the Crafting trial dungeon, can still work in high-level facilities for a fee. We get money, sell them materials, and hopefully, they will sell their products within Vuzgal. Even if they don't, if we can make Vuzgal a holy land for crafters, we'll reap the benefits many times over," Erik said.

"Another academy?" Jia Feng looked at Erik and Rugrat.

"It would be like an outer feeder academy. We screen people through it, pull them to our side and to Kanesh Academy, or let them go. We send people up there to break through to Expert and they spread that information in Kanesh," Rugrat said.

"Okay, but for students, for staff, what are the requirements? There are a lot of people who are going to want to go. They've built up savings, resources, and skills. Down here, they're just another student, but up there, they have position, power, can show off to others. If a lot of them leave, well, Kanesh might become the weaker academy of the two," Jia Feng warned.

"For teachers and the internal running of the academy, we will need your assistance. As for students, they will have to rely on their own means if they want to reach the Fourth Realm. I see Kanesh as our main academy. We will always improve the conditions here first before anywhere else. The mana density is nearly two times stronger than that in Vuzgal, the prices are cheaper here, there are more books and less competition for the higher level workshops. The academies will need to adapt to the changing environment," Erik said.

Jia fell silent for a few moments before nodding. "If they truly want to go to the Fourth Realm, having them pay their own way will make them more motivated. We cannot take on everyone's fees."

Rugrat leaned forward. "With the teachers, we will be recruiting them to join the Vuzgal Academy, but we will need to evaluate them. Those who pass our tests, we should look at inviting them down to Kanesh Academy and making them Alva residents. All information from Vuzgal will be relayed and held in the library. Still, we're going to need some books, tools, and items for the academy."

"We'll need items to bring people to the Vuzgal Academy," Jia Feng said, showing she understood. "We can get the scribes to copy a number of books and send them over to Vuzgal to entice people to join. With the tools and resources, we will need to find out what they need, compile everything that we have. I'll have the department heads coordinate who they want to send: resources, tools, and other items. It will take some time to organize. While I think that the students should pay, will there be some aid for the staff to move?"

"Do we have ways to reduce the costs on the teachers and staff?" Erik asked Delilah.

"We can purchase monster cores from the traders at a set rate. Elise should be able to take care of that." Delilah looked at Elise, who tilted her head in acknowledgement.

"Instead of needing to pay immediately, we take the money from their wages until they pay it off, with no extra interest—would that be enough?"

"I think so." Jia Feng looked to Delilah, who turned to Erik and Rugrat.

"Okay, so that is pretty much the summary of Vuzgal, right?" Erik looked at Rugrat.

"Sounds right to me."

"All right. Egbert, anything to report?"

"The library has had to start using storage devices for all of the books. We need to expand the facilities soon. We are going through the books and items from Vuzgal but it will take some time to do so. I have worked with Delilah and the blueprint office to look at the development of the dungeon. We can actually increase the size of the floor now that we have the higher grade dungeon core. I have a few suggestions for this. If we can cut the rock into bricks with the dungeon core, we can use them later and it takes less time as we're removing less material. It will allow us to expand the amount of area for the Alchemy garden and farmland. Though I am being asked by most people about the lower floors. Now that we have cleared the Metal floor, people from every department are interested in heading down there," Egbert said.

"Glosil, what are your thoughts on allowing people on the Metal floor?" Erik asked.

"We have control over the beasts now—at least, it appears that way. I still would like it if Egbert is always watching over them and we have some of our military members on the floor as others are working there. At least for a few months until we're sure we control everything."

"Once we confirm all of the beasts are under our control, would that make you feel better?" Delilah asked.

"Yes, but a part of it is we just don't know those beasts." Glosil shrugged.

"It's your job to be paranoid. We'll have a rifle squad at least on the floor where others are. Have the military coordinate visits. In a month, Egbert and Glosil, I want you to meet together, assess the threat of the floor," Erik said.

"I ask that the people on the floor are no more than two per soldier I send down there," Glosil said.

"That's going to slow down anything that they do," Jia Feng rebutted.

"Slow and steady—better to be safe than dead," Rugrat said.

Jia Feng sighed and made a note.

"Anything else?" Erik asked Egbert.

"The dungeon in the Third Realm has reached peak efficiency. The only way they can grow more now is if they get new plants. The Sky Reaching Restaurant has gained fame in the Third Realm and Elise is running negotiations to expand into the other headquarter cities. We have finished filling the mana storing formation above us with Mortal mana cornerstones. With time, we will start to replace these with Earth-grade mana cornerstones. Removing the Mortal mana cornerstones, we can send them to Vuzgal to be used there. Though we might start running out of places to use them," Egbert said.

"Nice problem to have." Rugrat laughed.

"Well, we don't want to waste them. I don't think selling them would be the best idea. We just need to find a way to use them and not waste them," Erik said.

"Well, if anything, we can have people go back to those Crafting trial dungeons, plant a mana storing formation underneath, and then just mine out the mana stones that are created because of it," Blaze said.

"Mana stone mines—sounds pretty cool," Rugrat said.

"We're still far from that. We need tens or hundreds of them in Vuzgal still," Egbert warned. "That's all I've got!" He sat back and pulled out his newest novel. Bending forward, he was half in the book as he read.

The others in the room smirked, rolling their eyes and shaking their heads.

Erik didn't even bat an eye and he looked to Jia Feng.

"We've increased our student population. Right now, the issue is we have a lot of people in continuing studies. Though I think this will thin out some as people head to the Fourth Realm. The student grant system has gone well. Everyone below the age of sixteen has got a full education and those from sixteen to eighteen get two years of schooling for free, with the remaining years needing to be paid for by them. The Sky Reaching Restaurant and the healing house in Vermire have been great locations for people to apply their skills in real world situations. Though we have run into a small issue that Vuzgal could assist with.

"We have the largest number of high Journeyman healers and cooks. They are improving all the time but they need people to take that next step. If we can get Expert teachers, this would help. The main issue is not advancement—it's money. They earn good amounts for the First and the Third Realm, but if they were healing people who were in the higher realms, or cooking for higher level people, then they could make more money. With the Sky Reaching Restaurant in Vuzgal, we can adjust to allow them to earn more. Can we do the same with healing?"

Erik frowned and Rugrat pressed his lips together.

"I *really* don't want to charge people more for healthcare. For food, that is different; it's a luxury." Erik cleared his throat, clearly having some difficulty.

"Why don't we treat them according to their rank, kind of like the military?" Rugrat said.

Erik gestured for Rugrat to explain.

"Well, like a private, a corporal, and a sergeant have different pay grades. Can we have the same for Apprentice, Journeyman, then like the low, mid, and high level? Keeps it competitive but fair. Money is one thing but some people just like proving their skill and ability, being recognized for it. They show ability; they gain rewards and recognition. Nothing monetary, but can get more time with a teacher, access to greater tools or time in a high grade workshop," Rugrat said.

Erik looked to Jia Feng.

She thought on the people in the academy.

"How would we decide the pay across the different crafts?"

"The pay would remain the same, one pay for having a Journeyman-level skill and being employed for it by Alva."

"If they work two jobs with different crafting skills?" Jia Feng asked.

"I might be able to help you with that," Elise said.

Jia Feng winced internally. It was her job to try to remove problems for Erik and Rugrat, not add more work.

"Thanks." Jia Feng cleared her throat. "Also, we have found that people who trained in Kanesh Academy are looking for information on Vuzgal. I'm expecting that a number of our alumni will head to Vuzgal or return now that there are more opportunities of upward progression in all crafting areas. That's all I've really got."

"All right, Blaze, you're up." Rugrat drummed his fingers on the desk.

"Well, apparently I am being used to help the military in some way?" he asked with a raised eyebrow.

"Yup." Erik smiled slyly.

Blaze had a nonplussed look on his face as the corners of his mouth were raised in amusement.

"Okay, well, the Adventurer's Guild has continued to expand. We have been testing and watching them throughout. The first batch of Alva recruits are ready to be sent over, which should help increase numbers in Alva. Most of them are people who are from the military, crave to be in the military, or those who are interested in a craft but make their money fighting. We selected these people to bolster the strength of the army with veterans while giving people a way to work on their crafting skills. Even if they continue on with the Adventurer's Guild, they will be stronger and be able to take on higher level positions.

"We have been able to create deals with people in the Third Realm to protect trading caravans that cross between realms. They're high-paying jobs but send our people across the realms now. We're looking to expand more, picking out key cities that are along trading routes or in high-traffic areas. We have not expanded into the Fourth Realm. Protecting goods and traders there—most of the traders are allied or part of one sect or another. Through some research, that will need to be validated. Most guard forces have people who are at least level forty-five, up to level sixty. That is a big gap.

"I have put out contracts to farm more monster cores and have running buy orders with the Trader's Guild. We have set up contracts with traders and the academy for consumables and items, generating a nice little income. As I was told, I have been using everything that the association earns to improve our locations and find new ones. We have had some friction, a few fights here and there—bidding wars on different contracts. I don't think that much changes with Vuzgal, though it sounds like I should increase our recruitment speed and testing people."

"Actually, one thing that might really help you is Elan," Rugrat said.

"Yeah, good point," Erik agreed.

"You might have heard of Elan Silaz. He's Qin, Yui, and Domonos's dad. He ran a trading company down here in the First Realm." Rugrat's eyes scanned over to Delilah, who seemed to know what he was talking about. "He has since been recruited into our ranks. He has taken over running our information networks and expanding them. We should have probably invited him to this briefing, but he's training with the special teams to power level him. Elise, uh, actually, it might be an idea for the three of you to meet, share resources. The informants among the traders and the specialists in the different Adventurer's Guild have been great at helping us understand what is happening in the realms. Now we want to not only *know* what's going on, but *affect* what happens. He can consolidate our information networks, giving us greater reach. Instead of us all having our own information networks, we have one and it just becomes easier to manage.

"Anyway, getting back to the point." Rugrat looked up, trying to figure out where he had left off. "Ah! Information, moving places, gotcha! Okay, so, with his help, it might be easier to get contracts. They can help with recruiting, finding out the background of people. They can streamline things for us. So, everything is taken care of and we just need to set up shop and reap the rewards."

Elise and Blaze looked deeply interested.

"It would be nice to have it all in one place. It is kind of hard to know who is the right person to talk to about different information. Then there are the agents in the Adventurer's Guild who take over admin and deal with secrets with Alva, while informants just pass along information that they've heard on their travels," Elise said.

Jia Feng wasn't that interested, but she could see the possibilities. "Would it be possible to use his information networks to find more students and teachers?"

"With time, yes," Rugrat said.

"May I ask about this whole military training thing?" Blaze asked.

"I have it as part of my report," Glosil said.

Blaze nodded and sat back as eyes shifted to Elise.

"We're selling more than ever. With our controls in place, there are very few people defaulting on their payments. Looking forward to moving into Vuzgal and seeing how things are there. Vermire is under our control. Having some problems with the economy of the First Realm. We're starting to create a reporting system of different prices for different items in the cities. It has led to a massive amount of returns. We are now affecting the First Realm on a regional scale. I have been talking to the traders. We will need to add in controls to make sure we don't screw up the entire First Realm economy.

"Second Realm—we're expanding into lots of industry. Third Realm is hard to break into. We basically have people shifting materials for Alva for the Sky Reaching Restaurant, selling ingredients, and finished concoctions. Will take time to expand into Vuzgal—again, harder market to enter, but with time we should be good." Elise pursed her lips and looked up. "Yeah, that's about it." She looked to see whether there were questions before she turned to Glosil.

Glosil checked the pad of paper in front of him.

"The military is undergoing a complete change from the ground up. Basic soldiers will have training in melee and ranged combat, with a small focus on fighting with melee weapons and magic, and a heavy focus on fighting with their weapon system. There will be support elements such as those needed to build, upgrade, and advance equipment. Any upgrades that crafters can create in the academy can be applied to the military to earn compensation. So, new spell scrolls, defensive equipment, offensive equipment, clothing, pills, and concoctions—we will give rewards based upon these different items. We are recruiting personnel from the Fourth Realm, the Adventurer's Guild, and Alva.

"Vuzgal's defenses are being built up. The entrance into Alva has been sealed now that we have the teleportation arrays and the totem. Basic training will be carried out in Vuzgal; advanced training will occur in Alva. It is my aim to raise our military strength to fifteen hundred, a battalion strength force. With that, we can have one company in Alva, and three companies in Vuzgal. The next aim will be to create a regiment, which will have close to six thousand soldiers."

"That is more soldiers than we have residents." Delilah looked at them.

"We have enough room in Vuzgal to hold at least one hundred, maybe one hundred and fifty thousand people. Most Alvans come from Vermire currently, and they have a population of a few thousand. Vuzgal will be like the floodgates," Erik said.

"That is a lot of people to deal with. If we expand too fast, then we could lose control over Alva. There is a lot to deal with: housing, food, the academy, trading, and loans," Delilah said.

"A lot of people will probably remain in Vuzgal and while the soldiers are bound to us, there is a process before they and their family can go to Alva," Rugrat said.

"With Vuzgal out in the open, it is much easier for us to recruit people there," Erik said.

"Why are we keeping Alva a secret? Would it be so bad if others knew about us?" Jia Feng asked.

Erik took a deep breath before blowing out his cheeks, but Rugrat beat him to speaking.

"We haven't run into other dungeon masters. We don't know if they would care about us or not. What we do know is that we've got a lot of resources. In the Ten Realms, it doesn't matter how people got their power; it's just the fact that they have power. The Ten Realms is a war zone, and announcing that we are going to build Expert-level workshops has drawn the interest of people who are level sixty. What do you think a sect will do if they find out about Kanesh Academy? With Vuzgal, we have an opportunity to bolster our strength."

"Well, that kind of doesn't make much sense," Blaze added.

"How so?" Rugrat frowned.

"Well, we clearly expect Alva and its people to increase in strength with time. As it does so, then others will of course want to take it from us. At what point do we say that we have enough strength that if we reveal Alva there won't be an issue?"

Rugrat was stumped and Erik leaned forward.

"Okay, so when would it be okay to reveal Alva?"

"Well, we don't ever need to purposefully announce it. Though we can allude to the fact we know a secret place to train. Once we have complete control over Vuzgal, we should have a force that can defend and attack. We should have deep ties with the other associations at that time. Being open with them, allowing people to move back and forth between the associations and Alva, that would solidify our ties and using their position, not many people would think about challenging us," Blaze said.

"I hate using other people's strength to look after ourselves," Blaze said, cutting to the crux of their issue. "But as you said, this is the Ten Realms. Unless we're people from the Divine Realm, people will still want what we have, but they will just be scared shitless to try to take it from us."

Silence fell over the room. Erik and Rugrat had awkward expressions on their faces but looked at each other, sharing a thought with a glance.

Egbert even broke away from his book for a few moments.

"It makes sense. Doesn't feel right, but with everything we're doing, someone is sure to find out eventually," Erik said.

"Yeah," Rugrat agreed.

The moment stretched before Glosil cleared his throat and continued. "We have different associations and groups that are interested in purchasing weaponry from us. So that is something to think on."

"Elise, would you take a look at that? Use Elan's resources when he gets things going. We'll need agreements with them to make sure that they don't use them against us. Only the repeaters and armor at this time. Everything else, we keep to ourselves," Erik asked.

"I'll add it to the list," Elise said, making a note.

Jia Feng smiled and Delilah coughed lightly.

"Our population has increased. We're reaching nearly sixty percent of the dungeon's floor capacity. We are recruiting more people than before from across the realms. As Egbert talked about, we are looking to expand this floor. With more people arriving, we need more space for them. We have a large population that moves between the realms. It is hard to contact them at any given time, but many of them own some kind of property in Alva. Working with the blueprint office and Matt, we are planning for the expansion of Alva. With everything, unless we are able to reach other floors, we will be able to hold fifteen thousand people at our current size. With the expansions, we will be able to support forty to sixty thousand people.

"Though the farmers won't be pleased with those numbers because they don't have anywhere to grow their crops. The iron deposits that we found in the area have been depleted. We have a greater need for administrators and people to assist with the running of Alva, and it seems that the same can be said of Vuzgal. I would like to ask to recruit people from those in Vuzgal to assist us here. Also, a school to help teach administrators: simple management skills, understanding of more complex ideas like loans, mathematics, and general use information."

"Could we add that to the basic education?" Erik asked.

"We could, but why?" Jia Feng asked, confused.

"Well, we might know how loans work, how investments work, but the people of Alva might not. It is useful information that can help them in later years. The banking system is new and can be confusing to many," Erik said.

"Yeah, numbers can be a pain in the ass. Don't know how many times I went to the bank and came out cross-eyed." Rugrat shook his head.

"Comes from the guy who can hit a nickel from what, two klicks out?"

"I've been practicing, and that math is just simple: air, gravity, bit of heat—pain in the butt with the different planet sizes and gravity differential." Rugrat's words sounded as if they belonged to a different language.

"We could add it," Jia Feng agreed.

Erik looked to Delilah. She nodded.

"I also have some other problems," Delilah said.

Erik indicated for her to continue.

"We have a number of people who are barely paying their loans and they are looking to get items from the people of Alva. They had the bank extend the duration of their loan as well." Delilah's voice hardened.

"What do you think that we should do?" Erik asked.

"I think it is time that they remembered that they are living on someone else's land and while we want them to increase their strength, we aren't pushovers," Delilah said.

"How?"

"We don't increase the period of time to pay back the loans for them anymore; we treat them the same as everyone else. If their loan defaults, then they become serfs of Alva Dungeon and will be forced to carry out labor in the farms, the Alchemy gardens, or for other jobs that people who don't need an education are needed for. They will work five days a week there. Their food and lodging will come out of their pay, with the remaining money being used to pay back their loans."

"What if they can't pay for their loan because their house is too big?" Jia Feng asked. Most of the people who went to the academy had a loan of one kind or another to pay for their school up front.

"Then we will sell their house and put them in the cheapest housing available," Delilah said.

"What if they have a family?" Rugrat asked.

"The adults will be put to work and anyone who is seventeen years of age; anyone under that age has to attend the mandatory education anyway. If the child is under five years of age, then one of the adults will be allowed to stay home to take care of them. This was all written out in the loan contract. They either work off their debt, or someone else can pay it off for them, with their own agreement between them," Delilah said.

"When they're done paying back the loan?" Jia Feng asked.

"Then they will no longer be forced to work and the agreement will be torn up," Delilah said.

"Also, the people of Alva have started a project in the central park. They are building a monument from donated funds to remember the fallen."

Jia Feng knew about the project but most of the others in the room looked a bit stunned.

"From their own funds? We made the Wall of Remembrance." Erik didn't sound offended, just confused.

"Alva Army went out there to become stronger to protect them. The military is still protecting us. Even with high levels, people are taking advantage; they're helping others. Alva has come pretty far. This is a way for the community to come together and show their support for one another and show their gratitude."

Alva is not just a group of people thrust into the unknown. It's become a community. A place for people to raise a family, to call home from their long journeys, where they learn, and are taught. Thinking on it, Jia Feng didn't know another place like Alva in the First Realm. Nor did she know a group of people who acted in the same manner.

"They would like someone from the military to attend the ceremony," Delilah asked.

"Glosil?" Erik asked, deferring the question.

"For something like this, if it is okay, I would like to bring back some of the friends of those who were lost and attend myself," Glosil said.

Delilah showed some surprise in her eyes and smiled at Glosil. "That would work perfectly."

The atmosphere of the room had chilled with everyone thinking on those lost.

"Is there anything else?" Erik looked around. There didn't seem to be anything.

"Egbert, you get those formations all set up?" Rugrat asked.

"One more chapter," Egbert said, completely trapped in the book's pages.

"You always say that, come on, help us or else I'll only let you get one book a week," Erik said. One book a month was just cruel and unusual punishment.

"Whaa-aat?" Egbert's jaw opened to a comical size as he looked at Erik and Rugrat.

"Fun having a minion at times." Rugrat grinned.

"Highly decorated and respected marine recon sniper, and you still love damn kids' movies."

"Wholesome entertainment," Rugrat defended.

"They're pretty good." Erik nodded and focused on Egbert. "Formation, fire it up. Connect the Metal floor."

"Fine, fine." Egbert waved his hand.

The table was a circle; underneath, there was a clear floor. One could see the dungeon core below. The refined mana from the dungeon core was directed up into the formation that split it outward. It ran through the walls into the floor so that it could power the entire dungeon. Then it ran through the walls of the headquarters building and up into the formations that sent it up to the mana gathering formation on the ceiling of the dungeon's floor.

A display of the Alvan floor was displayed above the table. It rose up, showing a floor below. Unlike the times previously, now the map was of much higher quality. One could see what the floor looked like with the different features. There were even moving objects that had to be the creatures on the floor.

A few of them had seen the detailed version of the Metal floor; the others had all seen it before.

They took time to study it. Egbert showed off as he made it come to rest in the middle of the table.

"Unlocking the separating doors," Egbert said.

Doors that were underneath the dungeon core, covered by the mist of mana that was being pulled in by the mana gathering formations and drawn in by the dungeon core, opened. On the display, a thin tube started to appear, going down through the ground, reaching toward the Metal floor.

"There are formations that run down the length of the tunnel. Each of the floors are blocked off from one another through multiple doors. These sections are largely untouched and have formations to repair themselves. Now that they have power, we can open the doors and we can start to rebuild the different formations."

"So what will happen once we open all of the gates to the Metal floor? Will we be able to close them again?" Blaze asked.

"Well, think of these as the backup lines. There are other formations that run through the ground that connect the floors. Once we can use this backup way to connect to the Metal floor, we can direct power into the secondary formations, allowing them to repair themselves. Those that are badly damaged will need to be repaired by our teams. Once we have the floor under our control and the formations are restored, then we can close the main tube again. The tubes were how we built the other floors," Egbert added.

"Built them?" Delilah asked.

"We—the gnomes, that is—built these tunnels to move higher. We used the dungeon core to excavate out the floors. They were just camps, a way out of the Water dungeon that we found ourselves in.

"Once we got to the surface, well, our population was high and we didn't want to go out there. Our base was much stronger than the gnome nations and there were people who were coming from other places and changing the Ten Realms. So, using the dungeon core, they created blueprints, and with our help, we created floor by floor, building our own safe haven underground."

"Just the scale of it all is impressive. They had to be amazing builders," Erik said.

Jia Feng looked at the floor as the tunnels continued to open. She had only ever seen the Alva floor. The fact that there were another five floors underneath them and all of them were larger than the floor she was on excited her, eager to see what would happen as they came under the control of Alva.

"The last door is ready to be opened," Egbert said.

Jia Feng saw that there were other formations that were also tracing down toward the Metal floor. Some of them went farther than others; some were growing, and others were just lit up.

"I have a preliminary connection with the main command formation. Do you want me to establish contact?" Egbert looked at Erik and Rugrat, turning serious.

"Connect them." Rugrat's face split into a smile.

Power from the dungeon core to the mana storing formation reduced. Instead of going into the formations that would power the floor, they went into the tunnel. One could see the formations lighting up as the power traveled down.

"Okay, opening this bottom floor is going to let a lot of mana that has a Metal attribute back up." Egbert warned, "Opening the last door."

The door opened and the floors were opened up to one another for the first time in centuries. A beam of power descended from the ceiling and traveled through the air, down to the command formation that was waiting for it. The formation started to activate as power and formations that were across the floor started to come online.

A wave of Metal-attribute mana rushed up into the dungeon core.

Lightning flashed around and rumbled within the closed area. There was too much mana for the mana gathering formation or the dungeon core to handle, so the mana started to spread through the floor.

"Increase the density of the mana on the floor. Turn off the mana gathering formation on the floor and clear up that Metal-attribute mana,"

Rugrat ordered as he and Erik pulled up their dungeon interfaces.

"Formations are off. Metal mana being refined," Erik reported.

"All right, I'll try to direct the power into the formation, use it to add to the repairs. Egbert, can you stop that power from feeding back into here? We can adjust the mana flow of the floor later," Rugrat said.

"Working on the control formation on the Metal floor. There are some flaws. It is repairing. I am re-routing some of the formation so that it will function. We will need some more work later." Egbert looked down, seeing something that the others couldn't. "Okay, we have some basic control. The mana gathering formations are now working, so that should make sure that we don't take as much Metal-attribute mana. We are only sending mana down there, not pulling it up anymore. We will still have a higher ambient mana, just with the mana gathering formations up here and the dungeon core. Only a portion as much as what it was before. That was a bit intense." Egbert laughed.

"The secondary control formations are starting to come online—that's good. Okay, so there are some routing issues. Looks like there are formations that were destroyed over time. Not as bad as I thought, though. The links will take some time to rebuild."

"The formations are growing between floors. It's starting to repair itself," Elise said as everyone started to refocus on the display.

"Looks kind of like a tree growing roots down and another spreading branches above," Delilah said.

"When can we close the doors between the floors again?" Glosil asked.

"We can close them as soon as we have some of the linking formations connected. It should take a day or two to complete. I am focusing on rebuilding those formations now. If I can draw more power, then it would be faster," Egbert said.

"Well, we're not using it for anything," Rugrat said.

"All power that is not being used to sustain the floor is to be used to rebuild the formations to connect us to the Metal floor, then the formations," Erik said.

"Very well," Egbert said.

The pillar of light reaching up into the ceiling disappeared. The dungeon core headquarters continued to glow with power but all of it was now being diverted down below.

Jia Feng was a little stunned. "So we're connected to the Metal floor now?"

"That's correct." Egbert smiled.

"Well then, Glosil, when are you free to talk about allowing people down to visit?"

The council grinned and smiled. Even Glosil cracked a smile.

"I have one more meeting, but I'll pay a visit this afternoon to discuss?"

"Works for me." Jia smiled. She looked at the display showing the two floors.

A dungeon with two floors, a city, an academy—and for some reason, it just feels like we're getting warmed up. What else will the Ten Realms have in store for us?

7 Undercurrents in the City

Matt looked around Vuzgal. He was one of the few non-military people from Alva who were a high enough level to reach the city. The others were traders or adventurers, with only a few crafters who studied multiple crafts and had been able to increase their Experience with monster cores or by paying people to level them by adding them to a party and killing monsters.

Most of the city is run with people we have oath-bound but are originally from the Fourth Realm or higher and are looking for stability. We've only got a few of our own people in key positions. Which is why I'm running around playing so many roles! Wayside Inn manager, Sky Reaching Restaurant architect and manager again!

He rubbed his head as he felt a headache coming on.

"Hey Matt!" Yui called as Matt walked up to the castle.

Matt raised his hand in greeting. "I need a coffee."

"Don't you have a storage ring?"

"Hmm." Matt pulled out a coffee. "Holy Satan's guch! Shit, that's hot! Fuck, burnt my tongue." Matt blew on his tongue and the coffee at the same time. He hadn't spilled a drop even as he moved around in tongue-induced third-degree coffee-burn pain.

"Forget things stay the same temperature in there?"

Matt's eye twitched as he stared at Yui.

"Blow on it, makes it cooler," Yui added.

"Blow me. Why the hell are you so damn awake?"

"Been up for like five hours and got my dose already." Yui gestured at the coffee cup vaguely.

Matt grunted as he felt his tongue recovering. "Body Cultivation—burnt tongue gone like that," Matt said. His coffee had cooled enough to make it only mildly scalding. He let out a hot breath. "That's it. You still training?"

"Every day, all day." Yui stood at the doorway into the castle. "Let me know if you head out into the city. I can send some people with you."

"I'll be fine." Matt laughed.

"Dude, this might be our city, but it doesn't mean there aren't people looking to take advantage of us," Yui said.

Matt's easy smile dimmed before he shrugged. "Yeah, makes sense. Hey, have you heard of anyone selling summoning spells?"

"There's Abil's place, down Twelve and Baker Street, I heard."

"Thanks." Matt perked up. *It's been some time since I added another creature to my collection. Just spending my time working on blueprints and dating. What's a single guy gonna do?*

"All right." Matt noticed a group of Alva soldiers on panthers off to the side. "Where you off to? Aren't you training?"

"Seems that the associations started a pissing contest—gonna go and scare them with some undead!" Yui's smile returned.

"Well, have fun. Don't stay out too late and remember not to miss dinner."

Yui rolled his eyes.

"See you later."

"Later, sir."

Matt gave a half wave and continued into the Castle District, feeling sorry for the poor bastards who got in Yui's way.

He passed through the castle gardens. Nearly a third of it, the part where the worst damage was, was filled with construction.

It's called the Castle District, but it's bigger than my campus back home.

Matt drank his coffee, becoming human. It wasn't long until he passed through the administrative offices and reached the main office that ran all of Vuzgal.

The men and women there all looked overworked and tired, but they were filled with determined energy.

Matt felt a shiver go down his spine just looking at them. *Beware of the mass of white-collar workers!*

He sped up his pace unconsciously as they looked at him with hungry eyes. He could feel the heat in their gazes before he reached the main office.

"The acting city lord is only meeting with people with appointments. He is booked for the next three weeks," the man said as he went through various files.

"Dougie, it's Matt," Matt said.

The man looked up from his work. He had only become a part of Vuzgal a few months ago but was a quick study and had shown his ability.

With the needs of Vuzgal, Hiao Xen focused on running the city, while his wife was handling recruitment and screening the different people. She also ran classes for the people who entered Vuzgal. With the city's prosperity, throngs of people from other realms applied to join Vuzgal. There were plenty of opportunities and mana stones to be made.

For those in the Fourth Realm, if they could find security in one of the most prosperous cities in the Fourth Realm just by working, they were more than willing to do it.

I wonder what will happen when some of them start to disappear, being recruited to Alva?

"Sorry, Master Richardson!" Dougie nearly jumped out from behind his desk. The man routinely turned down the heads from the different associations and high Journeyman-level people, but became flustered in Matt's presence.

The universe is a weird, weird place. Still have no idea why the Ten Realms exist and why we're all here.

Erik and Rugrat might be increasing their strength so that they could protect those who followed them, to push their own limits, and chase that ever elusive pinnacle. Matt, though—he only had questions. *What was the Ten Realms? Why was he here? Was it random? Did some god descend from the sky and pick him? Was he actually reincarnated?*

He shook his head with a smile and waved Dougie down. "Don't worry about it. I just wanted to make sure that I'm on time for the meeting," Matt said.

Dougie checked his timepiece. Timepieces were normal for those in the higher realms and the associations. The number of hours in a day might change from one realm to the next, but the timepieces allowed the associations to run smoothly and stay on the same timeline.

"You're on time, just a few minutes early. I will see if he is ready." Dougie sent a sound transmission, quickly receiving a reply.

"He is just finishing up some work but he is ready for you." Dougie pressed a button on his desk to disable a defensive formation.

"Thanks," Matt said as the door opened.

He looked around the room and laughed to himself. *I wonder if anyone has told Hiao Xen that all of the government offices are actually located in the concubine quarters of the castle. All of the rooms here were closer together and didn't have all of the grand extras of the other rooms.* Matt barely held in a snort, masking it as a cough. *Or the fact that his office is actually the bedroom of the empress. I don't even* want *to think what a blacklight would pull up in here.*

Hiao Xen sat at a big desk. Behind him, four sets of tall windows looked out over the city. The city was built on a rise that reached up to meet the valley where the dungeons were found. The castle's height allowed it to look over the growing city. The emperor's chambers looked over the valley, and the public areas offered a view of the city. The castle's original offices had actually been destroyed by the pillar that had fallen on the castle.

Those offices were being renovated to create Vuzgal's own academy and all of the construction outside was geared toward this.

The new tier-three crafting buildings in the city were taking time to build, but every resource was devoted to completing these crafting facilities.

Matt had designed them personally, from the different pavilions, to the growing library, the internal gardens and living quarters.

Formations had been moved around the castle complex to draw in more mana and hold it there. To anyone using mana, it was a holy land. Its mana density was only rivaled by the mana formations in the valley where the Alchemist Association raised ingredients.

Although they were making massive profits, the cost of the materials to make tier-three buildings wasn't small. In the dungeon, they could directly upgrade the buildings: simply pay the fee, put the materials together, and bam! Upgraded facility. In cities, it was more like building on Earth. You needed materials, craftsmen, and the kitchen sink to build the damn places. If they wanted to increase the grade of the place? They would need to tear it down and build a new one, or make a new one and then they would probably leave the first because it still served a purpose.

Though I've heard that if someone is able to combine the techniques of spell scrolls with blueprint designs, then they can upgrade and change a building with a special blueprint design. It would save a lot of time and resources to just upgrade the existing structures.

In Vuzgal, they were focusing on tier-three workshops. To build tier-four workshops in a city, they would need to ask mid- to high-level Experts or Master crafters to assist. The cost for them to work on something mundane as a workshop would cost months' worth of Vuzgal's income.

Which was probably why Delilah has been asking me to buy extra materials, so that they can be funneled to Alva Dungeon for when they upgrade the workshops there.

"Sorry, just finishing this one up." Hiao Xen quickly finished writing on the report. He took out a stamp and slammed it on the report. The report turned into motes of light and floated out of the window.

"Light-paper," Matt said.

"Useful material—once enchanted, it can act as a messenger system of sorts, going between two people. It can only be sent with a stamp and then opened with another stamp," Hiao Xen said in approval.

Matt nodded. It reminded him of messenger systems on Earth, but it had magical paper moving between people instead of an internet connecting them across the world. The light-paper would float across the city as motes of light. With so many communications being sent, you could see clouds of light moving across the city, or shooting off into the distance at night.

Looks pretty, but I bet the poor bastards in the castle wished they could get some sleep instead of being stuck here all night.

"No worries." Matt took a seat. They'd gotten comfortable with each other over the last couple of weeks. Everything that was planning-related went through Matt before it was finalized, and he or his apprentices had designed every major building in Vuzgal.

Work was only increasing and speeding up.

"Through my contacts, I was able to find around three hundred people for the Sky Reaching Restaurants." Hiao Xen pulled out a file from his storage ring and passed it over.

"Okay, I'll pass this off to Jo. She can sort through it and give it the final okay before sending them to the Third Realm for training. It will still be a few weeks before we're able to open up the second Sky Reaching Restaurant location unless we can recruit more people."

"What about just opening up the stores?" Hiao Xen asked.

"Why are you so interested in the Sky Reaching Restaurant?" Matt laughed.

Hiao Xen sighed, leaning on his hands. "Every single conversation I have seems to come around to the Sky Reaching Restaurant—when will another location open, when will there be more food?" His eyes narrowed as a dull expression covered his face. "You know how annoying it is talking about ingredient yields with the head of the Alchemist Association and the rent, then having him segue into the Sky Reaching Restaurant? We had discussed all of that in a meeting before, so he was just using the meeting to find out about his favorite restaurant!"

Hiao Xen had a pleading look on his face and Matt couldn't stop himself from laughing.

"The stores are a good idea. It is much easier to hire people to sell items than get cooks and chefs and train them up to the standards of the Sky Reaching Restaurant," Matt said.

"Thank you. It should keep me out of at least twenty percent of my useless meetings."

"Well, you'll be pleased to know that the last Wayside Inn has been completed. I have people surveying the outer city, and there is another group that is looking at the road to repair it. I talked to the people to the east in the Chaotic lands. For some reduced taxes, they're willing to put resources toward doing up the roads." Matt pulled out a contract and passed it to Hiao Xen as he kept talking.

"The defensive bunkers around the outer city are complete and manned.

The undead are working on the upgrades within the castle. Primarily the academy. The facilities for admin and living quarters for the admin staff and their families should be completed within the week. The rest of the apartments, grounds, and such should be completed in two weeks. Academy should take no longer than a month.

"I have been able to get some alchemists to replant the gardens. They will increase the mana in the area and secrete relaxing smells. Some landscapers are working with them to create small gardens to give people a place to hang out. It'll be pretty sweet.

"The places that are in town, they'll take another two months to be completed. I checked with the alchemists; their walls are all completed now, so no one can get into their areas."

"The Blue Lotus location just finished completion. They're going to have their first auction tonight. Are you coming?" Hiao Xen said.

"They usually have some good items, but I've got a date and some beers calling my name so I'll take a rain check." Matt smiled. People were all looking for him but he was always on the move. Not many knew what he looked like, so the guy with the odd hat and beard was able to hang out in different bars, drinking with his buddies instead of getting trapped in asinine conversations.

The two of them went over the main topics, before Matt hurried off, leaving Hiao Xen looking at his mountain of paperwork as two new reports made of light reconstructed themselves on his desk.

"Why the hell did I agree to this job?" Hiao Xen muttered as Matt left the room.

Matt waved to Dougie, but he was head down in work as well. Matt quickly headed down out of the castle and through some side streets, reaching the crafter's district that made up the center of the city.

"Bit lopsided right now," Matt complained. Forces in the west were still stuck in battle while the Chaotic lands to the east were reaping the greatest rewards with trading caravans riding toward Vuzgal. The one problem was that they were going through the roads that the Blood Demon sect had been on. The army had fixed the roads, but just enough for them to pass. Performing thorough repairs was one of Matt's projects.

Matt took his time walking, listening to the conversations around him.

"A capital city in the middle of the forest with no one around—just how lucky are the city lords?"

"Lucky? I heard that this place was cursed. Those skeletons that do the work of the city? They've been fighting here for hundreds of years!"

"They're just big laborers, though!" The first laughed.

"Laborers? Do you know how strong they are? They're like level fifty and sixty, some of them!"

"I hear if you join the military then they will help you level up your cultivation and overall level to level forty-five!"

"Level forty-five? Most fighting forces start at level thirty. They don't have many people. Must be pouring out mana stones to get people to level forty-five!"

Matt turned the corner, passing a tailor shop.

"Vuzgal? Should be called a paradise for crafters," one said.

"I heard that the associations are all thinking about opening recruiting here. If they do, not only can you get access to the dungeon with its workshops, you can join an association."

"The biggest fact isn't the associations—it's the workshops. I have a cousin working in the castle. He said that if this is a paradise, then inside the castle is a holy land. And their requirements to let people in aren't about crafting skill, but rather one's willingness to learn!"

"Are they recruiting? I should go and look!"

"I'll come too!"

"What are you talking about?" the tailor of the shop asked as he walked forward.

"Uh!"

"Going for drinks later!" the quicker-minded one blurted out.

"Focus on your work! It's so hard to find good workers," the man complained.

Matt grinned as he passed a tea house.

"It might cost a lot to reach Vuzgal, but they have thought ahead. With the Wayside Inns, it allows a great number of people to visit for only a few days and then leave again. The taxes are low and the city is built with crafters in mind."

"The city lords even leveraged the associations into supporting them. I heard that they charged the later adopters more." Another trader laughed.

"Each of the associations have their own headquarters here, but Vuzgal has become the most powerful city not ruled by the associations," the first said.

"How can you say that? It is only a tenth the size of some of those headquarter cities."

"It is for now. It has only existed for a few months, but there is still more land for sale and there is plenty room for them to expand," the first trader said wisely.

Matt simply smiled to himself, looking at the construction and the buildings that were rising all over the city by the minute.

"Commander," a girl in the large column of people called out as she pointed to the sky.

Bai Ping looked where she was pointing, shielding his eyes. He saw the pillar sticking into the sky.

Finally.

"If we pick up the pace, we should be there in an hour," he said.

The pillar had been covered by the tree coverage and it was only by chance that the little girl had seen the pillar.

The men and women in the group had relieved looks on their dirt-covered faces.

They had been living in a simple city, Ulinheim, with only a few hundred thousand people. They were the rejects from the different sects. They had neither backing nor innate abilities.

So they had carved out a life for themselves in the inhospitable mountains away from dungeons that drove the people of the Fourth Realm crazy.

They had focused on farming and other simple crafts, selling to passing caravans, or sending people to a nearby city as traders.

Then war broke out in the mountains. Different groups fought one another, and Ulinheim, which was in a pass, was suddenly in the way of an advancing army.

The city of one hundred thousand had been attacked in the night.

Bai Ping had only escaped with his sisters, his uncle, and cousins. His uncle was badly wounded and, being the highest ranked guard, Bai Ping had taken command. They had gathered together as many people as possible and then set off to the east, toward Vuzgal. It was a neutral city. As long as they got there, they could try to find jobs, or they could teleport to other places where they had family members.

Bai Ping's family had all been guards. Each of them was strong, but it was incredibly hard for them to increase the strength of their Body or Mana Gathering Cultivation, so they were dismissed by others. They had been a community pillar in Ulinheim, but now in their group of fourteen hundred, there were just eighty members of the Bai family.

Bai Chang, one of his cousins, jogged up from where she had been guarding.

"Uncle isn't looking well," she said with a look.

"We'll be at Vuzgal soon. We can try to get a healer to look at him there," Bai Ping said.

Hiao Xen let out a heavy sigh as he looked at the Blue Lotus from within his carriage.

The streets had been cleared and repaired; buildings had been torn down or repaired as if they had never been damaged.

He knew that beyond the central district, roads were still being repaired. The buildings weren't being rebuilt, just left. Only the crafting workshops were being repaired, or stripped and their materials used to build other crafting areas of Vuzgal.

Already people are looking to buy more land within the city. Once the auction house is built, we'll start selling off some more tracts of land. The prices have increased dramatically. People are filling up the Wayside Inns. Those who bought land before are holding onto it, preparing to build compounds and manors upon them.

People were running back and forth. There was plenty to be done and only so much time in a day. There were plenty of jobs to be had. The military and the administration of Vuzgal were both recruiting. Even taking on odd jobs for people who were working or living in the city was enough to sustain new people entering the city.

The Vuzgal bank had opened its doors, allowing people to invest their mana stones there and awarding large loans to others. The injection of funds allowed people to quickly create and grow business ventures. New trading houses were working out of the Wayside Inns and renting space along the main roads.

Adventurers came through to go to the dungeons; crafters filled the streets. Each group assisted and drove the others.

They reached the Associations' Circle. It was down the road from the castle compound. The main street ran into a large roundabout park with small shops and secluded areas for one to get away from the busy city. There was even a large pond in the middle of the park.

Around the outside of the roundabout, the main road ran from the castle compound, through the inner city and outer city splitting into the west, north, and eastern roads.

In a circle, one could see the grand buildings: The utilitarian Adventurer's Guild with their main administration building, and attached hostel and store. The Crafter's Association's different segmented buildings, each supporting a symbol for the different associated craft. Their main admin building rested in the middle, with the Crafter's Association emblem carved into its wall.

The Alchemist Association with their compound, their administration building at the front with other buildings visible inside the walled compound. Then there was the Blue Lotus building, created from blue, gold, and white stone—a lotus flower blooming.

Each of them take up a quarter of the area. The size and grandeur of the buildings reflect the power of the administrators and how powerful they think that the area they are in is. These buildings are comparable to the ones you would see for a regional headquarters. I wonder what we'll need to do to get this to an outer headquarters location standard. Hiao Xen smiled to himself, remembering the humble buildings that had been erected when the associations started to arrive. Behind their main fronts were walled compounds for people to stay in from their association. The Crafter's Association's quarters were growing to be as big as their administrative building, with crafters wanting to join in on the trial. They were expending a massive amount of resources to build Expert-level crafting areas to be on the same level as the proposed facilities in Vuzgal and the Crafting trial dungeon.

The front of the Blue Lotus was filled with guards keeping people back and checking invitations.

Hiao Xen's carriage came to a halt.

Everyone looked at the guards sporting their strange armor and helmets. Their new glasses made it hard to see their eyes.

Lieutenant Yui had assigned them to assist Hiao Xen, augmenting his personal guard. They rode on their sleek black panthers, completely armored, with their repeaters mounted on top.

It might be a bit over the top, but it sends a message, and a powerful one.

Hiao Xen stepped out as the guards with him looked around.

People called out as they saw him leave his carriage and walk to the entrance.

Two of the Vuzgal guards followed, scanning the area as they moved. There was something cold and calculating about them—a difference between them and others that made them seem predatory.

Yui and Erik explained that before they took Vuzgal, they had just been Alva adventurers. Then, with taking Vuzgal, since they had a city and they wanted to look good in the eyes of the associations, they called themselves the Alva Army.

Sects have forces as powerful as them, but what group of adventurers coming from the Earth realms could be so powerful? Then there is the matter of just how they took Vuzgal. No one knows how, and they're not talking about it. Though taking the city might explain how they have such high levels. It doesn't explain how they became professional soldiers with high Mana Gathering Cultivation and Body Cultivation, or have so many open mana gates.

Hiao Xen knew that Erik, Rugrat, and their people were keeping secrets from him. That didn't mean he was going to look into them. If they weren't telling him, he trusted there was a good reason not to. They didn't pry into what he knew of the Blue Lotus or push him to use his authority. It was a careful dance and Hiao Xen made sure to do his job and carry out what they asked of him.

He was about to present his invitation when the vice leader of the location personally walked up with a wide smile on her face.

"Manager Hiao, it is good to see you," she said with a light laugh.

Hiao Xen smiled. He could see that she was very good at her job, as he already started to feel comfortable around her. A few months ago, he would have found it hard to get an audience with her. Now she was taking the chance to talk to him, ignoring others.

Hiao Xen cupped his hands in greeting. "Miss Shriver, it is good to see you. I am sorry that I have not been able to see you."

"You are a busy man, running one of the largest cities in the Fourth Realm. I can understand that getting a meeting with you can be incredibly difficult." She gave him a small bow, lower than his, speaking to his new position and she easily looped her arm into his. "Come. I will take you personally to your viewing box."

The guards looked on, unfeeling expressions on their faces. Half of them were originals from the Alva Army; the second half were personal guards Hiao Xen had brought over.

Some of the Alva guards looked over. Miss Shriver lit up the room with a smile and her looks.

They looked away, focused on their job.

Hiao Xen's guards had seen everything, checking her over with professional interest and then checking the surroundings as they were led to a grand elevator built on formations. They rose up, looking out of the elevator over the main lobby.

"Have you told her the truth of the matter?" Hiao Xen's voice dropped as his expression turned conflicted.

"Zhen Fu is a respected Expert-level tailor and she has a large pull with other Experts. After all, everyone needs clothes."

Hiao Xen's expression turned neutral and Miss Shriver tried to look through that expression and find out what he was thinking.

You must treat everyone equally; that was what Erik said. She is an Expert-level crafter so I will have to humor her for this meeting, but we will have to see.

The elevator stopped and Miss Shriver guided him to a door. The guards followed and they studied the guards who stood on either side of the door in front of them.

Miss Shriver walked forward, defusing the tense atmosphere as the door opened for her.

There were a few guards in the back of the room and then a woman sitting in the only chair in the room, smoking something.

Her robes flowed over the chair, dragons and tigers weaving between lilies. They were so vivid that it looked as if they were truly running across the cloth, with the light playing over them.

"Expert Zhen, this is Hiao Xen," Miss Shriver said.

Zhen Fu took another puff of her smoke.

Hiao Xen crossed his arms, frowning as he tucked them into the sleeves of his robes. He had Experts looking for meetings all the time. He ran a city that had no less than ten Experts within it and more who visited regularly.

Bowing to her would not show his impartiality.

Zhen Fu let out a lazy stream of smoke as Miss Shriver continued to bow.

Hiao Xen looked past Zhen Fu and over the massive auction house that the Blue Lotus had created. There were ten floors in total, with the ground floor covered with people talking to one another and greeting their neighbors. Each of the people down there controlled a powerful faction that could be called pillars for any city they decided to settle in. The remaining nine floors were filled with private boxes. The lowest people were city lords of the lowest grade, with the mid- and high-level city lords above them; sect leaders in the third tier to the sixth; with the middle managers of associations in the seventh; with their more powerful figures in the eighth and ninth. On the tenth, there was only one box: the box reserved solely for the leaders of Vuzgal.

Its construction might have only been completed in a few months, but it was the largest auction house that Hiao Xen had been in and the most opulent. He couldn't accurately estimate the cost of the building.

Zhen Fu finally let out an irritated exhale of smoke, giving Hiao Xen an aggravated side eye.

He stopped surveying the auction house and looked back to her, his expression calm.

"You have been rented out to the city lords but you already think that your standing is much higher than before!"

Hiao Xen stood there, her words not affecting him in the slightest.

"I have sent two messengers to your office in order to get access to the dungeon, but they have both been denied. Have you forgotten your roots?" she said in a dangerous tone.

"There are rules in pl—"

"I do not care for your legal speak. Get me access to the dungeon and to the facilities within the castle or else don't blame me for being unkind!" She turned her head to face forward again as she took an irritated puff of her smoke.

"You will have to follow the same process as all others. Just because we share the same background does not mean I can give preferential treatment. I will not tell the city lords about this unless they ask, which is the only grace I can give you. I hope you have a good day, Expert Zhen." He cupped his hands and turned to leave.

Zhen Fu choked on her smoke as she tried to talk.

Hiao Xen got to the door. The two guards there blocked him, their power overbearing and pressuring Hiao Xen.

"Move out of the way or else I'll have you kicked out of Vuzgal," Hiao Xen said to the guards, not showing any weakness to them.

They stood there, as Zhen Fu got herself under control.

Hiao Xen tapped his sound transmission device.

There was a noise outside before the door opened.

The guards looked to the door as the Alva Army guards held their rifles, ready.

"Acting City Lord?" one of the Alva Army asked.

"Meeting ran longer than I thought," Hiao Xen said.

He walked out of the room, and the guards moved out of his way.

"Very good, Hiao Xen, very good!" Zhen Fu said, her fury clear in her words.

"I hope you enjoy the auction, Expert Zhen." Xen left the floor and went to the elevator.

Miss Shriver didn't know what to do. She had an idea of what Zhen Fu wanted when she had recruited Miss Shriver's help.

I didn't think that he would be so unyielding. If he just allowed her access to the workshops and materials in the castle, then he would have gained a supporter. Instead, he slapped her face.

"This Hiao Xen forgets his position. He is only a lowly half manager in the bottom of the Fourth Realm!" Zhen Fu said, letting out her fury and stomping her foot. "It looks like it will come to this elder to teach him the truth of the world!"

Miss Shriver wanted to say something, to calm Zhen Fu and try to de-escalate the situation when she saw movement on the highest floor. Hiao Xen sat in the highest seat in the auction house. An attendant came up, giving him a tea as people in the auction hall all looked to him.

The acting city lord was the most powerful figure within Vuzgal, but it was normally impossible to see him as he was dealing with running the actual city.

Hiao Xen took a tea from an attendant. Seeing the stares and people talking about him, Hiao Xen raised his cup and smiled to them all.

Others bowed and smiled back to him.

Zhen Fu had arrived just a few days ago, but Miss Shriver had been here ever since they found out about the crafter dungeon and the two extra hidden dungeons in the valley.

She had seen Hiao Xen enter the position of acting city lord.

I thought that he was in over his head. But he has been totally neutral in his treatment of everyone. Now, not even the guards from the associations dare to accept a bribe for the fact that they will be kicked out of Vuzgal. The Alva Army is a mysterious organization and the profits as well as the bank have driven people from across the Fourth Realm to call Vuzgal the upcoming trading capital of the Fourth Realm. Is his unwillingness to get into the political games of the associations and running the city a weakness or a strength? I will have to make sure to protect the Blue Lotus. No matter what Zhen Fu decides, this could be seen as a test of sorts to see his resolve.

"There he stands, thinking himself a lord above us all. I, Zhen Fu, will not let anyone stand over me! I might not have fighting strength, but there are plenty who owe me a favor or are willing to act in my stead. Let's see what he does when he draws their ire." Zhen Fu had a malicious look in her eyes. As she smoked, the corners of her mouth curled up into a cruel smile. "Watch—I will play you to death, Hiao Xen. Not even the Blue Lotus will willingly accept you back into our ranks.

"Miss Shriver, get me the names of the Experts in Vuzgal. Hiao Xen will come back, begging for forgiveness on his knees. Power doesn't come from one's skill—it comes from one's ability to move others! You should learn it well." Zhen Fu waved her hand, dismissing Miss Shriver.

Miss Shriver bent lower in her bow before she left. As soon as she was past the guards, a conflicted look appeared on her face.

I don't know what will happen in the future. The Hiao Xen of the Blue Lotus would have done her bidding, but now he refuses to budge. It's said that he might even have the ear of Elder Lu from the headquarters. I need to report this to the manager.

As the sun had lowered, they got closer and closer to the pillar standing over Vuzgal.

Bai Ping felt relief as the road ahead opened up. The trees gave away to cleared ground. It was patchy, with ditches and hills, signs of a battle not long past showing. Closer to the wall, the ground had been leveled out. Mages could be seen walking around with groups of knights, repairing the ground.

Everyone felt relieved seeing the capital.

Why haven't they repaired the walls? It looks as if they're even tearing them down in some places. Bai Ping and the others continued along the road that curved toward the massive gates of the capital.

"Riders!" someone called out from the rear.

"Move to the side to let them pass," Bai Ping said in a tired voice. The fighting, the journey across unknown terrain with fourteen hundred people relying on him, and the pressure started to lift as he continued to march. He could just envision collapsing on his bedroll; even a nice piece of ground would be enough.

Why would there be riders coming all this way? Are they going to Vuzgal as well? Something in the back of his mind made him frown and forget his bedroll.

"Bai Chang, go and get the guards together. Watch those riders," Bai Ping said.

Bai Chang looked as though she wanted to argue. They were in sight of the city, after all. "Yes, Commander." She moved to the rear.

People started to talk in excited voices with one another, repeating rumors that had grown on the journey. They picked up their pace and lifted their feet up.

Why are they taking down their wall? Are they that confident of not having anyone attack them? Bai Ping was still confused as they kept marching.

A blast of light appeared from the rear of the group as the riders attacked with spells and ranged weapons.

"Attackers!" someone yelled as others screamed.

The tide of people sped up as they pushed forward.

"Shit! Everyone, get moving toward the city! Guards, with me!" Bai Ping yelled.

People broke out into a run as they rushed along the road. Some ran over the uneven ground, trying to get away from the riders.

Bai Ping could hear them pleading with the people of Vuzgal to help them. He focused on the rear, seeing the rear guard firing arrows and spells at the riders. They killed a few, but their armor was strong and they were higher levels. Bai Ping's body froze up for a second.

They're going to kill us.

He had to force himself to breathe as he drew his sword.

I'll try to buy them some more time.

He looked at the other guards. They weren't strong, barely as capable as the soldiers of the sect armies, but it was their families and friends who they were protecting.

What was their life if they could save a few more of the villagers they swore to protect?

"With me!" Bai Ping yelled as he charged toward the rear with the guards. They were tired and broken, but they still had their honor and their fighting spirit.

They had been losers all of their life—what was one more loss to them?

"Archers and mages in the rear. Those with spears and shield, up front—cover the road! Swords and melee fighters in the middle!" Bai Ping organized them as they ran. People were hit by arrows from the riders or spells, crying out or just dropping to the ground soundlessly.

Bai Ping yelled louder, trying to not look at those who dropped and drowning out the screams of the wounded.

Sergeant Sun Li was taking a break from training and was on patrol of the outer defenses.

Vuzgal's walls were opened, making it seem to be inviting people in. The pillars that were part of the walls remained and there was a low wall that soldiers could use as cover and fire over. But the fifteen-meter-tall and six-meter-wide walls were now building materials to rebuild Vuzgal's buildings, create the Sky Reaching Restaurants, and the Wayside Inns, and fix the roads and the amenities that ran through the city.

Only when someone got close would they see that in the rise leading up to the small wall, a multi-layered bunker system had been buried into the ground. The tripwires, barbed wire, and obstacles were constantly being worked on. It was a great way to teach the recruits to pay attention and built character with physical jobs.

He passed one of the skeletons that was being fitted with new armor and weapons. Apparently, they would grow in strength with time, but otherwise, better weapons, armor, and concoctions applied to the bones assisted them in the short-term.

They were the backbone of Vuzgal's defense until more recruits were able to become soldiers.

All of them had sworn oaths that would keep their lips sealed, but still none of them had been sent to Alva yet or learned about it.

Until they graduated their course, they were just recruits and could fail out at any time.

The sun was starting to go down and the lights of Vuzgal came on. The city never slept, with crafters working around the clock. Bars and cafes were filled with people from across the Fourth Realm. People celebrated their success or drank away their worries. Agreements were made and trades agreed to. Weary travelers arrived, and others went home.

The Blue Lotus was a hive of activity as the first auction was underway. There wasn't one spare seat in the entire building. Everyone was interested in seeing what the Blue Lotus would bring out.

Sun Li felt as though he were seeing the start of something great, something he couldn't imagine where it was going to go.

He ducked as he passed from one bunker to the next.

"What is that?" one of the sentry teams said as they looked out from the bunker over their heavy repeater position.

"It's moving—a group of people?" the other asked.

Sun Li went up to their position.

"Sarge," one said in greeting.

"As you were," Sun Li said. He used a new spell, enhancing his vision and making it easy to see through the dim dusk light.

He could see the group of tired travelers coming out of the forest from the west. "Looks like refugees from the west. Seems we're going to have a few late-night arrivals. Send word to the reserve force. We'll need their help to process everyone into the city. Must be a few thousand of them."

One of them started to pass a message back through command via sound transmission.

Sun Li was about to head off and gather some soldiers up to help with processing them all. With fifty or so trained military personnel and over two hundred being trained, there was only twenty or so trained military personnel within Vuzgal.

They were spread *thin.* Thankfully, with the undead knights and mages, they had an extra five thousand.

The associations took off some of the stress with their presence and the guards who were there to defend the associations' interests. They wandered the short wall instead of the bunker system.

Fat chance that they'll help. Unless it is a threat to their associations, they won't step out.

Sun Li didn't hate them for it; he understood their position. They had their own orders and priorities. *We need more damn soldiers. Wait, was that a flash?*

He looked over to the group coming along the road. He saw more flashes as people started to run.

Instinctively, he knew that they were being attacked.

"Someone wants to start fighting outside our gates?" Private Lee said, his voice heated.

"Sound the alert." Sun Li raised his sound transmission device to his lips. "Lieutenant Yui, this is Sergeant Sun Li. Message, over."

"Listening. Go on," Yui said back.

They still didn't have radio procedure down completely.

"There is a group of people coming down the western road. They entered the open area in front of Vuzgal. It looks like they are being attacked from the rear. The group is now fleeing across the open fields and down the road. What are your orders?"

"Are they within our borders?" Yui asked.

"Yes, sir," Sun Li said.

Sun Li found himself connected into a command channel.

"I am deploying flying undead to survey the area and give us updates on the battlefield and be ready to engage the enemy at long range. Sergeant Sun Li, you are to take a rifle squad and mount up with mounted undead knights to engage those who are fighting within our lands. Understood?"

"Understood, sir!"

"Sergeant Hall, you will coordinate with the front lines and provide mortar support. If they start running, I want you to chase them right off our road with your mortars. Sergeant Acosta, move to the front lines to take over the management of our line defenses. All other sergeants are to ready their forces to move if necessary. Understood?"

"Understood!" They chorused back.

"Get to work." Lieutenant Yui closed the channel as Sun Li opened another to his squad.

"All right, ladies and gents, form up at the main gate. We have a mission."

He ran through the bunkers. Skeletons that had been working across the city stopped what they were doing and gathered into formations. Those at the walls readied the ballistas they were manning, and scanned the area, looking for threats and acting as sentries that would cut down anything that moved.

Sun Li left the bunker system, running through a trench and up into the dusk.

He opened his beast storage device. His panther appeared and he jumped onto her. He hooked his feet into his stirrups and checked the repeater mounted on her back. He pulled back the dual cocking mechanism, loading the dual heavy repeaters.

He saw the rest of his squad streaming in from their positions, riding their panthers through the streets. People rushed to clear a path as they thundered past. Those who didn't move fast enough, the panthers would jump over, or jump on the walls, leaving marks behind as they rushed forward with their grim-faced riders.

Sun Li looked up as aerial mages shot overhead, gathering mana as they cut across the skies and looked down at the fighting.

From the bunkers and in the city, beasts of all kinds made up of bones appeared, draped in armor. Atop, knights rode; they fell into columns, streaming together as they reached the gates, which were being opened by two massive death knights.

"Corporal Stenbock, is everyone here?" Sun Li asked.

"Just waiting on Webb and Shao. They were posted the farthest away," Stenbock snapped off as her panther pawed the ground.

"Okay, everyone listen up! Make sure that Webb and Shao hear this too!" He raised his voice so that they could all hear him.

"There is a group of people coming from the west road—look like civilians, cannot confirm if they are or not. For some reason, it looks like they were attacked from behind. We do not know if either of these forces are friendly or if this is some kind of ruse. Do not trust anyone other than our people. We have mortar support if we require it. If something feels off, let me know. Stay with your fire team. Make sure you are partnered up! Our objective is to make the two forces disengage from one another. Objectives may change on the battlefield, so listen for new orders. Once we have separated the two forces, then it will be our job to contain and process them if need be, or engage them if they have hostile intent. Understood?"

"Understood!" they replied.

"Good!" Sun Li saw Webb and Shao rounding the corner. He gestured Corporal Stenbock at them. She moved over to them as they started to go through the gates, rows of the undead moving with them in formation.

Hiao Xen had invited the leaders and people of high standing and power from Vuzgal to meet and join him on the tenth level, allowing them to talk to one another easily.

The lights in the auction house dimmed. Hiao Xen looked down on the stage. Everyone moved to their seats as the auctioneer, an older man with a refined bearing, stepped onto the stage.

"Hello, everyone, and welcome to the first auction hosted by the Blue Lotus in Vuzgal. Today we have brought out some of the finest items I have laid eyes on to commemorate the event!"

People clapped, their eyes glowing as the older man smiled calmly.

"We shall start with the first item!"

A cart was rolled out onto the stage as Hiao Xen got a sound transmission.

Who is sending me a—

"Lieutenant Yui?" Hiao Xen asked, his brows locking together.

"There is a group of refugees headed for Vuzgal. They were attacked as they entered the area outside of Vuzgal. Sergeant Sun Li is leading his rifle squad and supporting mounted undead to sort out the situation and if needed, render support," Yui reported.

Hiao Xen wanted to say something to dissuade him. After all, they were the guarding force of Vuzgal; if they got into a fight to look after some refugees, then people might look on them badly. Though he also knew that although Yui was technically under his command, on something like this, Erik and Rugrat would back him fully.

"Let me know if I can be of any help," Hiao Xen said.

"Will do. Yui out."

We can spin it to show our strength and show that no one is allowed to fight on our land without our say-so. That way, people won't think we're soft. I will have to look into the refugees. We can't take in people who aren't willing to do any work when there are people trying to enter Vuzgal paying tens of Earth mana stones. Though it could help with the recruiting work if people who are looked down on by other groups come to Vuzgal to do our tests. I should think about putting up testing centers in other cities—maybe talk to the associations about it?

The Fourth Realm was a violent place. Even knowing that there was a fight going on outside of the city, Hiao Xen had confidence in the Alva Army to protect the city, so he dismissed it from his mind. That was Yui's area of expertise; his was completing the tasks he had been given by Erik and Rugrat.

Bai Ping let out a yell, sidestepping a fellow guard to land a hit on the rider's beast.

The beast let out a pained cry and tilted away from the attack. Its rider swung their spear, striking the other guard and sending them flying to the side as their mount plowed into another guard, who let out a scream as they rushed on by.

Bai Ping didn't have time to look as he hacked at another mounted rider and hit them. The power from their charge turned his sword, making him grunt in pain as his shoulder informed him it was no longer located in his socket.

"You have entered the territory of Vuzgal. Place down your weapons or you will be fired upon. You have ten seconds to comply!" A man's voice cracked through the air.

Bai Ping turned and looked where it had come from. He saw an army from hell. Undead riders with their glowing eyes rushed down the road and came out across the plains to encircle the civilians who had fled, as well as the attackers.

Do they think that we are trying to attack them? Bai Ping thought in fear.

The commander of the attacking mounted forces altered their direction, moving to clash with the undead.

"Anyone who dares to interfere will be destroyed!" the commander yelled back. As his people formed up and charged forward, Bai Ping's heart dropped.

He knew just how strong that army was. They had gone through the shield and spear guards that made the rear guard without pausing, killing guards with a flash of a blade or the jab of a spear.

Bai Ping and his guards had maybe killed ten of the mounted attackers; they had killed nearly fifty guards, killing civilians as if they were annoying flies.

They don't see us as a threat. If they can finish off the Vuzgal force, then they can kill us without issue.

"Time's up." The Vuzgal commander's voice was emotionless and there was a noise from above.

Bai Ping looked up to see undead mounts coming from the sky. Mages, who had prepared spells already, released them upon the charging attackers. The road was turned into a hell.

Meteors formed and shot into the attackers, exploding into flames and rocks. Shards of ice rained down. Lightning moved like a snake through the clouds above, causing the road to explode. In seconds, the organized group of attackers was in chaos.

Smoke covered the battlefield as the spells reaped lives. The attackers diverted, trying to spread into the woods to the north and the open ground to the south to get off the road.

The formation of undead had opened up at some point and a force on panthers was revealed. Bai Ping could see it as he was on the side of the road, but those on the road couldn't see the force.

Bai Ping's stomach dropped at the smooth flow of movements and organization as weapons on top of the panthers fired again and again. Large bolts shot into the clearing smoke, cutting down mounted attackers.

The smoke cleared as the Vuzgal mounted forces, human and undead, cut through the mounted attackers. As the smoke cleared and they were being torn apart by the Vuzgal guards, the attackers had lost all of their morale and now turned and ran as fast as they could, looking to escape.

They rushed down the road, avoiding everyone. Bai Ping saw the fear in their eyes, a complete change from the disdain and confidence they had when cutting through his group.

"Put your weapons on the ground and wait to be seen to. Emergency medical aid will be provided. Again, put down your weapons or we'll take off the limb holding it," the man said.

Bai Ping looked to the other guards, all of them silently asking him what to do.

He tossed his blade on the ground.

They gritted their teeth and did the same.

Now we just see what the people of Vuzgal are like.

They were separated into groups. There were people among the army who used different healing spells and items they had to put the wounded together and patch them up.

The smaller cities wouldn't be willing to try to heal them, only move them to the side of the road so they didn't clog it up.

Skeletons acted as guards, each of them standing like statues. But when given orders by the Alva Army, they moved to obey.

They cleared the battlefield and started to work on the road. Some dug dirt; others packed it down.

The army moved systematically, dealing with the wounded first as another group interviewed the refugees according to what they wanted to do. They were given different passes accordingly.

The wounded were all stabilized, with even those who were on death's door recovering. Still, there were nearly a thousand people who had been killed by the riders.

"Bai Ping?" a woman asked, looking at the group of people that Bai Ping was part of.

Bai Ping's stomach tightened but he stood up, the guards looking over as the woman checked the sheet of information that she had.

"Follow me," she said.

He did so, reaching a man who sat on a chair. A large panther lay down lazily behind him.

He petted the panther, which cracked an eyelid to look at Bai Ping before closing it again, looking at something more interesting in the forest.

The man pulled out a chair and put it on the ground. "Thanks, Corporal," the man said.

"Sir," the corporal said and left.

The man waved to the chair.

That voice—is he the leader of this group? The one who was yelling at the riders?

"Bai Ping." The man looked him over.

Bai Ping didn't feel as though there was much of an age difference between them, but something about the movements of the other man, something in his eyes added years to him and made Bai Ping think that he was a dangerous man to cross.

"Your city destroyed, family broken, you took three days to collect people from the city, gathering fourteen thousand people and struck out for Vuzgal. Nearly two weeks of hard marching, with everyone a low level and the weakest of those in the Fourth Realm, many of which who aren't even level thirty, but were stuck in this realm because of their birth." The commander let out a mirthless laugh.

"You know, in the lower realms, everyone thinks that being born in a higher realm gives everyone an unfair advantage. They forget the part where everyone is born at level one. That, yes, in the higher realms it is easier to get more resources and that the higher mana will make one's body a bit stronger. It also means that more children die who are not from the groups that have the resources, the mana and the environment so harsh that they can't survive for more than a few years. First Realm or the Fourth, you need resources in order to get stronger. Few of the people in your city had enough money to get enough Stamina concoctions or ingredients. Even if they wanted to, how could they descend to the lower realms to live a comfortable life?" The man let out a sigh and sat forward, shifting his armor around without conscious thought.

"My name is Sergeant Sun Li. I would like to offer you a job."

Bai Ping choked up as he nodded, unable to speak. He had seen the might of the man on the battlefield.

"Join the Vuzgal army. Training will take three months, but you'll be well cared for, with food and shelter. We're looking for more recruits right now," Sun Li said.

"Why?" Bai Ping choked out.

"Why? Good question. Mostly because it takes balls to do what you did. You could have left everyone behind but you didn't. I don't care about your strength or your ability. That can be learned or increased with time. What matters is character. You seem like the kind of person who has the right stuff. Vuzgal might be the chance that you all need. We are recruiting people to be taught all of the crafting professions, the military, administration, and countless other jobs needed to run the city."

"Wouldn't we bring shame with how weak we are?" Bai Ping asked.

Sun Li smiled and then started to laugh before he snorted and fell into a sigh.

Bai Ping didn't know how to react and just sat there, his anxiety growing, thinking he had pissed off Sergeant Sun Li.

"There was a time that I was weaker, *much* weaker than you are now. Levels, cultivation—they take work, but with the army, you at least have a guide and information on how to increase both."

Bai Ping sunk into thought as Sun Li pulled out a piece of paper, a contract.

On it were terms listed for joining the Vuzgal army.

"Think it over," Sun Li said.

Bai Ping took this as his dismissal. He bowed to Sergeant Sun Li and then headed back to the group of people he was with.

He shared what he knew as group by group went to the border officers, a strange group of people who asked what they were doing, where they were staying and so on. There were also recruiters. These people worked to find them a job suitable for those who were interested.

Bai Ping stood in front of one of the recruiters and passed them the contract Sergeant Sun Li had passed him, with his sign on it.

"You'll report to Barracks E for testing. Here is a tag for the apartment you will be allowed to use. While you are training, your family can use this. If you fail out of training, then the premises are to be cleared out in forty-eight hours." The recruiter pulled out pieces of paper and information.

"Understood," Bai Ping said.

"Good luck," the recruiter said with meaning, passing him the papers. "Next!"

8 Adjusting to New Roles

Lord Aditya looked over Vermire. It had never been more prosperous. *I've never been so at ease. Even if someone was to challenge us, I find it hard to understand how we would lose. We used to accept all the people who came to our outpost; now we can pick them and are removing the cancers in the outpost. The people are stronger than ever. With the best of the new people being sent to Alva, then the power backing us only grows.*

Aditya touched his hand to the letter that was inside his jacket.

"You called?" A woman's voice came from behind Aditya.

He turned to see one of his "guards." She didn't look special, rather unremarkable, which was the best for her position. She was the person in charge of the information collected from Vermire and its sources.

"Miss Evernight, I was wondering if I could pass this to you." Aditya took out the letter from inside his jacket and passed it to her.

She frowned and then opened the letter. Her expression changed. It was the only time that Aditya had seen that happen and took it as a small victory.

"Well, this explains why you have opened lines of communication with the other outposts. We knew something was going on."

Aditya smiled. *If they didn't trust me, then they would already know the contents of our meetings. They must trust me more to not keep me under complete observation.*

Aditya straightened up a bit. "If we can unite the outposts and create an outpost or even a camp in the middle of the Beast Mountain Range, it would consolidate our power. It would allow us greater access to the other outposts. Over a period of time, it would be possible to make their strength ours."

"You don't think that they will fight back?"

"Some might, but our strength is much higher now," Aditya said simply.

Evernight smiled. It was a cold thing.

"Seems that you have been putting the cultivation resources and weapons to good use. I will have to pass this information to my leaders for confirmation. What resources will you require?"

"Information on the different outposts would be helpful so we know what we're dealing with—who are backed by which powers, which will come to our side, what it will require for others to join us. For the military side of things, we should have that covered at this time. The guards have tripled in size and strength. Unlike most people in the Ten Realms, they have created their foundations and gained Body of Stone and cultivated their mana into Vapor."

The woman studied Aditya and then nodded. "I will pass your request on. Is there anything else?"

"No," Aditya said.

She bowed her head to him and left without a backward glance.

Aditya had a bitter smile on his face. He was looking to impress these people but he didn't know whether it even registered to them. *There was a time that I wondered whether they were using the dark arts on those people, until I saw them working in the healing house. To go from simple farmers and people without anything, to healers capable of dealing with the worst wounds in just a few months...what kind of monsters are they?*

Instead of feeling scared when thinking about them, he could only smile as he tapped his foot against the floor.

He might call them monsters but they had taken him down a path he never thought he would be able to step upon.

I wonder what their plan is for me.

Erik turned in his chair, cracking his back. Rugrat was down in the Metal floor still, working with the different smiths and crafters checking over the different resources on the Metal floor. From alchemists and tailors to smiths and formation masters, everyone wanted to see the new floor.

"Looks like we'll have to build some more infrastructure down there. The lighting situation is a bit of a pain. We'll need to add in a day and night cycle like with the first floor if there are going to be people living down there." Erik read the report from a team of people from the academy and the council who were sent down to assess the floor. The military was down there too, but they had different priorities. "Sounds like a job for the blueprint office."

Erik smiled and shook his head. *I never thought that I would have a city's worth of resources at my beck and call.*

He wrote on light-paper, sending a message to the blueprint office.

He checked the pile of reports and picked up the next one on his desk. "No wonder Rugrat stayed down on the Metal floor to assess it. He didn't want to do all of the paperwork."

There was a knock at his door, interrupting his line of thought.

He looked up and put the folder down. "Come in."

The door opened and Delilah smiled to him, shutting the door behind her.

"Delilah, what can I help you with?" Erik smiled. He felt bad for having dropped her off in Alva, and then when he returned, he'd had Egbert make her the head of the entire dungeon.

Though that kind of was Elise's idea, he reasoned with himself.

"Teacher, I think we need to talk about roles." Delilah's smile slipped and her expression turned serious.

"Okay." Erik sat up. She might be his student but she had stepped into her role as the council leader well.

"You need to leave more things to the rest of us," Delilah said.

Erik made to open his mouth but she stopped him with a look.

"You and Rugrat have been so concentrated on different parts of Alva, you have not been able to develop yourselves," Delilah said.

Erik opened his mouth and closed it.

I want to increase my strength; I have new ideas for how to increase the speed that I work on concoctions. I have a good amount of medical knowledge, but that doesn't mean I am an amazing healer. I need to take my time and check what I know from Earth to what works in the Ten Realms. Then there is cultivation. I have my Body Cultivation but now I am using firearms—should I increase my Mana Gathering Cultivation instead? Though Vuzgal is undeveloped, there is so much loot, information, and resources that has just been added to Alva. Everything is growing.

"You and Rugrat are the leaders of Alva and you will always be. But that doesn't mean that you need to be here all the time and it doesn't mean that you need to manage everything all of the time. You have us here for that. We are the people who take your ideas and turn them into reality. Will we mess up? Probably. Though we need your strength to advance, the military can train people up. Once you have laid down the foundations, then they can grow. With you two, if you can go to the higher realms and bring back more information and more resources, then Alva will grow off that."

"I never thought that I would be leading a city or that I would have a dungeon under my command. It kind of just happened. I feel like we're just dropping this all on to you—the council, the people of Alva—and it doesn't feel right," Erik said.

"It might not feel right, but you are Alva's strength. The stronger that you get, the further that you go, the further you can pull all of us along. We need you and Rugrat to be our guiding lights. You lead and we will follow. Does that mean you should go off right now and try to ascend all of the realms in a mad sprint? No. It means that you shouldn't be worried about us when you are out there looking to increase your strength. We need time to consolidate. We have made a lot of gains, but it shouldn't hold you and Rugrat back. What is the use of the academy of having all of these people around you if you don't use us?"

Erik frowned and let out a breath through his nose. Delilah started to fidget nervously before Erik spoke again.

"I can't say that I like it, but I can understand it. Rugrat and I weren't high-ranking officers or leaders; we were just basic soldiers. We're used to being hands-on with those under our command. We know how to train people to be soldiers, but we need the leadership to grow themselves." Erik let out a heavy breath and laughed, feeling tired and also as if a big weight had dropped from his shoulders. But it was replaced with a new worry.

Delilah seemed to deflate. It seemed as though asking Erik all of this had taken a lot out of her.

He smiled, knowing that she was looking out for him and for the future of Alva.

"You've grown a lot while I've been gone," Erik said with a self-deprecating laugh.

Delilah smiled beautifully as Erik's now relaxed mind started to work.

"We'll do as you say."

Delilah nodded. "So what will you do then?"

"Now that I'm not commanding the Earth floor operation, you're already trying to find things for me to do?" Erik asked with a smile.

Delilah rolled her eyes and shook her head. "You know what I mean!"

Erik chuckled and picked up a pen, letting it slide through his fingers and the base hit the desk before he picked it up and repeated the process.

"My mana pool is currently too small right now for me to open my final mana gate. Though, with tempering my body, I can increase my durability; then, using different pills, mana stones, and the dungeon core, I should be able to open my fourteenth mana gate.

"To temper my body and reach Body Like Sky Iron, I need to temper myself with the Earth element. So I need to wait until the Earth floor is open, or go and find some pills and concoctions to complete it. I fight with my fists but the more I do, the more I'm realizing that I can't match the people in the Ten Realms.

"So, that means I need a combat instructor and I need to increase my Alchemy abilities.

"Elan Silaz needs time to work on developing information sources, see if we can find any more people from Earth. I feel like I'm saying Earth a lot. Then there's also the factor of increasing our number of crafters and the level of people in Alva. Which also falls to Elan Silaz to act as our purchaser of monster cores so people have access to cores they can use to increase their levels. The military have a lot of short-term gains with fighting and killing creatures, but the crafters have a lot of long-term gains working on their craft. It will take them longer, but breaking through certain crafting bottlenecks, they'll be able to increase their level dramatically. We can use the Trader's Guild and the Adventurer's Guild in the different realms to also help the crafters increase their levels, take them out on level-grinding parties."

"It will cost us a lot," Delilah said.

"We make the options available to them—it is up to them whether they take them or not. Private companies can add it into their recruitment. Say they need a trader for the Fourth Realm. They just say that they must be at least level twenty and they will boost them the rest of the way. It's like how someone joining the Alva military doesn't have a level requirement, but we will increase their Mana Gathering and Body Cultivation so that they can deal with the training and so that they will all be pushed up to the same level when they begin training. Before, that cost was high, but as we have learned more, most basic medics can do the cultivation increases. We've grown Alva—now it's time we let our people spread out and solidify their gains."

"What about the Fifth Realm?" Delilah asked.

"It will be there at the end of the day, but we have time on our side. We can wait and see what Elan can learn before we challenge it," Erik said.

"Okay," Delilah said.

"How has your Alchemy been going?"

"It's progressed. With the access to resources and the rooms, I use it to relax. The systems of Alva are improving to take the load off one person and spread it out a bit more," Delilah said with a wry smile.

"What level have you reached now in your Alchemy?"

"Level sixty-seven," Delilah said modestly, but Erik didn't miss the pride in her eyes.

I'm still level seventy. I've been making concoctions that work instead of trying to expand my abilities. Old Hei said that with assisting him in making that concoction, I needed to work much harder to increase in level once again. After all, Expert is only five levels away.

Erik called up his own skill.

Skill: Alchemy

Level: 70 (Journeyman)

Able to identify 1 effect of the ingredient.

Ingredients are 5% more potent.

I have been stagnant for too long. I need to work on my skills. If I can achieve Expert, who knows what I might get for a reward. The concoctions that I could make!

Erik laughed. "It looks like you're right. I haven't been focusing on my skills and personal strength—my student is able to kick my ass already!"

He gave Delilah a wink. "So, would you be interested in meeting your grand teacher?"

"Grand teacher?" Delilah asked, confused.

"He's much more powerful than me in Alchemy, but he'll take any excuse to get away from his duties and work on new concoctions and Alchemy!" Erik smiled.

Blaze looked at the men and women in front of him, studying them all and being studied by them. Each of them were a higher level than him, but there was no disrespect or disdain in their eyes as other high-level people in the Ten Realms might look down on him.

Some of them were stationed in Vuzgal, some in Alva. With the totem, they were able to come down to complete training.

"You have all been selected to participate in the leadership course. I will be overseeing the course, but your teachers will be Acting Lieutenant Blaze, First Sergeant Rugrat, and Major West. An officer in the Alva military is different than the role that officers play in other militaries. They are not only the overruling power and leader—they are the teacher of the unit. You will all be acting officers until you complete your training to be scouts, mortar operators, mages, engineers, medics, and members of the close protection detail. *If* you do not perform as needed in your training for these different roles, you will be stripped of your officer ranking, dropped down to a noncommissioned ranking in line with what you have been taught so far, and only when you have completed your courses will you be able to apply to become an officer once again.

"You are being given one hell of an opportunity here. If you complete all of your training and there are no major screw-ups, then you will become officers, with a probationary period of six months, where you will be reviewed and checked to make sure you can carry out the duties of your rank. All others will need to claw their way through training to gain the rank of sergeant. Then, as they reach first sergeant, they will go to officer school to train to be an officer. You're jumping several steps so the slightest screw-up, the slightest issue, you will be busted back down and will need to redo." Glosil looked at the men and women there. All of them stood straighter, brimming with fighting spirit.

He's become more of a leader, certainly more of a hard-ass, but if they screw up, there are lives on the line. Blaze hid a smile, impressed with Glosil's growth.

He nodded to the people in the ranks and then marched around and joined the formation, creating a stir.

"Looks like everyone is here for the course," Blaze said in a loud voice, pulling their attention back onto him. "It is my job to make sure that you are ready to lead troops. I will teach you basic tactics, how to position your forces, how to create a battle plan, and pull your shit together when you actually meet the enemy and have to adjust everything on the fly. How to work with them and be a leader. Captain Glosil will be assisting me in teaching you combat tactics based upon your new weaponry and skills. First Sergeant Rugrat and Major West will work with you to incorporate all of the assets within your units. You will be training here in Alva and in Vuzgal. Once we have completed training, you will be tested, commanding real troops in battlefield simulated situations, defensive and offensive. Once you have all been tested, you may be qualified to become an officer or dropped back down to noncommissioned officers to retest."

Blaze looked at them.

"Okay, gather around. The first class will be on positioning. Positioning yourself and those under your command is key to winning the battle. Knowing where one another is prevents you from attacking your own people and can allow you to react faster and more effectively when you are in combat."

Delilah sat in her office, looking over an urgent message.

There was a knock at the door.

"Elan Silaz to see you, Council Leader," her secretary reported.

"Allow him in," Delilah said. She didn't get up from her desk as Elan walked into the room.

She had met him in a perfunctory sense, but that meeting had been hosted by Erik. Now Elan was reporting to her. He was nearly three times older than her but she was the senior. It was an odd feeling as she knew his daughter and sons all held high positions as well.

It doesn't matter the person's position; their character and their ability matter more. She remembered Erik's words, made bolder by the faith that he, Rugrat, the council, and the people of Alva placed in her. She sat up and looked at Elan.

Her aura was peaceful and calming. She had only opened ten of her mana gates, but she had formed her core as well, slowly compressing more mana. It gave her something to do when she was working as the council leader. It gave her an otherworldly air.

Elan stepped into the room and bowed to her.

"Please, take a seat." She held out a piece of paper.

Elan took it and then sat down.

She waited for him to read the letter completely.

"Lord Aditya, while not completely trusted at this time, has proved his loyalty time and time again. He has tied his outpost to our Alva, acting as our agent. The relationship was rocky to start but it has grown stronger with time. Are you up to date with the information in the First Realm?"

"I might be lacking in some respects, but I have a good understanding," Elan said.

"Very well. I do not. What do you think will happen if we act out this plan?" Delilah didn't want to appear as if she did know what was going on, or else she might miss a key part.

"He wants to gather all of the outpost leaders together and then form this city in the middle of the Beast Mountain Range. It will stir things up. There will be those for it, against it, and neutral. It will give us a more complete understanding of the outposts around the Beast Mountain Range. Then, with clearing out the Beast Mountain Range, people might come together or they might fall out—same when forming the central outpost. People are greedy. There will be a lot of interests involved. Some of the outposts are part of nations, or other groups. Some of them are independent. Whoever controls the outpost city will become the leader of the connected outposts, in a large way. There are a lot of things that can go wrong, a lot of subterfuge that can happen." Elan held his chin. "Which I think is the reason that he has asked for our help."

Delilah moved her head to the side, allowing Elan to clear his thoughts.

"Right now he hasn't said anything to anyone. This is just a plan that he has and he's seeking approval as well as intelligence resources on the other outposts. We have decent coverage on the other outposts. If we focus on developing more sources in key positions, we can know what the outpost leaders are thinking. We have the advantage of surprise: we find out their weaknesses, know about their fighting forces, how each of the outposts operate."

"How does this help his plan?" Delilah interrupted.

"The more we know about the outposts, the greater reach we have. It allows us to use different methods to influence this plan. We can bribe, blackmail, and guide people into an alliance with Vermire. Then, using those same people again, we can merge those outposts with Vermire, taking everything."

"Building the outpost in the middle of the Beast Mountain Range is not the goal—controlling the outposts is. If they're focused on the outpost being built, then they won't think about themselves. We use it as a way to flush out the outpost leaders, use it as a test to see what they really think. Bring the rats out," Delilah said.

"Right." Elan smiled, pleased with her leap in judgement.

"Okay, so we will need to develop information assets in these different outposts to get to know what these outpost leaders are thinking. Then we give Aditya the go-ahead to start meeting with outpost leaders." Delilah studied Elan, making a decision. "At the same time, present names to my secretary of people from your trading house who you think would be assets to Alva. We need to grow and rapidly. I will not accept people trying to make competing groups that create friction."

Elan had a grave look on his face, looking at Delilah. Even at three times younger than him, she had a presence that he had only faced a few times before.

"I will present names to them shortly. I will only pick those I think will be loyal to Alva first."

Delilah held his eyes for a few more seconds, as if weighing his character. "Good. You may leave. Keep me updated." She turned to the papers on her desk once again.

9 Crafter's Path

"So what are you going to do?" Rugrat asked Erik as they walked out of Alva and toward the barracks on the outskirts.

"I'm going to head to the Third Realm. If I want to advance my cultivation, then I'm going to need to make some powerful concoctions." Erik smiled. "What are you going to do?"

"Vuzgal! Isn't it the best place for crafters, after all? I think with Tan Xue there, we can bring over some more smiths from across the Fourth Realm. With the workshops and the materials, I'm excited." Rugrat grinned.

"How does Taran feel about being left behind to run the smithing department?" Erik asked.

Rugrat coughed, looking a bit embarrassed. "I'm sure he'll be fine with learning the secrets of the Metal floor. We've only touched the surface, and he has all of Tan Xue's notes, Expert-level blueprints, and then the Expert-level workshop all to himself."

"Have you asked him or Tan Xue?"

"Nope."

Erik let out a tired sigh.

"You might want to do that before you kidnap one and force the other into their old job."

"He ran the whole academy for a while, they'll be fine," Rugrat said.

"So you think that he's going to reach Expert in smithing before you?"

Rugrat snorted. "He can try! I've got five barrels of Alva shine on the line."

The corner of Erik's mouth lifted as he shook his head. "When are you heading to Vuzgal?"

"In a few days." I have to talk to the two of them first, want to take Taran up there to take a look around if he can get the free time, before he takes over as the head of smithing in Alva. I talked to Jia Feng, she's getting a group of crafters together to fill out our ranks.. A lot of people who left Alva searching for information and experience are congregating on Vuzgal now." Rugrat yawned and stretched.

"I had heard that people were buying monster cores like crazy," Erik said.

"Yeah, Elan has been doing a swift business, got his hands on a few Earth-grade Mortal cores. They're only up to the lesser level, but still they cost nearly thirty mana stones down here. Boosting one's level with monster cores is no cheap thing. Though most of the crafters' expenses are low and the money they make is high, so although it's difficult, it's not impossible for them to purchase the monster cores."

"Yeah, I grabbed a set of them. We only consumed up to the Mortal common monster cores. I kept at least one Mortal greater, grand, and variant grade core and got an Earth lesser and common core. I haven't reached a bottleneck right now, but they might come in use." Erik pulled out a box.

"What is this?" Rugrat asked.

"I got you monster cores as well. I knew that you would forget otherwise," Erik said.

Rugrat coughed, an awkward look on his face as he took them.

"Were you just feeding them to George?" Erik asked as a thought struck him.

"Well, he's a good boy and I didn't think I had much use for them…" Rugrat trailed off.

Erik opened his mouth and then closed it, thinking of the monster cores he had purchased for Gilga.

Never mind, best not to try to think of how much I spent on treats, uh, monster cores.

Erik cleared his throat as they reached Glosil's office in the barracks and knocked on the door. Rugrat put the box away and stood straighter.

"Enter," Glosil called from beyond the door.

They walked in and Glosil looked up.

His expression cleared, seeing it was them.

"Don't worry, just here for a casual chat." Erik stopped him from standing and saluting. "How are things going?" he asked as he and Rugrat took seats in front of his desk.

"I have been collecting information on the Alva Earth floor." He let out a sigh. "The formations are busted to hell. We were able to bring more of them online once we fired up the main command formation on the Metal floor." Glosil pressed his lips together and put a map on the table. "Still, it's not much."

"Do we know, roughly, what level the creatures are down there?" Rugrat asked.

"Twenties to low forties. Increasing the upper limit just due to our limited information. Going to create a beachhead camp and then advance from there, bring the formations online to gather more information before pushing forward."

"Sounds like a good plan. How is training and the reorganization of the military going?" Erik asked.

"In two weeks, the first class in Vuzgal will graduate—just over two hundred new privates. A new class will start right afterward. The staff in Alva will finish training the two hundred recruits here and then be shifted to Vuzgal to train the excess recruits we have there. Yesterday, Tiger Company completed their training and are all scout qualified. Next week, Rugrat will be taking command of the officer training class from Blaze." Glosil looked to Rugrat, who nodded.

"Blaze, Erik, and I sat down and confirmed the training schedule."

"They won't like us, but they'll have earned their spots," Erik added.

"I look forward to it, seeing as I'm in the class," Glosil muttered.

"You volunteered and it shows that you're willing to learn—sets a good example and makes you closer with the rest of the officers," Erik said.

"If the training ends in Vuzgal in two weeks, doesn't that mean that their vets will start training as medics, engineers, and mages?"

"That is correct. In a month, we will be able to have people trained to fill the positions of a combat company, minus the close protection detail. It won't be full, but we'll have the skeleton."

"Someone sounds eager." Erik chuckled.

"Well, it looks like you have things in hand." Rugrat slapped his hands on his legs to a random beat. "I will be heading up to Vuzgal tomorrow."

"I will be heading up to the Third Realm and then heading to Vuzgal to take over the officer training."

"We will be executing our attack on the Earth floor in three days with Dragon Company." Glosil checked his paperwork.

"Looks like we've got plenty to keep us busy," Rugrat said.

"And keep some of us out of trouble," Erik added.

Elan sat down in the bar. He wore simple trader's clothing, his face dirtied up. A smile appeared on his face.

"Good to see you. It's been too long," he said with a laugh, reaching out his hand.

The other trader followed along and laughed. "The days fly by when you're on the road!"

A barmaid came over, smiling as she saw the two traders reunited. "Drinks or food?"

"Two of your Jales, please." Elan tossed out a silver coin.

The girl snatched it up and hid it in her sleeve with a wide smile. "Coming up!" She rushed off.

Elan looked at the other trader. It was their first time meeting, but the trader was someone who people from Alva had cultivated into an information source. "You have something for me?"

"Everything seems calm right now. There are a few nations that are looking to insert trading companies that they own into Vermire to take over trading and then the city." He laughed and patted Elan on the shoulder.

Elan laughed as the drinks came back and the girl put them down.

"Let me know if you need anything else!" she said with a bright smile and left.

The two of them grabbed their smoky glasses filled with what looked to be clear water. They cheered and took a drink of the refreshing drink that tasted remarkably like fruit.

"Dangerous, that," Elan said as the man passed him a bundle of scrolls. Elan took it into his storage ring.

"That's when you know it's the good stuff," the trader said, his eyes scanning around. "There are talks of some of the healing houses moving to other outposts to pull people away from Vermire as well."

Elan seemed to weigh the information as he took another slow drink, watching the trader out of the corner of his eye.

He didn't say anything else, watching Elan nervously.

Elan took out a clear potion bottle covered in runes. The potion was red, with golden flakes that were stirred up with the slightest movement. "This should help your grandson," Elan said.

The man looked at the potion. Even as a veteran trader, he didn't seem to believe what he was looking at. "How?" he started. But then he looked at Elan and shook his head, a self-deprecating smile on his face. "I know better than to ask."

Elan nodded as he reached out more; the trader took the potion under the table and then grabbed the drink, taking a deep gulp.

Elan passed over his sound transmission mark. "If you hear anything else, let me know. There are plenty of rewards that might be hard to find in the First Realm," Elan said with meaning.

"You have my word," the trader said.

Elan smiled, the serious atmosphere dissipating as he raised his glass. "To your grandson and your family's health!"

"And to yours as well!" The trader's smile was now totally genuine as they clinked glasses and finished off their drinks.

Elan headed through Vermire. Once he had become a person of Alva, Vermire was like his backyard. Lord Aditya didn't hide anything from him.

Elan had taken control over all of the spies Lord Aditya had raised, then those from the different Alva traders, and the Adventurer's Guild.

The information network was vast, so his last few weeks had been spent going through the totem. He had gone to the Second Realm before, but it was his first time going to the Third Realm. What was something that he thought he wouldn't be able to do in his life had almost become an everyday norm.

The Adventurer's Guild and the traders in the higher realms had created extensive information networks. Most of them were looking for jobs, but a few of them had access to information that was useful to Alva. That would allow them to advance their reach and their ability, or escape issues that might appear.

Seems that more people are looking to gain some control over Vermire now that they've seen that they can be a powerful player.

He moved through different alleyways. Using the formations in the city, he could tell that there was no one following him. Still, he changed his appearance twice, a skill he had learned from some shadowy figures.

Then he reached the lord's manor as Elan Silaz. He presented his documents and was allowed in. He waited for some time before he was admitted to Lord Aditya's office.

Lord Aditya's leg had been healed long ago and even more than that, he was now walking down the path to temper his body. He might have gone against Alva unknowingly in the beginning, but now he was one of their most loyal subjects.

"So, how does the recruiting go? I heard that you were able to find some Apprentice-level crafters not long ago."

Both men would have been stunned with these words not long ago.

"Don't you find it strange when talking about Apprentice crafters as if they're common cabbages?"

"Get used to it." Aditya shrugged.

"Finding Apprentice crafters in the First Realm isn't easy. Thankfully the only requirement is motivated people, which are a lot easier to find." Elan pulled out the scrolls he had gotten from the trader and put them out on the table between two couches.

"What's this?" Aditya asked.

"A potential problem, kind of." Elan started to read the documents, looking at the files that contained information on the healing houses first, and waving for Aditya to join him.

Aditya took the files on the different trading conglomerates and their actions, as well as different healing houses that outposts were talking to.

The two of them fell into silence for some time.

"Those ungrateful pricks," Aditya said as he flipped pages.

"Hmm?" Elan asked, his eyes not leaving the scroll in his hand.

"There are a few traders who are trying to get their leaders to move in on the other outposts in the area, to have them take over and then create direct competition with us. They're gathering support. Then there are other traders who are offering to increase their prices when dealing with us for goods like food. Otherwise, we can't support our people. If they increase the prices, then others will do the same. At that point, people might question if I was to try to buy food from Alva, wondering where I got it from."

"You have stocks of food here, though, right?"

"Yes, enough for the original Vuzgal to survive a year on. But now, with the new population increase, it would only last for four or five months," Aditya said.

"Let them increase their prices. People will be angry and pissed off, then you privately sell your stock, for the people. Show that you want what is best for them and you're selling your own stock at only a slightly higher price than before. They will look like robbers taking advantage of Vermire's people and be driven out, while your popularity will increase among the people of Vermire," Elan said.

"Well—" Aditya thought it over before he let out a small laugh. "When it comes to things like business, I've still got a lot to learn!"

Elan smiled.

Aditya realized that he was a frog at the bottom of his well, but he was actively looking to improve the way that he dealt with things. He was still a young man by Ten Realms standards.

"They're also looking to add additional taxes for anyone who comes from our direction because of the threat to their people on the roads and having to put out their soldiers to clear the trade routes. Some are directly looking for the militaries to pressure us. Now, the pressuring us with the military won't work, because we're a neutral ground for all nations. If the military tries to pressure us, then the other nations will quietly but firmly show their displeasure," Aditya said.

Elan took a few minutes, finishing the line he was reading before replying. "Are you trying to impress us with your plan to make a trading city in the middle of the Beast Mountain Range?" Elan looked up at Lord Aditya.

"I do as I am ordered," Aditya said.

Elan's expression turned into a smile. "Well, I can tell you that my official job here is to expand the information network that we have into the other outposts and to see just how valid your idea might be. Then it will be up to the leadership to decide what we do." Elan picked up a new scroll.

Aditya's face split in a wide smile.

Elan knew his history and how he had come to the attention of Alva. Now he remained as the lord over Vermire Trading Outpost, one of their people. He was a lord in name only, but they had entrusted him with a great number of secrets and revealed more power than a simple group in the First Realm should have.

He'd kept his lips shut and worked hard to do his best. With them looking at his plan seriously, it showed that he had gained a heavy measure of their trust.

Seems that the healing houses are getting nosey again.

"Is there something wrong with your scroll?" Aditya asked, looking at Elan's sour expression.

"It looks like the healing houses are a bit pissed off with how low the Alva Healing House's expenses are. They also are confused by their techniques. They're gathering information on them right now, but I don't think that anything good will come from it." Elan sighed.

"I guess this is part of the price of success? As soon as you have something, then others want a piece of it." Aditya let out a dry laugh.

"Well, at least we have the drop on them so we can prepare ahead of time. I would also suggest that when the food prices are increased, create an area with greenhouses to grow food all year round," Elan said. "Shows the people your sincerity and that you're looking to avert disaster and take a step further in becoming a completely independent city."

"I haven't told you yet, but with our permanent population and our size, we officially became a Ten Realms-recognized grade-two town the other day," Aditya said with pride.

"Congratulations." Elan smiled. "Only two more grades and you'll reach city status!"

"I never thought that I would control a city—still doesn't feel real," Aditya said.

"There's still a long way to go."

"And many problems to be dealt with!" Aditya chimed in.

Elan snorted. "Well, at least it keeps us both in a job."

Fehim was walking through the Alchemy plants, stopping as he reached the center of the garden where the silverlight tree had been replanted.

He liked to tour the garden every so often.

"Checking up on the others?" Erik, who sat on a bench facing the large tree, asked, turning his head to look over at Fehim.

"As the Alchemy department head, it's only natural," Fehim said with a smile. He moved over to Erik and bowed.

"No need for that, Fehim." Erik waved him off and indicated to the bench.

Fehim smiled and sat down on the bench, looking at the tree with Erik. There was an Alchemy book open in his lap.

"Seems a little different." Erik looked at the silverlight tree. Instead of being silver and green, its main trunk looked to be made from polished silver and looked fragile, as if a stiff breeze would cause it to snap. The leaves hung down in myriad colors, mingling with one another, random but beautiful.

"Well, that might be because we got the tree type messed up. It *was* a silverlight tree, but now it's an ever-silver tree. Known to people as a mana tree. It can live in any environment that has a truly massive amount of mana, but only one in ten thousand will reach maturity because they are incredibly fragile and it has interesting mana requirements.

"When you brought it, it was silver and green, due to its structure being changed by the mana that they absorb. So when it was in the dungeon, absorbing just two types of mana, it took on characteristics of them both. So when it was exposed to other kinds of mana, then it started to change. We took it around the garden, balancing out all of the different attribute manas that it consumed and then it changed into its current form.

"From what we've been able to learn, when it reaches maturity then silver fruits will appear on its limbs, showing up once every five years afterward. These fruits are called silver fruits. Someone's naming scheme isn't that amazing," Fehim said dryly.

Erik smiled. "What will they do? Can they be used in a concoction? And what does the tree do with the mana? I can sense it pulling in mana but not letting any out?"

Fehim grinned. "The silver fruits randomly increase a person's attributes by one to seven points."

Erik looked at the ever-silver tree with a new appreciation.

"I haven't been able to find out about any concoctions that use them. I think few people would try to experiment with something so powerful. I've been searching for more information discreetly but they're incredibly rare and even the one that you brought wasn't in good condition. It would have died in a few months or years—even now we have to monitor to make sure that the trunk doesn't snap. We've been trimming back the branches so there's not as much strain on the trunk. It will mean a lower yield, but as long as we can grow the tree, there's a possibility that it will create a bud that we can plant and grow into a second ever-silver tree."

"What protections have you put into place?" Erik asked.

"There is a defensive formation around it. Qin worked on it personally. It is powered by the dungeon and there is a mana barrier as well. Someone will be alerted as they get close to the tree. If they keep going, then the defensive formation will toss them out. Second time, it will attack to disable. If someone attacks, then the barrier will block and the formation will attack," Fehim reassured Erik.

"Well, we should get a good harvest in five years," Erik said.

"Four, nearly three years," Fehim corrected.

Erik looked to Fehim and raised his eyebrows. "Huh. Time seems to have sped on by."

"It has," Fehim said.

"Are you afraid of losing your position as the head of the Alchemy department?" Erik asked.

"You going to fire me from it?" Fehim asked.

"Nothing like that." Erik shook his head at Fehim's easy smile.

"I will probably lose the position soon, but, I am quite a bit older than most of the students and I started learning later on. I care more about the ingredients and my skill lays in assisting alchemists with their concoctions, not making them myself," Fehim said. "I knew that others would surpass me eventually. If Delilah was not the council leader, then she would be the department head."

"Not many people would be as willing to give up their position as you," Erik said.

"We are growing. Alva has tens of people coming from across the realms every week instead of every few months. About four-fifths of those people are choosing to live in Alva. People are working harder than ever so that the people who just joined Alva don't take their position. It creates competition, and there are some inner frictions, but all areas of Alva have handled it well, turning it into action, instead of nefarious rivalry."

"It's much bigger than when we started," Erik agreed.

"And like our gardens, it will continue to grow faster with each passing year." Fehim cleared his throat, making Erik look over.

"About the lower floors."

"Not you too." Erik snorted.

"We have plants of different attributes up here. Although I wish to keep a garden here, with the need for more housing, I can see that we can't keep expanding the garden all over the place. Also, I am told that the mana density on the lower floors is higher and we have gotten samples back from the Metal floor already. Are there really floors of all different affinities?"

"Don't care about your position but passionate about your plants," Erik said dryly.

Fehim shrugged, a light smile on his face.

"Under the Alva Dungeon floor, there is the Metal floor, the Earth floor, the Fire floor, Wood floor, and then the final Water floor. Each of the other floors is many times larger than the current Alva floor."

"We could grow so much down there, raise different attribute plants. We would have a hard time on the Earth floor—the farmers are going to want to work there. Maybe with the higher Earth mana, they would be happier with a smaller plot of land. They care about growing things in mass instead of increasing their potency. Wait, is this why you're holding off increasing your Body Cultivation?"

"Partly," Erik said.

"You used the battlefield dungeon as a way to get down to the Fire floor in order to temper your body in the heavy Fire-attribute mana?"

"Right. For my next tempering, I require to temper my body with the Earth attribute mana, then Metal, Water, and Wood. Each time, I will require stronger concoctions and higher concentrations of mana to allow me to temper my body completely. From what we've learned, we know that there can be partial temperings and complete ones. Partial will allow us to complete the quest and some will remain there; others will continue to temper one's body completely, removing any and all weaknesses. It requires a lot more resources and power, but there are greater benefits later on."

"One can become stronger immediately but weaken his gains later on." Fehim nodded.

They fell into silence.

"So once the Earth floor is cleared, will you attempt to temper your body once again? We already have the Metal floor—that will be two temperings complete, right?"

"Yes and no. I can feel that I will need powerful aids to complete my temperings. I will talk to my Alchemy teacher to see if he knows what can help me to overcome my remaining boundaries. Body Cultivation requires a lot of resources to cross, no matter what. Mana Gathering Cultivation requires a lot of work over time, but it is possible to increase through sheer tenacity," Erik said.

"Both paths take us beyond the realm of just humans, touching upon the power of the Ten Realms in different aspects," Fehim said. "I'll keep an eye out in the books from Vuzgal for any information on cultivation aids."

"Thank you, Fehim." Erik looked at him and then back to the tree. "I wonder what it will look like in three years."

"Bigger, I would guess," Fehim said seriously.

Erik couldn't help but laugh and Fehim joined in.

Rugrat showed off the new tools in the workshop: routers, band saws, sanding belts, table saws, and drills.

"This will make things a lot easier. Instead of taking hours for the new blacksmiths to sharpen blades, it will take them what, a few minutes?" Taran said.

"With the routers, I think that the formation masters would be interested," Tan Xue said.

"I sent off a bunch of the routers to them. They can just use gems and mana stones in order to power them instead of having to use their mana all the time to make mana blades and other tools," Rugrat said.

They looked at the machine shop. It hadn't taken Rugrat long to make everything, using parts and items that they had already. With the rotating formation, his mana blade, and refined metal.

"It should increase production on different items. Though we still haven't reached this factory stage level of assembly. Even with ammunition, we are casting the rounds and the cartridges, which is done by hand," Taran complained.

"Haven't you been working with Matt, the blueprint office, the Alchemy department, and the formation masters to make a machine that will make the cartridges and the rounds for you?" Tan Xue asked.

"Yes, but it all takes time. The mortar rounds need a process, as well as the grenade launcher rounds." Taran sighed.

Rugrat snorted and then looked at them both. "We had none of this a year ago. Like, look at how far we've come. Sure, we've got further to go but we've done a lot. You've both done a lot. If it wasn't for your efforts, we wouldn't have gotten to this stage. We are producing rifles at a breakneck speed. Once we can incorporate the machines in this machine shop into production, then it will only increase. When we started, no one would think about four different departments working together in tandem.

"This is what Alva needs—people sharing information, working together, to take what we have already and combine it together to increase their effect. Alchemy concoctions used with needles and intravenous needles.

Healers working with tailors, alchemists, and smiths to create sterile plastics. Alchemists working with farmers to make more potent, plentiful, and powerful ingredients as they discuss preparation with the cooks." Rugrat looked between them both. "You've done something incredible here—don't let anyone tell you any different."

Taran and Tan Xue looked away, awkward with the praise.

Taran cleared his throat. "Well, if you have some more secrets about making it into the Expert realm of smithing, then I would think you were proposing!"

"Don't worry—I'm sure you'll make it to Expert only a few years after me." Rugrat's winning grin appeared as Taran faked throwing a punch. Tan Xue snorted and shook her head, the serious atmosphere from before disappearing.

"Though I did want to ask Tan Xue about a few things Expert related. Beers?" Rugrat said.

"Well, seeing as we've done so much work as you've said, it would be impolite not to accept your offer to buy a few rounds." Taran cleared his throat and walked ahead.

It took Rugrat a moment to figure out what he said as Tan Xue moved to follow Taran.

"You coming there, slow stuff?" she called back to Rugrat.

"I didn't say anything about buying a few rounds!" Rugrat said, moving to catch up with them.

They reached the Spitting Boar, one of the new bars that had appeared in Alva. It looked over one of the parks and stood three levels tall, with the top level open to the rest of Alva.

They went to the third floor, grabbing drinks and moving to a table.

"So I've explained a lot of this to Taran already. I made it into the Expert level of smithing. I'm not really sure how. Though I have a feeling it didn't have to do all with knowledge, but the application of that knowledge. Right now, I feel like I am in unknown territory, so I haven't been talking about it much. I don't want to send people off on the wrong path. It feels like there is a boundary around me, like there is something I don't know that is stopping me from progressing. At the same time, I feel like if I figure out what is holding me back then I will be able to increase my ability in smithing a lot." Tan Xue took a big gulp of her beer.

"Okay, well, when you made that first Expert-level item, what did you think? What did you do differently—materials, tools? Why were you making the item you were? What were the deviations from the plan?" Rugrat asked.

Taran and Rugrat focused on her and she looked up, closing her eyes to picture the whole process.

Rugrat pulled out a notepad; Taran did as well. They forgot about their drinks in a rare moment and declaration of interest in Tan Xue's words.

"I was really tired. I was just looking at my hammer and hitting it on the metal. I was focusing on using the vibrations of my strikes to increase the strength of the sword. I think it was a sword. Though I kind of tunneled—my mind started to think on my hammer. I knew it so well, how it had formed. I looked at it and I thought that it was interesting how I was working on a new weapon with an old tool that I had created. I thought about the cycle of weapons—hewn from the earth, then refined and combined with other elements and turned into tools. I thought how I was creating a resonance in the weapon with my hammer, how I wondered if I could create a resonance in my hammer's different elements and if that would transfer that change over to the sword.

"I focused on the hammer. Instead of using the hammer to attack the weapon and create the right vibrations, I started to alter how I used the hammer. I changed the mana flow through my body, the way my muscles moved, achieving a resonance with the hammer."

Tan Xue opened her eyes, stunned but also at peace.

"I realized that I am the creator. I always used the hammer to form, but it is I forming the weapon, with the hammer as a medium. That without a smithy, without a hammer and a forge, I could create a weapon. My body is the smithy. It is my truth, my realization. At the same time, using my body instead of my hammer to create the vibrations was a form of technique. I don't know what it means… I have to get back to my smithy," Tan Xue said, her eyes glossed over.

"Tan Xue, I need you to come to Vuzgal, if you're okay with that."

"Huh, what?" Tan Xue jolted in her seat.

"We need a high skilled crafter in Vuzgal if we want to attract people to the academy and make sure that any of the high skilled crafters that we hire will listen to us," Rugrat said.

"I have projects, classes, I run the smithing department for the Kanesh Academy," Tan Xue said.

"Well, umm, Taran, would you be interested in taking over as the smithing department head in Alva?" Rugrat asked sheepishly.

The two smiths looked at one another, their eyes narrowing as their turned their stares on Rugrat.

"How long have you been sitting on this plan of yours?"

"Uhh, a few days… maybe weeks," He muttered into his drink, taking a big swig to cover over the embarrassed look on his face.

"So you want me to go up to Vuzgal so we have the authority to negotiate with other expert crafters and establish ourselves and Taran will take over the department in Vuzgal. Anything else?" Tan Xue pressed.

"Well, there will be a group of crafters that will be heading up to the higher realms, and," Rugrat coughed. "You would be the head of the Academy."

Seeing the look in her eyes he talked quickly.

"Don't worry you would be a figurehead! There will be a staff and people that will help with the day to day running of the academy, like all of the assistants and helpers that are in the Kanesh Academy. You would get a bunch of resources, time in the crafter trial. Umm blueprints, the best of the best! There will be expert level crafting rooms too you'll be able to go outside too!"

A look from Tan Xue made Rugrat close his mouth.

She sighed and looked to Taran.

The bulky man shrugged.

"You've been running the smithing department by yourself pretty much this entire time anyway. You're well suited to it and with the extra resources you should be able to reach Expert soon. Are you okay with it though?" Tan Xue asked.

"I didn't think that I would like teaching others, but, I've come to enjoy it, seeing how excited they are, I don't mind being a teacher. Also I have five barrels of shine on the line, I'm not losing to him," Taran looked at Rugrat.

"I'm, just a half step away!"

"A half step too slow," Taran grinned.

The two of them looked at one another, grinning like idiots. Excited at the challenge set down between them.

"Alright, I have to go and pack," Tan Xue said, draining her drink and then standing. Next time, a little bit more warning would be nice."

"Yes Academy head!" Rugrat said, raising his glass to her.

She snorted and rolled her eyes, a smile pulling at the corner of her lips as she nodded to Taran.

"I'm sure we'll keep in contact," He assured her.

"You'll try to escape Alva more often than not," She filled in for him.

Taran just chuckled.

Rugrat, seeing them both he realized how just a few short years ago he had never met them, but now he couldn't imagine a life without them in it. Sure they fought and complained at one another, but they were his brother and sister, even if none of the same blood flowed in their veins.

Hiao Xen sighed as he got the latest information from the Stone Fist sect through his sources.

The Ice Empress of the Elsi clan had publicly shamed the Mai clan and Young Master Perkins by using the marriage ceremony to escape the city.

The Stone Fist sect had been angry, with multiple elders voicing their anger. The Ice Empress joined the Fighter's Association, with many of her disciples who held powerful positions within the Stone Fist sect joining as well.

Others broke off their ties with the Stone Fist sect.

"Just what the hell is happening over there?" Hiao Xen asked the air. "I hope that Erik meeting her didn't have a part to play in all of this."

He put the message to the side when there was another sound transmission from another source in the Fighter's Association.

"Benny, what's up?" Hiao Xen asked.

"You been looking for more information on why the Ice Empress joined us? Here's a message she just sent out to the entire Stone Fist sect," Benny said with a gloating voice.

Hiao Xen received a second sound transmission.

"My name is Mira Elsi. The other day, I was supposed to marry Young Master Perkins. I did not wish to shame the Mai clan, but actions cannot be undone. I made a promise, a contract with the Stone Fist sect and my own

Elsi clan when I returned. For years, I thought that this contract had been carried out by both parties. I was wrong. The Stone Fist sect and my own Elsi clan worked together to break the contract. I left my children for the sect, only to find out that they sent down assassins to poison my children. Even at this point, I do not know what their current condition is. They used formations to make sure that I wouldn't find out about the broken contract until later. It would probably have been years after I was married to Young Master Perkins."

Hiao Xen could feel the cold fury in her voice as she talked. He gritted his own teeth in anger, thinking about what would have happened if the same thing happened with his son.

"With the contract broken between us, I was free from the sect and my clan. I passed word to my followers, a number of whom believed as I did, that a clan or sect that does this to their members, treating them like goods instead of like their fellow sect members, does not deserve fealty. With this information, you, too, can break your contract with the sect as they have broken their own rules and their word to us."

The sound transmission ended.

"So, I guess that tells you what happened," Benny said.

"Is the Fighter's Association going to do anything?" Hiao Xen asked.

"Officially? No, of course not. We wouldn't meddle in any sect issues. Unofficially, it's pissed off a lot of people. Most of us were independents who joined the sect for the protection and the ability to increase our cultivation and combat fighting skills. She's a powerful fighter, but they were going to use her to try to give them another person with the ice emperor constitution. Went so far as trying to poison her children. It's pissed off quite a few people over here. So it looks like there might be a cleansing." Benny's voice lost his joy and turned serious.

"I'm reminded by the second name that some people called the Fighter's Association the Sect Monitors," Hiao Xen said.

"Breaking one's word isn't a light thing. We're all people here. Sure, we fight one another all the time—sometimes there are just people who need to die. For the most part, we need to clear those pieces away, or else the Ten Realms will have a bunch of useless groups."

"Why do you monitor the different sects and judge them?" Hiao Xen asked.

Benny laughed as Hiao Xen sighed, smiling. He knew Benny wouldn't give him a direct answer.

"I heard you're working in Vuzgal now—acting city director. We'll have to have a drink soon! If you want to know more, you should increase your standing in the Blue Lotus. There's still much you don't know about the Ten Realms," Benny said mysteriously.

"Seems more like I'm corralling children around, but you're welcome anytime," Hiao Xen said.

"Talk later!"

The channel went dead as Hiao Xen sat back in his chair and steepled his fingers.

"Unless she says something, there is nothing to link Erik to what she did. If he did something and we said it, we'd piss off the Stone Fist sect and it would look bad that we're meddling in other people's affairs. Though it would also make the Fighter's Association closer with us." Hiao Xen thought through different scenarios before he shook his head and stood, stretching.

"I don't even know if it was Erik who passed her the information. Let's just see what happens."

He looked out over the gardens. They had transformed. There had only been a few buds with plants of heavy Earth and Metal attributes; demonic-looking plants had covered the city.

"Even though most of the city was damaged, the mana gathering formations were buried deep and the mana here, although it was heavy with Earth and Metal mana, it wasn't as heavy as we thought. In fact, there was a lot of pure mana in the area. With the higher mana, it allows people to focus their mind more as they feel more relaxed. It also increases the power of people's spells. Just for these points alone, a lot of people came over. If someone was to grow up in this environment, with us cleaning up the mana with different attributed plants and grasses to convert the mana from just Earth and Metal to Fire, Water, and Wood, they'd have a much higher advantage over people from other cities."

Hiao Xen smiled as he looked over the odd plants that were slowly helping to restore the balance within Vuzgal and were growing voraciously.

The apartments for the administration of Vuzgal had been completed and the grounds restored with Alchemy plants.

The head of the Alchemy Association seemed interested in them when he came over last.

He was proud of all that Vuzgal had become and knew that this was only the start of their path.

He took in a deep breath, taking in the fresh air. He rotated his mana, revitalizing himself, and he turned back toward his desk. He had just sat down when there was a hurried knock on his door.

"Come in," Hiao Xen said.

Dougie walked in, frowning but also with his fists clenched together. He held a report. He quickly closed the door behind him and walked to Hiao Xen's desk.

His unnatural expression focused his mind and he forgot his earlier peaceful thoughts.

"Someone is stirring up trouble in Vuzgal. The craftsmen we hired through the associations, they are taking breaks and barely doing their work. The foremen mentioned the delays to me. Construction has essentially come to a halt. The work on the castle has stopped completely. Only the work on the workshops in the city has continued. There are people who are trying to renegotiate their contracts, applying pressure that they won't keep working. Also, a high number of crafters have started bad-mouthing the Crafting trial dungeon, saying that it is not the best atmosphere to work in and that we are demanding too much. Others have left the workshops, saying that they're subpar, but they're still paying for their time so people can't access the workshops even if they're empty. They are saying that we don't even have Expert-level crafters, so how can we say that we know anything about crafting. They're saying that a council of crafters should be made because we are taking advantage of them. The crafters are hanging out in the bars and other places, bad-mouthing the people of Vuzgal."

"Who is behind this?" Hiao Xen asked. His relaxed expression from before had disappeared.

"It looks like the Expert crafters who are close to Zhen Fu are the source of these issues. None of them have hidden their hands," Dougie said.

"Well, it looks like she really intends to go head-to-head with us." Hiao Xen's expression was complicated. "Collect the names of the people who are acting as their mouthpieces and those who are renting the workshops but not using them, as well as those who are exerting their influences for Zhen Fu.

Do it over the next three days. I want all of the names.

"Once we have them all, add in a new clause for the workshops. If someone rents a workshop and they don't show up, then their slot goes to someone else after ten minutes. If they appear but aren't using the workshop or working on their own projects after twenty minutes, they're to be kicked out. Also, people using the workshops must go through an interview. Independent or from an association or sect—it doesn't matter. Make sure that they're actually there to work. We can't waste the time in our workshops. Work with the crafters we have pulled to our sides and use this as a recruitment. See how driven they are and check that their words meet with their actions before offering them a position within the Vuzgal Crafter's Association." Hiao Xen saw that Dougie's face was strained.

"What?"

"There are a number of crafters who wish to increase their remuneration, or they will walk. Others have already left."

Hiao Xen stood, letting out an angry breath as he held his hands behind his back.

This is something that I need Erik and Rugrat to make a final decision on. This could be seen as a test of my abilities. If I ask them for help at the first obstacle, won't it look bad on me?

"If they are willing to pay out their contract, let them. Our recruitment must not be that good if people are already willing to leave. Talk to the recruiters and express my displeasure. Make another recruiting department. Model it after the Vuzgal army's recruiters. It doesn't matter one's level or their skill, only their dedication. The recruiters aren't looking to just fill positions but people who live for their job. The army has veterans as recruiters as they have a sense and knowledge about who will make a good soldier and those who can be molded into one.

"We should do the same with the crafters. Those we trust, we offer them a recruiter position. They can do that instead of teaching and they can get more resources to incentivize them and allow them to improve when they're not dealing with recruiting. We should have a number of people for general crafting recruiting, then have recruiters for each of the different crafts we work with. Filter out the crap. If we only have five crafters instead of fifty, but those five are more determined, we aren't wasting resources on those who will just leave at the least problem."

Dougie had pulled out a pad of paper and recorded down everything that Hiao Xen had said.

"We have only been passively recruiting at this point. We should also have our recruiters go to different cities and see if they can't draw in some independent crafters. Send them to the lower realms. If level and Experience isn't an issue, as Erik and Rugrat have said, there are hundreds of people who would be willing to learn from us, especially with the ability to pay off their contract and the freedom to leave, instead of most sects that one is bound to, who then make all of their decisions for them. People there will be much more willing, though don't tell them that we're from the Fourth Realm. Just recruit them solely based on their interest in crafting." Hiao Xen, pacing, felt a new energy fill him.

"I feel like I might thank Zhen Fu by the end of this. It's made me look at things differently. The outside influence will only filter out more people who are only wishing to use us and not give anything back. If they not only learn but help make products and support Vuzgal, then sending them on to learn more should be celebrated instead of those who learn and then are bought out by some group."

"There have also been a number of people who had left the Stone Fist sect who have expressed interest in settling down here," Dougie said. His shock had calmed down and his mind was able to think of other items of interest.

"We don't discriminate. As long as one obeys the rules and doesn't create trouble, they're more than welcome to come to Vuzgal," Hiao Xen said.

"Yes, sir. Just wanted to check."

Hiao Xen smiled. It seemed that Dougie had seen through it, just as he had.

"Make sure that all of those names are recorded. Get all of our ears in the city, from the Sky Reaching Restaurant and the Wayside Inns, crafting workshops and guards. I want to know just who we're dealing with here." Hiao Xen stopped his pacing.

"I will have it done," Dougie reported, straightening up. He felt his dismissal, bowing to Hiao Xen and leaving.

Nothing is ever easy!

10 Lord Returns

"Have fun and don't make too much trouble," Erik said as he shook Rugrat's hand.

"I'm interested to see what Matt and Hiao Xen have been up to while I've been gone," Rugrat said. "Have fun in the Third Realm."

Erik nodded and Rugrat turned back to the forty or so people with him. There were people from every academy department represented. They would make up the core of the teaching staff.

The academy's construction was nearly complete, with the final touches taking only another week and a half before it was done.

In a couple of months, a competition would be held among the departments. The winners of the contests would travel to Vuzgal or to the Division Headquarters in the Third Realm to expand their horizons. Everyone was working hard to get the opportunity to see these new places.

The departments were filling up, with hundreds of people now attending the academy.

Just the people we're taking in is more than all of the students the academy had when it first opened.

Rugrat looked at Tan Xue. "Ready?"

"I'd be better prepared if you told me sooner," She said darkly.

Rugrat let out a forced laugh and looked to Taran who was coming with them to see Vuzgal. He would only be there for a few days before he needed to return to Alva and take over his old position as the smithing department head.

Rugrat turned and accessed the totem.

You have reached Level 50, meeting the requirements to ascend to the Sixth Realm.

Do you wish to ascend?

YES/NO

His level hadn't increased since he left Vuzgal, remaining at level fifty-seven, just a few levels ahead of Erik as he opened all of his mana gates and unlocked the Mana Gathering Cultivation stages, like the Body Cultivation.

"Nope!" Rugrat went on to select Vuzgal.

He winced at the amount of mana stones that were required and light enveloped them all. Alva disappeared as the noise of a growing city and a cool breeze rolled over them.

The area where the other totem had been had already been turned into warehouses and sorting houses.

There were people using the totem constantly, moving across the Fourth Realm and even on to other realms.

Sky Reaching Restaurants pushed up into the sky and the castle had been fully repaired, looking nothing like it did when Rugrat had first seen it. The pillar stood above it all, looking down on the city.

It was as if time had gone backward to before Vuzgal's final war.

Still, there is a lot more building that needs to be done. We've still got a lot of land to develop. What will this look like once we have people populating all of Vuzgal?

"Move on, don't clog up the totem!" a guard yelled. He wore the emblem of the Fighter's Association, a bored expression on his face.

Rugrat moved forward, leading the group. He was about to walk through the gates when a few guards stood in front of him.

"Everyone has to pay the toll." The woman's eyebrows pinched together.

"Be kind of dumb to pay myself," Rugrat joked.

The woman didn't seem to think it was funny.

"Uh, you don't know who I am?"

"Even Expert-level crafters have to pay the toll," the woman said.

Rugrat dug around in his storage rings. "One second," he said as people started to get annoyed with the hold-up as the group milled around.

"There you are." Rugrat pulled out a medallion for Vuzgal.

It was a simple round design, showing the inner city walls, topped with pillars for the mana barrier and the main castle with its pillar on top.

The medallion was made from mana stone and reinforced with a special gold. Most would have stars above the medallion. One star was the sign of Hiao Xen, while two stars were the heads of different controlling bodies within Vuzgal that managed the city.

Rugrat's didn't have any stars on it.

She took it and used an identification key on the medallion.

Her expression changed as she quickly came out of the booth she was in and knelt on the ground, bowing to him.

"City Lord, I am sorry for my grave mistake!" She held up the medallion.

"No worries. I've been dealing with other things so I haven't been around much." Rugrat took the medallion as he laughed awkwardly and pulled her to her feet. "Keep up the good work." He smiled.

She cupped her hands and bowed. "Thank you, City Lord!" she said. Others looked over as Rugrat coughed at the scene.

He waved for the guards to move aside. They did so and Rugrat scurried away before people could see his identity.

I wanted to surprise Hiao Xen—how will I do that now?

They left the totem and headed through the city.

As soon as they were away from the totem, Taran and Tan Xue burst out into laughter. The others from Alva all smiled or chuckled.

"What? I was busy with other things!" Rugrat complained.

"The lady at the totem doesn't even know who you are—you sure we're in the right place?" Tan Xue snorted and put her hand on Rugrat's shoulder to steady herself.

Rugrat's head sunk down, a nonplussed look on his face as he resigned himself to accept the word-based abuse.

Rugrat took them toward the first crafting districts. There were people trying to work on the buildings but there were others just lying around the place, making it hard to have any progress and increasing the build time considerably.

"These will be where the new tier-three workshops are built." Rugrat frowned at the odd atmosphere as people moved around.

"Maybe in three years' time! If the city lords think that we will work on an unsafe jobsite, they're kidding themselves! We're worked to the bone. Only when they acknowledge their misdeeds will we renegotiate with them!" a worker said, overhearing them.

His gloating smile froze with the collective murderous intent that came from the group.

Rugrat stopped the people from Alva from talking with a look. They all stared at the person who had talked.

Talking shit to a group of people who have Body Cultivation and Mana Gathering Cultivation?

Rugrat quickly moved them on to the crafting workshops, most of which had people loitering outside. There were guards here, trying to move people, but they weren't putting their full effort into it.

The guards and the people who are causing the problems are from the same associations. The guards might have a high position outside of the association, but inside it, the crafters, even with their low levels, have a lot of power.

"I paid for an hour. So what if I'm eleven minutes late? I shouldn't have it given to someone else! Does the government of Vuzgal not care about their customers!"

"What do you mean that I wasn't working on my craft! It takes hours of thinking to come up with a plan!"

"You were sleeping!" someone from the workshop said.

"Says you!"

"This kind of atmosphere is good for no one to work in," Taran said.

By now, all of the people from Alva felt that there was something wrong.

They went to the gates that led to the valley. It had changed. There, people from the Alchemist Association watched the gates with annoyed expressions as they looked at crafters and others making a ruckus outside.

"The conditions in the Crafting trial dungeons are horrible! No light, bad water, and the bathrooms don't function! How are we supposed to work in such conditions? For one Earth mana stone, this can't go on! We demand that the cost is decreased. For us to pay for these conditions, it's outrageous!"

"Move! Coming through!" a group said, trying to get to the doorway. People mobbed them and crafters from all ranks gathered around them, making it hard to move.

"Going to the Crafting trial dungeon will only lead to despair!"

"Turn back—it is for your own benefit!"

The Alchemist Association didn't interfere, not leaving their guarding positions. They couldn't.

"You want to cause trouble with the Fighter's Association!" one woman yelled as the mana in the area was stirred up.

People moved away and the party passed. Another group of crafters tried to get to the gate but were mobbed by the people.

"Come, fellow crafters! You might be independent but we all work together!"

"Work for yourself! Get out of my way!"

"We are looking out for your best interests!" another from the human wall said with fake smiles.

"Then pay me back for my ticket! Get out of my way!" another yelled.

"Don't you see we're helping you? You'll thank us later," another man from the wall said.

Rugrat looked at it. Instead of showing anything, his face had gone blank; his aura had retreated. Only the mana around him shimmered slightly.

George was in his small form. He raised his head. Flames started to appear around his body.

Rugrat reached up and patted his head.

"We'll go to the castle and see what is going on." Rugrat's voice was calm. His thoughts had broken down linearly. He needed to know what was happening, and then come up with a solution to deal with it.

I hope that this is not due to Hiao Xen. No matter what issue arises, even if it weakens us now, this needs to stop.

They moved toward the castle. It stretched up into the sky, looking out over the rest of Vuzgal.

Rugrat saw another group outside of the main gate.

"Move aside or be *removed*!" a man yelled.

"See, the guards only resort to violence!"

"We just want to tell people the truth of your crafters! You don't even have high Apprentice crafters! How can you teach crafting?"

"This is a city of crafters but you don't know the needs of us crafters! Look at the condition of the workshops and the Crafting trial dungeon!"

"Like we can control the dungeon!" the man shouted back.

"Bring in the council of crafters!"

"Yeah! Representation for the crafters!"

"For the crafters, by the crafters! Vuzgal needs crafter oversight!"

"Crafter council?" Rugrat repeated these words, feeling as if he had locked onto a target finally.

His eyes moved to the people trying to force their way through the group.

"Allow them through," the guard said.

The crafters and people milling around shot them dirty looks as they headed for the castle, lowering their heads in shame.

Rugrat walked forward. The people of Alva all held their heads high as the group found a new target.

"Look to your future! Don't be blinded!" one called out.

Rugrat had reached the end of his patience and he extended his hand. Mana rolled toward him. This was his city, his dungeon, and he had a body of mana. People stumbled backward as they felt the mana reject them. Those who had weaker Mana Gathering Cultivation felt the mana being drawn from them. Others felt as if they were being choked, their mana cut off.

Rugrat cast one of his first spells, fueling it with the power he drew in. A massive spell formation appeared underneath all of the crafters.

"Silence." He cast his Silence spell. The area went quiet. "That's much better."

He walked forward. The crowd opened their mouths but no noise came out as Rugrat and the group moved.

Instead, they used their bodies to try to stop them.

Rugrat walked into them. They were only crafters. Although they were powerful in their craft, many had let their cultivation slide. The people in Alva focused on their cultivation, religiously working to increase their strength day after day.

They forged a path through the crafters. Seeing that they wouldn't be able to stop this new group, the crafters cast them dark looks that promised retribution as they stepped out of the way.

His eyes moved to the chests of the different people gathered.

Blue Lotus, Formation Guild, Crafter's Association, a few random sects thrown in, a few from the Alchemist Association but they're at least trying to hide their badges.

"Sir!" the guard yelled out and saluted Rugrat. He was one of the men from the Alva Army.

The others straightened as Rugrat marched through the gates with the crafters following him.

"Looks like things have changed around here—some good, some bad," Rugrat said.

"Sir." The man's face darkened as he had a hard time putting what had happened into words.

"Let the others know that we've arrived." Rugrat walked past the recruiting stations, and the crafters from Alva continued to follow him as he took them into the castle.

People looked at Rugrat and his group as they walked through the administration area of the castle.

Rugrat marched at the head. George rested on his shoulder. He looked lazy but Rugrat could feel the coiled energy within him.

Can't have you mauling protestors now, Rugrat told him. George had barely restrained himself from leaping off Rugrat's shoulder and charging into the crafters who dared to block his master's path.

He understood some human language and the actions of others. Though he had beast thoughts instead of human. Creating dominance and asserting power were as far as his thoughts went to resolving the situation.

Rugrat quickly reached Hiao Xen's office.

"Sir, Hiao Xen is not—" the secretary started to say.

"Find them lodging and someone to show them the workshops." Rugrat walked up to the doors. The restraining formation and locks on the doors were useless as the medallion in his pocket unlocked them.

He opened the doors to find a ragged-looking Hiao Xen working at his desk.

"Didn't I say I wasn't supposed to be disturbed!" Hiao Xen yelled as he looked up. "Rugrat?" Hiao Xen asked as his brain caught up with his eyes.

Rugrat closed the doors behind him and locked them. "What the hell happened?"

He turned toward Hiao Xen, who slumped back into his chair, showing the fatigue of the last few days.

"Zhen Fu. She's an Expert-class tailor from the Blue Lotus. She wanted me to give her access to the dungeon and to the castle workshops. I denied her. I guess she took it as a slight and then she started talking to the other crafters. As she says, everyone needs clothes. It looks like those she spoke to are others who are Experts as well." Hiao Xen let out a cold laugh.

"So all of this is because you didn't give her access to our resources and let her jump the line?" Rugrat asked.

"I swear on my oath to you," Hiao Xen said. The golden light fell on them both, confirming the oath.

"You did good. Now, tell me what you've done in the meantime." Rugrat's face was still impassive as he moved to the desk and sat down. Even though he was on the receiving side, Hiao Xen was clearly the subordinate.

Rugrat took on the role of leader, leaving the funny business at the door.

"I added in new rules to the crafting workshops and the Crafting trial dungeon. In response, they had people start lazing around the construction site, making it unsafe. They started all of this propaganda about us not being a city for crafters. They used the fact that we don't have crafters as a reason we can't raise other crafters. Using their bodies and their words, they have essentially stopped all crafters from working and there are only a handful of people who have the guts to apply to join the administration department. It is hard for us to leave the castle. We were able to use the Fighter's Association guards at the totem to resolve the issues there—few of the associations want to get on their bad sides.

"Otherwise, the guards from the other associations are in a tough position because they're enforcing our rules against their own people who have a higher standing in their association than them. I didn't want to use the forces training the Vuzgal army because of the focus you and Erik have placed on them. Also, if they made an issue with them, then this could blow up."

"Smart. It's just that they have people and reputation on their side and they've stalled the city. Do we know all of the players involved?"

Hiao Xen pulled out a stack of paper and put it on the desk. "These are the names of all the people Zhen Fu or her fellow Expert crafters have pulled over to their side."

"Good." A plan started to form in Rugrat's head. "Sometimes one needs to just cut the infection out so it doesn't fester."

"What was that?" Hiao Xen asked.

"Nothing." Rugrat sent a sound transmission.

A moment later, Tan Xue and all of the crafters who would become the department heads in Vuzgal opened the door.

"Rugrat?" Tan Xue asked.

"Come in. Close the door behind you," Rugrat said.

"I'm sorry, sir!" the secretary said.

"Dougie, just do as they say," Hiao Xen said.

"Yes, sir," Dougie said, sounding confused.

The door closed behind the crafters, who walked up behind Rugrat.

"These are the new teachers for our own crafting school. Each is at least of the high Journeyman level," Rugrat said.

Hiao Xen nodded.

"None of them are older than thirty-five, and Tan Xue is an Expert smith," Rugrat said.

These words made Hiao Xen choke on his spit and have a violent bout of coughing. "Thirty-five?" he managed to choke out.

"Yup, we might be young, but we've got drive. As long as we work together and we're driven, then we can cross more barriers than you'd think." Rugrat smiled as he stood and looked at the crafters.

"I need all of your help. Today, you will familiarize yourselves with the workshops within the castle. Tomorrow, I want you to display all of your abilities." Rugrat pulled out Heart Calming pills that Erik had made him to help with his smithing.

He passed them out to everyone within the room, their eyes shining.

"Show the world your strength with your skills. Materials will be provided as needed. Show me what you can do." Rugrat looked into each of their eyes, the corner of his mouth pulling up slightly.

The crafters all showed their fighting spirit. They had been bottled up, working within Alva to display their skills. For many, this was their first time that they were in a city with their crafting skills.

They wanted to see just how far they could push themselves and the items that they could make.

Associations, bah—we'll show them the strength of the Kanesh Academy!

Rugrat turned back to Hiao Xen. "They've been stopping people from joining, saying that we have no way to create proper Journeyman and Expert-level crafters; showing them that we have an Expert-level crafter already and a fully developed bunch of Journeyman smiths? I think that'll be a nice kick to the teeth." Rugrat grinned.

"Then we just need to find other Expert crafters—we show that we don't care the level of people but their determination. We open up the training fully. I can see if we can't get some teaching staff. They'll be Journeyman level, but with time in the Expert-level crafting rooms and being around other crafters, I'm sure they'll be able to make Expert sometime soon."

"They'll all be low level," Taran said.

Rugrat used his sound transmission so Hiao Xen wouldn't hear.

"Even better—shows how we have high-level crafters even at a young age. We should bring a few of the younger students who have done well on a trip," Rugrat said. "Give them an incentive, allow them to improve and we increase their levels passively because of it. If the Kanesh Academy is the placc that people go to learn, then this is the place where people go to make!"

"This will show our crafting ability, but then what about the people disrupting the city?" Hiao Xen asked.

"Summon all of the association heads here. They have three hours to comply. I wish to see them all." A chill pervaded the air.

"I will see to it." Hiao Xen started to send out sound transmissions.

"Who does he think he is?" The head of the Vuzgal Blue Lotus, Lang Bo, harrumphed as Nadia Shriver sat across from him.

"Acting city lord—does he think that will mean anything when he returns to the Blue Lotus?" Lang Bo said flippantly, before he waved to Nadia.

"Go in my place. He *summoned* me to a meeting in three hours? I have much more important things to deal with. He is undoubtedly unable to deal with the current situation and is looking for our help now. Make sure that you get good conditions from him. Zhen Fu's influence is no small thing. She will only be pleased by him kowtowing and becoming the head of this council."

Nadia knew the true purpose of the council was to pull power away from the leaders of Vuzgal and turn it to the power of these high-level crafters, who would then use the workshops and resources of Vuzgal to increase their position and their skill level.

She kept her mouth shut as she cupped her hands to Lang Bo. "I will do as you say." *It's unfortunate that Hiao Xen ran into Zhen Fu before he was able to build up his network and his power base.*

She left the room to prepare, going to her office—only to run into Zhen Fu on her way out.

Head Lang Bo must have told her.

"Expert Zhen Fu." Miss Shriver bowed to her.

"I heard that Hiao Xen had the audacity to order our head around. I wish to see just what *tricks* he is up to," she said, not hiding the information.

"Of course, Expert Zhen Fu." It wasn't as if she had the power to order her otherwise. *Tricks? You mean the ways that he has tried to keep Vuzgal running?* She wisely kept these thoughts to herself as they went to the awaiting carriage.

Zhen Fu ordered the driver to slow down, bringing them precariously close to the deadline they were supposed to meet Hiao Xen.

The groups that had been making a mess of Vuzgal moved aside respectfully, cupping their fists.

Miss Shriver didn't say anything at their clear deference toward the associations and the Experts who had tagged along with different heads or deputy heads.

The same thing happened at the castle when they gained access.

Miss Shriver felt that she was more of an attendant rather than the representative of the Blue Lotus.

A guard frowned, looking at them both. "Neither of you looks like Lang Bo," he said.

"You dare to look at us with those eyes!" Zhen Fu said, going into a rage looking at the low-level fighter.

His eyes moved to her. There was no emotion in them, her rank meaning nothing to him.

"I am Deputy Head Nadia Shriver," Nadia said.

The man let out a huff and waved a woman guard forward. "Escort them to the meeting hall."

As they passed the man and followed the woman guard, Zhen Fu opened her mouth.

"I will see you in the streets. No one, not even the other beggars, will help you and your family," she said as she passed, flashing her Expert-level tailor badge.

Nadia couldn't do anything, but the man, instead of apologizing or getting angry, just shook his head and continued to look out on Vuzgal.

In Zhen Fu's eyes, only those who were of a higher position than her or of the same status were worth her time. All others were subservient and they should act as such, or else she would ruin their futures.

She was petty and cruel; one only needed to look at how she had motivated the different groups within Vuzgal. She saw the city, with a lower level non-crafting manager placed above her, and she couldn't take it.

Was her outrage all a pretext so that she could take control over the city, to wield its power as she sees fit?

A chill went down Nadia's spine. She felt as though she had started to see another side of Zhen Fu: a cold, calculating woman who played with people in her hand as if they were dice.

Zhen Fu looked over the castle as if it already belonged to her.

Forcing the council of crafters upon them will be the first step. Then I will slowly choke them out and establish my rule over Vuzgal, making them deal with the running of the city while I deal with how power is exchanged. Other than the headquarters for each of the associations, Vuzgal will become the most powerful place in the Fourth Realm. After all, the reason I came to the Fourth Realm from the Fifth was not because of the fighting, but for the ability to earn greater rewards than possible in the two higher realms and not have to compete with others while doing so. A mid-Expert-level crafter in the Fourth Realm is akin to a god.

She smiled to herself. She had manufactured this situation. The other Experts she had contacted willingly supported her with the promise of positions and resources. Other Experts didn't want to get involved and took a neutral stance but none of them dared to stand up to her.

The rebuilding is rough, but with the help of a few Journeymen builders, it will be more suitable.

The woman leading them opened a door for them into a meeting room. The heads of the other associations were there.

The Fighter's Association head sat there with a bored look on his face. The Alchemist Association head looked perfectly relaxed. The Formation Guild, Crafter's Association, and Healer's Association all had confident looks on their faces. They had all brought Expert-level crafters with them; the Fighter's Association head hadn't brought anyone with him and the Alchemist Association had the deputy head with her.

They looked over at their entrance while the Expert-level crafters who had tagged along rose and cupped their fists to Zhen Fu.

"Please, please take your seats." She smiled, already taking the momentum of the meeting away from the lonely looking Hiao Xen, who sat facing the associations.

Zhen Fu's eyebrow rose. Although Hiao Xen looked tired, he didn't look broken yet. *When you return to the Blue Lotus, I will turn you and your family into my playthings. Otherwise, wouldn't others think me weak?*

She sat down on the main seat, forcing Nadia to sit in the aide's seat, making herself the head of the table.

"So, what is this meeting about?"

"Banishment." A voice came from Hiao Xen and an illusion spell dissolved behind him, revealing two chairs. One was empty; the other showed a man sitting back in it, holding up his head with his hand.

To his side, there was a wolf with fur that looked like moving flames. It was lying down but it was as tall as the man's chair.

You dare to sit there and stare down on me! He must be one of the city lords.

"I don't think that Hiao Xen deserves that. He was in over his head. The crafter's council will, of course, be willing to make sure that the crafters and

Vuzgal continue to develop seamlessly." She smiled, unaffected by the theatrics.

"Ugh—talking. Sometimes it's just so useless," the man said, a bored look on his face.

Her eyes thinned dangerously. "The council is the *only* group that can return order and prosperity to Vuzgal," she said.

"Silence." The mana in the room stilled under the man's command.

A spell enveloped her. A silence restriction fell on her body, making her unable to talk. The talismans and enchantments written into her robes tried to fight the restriction but they didn't have the power to break the spell. The man sat there, looking at her as he poured out a seemingly inexhaustible amount of mana.

"You dare attack—"

"Too much talk," Rugrat said, using a silencing spell on the other Expert-level crafters in the room. "Don't you find it interesting that the troublemakers in my Vuzgal show up to this meeting? It seems I will need to add Lang Bo to the list."

How is he able to cast Silence on all of us? It is a simple spell and doesn't take much mana, but all five Expert-level crafters are restrained by him.

"What do you mean by this?" the head of the Healer's Association stood and demanded.

"I mean to run Vuzgal," the city lord said simply as he pulled out some documents and wrote something down.

Hiao Xen looked at him in question as well.

I will tear you apart! I will take Vuzgal from you, and I will make you watch from the pillar as it grows in strength and I become its queen!

Zhen Fu's anger had reached its limit as her last defensive talisman failed, the silence spell keeping her restrained.

Nadia wasn't sure what she was seeing as Zhen Fu gripped her armrests, her nails digging into the wood.

"By attacking our crafters! I thought what I heard in the streets wasn't true. It seems I was mistaken," the Healer's Association head said in a derisive tone.

"Congratulations, another winner on a one-way ticket." The man wrote down another name and stood, clapping his hands.

"Now, seems some of you have forgotten the agreements we made. You were supposed to supply guard forces that were to aid in dealing with the security issues of Vuzgal. You were allowed to use the services of Vuzgal freely, as anyone in Vuzgal is allowed. Vuzgal is a sovereign land and you're all renting a plot of it. Seems that you thought this meant you owned it or something." The man laughed as if it were a rich joke. "You also agreed to punish your people in a way we agreed upon if they created trouble. I'll be waiting to hear from your headquarters on how they deal with the troublemakers who have appeared in my city."

"Who do you think you are!" the Formation Guild head demanded.

"I'm fucking Rugrat and this is *MY CITY!*"

The mana in the room was no longer still as Rugrat's voice filled the room and spread to the city. A pressure came from him that restrained the very mana in their veins and made it feel as if they stood in the presence of a war god. His voice turned deeper as he looked at them all, his eyes glowing with power.

"Vuzgal will remain a place free for all to visit, no matter your sect or your association. Those who create trouble or go against our laws will be punished."

Nadia realized that his voice was ringing through the entirety of Vuzgal.

"To those who wish to spend their idle time stopping people from getting to the dungeons, from being able to work, trying to oppress others with their actions and words, disrupting Vuzgal and its residents' lives..." The man dropped the papers he had been working on and added another name—the name of the Formation Guild head.

Rugrat placed his hand on the thick bundle of papers. "I banish you from Vuzgal. You will never again be allowed to step onto Vuzgal's territory. Crafters, traders, fighters, people from all walks of life are allowed to visit, but troublemakers, those who disrupt others or the running of the city, will be banished. I banish those listed as disturbing the peace in Vuzgal. This is effective immediately."

With Rugrat's voice dying down, a light flashed through the documents under his hand. The heads of the Healer's Association and Formation Guild as well as Zhen Fu and the other Experts stood and started to run out of the city. A flood of people who had been doing their bidding fled as well.

A city lord's compulsion. This is why city lords are called gods on their own land. If they are in a war, they can't do anything, and if they are given the city by a higher power, like a sect, king, or an association, then they can't banish anyone sent down by that higher power. To do this against the associations, and to tell everyone in Vuzgal about it publicly…

Nadia was rooted to her seat. People only had a few choices when they were being banished: which direction to run, and to use a totem or not.

This was one of the benefits that the Ten Realms gave to city lords. This alone was a powerful draw.

"I am sorry about these disturbances that have been going on the last few days," Rugrat said sincerely. His voice no longer echoed over the city as he looked at the remaining people around the table.

"Vuzgal hopes that with time we will be able to restore your confidence in us. We invite you all to come tomorrow, when we will be allowing people to come to view our workspaces within the castle as a preview of the workshops we are building in the city and as a friendly exchange between crafters. Also, I was wondering if the Fighter's Association would assist us in building a Battle Arena, a place for people to trade pointers and to have weekly tournaments."

With Rugrat's words, the remaining groups perked up. With one hand, he offered banishment; with the other, he finally revealed the strength of Vuzgal and offered a way to grow together.

The Fighter's Association head, who had been interested in the Experts being kicked out, showed a smile on his face. "Someone who is straightforward—are you sure you're not a person from the Fighter's Association?"

"I wish it was as easy being the city lord as it was fighting." Rugrat smiled.

Nadia was having a hard time matching the man before to the man now. The two of them seemed to be different sides of the same coin. *Vuzgal is not simple, but what will the blowback from this all be? Just who did they banish?*

"I know that you all have a lot to attend to. I hope to see you tomorrow, if possible. Vuzgal should have returned to its regular operation then." Rugrat smiled as they stood and made to leave. Then he stopped and looked at Nadia.

"Tell Elder Lu that City Lord West is in seclusion, working to create the concoction he is looking for. Tell him that I am getting tired of dealing with Blue Lotus issues."

Nadia's body trembled. She knew that the Blue Lotus was in the wrong here. She had heard that Elder Lu had visited in the past, but she didn't think that it was *the* Elder Lu who commanded the Blue Lotus in the Fourth Realm.

She made sure to cup her fists and bow to him.

He nodded and headed off.

She breathed a sigh of relief before she left, marching toward her carriage, her face pale as she rushed to see what state the Blue Lotus was in.

Rugrat let out a breath and slumped to the ground, a few steps down the corridor from the meeting room.

Hiao Xen moved to grab and support him. The mana usage had been heavy as he restrained Expert crafters and then used a sound amplification scroll he had activated earlier, as well as his mana domain to stun the remainder and pass on his message.

"Just lower me down. None of them should see me here," Rugrat said.

George padded over. At his full height, he looked down at his master.

"Damn, that sucked," Rugrat said from the ground. "Don't worry—just need to recover my mana."

George looked at his slumped master and yawned, heading down the corridor.

"Some solidarity would be nice!"

George let out a yowl.

"Do you only think about food?"

George's yowls came from the hallway he was walking down.

"Are you sure that banishing them is the right idea?" Hiao Xen asked Rugrat, squatting down next to him.

"First, it shows our strength. Second, it shows our neutrality. Third, we've set a precedence for anyone who tries to disrupt Vuzgal, or step on our heads with their rank. We don't care who you are or your backing; Vuzgal will continue to operate. If they want to try to get back at Vuzgal, what can they do? They can stand in front of all the totems, checking where people are going? If they send people to cause trouble, you just banish them as well. Then, instead of us wasting resources, they'll be running into a wall. The associations have contracts with us; if they break them, then they're just letting people from the other sects and independent forces take their spots at the workshops and the Crafting trial dungeon. We can also frame it to show their real feelings, how they made a contract but are unwilling to follow through. Looks bad on them and people won't trust them as much. Even if they block us in the short-term, the amount it will cost in the long-term will only mount.

"With time, we can raise Expert-level crafters or hire them. I have faith in this. So what is kicking out a few Experts who are trying to take over the city? There are more to be found. Maybe you should make sure that the other crafters know this. As long as they don't cross our line, then they can craft to their heart's content."

"Okay." Hiao Xen was a bit shocked by how far Rugrat had thought ahead.

"Even if it comes back on us, it was worth seeing their pissed-off expressions. Some people are just pricks." Rugrat laughed as he pushed himself up onto his arms and started to get up.

"Did you just think of all those reasons after you banished them?" Hiao Xen asked, coughing as he realized what he'd just asked.

"Yup!" Rugrat laughed. "Got to think quick on your feet when a gunny asks just what the fuck you're doing. Bullshit on the fly one-o-one!"

Hiao Xen started to massage his temples, trying to lessen the building headache.

11 Holy Land of Fighters and Crafters

Nadia didn't sleep well. She hadn't slept at all. She had spent the night with Blue Lotus personnel, demanding answers. People were outraged and calling for them to go against Vuzgal. Then everything had gone silent as Elder Lu's rage cleansed these naysayers from the Blue Lotus.

People were scared stiff as it was clear that the Blue Lotus's connection to Vuzgal was not a simple one.

She received a message from the headquarters that said that she was now the head of the Vuzgal Blue Lotus until someone else was sent over.

With it came a new transfer, the sub-commander of her guard. Olivia Gray was the leader of the Tareng guards and had been the person to fight beside the Vuzgal leadership against the Blood Demon sect army. She had been dismissed from her duties after remedial training and punishment she was being sent to Vuzgal. She had seen Erik and Rugrat from up close as well as their forces. While she had stepped over the line, she did it out of frustration and anger, lashing out at anyone in her way.

She was still a powerful fighter and a good commander, who had previous experience with the Vuzgal leadership, making her a useful asset. Still she was under strict orders, if she stepped out of line then her previous punishments would feel like nothing more than a walk in the park.

She would arrive in a few days. Nadia was hoping that she could get some more information from her to understand these new city lords.

The message indicated that she was also to talk to Hiao Xen and make sure that he and Rugrat knew the Blue Lotus was determined to work together with them in the future in an equal partnership.

So she now found herself with a group of crafters who had not been banished from Vuzgal going to the castle.

The different carriages went through a side entrance that was much larger than the main entrance into the castle.

Her mind relaxed as they entered.

"The mana density is much higher here than in the rest of Vuzgal. With this concentration of mana, all of the mana in the city must be concentrated here," Kaeso said with approval.

"With a higher mana concentration, people will find it easier to focus their mind and remove distractions and won't be as fatigued," Nadia said.

"Yes, Miss Shriver." Kaeso smiled. He was an Expert-level woodworker but had remained neutral in what had happened in Vuzgal and Zhen Fu had overlooked him. He was an older man, late to become an Expert-level crafter, and his resources were much less than others in the Blue Lotus. He didn't mind and lived a simple life teaching others woodworking and improving his own craft.

Although he was an older Expert crafter, he had seen a lot more of the Ten Realms than others and had a wealth of experience.

He was also the highest ranking crafter from the Blue Lotus remaining in the city, to show that the Blue Lotus wasn't slighting the Vuzgal city lord's invitation.

"There are isolating formations and mana gathering formations set up across the area, removing the outside noises so that people won't be distracted from their work. This was made by someone who has worked with other crafters before," Kaeso said as they passed the outer area, which had different workshops built up among multi-story buildings that were simple but elegant.

They reached an inner area, which was divided up into regions. There was a large library broken into several different lecture halls, with people rushing from class to class.

There was another area with several warehouses where people were taking out their daily resources.

Then there were workshops, ranging from Apprentice to Expert.

Classes were being conducted in these different workshops. It wasn't filled, but there were still hundreds of people who had applied. Vuzgal's population had exploded and there was no less than two hundred thousand people in the city, with a large portion of transient people who would come to trade or see the city, stay for a short period and then leave.

Still, Vuzgal had held onto a great amount of the property, developing it themselves or releasing it in batches. The landowner's house had turned into an auction house when spots opened up; the price of land simply increased too quickly.

The land would simply be too expensive for any small trading group. It would need a conglomerate or at least a mid-level sect to buy out even some small plot. Though those who dedicate themselves to Vuzgal can get lands paid for as long as they carry out their duties. They can also increase their levels and skills. I was blinded by Zhen Fu's actions, but with that removed and if Vuzgal is allowed to develop, then their strength will only grow. Yes, it might take time, but even Expert crafters are willing to offer lessons and tips if the conditions are right.

"The Apprentice to Expert-level workshops are all grouped together. Wouldn't the Expert-level crafters be annoyed by the distractions?" she asked Crafter Kaeso.

"It might be annoying to some crafters, but to those who want to teach others, this is the ideal situation as people can watch what they are doing and they can watch others in turn. I am more interested in how all of the facilities, no matter the crafting skill, are all together. Most sects and even the associations will group people based on the skill that they're trying to learn and make sure they all focus and discuss only their craft. In sects or associations that focus on one particular craft, their resources are dedicated to those who increase their ability with Alchemy or formations, as with the Alchemy Association and the Formation Guild. Here, everyone seems to be equal." Kaeso laughed, as if he discovered something as their carriage came to a stop.

Other carriages had come and students waited to take them around the different crafting workshops.

Nadia looked at Kaeso.

"Oh, sorry, I thought it might be ridiculous. After all, crafters can get rather full of themselves. Though if they're all trained together in a place like this, working together, then wouldn't they appreciate one another a bit more? Even the Crafter's Association has different schools and isolate their people. Though, if they're learning together from when they start, if they come from humble beginnings and they're given a chance, what would happen?" Kaeso asked.

She could feel that it was some kind of test. "Wouldn't they do everything to take advantage of it?"

"Yes, to some degree, but don't you think that they might also be much more loyal to the people who raised them? Were you born into the Blue Lotus or did you join?"

"I was born in," she said.

"I joined and I can tell you that I will die as a member of the Blue Lotus. They took a chance with me, and I was able to get to this position. I am an old man, but I hope that my students will be able to help increase the strength of Blue Lotus. Some might call me a fanatic, but, think—if just a minority of those who are taught by Vuzgal support it, and I mean fully?"

"They don't even have Journeyman crafters, though," Nadia said.

"With time, given their position, they will be able to invite others to assist in teaching their people, or directly hire them," Kaeso said as the door to the carriage opened.

They stepped out of the carriage.

"Hello Miss Shriver, Expert Kaeso." The student bowed to them deeply, his eyes shining as he said Jansen's name.

Kaeso smiled simply while Nadia stood there as he came up out of his bow.

"Please, if you come this way, we have some of the students and department heads giving a demonstration of their skills," the student said.

Rugrat accessed his interface before accepting the changes he had made.

The mana that was drifting stilled as it was being drawn in. Then, from the main pillar, a faint blue shimmer appeared and Rugrat felt his mind clearing with the heightened mana.

"Feels more like home," Tan Xue said.

"The mana density down there is much higher. It is a smaller space; there are a lot of powerful people and we have a large core and mana stones. Just by containing the mana in the dungeon and siphoning off a bit into the mana gathering formation and allowing the rest to circulate within, the effects are stronger. It'll be the same density inside the castle. The conditions in the rest of Vuzgal will have a much higher mana density than the wilds of the Fourth Realm, but lower than back home," Rugrat said.

"But for fighters in your Battle Arena, they'll be able to fight longer without the mental drain, crafters will be able to cast spells for less mana and craft for longer and at a higher level." Tan Xue let out a laugh. "You're one sneaky smith."

"In and out, undetected and unsuspected." Rugrat winked.

Tan Xue grimaced. "Be a lot less creepy if you weren't pulling your shorts out of your butt crack."

"It's really stuck in there. I thought I was hiding it well," Rugrat said, giving up all pretense of trying to "hide" his activities.

"You ever get sparks in there?"

"A man needs to commit to the look, or else it's foolish. And yes. And why do you think I always have a ladle of quenching water nearby? Thinking man, I am!"

"Pants! Use PANTS! Ugh, come on, that image isn't getting out! Is nothing sacred! I thought you just missed last week!"

"Nope, burnt mah nuts."

Tan Xue looked to the ceiling. Words—sanity—had failed her, while her imagination, the little devil, conjured unwanted images in her mind.

"Aren't you scared with banning the Experts that less people will come to Vuzgal?"

"Nah. Shows we're not scared of them, don't see them as important. They don't have as much weight to throw around and well, we'll have more of our own Experts soon! Also, with this kind of mana density, the facilities, you think that many people are going to miss out because we dealt with some assholes trying to move on us? It is the Ten Realms—strength is respected."

"Yeah, you're not wrong there. Guess with Alva, people care more about the work you put in and the person you are than just your strength."

"'Cause we're not—woo-hoo!" An ember split off from within the forge, which Rugrat's back was facing. He jumped up in alarm, his eyes going wide. "Grab the ladle!"

"No! You grab the ladle!" she yelled.

Rugrat jumped and ass bombed the quench bucket. A faint hissing came from his attire.

"Have they lost their minds?" Nadia looked up at the shimmering blue mana that fell over the city, the mana density increasing once again. "It must cost tens of Earth mana stones per day to increase the mana density like that all over the city."

"A fee that they can easily pay for with the entrance tolls, or the taxes they can earn on the increased manufacturing of higher quality goods by the crafters," Kaeso said. "Really, Zhen Fu and the others were too short-sighted. Others might call this wasteful, but how many crafters would want to work in this environment? Or fighters want to train against one another in that new arena and then fight in the dungeons? I bet the Alchemist and the Fighter's Associations are feeling rather pleased. Look at where the mana goes."

Nadia looked over to the valley, seeing the mana pass over the wall. The pillars that ringed the valley activated, allowing mana to drift down toward the valley.

"The city lord meant to increase the mana density to help the workers working on the workshops to accelerate their speed and revitalize the people and visitors to Vuzgal after these last few trying days," the student said in a humble voice with hints of pride.

Nadia smiled at the student, understanding where that pride came from.

"The crafting demonstrations should be well underway now, though Expert Tan Xue has probably just started," the student said.

"Expert Tan Xue?" Nadia's eyebrow rose.

"She is an Expert-level smith. She is twenty-seven this year." The student tried to be nonchalant, but their excitement showed through.

Nadia shared a look with Kaeso.

I thought that they didn't even have any Journeyman-level crafters, much less Experts. Just what the hell is going on in this city? As soon as I think that I know something, it gets turned on its head!

"Let's head over, shall we?" Kaeso proposed.

"This way," the student said.

"Could we go past the workshops that the woodworkers are in?" Kaeso asked.

"Certainly," the student said. "The healing workshop is actually a hospital. All issues from those who are employed by Vuzgal as well as the students and the military can be treated here. Also, people who are looking to have a private appointment can come and pay two coppers for healing. Attached to them are the alchemists who help out the healers, or medics if they come from the military."

"Who is the leader of the healing house?"

"That would be Department Head Kyle. He has extensive knowledge in dealing with different health issues and injuries.

"Then there is the Alchemy workshop. Ingredients are purchased from the Alchemist Association or grown in our very own growing areas. All of the plants within the castle will be changed over to ingredients that are meant to calm one's mind and relieve their fatigue. So a number of the Novices and Apprentices are out doing that while the Journeyman-level teachers are conducting lectures."

"Do they sell any of their products, like the healers?" Nadia asked.

"All products made within the academy can be sold to those in the academy, or will be sold by affiliated stores within the city. The higher level ones, I believe, will be auctioned off. I heard we can only make mid Journeyman-level concoctions repeatedly but not every time," the student said.

Nadia coughed, shooting a look at Kaeso.

It seemed as if the student didn't understand just how unique their situation was. Most sects of the Fourth Realm desired mid Journeyman pills and would use them as rewards for their mid to high-level fighters. This student made them seem as if they were just candies.

They slowed down as they got to the woodworking shop.

A woman was working with a formation powered lathe. With easy movements, she cut down the wood, rounding it out.

She took it and added it to a carriage wheel she was making. She attached the spokes all together and then the outer wheel, adding it to a carriage frame that was outside the workshop. It rested on stone as weights were piled up in the cart until the stone underneath broke, but the wheels and carriage were fine.

"Each of those spokes is practically identical, allowing them to be switched out as long as one has another one of them. Their strength is all balanced. One could lose three spokes probably before the wheel failed. Though the interesting thing was how they left space for enchantments. When they were working with the wood, they unconsciously injected mana into it, strengthening it and refining the impurities that were inside the wood, increasing its tensile strength. They only cut away the excess wood, as if revealing the spoke and wheel underneath. If you look, there aren't even any blemishes on the wood. Without these imperfections, the wood will be much stronger as there are no weak points. They also didn't leave any markings on the wood. Some people using a chisel will leave behind notches. Although not a big thing when starting, over time these notches might create a weakness and allow the spoke to fall apart.

"The inner wood was dark ocher wood, which has a high strength and is hard to work with, but then it doesn't rot over time. The wheel wood is green oak. It has a high strength, but it is also flexible, so when it hits stuff on the road, it will deform slightly instead of being purely brittle," Kaeso said, reviewing what he had seen to Nadia.

"It looks simple on the outside but it takes a lot of work to complete and understanding of techniques and materials. To the outside observer, the artist's painting looks like it was easy to complete, but to other artists they see the brushstrokes and the craft contained within," Kaeso said as Nadia's eyebrows pinched together in intrigue.

They went to the smithy, where the largest group of people were checking out the Journeyman smiths.

There must be about ten Journeyman smiths. It is one of the harder crafts to pick up in the lower realms. But to raise so many, and they look so young too…

They followed the student, who led them back toward a larger and more refined forge.

Inside was a woman working on a piece of metal. Her entire body thrummed with energy as the mana shifted around her and struck with her hammer as she worked at her anvil.

She had enhanced the metal already and was shaping it. Her mana flowed into the item as she first stretched out the metal and then brought it into rough shape. The blade vibrated but her tongs held it still.

She then placed the blade into the furnace, taking a breath before pulling out the blade and placing it on the anvil. Mana formed on the head of her hammer and she slammed it down onto the blade. The blade went from rough to polished finished, with traces of mana lingering in new lines and runes that had formed.

She struck down again; another section completed and runes and lines appeared perfectly.

"Is this imprinting formations through smithing?" Nadia said.

"I believe it is. One must have a good understanding of formations, but more than that, they need to have a greater control over their mana and their body and their knowledge of what they're smithing. If they make one mistake, then the item would come out as a failure. At best, it would drop a grade; at worst, one would need to melt down the metal and reforge it," Kaeso said.

"You said that she was only *twenty-seven*?" Nadia asked the student.

"Yes, Head Shriver." The student cupped his hands to her and bowed quickly, trying to peek over at Tan Xue.

"The Fighter's Association will send more people to fight in the arena. Others will come to see it—crafters will come for the atmosphere and for the resources and aid that they can find here," Kaeso said.

"What about the Experts who were banished?"

"If their leaders are smart, they'll make sure to keep them far from Vuzgal and try to mend their relationship. Although the associations' headquarters wield more power and have greater populations, the exclusivity of Vuzgal, with its cheap inns that allow everyone from independents to sect leaders the ability to lodge in the city, means Vuzgal is on the rise." Kaeso looked around the city, a smile on his face. "It wouldn't be a bad place to retire to."

"Well, you'd be welcome to stay," a man said from behind them.

They turned to see Rugrat standing there, covered in dust and muck, looking nothing like a city lord.

"City—"

"No need for that. Here I'm just a smith." Rugrat grinned.

Nadia smiled.

"We're always looking for guest lecturers and we have plenty of outer students—people who want to learn, but not sign anything permanent. We're more than happy if they go on to other associations or sects as long as they pay their fees. With our inner members, they will always be a crafter from Vuzgal, but that doesn't mean we can't partner with the other associations." Rugrat shrugged.

"Your outer students—is there specific requirements from them?" Kaeso asked.

"Outer have a contract that others can buy out, but they don't get as much resources and they aren't able to know many secrets. The inner students have access to more resources but they sign a contract binding them to us and to keep any secrets they might learn. Someone can come here, learn a craft and then prove themselves in Vuzgal. They might be recruited into our ranks, becoming an inner or core member, or they can join others—it is up to them. They can be independent, as long as they pay off their contract, which also acts as a student loan."

"Akin to sects, but you're freely accepting putting time into people and losing them to others?" Kaeso asked. Sects, didn't want to lose a single person, the more people they had the more power they had as they could get the sect or group more resources. They too had outer inner and core members, spending more time and effort on those that were inner and core members.

"Well, the loans won't be cheap, but yeah, if we increase the strength of the population, then Vuzgal will only have a higher number of crafters in it. With more people, we generate more ideas and sifting through thousands of people, we can find a few with true ability. Again, only the inner members are those we trust like family and we will raise with all of our strength."

"Bringing in independents—no, you would be creating them—as long as they were willing to sign the contract?" Kaeso said.

"Right." Rugrat smiled.

"In the healing house and in the tailor workshop, I saw a number of people from the army there. Are you allowing your military members to become crafters?" Nadia asked.

"Allow them to become? Although they do train in fighting, most of them are at least Apprentice crafters. Many of the older ones are Journeymen. The healers use the healing house as a place to prepare for what they might deal with on the battlefield," Rugrat said.

"I didn't realize," Nadia said. *If they're crafters as well, no wonder they're looking for people who are driven over those with a high rank. All of these people are young, incredibly young, but their crafting is on par with those in the Sixth Realm. Only there are Journeymen common, and Experts can be seen in every city. For the Fourth Realm, it will be a big deal.*

Nadia was impressed as she saw that they were making the most that they could from their position.

Elder Lu looked up from the report, looking at Zhen Fu sitting in front of him.

"Using my influence, it will only be a matter of time until people start turning on the leadership of Vuzgal. Hiao Xen has become too consumed with power. It is truly a sad thing seeing one of our own like that." She sighed, shaking her head.

"If we can get them to agree to create the council, then we can start to increase the Blue Lotus's power over the city." She looked up, offering him this platitude.

"Oh," Elder Lu said.

"Vuzgal will become a powerhouse in the future. If we don't stake our claim, then we will lose our footing there," she said, confused by his words.

He put down the report and rested his finger on it. "This is a report from Nadia Shriver, the new head of the Blue Lotus location. After you left, the people of Vuzgal were a bit shocked, others relieved. Some even started talking up about how if they were banishing Experts, then they would ban others they didn't agree with, calling it a tyranny. They were banished as well. Though, the day afterward, City Lord Rugrat opened up the crafting sector that has been under construction since Vuzgal was properly established.

"They are offering to take in students, teach them. And the associations, the sects—all of them are free to poach them, and even send their students there. Even with our academies, we only allow people in from the outside if their position is extremely high and then we place a number of restrictions on them. They would take in anyone as long as they prove that they really desire to be a crafter through a series of tests. Now, we both know it takes time to raise someone's craft to a higher level. Though they somehow have a low Expert-level smith who looks to be close to making it to the mid-Expert-level, who is twenty-seven years old. From her file, she was in the Second Realm just a few years ago and she was at the high Journeyman level.

"So, in a few years, they could churn out Novices turned into Apprentices or Journeymen. Rugrat apparently hinted at leaving it open for people to freely recruit them. A sort of open scouting to take them into other associations. That's not all, though. They've got the full backing of the Fighter's Association and the Alchemy Association and all of the people in Vuzgal right now. They increased the mana density of the entire city and the valley, and are actively working with the Fighter's Association to build an arena.

"Let us not try to make this something it's not. You saw the potential of Vuzgal and you wanted it for yourself. You are a low-level Expert but you use it to lord over others. Your clothes are akin to bribes, using them to draw other Experts and people of power close to you. We don't mind this in the least, but instead of making us closer to Vuzgal, you've only increased the distance. You want to talk about value? With the contributions of the military of Vuzgal, they saved our face of having an entire city we co-operated wiped out. They tore down a war-fighting legion with less than two hundred people. Then there is the nature of Erik West's contribution.

"His two contributions eclipse everything that you have done for the Blue Lotus several times over. Saying that you were doing it for the good of Blue Lotus? Do you know who allowed Hiao Xen to become the acting city lord?"

Zhen Fu's shock had turned to anger but she kept her mouth shut due to her position being well below Elder Lu's. She wasn't even able to utter a word as Elder Lu kept talking.

"*I* did. He handled himself well with the issues against the Blood Demon sect. It was meant as a test of his ability to lead and command. Now you have weakened his position within the Vuzgal government, slapped our own faces, and I have to find a new head for Vuzgal's Blue Lotus location. Don't worry about crafters. With the recent changes, there are a number of Expert crafters coming from the higher realms who wish to see this Vuzgal city, its workspaces and its dungeon," Elder Lu said dryly.

"You will be transferred to the Fifth Realm. There you will become an evaluator for half a century. You will scout out talents in the Fifth Realm to send on to our academies in the Sixth Realm. It is the hope that this will allow you to control your emotions better and to put the work of the Blue Lotus ahead of your schemes," Elder Lu said.

Zhen Fu looked as though the strength had left her at his words. The networks she had arduously built up over the years would all be destroyed. An Evaluator went around finding people of talent and recommending them to the Blue Lotus.

That was it, they weren't like teachers that could take people under their wing, gaining their loyalty and growing them into powerful supporters. All of their work was dedicated to growing the Blue Lotus' power, instead of their personal power and their job took them across the realms. Not allowing them to stay in one place too long to set up a power base.

"You have your orders," Elder Lu said, dismissing her.

She choked down her words, the contracts she had signed with the Blue Lotus made her unable to refuse.

She bowed her head and stomped out of his office. Elder Lu couldn't see the fury on her face as she walked away, but he could feel it.

An Expert crafter's anger wasn't all that remarkable to him, if she was a high level crafter or master, then he might care.

Elder Lu looked out of the large windows behind him. He let out a laugh and shook his head. "Vuzgal? Well, they aren't politically minded—maybe it will make a truly neutral city in the Fourth Realm?"

12 Investigations

Delilah and Erik were in the Alchemy workshop, Erik observing Delilah as she worked.

She drew out a handful of yellow and purple pills from her cauldron and presented them to Erik.

He checked them over and sniffed them.

"Good, though you have some basic issues," he said as she secured them in a pill bottle.

"You didn't pre-warm the cauldron enough. Don't you remember how I told you to warm everything evenly? You need to add heat inside the cauldron, outside and over the lid. You heated up the bottom more than the top and then the lid was only mildly warm. This led to uneven heating of the concoction. Metal also expands and contracts, so the lid fit, but because of the uneven heating, the lid and the cauldron had gaps between them, creating a higher flow of air into the cauldron. That was why when you were adding the bleeding crown with crushed frost berries, you lost control of your flames for a few seconds. It also reduced the efficacy of the pill because of the mana dilution that occurred."

Delilah lowered her head, angry at missing such simple things.

"Remember, we can prepare for as long as we want. Prepare your ingredients, your cauldron, and all of your tools for as long as you want. As time goes on, you'll get so used to them you can use them with instinct. If you're already working, most times it is too hard to try to adjust. Instead of concocting pills, I want you to learn more about your tools. Also, use tools that work for you; don't use them just because. This is your Alchemy workshop—make it yours.

"Also! Poison pills are going to be the hardest to give your enemy! Powder you can spread over a large area; potions you can cover your blade," Erik said before his voice softened. "Have you cleared away your responsibilities?"

"I have delegated as many of them as I am happy with. Otherwise, I will have people bringing information to the Sky Reaching Restaurant so that I can remain in the loop with everything that is happening here."

"Okay, then we will set off tomorrow." Erik stood.

"There is one meeting I have to attend. It is about the expansion of Vermire," Delilah said.

"Do you need me to be there?"

"Well, it is expanding Vermire. It's a large project. We are still making plans and gathering information at this point..." Delilah trailed off.

"Remember how I said that I wouldn't have given you the position if I didn't trust you? Well, I think that this is one of those situations." Erik smiled.

Delilah and Glosil looked at Elan, who was hosting the meeting. Behind him, there was a map of the Beast Mountain Range with the different outposts marked.

"I have been cultivating assets in the outposts around the Beast Mountain Range. We have complete coverage of the outposts, but entering the upper echelons of each of the outposts has been difficult. With some, we have been able to get access. Still, I am confident that we will be able to know what is happening in each of the outposts and gather information on the happenings of the outpost leaders to aid in operations proposed by Lord Aditya of Vermire. In total, there are forty-seven different outposts of varying size that lay around the Beast Mountain Range." He pointed to the map of the main mountain range in the shape of a coffee bean with a wavy line moving through it, with multiple valleys that dotted the craggy landscape.

"The proposed site for the main trading outpost is on King's Hill." He pointed to a central located green area at the bottom of the mountain range on the south side. "Glosil has more information on this. With the forty-seven different outposts, we have the preliminary results listed in the reports in front of you. There are seventeen lords we have identified who would be interested in joining in on this venture without too many issues. That leaves thirty others. Nine more would join with some pushing through my contacts. Another thirteen would remain neutral; we can possibly pull them in later. The remaining eight are our issue. They will go against it. Five of them have backing from some kind of nation that will not take kindly to this. Three are independents. All of them are large powers in their own rights."

"So we will come into conflict with them no matter what." Delilah frowned.

"I believe so."

"Will they resort to violence? What will their move be?"

"Some of them might. It depends on the five that are backed by different kingdoms. If they push for it, then they could fight us."

Glosil cleared his throat. "It is likely they will attack the outposts or the main force when they are at their weakest, reducing the outposts' strength so they can attack the outposts directly and take them over. It's what I would do."

"So we have to worry about them attacking our rear."

"It would be better to get them to fight the other outposts than not, in my opinion," Elan said, getting Glosil's frown and Delilah's perplexed look.

"Two things: if they attack us in broad daylight, then we can have the outposts become closer, fighting against this new enemy. Second, we don't have to worry about them in the future. In one move, we build the outpost and clear out the outposts that could be a large issue in the future. If they don't fight us, then they might turn to banditry, attacking our convoys, draining our strength over time," Elan explained.

"In one strike, we take out their power, take their outposts." Glosil nodded.

"Which would also be great trading chips for us. We turn those outposts into outposts controlled by the same council as the King's Hill Outpost. Then people see that joining us has far more profits than not," Elan surmised.

"We still have to win this fight. Nothing has happened yet. We don't know if we will be able to get all of those outposts on our side or not," Delilah said, wanting to pull Elan back.

"I just want to make sure that we cover our bases," Elan said.

Delilah nodded and she turned to Glosil. "What do you think?"

Glosil stood and moved to the map as Elan took a seat.

"The terrain of the Beast Mountain Range is a pain to fight through. In the First Realm, storage devices aren't that easy to find. To establish the first road to the outpost, I propose that we have the force gather in one location, made up of five parts. The main fighting force will fan out and deal with any threats as they advance. They will have a reserve force as well to support them. Another force will be there to finish clearing the path and lay down a road to move supplies and supporting forces through the terrain. Then there will need to be a support element to repair weapons, hold supplies, cook meals, and such. The last force will move up and down the road, carting supplies in from Vermire. Slow and steady, move forward, clear a path, build the road all the way to King's Hill," Glosil said.

"Seems rather simple," Delilah said.

"It sounds simple, but they'll need to have navigators who are checking where they're going all the time to make sure that they don't go off course. Need to send out scouts to check the terrain and the beasts. The beasts are going to be pissed off that people are going through their territories. The moving supply train will need to have a fighting force to keep the beasts from killing them. The reserve force will act like close-in protection for the workers and supply train with the main force. We need to know if we have mages powerful enough to make the road or make it by hand. If we don't have enough building materials, food, water, arrows, then this all grinds to a halt. This will be hard to coordinate. Throw in different military groups—it will not be a simple and easy process."

Delilah let out an impressed grunt. "I didn't think of all the moving parts behind it. Even the food and water will be hard to maintain, needing to support that many people."

"Yes, and there will be a lot of people—about five hundred for the main contingent moving forward, three hundred fighters, and two hundred support or builders. If they are given time to work together, then they'll work out the kinks."

"Though what if they're attacked by the other outposts?" Elan asked.

"We are very selective in Alva who we pick to join the military because of the secrets that they will be exposed to. After talking with my officers, we are thinking about bringing a number of the Vermire fighting force into the Alva Army. We have had time to watch them and understand them. What I propose is that we begin a training camp. We train them up as we would train up basic soldiers. That should increase their strength rapidly, but not to the point where it alerts the other outposts. They then in turn train up the remaining guards and increase their numbers."

"Much like the Adventurer's Guild?" Delilah asked. "Where they are trained up by the Adventurer's Guild, then they come here for training and the opportunity to join Alva. Some join the military, others join Alva. Others go back to the Adventurer's Guild with much higher strength than before and increase our reach."

"Correct." Glosil smiled.

"Once we've trained them up, what do we do about these other outposts? The guard force is only around one hundred people for each outpost. Each outpost might only send twenty to thirty people. Let's not forget that five of the possibly aggressive outposts have the backing of a nation that has thousands of fighters at their disposal," Elan reminded Glosil.

"The one difference with training up these Vermire forces is that we will train them to fight in combat groups—healer, tank, ranged, damage, and corporal commanding—to increase their strength in the field. The current force of Vermire is around four hundred guards. I want to increase that number to eight hundred, with the additional four hundred being trained in secret. We will need somewhere for that training to take place, as well as Vermire's help and our recruiters help to pull in more fighters to train." Glosil looked to Elan.

"To increase their fighting strength rapidly, there are a lot of people who would be interested in the First Realm. As for the training location, it shouldn't be too hard to find one."

"The role of this secretly trained force will be to be ready against the potential threat from the other outposts?" Delilah asked.

"They will act as a safety for us, a force ready to be used. I want them ready to attack the lords conspiring against us. We can sell items for home defense to allied outposts through our trading network."

"You have really thought this through," Delilah said, not hiding how impressed she was.

"We don't always need to be the ones fighting to win," Glosil said.

"It will make the other outposts thankful for the items, and hopefully bring them closer to us. What if they use them against us?" Elan leaned forward.

"They could, but for the majority, if they're coming over to our side anyway, didn't we just get money from them to defend the land we control?"

Elan couldn't help but laugh at Glosil's words.

Delilah smiled as well.

"The one thing I can think of, from the council's perspective, is that it might be a better idea if the first road to the outpost doesn't come from Vermire," Elan said. "Creates tensions, making it look like Vermire has all of the cards. It would be a good bargaining chip."

"I can work up the three outposts that it will be easiest to make a road to and from. Just need the blueprint office to work on it. Thankfully, they already create maps and are familiar with the area," Glosil said.

The two men stopped and looked to Delilah.

"Okay, it looks like you have this in hand. I do not want any exposure of Alva in this. Get this camp location sorted out, train the current force, and have them train the second hidden force. I want everything in place before Aditya moves forward. Elan, manage him. Let him start feeling out the other outpost leaders, start hosting some balls or something to get them to come over. Maybe a few auctions with powerful items? Figure it out and keep me updated." Delilah stood and the two men bowed to her. She nodded to them. "I hope to have a new outpost in no more than a month!"

With that, she left the room.

Elan and Glosil looked at each other with serious expressions.

"I look forward to working with you directly," Glosil said.

"Thank you, Captain," Elan said.

13 Formation Academy Competition

Qin and Julilah had been working continuously after meeting with the formation academy's head-Yan Zemin. They received plenty of formation plans and resources.

Not wasting any time they got to work, wanting to see their fellow Alvans as soon as possible.

They were progressing quickly, they could take two, sometimes even three days to build them if they didn't finish them on the first try.

Failure was its own kind of success as it showed them what they hadn't mastered yet, and what they still needed to learn.

"What is all of that noise?" Qin asked sleepily. They had fallen asleep in the larger formation workshop again.

Julilah made a noise of not wanting to be disturbed as she turned her head away from Qin.

Qin went to the door and opened it, letting the sun in. She held her hand out against the sunlight streaming in. She saw a few formation masters walking around the workshop and raised her voice to them. "What is all of that noise for?"

"The noise? You don't know about the formation master contest?" one said, shocked.

"Contest? That sounds familiar. Hmm, is that what Yan Zemin was talking about?" Qin yelled to Julilah.

Julilah only answered with another annoyed noise.

"Thanks." Qin turned back and closed the door.

She looked at the formation workshop. There were two designs that they were working on. Julilah's was a domain formation while Qin was working on another area of effect formation that was meant to be hidden in a talisman. It was a mana barrier, but highly miniaturized so it could act as a hidden protection.

Qin's detail work wasn't that good, so she was taking on projects that improved her deficiencies.

She let out a sigh. The projects were challenging and fun, but she missed seeing Yui and Domonos. She hadn't seen them in so long and only had a few days to see them before they went to the Formation Guild.

Once we've finished reading from the library and we surpass Head Yan Zemin, then we can go to Vuzgal. I wonder how Father is doing.

She laughed to herself. *Now we only need to get little Wren to join Alva. It's been so long since I last saw him.*

She woke up Julilah forcefully. "Come on, let's clean up. Then we can head to the library. We've completed all of the basic classes now, so if we can understand all of the books, that should be the end of our education here. You can see Tan Xue again."

That magical name made Julilah get up. She didn't look pleased by it but she was moving at least.

They cleaned up their workspaces and then headed to their rooms. After cleaning up and donning new clothes, they traveled to the library.

"Most of them are probably at the contest," Qin said as they looked at the empty library.

"Less people to compete with for books," Julilah said.

They headed into the shelves, breaking up and going for different books. It made it faster and when they started talking or working on formations, they could condense that information down and pass it on to the other.

They only had limited access so they didn't have many more books to go through that might be able to help them at their current skill level.

Elan had completed his control over the information network in the First Realm as well as the Second and Third Realm.

He had created four different levels of information: information on the Ten Realms from other sects and organizations. Information coming from the higher realms. And information that might be useful for Alva and its people. This was further broken down into information on threats or possible threats to Alva, their subsidiaries or their allies, and useful information to increase Alva's strength.

Lastly, information on people from Earth and estranged crafters as well as possibly recruiting them.

Finally, he was making sure that no information was leaked about Alva Dungeon.

"I'll need to develop the information networks in the Third Realm a lot more. We really only have the Sky Reaching Restaurant that gives us a lot of rumors and information. That said, threat-wise, there aren't many people who can threaten the restaurant and the traders all work independently and are all over the place. The threat is in the Second Realm with other mercenary groups not liking how the Adventurer's Guild is stepping on their toes, or how the merchants from Alva are pushing out aggressively and quickly becoming large powers in the trading world. The First Realm has threats, though our strength is such that just one member of the army could stand up to an entire sect or a kingdom with the tactics Erik and Rugrat have taught them and the gear that Alva creates.

"With building out the intelligence agency, even though I have been able to pull more people in to share the burden, it will take time. For now, our main focus is gathering information in Vuzgal and the Fourth Realm and compiling more information on the higher realms. As Erik and Rugrat advance through the realms, their strength and the power of Alva increases. With what the Expert crafters were doing, it was a play for power—they were using their position as a formidable tool. If we truly want to be stable then we need to be an existence that can compete in the highest realm." Elan shook his head. Even the words sounded insane to him. There was so far to go, but it was the only way to create true stability like the stability that the associations had.

Elan adjusted his seat. "Okay, so then I need to head to the Fourth Realm," Elan said. "Didn't think that I would have to use my new levels so soon."

He got a sound transmission from people placed in Chonglu.

"There were two strong people who just exited the totem before heading for the castle. I think that they're now fighting," the spy hurriedly said.

Elan closed the sound transmission, taking a moment before he sent a message on to Erik, who was preparing to leave the next day.

Qin and Julilah were reading when a librarian came up to them.

"Aren't you two interested in the competition?" the librarian, a kind-looking man with a long white beard, asked.

"Not really," Qin said.

The librarian coughed and his eyes bulged in shock, as he tried to display his high Apprentice-level emblem on his chest more prominently.

"You okay?" Julilah looked up from her book with a frown.

"Young ladies like you, aren't you interested in seeing the talents from the other academies? It is a great opportunity to meet others," the older man said, hinting heavily.

"Not all that interested," Qin said.

"There are girls and boys there." The man looked between them.

"What are you trying to say?" Julilah asked.

The old man sighed and shook his head. "You're young and free. This is a great opportunity to get outside and leave the worries of the world behind. A change of scenery is as good as a break!"

"Just got a few more books to read," Julilah said.

"You must go out and enjoy life or there will be little to remember and enjoy later on!" The man drew himself up to his full height.

"Well, books are more useful for us," Julilah said.

"Fine. I will let you borrow these books as long as you make an oath to return them and to go and watch the competition!"

"Okay. It would be nice to get some sun," Julilah said.

Qin let out a groan but the older man, getting their agreement, quickly took them to the counter and signed out their books, got them to give an oath and then sent them on their way.

Qin and Julilah were walking toward the competition, getting used to the sun outside, as the older man whistled and locked up the library.

"Telling us to go and enjoy life and our youth but he just wanted to close the library and have the day off!" Qin complained.

"Come on, don't you want to see people fighting with formations?" Julilah asked.

"They have formation fighting? Why didn't you say so?" Qin grabbed her friend's hand and led the way to the arenas.

Being the close students of Head Yan Zemin, they were quickly admitted and found some seats in one of the booths that was reserved for visitors.

Cai Cheng sat in the challenger box. There were three such boxes for the students of the different academies that were going against one another in the competition.

Cai Cheng was a genius within his academy. It was only his third year and he had reached mid-Apprentice rank. He came from the famous Cai family. Much like the Mao clan, they were a group with wealth and resources that they used to cultivate geniuses to gain high position within the Formation Guild.

Cai Cheng didn't see anyone from his current generation as his opponent. He wanted to use this competition to increase his momentum and gain favor in the head of the academy's eyes so that the head could apply on Cai Cheng's behalf to get him promoted into an academy in the Fifth Realm. There the association's power was much higher, the mana was less chaotic, and it was filled with academies.

It was a big change as the groups in the Fifth to the Seventh Realms turned from fighting one another and turned into crafters. Fighting competitions were still held, but dungeons and crafts were the main way to increase one's level. With the complicated nature of alliances, if there was one fight in the higher realm groups, then it wasn't impossible for an entire continent and millions of people to be drawn into the conflict.

The opportunities and wealth of information in the Fifth Realm were like heaven and earth compared to the Fourth Realm. All of the resources from the Fourth Realm that had any value were transferred to the Fifth Realm anyway for people to purchase or use.

The younger one was when getting to the Fifth Realm, the greater their achievements.

Cai Cheng was confident in his skills as he saw two girls entering a private booth and sitting down.

They wore simple robes, but they showed signs of newly formed women. Their eyes were bright and there was a presence around them that few girls would have at their age.

Their skin looked soft, making Cai Cheng want to cup their faces in his hands and look into those water-like eyes.

He took a moment, sensing their aura more. *They're a lower level than me, but with that confidence and the way they look around the arena, it is clear that they only have a limited interest here.*

"Who are they?" Cai Cheng asked one of his friends.

"It seems that Cai Cheng's eyes are similar to my own." Lian Ju spoke up, making Cai Cheng frown.

He looked at the other boy. He was just two years his senior, but he was just a half-step stronger than Cai Cheng.

"Lian Ju," Cai Cheng said in a low voice of warning.

"I'm not sure which one I would pick. Why don't I just have both of them! They would suit me well, don't you think?" Lian Ju asked with a raised eyebrow and laughed, his eyes never leaving Cai Cheng.

"Don't you think that they should go to the strongest person?" Cai Cheng counterattacked.

"I can only agree," Lian Ju said lazily, but his eyes sharpened.

Seems as if he is trying to probe me more.

"I find that competitions are much more fun if there is something to be won or lost," Cai Cheng said simply, staring Lian Ju down, a taunting smile on his face.

The others around them who heard the terms of their bet talked to one another, getting excited.

"Whoever places higher will have them," Lian Ju said.

"I agree." Cai Cheng looked away, as if Lian Ju was no longer worth his time, and his eyes fell on the two girls.

One was reading a book and the other had propped up her head and watched the battle happening below.

14 Retribution

Erik was having lunch and looking at his latest reports, waiting for Delilah to finish her work before they set off for the totem, when he got the sound transmission from Elan.

He listened to Elan's message. *People showing up from the totem and then heading to Chonglu's castle.*

He was up and running before his mind caught up with him. His chest tensed in fear.

Gong Jin, Simms, Xi, Tully, and Yang Zan were up and following him. Since Glosil took over, there was always a group with him. Special Team Two was in Alva; Special Team One was in Vuzgal with Rugrat.

They must be people from the Stone Fist sect coming to finish off the job!

"Roska! Bring your special team to the teleportation pad, now!" Erik yelled. His clothes pressed against his body as he ran at full speed, turning into a half blur. He moved through the dungeon, with people yelling out behind him.

He jumped up onto Gilga as the rest of the special team jumped onto their own mounts.

"Egbert, teleport to Chonglu!" Erik said, knowing Egbert would hear him anywhere in the dungeon.

We have to make it! Erik knew only too well how easy it would be for people from the Fourth Realm to kill someone from the First Realm.

Without needing a guide, it means that they must have been here before. Could they be the assassins who came down before and are looking to finish the job?

Erik quickly passed on what he knew in just a few sentences as they moved and checked their gear.

Lord Chonglu woke up to the screams inside the walls of his castle.

Ronhou stirred and let out a growl. With their connection, Chonglu's eyes snapped open. *Scents from that night!*

Chonglu got out of his bed, ran out of his room, and slammed through room after room, leaving his robe behind as Ronhou followed behind him.

"Protect the children and slow the attackers!" Chonglu yelled. He knew that the assassins would be able to defeat them in their current state.

"Yes, Lord!" Quinn said as he started to organize the people in the castle.

There were screams all around. Chonglu's world had turned into one goal: protect his children.

I can ban them from the city, but I need to know their name or be in their presence. Though if they just declare war on the city, it won't do anything! He gripped his fists, feeling useless and weak.

The door ahead of him was slammed open ahead. Felicity was there, dressed and wide-eyed, her maids around her.

"Come!" he said, moving for Feng's apartments.

Felicity was picked up by Quinn as the maids fell behind the stronger guards running after their lord with steely expressions.

The corridor they were in was filled with dust as a man stood up in the middle of the guards. His features and body were hidden underneath black robes, with no way to identify him.

"There you are." He locked his eyes onto Chonglu.

"Stall him and protect the lord!" Quinn yelled as he and the lord's personal guards kept on running.

"Ants!" the man yelled as people charged him.

His movements were quicker than the human eye could follow. Each punch deformed metal and destroyed flesh. Blades couldn't touch him as he moved forward.

Chonglu felt that the man was almost bored, savoring the growing fear in Chonglu, that sense of impending doom.

"I ban you from the city Chonglu!" Lord Chonglu yelled.

The man's attack paused for a half second, enough for someone to land an attack. The man was pushed forward by the spear jab, but his armor easily took the hit.

"I declare war!" he yelled as he turned back, yanking the spear from the user's hands as if dealing with a child, pulling him forward. He reversed the spear and stabbed back in one motion. The spearman, impaled with his own weapon, looked down at the weapon pierced through his armor and body.

He's no man but a demon! Chonglu thought as he heard fighting ahead of him.

"Feng!" Chonglu yelled.

The guards threw the doors open, showing a bloody scene beyond. They had charged a second black-covered man.

He moved his hand and combined it with mana, turning it into a finger art that shot out, sending guards flying with serious injuries as he marched forward.

Feng let out a yell and attacked.

Ronhou, seeing his actions, charged forward and bit the attacker's arm. His aim was thrown off, and his attack blew out a wall instead of hitting Feng.

The man snarled and punched Ronhou.

Ronhou slumped and Chonglu felt the contract between them disappearing.

The man shook Ronhou off and his eyes locked onto Feng. He moved forward, throwing his fist forward as he executed a fist art.

"Get back!" Chonglu used a secret technique, shooting forward to grab Feng and threw him back to his guards. Chonglu felt his actions were locked down and felt the fist seeking him out, leaving no room to escape.

"Die!"

Chonglu felt the attack strike him in the chest. His weak talismans were easily broken. He was only wearing simple armor after being woken up in the middle of the night.

He flew backward; his vision dimmed as he slammed into the ground, a green circle around him. He heard an explosion in the distance.

Erik lowered his rifle; the assassin looked at the bloody hole in his chest that was starting to repair and then at Erik with shocked eyes as he said two words.

But Erik could only hear the last part: "—gal."

The man dropped to the ground.

"Protect the children! See to the wounded! Yang Zan, I'm going to need your help!" Erik's voice rose as the tombstone appeared and Chonglu was revealed.

"Who are you people!" Quinn demanded as he looked at the five people swarming through the castle who had hidden their identities.

Erik tossed out a talisman to Quinn; then he took a knee next to Chonglu, keeping power going to the Hallowed Ground underneath him as he assessed him.

"You should know that I have the trust of Lord Chonglu," Erik said, using his Clean spell on Chonglu.

The guards stepped forward, ready to cut them down.

"Erik?" Quinn said, holding up his hand.

"Seems that you need a healer, good thing I was in the area," Erik threw off his cloak, as he got ready to work.

Quinn seemed to be having and internal debate.

"Either you let me help him, or he dies," Erik said, he didn't want to get stabbed in the back by a nervous guard.

"Do it," Quinn said and waved his guards down.

Erik didn't have any deep ties to the man, but he had healed his children and was invested in them. Seeing the passion and care from their mother, he couldn't just stand by. That wasn't the kind of person he was.

Yang Zan moved to him as Gong Jin organized the others to check on the other wounded and create a perimeter.

Roska appeared and dropped another body off covered in black.

"He's messed up internally. I'm healing his brain—massive internal injuries, bones turned into shrapnel inside his body," Erik said, thinking of possible treatment options.

"Check his head and heal his brain. Keep me updated on his status. Watch his Stamina," Erik rattled off as Yang Zan moved to put his hands on Chonglu's head.

Quinn took the children away. They were in shock and seeing the condition of their father wouldn't calm them and might only scar them.

"I've got a crack in his skull," Yang Zan said.

"Fix that first. Use Heal Bone. Don't need to do it all the way—only stabilize him," Erik said, studying Chonglu's body. It wasn't good as he had taken the hit to the chest. His bones had been shattered, shredding his organs and internals to different degrees.

"Make sure to conserve your mana." Erik pulled out IV bags that had been readied with IV tubing of different concoctions. He tore open the bag holding an IV needle and catheter that the healers had worked on with different crafters to create.

"Understood," Yang Zan said.

"The damage is too severe to use general healing spells—even focused ones won't work. Going to have to operate. Need to reduce the strain on his body." Erik talked to himself.

"Remove his limbs. That way we're focusing on the main body, not worrying about clotting or those issues in the limbs," Yang Zan said.

Erik thought his suggestion was insane; it went against everything that he had been taught. Just lopping off someone's limbs was never a good idea.

"If we do that and store them, we can reattach them afterward!" Erik tore open a bag with IV instruments and pressed his fingers against Chonglu's neck.

"Quinn, come here!" Erik yelled.

"Brain is holding stable. Stamina is dropping quickly. Heart has stopped. Lungs still collapsed," Yang Zan said as Erik found what he was looking for in Chonglu's neck.

"Putting IV into the external jugular vein," Erik said. He hit the vein on the first try.

"IV solution four parts Stamina, one part healing solution," Erik said. The tubing had been primed and there were no bubbles, allowing him to attach it directly into the catheter and let it flow into Chonglu's body.

Quinn dropped beside them and Erik used the Clean spell on him and passed him tourniquets.

"Open these up and put them around his upper legs and arm." Erik pointed to the places he wanted them with his right hand as he pulled out a tray of medical tools, using the Clean spell again.

He cancelled his Hallowed Ground, feeling his mana recovering, and took out scissors, cutting Chonglu's clothes to expose his chest.

"Stamina is starting to stabilize. We're really low—touch and go here," Yang Zan said.

"Make sure to take mana pills as needed, and concentrate on conserving. The more mana we expend, then we can't keep him going." Erik used a scalpel to cut Chonglu open. He didn't need to break his breastbone as he opened his chest. His heart wasn't beating anymore and he looked like a mess internally.

Erik stabbed a needle into Chonglu's heart and injected the small amount of healing and Stamina concoction held within the needle.

Chonglu's heart started to recover slowly and Erik turned to the ribs and breastbone, using his Heal Bone spell that made his bones glow. He fused them together, enough to make them stick together but not enough to make them recover completely.

"I'm done," Quinn said.

Erik put his tools to the side; using the Clean spell, the dried blood fell from his hands. He grabbed one of the arm tourniquets closest to him and yanked on the strap and then took the handle on the strap and twisted it, tightening it a few more times as he spoke.

"Don't be scared about hurting him! Tighten it up until you can't anymore and then turn it a few more times."

"Stamina drop!" Yang Zan said. "Brain can't go on just my healing spells. Thinking spinal or brain stem tap with Stamina!"

"Shit," Erik hissed as he massaged Chonglu's heart, pumping the Stamina and healing solution. The Stamina solution was replacing the blood or revitalizing it, while the healing concoction broke down the clots that were forming and repaired the damaged veins, arteries, and cardiovascular system.

The IV in Chonglu's neck was also working, but it was going down to the heart instead of up to the brain.

Erik massaged the heart, mechanically forcing blood through Chonglu's body. He used his Simple Organic Scan, looking through Chonglu's body.

"Blood now moving to the brain," Yang Zan said before he fell silent.

The two of them had turned off the outside world, their patient the only thing they were focused on.

Erik paused on massaging Chonglu's heart and it started to beat by itself.

Erik didn't have time to be happy as he looked at Quinn.

"They're tight," Quinn said, his face pale. He looked just at Erik, not daring to look down.

Erik checked the tourniquets and then pulled out a blade, using his Clean spell on it. "Okay, cut where I leave marks."

"Cut?" Quinn asked, alarmed.

"Do it or else his body will be strained trying to recover everything and then we could lose him!" Erik yelled and forced the blade into Quinn's hand, using the Clean spell again to make sure that his hands were clean. Erik took a new scalpel from his tools, cleaned it, and pulled out what looked like a perfume bottle. There was a healing potion on one end and a small air pump with a bendable nozzle.

Erik cut Chonglu's trachea and put the bending nozzle down and inside, squeezing on the little air pump.

The healing solution turned into an aerosol, spreading through the lungs, and started healing them from inside.

"Need to hold the healing solution. Body is in severe Stamina withdrawal," Yang Zan said.

"Condition otherwise?"

"Brain is stable. Heart is strong. Cardiovascular system is repairing, but internal bleeding is heavy, leaking all over the place—whole body is trying to recover instead of system by system," Yang Zan said.

Erik looked over at Quinn, who had removed Chonglu's first leg. One of the guards standing nearby took it from him.

"Looks like losing the leg reduced the Stamina loss," Yang Zan said.

"Hurry up, Quinn!" Erik said.

Emboldened by their words, Quinn worked quicker, removing the limbs.

Erik had a pair of tweezers and a scalpel. He removed the bone fragments throughout Chonglu's body.

Quinn watched over them as Erik and Yang Zan talked back and forth. Yang Zan kept Chonglu stable as he calmly sipped on mana potions. If he did one wrong thing or didn't notice something, then Chonglu's condition could collapse in a matter of seconds.

He used an airbag to make Chonglu breathe, using the aerosol healing solution only a few more times before he removed it and healed the trachea.

Erik fused the broken ribs, removed the bone fragments, and aligned his spine again. It was time-laborious work. They needed Chonglu to recover enough Stamina so that their stabilizing spells would be effective and they could continue to progressively heal him.

This kind of healing would be impossible back on Earth and it went against most of what he had been told to do as a medic.

Erik removed the last bone fragment. Chonglu still had massive internal injuries, but his lungs were being made to work with the air bag. His heart was working and pumping the mostly IV solution in his veins; blood was starting to be created again and although recovery was incredibly slow, it was happening.

Erik put down his tools and then started to stitch up the various injuries inside Chonglu's body. With them next to one another, less healing solution would need to be expended and Chonglu would recover faster.

Erik checked him over once again and rolled back onto his heels, realizing how much his body hurt from being stuck in just a few positions for hours, only moving quickly when there was an emergency.

"Check without healing spells," Erik said, as he used Simple Organic Scan.

Yang Zan stopped casting his Focused Heal on Chonglu's brain.

Erik and Yang Zan checked his brain and his body. It was still in critical condition, but now, with time and a very weak healing concoction mixed with a strong Stamina concoction, Chonglu would recover.

"Monitor him over the next hour and make sure that there are no issues without continuous healing spells. We can increase the healing concoction then and he'll recover faster," Erik said.

"Yes, sir," Yang Zan said.

Erik looked to Quinn, who sat in a chair, watching them. "We're going to need to move Chonglu and his family. If they stay here, another attack might be right around the corner."

"This is Chonglu," Quinn said defiantly.

"You think that you can stop people from the Fourth Realm easily?" Erik asked.

Quinn fell silent, gritting his teeth in anger.

"Sir, we stopped people from moving. We didn't want information to leak." Roska walked over from where she had been tending to the wounded. "Gong Jin has been in charge of security while I have been in charge of the other medics."

"Were you able to save many?" Erik asked.

Roska simply shook her head. She didn't need to say anything else.

"You did good. They're all to take oaths to agree not to tell anyone about us. Nothing is to leak about this incident. Tell the people that he was attacked, but he repelled the attacker and is leaving to meet with the king immediately. I will head to see Mira Elsi," Erik said.

"Are you sure that is a wise idea?" Roska asked.

"I don't see why it wouldn't be. I'll return within ten minutes." Erik walked over to the two corpses and waved his hand, collecting them both.

"What are you doing?" Quinn grabbed the hilt of his sword.

"You won't know who these people are, but I need them as proof. Trust me, the next person who comes will be Chonglu and his children's greatest shield." Erik jumped and flew through the window. It was mid-morning now; he had been working on Chonglu for unknown hours.

He flitted over the rooftops. People didn't even catch sight of him before he dropped into an alleyway. He changed his clothes and walked out to the totem, making it look as if he was just crossing the square before he disappeared in a flash of light.

Mira Elsi rushed over to Vuzgal when she got the message, heading to the designated Sky Reaching Restaurant.

She was guided to an empty floor. In it, there was Erik, wolfing down food.

Seeing her and her alone, he looked at the guide; they nodded to Erik.

"I need you to swear an oath that you will not reveal where any information I give you came from, or look into my background or the background of anyone I am associated with," Erik said.

"Why?" Mira asked.

"I have enough worries—I do not need you as well," Erik said. *Others have probably figured out we're not from the Ten Realms. As long as they don't figure out Alva, we'll be fine.*

Mira studied Erik some more as he continued to eat.

"This better be useful or the oath will be annulled," Mira said.

Erik waved his hand and two corpses appeared. "These two nearly killed your husband and intended to kill your children," Erik said. The oath came in full force, binding Mira's words and actions.

The room chilled but Erik wasn't affected by it and continued eating.

"I can take you to see Cai Chonglu," Erik said. Elan's information network was already starting to show some fruits.

Mira tensed at what he was saying but instead chose to take a knee and pulled off the wrappings of the different men and checked their storage rings.

"Does he still use his first name at banquets?"

"Never known him to have a banquet and it took quite a lot to find out his first name—only refers to himself with his last name."

She looked at him, studying him again before standing. Her words had been another test. "These are people from the Stone Fist sect," she said, a cold look in her eyes.

"I can take you to Chonglu. You can call on the people who are downstairs," Erik said.

Mira arched her eyebrow.

"This is my city, after all." Erik looked out of the window at Vuzgal. He was still surprised by the scenery; the city was growing faster than ever. Rugrat's actions were a master stroke, increasing the number of people within the city, many times over. People were already asking whether it was possible to increase the size of the city so that there would be more housing available.

"I would be in your debt." Mira stood and cupped her fist.

Erik could tell how hard it was for a proud person like her and one who had been betrayed by the people she trusted most to make such a statement.

"Follow me." Erik pulled on a hat that hid his features.

"Why did you do this for me?" Mira asked, unable to hold her question back.

"I didn't do it for you. I did it for your children," Erik said bluntly.

Mira fell into silence as she had the others with her and followed Erik.

They left Vuzgal through the totem.

Entering the First Realm, their mana moved slower and there were more impurities within it. Erik and the others felt awkward as their bodies tried to draw more mana in, but the First Realm didn't have any more mana to give.

Erik guided them away from the totem quickly and then through some alleyways before climbing to the roofs and heading for the castle.

The members of the special team and the guards were still there as Erik and Mira's people were escorted into the castle and up to where Chonglu was.

Mira, who always seemed to look at the world around her with cold eyes, let out a startled breath as she saw Chonglu's broken body on the ground.

"He just needs time to recuperate, we think," Erik said.

Quinn looked at the guests and then to Mira. Erik's words seemed to break him out of his reverie.

"My lady." Quinn dropped to his knee.

"Quinn?" Mira looked at him closer.

"While you didn't age, some of us did," Quinn said.

There was a noise and Mira turned and looked to see a young boy and girl.

Looking between them, Erik could see the resemblance.

The boy and girl looked tired and distraught. Tears, long dried, left trails on their faces as they looked at this woman.

Felicity rummaged around her neck and pulled out a locket as Feng looked over and then to Mira.

"Mom?" Feng asked.

Mira's ice empress exterior shattered and tears poured down her eyes. She turned into a blur, leaving falling ice behind as she dropped to her knee, hugging them both.

She tried to say words but could only cry and look at them both, studying and looking at them for any damage.

The group with her spread out to protect the castle.

Roska walked up to Erik. "We have the oaths. They'll think that we were sent by Mira," Roska said in a sound transmission.

"Good," Erik said and moved to one of Mira's people.

"He needs a mixed healing and Stamina concoction. It would be best if a healer also monitors him at the same time to keep him stable," Erik said.

Special Team Two gathered themselves up, their job done.

"Look after those two. They awoke their constitutions. Ice phoenix constitutions—should be powerful fighters in the future," Erik said as he left with the group.

"Thank you!" Mira yelled after him.

"Remember—none of this happened." Erik looked into her eyes.

Mira nodded as Erik turned and left with the special team. They used the totem to return to Alva.

Once they were safe he took a look at his latest notifications.

Skill: Healer

Level: 73 (Journeyman)

You have become familiar with the body and the arts of repairing it. Healing spells now cost 5% less Mana and Stamina.

45,948,136/56,900,000 EXP till you reach Level 58

My Experience gain wasn't much in terms of my overall, but still, everything adds up. I don't know what I'll have to do in order to push forward now. The fastest way is to kill things. With crafting, I can level up, albeit slower. Erik waved his notifications to the side.

"The way that I think of healing people has changed from when I first entered the realms. I would've never taken a person's limbs off unless they were damaged but I took them off to keep more blood in the body and reduce the strain on Chonglu. Stamina and mana play a much larger function than limbs. Everything can be healed or altered with time."

Erik spoke to himself quietly. He was a little scared with how easily he had changed his ways and adopted methods that any doctor back home on Earth would've dismissed as ridiculous. Magic, concoctions, and healing magic made it all possible.

15 Armaments

Rugrat looked at a formation on one side of his workspace and his original rifle from Earth on the other.

"Okay, I've adapted items in the Ten Realms to become weapons like those on Earth." He sat down on the stool in front of the desk.

"Though, that said, weapon technology on Earth still has room for advancement. Sure, the fifty cal machine gun might work as advertised a hundred years ago and a 1911 pistol does the same thing. Reliable is good, but reliable might not be the strongest. Gatling gun—good concept when it started, great gun. Then someone stuck a motor on it and then its rate of fire shot up and the heat was dispersed over multiple barrels to allow cooling.

"Earth weapons are heavy. They need a ton of ammunition. Ammunition problem is solved with storage rings. Though we still need to increase our production speeds. The weight issue by increasing Body Cultivation. Recoil can also be negated by increased strength, better aim with Agility. Which then gives rise to issues like the rounds aren't as powerful. With a higher reaction time and greater control over the human body, shooting at longer distances isn't an issue. But then you have to calculate where that round is going, change up your shooting table. I can do it, sure, but very few people understand math other than the sharpshooters who have mandatory tests and classes.

"Now the other issues with weapons: heat buildup, the amount of ammo that it can store. We've got repeating crossbows and bolt action rifles. They're good but reloading them is a pain in the ass. Also, although we're building out an ammunition factory, more rounds is always better than less rounds." Rugrat took out an M32 launcher and put it on the table.

"The charge is made of gunpowder, but then the explosive head is actually just a formation on the round. The power of the round, if it has a formation, isn't based on its speed or weight, but the material and the formation." Rugrat lapsed into silence.

"For artillery, we could make howitzers, but that is a hell of a lot of work. And if we improve the mortars, maybe got acceleration formations on the tubes, we could be hitting even farther away with greater lethality. Simpler, easier, still as deadly and with a higher rate of fire. Tube acceleration…if there was a way to do that, if we could accelerate the round instead of using gunpowder. Recoil won't disappear when you use a rail gun instead of a gunpowder round, but then, if needed, a formation can increase the power that it uses to fire. So say someone increases their Body Cultivation—their weapon shots are as powerful as they can handle without needing an entirely new rifle.

"Also say they're going up against a powerful opponent. Sure, they might bust their shoulder, but with some healing concoction, they could fight stronger opponents with much stronger defenses. With gunpowder weapons, we would have to keep on finding new powders, just like how I spent days with those rifles. With a formation, we just boost the power. So with magical rail guns, we don't need the gunpowder, so we can make larger and denser projectiles and cover them with stronger formations, filling or covering them in poisons.

"Also, if there is no cartridge, but only the projectile, there is nothing to extract and remove the spent casing. Just need a magazine to push the rounds up, then the magical rail gun part to send it hurtling forward. We could make the rounds smaller if we wanted. Have a long barrel for greatest acceleration…magazine fed. Bullpup or not? With bullpup, get that longer barrel without the greater length overall, though we can only really use stick magazines. Can't use drum magazines or you've got that sticking in your ribs, making it hard to aim properly.

"We won't go with bullpup—if we could make a truly universal weapon, then we could arm everyone with this. Everyone would be a machine gunner, a rifleman, and grenadier."

Rugrat leaned forward and started to sketch out what he wanted.

"It will look like the FAL. So standard forward mounted magazine, so if you have a drum mag, no problem. Put rails on the front to load up a grenade launcher. It won't be hard to modify the M32 parts to a smaller underbarrel version. I can make a suppressor—just be a band of metal that goes over the barrel with a silencing formation. I'll pass them off to Special Team One and they can help me in making and adjusting the regular sights on the weapons. We still need to look at different sights, like those with magnification and projection sights like red dots and holographic sights. I need to talk to Qin and Julilah, see if we can make the formations all socket-based so they can be replaced. That way, we can upgrade the formations without having to make a completely new rifle!"

Rugrat continued to draw out several more blueprints, adding to a list of things he needed to figure out, or get someone's help to figure out.

He got up and stretched.

He felt George through their connection. The wolf was bored, antsy, and trying to get Rugrat to head over to the dungeon that was to the west, near Aberdeen, that he'd located when they were running from the city.

Rugrat left his workspace and headed over to where Tan Xue was giving a lecture.

He waited until she finished before walking up.

"Seems that your open house idea really worked out." Tan Xue raised an eyebrow at the departing students.

"Wanted to make sure that you weren't bored." Rugrat smiled as he pulled out blueprints. "I was wondering if I could get your opinion on these."

Tan Xue waved him forward and they left the lecture hall and went to a private study. She took the papers from him and put them on the table. "It's always new weapons with you."

"Might as well be—been using them for so long." Rugrat shrugged. "Do you know if Aberdeen is still fighting?"

"Aberdeen?"

"The city to the west," Rugrat said.

"I have no idea. Ask Hiao Xen." Tan Xue looked over the pages of information still. "For the barrel, it would be best to use Earth iron mixed with enhancers that disperse heat. Then you can increase the rate of fire without fear of melting the barrel without *a lot* of punishment. Have you figured out the formations that you want to use on the barrel?"

"Nope. I was hoping to give that one to Julilah and Qin," Rugrat said.

"Good idea. Swapping formations should work but Julilah would be able to tell you more. This is also a lot less complicated than those other versions, without so many moving parts."

"The only moving parts are really the trigger that activates the acceleration formation and then the spring or formation in the magazine that pushes the new rounds into the rifle," Rugrat said happily.

Tan Xue held her chin as she kept reading.

"You sleeping well?" Rugrat asked suddenly.

"Yes, why?" Tan Xue looked at him with a frown on her face.

"Want to make sure that you're doing well. We spend so much time working on these different projects and not making time for ourselves, I just wanted to check that you're okay," Rugrat said.

"I'm fine," Tan Xue said.

"Seeing anyone?"

Tan Xue looked over to him with a raised eyebrow. "Do you want me to look at this blueprint or discuss my love life?"

"Bit of the old multi-tasking," Rugrat said.

"I haven't been dating, nor have I been looking for anyone. I've been focusing on my smithing and trying to increase my ability. I'm still young. We can now live till we're like four hundred years old and we haven't crossed forty years yet. We've got time." She cleared her throat.

"From what I can see, it looks like it would work to me, though you're going to need Julilah and Qin's help. Making the basic design will be easier than making the current rifles that the army is using. None of those small parts. The stock can be made of wood—the handle as well—the foregrip and body made of Mortal grade metal even while the barrel and this compensator at the front could be Earth grade. The barrels would be something that I think only a low Journeyman could make, but the body, a mid-Apprentice-level crafter with the right workspace would be able to bang them out. These new formation-based rounds, the simple ones, a low Apprentice-level crafter could make them. The formation bit would be a pain, but if we could use that casting method you've talked about or a press that could automate it all, I'd think it would be much faster than the gunpowder ammunition. No three different kinds of metals, then the primer and the powder and having to make sure that there's no static so the factory doesn't all explode."

"Simple and elegant," Rugrat said.

"Looks ugly as hell to me, but that's why I stick to swords, shields, and spears," Tan Xue said.

"Beauty is in the eye of the smith! I think?"

"You can't make a statement like that and then follow it up with 'I think!'. How many times have you been hit in the head with heavy objects?"

"The one thing that I am worried about is people taking the weapon and copying it. It will happen with time, but don't want it to happen too soon," Rugrat said.

"So something that will make sure that others can't use it, but then make sure that we can use it all the time?" Tan Xue said.

"Yeah," Rugrat said.

"I think you're worrying about the wrong things. On Earth, did you have any measures to make sure that people couldn't use your weapons?"

"No," Rugrat said.

"People here are going to be much stronger with the weapons than they are used to, either the bows they have, or their axes, or us with our rifles. It is not going to matter much. While we are training our people with multiple weapons, if they're just trained with one, then we have the advantage. Unless they're Sha, it will be hard for them to train with anything that is like our weapons," Tan Xue said.

"So I'm being paranoid?" Rugrat asked.

Tan Xue shrugged. "Some things we just can't keep a secret all of the time. We just have to pick the ones we care about. Adding in a protection formation would decrease the power of the overall weapon."

"Good point," Rugrat said. "Now, the other problem is how to deal with the people who are interested in buying the weapons that we have already."

"Why don't we sell off our excess and make an agreement with them to not fight us and we won't fight them? Be a way to create an alliance. I did it with people in Hersht—a good way to get some protection."

"If we were to give them some more of the simple repeaters without sockets and such, it wouldn't be that hard, just need woodworkers and smiths to make them. Apprentice and low Journeymen could do it. If we sell them at a low enough price, then they'll just come to us to buy them, give us a continuous albeit small income," Rugrat mused. "Need to think on it some more. Now, want to make one of those semi-autos with me?"

The formation competition continued as Qin and Julilah sat in the stands, reading their books.

"Why can't the workshops be open even? Do you think the sect would be willing to let us use their workshops?" Julilah asked.

"We don't want to owe them more favors," Qin said.

"Well, what are we going to do?" Julilah sighed. They had been reading books for three days.

"I think that we've almost finished with all of the books we can get access to and are useful in the Formation Guild. Once we've read them all, then we can head to Vuzgal. They've got formation workshops there," Qin said.

"We could see Tan Xue and the people from Alva," Julilah said, her eyes shining.

"Quiet down. It's time for the semifinals," Qin complained.

"How will me talking disrupt what you're seeing?" Julilah whined.

Two challengers stepped up to the platform. One wore a green emblem, the other a red, showing the academies that they came from.

"Who are they, anyway?" Julilah asked as the two people stepped up on the stage.

"The red people are from the Tiston Academy. The one with the green is from the Vrajeik Academy. The Tiston Academy's students have been stronger in their formations' power but the Vrajeik are powerful formation fighters. In a battle, it is not only the formations that one has prepared, but how they're able to use them that will impact the fight," Qin said.

"Okay." Julilah looked up to see what would happen.

The referee started off the round.

The two competing men threw down their formations. The Vrajeik attacked directly with his formation, a lightning attack striking at the Tiston.

Their formation clashed with the Vrajeik. Their attacks collided as the Tiston member's formation was a touch stronger, but the other formation master activated formations that were on his equipment. He charged forward, his body enhanced; a shield flared to life as they burst through the clashing energies.

The second was just throwing out their second defensive formation as the enhanced Vrajeik man appeared. They weren't attacking and quickly entered their barrier and struck out with their fists.

The Tiston formation master was a formation master first and was taken by surprise as they were thrown backward and fell outside of the stage.

People cheered from the Vrajeik side as the man on the stage showed a pleased smile.

"He combined his actions with his formations, working against the formation master's natural inclination to make just formations and leave the fighting to their guards." Qin nodded in approval.

"A weapon is only one part of the equation; the person who uses it is the other. If the fighter and the weapon are better suited for each other, then their power will be much greater," Julilah said.

"Just when did you start sounding like some old sage?" Qin complained.

"So how were they?" Julilah asked as people were talking about the match.

"Above average. Powerful formations from the Tiston Academy guy. No combat experience; the other doesn't have much, but it looks like he's sneaky. Formations were good, not excellent," Qin surmised.

"Such high praise." Julilah slumped back in her seat, pulled up her book once again and continued reading.

The next round was another person from Tiston and someone from their own Aojior Academy.

The Aojior Academy girl looked at the Tiston boy. The two of them bowed before the referee began the match.

The Tiston boy activated two formations at once. The Aojior used a defensive formation as she started to throw out formation flags to activate a secondary formation.

The Tiston boy took out a formation, smacking and throwing it. It was hastily done and Qin shook her head. The formation exploded as the other girl was activating the formation. The formation relied on drawing in mana to activate. With the mana being stirred up by the formation exploding, it wasn't able to activate and failed. A backlash of power caused the formation to fail. The boy threw out formation flags, stabilizing his defense as the other girl used a formation to send ice rain pelting down on the defensive shield. It shook but with having secondary formation flags, its strength was much higher than a single formation. It shrugged off the attack as the boy used a formation on the ground, casting Mana Bolt. The strength of the mana bolt increased in power under the formation's power; the mana bolt the size of a fist grew to be the size of a man's arm as it shot out and collided with the girl's weakened shield. Three hits took the shield out and the next spell paused in the air above her.

"Cai Cheng from the Tiston Academy is the winner!"

"I dedicate my win to Miss Qin and Julilah." Cai Cheng looked to the two girls and gave them a bow.

"I think he's hitting on us," Qin said.

"Both of us," Julilah said, her eyes thinning.

Everyone looked at the two girls in the boxes.

"Who you dedicate the win to is none of our business," Qin said, her voice carrying through the quiet arena.

Cai Cheng's bright smile dimmed but he stopped himself from displaying anything else. "I was in the wrong. Seeing two beautiful women and winning my match clouded my judgement."

Qin and Julilah nodded, leaving the topic alone.

The competition continued on and people laughed at Cai Cheng and talked about the two mysterious girls in the box reading books.

"Are you looking to date anyone?" Julilah asked.

"No, why?" Qin asked.

"Not even Erik?" Julilah said.

"You!" Qin turned and smacked Julilah's arm.

"What? I'm your best friend. You think that I didn't know?" Julilah laughed.

"Well, what about you?" Qin asked.

"There are plenty of cute boys here, but most of them have...what Rugrat would say is 'a stick up their ass.' All arrogant and showing off, but they aren't actually interesting people. Don't have anything to them other than their crafting skill," Julilah complained.

"What about Du An? Were the two of you going out?" Qin asked.

"No, I tried making it clear but he's as dense as the wood he works on!" Julilah complained and closed her book with a clap. "Let's go home!"

"Just like that? But we have the stuff from the sect," Qin said.

"Ugh, well, let's just go and finish that off," Julilah said.

"The workshops are closed here except those in the city," Qin said, revisiting their previous dilemma.

"Then we go to Vuzgal and we send everything back," Julilah said.

"Okay." Qin stood.

"That was quick," Julilah said.

"You suggested it and I want to see just what this Vuzgal looks like! Also, I got a message that Domonos and Yui are in Vuzgal, training up more soldiers. Though we should say good-bye to Yan Zemin—she helped us out a bit," Qin said.

They left the box and headed up toward the main box where Yan Zemin was located.

"What is your formation crafting skill at now?" Julilah asked.

"I'm at level sixty-five, so half-step peak Journeyman formation crafter?" Qin said.

"Oh, that's good," Julilah said.

"What level are you at?" Qin asked, her eyes thinning at Julilah's pleased expression.

"Oh, not much further, you know, I think just level sixty-six or so."

"How! You!" Qin said but they had arrived at the door to Yan Zemin's box.

The guards knew them and opened the doors, allowing them into the large room.

They moved over to where the three heads of the academy sat, talking to various people.

Qin and Julilah moved over to Yan Zemin. She had the fewest people around her, not one for small or useless conversations.

"Julilah, Qin," Yan Zemin said, looking at them both. "I hope you're not offended by young Cai Cheng's words."

The Tiston Academy head looked over with a dark expression on his face.

"No, we just wanted to thank you for your hospitality. We're going to head home," Qin said.

"The books and lessons were eye-opening. They've allowed us to solidify our foundations and opened up new paths to look into formations," Julilah said.

"Head Yan Zemin, you haven't introduced us," the academy head from Tiston said.

Yan Zemin frowned but quickly introduced them. "Julilah, Qin—this is Tiston Academy Head Gust Jorjens."

"It is good to meet you, Head Jorjens." The two of them cupped their fists but did nothing else. They turned back to Yan Zemin as if he didn't exist.

"These must be your direct students but they're incomparably rude," Head Jorjens said. The other elders all looked at the two girls and Head Yan Zemin in a bad light.

"We still have a few projects to complete for the inner palace, though we can send over a few people to deliver them and work on them from home," Qin said.

"Understandable. Vuzgal is a great place to work," Yan Zemin said.

There was a stir in the group. There were no crafters in the Fourth Realm who didn't know about Vuzgal now.

"Vuzgal? Are you perhaps from one of the crafting clans that has made a home in Vuzgal?" one of the elders asked.

"No." Qin and Julilah shook their heads.

Everyone started to look at them with curious eyes.

"We're part of the crafters who work for the city lords, the Vuzgal crafters," Qin said.

Quiet conversations started in the room.

"I have heard that Vuzgal is a holy ground for crafters. The dungeon only costs an Earth-grade mana stone and if one shows their talent in the city workshops or in crafting competitions, then they can win slots to enter the Crafting trial dungeon."

"The city is supposed to have workshops for Experts!"

"The mana density is incredibly high, the kind of atmosphere that would be hard to find outside of a Sixth Realm city, with formations in the workshops and the Battle Arena to increase the concentration."

"That's not all. I heard that there is an Expert-level smith who is less than forty years old!"

Yan Zemin grimaced and shot those talking a look.

"Are you sure that you wouldn't be interested in the Formation Guild? With your talent, you could get the same resources as those in Vuzgal. We also have more Experts and teachers with an in-depth understanding of formations," Yan Zemin said.

"Thank you for the offer, but we've already made our oaths," Qin said and Julilah nodded.

"Very well. Make sure you return any borrowed items and I hope that you will think of the Formation Guild if you don't wish to work for Vuzgal anymore."

Qin and Julilah finished up their good-byes and left the box, heading to the library to deposit the books that they had been reading.

"With the books we bought, the other formation masters should be able to gain a greater understanding of formations. Should see an increase in the formation department's strength!" Qin said.

"You just want us to beat out the other departments in raising an Expert-level formation master," Julilah said.

"And you don't?" Qin asked.

"Don't worry, Department Head. I'll soon be able to become the Expert formation master our department needs!"

"You! Are you trying to take my position as department head!" Qin bugged her friend.

"You'll need to fight harder if you want to keep your position. Re-election is up in six months!"

"You're really going for my position!" Qin said.

"May the best formation master win!" Julilah said, putting down her playful challenge.

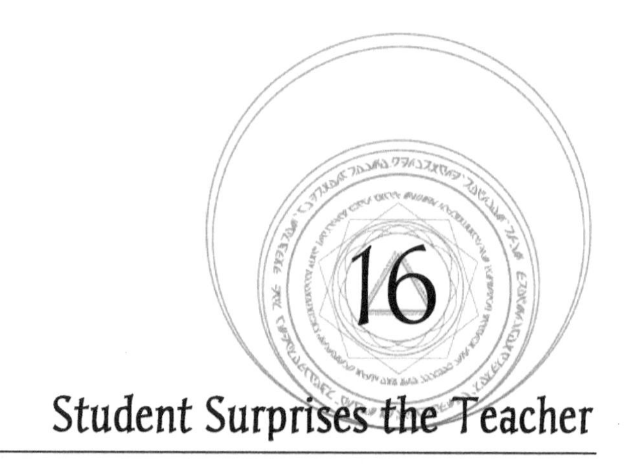

16

Student Surprises the Teacher

Erik checked his new gains from the last couple of days.

With the issues in Chonglu, their original departure for the Third Realm had been pushed back.

Delilah let go of her mother and looked at the rest of her family and the council members who had gathered to see her off.

"Time to go," Erik said to Delilah, seeing how hard it was for her to say good-bye, even for a short while.

Alva had grown rapidly over the last year. But now all of the different departments worked like a well-oiled machine, building places for people to live, creating apartment buildings as Matt called them, setting up people to get an education and then on to jobs.

Delilah was proud of what they had been able to establish here.

"Be safe and remember to write home every so often," her mother said.

"I will." Delilah looked from her to the rest of her family before she turned toward Erik and the groups of people saying their last good-byes and stepped into the area around the totem.

"Keep the lights on," Erik said to the council leaders Jia Feng, Glosil, and Egbert.

He used the totem. Alva disappeared and the noises of the Third Realm Division Headquarters filled Delilah's ears.

Erik smiled as he pulled out a badge and put it on his chest, marking him as a mid-Journeyman alchemist.

Erik led Delilah toward the Division Headquarters that towered over the city.

Erik presented his medallion at the entrance and his identity was verified. A guide came up to them and took them through the Division Headquarters and into the inner areas.

Delilah followed Erik, reaching the heart of the Division Headquarters.

Medicinal ingredients infuse the air from their repeated use. The mana is much higher here as well, not quite on the standard as the density in the Expert-level crafting rooms, but it covers a much larger area and is closer to the mana density one would find in an Apprentice-level crafting room. These are just the general areas. I wonder what their training facilities are like.

Delilah's interest increased as she noticed the differences in the headquarters compared to the city that had grown around it.

They took an elevator driven by formations that took them near the top of the Division Headquarters. They came out and were greeted by guards standing in front of a large door.

By their strength, the weakest among them is in their mid-fifties level and the strongest is just over level sixty. Delilah studied them some more, trying to guess the level of their Mana or Body Cultivation.

Just these guards have the same strength as Alva's soldiers. I thought that they would be unstoppable in the Ten Realms. Delilah let out a self-deprecating breath. *There is always someone higher and the power of the associations isn't something that can be ignored.*

"Captain Khasar, I hope you've been doing well," Erik said, greeting one of the guards at a pair of large doors.

"It is good to see you again, Journeyman West. He's waiting for you," Khasar said as the doors opened for them.

Delilah looked at Erik. He seemed to have changed. He had been dealing with the administration of Alva and Vuzgal these last few months, only taking a break to go into the Metal floor.

Now she saw a different side of him: not the warrior, or the leader, but the student. He was more relaxed and excited, but no less determined or driven.

Maybe that is his strength—everything he does, he puts all of his effort and energy into it.

She followed Erik into the large room beyond. There was a small garden in one corner, a workspace in another, then a full wall of windows looking over the Division Headquarters and the lush forests below the mountaintop city.

Delilah smiled to herself as she felt the mana density of the room.

Nicer, but still it is about a third of the mana density in Alva Dungeon. Being outside of the dungeon, she started to remember the benefits and the aids that one could find in Alva.

I've become so used to it, numb to these advantages I hold. I'm always a little stunned by the people who come from the other realms. To them, Alva is a paradise. She paused as they crossed the massive room. *Alva is our home.* She felt shaken to her core as she *really*, truly believed that. A smile spread across her face. *It is only when you're away that you learn how valuable the thing you left is.*

"I was wondering how long it would take you to show up, Mister City Lord." An older-looking man laughed as he looked from his desk with a wide smile.

"Old Hei, this is my student Delilah," Erik said.

"Student! Looks like you are growing up some." Old Hei laughed as he turned his gaze to Delilah.

"Student of healing or Alchemy?" he asked Delilah.

"Delilah greets Grand Teacher, and of Alchemy." Delilah cupped her fists and bowed deeply.

"What is your skill level?" Old Hei asked in interest. "Don't worry, Erik. I won't ask you to bow. We both know you mess it up every time."

"I should be around level sixty-eight." Delilah tried to hide the smile forming on her face as Erik coughed awkwardly and looked out the windows.

"Level sixty-eight! So close to becoming an Expert! Those last levels are the hardest." Old Hei then looked over to Erik, who had an awkward expression on his face.

"Erik, what is your current Alchemy level?"

"Seventy." Erik coughed slightly.

"You haven't been able to improve your Alchemy? Or you have been doing other things?" Old Hei asked.

"Other things," Erik said.

"I heard about some of it," Old Hei said dryly. "Guess I should call you City Lord West now?" Old Hei grumbled. "Please rise, grand student."

Delilah rose to see Old Hei had walked around his desk, with his arms crossed and a mocking smile.

"It was an accident?"

"Yes, you accidentally took an ancient undead-infested city, then gained the support of all the associations. I hear that you banished a bunch of Expert crafters, are building an academy, and have plans to build a Battle Arena, auction house, and are quickly becoming a capital of crafting and mercantile trade in the Fourth Realm." Old Hei let out a laugh and shook his head, uncrossing his arms. "May your life always be filled with interesting times. You know that the Alchemist Association wants me to barter with you to get better terms, right?"

Erik scratched his head.

"You think I would do that...just, if you could get me some more of those little shrimp tempura from the Sky Reaching Restaurant, mmm!" Old Hei closed his eyes as if tasting them all over again.

"You're looking well for someone who eats over at the Sky Reaching Restaurant so much. I have heard the management say that they should give you a free meal every ten as you're there every time you can get free, or have it delivered," Erik said.

"I appreciate food." Old Hei shrugged and then winked at Delilah.

She smiled at the back and forth.

"Come on, we have a lot to catch up on. I got a few things." Old Hei guided them toward a balcony that looked over the city.

"You must try these eggs Benedict, just marvelous." Old Hei served food before they settled down.

He was not what she was thinking one of the Pill Heads of the Alchemist Association would act like.

"Your healing?" Old Hei asked.

"I got to level seventy-three just a few days ago. It was a complicated surgery, bringing a man back from the brink."

Delilah had heard about the incident with Lord Chonglu. Others didn't think that he would have survived but Erik and Yang Zan had pulled off a small miracle, keeping him alive and repairing his body.

"I have been hearing what happened in the Fourth Realm. Between fighting the Blood Demon sect and establishing Vuzgal, were you able to practice and read?" Old Hei asked.

"I was able to do some Alchemy," Erik said weakly.

"Anything that pushed your boundaries or concoctions that you knew already?"

"Concoctions that I already knew." Erik didn't hide anything.

Old Hei nodded knowingly. "Okay, well, before I can teach you both, I need to know what your ability is. I want you two to create a concoction. Delilah, make this for me." Old Hei passed her a few sets of ingredients and a formula.

She took it and studied the contents. It was a water-breathing concoction.

She studied it and then used her Journeyman book, looking up information on the concoction, adding in a new entry on the concoction and notes on it that would be useful to her.

Erik and Old Hei left her to it, talking among themselves. Erik talked about the issues that he was having while Old Hei offered pointers.

She tuned them both out as she studied. *I don't want to let Erik down.*

After a full half hour of study, she nodded to herself.

"May I use your workspace?" she asked.

"Please, go ahead," Old Hei said.

She went to the workspace, checking it was clean and in order. She put down her cauldron over the flames, adjusting the flames to start warming the cauldron. She moved to the bench and started to prepare the different ingredients.

She prepared them all and then sat in front of the cauldron. She injected her mana into the flame formation, adjusting the flame and getting used to the flame formation.

Take your time and get to know your workspace. Erik's words sounded out in her head. She understood the formation, saw that her cauldron was fully warmed, and took time to calm her mind. Circulating her mana, she reviewed the steps of the formula and her own notes.

With a flick of her wrist, the first ingredients, a red-blue-green mixture, was poured into the cauldron.

She didn't notice Erik or Old Hei, who had moved closer and were inspecting every action she took.

Her mana covered the cauldron as her tools talked to her, letting her know what was happening on an almost instinctual level.

The water-breathing pill had long roasting phases where one just needed to monitor what was happening in the cauldron, making sure to not heat it too long or too short, and to maintain a good temperature.

Her teacher and grand teacher watched on, not saying anything as they made their own observations.

It took her nearly two hours before she allowed the flame underneath the cauldron to dim and she pulled out the pills inside.

She stored them in pill bottles and presented them to Erik and Old Hei with a frown.

"What? Do you think you could have done better?" Erik asked, reading her frown perfectly.

"When I was adding the pulp extract from the Liole shoots, they were not processed enough and thus when combined with the other ingredients, they didn't combine properly," she said.

"Anything else?"

"I should have used the centrifuge longer when working with the Sera roots. They didn't separate out fully, so there were impurities added into the concoction." She saw Erik waiting for her to say anything else.

"Otherwise, there were a few times where my technique was lacking. I should have used four flames as one to heat everything evenly instead of the two-flame method. I didn't take into account the long brewing time fully."

"Good. You have been able to accurately pick out your major flaws without us saying anything. If you were to do as you said, then you would have produced peak Journeyman pills, instead of just half-step peak pills," Old Hei said.

"Though you took your time in understanding the ingredients, your concoction, workspace, and the formula. Taking your time greatly improved the success rate and strength of your concoction," Erik said in approval.

"As for issues, you were using the dragon chasing flame control method. Using a two-flame method is good when you need to heat a small mixture. The water-breathing pill I gave you creates a lot of volume, so with a two-flame method it will be hard to control everything that is going on—heating the new ingredients and also maintaining the temperature of the main combined group of ingredients.

"You also positioned your hands on your knees. It keeps a lower profile, yes, but when you need to move your hands in order to coordinate the movement of the flames, having space is essential. Keep your hands raised in front of you and not resting them on your knees. You'll have a wider range to move through so your mobility is not limited.

"You have been working with someone to prepare your ingredients. This is fine, but even if someone prepares your ingredients, you must know everything about them. You made a few lazy mistakes that come from not preparing ingredients in a long time. That said, I think your biggest issue is not your skills—I think it is the limited formulas you have. For you to produce mid Journeyman-level pills on your first try with this formula, it is rather impressive. I think that unless Erik improves quickly, it won't be long until you beat him to the Expert level." Old Hei smiled and pulled out another formula.

"And this one is for you. Get yourself ready and pass me your notes," Old Hei said.

Erik sighed. He passed his notes to Old Hei and changed positions with Delilah.

Delilah sat with Old Hei, who reviewed the entire process she had gone through, going through every detail he had noticed.

He invited her to discuss it as Erik reviewed the formula and started his preparations.

Erik was halfway through his concoction when he stopped and poured out the contents and started all again. He did that two more times before he seemed satisfied.

Delilah's emotions were jumbled up, seeing him pour out his ingredients so many times. She felt that she had surpassed him, but felt it strange to surpass her own teacher, who had been like a Alchemy saint when she had first met him.

"A teacher's greatest achievement is to have their students surpass them. I am an Expert-level alchemist but I have faith that both you and Erik will surpass me in the future. At the rate you two are increasing your level and your information, it shouldn't be too long." He laughed. "The one piece of advice I have is to make sure you not only do Alchemy, but learn it. Read books, talk to other alchemists, see how they work. If you merely replicate what others have done or continue down your path and don't take inspiration from others or listen to others, then your path will end in the Expert realm. People say that an Expert alchemist can make a concoction from simple household ingredients. Now, that concoction will not be very strong and it will take a lot of effort to complete but it is possible. An Expert-level alchemist must have a great amount of knowledge.

"In the Journeyman stage, one gets their crafting book and can have the capability to store a great amount of information and never lose it. An Expert turns that information into action. They draw out power from ingredients and concoctions that lower level crafters can't. To get to the later levels of Alchemy, one isn't just copying others' formulas; they are forging their own path of Alchemy. When someone becomes a Master, the information is their base but they don't need formulas as they are able to analyze ingredients with a glance or a sniff and create concoctions freely."

"What about those who can call down the stars of the realm?"

"Those who can call down the stars when creating a concoction can create concoctions that contain a spirit. These concoctions, with time, will only grow stronger and can gain their own consciousness. Those concoctions can change a person's fate, their very stats and their cultivation." Old Hei chuckled. "Even I only know information about the peak Expert-level crafters. Instead of just making recovery pills, Experts make enhancing pills that allow one to increase their fighting capabilities, increase their cultivation and so on."

"Could you increase someone's Body Cultivation with just a pill?"

"In the clans of the Fifth Realm, there is the Gray Stone pill which will allow whoever takes it to increase their Body Cultivation directly to Body Like Stone," Old Hei said. "Oh, it looks like Erik is nearly done."

Erik tapped the side of the cauldron. Three pills shot out and into a bottle he had prepared.

17 State of the Realms

"All right, I hope you've all been paying attention to training, because we have a mission," Second Lieutenant Yui Silaz said as he looked at the orders he had just received.

Tiger Company had been reorganized. They were still called Tiger Company, but now they were Tiger Company's First Rifle Platoon. It acted as a promise that with time they would grow to create a full combat company.

"Sergeant Acosta!"

"Sir!" Sergeant Acosta, who stood at the side of the briefing room, stood at attention.

"You and your Second Rifle Squad are to head to the First Realm. Your mission is to train up the Vermire guard forces into a specialized combat company!" Yui smiled as he saw Sergeant Acosta just keep the displeased look off her face. "Once you have completed training with the guard force, you will then need to train up a green unit of new recruits. All of this must be done in secret and they must be to a high standard. I have heard word that Captain Glosil is looking at the Vermire guard force to add some of their members to our ranks!" Yui held Acosta's eyes. "We only take the best troops, so I hope that we can take them all."

"Yes, sir!" Acosta said.

He could see the fighting spirit in her eyes. "Good! First Rifle Squad will be your support." Yui looked at Sergeant Song-Min, who came to attention and nodded, acknowledging his orders. "Get your bags packed and move out in packets by tonight. Report to Captain Glosil for further orders. Third Rifle Squad will continue to man the defenses and police Vermire. That is all!"

Elan poured the tea down his neck as he stood when Rugrat came into the room.

"Don't worry about it." Rugrat waved him back down to the meal and tea that had been set out in front of him.

He had been working so much the last week that he had forgotten to eat. When he arrived, Rugrat heard he was there and got food sent to him as he was finishing up cultivating in the main pillar of Vuzgal.

Elan swallowed and cleared his throat. "Was the manual on the mana cores useful?" he asked first.

"It's made it a lot easier for me to compress and clear my mana while increasing the speed and amount of mana I can draw in at one time," Rugrat said, not hiding his excited smile. "Were you able to find more information on Mana Gathering Cultivation?"

"I was only able to find a few pieces of information on Mana Gathering Cultivation and Body Cultivation." Elan didn't hide anything as he took out a collection of books and put them on Rugrat's desk. There were only seven books, but they were worth more than three times their weight in Earth mana stones.

Elan didn't hold any jealousy passing them over. He knew how Rugrat had people copying the books already and freely shared everything with the people of Alva.

He had read them on the way over and made some notes that could help him increase his cultivation with time.

Elan was trusted by Erik and Rugrat completely and he made sure he did everything to show his loyalty—not out of fear, but wanting to show them that he was worthy of that trust.

"What have you been able to learn otherwise?" Rugrat took his seat and invited Elan to do the same.

"I was able to gather more information on the Fifth Realm. It would be apt to call the Fifth Realm the 'admission realm.' Once in there, there are massive competitions everywhere, to test the people of different sects and the people who have made it to that stage. If one can get good rankings, they can get the interest of powerful sects and associations. This applies only to crafters. For fighters, the Fifth Realm is pretty much useless to them, but the Sixth Realm is a holy land. I have heard rumors that the Sixth Realm is covered in large-scale dungeons where people can go to increase their fighting skills, acquire ingredients, and more. Some of the dungeons even have tests that one must go through in order to complete and can gain rewards upon completion

"Sects control massive tracts of lands. Fighting between them happens, but it is limited because any loss is large. So there are more competitions to establish standing within a sect, standing between sects, competitions over plots of land and resources."

"So betting on a whole new scale?" Rugrat asked.

"Pretty much," Elan said. "The Fifth Realm is dominated by Journeyman-level crafters, with most being at least an Apprentice in another craft. The teachers are half-step Expert, or Experts up to the middle grade. The Sixth Realm has at least Expert-level students, with the teachers of the Expert middle and administrators of the high grade. Levels are gained through cultivation aids, monster cores, and increasing one's crafting level. Most academies work on a credit and mission system: one needs to complete a number of missions and they get credits that can be used to buy different items from the sects or they can use it for classes, to meet with tutors. It replaces mana stones within the realm."

"What can the independent students do?" Rugrat asked.

"They can join a sect to be taught and live in one of the outer cities, which are basically simple cities at the edges of different sect's influences. Sects recruit from these, or they use them, treating them like their personal property, allowing them only to exist because they're more useful alive than wasting the effort to kill them. If someone has influence, then they can enter an academy and learn from them as long as they are willing to pay the price.

They will not get as much access as the other people in the sect; their credits will be worth less and the products sold by the sects will be more expensive. Prohibitively so." Elan paused.

Rugrat tapped his fingers on the desk, frowning. "Okay, so they're using the dungeons, but do they own the dungeons, or are they just working around its limitations, killing all the creatures in it as soon as they respawn?"

"I am chasing down some leads but I am not sure at this time," Elan said.

Rugrat smirked and nodded. "Good work."

"Thank you." Elan bowed his head.

"Anything else about the Fifth Realm?"

"Not at this time but I am building more contacts, some that are returning or go back and forth more. I can get an idea of what is currently happening in the Fifth Realm and get to know when these different competitions are happening, if we want to allow people to enter them. Though, we should be careful. If we draw too much attention, then people might start looking at us as an annoyance. We need to grow in strength. With our contracts with everyone, there is a loophole that I only discovered through a source. As long as the people attacking us call themselves the real rulers of Vuzgal, then they will be able to take over without the association needing to step in. They likely won't try to, either."

"Why?"

"The associations want to do business with the best partners. Strength rules in the Ten Realms. If we can't hold our position, then the next group that comes should be stronger and they already have a contract established, so their returns should be greater with this new group. It's not like they will go up against the associations," Elan said.

"Would the associations try to take us out of power?" Rugrat asked.

"I don't think so," Elan said, not feeling one hundred percent about it. "See, they understand that in these kind of things, it is best to have a neutral party in control so that all of the associations are treated fairly. They won't stop someone but they won't actively support either side. To them, we're just a minor convenience. If there is someone else more convenient, they'll take it. It has happened before."

"Is there anything that you have to report on Vuzgal?"

"There are different groups trying to work together to affect prices in

Vuzgal. There are groups recruiting from here as well. Crime is low. Most people are powerful and they are keeping their darker activities in places where they have more power."

"The other realms?"

"We are firmly entrenched into the Division Headquarters now and can get information across the Third Realm. A number of books and pieces of information have been recorded down and sent to Alva's Alchemy department. We have no issues there. In the Second Realm, a group of people from Alva have turned into bandits. They are going against the government there and are turning it into their own land, fighting against the forces there." Elan looked at Rugrat. A flash of anger showed on his face before his eyes became cold and his expression deadly.

"I have a full report on it here. They have been going to the Second Realm with their weapons and armor. They recruited some local people, started stealing and then they turned to bigger things—stopping trade caravans, attacking military groups. They would return to Alva to increase their strength and purchase supplies. There are only eight people who are actually from Alva, while there are around four hundred people under their command." Elan took out several pieces of paper and gave it to Rugrat.

Rugrat took it with an ominous expression before he put it to the side. "Anything else from the Second Realm?"

"No, the Trader's Guild and Adventurer's Guild have made progress in the First, Second, and Third Realm and are making progress in the Fourth Realm with rapid success. There are a few people skirting taxes but I have sent information to the treasury and a report for you and Erik." Elan passed him another report and then took out another.

"This is a profile on Tanya Kvist. I believe that she is someone from Earth as well. She spends most of her time in the forests of the Third Realm but she has a creature with her. She calls it a dog. It is smaller than most beasts. We're not sure if it is called a Doberman or Tetsu," Elan said, perplexed.

"She's from Earth? What is happening with her right now?" Rugrat asked.

"Someone took her Doberman and she is working out how to get him back," Elan said.

"Who did?"

"The Northwind sect in the Third Realm. They want to raise new beasts from him because he is loyal and powerful while not increasing in size as he gains strength."

"Assholes—steal a person's dog?" Rugrat said. George growled in agreement. "Do a threat assessment on the Northwind sect."

"Already have," Elan said as *another* report appeared in his hands. "They're not a real threat and we can keep our hands clean. They won't know who did it."

"All right, I want you to make sure that she and her pup are safe and that none of this links back to us. Get her somewhere safe for Erik or me to meet her. Tell her that the United States is nice this time of year," Rugrat said.

"Got it." Elan made a note, not having any idea what Rugrat meant.

"Now, anything else?" Rugrat asked.

"I will need to use one of the special teams in order to carry it out," Elan said.

"You'll have them," Rugrat said.

"Should be it," Elan said.

"Good work. Keep it up. I'll read these reports, and take those books down to the scribes so that they can copy them out."

"I can do that." Elan collected the books back up. Dismissed, he headed out of the office.

18 Family Reunited

Tanya was down on the small rise, looking down at the bandit camp. Tents had been thrown together from one side to the other; there was all of the loot that the bandits had been able to gather among them. There were cages filled with people, beasts, and other valuables.

One cage in particular contained an angry Doberman that was pacing around, barking, and growling at his captors.

The captors laughed and jeered, hitting the bars and taunting the Doberman.

"Stop, Tetsu," she whispered to herself. Her fist tightened and turned white around the dagger in her hand. She wanted to run down there, free Tetsu, and escape into the darkness without anyone noticing. But she knew that would not be an easy task. She averted her eyes and looked at the sentries. She had been watching them for hours now, getting to know their habits and their routine. She checked her storage ring and her muddy clothes.

Her Tomas Ledin shirt was tattered and torn; one could see the attempt she had made to repair it over time. Thankfully, her stylish combat pants and combat boots she wore had come in useful for once instead of just making a statement to the masses.

She tracked the positioning of the lookouts once again, firming their locations in her mind.

Then, before she could stop herself, she moved forward, coming down off the rise, surprised that she had been watching the camp for hours.

"You know, this might be easier with a little bit of help." A voice came from beside her.

Tanya nearly jumped off the ground, her heartbeat racing as her blood ran cold.

"Don't worry. If we wanted to kill you, we would have done it long before now. After all, you didn't even know that we were here." A woman walked forward out of the bushes, looking at her and cleaning her fingernails with a knife.

Even when looking at her, Tanya had a hard time concentrating. *Just what kind of spells is she using to make it so hard to detect her even when she's only five feet away?*

"I have been told to tell you that the United States is nice this time of year." The woman looked at her, waiting for a reaction.

Tanya looked at her in alarm. "United States?"

"Ah, so you do know it." The woman nodded, confirming something. "My employer would like to meet with you. He'd also like to help you and your Doberman Tetsu out."

"Your employer? Just who are you?"

"I'm someone who can help you out," the woman said with a mysterious smile.

"What do you want with me?"

"I don't want anything with you. My employer just wants to meet with you and have a chat about Earth."

"Are they someone from Earth as well?"

"Now that is a question I can't answer."

"How do I know that I can trust you?"

"If we make an oath on the Ten Realms, the light from it will be the signal to my friends. They're already in position."

Tanya looked at the lookouts who were still patrolling the area, thinking about her options. It was clear that this group already knew what her plan was. If she didn't agree with them, she didn't know what would happen.

At least I will have a binding oath if I agree. Haven't I been searching for other people who might be from Earth as well?

She debated it over in her mind before she let out a pressured sigh.

"I, Tanya Kvist, swear on the Ten Realms, that if you save my Tetsu then I will listen to your employer's terms and go with you without fighting. If either myself or my Doberman Tetsu are threatened or attacked in any way by yourself, your employer, or any of your associates, then your life will be forfeit. Do you agree to these terms?"

"Tian Cui so agrees to these terms. You and your Doberman Tetsu, to the limit of my abilities, agree to meet with my employer and I will see that no harm comes to you before and during the meeting with my employer. You are free to leave at any time if you so choose."

Light of the Ten Realms gathered around them as the oath was confirmed, binding the two of them together as well as their terms.

"Now it's time for the fun stuff." Tian Cui grinned. As a light came down, there were sounds of alarm within the camp.

From her vantage point, Tanya had a good view everything that happened in the camp. People started to gather together, facing where the light had come from.

Tian Cui grabbed her hand and with a feat of strength, pulled her over her shoulder and ran off into the forest. Tanya could only see Tian Cui's feet as she moved through the forest with ease.

Tanya heard an explosion go off, followed by the clash of metal on metal. It seemed that the battle had begun in the camp.

I was looking over the camp for nearly a day and a half and I didn't even notice them creeping up. Who are these people?

Gong Jin saw the signal from on the hill, got up and started jogging, low and fast, close to the ground with his rifle ready as he scanned the area.

Han Wu's grenade launcher fired overhead and landed in the middle of the camp, where the bandits were sleeping and living. It only took a few grenades to cover all of the sleeping quarters that were far away from the loot stored on the other side of camp.

Gong Jin cast Detect Life on himself, seeing through the camp and all of the people inside.

A bandit on watch was cut off as Imani's Silence shot took him in the neck, killing him and dropping him to the ground.

Gong Jin took a running jump and cleared the wall. He came down, dropping to a knee as he aimed and fired, working the bolt action on his rifle.

Imani provided long-range support with Han Wu, while Yang Zan was on Gong Jin's right, reloading his rifle.

Gong Jin surveyed the camp. A bandit tried to run, only to have Imani find him with her rifle.

Gong Jin and Yang Zan swept forward into the camp. The sleeping quarters were a smoking mess, with broken tents and temporary homes mixed in with what remained of the bandits.

It was a scene of destruction.

An arrow shot out at Gong Jin. He took it on his armor and he fired back at the archer. The round dropped them to the ground and they breathed their last.

Gong Jin's face was grim. This was his reality. Although there were good times, he was the tip of the spear, which meant that he would see the worst of people time and time again, and most times when he was sent out, it was to kill someone else.

"Clear," Yang Zan said.

"Clear," Gong Jin said.

"Clear," Imani reported via sound transmission.

"All clear. Looking outward now," Han Wu said.

Imani and Han Wu left their overwatch positions and entered the camp as well.

There was a knock at the door and Gong Jin walked over to it.

"Knock, knock, anyone there?"

Tian Cui came to a halt and let her down, before leading the way toward the camp. The noise had stopped some time ago.

"That should be it," Tian Cui said.

"That should be it?" Tanya asked in confusion.

"Trust me. Whenever one of Han Wu's explosives goes off, it pretty much ends everything," Tian Cui said flippantly.

"Han Wu?"

Tian Cui didn't respond; instead, she walked out of the underbrush onto the road leading into the camp, right up to the front gate. Tanya was hesitant to follow her as there were over sixty different bandits within the camp.

"You do know that these bandits were actually contracted by Lord Adda, right?"

"I have my suspicions." Tanya would have to be blind if she didn't see how the different lords' beast tamers and other people of the Ten Realms looked at Tetsu.

"Welcome to life in the Ten Realms. If you have something that others find interesting or could be useful to them and they can get away with stealing it, then you're as good as dead."

Tanya made a noise of agreement, nodding her head slightly. Before she could say anything, Tian Cui had reached the front gate of the camp and knocked on the front door.

"Knock, knock, anyone in there?"

"We were wondering when you would show up for the party!" A man's voice came from inside.

"Well, hearing all the noise you guys were making, it sounded like a heck of a good time," Tian Cui said, sounding sour at missing out on a "party."

There was a slight grunt and scraping as something was tossed away, hitting the ground with wooden noise.

The doors squeaked. A man in full plate armor walked through. In the camp's flickering light, he looked terrifying. There was a grim look on his face and blood on his armor.

"Hello, Miss Tanya," the man said with a nod before looking to Tian Cui. "We still got a lot to clean up. Why didn't you go help out Han Wu?"

"'Cause he always makes a mess wherever he goes?" Tian Cui let out a suffering sigh.

"I've got to say, I think I'm improving!" A shorter man brought up a weapon, pointing it into the air.

The others started all talking, addressing the man. Tanya wasn't even listening to any of them. The weapon in his hands looked like what she saw in foreign movies and in videos back on Earth.

It basically confirmed what Tian Cui had already said and asked her.

She was afraid to look too closely around the camp. The grenade launcher in his hands must have been used on the living quarters, which was now nothing but a series of blown-out craters. There were only a few remaining people, who had all been killed in various ways. Other than a few fires that were slowly dwindling, there was nothing else left of the bandits who had once called this camp home.

It was hard to come to understand it. It happened all so suddenly. Tanya ran across the camp as a sudden fear filled her.

Tetsu! she thought in a panic, fearing that he might also be one of the casualties brought about with the man's grenade launcher, or being a casualty from the other fights. She knew how easy it was for bystanders to be caught up in a large fight.

She ran over to the cages as the people within the camp yelled out to her. She didn't listen to them, instead stomping right in front of the cage where Tetsu had been locked up.

She looked inside. Seeing those familiar eyes looking back at her, she couldn't help smiling as she called out his name.

"Hey, Tetsu. Come here, boy. Come on." Tetsu, recognizing her, padded over to the bars of the cage. "Who's a good boy?" she said, feeling a rush of relief as she patted and scratched Tetsu.

She moved to the lock and used a simple unlocking spell that she had learned from the game master compendium that she had been reading from, plotting out her next game session when she was teleported to the Ten Realms. It had become her most prized possession.

Tetsu greeted her eagerly, his tail betraying his excitement at seeing her again.

"Oh yes, who's a good boy?" Tanya reached down as he gave her sloppy kisses. She half-heartedly tried to stop him, laughing as she stood.

"Sit!"

Tetsu did as she asked and she brought out a treat.

"Shake hands." She reached out her hand and he raised his paw. The two of them shook hands before she tossed him a treat.

She turned to look at the group. Tian Cui was only a little bit away while the rest of the group was clearing the camp of any remaining loot and changing the appearance of the camp.

There were a few people with certain items.

"What are those for?" Tanya asked.

"We can't very well make it look like we came in to clear the camp or draw attention to you. There are few groups in the area that we don't agree with their practices. So, we'll make this look like it was them who took the camp," Tian Cui said.

The others worked quickly and efficiently and it wasn't long before they were finished laying down the new evidence and removing all signs of their involvement.

"Let's get going," the man in full plate armor said.

"Where are we going?" Tanya asked.

"Somewhere—well, you have your secrets and we have ours," Tian Cui said. "You'll need to store your pet and we'll have to blindfold you for the trip."

"I made a deal with the devil. I guess it's now time to pay," Tanya said, resolute in her decision.

She stored Tetsu away before Tian Cui put a mask on her. She smelled something on the mask, making her nose itchy and causing her to sneeze. Her head started to feel heavy and her vision blurry.

It must be some kind of sleeping powder or Alchemy concoction! Tanya thought in alarm. But she didn't have any strength left in her body as Tian Cui grabbed her once again and threw her over her shoulder.

If she meant me true harm, then shouldn't I be dead?

This final thought comforted Tanya before darkness took her.

Chonglu open his eyes and looked around in a state of confusion.

His eyes came to rest on Feng and Felicity, who had passed out beside him in their chairs. His chest tightened in those last moments when he'd been hit; he thought that he would never see them again. He reached out to pat their heads, only to find that his other hand had been captured. He looked over, thinking that he had been shackled, only to find his hand was entrapped in another's so tight it was like a vise. Tears appeared in his eyes as he turned over to face someone he never thought he would ever see again in his lifetime.

His emotions were a mess. If she was here, then he didn't know what had happened in the Fourth Realm; he didn't know whether the assassins would come again. All he did know was that he wanted to savor every last second and look at her face again being so close.

"Mira." He spoke in a soft whisper, as if speaking too loud would make her disappear.

She tensed, ready to draw her sword as his hand held onto hers.

It felt as if a lifetime had gone by. She feared that the person that she had been with him was gone, destroyed as she had to adapt to her new existence within the Stone Fist sect. She didn't know whether she was the woman he fell in love with anymore.

Memories of the time that they spent together, of the love they shared...she saw their two children in her mind. Her stiffness and cold exterior started to crumble and tears fell onto the floor. She let out a wail and grabbed onto Chonglu, burying her head in his chest.

Chonglu wept as he wrapped his arms around her, trying to bring her closer. He buried his face in her hair. Tears streamed down his face as he laughed and cried, unable to control his emotions.

Feng and Felicity were woken by the noise. They looked over to their mother and father hugging. They had been too young to remember their mother before she had to leave. They had seen the burning emotions in her eyes when talking to them, and then her cold manner when dealing with others. When seeing her with their father, they finally let go of their apprehensions. Tears fell down their faces as they grabbed onto Mira and their father, all four of them holding onto one another, crying and laughing.

The guards in the room looked at one another and then silently moved outside to give the family some time together.

"Well, Robertson, you did as you promised," Lin Chan said as she walked down the column of carriages headed onto one of the loading docks of the massive growing city Peli.

The city looked more like a nest than a metropolis. Supporting plants were woven together, creating floor upon floor and maximizing the growing room of the city. The city had walls to stop creatures from entering and large fields beyond, a teardrop of green above it all.

Plants worked like machinery to lift and lower, replacing formations and other devices seen in other cities.

"The Alva Adventurer's Guild is happy to provide," Robertson said. He was a short man with a black and gray beard, part of his heritage rather than his age.

He had a roguish glint to his eye and his armor, although well maintained, showed pitting and scarring from battles and training.

Lin Chan smiled and nodded. "Your payment." She took out a storage bag and passed it to Robertson.

He took a look inside before he held out a hand. "Good to do business with you."

"And with you."

They shook hands.

Lin Chan met up with the rest of the traders and Robertson turned toward the twenty or so rough-looking Alva adventurers who were stretching and complaining now that the employer was out of earshot.

"All right, let's get some rooms tonight. We'll head back to Alasam tomorrow and use the totem there to head to the Third Realm again," Robertson said.

"What about the loot?" Virion asked.

"The loot stays with me. We'll distribute it when we get back home," Robertson said.

There were groans and half-hearted complaints.

"Come on, let's go and see if we can't get some rooms for the night!"

In a high-class bar in Peli, a group of people were gathered around a table. They were sipping their drinks slowly, looking around, as if waiting for something to happen.

Another man, wearing similar clothes to them, walked into the bar, ignoring the other patrons. He quickly climbed the steps to where the group sat overlooking the entire bar.

A man sat at the head of the table.

As the runner reached the table, he held back his words, waiting for permission.

"Did you find out where they're staying?" the man asked in a quiet voice.

"Yes, Master Kernys. They're staying in the Copper Roost," the runner said in a low voice. The others looked around to make sure that no one else heard him.

"Are you sure that they have the cultivation resources with them?"

"Yes, Master Kernys."

"Go and watch them. Tell me when they move. With those resources, we can breakthrough and draw the eyes of the elders. When the next tests for those heading to the fourth realm come around we will be able to advance quickly." Kernys said.

The people around the table all smiled. The Fourth realm was a place where fortunes were made.

"Yes, Master Kernys." The runner's eyes filled with excitement as he ran back out of the bar.

"What about the Alva Adventurer's Guild? I'm told that they have big connections," a woman at the table asked.

"We are from the Willful Institute—we take what we want, when we want it. They might be a force in the Mortal realms, but in the Earth realm they're nothing. Our Wilful sect is able to reach into the fourth realm and a number of our members have reached the fifth realm and entered sects that have a powerful standing in even the Sky Realms."

19
Fighting Art Basics

Old Hei was dealing with matters pertaining to the Alchemist Association and Delilah was "having lunch" at the Sky Reaching Restaurant. Which actually meant that she was dealing with the reports from Alva that needed her attention.

Erik had been working on his Alchemy for a few days and was getting antsy. He had a lot of knowledge, but now he needed to work on the practical knowledge, to practice his Alchemy over and over again. It was dull and boring but there was no way around it.

He had taken a break to train in fighting and was off in a private training square, one used by Old Hei's personal guard.

He was focusing on channeling mana through his body. When he did so, his movements surpassed his boundaries—his movements quicker, his reaction time lightning fast. He could jump several meters with ease, and fall the same distance without having to bend his knees.

"I don't think I've seen someone with such a high degree of control over their body," Khasar said.

Erik looked over. He had noticed him there, but he had been so wrapped up in practicing his fighting style that he hadn't paid him any attention.

"Thank you," Erik said.

"Though I don't understand why you don't use your mana to affect the environment around you," Khasar asked.

"Affect the environment around me?" Erik asked.

"You don't know it?" Khasar asked.

"My knowledge of fighting styles in the Ten Realms isn't all that deep," Erik admitted.

"This would make sense." Khasar nodded before he stepped out into the training area. "There are three main types of melee type attacks and fighting styles: inner, that allow one to control the strength within their body." He executed a punch that let out a blast of air that sent the dust on the training square rolling away.

"Then there is inner and outer, where a person has control over their body and the mana within it and then use mana on the environment around them to increase the strength of their attacks."

He turned and punched. There was no rush of air; there was no sound, but Erik felt a blast of air go past him. It was much stronger than the first punch, where the power had spread into the air with barely any of that wind reaching Erik.

Khasar stood straight.

"Then there is domain. This is created when someone's senses and reactions are so fast and strong that within a certain area they control everything within it. A person with a domain will be able to kill someone who is next to them as fast as someone who is at the edge of their domain. Only others who have a domain or have incredible reactions can hope to defeat them. Otherwise, only special weapons and taking time to grind them down will stop them."

"Isn't this inner and outer?" Erik used Mana Blast. A shockwave of mana emerged from his hand.

"While that is *terrifying,* that is not inner and outer; that is merely the mana within your body being forced out in a concentrated blast. When I executed that technique you saw, I created a layer of wind mana around my hand so that it wouldn't have any resistance as it moved forward. Then I moved mana through my different mana veins in a special circulation, allowing my attack to not disperse immediately. Altogether, I executed a fist art. There are palm arts, finger arts, leg arts, even head arts, as well as saber, sword, spear, and bow arts. These are all physical weapons. Through understanding one's body and their weapons in detail, they can execute impossible techniques, increasing their damage, attack speed, and so on," Khasar said. "I can see your skeptical look. I'll teach you a movement art."

"Okay," Erik said.

Khasar blurred so fast it looked as though he had *teleported* over to the other side of the training square. He stood there with his clothes settling back down as the dust only under his feet was swept up. There was no trail of him across the training square.

"How?" Erik asked.

"I will impart the technique to you—not only the movements that you must do with your body but the way that you must move your mana in order to use the full power of the move," Khasar said.

Erik nodded as Khasar passed on to him how he should move the mana in his body and how to do it in time with his movements.

Erik checked it over a few times and asked Khasar a few questions.

"Okay, now we won't learn without doing. Give it a try," Khasar said.

Erik followed the circulation method he had been told and felt a tearing pain in his body. He started to move forward and then accelerated suddenly, tripping and rolling. He stopped circulating the technique.

"Try running and *then* circulating your mana. That way, you don't have to get the timing of the two lined up right as you start," Khasar said.

Erik started jogging and then incorporated the technique. He would shoot forward, and then stop circulating the mana so his body was going fast. But his perception was too slow and he would go down in a shambling mess.

He kept on doing it again and again.

Finally he started to get the timing of the two parts together. The air stopped whistling past him and he started to glide through it.

If he got the timing wrong, then his body would hurt with all of the built-up energy having nowhere to go, causing a small rebound.

The rebounds happened less often and the pain stopped appearing as Erik got the hang of it. He only stopped after he could sync up the running with the circulation without issue, though he was unable to stop, causing him to tumble and crash after his sprints.

"Seems that I was just a frog in a well," Erik said, using a proverb that he had heard all too often in the Ten Realms.

"It is good to understand there is always more to learn," Khasar said. "Now, get up. Let's see if you can do it again."

"Sound like my old drill instructors." Erik got to his feet, shaking his body.

"Now you've got the part about starting, we just have to work on the bit about *stopping.*"

Erik blurred, leaving the corner he had been standing in.

"Left!"

Erik went to the corner designated left.

"Forward!"

Erik moved again.

"Right!"

Erik didn't even make it to the forward corner before he was moving to the right corner.

"Back! Left, forward, backward!" Khasar kept on calling out the changes again and again.

Erik had to switch where his momentum was going, change the resistance on his body. The first time Khasar had done this, Erik had been practically standing in the same spot. There were so many things to think about, he got nervous and messed it all up.

It was kind of like driving for the first time: someone would be trying to change gears, do the clutch and the gas, then braking and then turning and signaling and watching everything that was happening around them. It was just so much information that a person was not able to easily process it. It was only when some of those functions became almost as easy as breathing that instead of having to worry about the clutch, the gears, and the gas, that they instead focused on the mirrors and the indicators.

It was about practicing them over and over again until it got to the point that all of the different moving parts flowed together and Erik was able to move in any direction without issue.

Now he was able to get a few meters in any direction before he had to change directions.

"Okay, that should be good," Khasar said.

Instead of flopping down, Erik focused on his breathing and drank from his canteen.

"You've got plenty of Stamina and mana, which allows you to fight longer and go further than most people and you improve quickly. It shouldn't be long until you're executing even basic fighting techniques and then you can get into the named techniques," Khasar said.

"Thank you," Erik said.

"Aren't we both people from the Alchemist Association?" Khasar smiled. "Just don't get arrogant."

"Like the others?" Erik smiled.

"Looks like you are learning something." Khasar left Erik in the training square.

After Khasar's lessons, a lot more of the information that he thought was just fluff in the different technique manuals he had seemed to make sense.

He closed his eyes, remembering the One Finger Beats Fist technique. It was still the most advanced technique he had. All the other techniques he hadn't paid attention to, just thinking that they were fancy names for something that had no actual way to increase his fighting strength.

He focused on the images he had been shown with the One Finger Beats Fist technique.

With his eyes closed, he started to practice the One Finger Beats Fist. He started to circulate his mana in accordance with the mana circulation technique. There was a rumbling noise from within his body as power gushed out of his mana channels and his finger, making him let out a wet cough. His arm and finger felt incredibly tired and sore.

They started to recover but Erik took time to recover.

"Too much power too fast. I need to slow it down and decrease the amount of power that I put into each attack or else I could really hurt myself."

Erik focused on the control. With his healing and Alchemy skills, his normal control over mana was much higher than others.

After ten minutes, he struck out with his finger. The light around him seemed to become darker and his finger became brighter as all of his strength was directed through his finger. The air was disturbed; reality wasn't bent, but a small hole as big as a finger appeared in the stone where he had struck out. A crack appeared through it.

Someone could easily underestimate the power of a single finger, just like those opponents I saw in the visions. I used it before when attacking people, attacking their weaknesses. As long as I was able to dodge the main attack and met them head on with this finger technique, then I could catch them off guard and hurt them.

His entire body seemed weaker. "It draws power from my entire body. If I was to go all-out, then I would need time to recover as my Stamina would drop a lot and I would feel weak for some time afterward. I should take this time to increase my knowledge of fighting techniques. As Khasar said, I have a lot of Stamina and mana. If I can leverage those to fight for longer, or use them suddenly in an attack—" *I've only cultivated and refined pure mana into my body, making it stronger and denser than others.*

Erik felt as if he had tapped into a new unmined strength that he had been standing in front of, but he had been looking at it from the wrong angle.

Erik shook his head. His biggest barrier had been his perception of just *how* people should fight with their bodies. For his entire life, he had been taught to punch and kick. Using mana to increase his strength was one thing, but to change the environment around him in order to increase the attack power of his strikes…it just wasn't something that was possible on Earth. People were all just fighting against one another, against the world. In the Ten Realms, it would work with them in order to defeat their enemies; it was just figuring out the right way to use that power in order to aid their own attacks.

There was a knock at the door.

Glosil looked up from his papers. "Enter."

The door opened and Sergeants Acosta and Song-Min walked into the room, coming to attention in front of his desk and saluting.

He returned the salute. "At ease. Take a seat."

They sat down and looked at him.

Glosil observed them. Since he had last seen them, his training program had gone into full effect, with Dragon Company's members taking over the majority of training while Tiger Platoon worked to maintain combat effectiveness, improving their defenses and working within Vuzgal.

Hopefully we should soon have more of the police force that originated in Alva in Vuzgal to take over. They have better training to deal with these conflicts.

"All right, so you've probably got the broad strokes. Now, here are your orders." Glosil took out two folders and passed them over. They included maps, key information staging areas, and such.

"Song-Min, your group will focus on providing security, making sure that no one learns of the training and make sure that no one gets information out about the camp. Acosta, it will be your job to train these people up. There is a breakdown of the groups. We won't be looking to make rifle squads or platoons. Instead, we want to turn them into parties. We don't want to give them repeaters or rifles; it will point right to us. If they are just using their original abilities together, it will be harder to trace. They'll be more organized, better at working together and higher skill levels. That should be enough."

"We heard that they might be joining the army?" Acosta asked, looking up from her open folder.

"This is a possibility. Use this opportunity to evaluate them."

Acosta and Song-Min nodded.

"Now you are probably wondering why are we training them up in the first place and what this second secret group is about. Well, our current plan is—"

Lord Aditya walked into his office and saw Miss Evernight standing to the side; a man and woman looked out of the large windows looking at Vermire, their bodies turned so they could see the door as well.

They glanced over to him, studying him as the door closed behind him. One of them activated a formation to stop noise from escaping.

"I am Sergeant Blue. This is Sergeant Red. We're here to train up your people. Our higher-ups have reviewed your plan and made some adjustments." The woman stepped forward.

"Okay." Aditya's heart sped up. *Does this mean that they've accepted my plan?*

"We are still gathering more information on the other outpost leaders but in the meantime, this will allow you to increase your guard force in numbers and strength. Also, your guards will have the opportunity in the future to join our ranks."

Aditya felt pain inside. He had spent a lot of time and effort on his guards. *I am just the manager of Vermire now.* He calmed his heart and the pain lessened as he nodded. "What can I do to help?"

"You'll need to cover how we're moving troops around and training them," Sergeant Blue said.

"Okay. I'll need some time to work on that. I can send them out to train in the Beast Mountain Range. If I have two forces, then I can move them around so there are the same amount of people on the walls and patrolling even if there are half of them out and training. What will their training involve?"

"Okay. We need to come up with a concrete plan, as well as look over the people you wish to hire who aren't from the guard force. We will be training the guard force, though they will need to train the new recruits. We will take care of security, but we don't want to be revealed. Our higher-ups do not want us to be seen in this conflict. Others might question it after what happened in the last conflict Vermire was involved in." Sergeant Blue looked to Miss Evernight, who nodded seriously before looking at Lord Aditya.

"We have a lot of work to do."

20 Bandit Clearing

Tanya woke up suddenly. She still had a hood on her face and she looked around in alarm.

"Will you take the hood off her?" a man asked.

His accent was familiar. She had heard it in movies and on the news from time to time. *Redneck?*

The hood came off her. She saw that there were only three people in the small room: Tian Cui, herself, and a new, larger man who wore body armor.

He looked like one of those people she had seen in war zones as he held the straps of his vest, looking at her.

"Well, we're a long way from Earth." The man stepped forward and grabbed a chair, sitting down opposite her. "Cui, hands?"

Tian Cui sighed and then cut the bindings, releasing Tanya.

She rubbed her wrists, looking at the man in front of her. "Are you from the South?"

"Southern United States, yes, ma'am. And your accent—European?"

"I'm from Sweden," Tanya said.

"When did you arrive in the Ten Realms?"

"A while ago. Are there other people from Earth here?"

"You're the first we've tracked down so far," Rugrat said.

"Others came through too?"

"Yes. My friend and I arrived here some time ago, we met up with another person from Earth too, he joined us as well. Don't you know about the Two Week Curse?" Rugrat asked.

"What?"

"Get infected by magic and then two weeks later, have magical fireworks and poof! You disappear from Earth and arrive here," Rugrat said.

"Oh. I didn't hear anything about it," she said.

"You must have been one of the first people to make it into the Ten Realms then. It had been going on for months when we arrived, which must've been like two—three years?"

"We?"

"Came in with my battle buddy Erik. He's in the Third Realm right now with the Alchemist Association. Enough about us. This is about you and your future," Rugrat said.

"You sound like some kind of recruiter."

"Had to do a couple of years of it…not my proudest moments," Rugrat muttered before clearing his throat.

"Now, my existence, the existence of these fine people and the information that I am about to tell you, you will never repeat to anybody unless I give you face-to-face permission, understood?" Rugrat asked.

"I understand." Tanya nodded.

"Good! Well then, you do an oath on that, and I'll do an oath on not hurting you and telling you the truth, nothing but the truth. Oaths make the realms go round, you know," Rugrat said.

Rugrat looked at Tanya as the light of the oath disappeared from the room. She was petting Tetsu. George, in the corner, sniffed him, the two of them getting to know each other.

"No fighting now," Rugrat warned them both as he saw them out of the corner of his eye.

Rugrat saw George's expression and only opened his eyes to enforce the point. George seemed to get it and went back to what he was doing.

"So tell me about you. Who are you? What did you do before this? How have you been surviving until now?"

"Tanya Kvist. I was a factory worker. I did it mostly to pass the time. I was planning a game night when I was teleported here, I guess? I have a game master book, so I looked up stuff in that book, tried to connect some stuff to what is going on here. I was able to make some spells and then I've just been increasing Tetsu's strength. He gets a lot of attention.

"I made my way through the First Realm, killing and eating, providing for us both. The Second Realm, I tried my hand at a few different things. I am a Novice in a lot of different crafts."

"Any you're particularly interested in?"

"Not really. I like learning about them, but doing them? It's way too many steps ahead of me."

"Okay, so these spells?"

"A few healing spells—one to get rid of disease. Tetsu was sick. Night Vision because it's an asset. I wanted to build myself up as a ranger. I got good at making traps and hiding them to weaken my prey before finishing them off, or the traps dealt with them. Then I came to the Third Realm. Someone wanted to buy Tetsu, was an alchemist-to-be—got all pissed off and I've been running ever since. Then I went into a city again to get supplies and the lord of the town, Lord Adda, found out that I was here. Wanting to get on the alchemist-to-be's good books and the sect that backs him, he sent out his bandits to come and capture me. He didn't want to do it officially, or else his monarch might know and then his monarch would use Tetsu to get into their good graces instead of him."

"So, not an easy few years," Rugrat said, his voice turning softer.

"Easy? No." Tanya snorted and shook her head.

"Well, I guess it is time for me to say my part. Okay, so Erik and I control a dungeon in the First Realm that has an academy that has a lot of books on any crafts you could possibly want. We're building a network of adventurers and fighters through the lower realms, feeding them into the dungeon to make them soldiers, or our agents as they get to higher levels. Got hospitals and healthcare. Food and all the good stuff. Also, we've got a *ton* of traders. They're everywhere as well; have branches through the Trader's Guild and the Adventurer's Guild as well as through a restaurant—great food, by the way.

"Oh, and we own a city in the Fourth Realm. Got an in with a few of the associations, but they're all two-faced and although the people we're talking to might like us, the organization is big so we don't know if there is someone higher in their chain of command who won't like us one day and then we've got a big old problem. Now, I have to head to the Second Realm to deal with something, though we will be meeting up with some of our people there.

"Now, this is an option, but we want you to come back to Alva. Give it a look around. If you don't like it, then you are free to go on with your life as you want, or you can join us. We've got a lot of people from the Ten Realms, but you're the second person we have met who is from Earth, though we do suspect that there is someone else who controls a powerful sect or group who might also be from Earth."

Tanya stared at Rugrat for some time. "Well, you guys have been busy."

"Erik would say that it is a good way to keep us out of trouble." Rugrat shrugged.

Tanya let out a soft snort, before she looked at Rugrat, studying him. She would be placing a lot of trust in him, but so far he and his people had all been good to her. She thought back to the camp, to the destruction that she had seen.

"What do you want from me?"

"Want? No idea. But we think that it would be better if we brought some Earth thinking, melded it with some Ten Realms know-how and maybe we'll be able to do a few things that neither would be able to," Rugrat said.

"Like what?"

"Well, you were a factory worker, right? We have a few factories that are up and in operation but they're not all that efficient. You have seen how a factory works and you could go in there and alter things so that the factory *would* work. You said that you altered spells and created them. We have people who are able to make magic scrolls and formations, but that's a lot easier than doing it with spells. Weaving spells together is hard as well as dangerous, but the benefits would be great. As long as you're safe while doing it, then we could open up a whole new area of study," Rugrat said.

"So there's nothing really set, just try my hand at different things and if I am good at something, then I can do it if I want?"

"Although Erik and I control Alva and Vuzgal, we allow the people of Alva to work freely. If we force them into jobs, then they're not going to do very well and it will come to bite us in the ass. We want people to work together, for there not to be any barriers between crafters. Who knows? A few crafters might get together and then they can create something that they would never be able to create by themselves."

"What about Tetsu?"

"Well, he is your pet. You can probably pay the pet stables to look after him if you need, but otherwise you can look after him. Just make sure that you clean up after his mess." Rugrat sighed.

"That I can do." Tanya smiled.

"Good." Rugrat stood and he shifted his body armor around. "So, are you in or are you out? You can take your time. There isn't really a rush, but I need to go and deal with something."

"I'm in," Tanya said, taking another jump.

"Well then." Rugrat reached out his hand.

Tanya stood and took it.

"If you go and you don't like it, you can take an oath of silence and leave. If you go and you do like it, as long as you pass the tests by the new resident staff, then you will take the Alva citizenship oath and you're one of us," Rugrat said.

"Okay," Tanya said.

"Well, let's get a move on." Rugrat turned and Tian Cui opened the door. As they left the room, George and Tetsu followed behind. They saw the rest of the team checking their gear, reading, and playing a card game.

"Okay, let's head off to the Second Realm," Rugrat said.

They left the warehouse some ten minutes later and headed to the totem.

"I don't have any mana stones," Tanya said as they got close.

"No worries. It's not that much," Rugrat said.

"Not that much?"

"Well, it used to be. Things change a lot around here. You start to get used to it," Rugrat said.

They used the totem and appeared in a new city, where they passed through security and went to a tavern. Rugrat and Gong Jin headed off to a meeting as she went with Tian Cui to a shady corner.

A merchant appeared, wearing fine robes.

"Tian Cui!" The merchant smiled.

Tian Cui broke into smile as well, laughing, and the two of them hugged.

"So this is where you've been. Did I scare you off after you confessed?" Tian Cui winked.

The merchant gave a cough, looking embarrassed. "There were good opportunities and I needed to make some coin." The man looked away and blushed.

"Oh, well, maybe if you asked again instead of running off, you might get a different response," Tian Cui said.

Tanya looked off into the night, trying not to be *too* much of a third wheel.

"Hurry up to Vuzgal. I'll be in Alva next week probably, though," Tian Cui said.

"Just finishing up here in the Second Realm. I've been hearing about Vuzgal. Is it everything the others are saying?"

"Everything and more. There are thousands of Mortal stones flying around that place every day. I don't even know how much is going per month and there are people buying all the time. The original plots are now selling for fifteen times more than the first people bought them for."

The merchant let out a low whistle.

"But then, that isn't what we're here to talk about. You're heading back down, right?" Tian Cui asked.

"Yeah." The merchant nodded.

"Rex, meet Tanya. Tanya, this is Rex. We lived in the first Alva together. He's had a crush on me for as long as I can remember."

"Thank you, Tian Cui." Rex reached out his hand, shaking Tanya's.

"Good to meet you." Tanya had stored Tetsu away; she didn't want to draw any unwanted attention.

"She just needs to get down to the First Realm and then join up. Make sure that the citizen people process her," Tian Cui said.

"All right." Rex nodded.

"See you later. Got to go and deal with some problems." Tian Cui sounded tired all of a sudden.

She said her good-byes and Tanya was left with Rex.

"They move fast in the special teams. They're jumping across the realms all the time and work directly for Erik and Rugrat on most operations. They're the best fighters we have, which puts them in the most demand," Rex said. "Let's get you some food. We leave for the First Realm in the morning."

"Okay," Tanya said. The last few days had been a whirlwind. She was looking forward to some point where she could just put her feet up and relax.

Rugrat and Gong Jin were sitting in a bar when a woman walked up and sat down opposite them, passing Rugrat a package under the table. It went into his storage ring.

"Give me the quick version."

"Came here, started as traders, saw others with more, started taking it, got away without problems. Got bold, started to do it more often, hired people to help them take on bigger jobs. They have a backer. They've got powerful weapons and they are moving their goods, though I haven't heard anyone that is buying," the woman said. She was a local source and not someone from Alva, so Rugrat and Gong Jin filled in the blanks in her story themselves.

"How are they working now?"

"High value goods, people who are worth a ransom, or that they can sell as slaves—it doesn't matter to them. They'll hit any caravan they can find, making the southeast a dangerous place to be," the woman said.

"Has anyone tried to take them down?"

"A few of the traders banded together to fight them, but they weren't strong enough. A city lord put a bounty on their heads, but then the bounty hunters' heads were found in front of the city a few days later. They're strong and bold. Brings them a lot of rough people to do their bidding and no one has been able to challenge them."

"Got it." Rugrat passed her a small sack of money. It disappeared into her storage ring and she left the tavern.

Rugrat and Gong Jin looked at each other.

"What are you thinking, boss?" Gong Jin asked.

"See what merchant convoys we have in the area, that we own. I want them to act as bait. Use people only from Alva—I want to keep this contained.

"They go in, we spring a trap, capture the bandits, group by group, clean them out, take out their strength, silence them and then put them to work for the rest of their lives as labor. We take down the people from Alva and we do the same with them."

Rugrat saw the question in Gong Jin's eyes.

"If we can't capture them and it is a risk to ourselves or to the bait, we kill them, last resort," Rugrat said.

"Yes, sir." Gong Jin nodded, taking a few moments to build up some courage. "You and Erik gave us a whole new life. We had no idea that this would happen. Just letting it go on would only set a bad example. At the end of the day, we're just people and people make mistakes."

"Thanks," Rugrat said.

"Now please don't court-martial me for talking out of place."

Rugrat shook his head and laughed, feeling a lot less tense as they headed out of the tavern to brief the others and put their plan into motion.

"I don't like it," Elise said.

"You said that ten minutes ago," Ray, the carriage driver, said as they rolled on. Ray was one of the later generation Alva residents. He was a reliable man and was the leader of this convoy.

But hearing what they were doing, Elise had raised her doubts with Rugrat. When they hadn't budged, she had then added herself to the convoy.

"I just don't like the fact that there are only six of them but there are supposed to be a hundred of these bandits, maybe even more than that," Elise said.

"You heard it as well—they defeated an army numbered in the thousands. A few hundred isn't much to them and they're not looking to kill them all," Ray said.

“It’s the fact that we have to do this that is wrong,” Elise said.

“Yes, it is,” Ray said.

They lapsed into silence.

Rugrat looked over the land from on top of George.

“I’ve got movement.” Using a long-distance Detect Life scroll, he saw dots moving on the horizon.

The group was quickly setting up. There was about fifty of them.

Rugrat marked their position and then sent the information via his sound talisman to the rest of the special team.

He grabbed a crossbow with a canister mounted on it.

The rest of the special team were using the cover of the forest to move around, Rugrat giving them information so that they remained hidden. They worked their way from the rear to the front, knocking out and incapacitating the bandits.

“Remember, don’t take them all. Let some escape,” Rugrat said.

The trader convoy started to enter the area that the bandits had prepared.

Bandits emerged around Elise, yelling as they came out of their hiding spots.

Han Wu, who was hiding in the convoy, fired his grenade launcher. The explosions went off, surprising them and stunning them.

“Get them!” Elise yelled as the merchants showed their armor and jumped down from the carriages.

The sudden reversal made the bandits rethink as they saw that there weren’t as many on their side as they thought. It looked as though some of their members had run off.

They turned and charged away in a panic.

Elise waved her hand, slowing the merchants. “Check for wounded!” Elise yelled.

The merchants checked their bodies, and then looked around.

“Don’t worry—I didn’t hit anyone,” Han Wu said. “All noise and flashes.”

"While we had to do the real work," Yang Zan said as he dragged several bandits out of the forest.

"Go and help them." Elise looked up, seeing the small spot in the sky that was Rugrat tracking the bandits as they ran.

Viggo had been a farmer with big dreams. He had done everything to try to get away from Alva to set out on his own path and show them just how well he could do.

When the attack came on the village, he had fought and his passion to do more with his life had burned brighter than ever.

Once they went to the dungeon and he started to see the traders heading out and coming back with massive rewards, he saved up and paid for people to help him increase his level.

He reached the Second Realm and started trading. He made some good money but it was only a small profit.

Then a trader slighted him—said that he was just a small fry, that he would never amount to anything. He didn't take that so well and when the trader left the city, he led his friends and a few people they had convinced to attack the trader.

With the weapons and items from Alva, they were able to win over the traders.

Then they had returned to Alva with those same carriages, showing off just how they were incredible traders.

It was too good, so they had continued. They could buy gear from Alva and then sell the items they got without it ever being traced back to them.

"Don't worry, it won't be long until we're the biggest traders in all of Alva and then we can do what we want. Doesn't Elise take what she wants and no one says anything?" Viggo said to his fellow conspirators as they sat in a hall enjoying food and drink they had looted from the latest caravan.

"I heard that Erik and Rugrat were able to take a city in the Fourth Realm, though." One of the others spoke up.

"Shut up, Otto! So what is a city? We could take several of them without effort!" another yelled, throwing food at them.

Otto grumbled and smacked the naked woman beside him. She cried out in pain and the five's eyes turned to her.

"Ah, Otto, you were too rough. Look what you've done now—you must have broken her face," Viggo said in mock-sadness.

The woman held her face. Tears streamed down her face as she looked at the other slaves, who all looked away.

"We were stepped on our entire lives but we never screamed, we never yelled. Aren't you strong enough?" Viggo said.

The other sniggered as Viggo moved closer, half crouching as the woman whimpered.

She covered her face with one hand and raised the other feebly, to defend.

"Ah, seems she does have some fight in her." He laughed and grabbed her arm, breaking it.

She cried out again as she dropped to the floor.

"Don't you know anything!" Otto yelled and broke a knee cap.

The woman's screams were disjointed because of her broken face.

"Lord! Lord! We were attacked, Lord!" a man yelled as he rushed into the hall.

Viggo and the others looked up, their expressions offering death as the man came to a halt and dropped to his knees.

"We attacked a caravan that you told us about. When we attacked them, it was like they knew. They had powerful weapons and everyone was wearing armor. It was a trap. They must've killed most of our people. We fled, but only a fifth of our number were able to make it back," the man said in a panic.

"The lords are getting bold!" Viggo yelled and stood up to his full height. His belly appeared underneath his armor and he was covered in gold and jewels.

The woman was still whimpering, unable to do anything but just lie there at their mercy.

"I hate broken things. Kill her." Viggo stepped forward.

Rugrat looked over the outpost. It must have been a small village at some time. Maybe it was a way station to another city that had found better trade routes, or a farmers' town that had been claimed by the desert.

Its past didn't matter now as Rugrat saw the three hundred or so people who were moving through the town. About three hundred people were locked up in cages. Goods were stored all over the place, with carriages being looted and their items checked before they were repacked again.

He watched as chained people were herded into cages that were dirty and filled with filth. The bandits didn't see their victims as people anymore, just new loot to be sold for a profit.

"Elise, you're going to need more people to help deal with this issue." Rugrat's voice was cold. He had long moved past the point of making jokes, seeing this all and knowing that this was done by people under his command.

There was no more mercy in his heart.

Gong Jin and his team had been moving according to his directions and they were now coming in from the north, farthest from the main hall where the fastest man was running toward and only had a few people in it.

Rugrat was watching everything that happened in the camp as he pulled out a scroll.

He saw the woman being hit as he activated the spell scroll.

Spell Scroll: Demon Chains-in effect

Everyone within a target area of 200X200m is captured by unbreakable black chains that will last three hours, or can be broken by someone Level 35 or higher.

Black chains appeared across the city. Everyone was chained in place, unable to move, only struggle.

Otto was just a few feet from the woman, staring into her fear-filled eyes as the demon chains held him tight, making him unable to move.

"What is this!?" he demanded.

There was a crash from above. The tattered ceiling fell apart and light shone in. A massive wolf with flames across its body dropped to the floor, taking up the entire space.

"You are charged with betraying the trust of Alva, carrying out acts of violence, acts of slavery upon others for your own personal gain."

The man's voice made the mana in the room quiver. Viggo felt his mana stop in his mana channels.

The five all looked up at the voice. They knew it. They knew it well. It was Rugrat.

"Dungeon Master, we were just looking to bring more strength to the dungeon! To bring in more money for our families!" Viggo said, already pleading with him.

"You will serve Alva for the rest of your lives as forced labor. Your crimes will be judged by the people of Alva." Rugrat used a Silence spell on them all, making them unable to talk as George got smaller and he stepped off.

He walked forward. His hard expression and his sand-dusted armor showed the hard edge he had rarely revealed to the people of Alva.

"If there was no one watching, I would mount you on a pike and tie weights to your ankles so that every time you moved, every time you struggled, you would slowly sink down farther. You wouldn't die from your injuries. Your infections would kill you—your own body poisoning yourselves." Rugrat manipulated the mana so his voice only carried to those five, who had wide eyes as they saw the uncaring look in Rugrat's eyes.

He stepped forward and bent down to the girl they had been hitting. He took out a potion and fed it to her; she let out a gasp as her body started to repair in front of their eyes.

"Miracle potion," one of the slaves said.

"Just a potion. Are any of you injured?" Rugrat asked.

The slaves looked away and shook their heads. They had been cowed over the days or weeks they had been controlled by Viggo and his people.

Viggo felt some triumph seeing their sheep-like expressions. *As long as I am alive, there is a chance that I can make a comeback! The people of Alva are soft. I can use them to release me!*

Elise looked over the city. The bandits were to one side and the slaves on the other. They looked at one another, looking at Elise and her people with fear, but accepting their aid.

I can't even begin to imagine what they've been through. Elise thought of the slave pits.

Rugrat came out from the slave pits carrying a young boy, who was in bad shape. He passed him off to Yang Zan.

"He was at the bottom. His mother and father were killed in the attack. The others tried to help him but he got sick," Rugrat said.

"Understood." Yang Zan looked over the young man and started to organize those who had basic medical understanding and got them to work.

Rugrat stepped over to Elise.

She blinked and looked to the side as the wave of smell hit her.

"Yeah, it's not good in there," Rugrat said.

"I had no idea that—" Elise said.

"I believe you, but we need to make sure that something like this never happens again," Rugrat said.

Elise felt as if the energy in her body had been sucked out of her and could feel the pit in the bottom of her stomach.

It is my job to not only grow the traders, but to watch over them. If it wasn't for Elan's information network, then we wouldn't have found out about what was happening here.

Rugrat headed off to deal with something and Elise watched his back. She knew that underneath his jokes and games, there was another side of Rugrat, a ruthless side that would destroy himself to complete his mission, that could turn off his emotions and deal with the task ahead of him.

She had forgotten about it after not seeing it for so long. She saw the same coldness in the expressions of the special team as they worked, detaching themselves from their work.

I have been in the lower realms for too long. I don't know what is happening in the Fourth Realm and I'm out of contact with Alva.

Elise promised to go back to Alva more and go to the Fourth Realm, not to build her business, but to understand just what all of the traders were doing so that when someone asked, she could give them an answer.

I focused on expanding so much that I lost sight of some of my responsibilities.

Robertson and the team were laughing and joking as they left Peli.

"Thankfully we have some spare cure poison and healing potions for all the hangovers," Virion said as she walked beside Robertson.

"Yeah. We'd be in one hell of a mess otherwise." Robertson chuckled.

They left the shade of Peli behind, looking at the massive grown city as they passed through the fields.

Peli was a city in the Second Realm, but it was settled by a few families from the Third Realm. In the Third Realm, their power was limited but in the Second Realm they were like kings, controlling an entire city. With their practices, they turned Peli into a growing city that did regular trade with the Third Realm. Wanting to protect the city, they didn't build a totem within it and created a sister city, Alasam, with a totem.

Most of the trade happened there, but the higher quality goods and the major suppliers were still in Peli. Lin Chan traded with them directly but the route between the two cities was plagued with bandits and her load was too valuable to leave up to chance. When returning, she would have the protection of Peli to Alamas.

Although it was a Second Realm city, its close connection to the Third Realm made it so that no bandit was willing to attack a Peli-protected convoy.

"What are you going to do when we get back to the Third Realm?" Virion asked.

"Cultivate—increase my Body Cultivation and then apply to challenge the Elite's test," Robertson said.

"The Elite test? Again?"

"I can do it! I know that I can!"

"It takes brains, not brawn." Virion sighed.

"Well, it takes stubbornness, too. You've met the guild leader, right?"

Virion snorted and nodded. "Guess being as stubborn as a metal mountain is true."

The group were relaxed as they left the fields behind and moved into the mountains that surrounded Peli. Great waterfalls fell down as they walked up the gradual slope and through the defensive outposts and into the rolling forests that covered the path to Alamas.

"Who's there!" one of the rangers in the group yelled out, pulling their crossbow. The others grabbed their weapons, looking around, wondering whether it was a prank or not.

"Stop messing around, Kujo," someone said as they straightened up.

"Someone is watching us, following us," Kujo said.

Robertson looked around. He had an uneasy feeling.

He looked around and there was a whistling noise. He threw himself to the side as arrows came from the trees. Three were hit and they cried out in pain. Kujo got several arrows, falling to the ground. His blood stained the ground.

"Ambush! Get into a circle!" Robertson yelled. "Mages, smoke them out!"

The mages started to cast. Another one was taken out with arrows before their attacks shot into the forest; two of them used detection spells that lit up all of the attackers.

The archers didn't need orders; they shot out at the silhouettes that were now highlighted in the forest.

Only a few of the silhouettes disappeared as they were killed. The others dodged or blocked as the ambushers jumped out of the forest.

"Well, I must say that you are better than I thought you would be." A man pushed back his hood. He had pale skin and hair, with red eyes.

"We're from the Alva Adventurer's Guild. Do you know what will happen if you kill us?" Robertson demanded, trying to gain time and looking for a way out.

"Yes, some little mercenary group, I know." The man opened his cloak so Robertson could see his sect emblem. He smirked. "Do you think my Willful Institute will care? Do you think that your guild would dare to come after me and my companions if we were to slaughter you all?"

The man stepped forward, a vicious look on his face.

A mage used their spell staff. A golden eagle appeared and shot forward. It flapped its golden wings that shot out from its body, sounding like metal darts as they struck the ground.

"Run!" Robertson yelled. The group turned and ran, taking the dead into their storage rings as they did so.

"Tricks." The man snorted.

Robertson looked back to see the man racing forward with several others.

"Virion, make sure that they get out of here." Robertson took out a pill and threw it into his mouth, then took out several spell scrolls. He passed her the storage bag and his storage devices.

"Robertson," she hissed.

"Don't let them down and let the guild leader know." Robertson smiled. "It all has to end one day."

Robertson felt the pill turn into energy within his body. He took several spell scrolls and activated them. Power swelled in the area as the ranged fighters shot back and forth between the groups. A mage lay down a smokescreen, making it harder for the Willful Institute.

"He's using a spell scroll, defensive scroll!" one of the Willful Institute members yelled out as they drew out defensives scrolls.

"We can make it!" Virion said.

"You damn well better," Robertson said as the power flowed through him.

His body started to grow, to become withered as he used his life force to complete the change. Powerful forces of death and life worked within his body, increasing his strength massively at the cost of his future days.

Kernys couldn't see anything ahead. The tracker beside him was unable to confirm where the mercenaries were.

"This damn smoke," Kernys hissed. "What is that!"

"Ahh!" A wet noise sounded as Kernys slowed his pace.

The fog cleared a bit and the light shone behind a man who glowed in alternating black and white as power fluctuated wildly around him.

His mana shield blazed with white flames while his sword was covered in black flames. One of his eyes was black; the other was white.

He stepped forward and shot through the fog, creating a tunnel through it.

Kernys was able to raise his sword to block, but he was tossed backward. He used his Agility to recover but the tracker was cut down by the white and black man in just two blows.

The tracker was the real target!

Kernys gnashed his teeth as the man tilted his head to the side with a peculiar look on his face.

He shot into the fog once again. There was the sound of fighting and Kernys rushed forward, to find dead bodies.

He found the man, who turned away from the woman who had spoken up in the meeting. Her face was covered in regret as he withdrew his blade.

"Ahh the sects, the overlords, and dominators." The man shot at Kernys, who was able to put his blade up in time and move to the side.

He has incredible strength. With whatever he's used, he has strength that people with Body Like Stone would be able to harness. Kernys assessed and prepared himself.

I just need to work him until the effects wear off, or gang up on him with others.

"Come here! I have him cornered!" Kernys yelled.

"Oh?" The man's head turned and that same creepy smile appeared. He ran to the side but Kernys was there to stop him.

"You might be strong, but your techniques are weak, old man!" Kernys sneered as he halted the man's movements.

"Rat!" the man yelled out.

Kernys deflected the attacks, but he was weakening as the man used his shield. Just as it was about to crush Kernys's side, a green eye appeared at the point of impact and the man was hurled backward.

Kernys felt the medallion his mother had given to him crumble. He didn't have time to think as he ran forward and slashed, hitting the man's side.

The man distanced himself and got up, but there was a cut on his shoulder.

An archer fired arrows and the man defended. There were two others, one with a sword and the other with a spear.

"Space out and hit him from the sides. His strength is high—watch for his attacks!" Kernys yelled, a vicious look in his eyes.

"I'll break every bone in your body. I'll kill you slowly and then take your skull and throw it into my toilet!" Kernys yelled.

"What does it matter when I'm dead?" The man took a sword hit on his shield. The spear attack raked his side. He traded the hit as he stabbed at the swordsman.

They had a defensive artifact as well, but it was only a simple shield. He broke it easily and plunged his sword into the sect member's side, tearing it back out as they collapsed.

He let out a grunt as an arrow pierced his shoulder blade.

Kernys rushed forward but the old man blocked his blade. The spear user tried to angle himself to get a blow on the old man, who pushed Kernys back.

Kernys charged forward again, this time using his sword and distance to play with the older man.

"You think that we're the only group to ambush you? There is another group down the road, waiting for your people. None of them will make it! No one will know of your fate!" Kernys boasted.

The old man laughed. He seemed to be free of all worries. "We may die here today, young one, but I have faith in the guild and in my guildmaster. So what if you live in the Fourth Realm—you do not rule the Mortal realms!"

The man launched a full attack, leaving himself open. An arrow whizzed by his head. The spear missed him and Kernys was too slow to stop him as the man slashed his armor, breaking bone and making Kernys let out a hiss of pain.

The man paused for a second, and the spear man pierced through his leg, making him cry out as the archer put another arrow through his armor.

The black and white features were even stronger than before. The man used his explosive power, reaching the spearman and slamming his shield into their face. He threw his sword. The archer didn't seem to believe their eyes as the sword impaled them. The spearman dropped to the ground as the man bashed their head with the edge of their shield.

Kernys ran forward. The man tried to dodge but Kernys raked his back.

The man got back to his feet and faced Kernys. He was covered in blood as the power around him dimmed.

Kernys sneered as the man took out a token and snapped it. A glow of power appeared around it before disappearing.

"What did you do?" Kernys yelled.

"I'm not sure." The man threw a pill into his mouth, smiling. His eyes rolled back and he dropped to the ground.

Kernys was stunned as the man's power dissipated and he could tell that he was dead. The fog lifted from the fighting, but there were only a few of his sect members remaining, with only the one mercenary body.

Kernys let out a yell and kicked the man's corpse, the mocking smile still on his face.

21 Viewing Hall

Qin was off seeing her brothers and her father, who was in the city, while Julilah brought Tan Xue breakfast. She had worked through the night again.

Julilah sat there, watching her work as she had so many times and ate her food. She found the noise and the heat relaxing.

Her mind returned back to her old memories, to her old life in Kaeju.

She let out a sigh as Tan Xue finished what she was working on.

"Julilah!" Tan Xue said, surprised to see her there.

"I brought you breakfast," Julilah said.

"There's no need for you to do that. How long have you been there for?" Tan Xue put the work to the side and sat down on the seat next to Julilah.

"Only a few minutes. I got your favorites," Julilah said.

Tan Xue looked at the carefully made breakfast, unable to hide her excitement or hunger. "I remember when you tried to bribe me with these to teach you smithing."

"You would only eat them if I accepted your money," Julilah said.

Tan Xue snorted, looking at Julilah with a smile, and started eating.

"I'm glad that I had you," Julilah said.

"Where is this coming from?" Tan Xue asked.

"You know how my dad wasn't there and my mother made money through *pleasing* men. You listened to me and talked. You might not have wanted to teach me smithing because you didn't want others to use me, like they did with you, or have people threaten you with me," Julilah said.

Tan Xue paused her eating and looked down at her meal.

"Thank you. I don't know where I would be without you there," Julilah said.

Tan Xue looked up with tears in her eyes as she sniffed and looked away.

Julilah didn't let her get away and hugged her.

"You...you can't surprise me like that," Tan Xue said off to the side.

"I just realized I never said thank you for everything," Julilah said in a small voice.

"Come on, can't have us both crying in a smithy!" Tan Xue said.

Julilah laughed and they wiped their tears, feeling all the lighter for talking.

"Come on. We should do something today," Tan Xue said.

"What?" Julilah asked.

"Don't sound so alarmed. You think I don't know how you don't like big crowds and being stuck in awkward situations?" Tan Xue said as she shoveled food into her face.

"So where?" Julilah asked.

"The Viewing Hall!" Tan Xue said.

She finished off breakfast quickly and the two of them had tea, catching up. Tan Xue wouldn't tell Julilah anything else about the Viewing Hall.

They left the smithy and then went into the depths of the crafting area. They entered a building with a special key and they took the stairs down to an underground area with different rooms in it.

"This is the Viewing Hall. It is a new addition to Vuzgal. The Crafting trial dungeons are all fitted with recording devices that record what different crafters are doing. All of those recordings are stored here and there is a second Viewing Hall that will be located in Alva."

"Recordings of Experts?" Julilah asked.

"Yes," Tan Xue said as she took Julilah to a room. "Put some of your blood on this key—it's your key—then insert it into the wall. Then you will be able to access the recordings and the door will seal."

Julilah put some blood on the crystal-like key and put it into a glowing hole.

A screen appeared in front of her, asking what type of crafter she wanted to see and what level of expertise that they were at.

"Luis, Expert-level formation master," Julilah said out loud. Her view changed and her body felt different.

"It's not just a recording, but Erik and Rugrat call it a simulation!" Tan Xue said.

"I can't control my movements!" Julilah yelled out.

"Don't worry. Try to emulate them. You're not really here. We're in a shared space that makes it as if we're inhabiting their bodies while they're crafting," Tan Xue said.

Julilah steadied herself and started to follow what Luis was doing.

His movements were simple, but she could feel her movements, and the way that he was moving, incorporated more than just simple movements.

Forgetting her misgivings, she started to concentrate on the movements, understanding why he was doing what. With just a recording, she might be able to see his movements, but being inside the recording, she was able to understand that what was happening on the outside could be misleading.

She relaxed, her mind focusing with the high mana within the Viewing Hall. She fell into a trance-like state, combining her knowledge with the techniques she was practicing, matching the two together.

Tan Xue stood off at the side, watching Luis/Julilah working on the formation, a proud smile on her face. She focused on what they were doing, frowning from time to time when she saw something new she didn't understand.

The light dimmed and Rugrat looked over Alva again.

He let out a tired sigh. More houses had been built; there were more mana stones above the dungeon; students of the academy and the military moved around, talking to one another, focused on their studies or talking about the latest news from the other realms.

Most of those who had been slaves had taken oaths of silence and generous payouts to continue on with their lives. A rare few wanted to go and visit Alva.

They had shifted the bandits to other trader groups from Alva, to be used for labor as they were needed. They would be brought back to Alva for trial.

"Ah, so back for a while?" Egbert asked, settling down in front of Rugrat.

"You been flying around again?"

"It is the easiest way now that there are all of these pesky buildings in the way," Egbert said.

"I wanted to test out something with the answering statue," Rugrat said.

"Elan sent word. It is on its way to Vuzgal now."

"Of course it is. How is the Crafting trial dungeon?"

"It's operational, as is the new Viewing Hall," Egbert said.

"How have things been?"

"Calm. The recruiting has calmed down. People don't want to draw too much attention and I think what happened in the Second Realm will only serve to make people want to bring less people in. Still, we have an impressive amount coming in every month, a few hundred now. We're up to around twenty thousand people who are Alvans, or are being vetted to become people of Alva."

"The Metal floor?"

"It is under our complete control. I have a few materials that we still need to identify..."

"Give them to me and I'll see if I can find out what they are from the people in Vuzgal or through Elan," Rugrat said.

"Thank you!" Egbert passed him a storage ring with them inside.

"Also, Glosil has a plan to take the Earth floor," Egbert said.

"Good. The sooner we control all of Alva, the better," Rugrat said.

Rugrat saw Glosil, Blaze, and Elise approaching him and Egbert went quiet.

"I want to head up to the Fourth Realm. Vuzgal is the center of trade in the Fourth Realm and I want to check on operations there," Elise said.

"I want to learn more about the associations and also fight in the Battle Arena," Blaze said.

"And you both have people to cover the other realms?" Rugrat asked.

"Yes," they both said.

"Very well." Rugrat nodded and looked at Glosil.

"I have come up with a preliminary plan. I wanted to get your consent to it and then I'll coordinate with the rest of the military to carry it out," Glosil said.

"Let's head to my office and talk about it more," Rugrat said.

"You're not going back to the Fourth Realm?" Blaze asked.

"I'll be a day or two, then I'll join you. Don't worry—Hiao Xen has everything covered," Rugrat said.

As soon as he and Glosil were in the dungeon headquarters, Rugrat's face fell. He grabbed a seat, pulled out a nutrition bar and started chewing on it.

"Rough?" Glosil said.

"Trusted them to do the right thing. Instead, they created a criminal organization and they were using Alva to peddle their goods." Rugrat shook his head in anger. "Don't know how many they sold into slavery or how many they left dead in the Hersht sands. But we're not here to talk about those pieces of shit. Your plan?"

Glosil cleared his throat and called up the glowing floor plan of the Earth floor.

"We know that the closer we get to the center of the room, then the higher the Earth mana attribute and the higher the gravity. So we're going to need to take people who have tempered bodies that can handle that kind of pressure. The floor is an overgrown jungle—limited sight lines. Animals could be everywhere. We don't know if there will be a king of the floor or if there will be different creatures fighting one another.

"I wanted to make it quick and fast, but I realized that it would only lead to more mistakes. We need to know just what we're dealing with before we charge in.

"I want to send in a group to establish a position around the teleportation formation, make it ours and hold it. Then we push out from there toward the core, use bases to support one another and send out scouts to learn what is happening on the floor. Then we move forward, creating camps as we need to support one another over formations in the floor. We repair those formations, slowly regaining control over the floor before we strike the center. This is only if the situation is bad and hard to handle. If it's not that bad, we can send in a strike force through the floor with support and they retake the main commanding formation, repair it so we can once again extend the dungeon's influence over the floor. Egbert's words gave me an idea. It's risky, but could speed things up."

"What?" Rugrat said.

"The gnomes used to drop the core down and used it like a drill. It would take command over an area, change it and turn it into a floor and then it kept on going. If we can drop the dungeon core down, then you and Erik could change the floor, rebuild it, repair the formations much quicker," Glosil said.

"I want more concrete information before we do something like that. If we drop the core, Erik and I need to be close to it, so we would need to take it to the floor and then do these changes, which can take a lot of power and resources. We go with your first plan for now and use the second as a backup," Rugrat said.

"I just don't want to put the dungeon core at risk. If we lose it, or something happens, it wouldn't be good. We might be able to replace it with one of the cores from Vuzgal, but then we'll lose something—the Crafting trial dungeon, or complete control over Vuzgal and its undead force. I really like having an army of undead to call on to back our people up with."

"Okay." Glosil nodded.

"Now, establishing this beachhead—how will you go about it?"

"Beachhead?"

"It's a term for entering enemy territory, their beaches, and creating a defensive position from where we can launch further attacks or operations," Rugrat said.

"Okay, well, taking a look at the landscape, I thought it would be best to have close-in weaponry and then move in mages, with artillery. The ceilings are tall, but we would need much smaller charges so that they don't hit it and rain down rocks on us, which means that we're not going to have an awful lot of range," Glosil said.

The two of them bent over the plans, discussing the upcoming operation.

Delilah walked into the library of Alva. She'd snuck out of the Third

Realm to come down. With the totem in Alva, it now made it incredibly easy to reach. People from all walks could be found here. Any of the books people could read for free, but people had to pay a membership fee to rent the books and take them home and each rental had a time limit on it.

The library was the largest building in all of Alva, the home of Egbert and his librarians. The librarians were some of the strongest mages. They had a demure appearance and shared a joy of finding new knowledge and showing people the path to new information that would help them to increase their abilities.

They all wore simple brown and green clothes. Each of them had cultivated their mana to a high degree, some of them surpassing Rugrat's own cultivation, opening mana gates and using what they learned and the resources of Alva to increase their power.

Egbert also spent the most time with them and could easily pass them on tips and tricks or guide them to books that would aid their pursuits.

Delilah liked going to the library. Here, the people of Alva learned. She reached the front desk where librarians sorted out books and assisted patrons.

The man at the desk stood with a smile as he greeted Delilah.

"Where is he hiding?"

The man's smile faltered for a second before sighing. "Novice area, fiction."

"Thank you." Delilah weaved through the bookcases, seeing people in the aisles looking for books, putting them back; some were at desks piled high with books, working feverishly, or others who were reading one book at a time.

She reached the fiction section and passed people smiling or laughing silently to themselves. Others gripped the next page, ready to flip it over in a moment, not willing to break that immersion, the story gripping them tight.

She headed back into the shelves. Here they had been positioned to make nooks and crannies for people to get lost in and hide from others.

She looked at the people's hands until she found a robed man who had bony hands.

He sat on the edge of his seat, holding the edge of the page.

She could see inside his hood, his jaw half open, captured by the book.

The Wealthy Merchant's Scion and the Shapeshifting Woman. Sounds kind of fun. Delilah coughed as she realized the train of thought she was going down.

"End of the chapter," Egbert said, not looking up.

So he knew that I was looking for him at least.

She sat down and pulled out reports, absorbing information books and then marking down reports and adding notes.

Egbert let out a noise as he carefully put a bookmark in the book's pages, taking a moment to leave the world he had been in and return to the library.

"Okay, so what do you need, Miss Council Leader?" Egbert pushed back his hood, not trying to hide his appearance anymore.

"Alvan bandits," Delilah said, her voice turning cold.

Egbert's eyes flashed and his expression turned grim. "Okay, what about them?"

"We need to try them. The police force we have is only growing up now. It is spread thin. I've already ordered them to make up a group of officers who would be in charge of going around the realms and checking in on the people of Alva, make sure that they aren't up to anything nefarious. They would be trained up by Elan and his people but they would operate in the light while Elan operates in the dark. Still, it doesn't deal with the bandits we were able to arrest," Delilah said.

"And what do you need from me?" Egbert asked.

"I need a judge, someone to listen to the different sides and render a judgement fairly," Delilah said.

"So, me?" Egbert asked.

Delilah nodded.

Egbert was quiet for some time. "Yes, they need to be punished. And I will be following the Alvan laws?"

"That is correct," Delilah said.

Silence filled their nook, the lighter atmosphere from before shattered.

"I heard that you have the newest Earth arrival, Tanya, working here?"

"She has a different way of looking at the Ten Realms. She is studying magic, trying to get a greater understanding of its underlying principles and ways to effectively use it. I have tentatively named her as the head of the pure magic research division, though I've not told anyone."

"How is it different from the spell research division?"

"The spell research division looks at taking spells that we already have and combining them with others to increase their strength and create techniques. They are working spells together. If we can understand the basis of magic, then it will have a multiplicative effect upon the power of spells. We could reduce the amount of power needed, spell casting time, and increase the effect. Spells are useful to those who have the mana capacity and mental aptitude for it. In Alva, nearly everyone can cast at least basic spells but out in the realms, there are a lot of people who don't cast spells. Learning about mana and magic doesn't just affect spells; it effects formations, spell scroll making, woodworking, smithing, tailoring, Alchemy, farming, cooking, every craft, as well as Mana Gathering Cultivation and, as we have found out recently, Body Cultivation."

"You think that it could be that effective?"

"I'm not sure how effective it will be but I think that if she makes the right breakthrough, then all magic in Alva could take a qualitative leap forward."

22 Training Demon

Delilah rubbed the sleep from her eyes as she walked out into the courtyard of the residence that she and Erik were living in.

He was in the middle of the courtyard, with Khasar watching him.

Erik breathed heavily, his body covered in sweat. His body dropped but in his eyes there was an excitement, a willpower that demanded more, that pushed him past his boundaries, almost as if he were hungry for more to increase his strength.

"Come!" Khasar said.

The two of them shot toward each other. She felt as if there should be a rush of wind, but there was only a small amount of dust being stirred up. The control over their strength was impressive.

They clashed and their hands and fists shot out as they fought on the ground or in mid-air, their movements taking them around the courtyard.

Khasar seemed to be playing with Erik.

Delilah could see his building frustration. But instead of lashing out as she had seen younger fighters do, he refined his ability. He drew more mana into his body; his skin started to glow with power; his muscles started to increase in size and his eyes turned colder, the mana serving to focus his mind.

The mana drifted toward him, cutting it off from Khasar.

Khasar showed a bit of shock before he laughed. "A few more secrets! Yes, I knew that you had more power!"

He started to draw on the surrounding mana as well, buffing his strength.

Khasar hand cut through the wind like a blade, silent and deadly.

Erik jumped to the side, getting underneath the attack that left a shining line through a pillar. He used his hand to toss himself behind Khasar. He landed on his left foot, planting it and spinning around as he lashed out with his right leg.

Khasar was there already. He floated away from the attack. Erik pushed off the ground and blurred. The two of them connected with hands and fists.

Khasar grabbed Erik's hand, opening him up, and he pushed his palm forward. The space around Erik became solid, sealing him in place. Khasar's hand blurred as several hands appeared over the one as he struck Erik.

Erik was sent flying backward. He slammed into a wall like a cannonball, spurting blood.

Dust was thrown out and Delilah rushed forward in a panic. "Teacher!"

There was an awkward look on Khasar's face as he moved forward too. "I might have used too much strength," Khasar said.

Erik was on the ground. Behind him, there was an impression of his body and a handprint that covered his body, imprinting on the wall.

Blood fell from Erik's lips and his eyes were closed.

Delilah ran up to him, to see his lips moving.

"Multiple hands, manipulating the space around me as if it were tangible. The hands were closely packed together, disrupting and focusing the wind, creating a sort of air cannon, like being in front of a jet when it passes through the sound barrier…overlapped over one another, combining the effect of the air with the physical abilities of the hand." Erik's eyes snapped open.

"That was incredible!" He started to stand.

"Ah, body." Erik used a healing spell, helping his impressive healing abilities. His body started to repair itself, faint heat vapors rising up from his body.

"Teacher, are you okay?" Delilah asked.

"Never felt better," Erik said.

Khasar smiled and shook his head.

"That technique there—you used the movement technique on your palm, moved it really fast, contained the air and then unleashed it in one shot, right?" Erik asked.

"Yes," Khasar said, surprised with his accuracy.

"If you could throw some water in there, then it wouldn't just be powerful shit—it could go through people, or rocks or something. Toss it out of your storage ring." Erik held his chin.

Khasar's brows pinched together in thought and then he threw his palm out. He had let out some water from inside his storage ring. His hand blurred and then a part of another poor pillar was torn apart and the water droplets cut through a wall behind it.

"Will you two stop destroying our house?" Delilah growled, seeing the new destruction and noticing all of the scars and cuts that were left on the different pillars and walls. *I'm surprised that this place hasn't collapsed already!*

Khasar let out a cough and Erik looked around.

"Oh, sorry. I was focused on training so I didn't notice." Erik looked meekly at Delilah.

Delilah could only let out a sigh. *He means well but he is so focused on increasing his power that he forgets about everything else.*

"Well, if there are damages, I'm not telling Grand Teacher," she warned.

"I have some friends in the maintenance hall. They should be able to fix this up. But we should maybe take our practice to the private training halls?" Khasar said.

Erik nodded.

"I never thought to combine water into the technique. With it, the strength of the attack increases more!"

"Well, if you could use heat, then you could superheat it into steam. Or maybe use another medium, like iron and then superheat it into plasma? Then that would suck big time."

"Plasma?"

"State of matter, I guess?" Erik said.

Khasar smiled, clearly not understanding what Erik was talking about.

"How were you able to hold me in place, though?" Erik asked.

"Ah, space sealing. It is something that only higher level people who have a high Body or Mana Gathering Cultivation can do. As one increases in level and holds more power of the Ten Realms, then they can alter the natural realm to a greater degree, like how people who are over level fifty can walk in the sky because the ambient mana can keep them up. When someone has a greater cultivation, then they can bend the rules of the Ten Realms more; they become a force of their own intelligent nature in the Ten Realms. The technique that I used is a palm art, Air Sealing Thunderous Palm."

"These techniques rely on just the environment and your own body. When you're attacking, you're using the influence you have over the Ten Realms to bend it to your will to create these techniques. The Ten Realms isn't fighting with you—it's working with you," Erik said in a moment of realization.

"It's best to think of the Ten Realms like a beast. When you're small and powerful, it doesn't look at you at all. When you get stronger, then it is more amenable to helping you. You show this power with your increased stats, more mana, more physical abilities, and such.

"There are many ways that people learn to control their power and that over the Ten Realms. When fighting, you react instead of thinking things through, allowing you to pass this boundary. You can meditate on the Ten Realms, create within it, or test out your limits in your own way. Everyone gains control in their own way," Khasar said.

Delilah listened to their conversation. *I just saw them fighting, but is it possible that them fighting allowed Erik to have a greater understanding over the Ten Realms, an understanding that could increase his abilities overall?*

She looked at Erik, who nodded.

"Information builds the platform, but it is only through using that information that we can affect change," Erik said.

"Seems like you are learning," Khasar said.

Delilah saw Erik's eyes light up. Just as he opened his mouth to ask for another round of fighting, she cleared her throat.

"Grand Teacher wants to see us both. He said that he wants to create a high-level pill and needs assistants," Delilah said.

"Very well," Erik said. "Thank you for teaching me." Erik cupped his hands and bowed his head slightly.

Khasar returned it. "It is the least I can do if you're not willing to take protection from the Alchemist Association. I don't think you realize just how much they value you."

"I've forged my own path to this point—I don't want to start relying on another's strength. I do know when to ask for it, though," Erik said.

"Don't forget that," Khasar said.

Khasar departed and Erik used a cleaning spell and took a sip of Stamina potion.

"That's the good stuff. I finally got the taste right, just like espresso," Erik said with a satisfied sigh.

"Are you sure? You have been tasting every ingredient you can get your hand on," Delilah grumbled.

"You can do it, too, if you want to get the Reverse Alchemist title!" Erik laughed.

Delilah screwed up her face in displeasure. "I wish you didn't tell me how you got that title. It sounds horrible."

Erik shrugged.

As they walked through the Alchemist Association, different people greeted them. They nodded and cupped their hands in return.

Erik was still awkward with it, but it was the effort that people appreciated.

He took a look at his stats and his skills.

Name: Erik West	
Level: 57	Race: Human
Titles:	
From the Grave II	
Mana Emperor	
Dungeon Master III	
Reverse Alchemist	
Poison Body	
Fire Body	
City Lord	
Strength: (Base 36) +41	770

Agility: (Base 29) +72	555
Stamina: (Base 39) +23	930
Mana: (Base 8) +79	870
Mana Regeneration: (Base 13) +58	36.50/s
Stamina Regeneration: (Base 41) +59 21.00/s	

Skill: Hand-to-Hand

Level: 61 (Journeyman)

Attacks cost 20% less Stamina. Agility is increased by 10%.

"Something bothering you?"

"My hand-to-hand hasn't increased. Khasar said that it would only increase if I defeated my opponent, or if I were to display a technique. I guess it is like spells: if you create a powerful spell and use it, then you can get Experience. The same must go for techniques," Erik said.

They made it to Old Hei's training quarters. The guards let them past and they found Old Hei reviewing a formula and checking the various containers in front of him, checking the ingredients contained within.

He looked over as they came in. "Good morning!" Old Hei said.

"Excited to be making a new concoction?" Erik asked.

"Of course! Never mind the administration! I came here for the resources!" Old Hei laughed.

Delilah rolled her eyes. "And everyone else thinks that you're alchemist sages."

"We're all still people." Old Hei winked as he put the items back into his storage ring. "Come on, let's have breakfast and discuss!"

They went out of the training room and sat on a balcony, suspended some thirty floors above the ground. It was a small garden with formations placed down so only a slight refreshing breeze rolled across the balcony and it drew in mana to nurture Old Hei's personal plants.

They sat down at a table filled with delicacies that had been specially prepared by the Sky Reaching Restaurant.

Instead of using ingredients to make concoctions, they combined them together to create meals that although they wouldn't give an immediate boost to one's stats, the effects lasted much longer and tasted a lot better.

"So how have your supplemental classes been?" Hei picked up different delicacies from the table and placed them on his plate.

"I have been attending the information lectures to increase my knowledge as well as purchasing information books and adding them to my skill book. As you said, I tested out the different ingredients to make sure that my own findings matched those of the different ingredients found in the books," Delilah said, also taking different pieces from the array of food.

"Good. Then, next, you should work in the gardens, tending to the different plants there and caring for them, to increase your practical knowledge," Old Hei said.

Delilah had a sly smile on her face as she nodded.

What would Old Hei think if he knew the kinds of ingredients we had growing in Alva, or in the dungeon hidden underneath the Sky Reaching Restaurant? Erik's eyes flitted over to the tower in the distance. It was the second tallest building, shorter than the Alchemist Association buildings.

"How have your concoctions been going, Erik?"

Erik grimaced, letting out a strained smile. "Not that good," Erik admitted as he put down his tea.

"Oh, why?" Old Hei put down his chopsticks and looked at Erik with a serious expression.

"I have been focusing on making concoctions to temper my body with Earth mana. My control is good and I can make mid Journeyman-level concoctions with ease. High Journeyman concoctions are harder, but it is when I am making half-step Expert concoctions I find that I am lacking in mana," Erik said.

"Lacking in mana? What is your Mana Gathering Cultivation?" Old Hei asked.

"I am close to forming my mana core," Erik admitted.

"Close to—how close?" Old Hei's tone dropped as his eyes narrowed and he raised one eyebrow.

"I could break through at any moment but I am suppressing myself."

"Why?" Old Hei asked, a bizarre look in his eyes.

"Like Rugrat, I want to be able to refine out all the kinds of mana that I absorb," Erik said.

"You—" Old Hei smacked Erik on the back of the head. "Weren't you listening to *anything* I said about body tempering? The Mana Gathering Cultivation system, once reaching the core stages, is not about the elemental attribute mana, but rather removing the impure mana within one's body and compressing it constantly to increase one's available power. Which is then released through one's body in the Mana Heart stage." Old Hei looked at Erik, who nodded.

"With the Body Cultivation, after going through the foundational temperings of Body Like Stone, one then tempers their body with high affinity mana, incorporating it into their body, *storing* it in their body. Mana Gathering, those impurities are a poison; Body Cultivation, they're a strength. Now most either go down the path of either one. If you want Body Cultivation, the more impurities the better; Mana Gathering, the less impurities the better.

"Rugrat's body purifies the mana and allows it to enter his body, increasing his Body Cultivation without him knowing it. But it is at a low rate; most of it is just released from his body. Now, if you were to absorb mana, it would hurt like hell, but it would temper your body, becoming a nourishment, drawing that mana out of your mana channels and your core. Now look into your mana drops and your channels, look for any Fire-attribute mana."

Erik turned his gaze into his body. There was no Fire-attribute mana to be found within his mana channels.

"Now look into your muscles." Old Hei guided Erik.

Erik examined his muscles. There in the muscles he could feel a hidden heat, an explosive power within his muscles.

He had studied the changes in his body, but since the last time he had checked, the power of Fire within his muscles had only increased.

"What?"

"Do you remember what part of your Body Cultivation quest said? Look up your title," Old Hei said.

Erik did sheepishly, having a bad feeling.

Title: Fire Body

You have tempered your body with Fire. Fire has become a part of you, making your body take on some of its characteristics.

Legendary Fire resistance.

Increased control over Fire Mana.

Physical attacks contain Fire attribute.

Can completely purify the Fire attribute in Mana.

"Can completely purify the Fire attribute in mana," Erik said.

Old Hei focused on him and blinked a few times as if having trouble digesting just what he had heard.

Delilah rolled her eyes and poured Old Hei tea before herself as Erik had already served himself.

"Now, you know most people don't get a title for increasing their Body cultivation, only someone who maniacally tempers their body *completely* is able to do that. You know, I thought that someone who did that might, you know, read *everything.*"

"So you're saying that I should break through?" Erik asked.

Old Hei took a few moments, looking up to gain strength before he continued.

"If you will do no less than completely temper your body and get these titles, then you could cultivate any and all mana and it would increase your Mana Gathering Cultivation and increase your Body Cultivation. You could use the concoctions and then also cultivate the Earth-attribute mana, directly injecting it into your bones, and refining the remaining mana into your core. Then, as you reach the next stage of Metal, you can use the Metal element mana in your core to increase your Body Cultivation all the way, so that it then stores that power within your body, instead of in your core. If you do not get the titles, then you should increase your Mana Gathering Cultivation with pure mana. But knowing your insane focus on completing everything, I doubt you'd want to do that," Old Hei said.

"So I should compress and form my core, then draw in any kind of mana to compress my core, to use it later to temper my body?"

"Yes," Old Hei said, sounding pained at having to explain everything to Erik.

"Though I think I had a breakthrough," Erik said.

Old Hei sipped his tea and waved for Erik to continue.

"I thought that techniques were just ways to create concoctions, and they are, but I didn't realize that a part of it was actually using the Ten Realms to help, combining physical actions with using the power of the Ten Realms."

Old Hei cracked a smile. "Oh?"

"What are you hiding?" Erik asked.

"Well, I guess you would find out after getting this far, but if you want to concoct Expert-level concoctions, then you will most likely need to use techniques to control the powerful forces at play," Old Hei said.

Erik thought back to when he had assisted Old Hei with the Mana Channel Revitalization pill. When he had been watching, he hadn't reached a high enough understanding to figure out just what Old Hei was doing. Now, with his new knowledge, thinking back to that scene, he saw discrepancies with the mana he was using, his movements, and the way that the ingredients reacted.

Erik closed his eyes, using his skill book to recall everything that he had seen that day, comparing it against the other times that he had seen concoctions being made.

"Techniques are part of using external mana," Old Hei said.

"Alchemy blends the movements of the body, the control over one's own mana and techniques of these both to create alchemical concoctions," Erik said.

"Right," Old Hei said.

Erik felt as if he had many revelations today. He started to jot down notes on a pad of paper. He had progressed far but he'd been able to surpass a big barrier to his progress.

Erik put his notes away and calmed his mind. He looked at his mana core. It was on the cusp, the last two mana drops opposite the three other combined mana drops.

He retracted his senses, a look of excitement on his face. "Thank you, Old Hei," Erik said.

Old Hei waved off Erik's thanks. "Aren't you helping me in making a high Expert-level pill? If I can make it repeatedly then I can head to the higher Realms!" Hei grinned.

Erik only smiled. He had long ago accepted that there was no way that he would be able to thank Old Hei for his help and would help out the other man in any way possible.

"Make sure that you take care Erik, while in the lower realms you have a lot of power, its nothing to those in the higher realms. The Ten realms are unforgiving."

"Do you know something about the higher realms?" Erik asked. Information on higher than the seventh realm was limited, what they knew of the seventh realm was spotty by itself.

"I know only what I've seen," Old Hei said in a deep voice.

"Old Hei, it sounds like you're just talking in riddles now." Erik chuckled, trying to lighten the atmosphere.

"Maybe I am—I hope I am—but don't you find it odd how the Ten Realms seem to actively be pitting us against one another so only the strongest make it to the top? The first thing you saw, didn't it say, 'Fortune favors the strong'?"

Erik sunk into thought with that.

Old Hei let out a sigh and patted his shoulder. "I know that look."

"What look?"

"There are two ways to look after the people you care about. One: have something that everyone wants but can't get, and Vuzgal isn't that. If someone took over and the associations liked them more, then they wouldn't be opposed. The other option is to become strong enough that no one else would dare to touch your people out of fear of retribution. Before that mess with the Blood Demon sect, it was nearly seven hundred years since someone even *tried* to anger one of the associations."

"Do the associations really reach the Tenth Realm?" Erik asked. It hadn't been spoken but he'd assumed so.

Old Hei looked at Erik and shrugged. "I'm just a division leader of the Third Realm. There are plenty of Expert-level crafters out there."

Someone who controls a third of an entire realm doesn't really know what happens in the highest realms.

Erik's expression was grim. The path so far hadn't been easy, but that didn't mean it would be easy in the future either.

"Where are we going?" Pegleg Jim—still called that despite the fact he was no longer missing a leg—asked Pan Kun.

"I just have our orders," Pan Kun muttered in response.

Pegleg Jim lapsed into silence as the group moved through the forest.

"Why all the secrecy?" Jim asked.

"Did all the questions come back with getting your leg?" Pan Kun complained.

"Just askin'," Jim muttered.

Pan Kun rolled his eyes before letting out a sigh. "You know how the lord has been secretly gathering more people to be guards, train them up a bit to act like us and then send us out? Well, he has a plan for something, and we're going to learn about it." Pan Kun stepped forward. The forest fell away and he was in a large clearing, looking at rows of tents. There were already some people lined up, being yelled at by others who Pan Kun had never seen before. But his instincts yelled at him that they were dangerous.

One of the unknown group headed over. The man looked them over as if he had found a new and unappealing fungus. "Move it! Get into line! Officers to my left, guards to my right! Hurry up about it!"

The others looked to Pan Kun, whose face paled as he followed the man's orders. *These must be people who had taken command of Vermire.*

Two more of the fearsome people came out, assisting the first in getting everyone into line and assembled, gathering them with the original group. Others were pulled out of the forest. More of the frightening people, these ones on mounts, dragged them into formations. They moved the guards as if they were just children.

Pan Kun looked around. Lord Aditya had hinted that they would get support. *What kind of support is this?*

Everyone was gathered up and everyone was checked. They weren't missing anyone.

A woman stepped out in front. She had a cold, dull expression as she looked them all over.

"We have been hired by your lord to teach you how to fight a true battle. You will be broken down into fighting teams of five people. You will be taught how to fight and coordinate in these groups, how to fight and coordinate in a fighting squad of three fighting teams and a leader. We will form you all the way up to a fighting company, where you can all fight together, executing orders fluidly, and exert your greatest strength. I don't have time to deal with your complaints, your bitching. You don't have the time to do it either. Lord Aditya has a plan to unite the outposts and create a central outpost on King's Hill. Listen to the directions of myself and my people and we will increase your combat capability as a team. About time we got started."

She looked to the others with her; they called people over, quickly dispersing and breaking the groups apart.

Shit, this is going to suck, Pan Kun thought as he heard his name being called.

23 Alva's Will

Glosil sat in the command center of Vuzgal, talking to Domonos and Yui. He had just finished presenting their plan and they looked over the information, asking several questions before they fell silent.

"Any more thoughts?" Glosil asked.

"None, Commander," Domonos said.

"No, Commander," Yui followed a half second later.

"Very good. Then the plan will be for you to finish your current training of the forces here. Once that is complete, we will begin training for the operation. I intend for us to take four sections as well as the special teams in the first wave, with our remaining forces coming in and erecting the camp that will cover the teleportation formation. From there, we will then move into phase two," Glosil said.

"We have been able to build up a fighting force numbering close to six hundred in strength. All of them are sworn to Vuzgal and without knowing it, they are sworn to Alva as well. What if we were to bring some of them back to Alva to train there?"

"What are you proposing?" Glosil asked.

"A new training program. Those who are training will be part of the reserve army; those who have completed all of their basic training will become part of the Vuzgal Defense Force; those who have not only completed their training but have been accepted as personnel of Alva will form the First Army. They will become people of the Alva Army just like us, get access to the academies and train in Alva for part of the year, or protect our people, operating in the Adventurer's Guild before being rotated out to operate in the Fourth Realm to temper their strength. Whether that is secretly in the Battle Arena, or by joining in with fights against groups that we see as a possible threat," Yui said.

Glosil held his chin in thought.

"You bring up a problem that I have been thinking on for some time. We will try your method. Each of the current members of the Alva Army, or the new First Army, will select two or three people from the Vuzgal Defense Force to become part of the First Army. While this training session is coming to a close, we will reform the First Army to incorporate these new members. Also, I want a list of names of people who will be staying behind to train up the soldiers here. They will pick from the forces that are left to fill out their training staff," Glosil said.

"We want to keep the training going?" Domonos asked.

"We have more than five thousand applicants who are sitting in apartments that we have built and are eating subsidized food we are giving them. We need to train them and find out who is here just for those benefits and who is here to be part of the military. Already our budget is dwarfing the size of others. We need to prove our worth to the people of Alva and to Erik and Rugrat. We are not the only people who can train these new soldiers."

"We were too short-sighted," Yui said.

"It is my aim to grow our military force to ten thousand this year and to triple that by the end of the next year, with each of them being the standard that we were when we entered the Fourth Realm and the members of the First Army being as strong as we are right now. I'm going to need your help to complete that goal and we will have to raise up a complete command structure. My aims are high, but I think we can complete them."

"Yes, sir!" Domonos and Yui nodded, eager to face the challenges ahead.

Glosil smiled and nodded. *I must prove to Erik and Rugrat that I deserve this position. They've given me a chance to prove myself and I can't let it go to waste, for them or for the future of the military and the soldiers who obey my orders.*

Miguel was sitting down and having tea, studying a piece of cloth in his hand. The finely woven piece had two small and colorful birds circling a small tree, playfully chasing each other.

Miguel smiled as he let the cloth glide through his fingers. The two birds seemed to let out excited chirps as they moved through the cloth, circling the tree that swayed lightly in the summer breeze. Its leaves danced with a shimmering light, capturing one's interest.

Miguel had a light smile on his face as he moved the cloth in his hands while he drank his tea.

There was a knock at the door to his private tea room.

Miguel grimaced, his reverie broken. "What is it?" He stuffed the cloth back into his storage ring.

"There is a man here. He wishes to talk to you about joining his crafting academy," the woman on the other side of the door said. The woman paused. "He says that he has Linor worm silk."

Miguel's body shook as he stood, nearly knocking over his tea. "Bring them to me!"

Linor worm silk? Do they know the significance behind it? Are they brave to go up against that witch Zhen Fu or do they simply not know about her threat?

The door opened and a young man appeared. He cupped his fists and bowed his head.

"Expert Tailor Miguel, it was hard to find you. My name is Hiao Xen. I am the acting city administrator for the city Vuzgal. I was wondering if you would be interested in joining our crafting academy?"

"Vuzgal." Miguel repeated the word slowly. He had been following what had happened there. There was no crafter in the Fourth Realm who hadn't heard about what was being called the crafting city. He had also laughed and drank for two days and two nights, outside of his normal character, when he had heard of the punishment that they had landed on Zhen Fu—the way that they had kicked her and any who supported her schemes out of the city, including Expert crafters.

He had lamented that the city might die due to this, but it had flourished. Its mana density increased and the city lords had revealed some of their crafting strength.

"I have some fine tea that I was able to procure from the Sky Reaching Restaurant. Would you allow me to pour you a cup?" Hiao Xen said.

"Please," Miguel said, realizing that he had kept the acting administrator standing at the doorway to his room.

The doors closed behind Hiao Xen. He took a seat and took out two glasses, pouring one for Miguel and one for himself.

"To good health and to a prosperous future—without Zhen Fu around." Hiao Xen let a grin slip out as he drank the tea.

Miguel let out a slight chuckle, raising his cup a bit higher in salute to the toast before he took a sip.

The flavors spread over his tongue and filled his mouth. The rich aroma turned into flavor as he took his time tasting it before he consumed it. The warmth spread through his body.

He felt his mana reacting, causing it to circulate faster, increasing the mana that he drew into his body.

This is tea? It could be called a Mana Gathering Cultivation tool by others! It brings clarity to the mind with the increased mana and the mix of invigorating herbs and leaves.

"Good tea," Miguel couldn't help but say. He took another sip, sighing and closing his eyes to take it in more.

His mind was calmed and his spirit rejuvenated. He opened his eyes, laughing awkwardly as he realized he had made Hiao Xen wait again as he had enjoyed the tea, feeling thankful for the other not ruining the moment.

"I was carried away," Miguel said.

"I can understand. Good tea like this would be wasted on those who didn't take time to fully enjoy it!" Hiao Xen filled up Miguel's cup more and then his own.

"As the lady said, here are two cases of Linor worm silk thread." Hiao Xen took out two specially made boxes.

Miguel took the boxes, trying to control his agitation as he looked inside the boxes. *The mana density of these threads is of the high grade, with little mana lost in their handling. With this, I will be finally able to finish my Sparrows Flight masterpiece.* He unconsciously rubbed the storage ring he had put the finely sowed piece of cloth away in. *The cost of this must have been several Earth-grade cornerstones and he's just giving it to me?*

"We talked about the silk—using it as a ploy to draw you to work for the Vuzgal crafter's academy would be taking advantage. I hope you can accept these as a gift of our sincerity and a show that we want to work with you," Hiao Xen said.

"Thank you. These will be of a great help." Miguel put them away, knowing it would be rude of him to refuse and that Hiao Xen made it clear that there were no strings attached. This was just meant as a thank-you for meeting with him.

"The crafter's academy, what is involved with it?"

"It is a place where people pay to learn, or join by becoming a member of Vuzgal. You would be required to teach others, but then you would also get materials and a residence and the ability to access other resources that others wouldn't. This is a contract that is viable for five years. At the end of the five years, you can choose to stay and renegotiate your contract, or go on to other pursuits." Hiao Xen pulled out a contract and placed it in front of Miguel.

Miguel raised an eyebrow. "Most groups and sects like to work with verbal contracts enforced by the ten realms, allowing them to hide a number of terms and clauses within that would tie a person up. Being able to read a written contract clears up many of those hidden pitfalls."

"Most of them are trying to make you part of their sect. We only want to employ you. You can become a person of Vuzgal if you want, but that is your choice later on," Hiao Xen said.

"Why wouldn't you try to make me a person of Vuzgal right away?"

"You don't know us and we don't know you. This gives us an opportunity to get to know one another better and see if it would be a good fit. If we just hired people in directly all the time, then we would get people who didn't want to be part of Vuzgal, whose work would start to decline because they got comfortable or because they didn't like working with us or got stuck into a lifetime contract. Also, once the contract is up, it's not like you will be kicked from Vuzgal. As long as you have a residence, you can stay there as long as you want. You would have to pay to use the crafting workshops and the materials, but we won't stop you," Hiao Xen said.

"I'm impressed." Miguel took another sip of the tea and turned to the contract. He read through it. It was straightforward, without most of the clauses that other contracts contained: he had to teach people and in return he would be able to get supplies and use the different channels of the Vuzgal city.

If he wanted to, he could just sit in an Expert-level workshop and create goods, passing them to the people of Vuzgal and having them sell it for him so that he could focus on crafting, instead of having to deal with all the extra bits that took him away from crafting.

He started to feel excited for the first time in a long time as it was opening a new opportunity for him. He had been stagnant for so long, so focused on his masterpiece, but he had been denied at the last step by Zhen Fu, who had thrown up barriers to stop his rise.

It had been years since then but he had faded into obscurity.

With Vuzgal aiding me, I can make a comeback and step onto the highest stage of the Fourth Realm and the possibility of joining one of the academies from the higher realms isn't out of my reach. There is even a clause here that they will help me join the meeting of crafters that they host so that people who have gone to their school can meet and talk with associations and sects to give them more opportunities.

"If you need more time to review it, that is fine," Hiao Xen said, his voice calm and unrushed.

Miguel held onto the contract tighter. Miguel pulled out a knife and cut his finger, pressing it to the contract.

The power of the contract activated as it wrapped around Miguel.

"I agree!" Miguel said.

Hiao Xen was a little stunned with how resolute he was. He laughed. "Welcome to Vuzgal's crafting academy, Expert Miguel!" Hiao Xen raised his cup and the two of them drank their tea together.

"So I have most of the items you will need. Please place a drop of your blood on to this. This is a token that will allow you to enter the different crafting rooms as per your rank and give you access to the academy and Vuzgal and allow others to identify you and your craft." Hiao Xen passed him an emblem and then pulled out different books. "These are maps for Vuzgal with your residence marked on it, as well as the names of the rest of the staff. There is an administrator for each department that you will talk to. They coordinate the different classes and create the schedules, leaving you to teach and to craft instead of worrying about the operation of it all. I think that should be it."

Miguel took it all with a smile.

"I will be heading back to Vuzgal in three days, if you wish to come with me. Otherwise, you can head there at any time," Hiao Xen said.

"Very well. Thank you, City Administrator Hiao Xen, for this opportunity!"

The two of them once again touched glasses and took a measured sip from their cups, letting out sighs, both of them with wide smiles on their faces.

Erik went to the Sky Reaching Restaurant, but instead of heading up to one of the dining rooms, he headed to the hidden lower levels.

There were a few farmers still around checking up on their crops or on the animals that they had raised there.

I don't want to think what Old Hei might say about this. The mana density is high here and it is good to raise Alchemy plants, but, the fact is that the Alchemy garden in Alva is much more potent than the patch we have here.

Erik moved deeper into the growing area. There were vertical gardens on the walls and the floor had been turned into a series of rearing and growing areas, every inch utilized for maximum efficiency. One area had been cleared of crops, but there were farmers going through with machines and concoctions, using machines to stir up the soil and the concoctions to increase the nutrients in the soil so the next crop would grow even faster.

Erik found a bare patch of ground and looked around. The mana in here was much denser than the mana outside.

Still, he put down a mana gathering formation and took out some mana stones, breaking them to increase the ambient mana.

He closed his eyes and focused his mind, circulating the mana within his body. He drew in a massive amount of mana, compressing and refining, circulating it through his mana channels and pushing it towards his dantian.

The mana density increased in his dantian but he stored up his power, he wanted to breakthrough all in one shot.

He let out a refreshed breath he opened his hand an Earth tempering pill appearing between his fingers.

"Well, I feel that this won't be enough, but I should get an idea of how much power I will need to temper my body." He threw it back before he could think about it too much. The pill dissolved, its power reaching throughout his body.

Erik drew in mana from the surrounding area and focused it on his bones; it drew the power of the Earth pill with it.

His body started to crack and break underneath the waves of pressure released by the Earth tempering pill.

He gritted his teeth against the screams as his body started to collapse. His body tempering tried to fight against it, so as he was broken, he was repaired.

Erik cast Hallowed Ground and increased its potency, channeling all of his mana into it as it sped up the process of breakdown and rebuilding.

Slowly, Erik's size started to decrease and he started to return to his normal size.

He finished the first pill, still a half foot taller than he had been before.

He stared at the second pill, allowing his body to recover as he mentally prepared himself.

"Round two!" He took the pill and laid back down. He once again fought against the pain. *Embrace it! Get used to it! The more pain, the greater the result! Come on—you've got this!*

Erik chanted inside his head, fighting against the part of his brain that just wanted to give in, that wanted to just pass out, or stop the process.

Erik came up from round two and studied his body. *The effectiveness of the pills are starting to decrease. I'll need to make more powerful pills with a greater efficacy, or make different pills that are stronger.*

"Round three." Dull-eyed, Erik took the third pill and laid back down.

He took on the pain as he once again decreased in size. Once he reached his original size, he stopped shrinking but his body continued to break down and be rebuilt.

Erik was panting at the end of his third pill.

"Notifications," Erik said in a hoarse voice but nothing greeted him.

He looked down at himself. "Going to need new clothes." He was covered in sweat and a thick black slime that smelled bad.

He used his Clean spell, barely feeling any mana loss as he looked up at his notifications.

There was nothing there. He felt stronger, but it seemed that his tempering had not gone far enough, hitting a bottleneck.

Seeing he hadn't been able to increase his Body Cultivation, he collapsed into a dreamless sleep.

His foundation was stronger than most others, using the methods that other people used in the ten realms to increase his cultivation weren't able to reach his bottlenecks. He'd have to use more drastic methods to increase his Body Cultivation.

Viggo was escorted into the court. The building had been where many had taken their oaths of allegiance to Alva, where people were sentenced for small crimes, and to settle disputes before they got out of hand.

Now the room was filled with people all who were murmuring under their breath as Viggo and his group were brought out to the stand. They all sat down behind the desk. A scribe acted as their counsel, fighting for their case. On the other side, there was another scribe and two police officers who were part of the raid on the bandits.

Egbert walked in the back of the courtroom and sat down in the main judge's chair. He pulled out a quill and a parchment paper. "All right, let's get started, will we? For this case, we will be calling up people to the stand to talk about items pertaining to the case. You will be bound under oath to speak the truth and nothing but the truth, or else you will feel a great amount of pain. Let's get started."

A police officer was called up to the stage first.

"When we arrived, there were close to one hundred people living in cages and deplorable conditions, no access to food or water. They had been traders or people who were getting a ride across the desert and they had been attacked, beaten, stripped, and tossed in these cages. Many were suffering from broken bones, dysentery, and infections. Meanwhile, the bandits treated them as goods, preparing to sell them off as slaves to other groups that they knew. We have reports from those in the cages that the bandits would use them as they wanted, create fights between the prisoners and watch for enjoyment, turning their pain into sport."

"What were they doing with the goods and other items?" Egbert asked.

"They would take the items and they would sell them to our own traders where they could. They were using the funds that they gained to return to Alva and purchase more items to fight with and increase the power of their bandit group."

"Okay. I think that will be all of the questions that I have for you," Egbert said.

"Bring up Viggo," Egbert said.

Viggo was picked up by two police officers and taken over to where the police officer had sat.

"Do you agree to tell the truth, all the truth and nothing but the truth so sworn on the Ten Realms, with punishment of severe pain, akin to being struck in the face?" the police officer said.

"I do," Viggo said, feeling confident. He had been able to skirt his oath to Alva before; he had confidence in this.

"Viggo, did you kill people for your own profit?"

"No!" he said, thinking that it was all for Alva. But he cried out in pain as his face hurt.

"Still thinking that you can skirt oaths?" Egbert looked over to the man.

Alarmed, Viggo's eyes widened as the pain started to fade away.

"This oath is ingrained into you, not placed on Alva, so you can't skirt it with just thinking that you were doing it for someone else. Thank you for letting us know about that loophole as we'll be changing the oath of allegiance. Did you harm others for sport?"

"No." Again, Viggo yelled in pain as he felt as though he'd been punched in the face. So it went on: Egbert asked exact questions that only left yes or no answers and either Viggo told the truth or he lied. And from the pain and him crying out, he wasn't able to lie anymore.

"Do you have anything else to say?" Egbert asked.

I'll kill you! I'll get free of this and I'll tear you apart! Viggo shook on his chair, his rage clear to all.

"Next, Otto," Egbert said.

Otto was taken up to the seat. He agreed to the oath, his face pale and scared.

"We started out being traders, but we weren't too good at it. We didn't make much money. Though then we got into a fight with someone and we had all of their goods. So we sold them off, you know. The oath didn't work on us. It was 'cause we were defending ourselves and the people we were killing must be bad for the oath to not work," Otto said.

"Who told you this?"

"Viggo." Otto lowered his head, not daring to look at his old leader.

"So you killed the merchant and then took his goods. You sold them off?"

"Yes."

"Then you did it again?"

"Well, we were living well, bragging to others about how we were good traders, but then we ran out of money again. So we picked out a trader and then we followed them. Using the gear we had, it was easy to take them down. Then we hit more caravans. We found others who were willing to listen to us. Who were down on their luck like us. We just killed them in the beginning but then we found we could sell the people—more profit and less blood on our hands. We did it." Otto let out a cry of pain as his Alva oath took effect and he crumpled to the ground. His scream turned into grunts and whimpers.

"The next defendant," Egbert said.

He went through all of the bandits and then talked to the other police officer. Egbert finally laid down his quill. The courtroom was silent.

"Swearing an oath to Alva, you gain our protection, you gain our support and you are beholden to our rules. In times of need, we will aid you, but going against the rules and the oath that you have sworn? If it is a minor infraction, you will be excommunicated by Alva and given a silencing oath. With what you have done, the oath will be amended and revised so that if this happens again we will know about it sooner. I do not know how many people fell victim to you cruel individuals, and it will be impossible to help them all. I see no reason to allow you to continue to live. You are a plague and an infection that only harms. You will be executed. Your names will be stripped from all records. There will be no record of you ever existing—no legacy, no mention in history. Upon your death, you will cease to be."

A chill ran through Viggo. In the Ten Realms, a core part of their guiding principles was to create a grave for those who had passed away and to go and see them continuously, paying respect to one's ancestors, making sure to keep strict records of one's lineage. They would look to add to their lineage, setting up the younger generation to do better in the future.

"All of your items will be sold and the monetary value will be split up and passed on to the survivors of this ordeal, without taxation or stipulation. Alva does not accept rapists, murderers, and slavers. See that the sentence is carried out immediately." Egbert looked to the police officers and then waved his hand. A silencing and weakness spell fell on them all.

Viggo wanted to yell and scream; *this couldn't be right—there was no way.*

Egbert looked at them all with cold eyes before shaking his head in disappointment. He shuffled his papers together as Viggo and his people were hauled out of the courtroom and into a room, where one of the police officers pulled out a sword and stabbed it into the first bandit. They gulped like a fish as they died. The police officer moved forward, his sword like a machine, cutting them all down.

Viggo didn't have any time to accept his fate as that sword stabbed into his stomach.

He coughed as he felt the poison on the blade racing through his veins. He watched as the first man's tombstone was looted and the body started to turn into motes of light.

Fear and unwillingness filled him as the poison reached his brain.

24 Help From Afar

Elise looked over the city. It was like nothing she had ever seen before. "It's massive," she whispered.

"Yeah. All the more room for people to mess up in," Rugrat chimed in.

She shot him a questioning look as they continued on their way toward the counters that would allow them into Vuzgal.

Rugrat's Vuzgal medallion had the guard standing aside and saluting Rugrat. He made sure that his cloak covered his appearance as he waited for Elise to follow and headed off into the busy city.

"I've never seen a totem so busy before," Elise said.

"People here have a lot more money to burn. You've got to remember the people from the Sixth and Fifth Realms come down here to increase their skills. To them, an Earth-grade mana stone is just loose change."

"Loose change I hope to scoop up," Elise said with a devious grin.

"Do Alva proud." Rugrat put both thumbs up, a grin on his face.

"Shouldn't you be looking after these people? Aren't they your citizens, after all?"

"I only consider the people who are part of the military, the Vuzgal Crafters Academy, as well as the administration, as part of our people. The rest are people using Vuzgal in some way or another."

"That's a cold way to look at it."

"It's a realistic way to look at it."

Elise fell silent. Her mind had unconsciously turned to those traders who had become bandits in the Second Realm.

Elise looked around the city, seeing their Sky Reaching Restaurants that reached up into the sky. Wayside Inns dotted the landscape.

"Looks like the crafter workshop has finally been completed." Rugrat used his chin to gesture at the busiest sector. "It will be the only Expert-level workshops that we have in the city for some time other than the ones in the academy. Got to have more workshops of the Journeyman class very soon."

"Is that why you are selling off land so slowly?"

"Partly. If we sell them all in one go, then they're going to go at lower prices. We only have so much land that we can sell. With time, as we increase our position in the Fourth Realm, they'll sell for more. It is also a means of population control. We don't have the guards or the people right now to manage an entirely populated Vuzgal. With selling the land and buildings slowly, we control the flow of people. Those who were fast enough to buy land from us in the beginning will be happy to know that later on we will only be renting that out to other people."

"Renting it out? People won't be pleased with that."

"They might not be, but it keeps Vuzgal competitive compared to other cities. If someone takes a five-, ten-, thirty-, or fifty-year lease, then they will most likely build a house up on that land. Then when we come in thirty or fifty years later to reclaim that land, we can now lease it with a brand-new house on it."

"Driving them to build up Vuzgal." Elise let out an impressed noise.

They left the city behind and reached the Castle District, passing through the Associations' Circle. Within the circle, there were carriages of all kinds, as well as mounts and beasts. All the people who walked around were high-level crafters or traders with a significant backing.

There were several Sky Reaching Restaurants in the locale that these people would go and visit to conduct their business deals.

As soon as they entered the Castle District, Elise's body relaxed. "Feels like home." Elise sighed.

Rugrat only smiled and pulled down his hood to reveal his face fully. "Come on. I'll take you to Hiao Xen." He guided Elise through the Castle District, in through the administration offices and to a massive door.

"He's expecting you," the secretary said.

"Of course he is." Rugrat chuckled. "Thanks, Dougie."

The man smiled as Rugrat pushed on the door, opening it to reveal who Elise assumed to be Hiao Xen.

"I was able to get one tailor Expert. There are three other Experts that I am waiting to hear from. Additionally, there's a number of Journeyman crafters I have my eye on. The number of people attending the academy has only increased since you've been gone, as well as our revenues from those passing through the city," Hiao Xen said, not looking up from his work as he went through report after report.

Elise winced, looking at all of the work. *Thankfully I'm not a council leader anymore.*

"Sounds like you've been busy while I've been gone. Hiao Xen, this is Elise. Elise, this is Hiao Xen."

Hiao Xen looked up from his work to see that there was another person in the room. "I'm sorry for my rudeness. I didn't know that there was anyone else here," Hiao Xen said sheepishly, letting out an awkward laugh. He stood and reached out to shake her hand.

"It's no worry. I know how these two can keep you working all hours." Elise smiled, taking the offered hand. "Between us, I'm happier it's you than me!"

Hiao Xen's smile became a little more honest.

"Elise here is a friend of Erik and mine. She will be acting as our chair for the chamber of commerce, but in secret. We don't want any of the other traders thinking that she has an advantage over them—keep them competitive, if you know what I mean."

"Makes sense. It's always good to have a few feelers among the traders."

"Good. Then I will leave her in your capable hands to get up to date." Rugrat clapped his hands together.

"Before you go, Erik sent you a message through the alchemist association couriers that I was supposed to pass on to you." Hiao Xen pulled out a sealed scroll.

"Wonder what trouble he's got himself into now," Rugrat said, looking at the scroll and putting it away in his storage ring.

"See you later!"

Rugrat opened the scroll as he walked to his own quarters.

Words started to appear on the scroll once it ascertained that Rugrat was who he really said he was.

When he finished the scroll, it burned into ashes. He shook his hand with a distracted look.

"Crafting techniques?"

"Are you absolutely sure about this?" Mira asked.

"I'm sure, my dear," Chonglu said. "Look, I know that you're scared but there's nothing to worry about," he said, trying to console her.

"We could go to the Fighter's Association. They would have a place for you, a place for us," she said.

"Do you really want Feng and Felicity to grow up in the Fighter's Association?"

"Don't twist my words on me!"

"I'm not twisting your words—I'm just asking," Chonglu said, sounding perfectly reasonable.

She let out an irritated noise and stomped her foot, not looking like the ice empress that she was named after at all. As a wife and a mother, she was trying to do the best by her family.

"You all only just increased your levels recently. Shouldn't you take more time to get used to it?"

"Time for you to convince me to join the Fighter's Association? Remember, I'm not like you—I don't have any skills that they are particularly interested in. Also, I owe Erik and Rugrat. *We* owe Erik and Rugrat."

Mira let out a frustrated yell as all the fight seemed to drain from her. Even with her overwhelming power he didn't cower in the slightest, just waiting for her to calm down.

"I just want you to be safe," she said in a small voice.

Chonglu stopped checking his gear. He turned to her and took her hands in his. Even if she was many times stronger than him, she acted like a little girl.

"We're just going to ask if there is any way to repay them. Erik and Rugrat are good people. If not, they wouldn't have saved Fang and Felicity or me, or told you about us."

"I know. It's just that we have relied on so many other people to protect us but now I don't trust any of them."

"We all have to trust someone." Chonglu used his finger to raise her chin so she looked up at him. He was not going to quit surprising her. "Plus, it is a new adventure!"

"You are not going adventuring with my children!"

"Builds character!" he said with a devilish grin.

Mira's eyes narrowed and she grabbed his hands tighter.

"Ow! Ouch! Dear, you really need to watch your strength," Chonglu said in a strained voice.

"Oh, I'm sorry. I don't realize that sometimes." Her grip ever so accidentally tightened again before she released his hands.

"We're ready to go!" the guard in charge of the convoy yelled.

Mira and Chonglu hugged, pulling each other in tight.

She moved to the children, hugging them again.

They had tears in their eyes. They had only gotten to know their mother again and they were leaving.

"Don't worry. When you guys are all set up, then we'll see one another all the time," she promised.

The two children found it hard to reply, simply nodding as they tried to contain their tears.

Mira and Chonglu talked quietly to each other before he got onto his mount.

The gate to the house opened and the convoy departed, heading for the city's totem and Vuzgal beyond.

Rugrat was looking at the report from Glosil on the continued training as forces moved down to Alva, as well as moving people from the Vuzgal Defense Force into the First Army, which would replace the Alva Army.

Rugrat was impressed. It also changed his plans for weapons and equipment for the army.

"If we were able to give the highest quality equipment or prototypes to the special teams, the trained army will get standard and tested weapons. Those in Vuzgal will get the last generation of weapons. If we give everyone prototypes, if they go wrong, they go wrong in a big way. The higher level weapons take longer to make and might require more skill. As people advance, they'll get better gear and it means that the old gear and production lines don't go to waste as fast. So Expert gear for special teams, Journeyman for higher-ups in the regular army—mortars, rifles, grenade launchers. Then repeaters and the bolt actions for the Vuzgal Defense Force," Rugrat said.

"We built up so many weapons it would be a shame to remove them and the infrastructure that we built up in Alva to supply them with ammunition. Over time, we can transition them to the new weapon systems."

Rugrat smiled. "Sounds like a good plan to me." He signed off on the new orders and agreed to them as a sound transmission came in.

"City Lord, there is someone saying that they are called Chonglu and that you know them personally?"

"Where is he?" Rugrat sat up in his seat. Erik had filled him in on what had happened in the First Realm.

"It's not just him, sir. He has a girl and a boy with him as well."

"Send a map to my office."

"Yes, sir."

Rugrat cleared away his desk a little bit, but it wasn't long until there was a knock on the door.

"Come in."

Rugrat stood as Chonglu entered the room with his children. "Chonglu, Feng, Felicity—I didn't expect to see you all here," Rugrat said.

"We owe you a great debt. You saved my life and the lives of my family, and you brought Mira and us back together. There is no money or wealth in the Ten Realms I can possibly repay this kindness." Chonglu dropped to his knee, his children doing the same. "We offer our loyalty, our ability, and our lives if you will have them."

"There's no need for that!" Rugrat said hastily, pulling them back to their feet.

"Please, if there is anything that we can do for you," Chonglu said.

Rugrat let out a snort, seeing that they would not let this go easily.

Something caught his eye as he looked out one of the windows. Seeing the Battle Arena that was being built, an idea popped into his mind.

"Very well. There is a task that you can complete. You will need to sign an oath to Erik and myself, promising never to reveal any of our secrets on your life," Rugrat said in a grave tone as he leaned back on his desk, crossing his arms.

Chonglu nodded, about to speak again.

"Feng and Felicity will go to school. They will learn at least one craft as well as basic studies in all crafts. When they are sixteen, they will be allowed to do as they want and leave school. Chonglu, you will become the administrator of the Battle Arena. Your wife is a person of the Fighter's Association, which will make it easier for you to talk to them and have more power with them. Though you will be neutral in all matters there. This will be a test of your abilities and we will be watching you to make sure that you aren't doing anything behind the scenes. Also, before any of that, I will need to know how you increased your levels so fast that you're able to go from the First Realm to the Fourth Realm," Rugrat asked.

"Mira," Chonglu said. "She brought high-level beasts for us to kill, and then monster cores to consume, ascending us through her efforts."

"Makes sense. The Stone Fist sect has tried to attack you twice now—personal strength is the only way to make sure that others can't harm you or the people you love."

Chonglu gave a short nod and glanced at his two children.

"There might be secrets that you need to keep from Mira," Rugrat warned.

"There are always secrets in the realms," Chonglu said.

Rugrat nodded and reached out his hand. "Very well, I'll leave running the Battle Arena to you Chonglu," Rugrat said.

Chonglu bowed deeply to Rugrat.

"Come on, no need for that, you'll need to prove your ability," *And your loyalty* Rugrat mentally added as he helped the other man back up.

"Well, that will take some time to get used to, but we have time. I'll have Hiao Xen get the right contracts ready for you."

"But we don't want to go to school," Felicity complained.

Rugrat laughed. "I didn't like school much either, but trust me when I say that going through school will make you stronger, much stronger than your mom and dad. Also, you can choose to learn fighting and high-level crafts while still in school. You get to pick the things that you want to try out. Think of it as a test period. Afterward, you'll have to pay for it," Rugrat said.

Chonglu saw Felicity and Feng thinking on his words. They didn't seem as annoyed now, more contemplative.

"Make sure that you train up. The barracks and training areas will be made available to you, though you'll learn more about that when you agree to the contracts," Rugrat said. *Then you can open your mana gates and temper your body further.*

25 Next Leap

Tanya was passed off to a group of traders. They were rather simple in their clothes and ornaments, but everything they had was of high quality.

"So where are we going? Is this it?" she asked as they rode into a city she hadn't seen before.

"Nope," the trader said as he guided the beasts expertly through the city. There were four carriages in total. "This is just the entrance," he said with a proud smile.

"The entrance?"

"You'll see." He laughed.

Tanya pouted, hearing little yips from the small beast storage crate that was hooked on her hip. She stopped herself from laughing at Tetsu's new size and the cute noises he let out.

Seeing his pitiful eyes and his head cocked to one side, she couldn't help but feel sorry for him.

"We'll get there soon enough and you can get out and run around," Tanya promised.

He still didn't seem happy with her explanation.

They headed farther into the city and toward the totem there.

The leading merchant got off; the guards took their payment and opened the gate to the totem.

They circled the totem as the leading merchant selected a destination.

"Won't the beasts freak out?" Tanya asked. "Tetsu nearly jumped on me when we went through the first time."

"They've seen it so many times that they're used to it now," the trader said as light fell over them all.

The light disappeared and they were looking at a modern city with a spider web of crystals on the ceiling. A beam of light reached up into them, illuminating them.

"This is Alva, and those are the recruiters who will take care of your citizenship." The trader pointed to a booth where a handful of people were lined up, talking to two people who checked their tokens and their identity before getting them to swear an oath.

There were armed police officers nearby, watching everything.

Tanya looked at the city and then back at the recruiters as they moved closer, the traders leaving the area around the totem.

"Oh, okay, that's it." The trader talked to his animals as they came to a stop and he got down. Tanya joined him.

"One Tanya Kvist for you, sent down by Rugrat. Here is her information token." The trader pulled out a token and passed it to one of the police officers.

"Got it. You bring back any of that desert drink?"

"Should have some at the stall tomorrow!" The trader slapped the officer on the back.

"Will do. Welcome home!"

"It's good to be back," the trader said with a tired but happy smile. "Got to get back to it!"

The police officer nodded as he got back to his carriage and beasts, and he looked at Tanya.

"Can I take out my beast?"

"Sure," the man said.

Tanya let Tetsu out. He stood and stretched, giving a big dog yawn before he wagged his tail happily.

Tanya took out some treats, getting him to sit before she fed him.

"Interesting beast. Powerful even though he looks like a cute sucker on the outside," the officer said. "You're responsible for him, so if he does wrong, it will be on you. If he attacks others without provocation, then he will have to be put down. Understood?"

"Yes," Tanya said, moving to protect Tetsu.

"I have a beast of my own, but the rules are to protect everyone. And there are a number of powerful beasts here that could cause a lot of damage and loss of life if they turned aggressive," the police officer said by way of apology.

"Next!" a recruiter called out.

There was no one left, so the officer walked up with a token and Tanya.

"From the higher realms—information token," he said.

"Thank you," the recruiter said with a small smile. She put the token into a formation and information started to appear in front of her eyes.

The totem flashed again as more people left Alva. Those seeing them off headed back to their homes.

"Name?"

"Tanya Kvist."

"Very good. My name is Helene. To start, you will need to take an oath to Alva, then I can run you through what my job is here as well as opportunities we have here—housing, food, all of that. I am only qualified to recruit people as traders and offer positions as a trader, but I can give you general information on the academy and all other programs, or point you in the direction of those recruiters, a recent change that has happened."

"Why?" Tanya asked.

"Once you do a job, any job long enough, you get a sense for people who would or wouldn't be good in your field. Although we can guide people to do jobs that they aren't suited for, they don't need to listen to us. I'm a trader most of the time but since I got pregnant, I've taken to operating my business at a distance. There was a recruiter position, so it gets me away from the house and stops me from losing my mind," Helene said with a smile.

"Oh." Tanya smiled at Helene's easygoing attitude.

"So, would you like information on the academy or on the traders?"

"I would like some information on the academy. Sorry, I don't think that

I would be that good of a trader," Tanya said.

"No worries. It's not for everyone and we prefer that you're passionate about what you do! Now, there are stipulations for entering into the academy. You can pay to enter and pay for your costs up front, or you can take on debt and pay that off at a later date. There are classes on all of the major crafting skills, as well as classes on defending yourself with the barracks, though you will need to be a resident of Alva for a year at least or be close family of someone who is part of the Alva administration," Helene outlined. "I'm going to guess you don't have a place to stay?"

"I don't," Tanya said.

"Well, there are the Wayside Inns for those who don't have houses in Alva. Otherwise, there are a number of homes or apartments up for sale. You can buy these, too, on a loan from the Alva Bank."

"Could I hold off?" Tanya asked.

"Yes, but you need to have a residence within three days or before you sleep next. If you are found sleeping in a park to avoid paying for a place to stay, then you will have three days to find a job, or leave Alva," Helene said.

"That sounds a bit harsh," Tanya said.

Helene looked at Tanya with a quizzical look. "Most city lords simply force people into hard labor if they don't have money to pay off some kind of debt. We don't have the space to waste on people who don't contribute. If you have a skill that others don't, you can sell it. If you are broken, you can be healed. You can increase your cultivation. Yes, you take on debt, but as long as you pay it off, then the Ten Realms is open to you. This is a chance rarely seen by others."

"What if you don't pay your debt?" Tanya asked.

"You will then be given a job that suits your abilities to pay off your debt, then you can leave Alva freely."

"I guess, seeing the city, I couldn't help but think of the way things were in Sweden, but that is Earth and this is the Ten Realms. Here I don't have anything but what's in my storage rings."

Even back on Earth I was renting because I didn't' have enough money to purchase a place of my own.

Helene sat there, waiting on Tanya.

"I'll take the information and look on it. I heard that there are a number of factories here. Could I have a look at them, or know who the owners are?" Tanya asked.

"Certainly. I would suggest going to the Trader's Hollow. It is a tavern where the traders meet up and where records are kept of all the different traders. It is located in the warehouse district with the trading interface."

"I heard that there was someone from Earth other than Erik and Rugrat, a Matt?" Tanya asked.

"He can be found in the blueprint office, or someone there will know where he is." Helene smiled as she pulled out a book and placed Tanya's token on top of it all.

"Okay, thank you," Tanya said with a smile.

"Now it's time for the oath," Helene said.

"Okay," Tanya said.

Tanya walked into Alva. The people were kind and smiled openly. Most of them greeted one another in the street to have a quick conversation and make plans. A trading caravan headed out, with people waving good-bye.

She saw apartment buildings rising into the sky and houses being built on private lots. Farms surrounded the building areas. The building in the middle of the city stood the tallest, with only a large tower on the academy's grounds reaching its height.

It felt busy, without the people being cold.

"Hello. I was wondering where the factories might be?" Tanya asked.

"Sure. You must be new. Take this street and they're on the second street to your right." The man smiled.

"Thank you," Tanya said.

"No problem!" The man hurried off to his next appointment.

Tanya headed toward the factories. They were a series of long buildings. She couldn't see what was going on, but she saw their final products being put into storage items and loaded onto carriages.

"Cloth and clothes, though the majority are items for the military, judging by the extra police," Tanya said.

She headed toward the blueprint office, thinking as she went.

Tetsu was looking around, his tongue hanging out of his mouth as children let out excited noises and people looked at him in interest.

Tetsu wandered off toward a woman sitting on a bench.

"Hello there!" she said, startled.

"Tetsu," Tanya said with a displeased tone.

Tetsu looked back at her as if saying, *I did nothing wrong. Who can deny my power of cuteness!*

"May I pet him?" the woman asked.

"Please, go ahead," Tanya said.

The woman petted the triumphant Tetsu.

Big dog, soft heart.

"Sorry for keeping you!" the woman said, noticing that they were heading somewhere.

"No problem," Tanya said. "Have a good day. Come on, Tetsu."

Tetsu looked heart-stricken as Tanya walked a bit more and clicked her fingers.

"Come on, boy." She raised her voice slightly.

Tetsu padded after her and they continued to the blueprint office. She was nearly hit by a door as a man ran out.

"Sorry!" he yelled as he kept on going, taking off at a run.

"It's no—" Tanya's eyes went wide at the man's speed. *What level is he to be that fast!*

Tanya checked that there were no more human bullets coming through the door and entered.

There were people coming in, giving their requests to the servers, who were selling blueprints or taking requests to record blueprints or create new ones.

Tanya lined up to talk to the servers.

"What can I help you with today?" the person at the counter asked.

"I was wondering if I could talk to Matt? I'm someone from Earth as well. I just got here," Tanya said. In this place she didn't know, she just wanted to see someone who shared some similarities with her.

"Okay." The server turned and went into the back.

A few minutes later, a man with a hat on backward, a pencil stuck behind his ear, appeared.

"Hey!" Matt's face opened up into a smile as he came around the counter. Others moved out of the way and he saw Tetsu.

"Oh, who's a good pup! What's this handsome guy's name?" Matt reached down, petting and scratching the pleased Tetsu.

"He's Tetsu," Tanya said.

"Rugrat sent me a message saying that you're Tanya—is that right?"

"Tanya Kvist, Sweden." She put out her hand.

"Matt Richardson, Canada," Matt said.

"It's good to meet you," Tanya said, feeling relieved.

"Come on, let's get a drink. I want to hear your story!" Matt said.

They headed out to a bar. Matt got her a drink and they sat in the back corner and Tanya started telling her story.

"Then next thing I know, I'm in the Ten Realms, screens popping up and all of that kind of thing. I wandered for what must've been a day, found a road and then I got to a town. Everyone looked at me and Tetsu weird. They wanted to buy him from me, or take him. I could only get some food to eat with the items I had in my pockets, but I had been playing tabletops a lot and I had my game master book with me, so I got what supplies I could and headed out into the forest—felt it was safer there. I lived in a hammock in the trees. Others tried to find us, but I got a handle on some basic magic, learned some basic Alchemy, really just enough to know what to and what not to eat. Then started to hunt, make traps and stuff.

"Trained up Tetsu, who got stronger. He ate a monster core by accident. I thought that he would die, but instead he became much stronger. Defended me and caught our meals. I put all of my points into Stamina Regeneration and mana pool; only had spells over other people and with the higher Stamina, I didn't need to eat so much. Went to towns here and there without Tetsu. We lived in the forests, increasing our levels through killing animals and I came to understand spells more. Then we reached level ten and headed to the Second Realm. We were there for some time, but guess we got overconfident. I took Tetsu into more places. There were more trained beasts there, but with my low level, people caught on, so we went on the run," Tanya said.

"That's one hell of a story," Matt said.

"Yeah." Tanya took a drink from her beer, enjoying the cold, refreshing feeling with the slight buzz of alcohol. She patted Tetsu, who gnawed on some bone that Matt had got from the bar owner.

"So spells, huh?" Matt said.

"Kind of like cooking. Now, I'm not saying that I'm a good cook or anything but my grandmother—now that is a woman who can cook." Tanya smiled. "I found that spells were really just a combination of different affinity mana, combined together and then bound with your will to do something. Take a flame." Tanya opened her hand as a perfect blue flame appeared.

"Wind, fire, and wood: one part wind, one part fire and wood. Then creating a fireball: three parts air, one part fire, and two parts wood. Now, most would think just *fire* and most spells are like that, but they're weaker and more unstable, requiring a higher mana output to sustain them. The extra wind and wood increases the power of the flame and launches it, but it moves according to your will as you are the power, the mana behind it, creating it."

"That is incredible. But what about if you have pure mana?" Matt asked.

"Well, I don't have pure mana, but I would think that it's like a formation. The mana stone or the person is the power and the directions of the person or the formation create action. So instead of having to collect the tinder and then strike flint to create a fire, you would just say *fire* and it would be created. Spells are like a memorization, like when you are looking for a letter in the alphabet. Rarely do you know what comes before and afterward; instead, you repeat the *whole* alphabet, just like when you were a kid trying to remember where that damn letter is, even if it is inside your head. A spell, if you repeat it enough, becomes a part of your trained instincts. What I'm trying to do is bridge the gap, to make using mana as instinctive as breathing."

"That sounds entirely too complicated for my brain." Matt laughed.

"Well, the first step is to use mana in my spells. Then, from there, it's figuring out how to cast spells without needing to repeat the spells, whether that is in my brain or out loud, so it's as natural as walking, running, and as hard to forget as riding a bike." Tanya took a slug from her beer.

"If you're interested, there is someone that I would like you to meet," Matt said.

"Who?"

"Egbert? You there?" Matt asked the open space.

"Egbert?" Tanya asked.

"You'll like him—made from mana, I guess?" Matt sat back and sipped his beer as the door to the bar opened.

"Administrator Egbert!" the bar owner said with a big smile as people looked over to the skinny man in the doorway.

The man walked in more, revealing his appearance.

Tanya nearly choked on her beer.

"N-necro, lich?" she asked as the people in the bar all greeted Egbert. He didn't have a face but still, from his eyes and his demeanor, one could feel his emotions as he moved through the bar.

"Just undead, though he still has memories and can think, kind of." Matt grinned and drank.

It took some time for Egbert to reach the table.

"Tanya Kvist, the newest resident of Alva, I am Egbert, the resident skeleton of Alva, safeguard of the dungeon core, Erik and Rugrat's unfortunate lackey as well as the Kanesh Academy Library department head! A very interesting conversation the two of you were having!"

"He is part of the dungeon. Because we're in it, he hears everything." Matt shrugged.

"I would be most interested if you studied the books on magic that we have in the library. Ah, sorry, does my appearance—hey, what are you doing?"

Egbert looked down at Tetsu, who stopped his actions and looked up at Egbert and Tanya.

"Tetsu! Stop, uh, chewing on his leg." Tanya frowned, not sure how to admonish her dog.

Matt snorted in the corner, shaking his head as he eyed his beer, staying out of it.

Tetsu let go of Egbert's leg slowly and bowed his head, peering up at her with his perfected puppy dog eyes.

"Well, I was wondering if you would be interested in a position with learning the arcane. I find that we are altogether lacking in that area. We are taking the information for granted, following different spells, but as you say, there is a large loss of mana when there shouldn't be. I like to optimize. So would you like to be the first member of mana studies?" Egbert asked.

"Mana studies?"

"Looking into the core of the arcane and the magical instead of just taking others' word for it," Egbert said.

"What would be involved?"

"Well, you would be linked to all of the different schools within the academy. Everyone uses spells, but then you would be the closest to the contract department—they create magical scrolls and the magical contracts—and the formation department, who create formations, though basically you would have free rein to study anything magical," Egbert said.

"You can make a department like that?" Matt asked.

"I can't not make a department." Egbert shrugged. "Also, although we know the basics of Alchemy and smithing and learned the basics on formations not that long ago, we still don't really know the theories and basis of spells and magic. If we could get to know some of the secrets, decrease the amount of mana that we have to use even..."

Egbert's words caught Tanya up and she rubbed her storage ring. It had been what she had been studying all this time. She hadn't thought of it before, but she wanted to unlock the mysteries of the Ten Realms.

"In my games, I was always the person who was investigating so many times that the rest of my group made me the game master so that I would stop spending a session figuring out the rules of the world and bending them." Tanya let out a snort but her eyes were glazed over, remembering those sessions and the time she had spent reviewing spells that she knew, or that she had been able to adapt from her game book to use in the Ten Realms. "Maybe I can find out the truth of the Ten Realms and bend the rules here."

"So this is a technique." Erik looked at the book Old Hei had slid across the table.

"There are only a few of them to be found in the lower realms regarding crafting. Most of them deal with fighting. Otherwise, the recruiters in the Fifth and academies in the Sixth Realm have collections of them. I only have five different technique books and I have only completely learned four of them. This is the only one that I can freely lend to others within the

Alchemist Association," Old Hei said.

"Flame Puppeteer?" Erik read the cover of the book.

"The technique uses threads of mana to control the flames within the cauldron. The flames can alternate temperatures and allow one to work complex concoctions that need different temperatures and fine control," Old Hei explained. "Open the book. It is written by a magical scribe to immerse one in the technique completely."

Erik opened the book and started reading the first page, reading about the positioning of the body, the way one should breathe and focus. He was drawn in by the words, feeling the world slipping away. He started to see scenes where there was an alchemist sitting behind his cauldron. He had his hands next to the cauldron. With a flick of his hands, lines or mana strings connected between his hands; he threw in prepared ingredients, his fingers moving the threads of mana that turned into flames, their changes directly affecting the ingredients.

More were thrown in as the man's fingers danced. It was a beautiful display of Alchemy, of one's mana strength.

The technique simplified the process for the alchemist, the perfect tool for the job as the concoction didn't fight but worked with him.

Erik knew on some level that the scribe had somehow imbued the book with the ability for him to see what the transcriber had seen in greater detail.

Erik could feel that he was only scratching the surface of the technique; the mana strands were just part of it.

The alchemist's eyes were closed, but still he reacted with incredible precision without anything inside the cauldron missing his gaze.

The strands between his fingers twisted into shapes back and forth, as if they were alive. The control was incredible.

Erik closed his eyes as a pill appeared from the cauldron and the alchemist cancelled his technique.

"What did the alchemist do?"

"The Flame Puppeteer is a technique that allows one to control combining different sub-concoctions at the same time before combining them. Its ability to isolate and concoct is incredibly useful for concoctions that have ingredients that need to be freshly prepared, or sub-concoctions that need to be combined as quickly as possible so as to not lose efficacy.

"Could the pill be completed without the technique?"

"Yes." Erik opened his eyes, confused.

"What would the outcome be?" Old Hei asked.

Erik leaned forward and looked at the now closed book. "The efficacy wouldn't be as high. It would require a lot more mana and concentration. The techniques are like Alchemy tools."

"Correct. And there are right tools for everything. Remember, one technique might be good for just one kind of concoction, but it might not be good for all of them," Old Hei said.

"How can I get more technique manuals?"

"There are a few ways. Get a high merit and get them as a reward. Impress people enough to join an academy in the Sixth Realm, or go to a competition and compete. Or," Old Hei smiled at Erik's conflicted expression, "go to the Fifth and Sixth Realm and buy them at the competitions."

"I can just buy them?" Erik asked.

"Mana stones rule in the Ten Realms. Although the technique manuals will be incredibly expensive, don't you control one of the most popular cities in the Fourth Realm?"

"Oh," Erik said.

The two of them looked at each other before they both started to laugh.

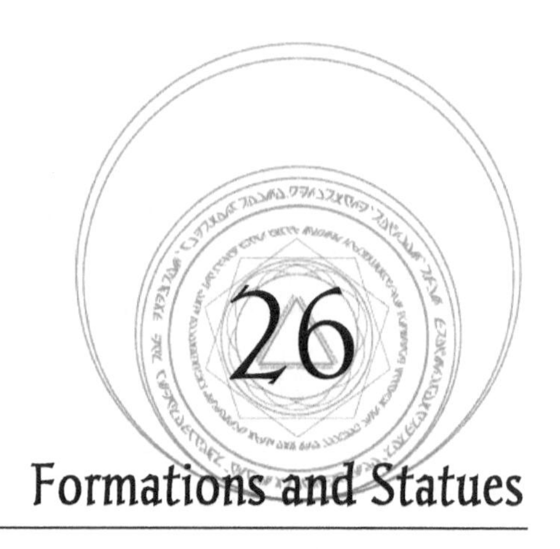

26 Formations and Statues

"That concludes formation power sources and interfacing with mana stones, ambient mana and gems!" Qin said, clapping her hands together.

The students in her class all started to get up, talking to one another about the lesson and heading to their next lecture, class, or workshop time.

Tan Xue and Rugrat wrote down notes. They walked up from the back of the class toward where Qin sat on her desk.

"You going to tell them or should I?" Julilah asked as she entered the classroom, walking over to them.

"Fine." Qin stood, some of her energy returning to her.

"We were able to complete the designs for the new rifle weapon system and Julilah was able to design a formation socket system for the grenade launcher and the mortar. She also added a formation socket within the formation so the shooter can pick what kind of warhead the enemy is hit by," Qin said.

Rugrat smiled. "Well, it sounds like we've got our next army upgrade ready."

Julilah smiled at the praise.

"I was wondering about having a mana stone in a formation and then also using ambient mana. Does that mean you would use the ambient mana first and then you would use the power of the mana stone? Could you, if you replaced the mana stones with a cornerstone, actually passively charge the weapon or armor?"

"Yes, but it would be a slow charge unless you're in an area with high mana concentration. And as it pulls in mana from one area, it would deplete it. So you might want to move around with it to draw in mana over a larger area," Qin said.

"Ah," Tan Xue said.

"Oh, Erik sent me a message the other day, something about techniques. Kind of been busy and it slipped my mind," Rugrat started.

"Techniques?" Tan Xue asked.

Rugrat let out an awkward cough as he realized that it might benefit her the most out of anyone he knew. He quickly told them everything that he had learned from Erik about techniques.

"And you didn't think to tell us? What else did you forget?" Tan Xue threw her hands up.

"Crap, answering statue!" Rugrat smacked his head as he turned around and made to walk out of the classroom, only to have the door slam open in his face.

"You don't have a trading interface!" Elise yelled, storming into the room.

"Huh?" Rugrat asked, his mind miles behind as he tried to pull the relevant brain cells together to spark inspiration.

"Trading interface! You know, the thing that we use to trade across the realms!" Elise made sure that the door was closed. "Can anyone hear us in here?" Elise asked.

Julilah grabbed a formation plate and stuck a controlling formation into the socket in the middle of it.

A distorted wave spread out, covering the walls, and all of their ears popped.

"Now they can't," Julilah said.

"Handy," Elise said with a nod and then focused her laser beams—uh, eyes onto Rugrat.

"A trading interface, like the one that can be found in Alva, the one that lets us trade with other cities. We can use that to trade with the other people of Vuzgal, offload our items we can't sell in the lower realms. We can set the descriptions of the different items to buy and sell there. We just tell everyone that they're from Vuzgal, make them want to come here in order to find cheaper goods," Elise said.

"That makes sense." Rugrat nodded.

"Then build the damn thing!"

"How?" Rugrat asked.

"Do you have a city building cornerstone? Like the interface that was in Alva Village?"

"I think I remember seeing something like that under the pillar," Rugrat said.

Elise pinched the bridge of her nose. "You have to access that interface. Then you can get a blueprint from it. Then you place the blueprint down where you want it, and build it just like anything else requiring a blueprint."

"While I'm doing that, I can put down the answering statue. All right, I've got to run, things to do!" Rugrat quickly left the room before he could get himself into any more trouble.

The women all looked at one another.

"Rugrat!" they said by agreement, shrugging before they collected their items and cleared out.

"Drinks anyone? Elise, do you know anything about techniques? Crafting techniques, kind of like fighting techniques?" Tan Xue asked.

"No, but Elan might know," Elise suggested.

"Good idea."

Rugrat was in the bowels of the pillar where he found the city interface. He had to chip some mana stones off it to get to it.

He accessed the interface, purchasing two of the city trading interfaces and put them into his storage ring before he took out the answering statue and placed it down.

Do you wish to fuse this answering statue with the dungeon: Vuzgal? YES/NO

"Yes," Rugrat said.

The answering statue flashed with runes before its base fused with the floor of the pillar.

The statue flinched and stood straighter, causing Rugrat to jump up and backward.

"Shit, crap, damn it!" Rugrat swore, trying to get himself back under control as he stared daggers at the offending statue.

There was no more reaction from it.

"Damn friggin' moving inanimate object," Rugrat muttered underneath his breath before he cleared his throat. "What is this place?"

"This is a dungeon city hybrid called Vuzgal by the locals," the answering statue said.

"How many people are in the city?"

"There are approximately 157,894 people within the limits of Vuzgal."

"Can you tell me the contents of books that are not located within the Castle District?"

"Yes."

"What must happen in order for you to get the information from a book?"

"I will only know the information from a book if it is in contact with an area that is under my control."

"So if I put a book down, then you can read it?"

"No."

"The book's information, can you copy it?"

"No."

"Can you repeat it?"

"Yes." Rugrat smiled at the answering statue's answer.

"Do you retain that knowledge?"

"I do not understand the question."

"When you are not in contact with a book, do you know the words contained within?"

"I do not understand the question."

Rugrat took out a book. "What is in my hand?"

"An item referred to as a book, made of leather, wood, and ink."

"What is contained within the book?"

"Markings, part of the book."

Rugrat put the book down. "What is contained within the book?"

"Markings."

"What are those markings?"

"A line going left to right and then down halfway through the character with two small notches two and three-quarters down the main stem."

"What letters do the markings make?"

"T-H-E."

"What sentences do the markings make?"

"The art of smithing is more complicated than most think—"

"Bingo!" Rugrat let out a laugh. "Okay, so you see books as objects, not as books—"

"I do not understand the question."

"Oh, quiet, will you?"

"That is not a question."

"You don't see the words inside the book as information; you just see it as part of the book. A component. So you can repeat it with perfect clarity, but as soon as that book is gone, you don't retain any knowledge of that book. You're a talking photograph! Just need the right parameters to get you to say it instead of just give us a load of useless information!

"Now, if we were able to somehow increase your knowledge, add sort of filters to you, then maybe you could look out for other things. Maybe have images playing of people attacking one another and then you look for anyone who is committing similar acts and then would catch people attacking one another in Vuzgal."

The answering statue stood there, like a statue, not responding as it had not been given any questions.

"There's going to be a lot of figuring out, but then, damn, you can be our very own surveillance system." Rugrat made to touch the answering statue and then stopped. *The thing just plain old creeps me out. Don't think of the fact that you're in a basement with it all alone. Crap!*

Rugrat smiled and backed away, not wanting to turn his back on it, for fear that it might move or stare at him with some kind of evil intentions.

You're overthinking things—totally overthinking it!

He forced himself to leave the room normally, but made sure that he was half facing the answering statue so he would know if it moved at all.

As soon as he made for the stairs, he ran up them as fast as possible.

Not scared of a statue—just wanted to get some cardio in!

27 Expansion

Chonglu looked over the Battle Arena.

It was a grand structure with several floors. In the basement, there were training rooms where one could fight against puppets, train in solitude, or have private matches.

Few knew the details of these rooms; even the leader of the Fighter's Association in Vuzgal didn't know the complete details.

The mana density varied in the different rooms, creating five tiers of rooms from A to E grade. The E grade had the lowest amount of mana, having the same ambient mana as that found in Vuzgal.

The D grade had a five percent increase in mana density; C a ten percent; B thirteen percent; A fifteen percent. It didn't seem like much, but the mana density was as high as some of the higher grade training rooms in the Sixth Realm.

These training rooms practically burned through mana stones, but the benefits couldn't be understated. At the Vuzgal level of mana density, one's mind was calmed and they became more alert, increasing their ability to focus on their tasks and develop faster.

Increasing that by just five percent, the benefits increased to nearly double. People would work harder for longer without noticing it. It was easier to fall into a training trance and gain enlightenment.

At ten percent, even training in such an environment for an hour would be worth three days of training outside; twelve percent an hour was worth training for a week; at fifteen percent, one hour could be like training in the Fourth Realm for two weeks. Even if one was to just sit down and cultivate their Mana Gathering Cultivation, they could break through bottlenecks that had been holding them back and accumulate mana at a much higher rate.

A hidden but powerful benefit was the purity of the mana. With its higher purity, one didn't have to refine it as much to clear impurities.

The first floor was the ticket floor and the first sparring areas. People could purchase tickets to the training rooms, or they could sign up for tournaments. The Battle Arena allowed people to fight and settle their grudges. Even fights to the death were okayed as long as either side was not pressured.

It was smart adding this in. The Fourth Realm is a land of death; if people didn't have a way to vent their anger and killing intent, then it could cause issues within the city. This way the violence is at least contained, Chonglu thought.

"How are the preparations for the tournament?" he asked his assistant Dominque. She had been part of the Alva Army, but then she focused on formations leaving the army behind. Now she was Chonglu's assistant and one of the people who monitored him and what was happening in the battle Arena. While she followed his orders he knew that she was reporting to others on his actions. He wasn't offended, he would have done the same thing if he was in Erik or Rugrat's position. Still he was having a hard time understanding just how powerful those two had become.

"Everything is readied. There will be a total of six tournaments happening concurrently: those from level thirty to thirty-five, then thirty-five to forty, with a tournament for every five levels up to level fifty. Are you sure about the prizes?"

"I'm sure," Chonglu said.

"Giving the tournament winners a luxury suite in the nearest Wayside Inn, cultivation resources, and allowing them four hours a day in the B-grade training rooms with discounts on all Battle Arena products," she said, casting him a look.

"Right. To the winners goes the spoils. It should bring out a number of competitors and most of them will probably want to go to the A-grade rooms," Chonglu said.

He looked at the different stores on the first floor. There were stands that would sell potions; others, armor and weapons. "What about the arenas?"

"The one hundred arenas on the second floor are all prepared as well as the thirty on the third floor. The last parts are being added to the six arenas on the second and the formations of the main arena are being laid down," Domnique said, checking her notes.

Chonglu was about to speak again when he got a sound transmission.

"The Fighter's Association head has arrived," one of the arena guards reported. The guards, like the staff of the arena, were all people of Vuzgal and had sworn oaths binding them to the city.

"Very well. I will be there in a moment." The message disappeared in a flash of light.

"Our guest has arrived." He started to walk toward the entrance. "How about the second training floor?"

"It will be completed in another month. From the reports, the skeletons and builders should have enough done by next week to open the preliminary rooms."

"Good. Leave them wanting more and show that there is more to come. Once we're done with the second floor, we'll look at building the third floor. But we will only be allowed to build it if our profits are high enough."

"Yes, Manager Chonglu."

They reached the front doors where Head Klaus from the Fighter's Association was standing with a party of other administrators and powerful figures within his association.

"Manager Chonglu, it is good to see you!" he said at their arrival, with a wide smile.

"Head Klaus, I am sorry for the wait! The opening will happen in a few hours, but would you be interested in a tour of the facilities? If it wasn't for the Fighter's Association's help and insight, we wouldn't have been able to build this arena," Chonglu said.

"Your words are too kind. But I am interested in what you have done. The Battle Arena has become a recent topic of interest and my association is always looking for ways to increase our strength."

"There are a total of one hundred and thirty-seven arenas and we want to run a monthly tournament with the highest placed members getting exclusive benefits. The first one hundred arenas are built just for smaller spars for the public to view. The thirty exclusive arenas people will need to pay for and the fighters will get a percentage of the profit. The same goes for the six side arenas. The main arena will draw in people from across Vuzgal to see the strongest in the city go head to head. Each is specially built with reinforced materials and extensive formations so that the fighters can unleash their power while the spectators remain totally safe. Betting will be allowed on site, and there are items from the Vuzgal crafters that will only be for sale here. Though, I think you will be mostly interested in the lower level training rooms." Chonglu led them into the basement and showed them the training rooms.

When they returned to the first floor, Head Klaus could only laugh. "I thought that the Battle Arena would be merely for show, but I was too short-sighted. Vuzgal truly puts all of their effort into every endeavor!"

"We aim to please." Chonglu showed a pleased smile. "Could I invite Head Klaus to open the Battle Arena with me?"

"Certainly!"

They headed out to the front of the Battle Arena. All of the shops were empty of customers, with staff ready to greet customers, eagerly waiting the grand opening.

The group walked out in front of the building and people looked over.

It looked as though there were a few hundred people, most of them from the Fighter's Association, dungeon divers or guards who had the day off from their regular duties.

"Hello, everyone. My name is Manager Chonglu of the Battle Arena. It is my great honor to announce with the esteemed head of the Fighter's Association, Head Klaus, the opening of the Vuzgal Battle Arena!"

People clapped and cheered. It was a bit subdued but Chonglu's smile only became wider as he wondered what the nobles and fighting sects would think.

"As a thank-you for coming to our grand opening, as long as you visit the front desk and register, then for the next month you will be able to buy a membership at a twenty percent discount! Now, I know you didn't come to hear me talk!"

He went over to Head Klaus and they stood in front of a ribbon. They were both given a set of scissors. They snipped the ribbon as the people clapped.

Klaus laughed and he shook hands with Chonglu. "Well, let me know how much memberships would be for all of the Fighter's Association members!"

Chonglu laughed with him, a pleased look in his eyes as others talked to one another, hearing their words.

"Please, come to my office. I have some fresh tea in and we can discuss it!" he said.

Those there for the grand opening streamed through the doors, seeing all kinds of counters and stores open. There were information boards across the floor. People stopped and read them, leading to excited discussion.

"Training rooms with higher mana density?"

"We can create private fights and choose the mana density, even invite people to come and view them?"

"Tournaments every month for all level ranges?"

"Look at those weapons! All of them are at least the mid Journeyman level and there are even low-level Expert weapons!"

"Formation sockets in armor and weapons? What are those?"

"Those memberships sound expensive—more like status symbols for the rich!" one scoffed.

"Or for training nuts," another chimed in.

"Look at these rewards for the first placed positions in one's level groups! Even the rewards for the top ten are incredible!"

"I thought Vuzgal only cared about the crafters?"

The sounds of the floor fell away as Chonglu, Domnique, and Klaus entered an elevator that rose up. Its sides were clear as they rose up, passing the first arenas that were walled-off squares with seating around them, then the second floor of arenas were spaced out more, with more seating. The third level of arenas was nearly twice the height of the first two floors, with much more seating and screens that would show the fight so everyone could see it perfectly no matter their seat. The final arena took up an entire floor and had nearly three times the seating as the third floor.

Chonglu's office was the second highest box. It looked over the arena on one side and then over Vuzgal on the other.

The Battle Arena was only shorter than the mana barrier pillars and the Sky Reaching Restaurants and Wayside Inns.

It took up a truly massive amount of land, being 300m by 300m. The area around it only had stalls for a further 300m in every direction in case they ever wanted to expand it.

"The view is even better from here than it is in my office," Klaus said.

Chonglu laughed the compliment off, but he was rather pleased with his office as well. *I only came to the Fourth Realm a week ago and I'm already managing this entire place. If the arenas were full, it would have thirty times the population of Chonglu.*

"Please, won't you join me in some tea? Or would you prefer something stronger?"

"Something stronger. This is a celebration, after all! I was serious about getting those memberships."

Chonglu walked to his desk, shooting Domnique a look. She bowed and departed, heading to manage the rest of the arena.

He took out two fine glasses and poured some of his highest quality drink. Hiao Xen had supplied him with a number of items, including supplies for entertaining different guests.

"Doing a deal for the entire association would be difficult, but what about a bulk membership package? One hundred of our gold membership packages at a thirty percent discount?" Chonglu asked.

"Thirty percent?" Head Klaus repeated, sounding as though he were thinking it over.

Chonglu passed him a drink and indicated for him to join him on his chairs looking over the city.

Klaus took the drink and sat down, sipping. "Mmm, good drink!" Head Klaus smacked his lips together.

Chonglu smiled. From Elan's information, he knew that Head Klaus appreciated his drinks.

"Thirty percent is the best I can do," he said. "I can make the times transferable between the one hundred memberships. So if one is not here, then their time can be given to others who are here."

"And with only one hundred spots, it would create competition with the members," Klaus mused. "Though I'll need something else to sweeten the pot," Klaus said.

"Well," Chonglu lowered his tone, "the A-grade is only our highest grade training facilities for now." He took a sip as Klaus gave him his full attention.

"S-grade training rooms will have a complete twenty percent increase of mana, though there will only be ten exclusive rooms." He dragged out his words, seeing the agitation in Klaus's body language.

"I could give the Fighter's Association first pick on one of the rooms every month and these rooms would allow up to five people to train in them at a time."

"I'll need a contract written up, but if it is as you say, we have an agreement," Head Klaus said.

Chonglu raised his glass. "Good to do business with you, Head Klaus!"

"And you, Manager Chonglu!"

The two of them smiled at each other. They touched glasses and took a satisfying drink from their glasses, looking at the growing Vuzgal.

Tan Xue was in the Viewing Hall again, reviewing some of the smithing Expert recordings. The recording ended and she frowned, opening and closing her hand on the hammer that wasn't there.

"It makes sense now. I felt that there was something missing. I thought it was just because I didn't have the skill with the hammer as the Expert's recordings. What I was missing was the other component of the technique, the mana circulation. No wonder I was getting different results in my smithing even when I was carrying out the exact same actions!"

Tan Xue sat on a chair and leaned forward, resting her elbows on her knees.

"I'm reaching the limit of what I can do just by myself. I developed my knowledge about ores, minerals, enhancers, formations, and using them all together, strengthening up my foundations. I still have much more to learn, but my biggest block must be not having these techniques to draw out greater power." She let out an annoyed huff and sat back against the wall. "There are techniques to increase the mana retained by the metal, techniques that work with the enhancers to make their effect stronger. Techniques to inlay formations into weapons at the same time, or to work specially enhanced metals that can't be worked with normal flames or tools. Rugrat said that there should be techniques in the Fourth Realm. I'm supposed to stay here for a few months to train people, but Rugrat doesn't have that restriction. I can send him to the higher realms and get a number of techniques."

Tan Xue stood up, a smile on her face as she walked out of the Viewing Hall with determined steps, right toward the military workshops which were all Journeyman or Expert level, where only people who had taken an oath to Alva worked on secret projects like the weapon upgrades. It was a new addition shortly after Rugrat returned from the Second Realm.

Erik looked haggard. He had been taking Stamina recovery potions and Mind Calming pills together to keep himself alert and energized as he focused on the Flame Puppeteer technique. His fingers moved; the air around them shook as the flames within the cauldron twisted and changed into different shapes, as if they were alive.

The cauldron started to shake as the mana in the surroundings was stirred up and drawn into the cauldron.

The cauldron started to settle down and Erik waved his hand. The lid of the cauldron crashed to the ground and he pulled out a jade box. The pills flew out of the cauldron and landed in the box.

Erik opened his eyes. A smile appeared on his face as he closed the box and laughed.

Flame Puppeteer

Expert

Your control over flames has reached a new level where you can control two flames as easily as you control one.

Second flame costs 3x amount of Mana

For learning an Expert-ranked technique, you gain: 1,000,000 EXP

46,948,136/56,900,000 EXP till you reach Level 58

Erik let a groan and allowed his body to fall backward. He pushed out his legs that had been numb, but as the blood returned, they started to ache. A wave of fatigue fell over him.

He had a look in the jade box. They were all Earth tempering pills. As high Journeyman pills, instead of being at their previous Condensed pill level of efficacy, these had reached the Inscribed pill level. Inscribed pills would never lose their potency and if they were in the right containers, then they could increase their strength. They were the second highest grade pill that one could create, under an Enlightened pill.

"And this is one of the weakest techniques." Erik looked at his skill increase again.

A fighting spirit welled up within him. It had been too long since he had tried to increase the efficacy of a pill. Enlightened was just a few steps away.

"With these techniques, even the weakest of our alchemists and our crafters will have a chance to become Experts. Only a few of them will be able to pass beyond, but that relies on their ability. If they have more paths to study from, they might have an easier time figuring it out themselves. We need to get more techniques."

"How are they looking?" Glosil asked as he emerged behind Sergeant Acosta and the training staff, who were eating together. They nearly jumped out of their skins as he smiled at them, waving them back down.

"At ease. Just checking in."

"Well, we've been working with them for three weeks now. They have the basics down. It took time to get them to start working as a team, but they've really started to become teammates. They've been able to increase their combat capability, without increasing their levels. They have a good handle on operations at the fighting team and fighting squad level. It will take more time to work on anything more advanced. I think three more weeks should do it," Sergeant Acosta reported.

"Very well," Glosil said.

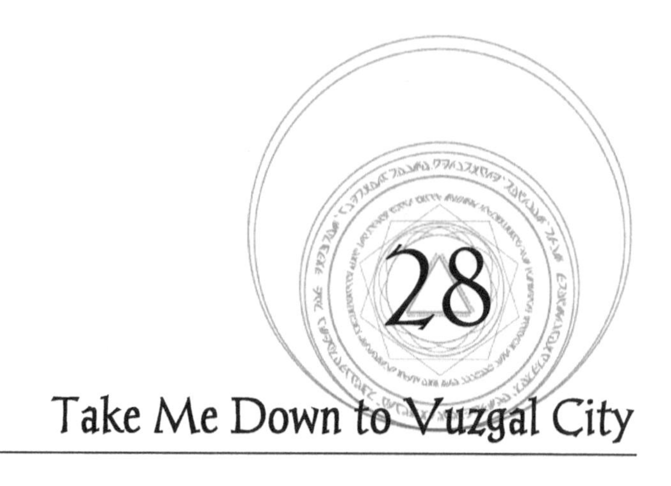

28
Take Me Down to Vuzgal City

"Where the grass is green and the girls are pretty!" Rugrat half-sung as he checked the barrel in his hands.

He attached it to the upper receiver of the weapon system and used a fusing rod. It was just a piece of metal with a fusing formation engraved into it. Applying it against the receiver and the barrel, the two fused together seamlessly.

Rugrat checked the sights on the weapon, putting it into a form that made sure they were lined up perfectly.

He assembled the clearing rod that extended from the receiver to the barrel. Cranking it backward would extract and eject the round in the weapons chamber if the round didn't work for some reason.

Then he lined the upper and lower receiver, pushing through pins, securing them to one another before he activated a fusing formation in the lower receiver.

"I was thinking of copying the AK design more, just have the top open up and then get in there. But with the two different receivers, even if we upgrade, the lower receiver simply supplies power to the upper receiver, so we don't have to make them again and we can just change the formations of the upper receiver. Change one part instead of the entire weapon."

"And don't forget whose idea it was!" Julilah said from the other side of the workshop, where she had mortars with deactivated formations in front of her.

"Stroke of genius, Julilah." Rugrat laughed.

He pressed the separating formation and the two receivers came apart again, just needing him to pop the pins out again.

"I heard that you might be in here," Erik said from the doorway.

"What are you doing here? Shouldn't you be in the Third Realm, doing Alchemy things?"

"Well, I was in the Third Realm. I mastered my first technique and I need to learn more," Erik said. "Want to go to the Fifth Realm?"

"Let me get my coat!" Rugrat said.

"Is Elan in?"

"He should be around. Why?"

"We can ask him what competitions are going on in the Fifth Realm and then get a guide to them. We don't really need to compete in the fighting but we can compete in mana stones to buy technique manuals," Erik said.

"But I wanted to see how my skills are compared to others," Rugrat complained.

"I'm not saying we can't, just that we take our time—we watch the competition, get information on the people we're competing against. Get a plan together before we do anything."

"Makes sense. Feels strange that we're literally picking out where we're going to ascend," Rugrat said.

"Safer, you mean?"

"I guess."

"Let's go and find Elan." Erik sighed.

"You want to go to the Fifth Realm, by yourselves, to find techniques at a competition?"

"He's getting good at this *repeat after me* stuff," Rugrat said.

"Yes. So, is there anything going on? We're not looking to compete and a competition that would have a lot of techniques even of the lowest grade would be a good start," Erik said.

"All right." Elan tapped on his sound transmission device.

After sending a few messages, he cleared his throat. "Okay, it looks like there is a general showcase going on in the city Arman—bunch of different sects showing off their people's skills. It means that there should be all kinds of people there trying to sell high-priced wares. There are a few auctions going on. If you give me two days, I'll be able to get more information on the organizers, get you a guide there and someone to talk you through the totem."

"Can I have a window seat?"

Elan looked at him in confusion and then looked at Erik.

"He's making an Earth joke about a plane, which is a flying beast, usually taken to go somewhere nice."

"With all of that information, it seems more like we're going on a vacation. I guess this is a plus of having a good information-gathering network," Rugrat said.

"Let us know when you have things organized. I'm going to focus on tempering my body. Rugrat, you said that you have a copy of that Mana Gathering Cultivation manual, right?"

Erik and Rugrat talked to each other as they walked out of the room.

Two of the most powerful men I have ever met, and they're not so different from anyone else. Sure, quirky in their own ways, and driven like hellhounds are coming after them, but good, decent people. Utterly insane and weird as hell, though. Elan smiled to himself and started to send out sound transmissions.

Erik and Rugrat headed down underneath the pillar and to the hidden underground city.

There were people from Alva here. With the power of the linked dungeons under Rugrat's control, they had transformed the area into a massive underground cave.

"So what is going on down here?" Erik asked.

"Well, we have the Viewing Hall down here. Then we've got people growing food for the Sky Reaching Restaurants, like the underground cave in the Division Headquarters. We're also building weapon systems down here. Half of the development happens upstairs but the assembly and building will happen down here once we finalize the new weapons and upgrades.

"Then, of course, we've got the resource farm that is happening underneath the Crafting trial dungeon. All of the resources from there are harvested and processed here before being used by our crafters or sold to our traders, who sell it across the realms. This is how we're able to support most of our crafters without needing to bring back resources from Alva. I was thinking of adding in training areas down here for the military—you know, work on their fighting abilities and we don't show others everything that we can do. There are people all looking at the training grounds, looking to understand the strength of our people," Rugrat said.

"It really is another city down here," Erik said.

"That's not all. Since Elan has been getting more information on the cultivation, I set up one of the dungeon cores from the secondary dungeons as a cultivation aid. We don't have to open all of our mana gates before we compress our mana core. It is harder to do afterward but not impossible. People have to pay to use the cultivation chambers but then they can clear out the impure mana within their body, replace it with the denser and pure mana refined by the dungeon core. The impurities grow the dungeon core; the pure mana grows their cultivation. Even if they just refine the pure mana into their mana channels, they'll experience an increase in Strength!" Rugrat said.

"Well, actually I found out something interesting for mana and body cultivators." Erik shared with Rugrat what Old Hei had told him.

"That's cheating!" Rugrat complained.

Erik just shrugged. "With a stronger body and higher mana capacity, it takes a lot more resources to cultivate both."

"Well, we don't have anything to do but wait for the next couple of days." Rugrat pulled out a book and passed it to Erik. "It can't be that hard to get to Body Like Stone, right?" Rugrat pulled out three pills.

Erik let out a light laugh seeing the pills. "It's always easier following in one's footsteps."

"Yes, it is. Now, you'll need to control that half-step mana domain you've got going on. It's as crazy as my Aunt Deborah's hair on a humid day!"

Elan was sitting in his "office." He switched between the Wayside Inns and Sky Reaching Restaurants so that he was never in one place for very long.

There was a knock at the door.

He looked up. The reports around him disappeared into his storage ring with a wave of his hand and he picked up the tea that was on the side.

"Come in," Elan said. The door opened to reveal one of Elan's agents, a woman called Verna Warren. She was one of the people who had joined the Alva military and found that it didn't suit her. She didn't know what to do, so she had gone on to be a trader. Then, as Elan was growing his information network, she became an informant before becoming one of his agents.

Elan had quietly set up a group within the intelligence agency that looked to actively recruit Alvans into the agency.

Only people who were sworn Alvans were allowed to join the agency. Otherwise, they would always just be informants for the Alvan Intelligence Agency. Those who joined were trained in stealth, poison, information gathering, and given the skills, spells, and gear to make them the best at what they did.

With them as the backbone of the AIA, they had expanded rapidly across the realms with different agents like Evernight controlling areas of interest or becoming part of the chain that passed information back and forth.

"Trader Elan, there is a scribe here to see you," she said.

Elan nodded. "Thank you, Verna. Show them in please." Elan took a drink from his cup.

She nodded and waved forward the others.

There were several men and women. Each of them were scribes but, being people of Alva, Elan could see that their cultivation wasn't simple.

Body tempering...a high level of mana gathering—they're good at hiding it. They've done what they can to enhance their sight for those long hours of writing and copying down information. Elan hid a smile.

Alvans and their tempering. Seriously, who would expect a scribe in the Fourth Realm to have tempered his foundation and reached Body Like Stone, or have opened eight of their mana gates?

Verna bowed to Elan and closed the door behind her. Elan activated a formation on the table and moved his jaw to pop his ear with the pressured feeling that came with it.

The scribes all bowed to Elan.

"No need for that," Elan said.

"You might not be part of the council but you watch out for Alva, protecting us. It is only right," the man heading up the group said.

"Just doing a job," Elan said. "And I would like to ask you your help in another task. Please, take a seat."

The four scribes sat opposite him and he pulled out cups and started to fill them, passing them to the others. They accepted the cups with both hands and afterward, Elan filled up his glass.

They drank together and relaxed a bit.

"Vuzgal has grown in scope and size in the last couple of months. I am in need of scribes to copy down information and create reports."

"Conditions?" one of the scribes asked. All Alvans were blunt and to the point; it was somewhat refreshing.

"You will be allowed access to high grade materials and your schooling paid for. You would work for three weeks and get a week off, rotating. You can leave with a two-month long warning. Access to spells and faster writing and scribing techniques."

"Tempering?" another scribe, a man this time, asked.

"Based upon your performance, you will be able to get pills and aids to increase your cultivation. All of you Alvans are cultivation mad."

The others simply smiled.

"Okay, so what does it entail?" Dang asked.

"You would be listening to a source that would relay information to you after their activities or during them. We just need to get them in close to get information while you can write up reports that one can assimilate, like information or technique books. You write and pass them on," Elan said.

"I don't think I am suitable," one of the male scribes said.

"That is no problem," Elan said.

The man bowed and left the room.

"Copy information?" Dang asked as the formation was re-activated and the door locked once more.

"Vuzgal's dungeon has a large area of influence. It extends over the city for the most part. If someone says something inside that area of influence, or they put down a technique book, then the answering statue will relay what the person is saying or can read out the information contained within different books. We have been recording down any information from different Expert or higher level books to add to the libraries.

"There is a lot of information on any given day and the answering statue's speed can be increased so only the fastest scribes can keep up with it, compiling a book in just a few minutes." Elan looked at the stunned faces in front of him.

Erik and Rugrat privately called scribes a printing press. They could use spells and techniques when writing to make them faster than a modern printer on Earth. They could also create magic spell scrolls, technique books, and information books, directly pouring information into one's mind.

Elan wanted to use them for this purpose. If they could write out information books, then the reader could directly assimilate the information into his or her mind, immediately getting up to date on everything that was happening, understanding in minutes what would have taken hours to read.

"Do you know where this answering statue is?"

"No," Dang said.

"Let's head down." Elan stood.

They headed out of the private room and went into the back rooms of the Sky Reaching Restaurant. Verna came with them, protecting and looking out for Elan.

They took a rising rune-covered floor, what Erik and Rugrat called an elevator, all the way to the basement. Then, with special medallions, a wall opened for them. They passed through several more doors before they reached a stone-covered floor. The floor and walls were smooth and sleek, though when stepping on them, one wouldn't slip.

They entered the dungeon proper. They were tens of meters underneath Vuzgal now. The area had changed. The alchemists and farmers had laid down their fields and there were beasts of the Vuzgal army that were being raised and maintained. A second ammunition factory had been created, as well as a complex of firearms and modern weapons facility.

Rugrat's new semi-automatic rifle, underbarrel grenade launcher, rotating grenade launcher, mortars, and formation sockets were all made down here.

Guards patrolled the area. Undead guarded each of the paths from Vuzgal. They were the strongest undead that they controlled, wearing a number of high Journeyman-level gear and being treated by alchemists and smiths to increase their overall strength.

There were very few entrances down to the underground but this complex was the base of Alva's strength in Vuzgal.

They stepped onto a speeding walkway. The runes moved the floor to make it faster to get around. Rugrat had called them airport walkways and played with them like a kid for hours after Julilah made them.

Simple, but effective.

They got closer to the Castle District and walls fell from the ceiling.

Each of the training areas and the Castle District extended their walls all the way down to the bedrock. That way, if someone got into the underground, they could still protect themselves and defend underneath themselves.

They passed the guards watching the gates and headed inward. There was a simple room, with a voice coming from it.

"With Flashing Footsteps, one must drive power through their legs and create light spells underneath their feet and in the direction opposite to the direction of travel. The light underneath their feet will levitate the practitioner; the force from the light blast will push them in the opposite direction. One must learn the spells Light Levitation, Directional Light Lance, Light as a Feather, or similar spells and understand them completely, combining them together into the Flashing Footsteps technique.

"Klaus, head of the Fighter's Association, and Deputy Head Inis—"

A voice was spitting out words at a rate that Elan could barely keep up with. He entered the room, seeing a statue standing there. Four scribes were in front of them—one furiously copying, the three others ready to write at any moment.

"—after all, you're the leader of the Fighter's Association here."

"Then shouldn't I be setting a good example? You know—heading into the dungeons, coming out victorious!"

"I'll see what I can do," the deputy head of the Fighter's Association said.

"Whoa!"

"You'll need to hide your identity if you want to go into the dungeon."

"Grogar the bold!"

"Are you sure you're okay? Did you hit something with your head this morning?"

"You! Hey, I'm the branch head!"

"Like when did that matter?"

Elan stepped back from the room, the sound being cut off, and the group looked at him.

"It is like an information gathering thing, able to pick up on anything that is happening within range of the dungeon. It is very literal, so you need to add in the correct terms to search through that information. If you want to gain information over a long time, then you need to add in priorities.

"We found out that the answering statue works with keywords. We were getting a lot of random conversations from the Expert crafters, so we added in these keywords, so if a tailor talked about a specific tailoring technique, we would record. If they were talking about the Crafting trial dungeon and their activities inside, we wouldn't as that is recorded in the Viewing Hall. We also found that if we gave the command to start from the beginning of the conversation, the answering statue would give us the information someone said in the last ten minutes. Past that, we couldn't get anything."

"What about if someone is using a formation to stop them from being recorded?" Dang asked.

Seems that you are the right person for this job.

"The answering statue doesn't make any noise, it just moves its lips."

Elan thought for a second. "Could it be mimicking what the person is doing?"

"We didn't think of that," Dang said. "If we had some people that were good at lip reading maybe we could figure out what they were saying?"

"I think I have a plan."

Elan explained the system that he wanted Dang to implement and expand on.

The answering statue could speak so fast it tested the speed of the scribes, spilling out information. It could also move its lips according to what someone was saying. With this, a second scribe with good drawing abilities was needed, creating an information book so that one could see what was being said.

"Okay, so we need four scribes in there at all times, then we need a second group to take the information collected and organize it. They will need to piece conversations together, piece the different books together. With the answering statue telling us which book or person the information is from, that will be easier. A group to compile that information and create several copies. Then we have another group going through the lip reading and translating that into conversation. And more people to send out items to the academy, items to the intelligence networks, and what is useful and not useful information," Elan said. The statue was simplistic but they could add in a number of commands and it would carry them out. It was just knowing what kind of orders they had to give in order to unlock its abilities.

"Sounds like a lot of work," Dang said.

"Ah, but then, with that, we can save the work of my agents, only send them out on high-priority tasks and the rest of them are free to work on other things."

"No wonder you're looking to recruit more scribes. I'm in," Dang said.

"Very good!" Elan smiled.

29 To the Earth Floor

"How are they looking?" Glosil asked Yui. Tiger Platoon was working with Dragon Platoon. They had taken over the teleportation pad in Alva and the farmers had worked with the alchemists to grow up an Earth-attribute forest around the pad.

There were different plants that would act violently if disturbed seeded in with them and then they used a section in the forest to simulate attacks by the beasts.

This created the closest simulation to what they might find in the Earth floor.

"I think that they're as good as they can be. I think they're starting to slack off with the training," Yui said honestly.

Glosil nodded.

They couldn't keep their attention all the time and once they had it down, then their minds would start to wander and they would assume that things in the training would remain the same way in reality.

"Incoming teleport!" the manager for the teleportation pad said.

"Clear the pad!" Yui yelled.

They moved out of the way. A few moments later, there were five new figures there: Domonos and some of his people from Dragon Platoon.

Seeing Glosil was there already, he headed straight for him and dismissed his soldiers.

They met with the group that was training as Domonos saluted Glosil.

Glosil saluted back. "How are things in the Fourth Realm?"

"Erik and Rugrat are planning to head to the Fifth Realm. They want to gain technique manuals. I went and saw them in the undercity. Erik told me about techniques and showed me their effects. They're very different from what we do currently," Domonos said. "They're like spells but can combine movements and mana together into attacks. Some can rely on just mana, or just on physical abilities. I recorded down everything Erik told me." Domonos tapped his storage ring.

"How is the training going?"

"The training staff is smaller but they're no less fierce. Seeding the new with the old was a good way to bolster strength. I don't feel like there will be any degradation in their training," Domonos reported.

"Good. We've been training with Dragon and Tiger Platoons. It has taken some time for the new members of the First Army to get used to everything here. I worked with your second-in-command and we reorganized the two platoons, mixed the old and the new in together. We have enough for another two platoons, bringing us up to a full company strength. I want to talk to the two of you about the chain of command for them. For now, I want to operate as two oversized platoons. Changing the chain of command now could only lead to more confusion before the fight."

Domonos and Yui nodded, understanding the sentiment.

"Are we still heading out tomorrow?" Domonos asked.

"That is the plan, unless there is anything that you two have that would make me push back the operation?"

Domonos and Yui shook their heads.

"Tomorrow it is. Make sure they're rested and well fed tonight. They're to remain in the barracks—don't want them getting into trouble the night before," Glosil said.

"Personal visits?" Domonos asked.

"In the cafeteria. Only two drinks per person."

"Understood," Yui said.

Glosil wasn't able to sleep at all that night. As morning came, he pulled on his body armor, pulling it tight and securing the Velcro. He checked the magazines, making sure that they were easy to grab and pull out.

He shifted around, checking the reassuring weight of the armor, before he grabbed gloves that had been made by the tailors to protect his hands and also give him full range of motion. He tilted his head back and put his helmet on, clipping the strap.

He checked the action on his rifle, putting a bit of oil on it before he loaded a magazine into his rifle and chambering a round.

His eyes found the mirror in his room. He looked at himself: the oddly patterned combats, the body armor, the knee pads, helmet, and gloves.

He looked like a dominating figure, as if nothing could stand in his way. But as he found his eyes, he could see the anxiety in them; he could feel the churning in his stomach.

If I fuck up, then people won't be going home to their families.

He didn't even know how to respond to his own thought as he looked for the answer. *I can't promise I'll bring them all home or any of that, because I know it would be a lie, to them and to me. I'll do my job, and I'll do it to the best of my ability.*

"Rugrat and Erik said that there would be times that I wouldn't be able to give myself an answer, times when I would feel the weight of responsibility, the lives that rest on my shoulders." Glosil let out a hollow laugh as he opened and closed his fist but there was no force behind it. He let out a shaky sigh.

"Let's get this done."

He didn't look in the mirror again; he turned and left his living quarters before he could think about hesitating.

He heard them before he saw them. The double-strength platoons were lined up in the parade square, checking on one another's gear and making sure all of their key items were on their person or accessible through their storage ring.

Some sat down, talking to one another; some section leaders briefed their people again.

Others quietly carried out their tasks.

Glosil walked out onto the parade square. Yui and Domonos saw him and met with him.

"Sir!" Yui saluted.

Glosil returned the salute. "Any issues?"

"Nothing much. Fighting nerves. Once we get going, they'll be okay," Yui said.

Domonos nodded with him.

"Move out in ten," Glosil said.

Yui saluted and Domonos came to attention.

Glosil saluted back.

They turned and headed back to their platoons.

"Grab your shit! Helmets on! Weapons ready! Section leaders, make sure all of your people are here and that they have the damn safety on their weapon!" Yui yelled.

"Move it!" Domonos added.

The two platoons quickly assembled, getting into their uniform ranks. The laughter and chitchat died down. Now it was time to go.

They assembled in record time and Glosil looked out at them.

"Let's go take back the Earth floor. Left! Turn!"

The platoons turned as one to the left and Glosil headed to the front.

"By the left! Quick march!"

Glosil led the company toward the barracks and the gates opened for them. The people of Alva waited on either side; they saw the army marching out of their barracks. Row upon row moved in sync, creating a powerful scene as they left the barracks and wove through the city to the teleportation pad. All incoming teleports had been stopped and the farmers had cleared out the forest around the totem.

A first-aid post had been created off the totem. People could be directly teleported back and rushed to the first-aid post to be stabilized and even completely healed. If it was more serious, they could be rushed to the hospital that wasn't far away to recover completely.

Egbert waited there for them, wearing gear that had been found in Vuzgal.

Niemm and Roska were there with their special teams.

"Any issues?" Glosil asked them as they traded salutes.

"Nothing to report. We're all good to go," Roska said.

"Let's do this then."

Glosil signaled to Yui, who sent up three sections.

They all went into the middle of the teleportation pad.

"Ready?" Egbert asked.

"Ready," Glosil said.

Alva disappeared and they appeared on a new teleportation formation.

Egbert cast a cleansing spell. A black wave spread out from him, removing all of the plants from the formation and for one hundred meters past it.

The special teams split and took up position opposite one another. Two of the sections moved into the open areas between the special teams, giving them an all-around defense, twenty meters past the formation.

The last section moved out and pulled out premade defenses from their storage rings.

"Teleportation formation is clear." Glosil knelt behind the defensive line, who were scanning the forest.

The teleportation formation flashed with light again as the remainder of Dragon Platoon appeared.

They quickly spread out as well, doing as they had trained—dropping off items to build a defensive structure around the teleportation formation.

The mages among them fused the different parts together, creating one complete structure.

"Movement!" someone called out and everyone looked over.

"Watch your arcs," Glosil said in a gruff voice.

Everyone looked back to the area in front of them.

"Beasts closing in!" Yui reported.

"Eliminate anything that seems to have hostile intent. *Only* shoot if you can see the target!" Glosil said for the benefit of everyone.

Glosil looked over to where the commotion came from.

A repeater gunner fired, his friend bringing him onto target as the beast was taken down quickly.

Other repeaters started firing at beasts that were moving in.

The teleportation formation flashed again and half of Tiger Platoon appeared. Domonos saw the situation and moved his people out of the teleportation formation quickly, holding them back as a reserve to the north of the formation.

As more of the beasts came, the rate of fire picked up.

Sharpshooters' rifles fired. The noise didn't faze the others anymore as they continued to play their role.

"Egbert, could you clear the east side a bit more?" Glosil said.

Egbert used the black clearing spell; the forest was cleared back and more beasts were revealed.

The sharpshooters, now with a clear shot, increased their rate of fire.

"Looks like they're turning back," Roska said.

A few grenadiers took the opportunity to fire a few grenades into the forest, clearing out trees and killing any nearby animals.

It only sped up their retreat.

"Phase one complete!" Domonos, who was in charge of the defensive building, said.

"Pull back to the defenses!" Glosil yelled.

They pulled back in an orderly fashion, as they had practiced time and time again. There was no relaxed look on their faces anymore; now it was the real thing.

They retreated into the defensive structure that was little more than a protective wall.

"Get us eyes," Glosil told Lucinda.

She worked with the other beast tamers and the few summoners, sending out their companions to search the area and get intelligence on the area.

"Move ahead with phase two," Glosil ordered Domonos.

He nodded and sent messages.

Watchtowers were built with mana barrier formations above them, covering the walls and the teleportation formation.

People moved out of the camp and threw up a second series of defenses. These were much stronger than the first and were laid out according to a defensive formation.

Repeater gunners got up into these watchtowers with the sharpshooters.

There were roars and noises in the distance. It seemed as though the Earth floor, which had recoiled from the new arrival of the First Army, now started to respond.

"Sir! The different regional beasts are all leaving their holes. It seems that they've noticed intruders and are looking to increase their domains!" Lucinda said.

"Ready yourselves!" Glosil barked.

Domonos looked to him.

"Continue with the second phase."

The second wall went up and beasts started to run toward the defenses. The First Army responded. The section leaders took over different sections of the wall, coordinating their fire and making sure nothing came close as they protected those working on the second phase of the defenses.

There was a disturbance in the distance but it was too far for Glosil to see.

"Lucinda?" He turned to the woman coordinating with the scouting forces.

"Two of the regional beasts met one another and they're fighting. They are beasts, after all," she said.

"I forgot that bit," Glosil said. "Is there a way to get more of the beasts fighting one another?"

"I'm not sure. I can ask those with summons to try to lure them toward each other."

"Do it."

Glosil moved to Yui, who was on the wall. "How are they?"

"Good. Now that we're actually fighting instead of waiting, they're reacting well. We might have too many on the defenses. If you could pull four platoons back, we'd have more room to move with, could help with building the defenses of phase two?"

"Pass the order," Glosil said.

Yui sent a sound transmission and the forces on the walls thinned out and Glosil got a reserve force back.

He moved into a watchtower, standing at the back to give the team in there room to operate as he looked over the battlefield.

The second defenses were a series of bunkers. The mages would shift the dirt and premade bunker sections were dropped into place, their design taken from Vuzgal. The bunkers were fused together, creating a large circular defense.

The work largely happened underground, with holes appearing and bunkers being placed down and fused.

The bunkers were laid out in a pentagram instead of a circle like the first phase.

"Egbert, can you help the people with phase two?" Glosil asked.

"I can create all of the trenches easily."

"Okay. I'll have the reserve force get ready and then fill in the trenches with bunkers," Glosil said.

"I'm ready when you need it," Egbert said.

"Domonos, have your people pause on phase two. I'm going to have Egbert clear out the remaining dirt and then have the reserve force move to assist in laying the rest of the bunkers," Glosil said.

"I'll get them to hold off." Domonos's channel went silent for a few minutes as work stopped outside of the first camp. The weapons fire was picking up more. The smaller beasts that were disturbed by the lords of the region were running away from the fight and now running away from the camp. The noise and destruction made them forget about even trying to attack the humans inside.

"We're ready," Domonos said.

"Egbert, do it," Glosil said.

Green lines appeared over the ground, trenches to the bunker system, leading in and out of the main camp so that they were never exposed completely when having to cover between the two.

The green lines solidified and then started to sink quickly, until they were at the right depth and the green lines disappeared.

"Done," Egbert said.

Domonos and all of his people got to work, erecting the second layer of defenses.

They were halfway done when a six-limbed creature came into sight. It looked like it was made of wood. It lifted its log-like head and let out a screeching chittering noise that made everyone flinch.

"Sharpshooters, alter your formation sockets!" Yui ordered.

They used different formation sockets, seeing which ones were the most effective at inflicting damage on the large beast as it sped through the forest, moving forward or sideways erratically.

Three more smaller versions appeared behind it.

"Repeaters!"

"As soon as it gets through the tree line, grenadiers," Yui said. "Everyone, watch your arcs—don't need more sneaking up from another side."

The creature rolled with the hits, but it was badly damaged. As it cleared the tree line, the grenadiers fired almost at the same time.

It was torn apart by the grenades.

The smaller versions were faster. Only one made it to the wall as pincers that lay along its back shot forward and stabbed at the defenders.

The defenders on the wall didn't panic. They attacked with their melee weapons. The beast's softer underside was torn apart and it died on the wall. They tossed it back onto the ground.

More beasts emerged from different sides but they dealt with it.

"Phase two complete," Domonos said.

"Get your people into the fight," Glosil raised his rifle to his shoulder and started firing at the creatures.

"Penetrate formation sockets and fire spells on weapons!" Yui said.

Different groups were using different formation sockets, it allowed the leadership to quickly see what was working and what wasn't.

People changed their formation sockets and the spells they were using. With the new combination, their lethality increased again.

With the added firepower, nothing got within two hundred meters of the camp as they established their dominance and cleared more of the forest through sheer destruction.

"Hold your fire," Glosil said, not knowing how much time had passed. He reloaded his weapon. He was covered in sweat and dirt from the fighting.

The beasts seemed to have enough of the fighting, having tested their strength. Those that survived turned and fled.

"Check wounded and supplies! Leadership on me," Glosil said.

The different commanders checked on their people. Yui, Domonos, Roska, and Niemm met with Glosil.

"Domonos, Yui—set up a watch. I want people in the outer and inner defenses, with some held back in reserve. Roska, Niemm—review the map. In three hours, if nothing happens, you'll move out to scout the area and location for Camp Bravo. Have a plan drawn up in an hour," Glosil said. "The reserve will act as a quick reaction force if needed. Issues? Questions?"

"Can we take Egbert with us? Be good if we need close-in support. With all the plants and trees, we can't use the grenade launchers effectively and we can't see that far," Niemm said.

"Granted." Glosil looked for anything else. "All right, see to it."

They broke apart and started to get to work.

Day one on the Earth floor.

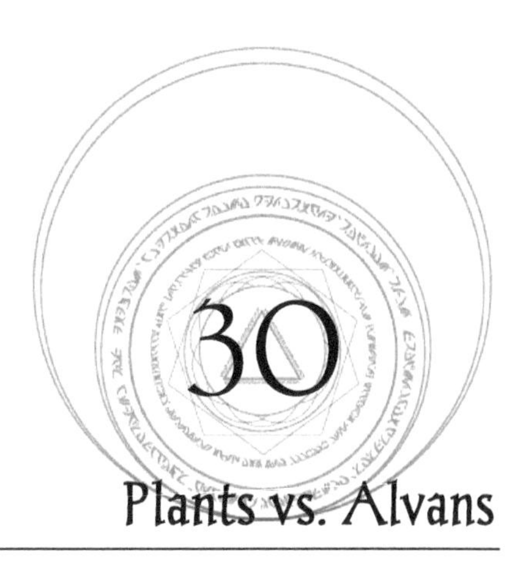

30 Plants vs. Alvans

"Well, at least it's quieter now," Storbon said, as they advanced slowly through the forest.

"Quiet makes me think that there's something hiding out there," Setsuko muttered back.

"Keep focused. We need to scout the location for the second camp. Keep your eyes open," Niemm said.

They continued forward silently, looking for any beasts hiding in the forest.

The farther we go, the greater weight on our bodies. It might be good to train in, but it only slows down our reaction time. The time delay and the extra force required is only slight, but in a fight, overestimating your own abilities can lead to problems.

Deni let out a grunt and jumped to the side as she fired at the ground. The forest seemed to come alive as roots raised up and lashed out at Deni.

"Shit!" Storbon fired his rifle and hit a root. It was torn apart but quickly started to regrow.

Storbon pulled out his spear and attacked.

"It's not a beast—it's a plant!" Deni yelled.

"Shit," Niemm hissed. "Start pulling back!"

They didn't question his orders and started to pull back in fireteams.

Storbon was running back as a vine hanging between trees hardened and shot out.

Storbon jumped to the side and blindly stabbed with his spear. His attack hit and cut the vine, but had failed to sever it.

Damn this high Earth attribute!

The vine started to regrow at a rate visible to the eye.

"Keep moving! Don't waste your time on the plants!" Niemm barked.

Storbon checked on Yawen and they ran again.

"Grenade!" Yawen yelled, tossing out a grenade behind them.

A sea of moving vines covered it quickly as they ran full-out.

The explosion cut the vines apart, leaving their dead lengths decaying.

"Rear man, toss down a grenade or formation plate!"

Storbon saw Yuli toss out a formation plate. A fire wall shot out. The trees let out creaking noises, trying to get away from the flames and cried out in anger. Those that hadn't even attacking before now joined in.

"Fuck!"

Storbon's world consisted of moving forward, checking on Yawen, and making sure everyone else kept up while tossing grenades and formation plates into the path of the plants' vines and roots.

Several vines came for him but he swept most back with his spear and used a Flame Burst spell, killing others to his rear.

The vines hit him in the chest. He used the momentum to be pushed back in the direction of the camp.

"Our strength increases the farther we go!" Tian Cui said.

"The plants are weaker with the reduced Earth attribute," Yuli added.

Storbon continued to cut his way through the forest and the limbs got weaker. There were more of them as there were more younger plants standing together.

"Egbert, we need some of that close-in support!" Niemm said.

Storbon heard rushing water and he ducked under a branch that shot forward. He stepped forward as another plant opened its flowers with a puff of smoke.

Storbon closed his mouth and held his breath. He shot forward, hoping he didn't inhale much as he made to pull out an antidote from his storage ring.

Several vines shot out at him.

Storbon distanced himself. His spear shot out, piercing the vines and using their own momentum against them before he slashed off the wounded vines. "Yawen!" he barked.

"I'm good!"

Storbon didn't even have time to look to his side as a small creature—blended in with the moss it was lying on—jumped forward, spitting acid.

Storbon sidestepped. The acid fell on his armor and he saw spiked vines whipping toward him, hoping to use the opening the beast had created.

Storbon smacked the beast with the butt of his spear. It turned into a moss cannonball, striking the spikes. The force pushed them back and the beast let out a squeal as it dissolved into the plant. The vine got larger as it absorbed its Earth mana like a tonic.

Yawen's sword sprouted flames as he cut the vine down. It dropped to the ground, writhing around.

"Move!" Niemm yelled.

Storbon kept running.

They were being attacked from every angle. The entire forest seemed to be working together to try to kill them.

The rushing water got closer until Storbon saw trees being torn apart in the distance.

"Cover your eyes!" Egbert's voice rang through the floor.

Storbon ducked, seeing water that had been formed into spinning blades cutting through the forest, carving a path through it.

His body went cold as one of the blades passed him by centimeters. He could feel the cold water vapor from the blade slamming into a tree, splitting it apart. More blades followed, the forces destroying any sign of the tree.

"Move!" Egbert said as the blades continued going. There were more blades behind but they were running down the sides of where the first blades had cleared a path.

Storbon looked at where the different members of the team were. They all started running and Storbon took up the rear to make sure that no one fell behind.

"Keep an eye out for any more attacks!" Niemm yelled as the spell started to fade.

Storbon looked behind him. "Damn. The forest is starting to regrow!" Storbon yelled.

The roots of the trees were starting to move through the soil. The trees moved into these new open areas to draw in more of the Earth-attribute mana, growing quickly. The path started to fade behind them, reclaimed by the forest.

The trees and plants started to move to claim the best spots.

Deni fired with a grenade launcher, tearing the plants apart and keeping their path clear.

They finally burst out of the forest and into the open area around the camp. They slowed down as they made it through the gate.

"Fucking killer forest," Lucinda said, trying to control her breathing.

Glosil marched over to them. "What happened?"

"The forest attacked us—the trees, the plants, a few small beasts all tried to kill us. The entire thing is one massive trap," Niemm said.

"Shit. All right, debriefing in ten," Glosil said.

"Sir." Niemm nodded.

Glosil looked at them all, checking that they were okay before he headed to the wall in the direction that they had come from.

Delilah sat in the Sky Reaching Restaurant, drinking tea as she read the latest request from Glosil.

"He wants to have the alchemists make a poison to kill the plants and the authority to do so?" she asked Fehim, who sat opposite.

"Yes. After further study, it looks like the beasts of the Earth floor are not the ones in power but the plants," Fehim said.

"What do you think about this?"

Fehim frowned and pressed his lips together. "If we use a poison on the plants right now, then they will allow the army to move forward. But afterward, we don't know how it will affect the plants that we want to put down."

"Do you have another option?"

"I was thinking explosives, but the amount needed would be massive. Though, fire is highly effective against Earth-attribute life-forms. Also, once fire defeats Earth life-forms, the Earth attribute only becomes stronger. Think of forest fires. Once a forest is destroyed, then the plants grow back even faster."

"So we need to start a fire?"

"We need to start a fire through the entire floor and make it spread rapidly, so I thought of explosives again and wondered if there was a way to make a concoction that is flammable rather than explosive and that will set fire to a large area. I talked to Matt. He said that there was a concoction called napalm, or a device called a fuel air bomb that used fire to clear a large area. He agreed with me—said that if a poison was used, there was no knowing what the effects might be on the land, on the plants and people if they consumed them. Said that there was a military that used chemicals; it was effective in war, but then the people in the area are still paying the price," Fehim said.

"Were you able to develop any of this napalm or fuel air bomb?"

"I haven't yet. I wanted to bring this to your attention as soon as possible," Fehim said.

"Create the poison as well as the fire concoctions. If you complete the fire devices within seven days, then we will use them. If not, then we will go with the poison," Delilah said. "We can't keep the First Army stuck in the Earth floor for too long. They have other duties."

"Understood." Fehim nodded.

"I'll motivate the alchemists here as well and see if they can create the concoction." Delilah stood. "It's good to see you, Fehim." She smiled.

"I wish it was for a better reason." Fehim stood and let out a dry laugh.

"Alva demands a lot from all of us," Delilah said.

Delilah walked up to the mission counter within the Division Headquarters. She presented her talisman that had been given to her by Old Hei. She had been given the temporary rank of probationary Journeyman alchemist. She was just waiting for an internal test within the Alchemist Association to get an official medallion from the association.

It wasn't enough to accept missions, but she could still create them.

"I wish to put up a mission, for a concoction formula. The concoction should be a liquid or a powder and it must be highly flammable, without being consumed too quickly. Is that possible?"

"That should be enough information." The woman at the counter smiled. "The reward?"

"Thirty Mortal mana stones, due within seven days."

The woman at the counter nearly choked as she looked at the medallion on Delilah's chest again. "Very well." She noted down the details and made a new posting.

31
Adventurer's Guild Bares its Fangs

Blaze was looking at his reports, checking the new contracts that were coming up. There were always some complaints from a trader who had had a perfectly safe trip but because the Alva adventurers hadn't begged and scraped, he reported them to Blaze. He swiftly tossed their messages in a separate bin. Their information would be collected and the association would never do work with them again.

He heard a commotion downstairs and then pounding on the stairs.

Blaze sat back in his chair as he grabbed the axe underneath his desk and ran his fingers over the button that would activate the formation that had been built into the room.

The door was opened by one of the Elites.

"Dammit, Din! I about near threw my axe at you. What's up?" Blaze asked.

"A group was taking a convoy from the Third Realm to the Second. They completed the job and were coming back when they were attacked. There are only four survivors," Din said, pulling off her scarf.

"Who hit them?" Blaze asked, his eyes focusing as he set his jaw.

"Looks like some group from the Willful Institute," Din said.

"That sect has been playing on my nerves time and time again." Blaze had heard the stories from Erik and Rugrat on their actions before. He didn't think that he would have to deal with them but in passing while he was running the association.

"They say enemies walk down a thin road together."

Blaze stood and looked out of the window that looked down on the training area. With their funds, they had been able to set up a headquarters in a regional headquarters in the Third Realm. They trained people from across the Mortal realms, with people hiring them out as guards, known as a status symbol to the Elites and deadly fighters to all others.

"What will we do?" Din asked, unable to remain silent.

"We send them a message asking them to look after this issue, then we see what they do."

"What about higher?" Din asked.

Blaze frowned. Din had been one of the few people who had gone to the true Alva to train. She had found a home there and acted as an agent of Alva and one of Blaze's direct subordinates within the association. There were more people heading to Alva to train every month. When they came back, they were changed; their strength in skills, cultivation, and combat standards were leaps and bounds stronger.

"I will inform them of the matter. There is no need to involve them at this time," Blaze said.

"What if the Willful Institute doesn't give a satisfactory answer?" Din ventured.

The air around Blaze seemed to congeal. He might be the leader of the Alva Adventurer's Guild but his strength had only increased. He continued to go for meetings in Alva, training there for a few days and spending all the coin he had on Body and Mana Gathering Cultivation aids. He had been able to open his twelfth mana gate and reached Body Like Stone.

"Then we inform higher," Blaze said.

"Who do they think they are? Demanding that we repay them for what? Dying? They killed twenty-four of our students as well!" one of the Willful

Institute elders yelled, slamming his hand against the table.

"I agree with Elder Tsi. This is not the first time that we have run into these troubles. Why do we need to lower our heads to some association? Are our students not people that have been accepted into sects of the Sky realm? They should be pleased that we aren't seeking retribution for the ones that they killed," Elder Dean said with a deep look around the hall.

"The ones who survived—I have heard that they made breakthroughs in their cultivation?" the elder head asked.

"Yes, Elder. That is correct," Elder Tsi said.

"Well, it looks like whatever they had was valuable. They attacked in the Second Realm, not the Third. The Alchemist Association won't care. There was no traders with them nor were they under anyone's protection, so it is only the Alva Adventurer's Guild we need to worry about." The elder head let out a snort and stood.

"Since they have asked for us to repay them, it looks like they want money. Tell them that if they want to continue to do business in the cities under our control, then they best remember their position. Those who carried out the ambush, see that they go to the Fourth Realm if they are able to. There is a new war brewing and the more bodies we can send the better. Tell this Adventurer's Guild that this was done because of them. Make sure that they know their position and threaten that these people will come back from the higher realms to deal with them if we ask."

The elder head walked out of the room, shaking his head. "If another one of you brings up a matter like this before me again, I'll have you stuck in meditation for a month to reflect on wasting others' time!"

32 To the Fifth!

Rugrat and Erik were underneath the pillar again. Rugrat was lying down, a grimace on his face. Erik had purchased tempering pills for him from the Division Headquarters and made those that weren't available for sale.

It was uncomfortable, but it was made to temper Rugrat's body without putting him in danger. Erik using poison to temper his body was much more painful and stressful. If he didn't have enough healing concoctions, or if he couldn't cast a healing spell, he could have died. These pills took care of breaking down Rugrat's body and rebuilding it.

Erik was on the other side of the room, located next to the formation that brought in all of the mana filled with all kinds of impurities.

Erik had read the manual on increasing the size of his mana core and reviewed it once again.

"Draw in mana through your mana gates; circulate and compress them before guiding them through your mana veins, compressing them from vapor, to mist to drops that when combined together will create your mana core," Erik let out a breath and shook his head, trying to relax and get comfortable.

He closed his eyes and started to concentrate, focusing on his mana system. With a thought, the mana resting in his mana veins was stirred up. It started to compress and flow toward his dantian. He compressed it as it went, combining the mana together.

Sweat started to appear on his head as he concentrated on keeping drops together, the energy held within his mana veins, within those few drops.

Erik smiled, thrilled by the challenge, by the power he felt within his body.

"Come on!" He pushed forward. The mana around him was stirred up, following the circulation path he had created.

It's like negative air pressure or when you siphon liquid from one tank to another—because I've pulled mana through here, it is pulling more mana through my mana gates and along my circulation path.

Erik focused his mind again and he continued to circle his mana drops and the small feeding streams of mana through his dantian. He used the liquid mana creating threads like yarn with them and he looped them around one of his mana drops and the three combined drops, he increased the power of the mana yarn exerting his own control over the drops as he forced them closer.

Sweat started to appear on his brow from the strain, it was harder each time to combine the drops.

Erik circulated the mana within his body, compressing through his mana veins, which was doing part of the work for him. Streams of mana could be seen entering his body.

It took all of his concentration to make sure that all of the mana was utilized, to make sure that it didn't become stagnant making him run out of mana.

It's like I'm manually having to control my entire circulatory system.

Erik continued for nearly two hours, finally the drop met up with the three combined drops.

There was a rush of mana through his body as more mana was drawn in, as the four mana drops were fused together, the fifth and final mana drop retreated as far as it could from the four combined drops. Erik felt a wave of fatigue rush over him, he released his control over his mana system and laid back. Holding his head, he let out a groan.

"Damn, that was about as fun as holding a damn plank for ten hours," Erik complained.

"Nrrghhff!" Rugrat grunted in the corner, staring at Erik.

"Oh, what are you complaining about? I did that already!" Erik said but he rolled over and went to Rugrat, checking that everything was okay.

"See, you're fine, ya big wuss." Erik turned his sight back to his mana veins and his mana core. The mana in his veins had calmed down but his mana core was darker, filled with impurities.

Erik paid attention to his mana core and felt the Fire-attribute mana slowly leaving his mana core and entering his body, tempering it.

He let out a cough as he compared how big his mana core was from before to how big it was now. It had barely increased in size and was actually reducing in size as the Fire-attribute energy entered his body.

It purifies my mana and makes my core denser. But losing even a little bit, even if it is for a good reason, hurts. I'll need to take some time to allow my four drops to stabilize and then attempt to combine my last mana drop, going to take a lot of power.

"It's not a battle—it's a war." Erik pulled out a pill bottle that contained the stronger version of the tempering pills. He held the bottle up and tapped one pill out. It rolled in his hand, looking like a small gumball.

Erik moved to a formation plate embedded in the floor and pulled out several pieces of paper.

"Okay, so if I turn this there and then put down this formation plate and then these flags around where I'm sitting, it should isolate the Earth-attribute mana." Erik read the instructions that Julilah had created and checked the formation plate that she had made.

He put it down and then set out formation flags in a circle. Then he moved to the main mana circle and turned a circular formation.

The mana had been collected and then shot down into the ground to the dungeon core hidden underneath. Now all but the Earth mana was being sent down into the dungeon core to be refined.

It was as though he had diverted a waterfall. When looking at the water falling, one might think that it wasn't that much water. But a jet of Earth-attribute mana *slammed* into the formation that he had laid down. It glowed brown as the Earth mana rapidly spread out like a geyser. It shot out everywhere before it reached the formation flags, where it stopped, like hitting an invisible wall, and started growing in density quickly. The air above the formation flags looked like a dust plume.

Erik looked at it, a bit alarmed, and then looked over to the restrained Rugrat, who was sweating and in clear pain, but he was looking at the formation and Erik.

Erik gave an awkward smile, having second thoughts about stepping into the formation.

Well, I can't bow out now—Rugrat wouldn't let it go. He's tempering his body and I already made fun of him.

Gritting his teeth, Erik stepped forward and stepped into the Earth-attribute formation before he could think about it too much.

The Earth-attribute mana started to enter his mana channels.

Erik sat down and pulled out an IV. He hooked himself up before pulling out the pill. The Earth-attribute mana rushed toward the pill, drawn in by it.

"Damn." Erik cast Hallowed Ground, increasing its strength, taking nearly all of his mana pool to do so.

Erik threw the pill back and swallowed it before he laid down.

His body started to break down and he couldn't even scream. Before, his body had been broken down; now it was as if it were crushed completely. The Earth attribute all around him was drawn into his body and he healed up, breaking it down further and further—his body, the healing solution in his veins, and his Hallowed Ground rushing to heal him up.

Erik felt the pill wearing off and he took another.

I need to make a breakthrough. If I'm not able to, then it will only be harder next time. Bottlenecks are like elastic bands: it's easier to break them in one shot, instead of stretching them constantly and then hoping it will break one time.

Erik's body cracked and broke again, but it was getting stronger each time. More of the Earth-attribute mana around him was drawn in, increasing the effects of the pills.

Erik's body was covered in blood. His skin cracked; his bones broke and rebuilt; his organs had shifted and every other breath brought blood up with it.

He had nearly passed out several times, but the aids he had laid down before kept him awake and functioning, keeping him alive when most would have died. If he gave in and passed out then he would've died.

Erik threw the second-to-last tempering pill into his mouth, scared that he would run out of pills.

Erik looked like hell as he fought the pain, repairing himself.

The pain started to fade as his healing aids helped him to recover.

Erik felt relief wash over him and his eyes rolled back. It didn't take long for him to recover.

"How do you feel?" Rugrat had finished his own tempering some time ago. Instead of moving on with his remaining temperings, he had stood watch to help Erik if he needed it.

Erik opened his notifications to see nothing.

It looks as if my foundation is stronger than I thought. If I want to temper my body more with the Earth element, I'll need stronger resources. If I could just heal it all away and grind out my temperings…

"It's been a long time since I healed anyone," Erik said to himself as he looked at his healing skill. After the initial race-like increases in his skills, the much slower level gain was a pain.

"There's nothing stopping us from building a few hospitals in Vuzgal. Even if they come through the totem, we should more than earn back the cost of running the place in sheer taxes." Erik gave it some more thought.

"It would be best if we didn't call it the Alva Healing House. The healing house in the First Realm has already created enough troubles. If we just say that they're Vuzgal healers, part of the crafters, that should deal with any issues."

Erik sent a sound transmission to Hiao Xen, leaving him a message before he settled down, feeling tired from everything.

And hungry, *really* hungry.

He pulled out food from his storage ring and started eating. He kept on stuffing food in his face.

"Damn, I'm so hungry! I hope I'm not hungry like this all the time or I'll spend all my mana stones on food!"

After eating for two hours, Erik pulled out a sleeping bag and rolled over.

"Tomorrow I'll increase my Mana Gathering Cultivation," he promised, closing his eyes and passing out in seconds.

Erik woke up the next day feeling relaxed.

He got up and saw Rugrat asleep off to the side.

With a few movements, Erik distanced himself and started to go through the new training regimen that Khasar had helped him create. He flowed from one position to the next, using his movement ability combined with his One Finger Beats Fist technique.

Khasar had shown him his own fighting techniques, and impressed on Erik that using someone else's fighting techniques would improve one's strength, but it would be limited. Your own created techniques were much stronger.

Techniques are not just a new way to punch or kick, they are a new way to combine your different movements and your knowledge into powerful strikes.

Khasar didn't teach Erik his techniques, instead he pushed Erik to fight him with his own ability, to push his body to the limit and see how he reacted.

He settled down after some time of training, with a better understanding of his body.

"Now just need to temper my body with Metal and I can reach the Divine Iron stage. With every stage, it becomes harder. With the Earth attribute tempering to reach Body Like Sky Iron, I tempered myself in small bursts. It increased my overall strength, but it was only a small amount compared to when I made an actual breakthrough. As I go, it will require me tempering my body multiple times before I can make it all the way."

Erik felt tired from the temperings, from the cultivation, but he knew that it would pay off with time.

He changed the settings on the formation that he had set up and then moved the circle on the main mana gathering formation. The air within the formation flags mixed together into a soup of colors, becoming a deep blue in color.

Erik took a step into it, feeling the density of mana nearly double.

All of the mana collected from across the city was being directed into this formation.

He sat down, crossing his legs.

Once again he pulled on the mana within his body, circulating it and drawing it into his mana core.

Erik flopped down sometime later, and he checked his watch. "Fifteen minutes. I increased and it's easier to control, a little." Erik took five minutes and then started to draw more mana into his body again.

He continued to do so until he heard movements from outside the formation. He looked out to see Rugrat setting up his own formation plate and his formation flags.

"Did you finish tempering your body?" Erik asked.

"Body Like Stone, baby." Rugrat grinned, before it turned into a frown. "Fricking sucked to do, though. Mana Gathering Cultivation is much nicer."

"Yeah, but the two of them working together—"

"Make them both harder, but yeah, it does increase your power," Rugrat said.

"How is your mana core?"

"I'm about to breakthrough to Mist Mana Core stage soon though!" Rugrat activated his formation and the area within the formation flags he had laid out filled with mana.

Hearing that, Erik was invigorated again. He was two stages ahead of Rugrat with the body temperings but he was still severely lacking in Mana Gathering Cultivation. His mana domain was only a quarter of Rugrat's. Erik had the same number of open mana gates, but as Rugrat had been increasing the Mana Regeneration and the size of his mana pool their entire time, his Mana Gathering Cultivation was leaps and bounds ahead of Erik's.

Rugrat turned to ask Erik a question, but the latter was already sitting up in his formation, drawing in mana from around him, trying to increase the size of his mana core.

"Good luck!" Rugrat jumped into his formation and started to compress mana into his mana core. The two of them waged a silent cultivation battle.

Erik and Rugrat got a sound transmission at the same time from Elan.

"I have been able to find you a guide to the city Arman. He will arrive in two hours."

"How many mana stones do you have?" Erik asked Rugrat.

"I don't know—a few dozen Earth grade and then a few hundred Mortal. I left most of them with the treasury," Rugrat said.

Erik looked in his storage rings. Everything he had amounted to five Earth stones and a handful of Mortal stones.

"We should collect as many as possible so that we have enough to compete in the auctions." Panic rose in Erik's chest. The funds of the bank were lent out most of the time, with them only holding a reserve on hand for the simplest of transactions.

Erik's eyes moved to the mana stones that were growing along the walls. "You contact the bank. I'll contact Hiao Xen."

Rugrat grunted as they left their cultivation areas. Erik put the mana gathering formation back to the way it had been. The mana in the formation flags was sucked into the mana gathering formation and sent down to the Vuzgal dungeon core.

Erik's sound transmission reached Hiao Xen.

"Erik, what can I do for you?" Hiao Xen asked.

"How many mana stones do we have extra that I could get?" Erik asked.

"Well, we don't keep much in the way of reserves. The mana stones are used to pay the people of Vuzgal, from military to admin, to the crafting school and building operations. Though the Battle Arena will have probably accrued funds at this time and I believe that Elise owes us a large amount in taxes," Hiao Xen said.

"Ah, thank you!" Erik said. He cut the sound transmission and sent one to Elise.

"Erik? Sorry, I'm doing a deal right now," she said.

"Taxes—have you paid them?"

"I…well, it was included in the price of the formation."

"Do you know where those mana stones go?" Erik asked.

"Straight to the treasury, I believe. Why?"

"No worries. Talk later!" Erik looked over to Rugrat.

"They have about fifty Earth stones that they can spare," Rugrat said.

"Crap. One more place." Erik sent a sound transmission to Chonglu.

"Chong—Chonglu, how has the Battle Arena been doing?"

"Mister West, it is so good to hear from you! The response has been incredible! We have sold out the ten thousand membership cards out already and we have thirty thousand applicants to fight in the Battle Arena. There are some people coming over from other cities just to fight!"

"Did you collect their fees?" Erik asked.

"First and last month up front, with the people entering the tournament paying an entrance fee," Chonglu said.

"Good! Have you sent it to the treasury yet?"

"Not yet. I was supposed to send it all over at the end of the month. The betting has already been fierce. We've made some good profit on that and the material goods and training items. The Fighter's Association came and saw me. They will be getting a membership package for one hundred memberships."

"Wow, okay, that's impressive," Erik said. *This Battle Arena is a real money-making machine!* "I'll be over soon to get the funds from you."

"Understood. I'll prepare them."

Erik looked to Rugrat.

"I just talked to the Blue Lotus. They were able to sell my items, so we have another few dozen Earth mana stones waiting for me there," Rugrat said.

"Well, I haven't collected my mana stones from them, and I already used the mana stones from the Alchemist Association from them making the Age Rejuvenation concoctions. With the Battle Arena money, we should have quite a few Earth-grade mana stones."

"Do you think that it will be enough?" Rugrat asked.

"I'm not sure, but where can we get more from?" Erik asked.

Rugrat pulled out a pickaxe and put it on his shoulder. "We're in a mana stone mine, and with how rare these things are, we need to get as many as possible."

"But the mana barrier," Erik said.

"We get the people in the undercity to take mana stones from the other dungeons and bring them here," Rugrat said.

Erik felt conflicted about it before he nodded. "All right."

"Okay! I've always wanted to mine for mana stones!"

"Use your mana blade. If you break them off all irregular, then we could get short-changed!" Erik said.

"Fine!" Rugrat sighed and created a mana blade in his hand.

Erik headed up into Vuzgal, sending a mental message to Gilly. Gilly, who had been roaming the Castle District, made her way over.

Erik jumped on her back and patted her neck as she took off, running through the streets and toward the Battle Arena.

The space around the Battle Arena was now as busy as the crafting districts. There were stalls everywhere, with people selling food and drink and people talked about the matches that they had seen or about their training.

There were people looking for sparring partners in a square outside the Battle Arena.

"Looking for a Journeyman-level archer to train, offering five hours in a C-grade training room!"

"Selling Stamina recovery potions and pills!"

"Want to make most of your training time? We have cultivation aids of all kinds!"

"Looking for fighting partners? Trust Vuzgal's premium sparring partner matching service!"

Erik passed them all and dismounted Gilly. They walked into the actual arena. It was packed with people at the different counters trying to join in on the new fights that were coming up.

Others browsed the goods within the arena. Only members and contestants were allowed to buy from the arena. The goods were of high quality and good prices so it drew a lot of attention. People who were training could have these items delivered to their rooms so they didn't need to waste any time.

"I am sorry but we have sold out of memberships!" someone yelled at the counter as a sign was put up.

"Sold out of memberships! How can this be?"

"We want to provide the best service to our members, so selling more memberships would only decrease the quality of the service. We are sorry!" the person said.

"Quality over quantity." Someone who had just bought a membership nodded.

"I was scared thinking that they might chase the gold instead of keeping their standards," another member said.

"I wonder how much we could get for lending out our membership," another said.

"Didn't you read the agreements? Only we can use our memberships unless we got them in some group deal," another said.

"How will they know?" the first shot back.

"You can try it, but don't come crying to me if it doesn't work!"

The ticket and betting counters didn't decrease in size at all, with people heading up to see the fights and putting their money on their chosen fighters.

Erik walked up to one of the guards. After the fiasco at the totem, Hiao Xen made sure that everyone in Vuzgal knew what Erik and Rugrat looked like.

The guard put his fist to his chest and bowed in greeting. "City Lord!"

"I'm here to see Chonglu. Could you take me to him?" Erik asked.

"This way." The guard guided Erik through doors into a VIP area and past others who were waiting, right to the elevator.

Erik stored Gilly away in her crate.

The guards all saluted and bowed to Erik as he stepped into the elevator.

As they rose up, Erik could see the arenas.

"Looks like the qualifiers have already started," Erik said as he saw the one hundred arenas filled with people sparring one another and putting on shows.

People were cheering and getting into the spirit as bets were being placed down on every fight.

There was a mage and a ranger going up against each other. The mage erected a frost barrier in front of themselves and they threw out sand golems that chased the ranger, who was dodging and rolling across the arena, firing their bow at the mage's barrier. It shook and broke in places, forcing the mage to concentrate on just his two initial attacks.

The ranger got to the mage's side and shot out an arrow.

The mage's worn-down mana wasn't enough to stop the arrow and it hit a barrier that appeared around them. The match ended, the referee stepping out as the mage dismissed their mana constructs.

They moved to the second floor. A few arenas had been blocked off with isolation formations as the people inside didn't want to reveal their fights to anyone. The fights that Erik could see were on a different level from those below. There were people running classes here and members who were testing out their newfound strength with one another.

Two people shot across the floor, sword and saber clashing with one another. The fighters—one man and one woman—smiled as they pushed back and forth. Their movements churned up the air and the ground shook with their attacks.

They must be in the high level forties to create that kind of disturbance in the arenas. Maybe we should look into beefing up the arena's strength again so it can deal with their power. With the new training floor that is being built, we could even entice Masters who are in the fifties.

The remaining two floors were clear, with no one allowed into them yet. The builders were still working diligently to complete them as quickly as possible.

Erik arrived in Chonglu's office.

"City Lord West," Chonglu said.

"Erik will do fine with me. Thank you for guiding me," Erik said to the guard.

They saluted and bowed, taking the elevator down, leaving Erik and Chonglu alone.

"Have there been any problems?" Erik asked.

"We haven't had any so far. With the Fighter's Association backing us and my own connection to them, I think that things should be relatively stable," Chonglu said with a smile, indicating to a chair.

"Good. Are you and the children settling in well?" Erik asked, as they moved to the chairs looking over Vuzgal.

"They're doing well with their classes. Felicity has become interested in woodworking. Feng still wants to fight, but all young boys want to be like the valiant heroes. I think that access to the Battle Arena's stands will only make that desire stronger." Chonglu laughed.

Erik smiled and nodded. "While I was working with the Alchemist Association, I came across a pill that I believe will be able to increase the strength of their bloodline. I'm not sure if it will work for your wife as well because I haven't examined her. It is a low Journeyman-level pill and it is called Winter's Rage. It is a berserk type of pill to increase one's strength in an emergency setting. It uses a combination of fire and ice type mana to increase one's power, with Felicity and Feng having their Ice Phoenix constitution it will have a different effect and should increase the power of their constitution. Your wife only has the Ice Empress constitution so the fire mana would hurt more than help her. Remember that they will need to temper themselves with ice and fire, the more the better."

Chonglu's eyes lit up as he stood and clasped his fists. "Thank you, City Lord West. We have brought you nothing but trouble but you have saved my children and myself, and given me this position. If you command it, my life is yours," Chonglu said solemnly.

Erik coughed awkwardly. "Please, sit down. I only did what I thought was right. We needed a manager here and you were a good choice for the position."

Chonglu let out a light laugh and moved to his chair.

"Have you been training as well?" Erik asked.

"I have been working with the training staff in the combat training rooms," Chonglu said.

"How are they?"

"They would be S-grade training rooms here at the Battle Arena. If not for having people rotate in and out, I think that most would still be down there. The focus one is able to achieve is unparalleled."

"Good." Erik nodded.

We've got the mana to burn. On the outside, we have them train in our weakest rooms and use their impure mana. The wasted mana turns into power for the formations and the dungeon core to consume, with the purest mana being channeled into the Vuzgal forces, from the academy to the military and the Alva residents. We can't give visitors all the benefits and not claim our own.

"I collected all of the available mana stones. I have the stones that I was going to use to pay back the bank for the startup funds."

"Best to return those to the bank and allow them back into circulation so that the Battle Arena can stand on its own two feet and turn into a new revenue source for the city," Erik said. "How many mana stones were you able to collect?"

"I was able to get one Sky mana stone and four hundred and seventy-three Earth mana stones and forty-nine Mortal mana stones."

Erik had a hard time containing his surprise. He had left Vuzgal and the different parts of Alva and their businesses to operate on their own. Most of the funds were liquid, moving from the businesses into the bank to be turned into loans and investments, keeping the money moving and growing the economic power of Alva.

I knew that we were making some money, but damn!

"Impressive," Erik managed to choke out.

Chonglu seemed a little daunted by the amount of money represented. "I have them secured away." He moved to his desk.

Erik stood and followed him.

Chonglu deactivated a number of formations, having to use his own blood and then Erik needed to use his talisman as well. The safe was made so that funds could only go in and not be brought out unless Chonglu, Hiao Xen, and the Vuzgal treasury director were there to do so. Otherwise it would require Erik or Rugrat to withdraw the funds.

There was a box inside. Erik looked inside. He could feel the powerful mana coming off a tower of mana stones piled on top of one another. There was no single Sky-level mana stone, but it was just the value of all the Earth and Mortal mana stones equaled one Sky-level mana stone.

Erik had a bracelet storage item and put the mana stones in there, adding them to the piles of other mana stones. The bracelet let him know just how many stones he had, creating organized stacks of them.

"Okay, keep up the good work. I'll see you later," Erik said.

Chonglu saw him out to the elevator and Erik descended.

He felt as though everyone was already conspiring to take his wealth from him.

He reached the bottom floor and called Gilly out again. They left the Battle Arena; he jumped on her back and took off toward the Associations' Circle.

He wore a doupeng to hide his identity.

Soon, his next destination appeared.

He dismounted in front of the Blue Lotus location. He felt mixed emotions looking at the building as he stored Gilly away. He had heard about the stunts that their Expert had tried pulling, how their leader had disrespected Hiao Xen.

They really put Hiao Xen in a bad position. Rugrat did the right thing, being ruthless with those who are ruthless.

Erik didn't hide how he was displeased as he walked into the Blue Lotus. The guards bowed to him but Erik didn't look at them, feeling cold to it all.

The air around him seemed to become cooler and the mana moved like a snake moving through grass—slow and condensed, as if ready to strike out at any moment.

People distanced themselves from him as he walked up to the VIP counter.

He put down his token. "Hurry up," Erik said.

The man at the desk gave a weak smile as he quickly took the token and checked it. "The branch head—"

"Too busy, hurry up," Erik said, not willing to see the replacement Blue Lotus head. He just saw the Blue Lotus as a cash cow, a professional relationship, with his only close ties being Hiao Xen.

"I don't think—" the man started.

Erik tilted his head and the mana twisted around him. He tapped his finger on the counter.

The man swallowed as his face paled. "I can take you to a private room and bring the items there?"

"Good," Erik said.

The man came around the counter and took Erik to a luxurious room.

Someone entered with tea but Erik waved them off.

The man quickly returned with an official-looking man.

Erik took the storage item the man was holding, dumping it out and then storing the contents in his bracelet.

"City Lord—"

"Good day." Erik turned and left the official and the man from the counter with sour expressions.

He left the Blue Lotus and walked across the road to the Alchemist Association. He felt the darkness from the Blue Lotus fade away as he saw the guards there.

He nodded to them in greeting as he walked in.

The Alchemist Association was filled with people wearing Alchemy badges. Erik's face relaxed and he smiled at the younger alchemist students walking around, talking to one another.

"I heard from my teacher that the ingredients grown in the Vuzgal gardens are up to twenty percent stronger than those grown elsewhere in the Fourth Realm!" an Apprentice alchemist said.

"We really lucked out. One can only find these growing conditions in the Sixth Realm!" a low Journeyman alchemist said.

"With the higher potency, my concoctions have become stronger," another low Journeyman alchemist bragged.

"Well, that's because you suck at concocting. Stop wasting such precious ingredients and give them to me!" the Apprentice alchemist complained.

"Become a Journeyman alchemist and you can get the same treatment as me!"

"Bah! So unfair!"

"Look, didn't we become Journeyman alchemists after coming here? It's not too hard!"

The Apprentice alchemist friend muttered dark words under her breath as the other two laughed.

Erik went to the counter and presented a token.

"The Alchemist Association head would like to invite you for tea if you have the time," the man at the counter said with a smile.

Erik thought about it for a moment before he nodded.

"Please follow me." The man came around and led Erik away.

The people in the Alchemist Association are arrogant, but they are all alchemists. Even with their infighting, they band together. The people from the Blue Lotus are no different, but they are all traders or people from different crafts, which creates more rifts and issues. Alva is made from a large mixture of people as well. We try to foster working together, which makes everyone stronger. Though there have been rifts and drama in different departments and among different people in Alva.

Erik let out a tired sigh. He wanted Alva to succeed so badly. Although he and Rugrat could guide it, it was too big for them to change individual parts.

Like what happened with the bandits. As times go on, we'll need to change our plans to make Alva the best it can be.

They reached the office of the branch head. He was waiting for them with tea.

The man from the counter departed.

"City Lord West, it is good to finally meet you. I am Isaac Paiva, the head of this Alchemist Association." The man smiled.

Erik took off his doupeng and gave a quick smile.

"Here are the mana stones that we have accumulated because of our deal. I have also included our payment for the next six months for renting out the valley gardens."

Erik took the storage box and started to transfer the contents.

"For your contributions and your ability with Alchemy, I also have an invitation for you to attend the Alchemist Association competitions within the Fifth Realm." He took out a letter and passed it to Erik.

Erik opened it and read the contents. He scanned the information. *Part of this is because of me being the lord of Vuzgal and giving the Alchemist Association concessions, but they still wouldn't let me into their academies if my skills weren't good enough. Old Hei has increased my skill to the point where I can head to the higher realms to learn, but then he is still in the Third Realm, working to increase his ability so that he can become a teacher in one of these academies.*

Erik gripped his fist in agitation, interested in heading to the academy to increase his ability. *I will make sure that Old Hei comes with me. Once I get the manuals from the Fifth Realm, then I can share them with him and hopefully he can break through his bottleneck and become accepted as a teacher in the Fifth or Sixth Realm!*

"Is there a time limit on this?" Erik asked.

"There is not, but this is only an invitation to a selection. You will need to pass that before you can be admitted into the academies in the Sixth Realm," Isaac said with a smile.

"What if I went directly to the Sixth Realm?"

"There are attendance examinations there. This letter would allow you to test there, but the people competing will be stronger."

"Makes sense—they need to check out my skill for real and then make sure that only the strongest are accepted. What happens within the academies?" Erik asked.

"You have a set amount of credits per semester. You can use those for classes. Then, as you contribute to the academy, you can get more of these credits to use on classes and even use them on manuals and ingredients, or other Alchemy related items."

Okay, so just as Elan reported.

"I have business to attend to today, but I will think on it. Is there a time

I need to apply?"

"There is a selection every three months and the invitation is good for one year." Isaac smiled.

"Thank you for passing this along." Erik stood and the two of them said their good-byes.

Rugrat looked at the mana stones in his ring. It was only a portion of the money that was going through Vuzgal every day. He had gone to the treasury and asked them to keep back what they could instead of issuing them to new loans, even for a couple of hours. He'd been able to get a few hundred Earth-grade mana stones.

He sat in Elan's office. The man was using his sound transmissions, calling in and sending out messengers, reading through pieces of information across his desk.

Instead of looking tired, he looked energized.

"You enjoy this, don't you?" Rugrat asked.

"Enjoy what?" Elan said as he continued to read. He knew that Rugrat wouldn't mind.

"The information, being in the know, in the middle of the web," Rugrat said.

"It is rather fun." Elan smiled slightly and kept on reading. "Information is power. With money, there is power as well, but with this, just a few changes, words in the right ears then it could mean a lifetime of wealth without having to deal with the issues that come with being a trader." Elan smiled. "It has been a long time since I have felt any real challenge. It has gotten my blood flowing again, being able to get to this stage. I feel like I am in my youth again and that anything is possible and I do not need to sit back and just hope for the world to stay the same, watching my children surpass me. Now we are all working together in different areas, competing with one another!"

Rugrat nodded, understanding his sentiment.

Erik opened the door to the office and came in. "George and Gilly are playing in the yard again," Erik said.

"Those two really are good friends for each other. Have you been able to find any pills to increase their strength?"

"One thing at a time. Once we have these arts, then we still have plenty to do. Elan, would you be able to look up academies that would be willing to take in paying students? I am thinking we support some people, like we did with Julilah and Qin, send them to the academies, increase their knowledge and then have them use their insights to teach our people," Erik said.

"There are a few places, but the cost is high and a paying student is only an outer disciple, so they get the least amount of access to the academy's resources."

"Failing that, we hire teachers and people from the higher realms."

"I can add it to the list." Elan sighed.

"Were you able to collect a lot of mana stones?" Rugrat asked.

"Take a look." Erik held out his wrist.

Rugrat looked inside, his eyes widening as he pulled back. "Damn."

"Right," Erik said.

Rugrat held up his necklace and storage item. He had trimmed the mana stones down in the pillar back pretty far. Instead of cutting them into stone by stone, he'd just carved out massive blocks the size of a person.

"I think that it should be enough," Erik said.

Rugrat nodded as he did some mental calculations. *Three Sky stones and 467 Earth, with 891 Mortal in total?*

"I hope so," Rugrat said.

"Your guide is a woman called Oilella. She should be able to take you to Arman. I have organized her through a trading contact, telling her that you're traders looking to go and see the sights. One-way trip. She'll cost eight Earth mana stones. When you meet her, say it's a nice day for a stroll in the rain. She will reply, I hear Arman is nice this time of year."

"Damn codewords," Rugrat complained.

Elan pushed a picture forward of the woman and the two of them memorized her features.

"They work," Erik said.

"What's the situation in Arman?"

"Arman is a competition ground. The city is tiny most of the time, but when the different sects in the area want to compete, they go to Arman to do so. The population of the city is about four hundred to five hundred thousand. With the competitions, the number of people in the city doubles to a million or more. This is a map of the city."

He pulled out a map; they took it and added it to their own maps.

"I have highlighted the different trading areas. Each sect takes over an area, with the traders who are allied with them setting up in there and neutral traders having a few other locations. These can be people who found a rare item but don't have anywhere to sell it, or they're not big enough to interest the sects, and so on.

"Then there are the auction houses. The Blue Lotus has locations within the academies and sect's headquarters as well as their own cities for trading. At Arman, it will be all local grown auctions. The sects may host their own, or the people of Arman will. The biggest auctions are held by the Black Willow auction house. It is an anonymous trading house. Everyone's identities are hidden unless they choose to reveal them. All kinds of objects are on sale there. The main competitions will involve formations, woodworking, tailoring, and fighting, but the main attractions will be healing, smithing, and beast husbandry."

"Beast husbandry?" Erik asked.

"Rearing animals, strengthening them, making them your own mounts—it is the beast tamer skill," Elan said.

"All of that is under beast tamer?" Erik asked.

"Don't you have the skill with Gilly and George?"

Erik and Rugrat looked at each other and shook their heads.

"I guess that makes sense. You didn't tame them; they willingly became your contracted beasts. If you were able to get a beast to submit to you, then you would get the skill. Having a beast bound to you and you bound to them with a soul contract means that you can raise other beasts but you won't be able to make a soul contract with any other beast unless yours dies."

"Where did you get all of this information from?" Erik asked.

"When I was younger, we raised animals and I learned about it. Just a passing interest—learned more of it as I got older."

"So there should be more manuals on animal husbandry and smithing and healing?" Rugrat asked.

"Yes, but it means that the competition for these items will be fiercer. I would suggest getting items not related to these three disciplines. They'll be cheaper. Then head to another competition with different main skill competitions and then get the books there," Elan said.

"Who are the groups there?"

"There is the Divine Sunset sect, who specialize in destroying everything. They're largely assassins, but they use formations in their attacks and beasts to increase their fighting strength. Golden Path sect is one of the sects that focus on crafting, or following the golden path, as they say. They have links to the associations. They're arrogant as hell, but they have the strength behind them to be so. The Agate Sword sect—formations, smithing, and swords are their main crafts. They're a sect of sword users. They also have a lot of healers and a few alchemists to help temper their fighters and make sure they don't die in training.

"The Soul Hammer sect: they cultivate the mind and heart. They're weapon making demons, woodworking and smiths. They're usually the winners of these competitions. Rarely talk to others or even one another. And the women of the Silver Garnet sect, the smallest of all the sects at this fight—they take women in and teach them the arts of crafting. They focus on beast tamer and tailoring skills to augment their illusion spells. Their strength comes from working together. It's said that they all have a similar constitution and look similar. Some say that they're all just twins of the original sect leader, created through some forbidden art. They've got formidable fighting formations, their clothes serving to enhance their magical power and the beasts to give them close range support. Pissing off one is pissing them all off.

"Well, that can go for them all. If you get into a fight or altercation, end it in a way so that they would look like they're sullying their reputation to deal with you. These are proud people. Reputation is more important to them than anything. Thankfully, you two are shameless, so you should be fine. Also, although they are arrogant, they put a lot more thought into attacking someone. These are all-powerful figures—they plan out their actions, gather information and plot before they act."

"So a smile now and a knife in the back later," Erik said.

"Saying we're shameless?" Rugrat asked.

"Exactly," Elan said, apparently answering both of their questions at once.

"Relationships?"

"They all hate one another in degrees. The Soul Hammer and Silver Garnet are close. Same for Divine Sunset and Golden Path. These two groups also hate one another: Soul Hammer against Golden Path, and Silver Garnet against Divine Sunset. The Agate sect is the strongest sect but they mostly keep to themselves, focus on developing their strength. On the surface, at least. They're playing a political game underneath: keep the other sects fighting, allowing them to use the competition to increase the strength of their people without getting caught up in costly rivalries, decreasing the strength of the other groups."

"Smart," Erik said.

"And dangerous," Elan reminded them and pulled out folders. "This is the basic information on the sects and a few of the important players."

Erik and Rugrat looked over the folders as well as the drawn images of the different people. There were elders, crafters who were held in high regard, different star students who were on the rise and had plenty of people looking out for them.

The list was long, so Erik and Rugrat split them up between them.

Elan worked on his own reports and continued to pass his orders and messages to his information network and agents.

"How is your network going?" Erik asked as he was reading.

"As you said, I used some of the people who decided that the military wasn't for them and others who were looking for a challenge, and had them build up their own networks or placed them into networks that were established but needed someone to maintain them. For other contacts, they don't even really know who they're working for. They think that we're another group and eagerly supply us with information, trying to get at people they don't like. The Fourth Realm has become our new base of power as there are people going to the Third Realm to get Alchemy products. People from the higher realms come here to fight and crafters from here move between the Earth realms with ease. A word in the right ear, the right pressure in the right places—we've extended our reach all the way to the Seventh Realm, where the Sha leadership is located."

"Oh?" Erik and Rugrat looked up.

"The leader of the sect has a strange interest in buildings and aesthetics. These are images of the buildings he lives in." Elan put forward an image.

"That looks…" Rugrat said.

"Pretty European. That's a lot of sandstone-looking building and then there's gold all over it. And the garden is all made to look pretty. Is there a formation in all of that?"

"There might be, but if it is, then it's probably buried underground," Rugrat said.

"Reminds me of that fancy French palace," Erik said.

"Fancy French palace? When were you in France?"

"Second wife."

"Ah! The V palace something?" Rugrat said.

"Versailles?"

"Wasn't that a battle or something from the First World War?"

"I think they made the treaty there to end the First World War," Erik said.

"So, then this guy might be French?" Rugrat asked.

"Old, old French. They're still using front loaders and he built a palace instead of apartments or something like it. Maybe they wanted a bit of France?"

"Or maybe they like role-playing period pieces?" Rugrat said.

"Well, it pretty much yells that they're from Earth," Erik said.

"And they started to appear nearly three hundred years ago." Rugrat sat back in his chair. "So this guy had to have come from Earth a long time ago."

"Maybe coming over here, time gets messed with?" Erik asked.

"That's pretty weak," Rugrat drawled.

"Right. Let's assume he came here a few hundred years ago."

"Then that would make sense. For them, this is modern. They only had front loaders around then. Also, if people disappeared from Earth, there wasn't news and internet so it might just be ignored and the information disappear," Rugrat said.

"Well…" Erik scratched his head and held his chin as he tried to find any flaws in Rugrat's logic. "Yeah, it makes sense. Though do we want to reach out, or wait?"

"Wait. Just because we're from the same place doesn't mean that we'll agree on everything. If we don't have the strength and he wants what we have, he could destroy everything we've set up in Vuzgal," Rugrat said.

"Keep them under observation but do nothing for now."

"Understood," Elan said.

"You memorized your people?" Erik asked.

"Yeah," Rugrat said.

"Fifth Realm?" Erik asked.

"Hell yeah." Rugrat grinned.

Erik and Rugrat stood.

"You'll find your guide in the Black Boar Wayside Inn," Elan said, giving them both waypoints.

"Call if you need us," Rugrat said.

The two of them walked out of the room.

Rugrat shifted his armor around, making sure it was on properly, checking his gear was all ready to go before he let his cloak cover it all again.

"Good?" Erik asked. He had done the same check.

"Yeah, let's git 'er done," Rugrat said.

They headed out and walked through the city. In their cloaks, no one paid them much attention—just two more people in Vuzgal.

"Vermire should be making a move soon to create that central range trading city," Rugrat said, using his sound transmission device so no one would be able to hear them.

"They have the necessary support?" Erik asked.

"Yeah. Jasper has even passed on his recommendation that we hire some of the guards, give them opportunities to go to the higher realms or join the First Army. Their strength is much higher than others in the First Realm and they're just restrained by the power there," Rugrat said.

"What's the plan with Vermire?" Erik asked.

"Make the city?"

"No, like the end plan. Do we want them to control all of the outposts there? Create a country? What?"

Rugrat drew in a breath through his teeth before letting it out slowly. "Have them take over the outposts, put them all under his control, and our control. Turn it into our territory, have them remain neutral on the surface, but underneath they're our agents."

"Makes sense. They can be our protection and our sword in the First Realm," Erik said.

"You talked about the healing houses...anything happening on that front?" Rugrat asked as they wove through people who came together and then spread out as they passed different stalls with intriguing items.

"I had lands set aside for them. Many of them have been busy studying. When we come back, I want to move them into the healing locations across the city and into the Battle Arena."

"What about the other healing houses or sects that deal in healing?"

"Most of them won't try to offer their services to people outside of their sect, much like how alchemists won't look to sell outside of the sect if they can help it, looking to improve their own strength before others. Never know on the Fourth Realm who might be your friend one day and your enemy the next," Erik said.

"So with us healing them?" Rugrat drawled on.

"With us healing them, then the healing houses will get more people to come over, like how the Healer's Association have the largest transient populations within the cities they've set up in and are one of the largest powers in the Fourth Realm."

"They didn't join the Associations' Circle, though?" Rugrat said.

"No, they didn't. We are a crafting city and for them, that doesn't bring as much business. The Battle Arena increases the number of people who are hurt, but still it's not as much as the big fights that happen all across the realm. They've positioned their cities in the middle of the lands that have the most conflicts."

"If we start healing people and bringing them here, will they get pissed?"

"We're just doing it because they're not. Even if they do, then they can create a branch here. They can't really affect us much. We've got alliances with most of the associations anyway and our supplies come from the traders. They would have to lock down the entire realm to try to cut off our supplies; then we could just get them from the higher realms. And we're a crafting city—we produce items and we've got a ton of raw materials coming in from the dungeons and the valley. The alchemists wouldn't be too happy with having their supplies cut off," Erik said.

"I guess it pays to have allies," Rugrat said.

"If we don't have the power, we need to leverage the people who do have power."

"That some Sun Tzu quote?"

"Maybe? No idea. Just sounded right." Erik shrugged.

They were near the Black Boar. There were all kinds of people looking around as they entered the city, taking it all in. Others were leaving or coming in, their expressions and actions showing that they'd done so tens of times before.

Erik moved to the side of the road. Rugrat frowned as he did so as well.

Erik waved to a server. "Two teas please," he said.

"West?" Rugrat asked.

"She's not going anywhere." Erik took a seat.

Rugrat took the seat opposite, looking over the people in the shop and then the people moving along the streets.

Traders were guided out of the totem defenses and sent down the larger transport roads, heading to the warehouses to unload their goods that would be shipped across the city.

There were people of all kinds, with clothes that spanned styles of the Earth realm: The cold-eyed fighters, the open-eyed youngsters. The hopefuls looking at their new future. Scions with money to spend, on top of their powerful mounts or riding in ornate carriages.

Traders called out goods while restaurants filled up with people who had just arrived or were awaiting their time slot to leave the city.

The light around the totem never stopped flashing as people entered and left in a constant stream.

There was a group of the Vuzgal Defense Force patrolling. They held repeaters and the special armor and helmets of the Vuzgal military.

The fighters looked at them with scorn or sized them up for a fight. But under it, there was a respect as they looked at their weapons and the two skeletons that walked behind them, one encased in powerful armor with a high Journeyman-level sword, the other wearing a mage's robes, rings, and finery.

"Even though we've been able to train them up, we'll need more time to increase their attribute strength," Rugrat said.

Erik followed his eyes over. "Yes, but we've expanded in numbers rapidly over the last couple of months. Once we increase their strength, we need to send them out to real fights. Otherwise, if we need them in a real fight, they'll only be guards."

"Who would we fight? We don't have any real big enemies," Rugrat said.

"We don't? What about the Willful Institute and the Stone Fist sect? The Willful Institute don't know who we are but after what they did to Domonos and they tried to kill us as well…" Erik said.

Rugrat's eyes chilled.

"Elan is looking into it," Erik said.

"What do we do if we destroy them?"

"Auction off the cities. We don't need them—resources we do," Erik said. "The Stone Fist sect must know that we did something, or that I did something. Mira acted after I met her and then when Chonglu reappeared again, here in Vuzgal, as the Battle Arena manager, with both of his children attending the academy."

"Will we need to deal with them or will Mira?" Rugrat said.

"If we can work with the Fighter's Association, even better—bring us closer. They're a group we want to have on our side. They raise the strongest fighters in the Ten Realms."

Erik went quiet as the tea arrived.

Erik paid the server and Rugrat took a glass.

"Thanks." Rugrat then sipped on the tea.

They fell into silence, enjoying the tea and watching the world go by in front of them.

"We were lucky enough to find the right people to manage all of this while we're gone," Rugrat said.

"Elise is developing the trade within the city and using the trading interface on behalf of the city to make massive profits. The Sky Reaching Restaurant is controlled by the cooking department. The academy is an arm of the Kanesh Academy in Alva. Yui and Domonos have been able to train up people to take over the training of new recruits, increasing the Vuzgal Defense Force and take in new members in to the First Army," Erik said.

"Who are able to operate on their own, clearing out the Earth floor. But I heard that they hit a problem?"

"Yeah, the creatures weren't the threat—the plants were. So they've been trying to create a napalm-like concoction with the alchemists to burn down the forests on the floor." Erik sipped his tea.

"You seem pretty calm about it."

"I read a report from Fehim. If they burn the floor to the ground, then it can clear it all for new plants to be grown. We've been losing farming land to building on the Alva floor. We can turn the entire Earth floor into one big farming area: Alchemy at the center, food on the exterior. The floor is almost twice the size of the Alva floor. Without buildings in the way, it'll be a lot easier to manage for the farmers and alchemists. Also, it shows that Glosil is thinking outside the box. Instead of fighting his way through, he's using the resources of Alva to make it easier on him and the First Army."

Rugrat sipped his tea and looked at the colorful street again. "What a damn life we live." Rugrat laughed, before his thoughts turned deeper. "What do you think we would have been doing back on Earth?"

Erik's hand stilled as he was raising his cup to his mouth. He continued the motion, draining most of it in a shot.

"Being a one-armed bandit," Erik said.

Rugrat grimaced internally, he'd half forgotten the state Erik had been in before they made it to the ten realms.

"My bad," Rugrat said.

Erik waved off his apology and let out a sigh.

"If I had all my limbs still, fighting for someone else's war, just trying to keep ourselves and our friends alive. Riding the adrenaline wave, trying to make the world a bit better with our actions, or at least safer for the people we're protecting. Maybe wasting away in Colorado, catching up on my fishing and hunting, reading a bit here and there. Maybe get a few dogs. Take up a hobby? I doubt it though, always thought that I would die with my boots on."

"Amen to that brother," Rugrat said, raising his glass to the other man in salute. He drank from it and the table became silent, each of them wrapped up in their own thoughts.

"We live for this, don't we?" Rugrat asked.

"What do you mean?"

"The fighting, the challenges, the crushing stress: the fear of failure, running that line of chaos and destruction. Somehow we made it to this point and got to this place but we're not sitting back, getting comfortable, raking in the mana stones. Instead, we're heading to the Fifth Realm, to see what's there, getting art books to increase our strength, our people's strength and go further. What're we gonna do at the end of it all?"

"Who knows. We'll find that out when we get there. There's still plenty of the realms to see, and I like helping out the little people." Erik drank his tea and put down the empty glass. "We aren't even halfway there yet."

Rugrat chuckled and finished his tea.

They left the tea shop and walked toward the Black Boar.

Rugrat saw Oilella first, nudging Erik as they moved across the tavern to a woman sitting back and sipping a beer. She had tanned skin from being caught out in the sun for too long. Her hair was pulled back into braids, with pieces of metal and jewelry weaved into them.

"It's a nice day for a stroll in the rain."

She smiled lazily as she put down her beer. "I hear Arman is nice this time of year."

"You ready to leave?" Rugrat asked.

"Yes. And the payment?"

Erik pulled out a bag that clinked as he put it on the table.

She looked inside. A glow appeared on her face as the surrounding mana increased slightly. She put it away.

"Shall we?" She smiled, pulling on her worn cloak and then pulling on a small pack with different items hanging off it.

She tossed a few Mortal mana stones on the table and adjusted the goggles on her head.

"After you," Rugrat said.

She led the way through the inn's bar and toward the totem.

"So first time to Arman?" she asked.

"Yeah," Erik said.

"Well, should be some good trading there with the competition, though still not as nice as Vuzgal. This place is the trading mecca of the Earth Realm—neutral, crafters all over the place, food, *real* food, Battle Arena, and increased mana. Though expensive place to try to get some land. The city lords won't even open it up, just renting it to people, but everyone is willing to pay it. Even have rent auctions. Those people who came in and got their places first could just rent out their land again—they could make a killing!

"Have you ever seen the southern wilderness? They say it's wild but there's just a lot of beasts. It's warm all year round. Even in the cold months, it's the same as the northern regions summer months!

"I heard that more of the Sky Reaching Restaurants will be opening soon—say that they had to hire enough cooks for them, but then only one in five people who applied made it through to become chefs. And most of them still aren't high enough skill level for the restaurants. I had a meal in there once. Took me two hours to eat one meal, just *so* good!"

Oilella kept on like that, continuing her own conversation for their benefit as Erik and Rugrat nodded and made noises as if they were listening.

Damn, she can talk more than my cousin Samantha!

They got to the totem. Oilella accessed the menu and destination with practiced hands.

Light surrounded them and they were in a new city.

A torrential downpour soaked Erik and Rugrat in moments.

Elan is probably laughing his ass off, Rugrat thought darkly as Oilella led them over to the gates leading into the city.

"Welcome to Arman and to the Fifth Realm!" Oilella smiled, perfectly happy in the rain.

Once they went through the gate, they went their separate ways. Erik and Rugrat looked over the streets.

Rain came down everywhere. The sun was still high in the sky.

"Damn. Feels like the Florida swamps," Rugrat said.

"I hate the humidity." Erik's shirt was already sticking to him even though he wore his waterproof cloak.

"Markets?" Rugrat asked.

"Let's check when the auction halls are open. They'll have the most valuable items. We hit those up when they're going on. In the meantime, we go looking for art and art manuals," Erik said.

"All right."

The two of them trudged through the rain.

"See those people with the red and yellow glowing crest?"

"The nuclear fallout-looking one?"

"Yeah, those are the Sunset boys. And the girls with the veils who are dry even with all this—they're the Silver Garnets. Left breast."

Erik saw the silver garnets that shone brighter than silver as they caught the light.

"I thought garnets were red and green," Erik said.

"Dude, really? This is the Ten Realms, after all," Rugrat said.

"Yeah, that was pretty dumb of me," Erik said.

They reached their first auction house, looking at the sign that told them about the items that would be up for auction and when the auction would be held.

They saw two groups yelling at one another.

"Soul Hammer and the Golden Path sect," Erik said.

"Seems like some kind of argument," Rugrat said.

"You came in and stole the Miod sand! We saw you prowling the area and you must've crossed the border and come into our territory to steal our sand!"

"Really? Who calls themselves a crafter and doesn't have tools to harvest some sand?" the other asked, looking down on the other man.

"You!" the Golden Path sect yelled as he drew out a hammer.

"Smith?" Erik asked.

"Ten bucks," Rugrat said.

"Really, you draw a hammer to fight us?" the Soul Hammer crafter said, his eyes dead and disdain heavy.

"You're the lowlife here! Repay back our sand and your trespass!"

"What is that saying? Fortune favors the strong? Well, I don't see anyone who is strong enough for me to give them my fortune."

"You!" The Golden Path sect group couldn't take it any longer and rushed the Soul Hammer sect, who drew their weapons as well.

The Golden Path had momentum, but the Soul Hammer looked at them with the same bored eyes. Although the Golden Path sect were filled with emotions, the Soul Hammers were devoid of them.

Mana was stirred up in the air and the rain was tossed back. The strength of the blows was enough to shake the Fifth Realm houses and clear the rain from the sky above.

Erik and Rugrat watched.

"Looks like a hammer art—heats up the hammer. Would be good when smithing," Rugrat said as the Soul Hammer man struck forward with his glowing hammer, only to have their opponent jump to the side and then send out a kick.

Their face twisted.

"Well, seems that they can still feel pain," Erik said.

"Who is creating trouble!" A voice called from above as a group arrived on beasts, wearing powerful weapons and armor.

"Shit! It's the Arman guards," one of the Golden Path members said as everyone distanced themselves.

"Time we were going?" Rugrat said.

They headed down an alleyway, not wanting to get caught up in whatever was next, making their way to the next auction house.

"Well, with the guards being strong enough to restrain the sects, it helps keep everything running and manageable here," Erik said.

"Well, I don't know if anyone that strong is really manageable," Rugrat said.

"You might have a point." Erik grinned.

"Why do I have to look after it?" Tan Xue asked.

"You're the highest level person in the academy," Taran said.

"Come on. But you're better at this stuff than me!"

"Uh, nope! I've got enough to deal with back home," Taran said.

"You just don't want to be the leader!"

"Look, Jia Feng is sending you a proper assistant to run things and you just need to be the power behind them. Don't you already get a ton of resources and aid?" Taran said.

"Yes, but!" Tan Xue wanted to complain more but she couldn't, making her just pout more.

"That's what I thought," Taran said.

Tan Xue groaned. "Why me?"

"We're not doing this again," Taran said.

There was a knock at the smithy door.

"Come in!" Taran said before Tan Xue could say anything.

The door opened to reveal Hiao Xen.

"I thought that I might be able to find you here. Experts Karlo Savic and Bai Guo are here. I was wondering if you would greet them with me, Academy Head?"

Tan Xue shot a look at Taran. "I won't get any smithing done!"

"Don't worry. I'm sure you'll get the first art technique books!" Taran waved her away as he looked at the item he was working on in the forge.

"Heartless!" Tan Xue said.

Hiao Xen nodded to Taran, who gave him a thumbs up.

"Who are Karlo Savic and Bai Guo?"

"Karlo Savic is a formations master. He fell in love with a girl he wasn't supposed to and his family turned on him. He has had many offers but he wants to just work and live with his wife. Bai Guo is a smith. He was a powerful figure, focused on his smithing, but there was a girl, a student who liked him, and he didn't like her back. She wanted to bring them together so she drugged him and said that he took her forcefully.

"Her family was powerful and they took it badly. It had been started and she couldn't stop it at that point.

"He had never been really liked. He had an odd personality. Those who wanted to see his downfall turned on him.

"His cultivation was destroyed. He was castrated. They used poisons for his wounds so that they're impossibly hard to heal. They mangled his hands and burned his eyes, scarring and cutting him so he would only hear people screaming in horror as he passes. It's not a pretty sight," Hiao Xen said.

"What did the girl do?"

"She disappeared. No one knows where she went. Some accused him of kidnapping her; others said he killed her. It was impossible because he was recovering from his wounds. Elan found him and we brought him here after he agreed to be a teacher."

"His wounds?"

"I don't know if they will ever be fixed, but then I have never seen a healer like Erik before," Hiao Xen said.

Tan Xue let out a sigh. It wasn't long until they reached a meeting hall for the academy grounds.

Waiting for them was Julilah and Qin.

"I guess that you have heard about the Expert formations master, Karlo Savic?"

"Is he here?" Julilah asked.

"Never interested in boys, but now you're chasing a married man?" Tan Xue tutted.

"It's not like that! And who said I'm not interested in men!?" Julilah said.

Immediately, Tan Xue had more questions she wasn't sure she wanted answers to.

"Don't hound him too much," Tan Xue said, leaving her questions unasked.

Karlo Savic stood as the duo entered the room.

"Expert Savic, this is Expert Tan Xue and the head of this academy," Hiao Xen introduced.

"Your academy is indeed impressive. I am looking forward to looking at it more," Karlo Savic said with a nod.

"Thank you. I know there are a number of people within the formations department who are eager to learn from you."

"Oh?" Interest sparked in Karlo's eyes.

"Our background in formations is not that deep but we have been able to raise a number of Journeyman formation masters who are eager to learn more and make that final step into the realm of Expert, as you have done," Tan Xue said. "Hiao Xen did inform you of the rewards that come with every person who you are able to assist in becoming an Expert, right?"

"I am sorry. I was in too much of a rush," Hiao Xen said with a short laugh.

"It is no worry. You are busy running the city," Tan Xue said. Everything that she was saying was part of a plan, one part to make him feel the competition from others looking to get his spot and then also show him the rewards for helping other people. One would cause him to grow, the other make sure that he wouldn't stunt the growth of others.

"With every Expert you are able to raise, you would receive six months of your salary as a bonus, including resources. These can be claimed immediately as resources or as supplies, as with all of the resources and mana stones laid down in your contract."

"Oh," Karlo said, trying to sound only mildly interested.

But Tan Xue could see the light in his eyes.

"Now, I would be a decent guide but Julilah and Qin are the top two formation experts and they would be more than pleased to show you around the academy and allow you to get to know one another," Tan Xue offered. *Ugh, sounds too much like a date. I don't want to think of Julilah on a date! Now I can't not think about her on a date! Who is this boy who she likes?*

"Thank you," Karlo said.

Hiao Xen sent a sound transmission and the two girls appeared.

"It is good to meet you, Expert Savic," they both said, cupping their hands and bowing.

"I'll leave you to it. Please let me know if you have any troubles," Tan Xue said.

"Thank you, Head Tan." Karlo cupped his fist to her.

She gave him a slight nod and then headed out of the room with Hiao Xen.

He guided her to another room.

Tan Xue opened the door and saw a man wearing red clothes. His face was wrapped, covering his features. His hands were hidden in his sleeves.

"Expert Bai Guo, my name is Expert Tan Xue. I am also a blacksmith Expert and head of this academy. I thank you for accepting our invitation. I believe that there is a lot that the students and I can learn from you," Tan Xue said.

"Another Expert blacksmith." Bai Guo nodded. "That will be good. I have lost the skills to smith, but with your ability then you can surpass my ability."

He sounded unemotional, as if passing on his teachings were a mechanical process.

"I hope that we can assist each other. Though I do not currently have any smithing arts."

"*Currently?* Which means that you have a way of obtaining them."

Tan Xue couldn't see through his bandages, but from the way they moved, she believed he was smiling.

"I might not be able to increase my smithing skill, but through others I can do so. The teaching, more than the benefits, are what interested me," Bai Guo said honestly. "I was a high-level Expert for forty years, and a mid-level Expert smith for fifty, a low grade for thirty. Now I don't have much time. With my cultivation crippled, my body is starting to fail and I have some eighty years left being in a high mana environment like Vuzgal, before the Ten Realms are done with me."

"Do you want to fight your former sect?" Tan Xue asked.

"There was a time that I wanted to burn them to the ground. I still despise them, but I guess it was because I cared more about smithing than people. I was aloof and arrogant. I kept away from them, aiming to improve. I stepped over people and used them. So when they had the opportunity, they all turned on me. My emotions...are complicated when it comes to them. There are certain people I hate, but this is my situation and I will not be able to change it anytime in the future. Maybe one of my students will be able to go on and make them apologize, but I have no expectations. Taking a step back from smithing, I realize how much I enjoyed it and didn't fully appreciate the enjoyment and sense of purpose it gave me. Now my new purpose is teaching others. I will not create issues with my old sect without seeking permission."

"That is good to know. I thank you for joining us," Tan Xue said, standing to let him go.

"Well, I have nothing that I am doing now, unless you have something else. What were those burning questions?"

"Well..." Tan Xue slid back down into her seat.

Hiao Xen stood and headed out of the room as Tan Xue started.

"I want to make a weapon with a formation in it at one time, just a simple one but I haven't been able to do it."

"How are you adding the formation?"

"Using my hammer and chisel."

"See, there are smithing arts to allow you to add a specific formation to a weapon. I believe them to be a waste of time—flashy practice to make an enchanted weapon in one shot. But there is a reason that the formation master and smithing skill are two different skills. Make the weapon, then add a formation. When you start and when you finish, the product may be very different; use all of your smithing skill, then all of your formation skill. Work the metal in the smithing portion so that it will be better suited for a formation, but do not make that the sole purpose.

"It's like an ornate sword. A sword is ugly but it functions. A sword can be beautiful, but because it has had so much metal removed, it is weak and prone to breaking.

"Formations augment and increase the power of the sword. The strongest metal, the perfect fire, the right enhancers—pour all of your smithing skill into it. Smith the ever-loving crap out of that weapon, then add in a formation that takes that weapon to the next stage. Some people say that Expert smiths can forge complete blades in one go. Yeah, a crappy one, maybe a Master-level smith or a Star-level smith could."

Hiao Xen closed the door behind him, leaving them to talk.

33 Opening Curtain

Erik copied down the last information of when the auction would be held, then he organized the auction times together and then put numbers over them according to the priority he placed on them.

Rugrat looked around, watching out for others. They were alone in a new city. One of them was always alert and ready to act if something happened.

"Okay, so it looks like most of the auctions are over the next three days. We can get a better idea of how much items will cost us if we go and wander the markets," Erik said.

"What's a bit more rain?" Rugrat grumbled.

Erik let out a dry laugh. "I wanted a second shower today," Erik said, following Rugrat to the market.

People stared darkly at the skies that seemed to ignore them, happily continuing its hot downpour.

"I don't think I have sweated in rain before," Rugrat said.

"Really? Thailand?"

"Well, maybe in Thailand. Hard to not, it's so damn hot all the time!"

"And you hated every minute of it?" Erik asked.

Rugrat grinned and pulled on his cowboy hat he had replaced his doupeng with. "Oh, it was some of the most fun I've ever had."

Rugrat moved to the side and wove into the crowd that was forming as they entered the marketplace. There were half-covered and erected stalls, with people pressed in together as they looked at the wares.

There were cultivation aids, spell scrolls, information and technique books. Rare resources, tools of all kinds and weapons.

"Any of these items would cause people in the First Realm to go nuts," Rugrat said in a low voice.

"We just need to make sure that we buy the right things."

Rugrat nodded and they continued looking through the market stalls, going from marketplace to marketplace.

Erik saw an older man, sitting underneath his porch covering, watching the world go by, a local to Arman.

"Sir, I was wondering if you could help me and my friend. We were wondering if you knew where the best place to get art manuals from would be?" Erik asked.

"Art manuals, you say." The man held his chin. "My memory is rather hazy these days. I'm sorry."

"Would this help clear it up?" Erik showed a box of thirty Mortal mana stones. Earth mana stones were something that only those from the Sixth Realm could easily pull out and was something that the upper middle management in the Fourth Realm might have. Most transactions were done with Mortal mana stones still.

"It seems that something is coming back to me," the man said.

Erik pulled out another twenty Mortal stones.

The man waved him forward and took the Mortal mana stones with a smile.

"Go to the Lee clan. They specialize in spell scrolls, but they always have a number of arts for sale. They increase the prices on the arts that are associated with the competitions going on, though!"

"Thank you," Erik said.

"I have heard some rumors, though," the old man said. "About technique arts."

"How useful?"

"Incredibly useful to people not part of the sect, and cheaper."

"The Ikazi baths?" Erik asked.

"Oh, so you know where, but do you know what they have on offer this time? Thirty might make me recall."

Erik passed over the stones and the man leaned forward, making sure that no one else was able to hear them.

"They're selling an Oleha plant. One that is said to come from the Grey Drake sect that can be used to increase a beast's bloodline strength. Many people will be bidding on this, so the other items will be cheaper." The man smiled.

"They're focused on the prize," Erik said and looked at Rugrat.

"We take the leftovers."

"Thank you for the time." Erik nodded to the old man, who smiled and went back to sitting back in his seat.

Erik and Rugrat headed off into the market.

Erik saw some ingredients he hadn't seen before and stopped at the counter. "A batch of these, please."

"Certainly!" The seller quickly packaged them up. "Twenty Mortal mana stones!"

Erik passed them over and took the ingredients.

"You still doing that thing?" Rugrat asked.

"What thing?" Erik asked as he took out the ingredient, balled it up, and put it in his mouth, his hand crushing the other ingredients. He screwed up his face. "Lemon, chilies—tastes like eating crayons and flowers!"

"That thing," Rugrat said.

"Build up my knowledge," Erik managed to squeak out between his face contortions. People gave him more space as he and Rugrat kept on walking.

"Increase the blood flow of a person, but be more effective with animals—would cause someone a chill and too much of it could create a poison that slows a person's reaction times greatly. Be horrible when used with food," Erik said as the information filled his Alchemy skill book. He felt a thread of information filter into his mind.

"Called lemur grass, actually pretty useful for animals that are hurt. Not as effective on humans and with our weaker constitution, can easily poison us instead of help."

"Damn you're weird." Rugrat led them both over to a stall that had powerful formations guarding different items.

"The Windwalking Movement art, how much?"

"This is an ultra-rare movement art that will allow one to walk on the wind and glide through the heavens! I will not be able to let it go for any less than ninety Earth mana stones!" The man made it clear that he would not budge on this matter. Though his attitude was that he was doing them a service, as if he knew that it would sell; it was only a matter of time.

"May we take a closer look?" Rugrat asked.

"I can swear on the Ten Realms that it is real. If it wasn't for my need to get a better healing art, I wouldn't be putting it up for sale."

Erik couldn't sense any disturbance in the mana around the man. When someone was telling a lie or annoyed, then the mana around them would start to move according to those feelings; it was unconscious and people who didn't have a domain didn't know it even existed.

Erik and Rugrat looked at each other.

"How can you prove it to be true?" Rugrat asked.

The man looked at Erik and Rugrat, as if assessing whether it was worth to waste more time on them.

"This is why."

The man jumped up, some fifteen meters into the sky, an easy feat for people who could make it into the Fifth Realm.

Instead of dropping back down, he glided like a leaf.

"Fucking paratroopers," Rugrat said.

"What?" Erik asked.

"I'll buy it." Rugrat pulled out the mana stones and put them on the counter.

The man looked at Rugrat in surprise.

"Swear it is the real one first, though," Rugrat said, keeping his hand on the boxes.

"I swear on the Ten Realms that this is the original copy of the Windwalking Movement art," the man said, his manner much more respectful as his eyes locked onto the boxes.

"Good." Rugrat held out his other hand. The man took the book out of the formation-enclosed space.

"Dear friend, I am sorry that I am late, but I saw the display of the movement art and I have a great need of it," a woman said. The crowd parted around her as she and her companions walked forward. All of them looked at Erik and Rugrat, assessing them, but not showing any overt threatening movements.

The man in the stall hesitated and Rugrat grabbed the book from his hands.

The seller coughed and smiled awkwardly, giving the girl a look, showing he wasn't a part of any of this anymore as he collected the Earth mana stones on his counter.

All of the people in the group wore a sword-like medallion that seemed to be carved from polished rock. Lines of various colors moved through the surface of the sword.

"Ah, young genius Hilia," Erik said, remembering her image from the pile of important people who would be at Arman.

The woman cupped her fist to Erik and Rugrat.

"I am sorry for my rudeness. I have been looking for a movement art to augment my smithing style and I believe that this art from the display might be what I need. One of my friends rushed to tell me about it but I was just a half second too late. For this, I am willing to pay twenty Earth stones above the price you paid for it as an apology and thanks."

Erik looked at Rugrat.

"I am sorry, but I'm in need of this manual as well. I can only hope that you are able to find another one," Rugrat said.

Hilia seemed to fight with what to say before she sighed and clasped her fist. "I can only blame my bad luck then. I am sorry for keeping you. Will you possibly contact myself or my master if you think of selling it?"

"Certainly. Good luck with the smithing tournament," Erik said.

Using a movement art to help with smithing, when you think about it, it makes sense. Like how I use a flame art to help me with alchemy. Using different arts and abilities together, it creates many paths to advance down.

Erik and Rugrat headed into the crowd, the book already secured in Rugrat's storage ring.

"Get information on who they are. There is no need to act rash. Maybe we can trade them something that they find useful," Hilia said to one of her followers in a low voice thinking that Erik and Rugrat couldn't hear her.

Erik was impressed. Here in the higher realms, there were many hidden Experts. Attacking someone without knowing their connection or knowing what they might be willing to trade wasn't much smarter than going in blind to it all.

They walked the market more. Erik and Rugrat felt the eyes on them as Erik discreetly tested the different ingredients that they came across.

Erik scanned around before his eyes fell on a guarded doorway. Above it, written in mana-infused words, was a sign: Lee Clan's Manual Store.

Erik nudged Rugrat and tilted his head at the building.

Rugrat changed his direction and they made it out of the people and walked up to the guard.

Erik felt him sweeping his perception over Erik and Rugrat but didn't do anything as he let them pass.

His gear was all mid Journeyman level and he was level forty-six, showing that this Lee clan had some background to have such a guard outside.

A formation seemed to separate them from the outside world, removing the noise and the heat. They looked around at the people touring the room, moving to counters and to offices that were hidden down different corridors.

"Hello, sirs, this one is Katrine Mae. Is there anything that I can help you with?" An attendant bowed to them. She wore a light uniform that served to enhance her beauty and hint at more.

Erik nudged Rugrat on reflex, stopping the spreading grin across his face.

"We're looking for fighting or technique arts," Erik said.

The woman's eyes lit up and her smile became brighter. She pressed her arms together, pushing her shirt's limits. "Please, follow me this way. We have plenty of items to interest you! Is there any specific craft or fighting style art you are interested in?"

"Any and all," Erik said.

"Certainly!" She took them over to a private room, waving them to comfortable chairs in front of a desk. She sat down opposite and pulled out several books. "These list the different kind of manuals. I can bring you samples from any of the manuals listed inside."

The books were small, more like menus. Erik and Rugrat opened them.

Forty Earth stones for a basic fighting art manual. Erik looked through the techniques and then moved to the next.

Woodworking arts, tailoring arts, healing arts, beast taming arts—Rugrat studied the stealth movement arts and the spell casting arts, alongside the archery arts.

Erik noted down a number of fighting arts as well.

Although it is good to have multiple arts for a craft, having too many arts when fighting will only lead to confusion. The greater the selection, the closer one can find an art to their fighting style and use it to increase their combat power. Is that the basis of the sects? Why they pull in people who are not only talented, but have an affinity for their sect? Sword sects pulling in swordsmen and focusing on them?

Erik made some notes and looked at Rugrat. "Do you have your choices?"

"One second." Rugrat flipped a page, going back and forth between some that had caught his eye.

"It'll be easier to tell its value with a sample," Erik said.

"Then I've got my selection," Rugrat said.

"Could we get a sample from the Lightning Fist art, the Cobra Kicking art, the Spinning Wood art, Flowing Threads art, Penetrating Healing art."

Erik and Rugrat named several arts, the attendant writing them down dutifully.

"I will require a deposit of five Earth-grade mana stones and I can only give you two hours to review all of the arts," she said with a sad expression. "These stones can be used toward your final purchase."

"That's fine." Erik pulled out the Earth stones and put them on the table.

She smiled and took them into a jade box. "I will return momentarily." She turned and left.

"Notice she didn't say we would get them back if we didn't want to buy anything," Rugrat said.

"Ah, looks like you're maturing in your older age—getting a bit wiser?"

Rugrat flipped off Erik. They didn't have to wait long before the attendant came back with a number of small manuals that were only a page or two thick.

Erik and Rugrat took the books and started to leaf through them. The words were brought to life; as they read, vivid scenes played in their minds, showing what the end result of the art would be.

Erik saw a woodworker spinning a knotted and ugly piece of wood that looked as though it deserved to be thrown into the junk pile.

The woodworker took her tools and jabbed them forward, shavings flying off the wood. In seconds, its size had decreased and the wood came to a stop. One could see that the disfigured wood had been reborn. A single staff lay in the lathe, emitting a powerful aura completely different from the wood from before.

"So it looks like it can refine and concentrate the power of the wood into its core; then she removed the excess and sealed that power within. It's like ingredients, refining them so that they are incredibly potent. It looks impressive on the outside, but there is a lot more going on, hidden workings that could be complicated or easy to understand."

Erik didn't want to waste mana stones but they needed to start somewhere. Erik moved onto the next art.

He finally came to the Cobra Kicking art and watched as a man moved freely through his attacker's stance, weaving through their kicks and punches before they raised their leg. A poisonous cloud appeared around their leg and it shot forward, hitting the opposing attacker.

The man using Cobra Kicking art lashed out again and again; the poison mounted in the attacker's body, reducing his ability to fight.

The Cobra Kicking instructor backed away, easily staying out of the other's reach before they crashed to the ground.

"Using their kicking art as a way to transmit poison into their opponent's body." Erik had his Poison Body and although it was good in a group fight, allowing him to weaken those in an area around him, or even kill them, when he was fighting beside his allies, he was unable to use it.

The attendant brought back teas and snacks for them as they continued to immerse themselves in the manuals.

There was a noise in the room and Erik and Rugrat looked up.

"I am sorry but the time has run out," she said apologetically. "Though I can extend again for another ten Earth-grade mana stones," she said with a wide smile.

"Do you have your choices?" Erik asked.

"Yeah." Rugrat put forward several art manual slips and put the others to the side. Erik added his own piles to Rugrat's.

"Could you price how much these would cost?" Erik asked.

"Certainly." She took only a few minutes, writing down a few notations. "Your total for these fourteen arts is 753 Earth-grade mana stones." She looked to be beaming at them both.

"These are much higher, though they're not as high grade." Rugrat pointed to different manuals.

"Ah, but they are in great demand. We only have a few of them left. If you buy these all together, then I can get you a discount of twenty mana stones," she said.

"Done," Erik said.

"I'll get those ready for you."

She headed out of the room and Rugrat sent Erik a sound transmission.

"We've got an auction starting in forty minutes, so might need to get a move on."

"All right," Erik said.

"Only been three hours and spent nearly a Sky mana stone already. Ballin'." Rugrat threw up rocker devil horns.

Erik shook his head. "*Fuuck.*" He sighed at the other's antics.

Minnie had always been diligent in her study of Alchemy. She was a good student and carried out a lot of missions. Unlike others, she didn't have a backing in the Alchemist Association to help her along.

Although she was a good student, there were plenty of others who were good students. To the outside world, getting into the Alchemist Association was like having your path set out ahead of you.

She had thought it would be like that as well. But once she was inside the association, she learned that the competition wasn't over; it just changed. Instead of just having to work for just one competition to enter the association, everyone was fighting all the time in different ways to get the eyes of others who could help them on their path to become a stronger alchemist.

There were a lot of good students in the Alchemist Association, but standing out was hard.

She enjoyed Alchemy but in the past, many of her products had exploded, set on fire, or turned into items of destruction instead of aids.

It made her unpopular with the Alchemy workshop students as they would need to clean up after her, time that they could spend studying or doing anything that was more fun.

After some time, just for fun, she started to look at these reactions and study them, just see what kind of destruction she could create. It had been a new outlet for her and she had become good at it. She had gone to different higher tier alchemists and tried to find classes that talked about these kinds of concoctions. Poisons and aids—those were what the Alchemist Association produced, not these fiery or exploding concoctions that were highly unstable.

So when she had seen the poster asking about a kind of destructive concoction, it caught her attention. She had thought it was just some kind of prank, but then she saw the seal and the reward with it. She had been surprised.

She slept on it a few days. She didn't want to admit to anyone that she had not taken the advice that the other alchemists had given her. She had been experimenting with the destructive forces of Alchemy after their advice.

The reward and hearing people talking about it tilted her decision.

If I can complete the mission, maybe then I can interest some people in supporting me. If not, then the reward is already high enough to interest me.

So now, she found herself in front of the mission counter with the poster's information slip in hand. She passed it to the man behind the counter with a letter that contained a formula inside.

"Thank you for your submission," the man said.

She nodded and headed back to her room. Dozens of others were applying their formulas against the mission. It had to be verified that it worked and then passed to the client, who would accept or turn it down.

Shouldn't have ever submitted that formula. Now the mission department will never take another formula from me again!

She was inside a workshop she had rented for an hour, working on different Stamina concoctions. They were very easy to make, but as people used concoctions instead of food to regain their Stamina in the higher realms, there was always a great demand for them.

She was about to finish up her latest batch when there was a knock at the door.

She frowned. "I swear I activated the sound-cancelling formation," she muttered and kept on working, just filtering out the last impurities and preparing her bottles.

There was another knock at the door.

She was getting annoyed now. *Why would they turn off the sound-cancelling formation? Is there some kind of emergency?*

The instability of her wavering mind made her forget her control over the flames, burning up the concoction within.

"Dammit!" she yelled, looking at the burnt sludge in the bottom of her cauldron.

Angered, she opened the door to her workshop with a dark expression. "What is it?"

"Expert Zen Hei wishes to speak with you." The guard raised his eyebrow slightly.

Her eyes went wide and her expression paled, not sure how to react.

"Please gather your items," the guard said.

She opened and closed her mouth but none of the words came out. She just bobbed her head and went back in the room. *What does Expert Hei want with me?*

She collected up her items without any conscious thought and went back outside.

"Please follow me." The guard led her through the halls.

She lowered her head as people glanced at them in passing. Seeing his armor and the emblem on his chest, one could see he was a personal guard to Expert Hei, one of the three Pill Heads.

Seeing her, a half-step Journeyman Apprentice, trailing after him, they couldn't help but talk.

"What could Expert Hei want with such a low ranked alchemist?"

"I heard that he doesn't take on students."

"Doesn't take on students? I heard that he has a personal disciple who has a student themselves. He helped Expert Hei create that Master-level pill!"

"Do you think that she did something to get his ire?"

"Is he looking to make an example?"

All kinds of thoughts and questions fell from people's lips as Minnie hid her hands in her robe's sleeves, nervously moving them around.

They reached Expert Hei's office and the guard opened the door. A woman sat at a desk, her brow creased as she looked through different books.

"Delilah," Old Hei said from where he was working on paperwork.

"Oh, sorry, Grand Teacher." Delilah—the woman—looked up from her work.

Expert Hei smiled but continued what he was doing.

Minnie was even more confused.

"You are the one who submitted the Long Burning Flame concoction, right?"

"That is correct," Minnie said, her mind having a hard time working again. *She was in the same room as one of the three Expert Pill Heads in the Third Realm!*

She snuck glances at him. He looked like a man just working at a desk, not what she had been expecting.

"You say that the concoction will burn hot and last for a long period of time, even in small doses, and it is hard to put out?" Delilah asked.

"Yes," Minnie said.

"I would like to commission you to make as much of the concoction as possible. I will provide all of the materials and pay for workshop time. I also hope I can observe you working on the formula. I will pay you one hundred gold per finished concoction, though I will need them all in three days," Delilah said.

With each batch, I can make thirty potions, which is three Mortal mana stones for every batch. I can make around sixteen batches a day, if I took mind calming concoctions and better grade Stamina potions. It's not a backer but with that many mana stones, I can increase my cultivation or I can get manuals and formulas that were out of my reach before!

"Okay," she said.

"Good. Then let's begin," Delilah said.

Erik and Rugrat wore masks that hid their identities as they were led into the auction hall. They weren't placed in a box but on the ground floor as they had only paid for the ground floor seats. As long as they were inside the auction hall, that was all that mattered.

A woman walked out onto the stage. "Thank you for coming and visiting our humble auction house. I hope you are all having a great day. Today, we have a number of items for sale, including treasures related to smithing and healing."

The people in the room shifted in their seats, looking at one another. They were all competitors in this room now.

She smiled, feeling the tension in the room increase. "Let us bring out the first item!"

With a wave of her hand, another gorgeous woman walked out with a handsome man, rolling out a cart onto the stage.

They pulled back the covering curtain, showing a pill bottle. A slight scent came from the bottle, calming one's mind and reducing the stress placed upon them.

"This is the Singular Focus One Dream pill. A pill that can increase one's abilities to their maximum, increasing their chances to create a high-level item. Pills and aids are not forbidden in the tournaments coming up this week. If you're looking to get an edge, then the Singular Focus One Dream pill can make your dream come true!"

People competing in the competitions, or those who knew someone who would be competing in them, all leaned forward.

"The starting price is fifteen Earth-grade mana stones!"

"It is a half-step Expert pill and it has a high efficacy. Fifteen mana stones is indeed not bad," Erik said.

"With the competition, people are going to bet everything on it. These kinds of aids will only increase in price," Rugrat said.

"Eighteen!" The first threw out their bid, aiming higher to scare off others.

"Nineteen!"

"Twenty!"

"Twenty-five!"

"Forty!" someone in the boxes yelled out.

"Forty-five!" another said.

"Forty-six!" the first person in the boxes said, after some hesitation.

"Fifty." The second person spoke as if money didn't matter.

"Any more bids? This is a rare opportunity that you won't see before the competitions start!" the auctioneer announced.

She counted down and struck her hammer, still pleased with the sky-high price.

"Sold to the bidder in the boxes." The woman bowed to them, unable to see who they were.

The pill bottle was removed and another item was rolled out onto the stage.

"A medical attenuator! Of the mid Journeyman level!"

"Medical attenuator?" Rugrat asked.

"Think of it like a medical scanner. They're a cool piece of diagnostic kit, but limited in the lower grades. They can basically find the point of injury in Apprentice level, then you focus your healing spells there—bingo, person healed faster. Higher grades, you can use to actually tell you what is happening inside a person. Though they're not as accurate as the Simple Organic Scan and the Simple Organic Scan doesn't take much mana." Erik shrugged.

"Why don't people use the spell?"

"Might have been lost. Spells are expensive and people like to hoard knowledge. Whole reason we're buying these manuals instead of checking them out of the library," Erik said.

"Really is kind of dumb," Rugrat said.

"Well, hopefully we can do something about that at least for our own people," Erik said.

They sat there, seeing different items pass by. Items increased in rarity and price as it went on. The auctioneer built up the atmosphere, slowing down to draw people and speeding up so that people's eyes were red with excitement.

"Damn, auctioneers can make a lot of money," Rugrat said.

"Why do you think we own so many of them within Vuzgal and the one within Vermire?" Erik asked through sound transmission.

Rugrat nodded, as if it were only natural.

"Today I'm able to bring you a great prize. After all, the competition will come and go, but it doesn't determine one's future! There are many treasures that can change one's fate and destiny! Today, we have Dasa Keri's carving tool!"

The cloth was removed from the top of a case with a flourish. Underneath, there was a simple-looking carving tool. It looked well-worn but one could see that sparks of mana moved along the blade and the handle.

"After using it for so long, Dasa Keri—who was rumored to have reached the medium Expert level—left an imprint upon the carving tool, raising the mid Journeyman-level carving tool to that of an imprinted weapon!"

Erik looked at Rugrat, who had his eyes closed, his hands moving as if he looked through a computer.

Rugrat opened his eyes and used his sound transmission device.

"An imprinted item is a weapon that has adapted to a user completely. If someone else was to use it, they wouldn't be able to use it effectively for its primary role, but they would be able to gain insights from the person who imprinted upon it. Only powerful people can do this. You can have special items to allow someone to imprint on a weapon quicker. Say a sword sect have a bunch of powerful members imprint their learnings into a sword; then, when someone is using that sword, they have a guide with the sword. Problem is that after the imprinting, it will eventually weaken," Rugrat said.

Erik and Rugrat weren't the only two talking. The room was filled with a commotion as people went back and forth, sharing what they knew with their neighbors.

"The bidding will start at fifty Earth-grade mana stones. One must increase the bid by no less than ten mana stones," the auctioneer said with a blazing smile.

Many could only sit back and watch what was happening. The amount of mana stones had long since passed their threshold.

"Sixty!"

"Eighty!" another called out. The auction hall turned silent.

"Ninety!" Another voice spoke up.

The hall went silent again as the different people bidding stared at one another.

"Should we bid?" Erik asked, through his sound transmission.

"We don't know how much imprint is left on it, and don't we have our own Expert-level crafters? With time, our people will increase this skill. Right now, the thing holding them back are those technique manuals—or a lack of them, really.

"With those and what we have already, it'll cost more, but the carving tool is good to raise only a few people's strength. With the manuals, we can pass them on to more people and increase the ability of all the people in Alva," Rugrat said.

"Look at you—thinking ahead," Erik said.

"Tan Xue would kick my ass if we spent all of our money on some formation carving tool."

Erik let out a chuckle and shook his head. A few people looked over to him.

"Don't draw attention. I am a tree, I am a tree, don't look at me!" Rugrat said.

"Is that how you got through recon training?"

"Yes, that and a liberal amount of dark humor, caffeine, and anger," Rugrat said.

"Sold for one hundred Earth mana stones to Formation Journeyman Huo," the auctioneer said to the pleased-looking older man in the higher boxes.

"Tools and techniques—one needs them all if they will break through into the Expert realm. Today we bring you an unknown healing technique manual. It was found in a hidden Expert's cultivation retreat. It boasts the ability to allow one to cast multiple healing spells at the same time, with decreasing one's mana cost by at least five percent and increase the power of the spell by ten percent. Though it is damaged, so we believe it is a half Expert-grade healing technique," the auctioneer said.

The healers all leaned forward and Erik raised an eyebrow. An Expert's retreat was a special cultivation area that an Expert created to get away from distractions to attempt a breakthrough in their cultivation.

"Useful?" Rugrat asked.

"I think so. If it can really do two spells at once, then I could cast a healing spell and then a Stamina recovery spell, so that I would just have to rely on the patient's ability to recover Stamina. Like with Chonglu—I would have been able to heal him in just an hour or less instead of taking several hours."

"Shall we?"

"I think we shall," Erik said.

"You sound like some kind of Dracula," Rugrat said.

"We will start the bidding at eighty Earth mana stones. Every increase must be no less than ten Earth mana stones."

Erik shot Rugrat a look as he raised his hand. But as he did, a voice drowned out the raised hands.

"One hundred!"

"There is a bid for one hundred Earth mana stones from Elder Mo of the Agate Sword sect."

The others who might bid on the item all cooled their bidding.

"One hundred and ten," a man in the Divine Sunset sect box said.

"One hundred and forty," the elder from the Agate Sword sect said back.

All others, including the sects, had given up on the manual.

"One hundred and fifty." Erik raised his hand.

The eyes in the room moved from the boxes to the people on the floor.

The auctioneer's eyes thinned as she looked at the hidden men sitting at the table. "If one does not pay the required mana stones promptly, then they will have to pay a fine and the item will not be given to them," she said.

"Ouch. I think she's saying that we're too poor." Rugrat laughed, sending his message via sound transmission.

"I understand," Erik said in a tired voice.

Her eyes stayed on him before she turned back to the podium and her smile returned in full force, looking at the two boxes. "Any more bids!"

"Shall we see if he has the strength in order to place such a bid? My Divine Sunset sect wishes to know instead of having numbers inflated," the elder said with a note of derision aimed at the auction house.

Falsely raising prices could be a great issue.

"You'll see in the end," Erik said, without looking behind him.

The elder turned to the people in his box; those in the Agate Sword sect talked to one another as well.

"What do you think they're doing?" Erik asked.

"From what I can read on their lips, they're looking into our background. They want to know if we're part of the auction or if we're wandering Experts, or just people trying to make a scene," Rugrat said.

"Your lip reading skills are impressive."

"Higher reaction time makes it a lot easier," Rugrat said.

"One hundred and sixty," Elder Mo from the Agate Sword sect said, looking at the two men for a reaction.

Erik raised his hand.

"One hundred and seventy," the auctioneer said.

"One hundred and eighty!" Elder Mo said again.

Erik rose his hand again. "One hundred and ninety."

Elder Mo fell silent and the Divine Sunset sect fell silent, using the opportunity to drop out of the bidding without being noticed, saving them from embarrassment.

"Sold to the man on the floor," the auctioneer said.

The whole auction house had a weird atmosphere as Erik and Rugrat sat there, people all looking at them as the next item was brought out.

"We only bring you the best of items. As the last item for this auction, we have the intermediary woodworking technique manual, called Infusion of Mana, a technique that is supposed to be able to combine wood together, increasing its overall grade or, through different mixtures, change its properties. For making tools, bows, spears, hammers, magical staffs, and formation flags, it is a must-have manual!"

Rugrat moved in his seat.

"We getting it?" Erik asked.

"I don't see why not," Rugrat said.

"Your turn," Erik said.

"We will start the bidding at one hundred and fifty Earth mana stones!"

The eyes turned to the boxes as they were the only people to have that sort of money.

"Two hundred," the people from the Golden Path box said.

"Two hundred and fifty!" the Soul Hammer box said.

"Two hundred and eighty," the leader from the Divine Sunset sect said.

"They're going all-out," someone on the floor said.

"Metal or wood—everything in the Ten Realms is built with these two items, from tools to weapons. An art that allows one to combine wood as if smelting metal, it could increase their strength dramatically."

"Thinking about it, only a big group could make the most use of it. There are so many combinations to make, you would need people to figure out all of the useful ones!"

"Do you think any of us can bid on something like that?"

The bidding had cooled slightly as the Golden Path elder spoke up with a pressured look on his face, staring at the other sect leadership.

"Three hundred and fifty," he said, his voice one of warning.

"Four hundred," Rugrat said from beside Erik.

Everyone once again looked at the mysterious pair.

The elder in the Golden Path sect smacked the chair and used his control over mana. It was an invisible force but it dropped like a hammer on top of Erik and Rugrat.

"A smith bidding on a wood item, interesting," Rugrat said.

Erik and Rugrat felt pressured underneath the hammer, but with their Mana Rebirth, they were much stronger than someone of the same level in terms of mana. Add in their Body Cultivation and their own control over mana with their skills, they were able to hold up under the pressure. It was difficult, but they kept their composure, acting as if it wasn't any problem.

"Do it again and I'll consider it an attack." Rugrat sent a thread of his own mana back. It was invisible and condensed, but it moved faster and pierced through the mana under the man's control, shooting past his ear and leaving a hole in the wall behind him.

The pressure on Erik and Rugrat disappeared as the Expert knew that the hidden mana attack could have very well attacked his body.

The people on the floor might not have known what was going on, but the different sects and the auctioneer knew what had happened.

"Are there any more bids!" she said, looking to cover over the incident, looking at the two men on the floor with new interest.

No one else bid on the item as she counted down. "That brings our auction to its conclusion!" she said. "Thank you all for attending and I hope you enjoy the tournament!"

Erik and Rugrat headed out to where they could collect their items.

A number of guards waited for them, awaiting the mana stones.

"If you could deposit the mana stones into here, then I can give you your items," the guard leader said with a half-smile as he held out a storage box.

Erik put his hand on it and deposited the mana stones.

The guard looked at the box and then coughed. An awkward expression appeared on his face before his smile became more real. "Please wait inside.

The items will be brought to you in a moment." He waved to a room behind the guards.

The guards moved aside. Their movements were awkward, as if they were not expecting to have to move aside.

Erik and Rugrat passed through them and into the room.

"They take a lot more precautions here," Rugrat said.

"Well, there are a lot of people from all over. To get to this realm, most people need backing of some kind. We just spent a lot of mana stones, so they're looking at us, just wondering who we are and what our background is. If we're weak, then they can pressure us like the people did in the lower levels. If we're not weak, they don't want to piss us off and have the people behind us put pressure on them. Everything that is done here is a tactical decision," Erik said.

"Still, they're willing to test others," Rugrat said.

"Yeah, but I think that we got through that rather well," Erik said.

Two of the women who had been with the items walked into the room and put down the goods.

Erik and Rugrat had a hard time looking at them straight on. They were incredibly pretty and seeing the awkward way that the two looked away only made them smile more.

"Please let us know if you need anything else," one of them said, her eyes flickering suggestively as the other played with her finger in her mouth.

"We'll—"

"Thank you for the offer," Erik said, speaking over Rugrat before his hindbrain got him into trouble.

They smiled and left the room.

Erik took the items into his storage ring. "Get some food and then we can head to the underground auction tonight."

Rugrat swallowed his complaints and focused on the task at hand, once again talking via sound transmission. "We've already spent about half of our wealth. These things aren't cheap."

"No, but the underground auction should have harder-to-find manuals and arts, and those aren't directly linked to the competition as there are other people coming from all over to bid on these items, simply using the competition as a cover."

They left the room and headed out of the auction house. People from the auction house bowed to them as they entered the streets and went to find somewhere to eat.

"Looks like we've got some people tailing us," Rugrat said.

"How do you know?"

"Check that mana around your body. You will feel a magical symbol attached to your body. With a surge of mana, you could erase it, but then people would be more suspicious."

"Well, we are trying to make people leave us alone," Erik said.

"That makes sense. I'm thinking like a combatant instead of some arrogant prick with money to spend."

Erik sensed with his mana domain there was an ovaloid around him where he could sense the mana flow and direct it easier, allowing him much higher control over mana outside his body.

He could feel all of the mana around him, including the linked mana that was resting on his skin.

Erik sent a surge of mana into it, breaking the connection and clearing himself of any tracking spells.

"What were you able to find out?" Elder Dai asked as he sipped on some tea. He wore the symbol of the Golden Path sect and was the same man who had pressured Erik and Rugrat with his mana aura.

"They got the items and then left the auction house. We had people follow them, but then their tracking spells were destroyed after they were affixed to their bodies. We have tried to compile information on who they are and where they come from. It looks like, based on the others who are tracking them, they shouldn't be from one of the other sects in the competition."

"So are they people from another sect? Are they from one of the associations? Or are they just on their own? We need to know their backer. We can't make a move until we do," Elder Dai warned in a grave tone.

The spy cupped his fists. "We know that they came through the totem. They did have a guide with them, though she has already left."

"Do we know where she went?"

"To the Fourth Realm, to Vuzgal."

"Vuzgal, the crafting city?" Elder Dai held his tea in mid-air.

"Yes, Elder."

Elder Dia let out a sigh and drank from his tea, but his eyes were open, thinking and analyzing before he came to a decision.

"Until we are able to find out what their background is, no one is to do anything. If she went to Vuzgal, she might have come from it as well. They could be two Elites sent by a sect that is fighting in the Fourth Realm, sent here to gather items to increase the strength of their sect. We might be strong in terms of crafting, but many of the Sixth Realm sects fight in the Fourth. We must be careful!"

"I will make sure to gather the information as quickly as possible and have people watching them and warning others in the sect to not cause issues." The spy bowed.

"Good." Elder Dai sent him off.

Other meetings with similar contents were being held in other locations in the city as the mysterious duo caused a stir within the upper echelons of the sect leadership.

"Hope you have a good lunch," Erik said as he cheered Rugrat's Stamina potion with his own and drank it.

Rugrat put it down and nodded with approval. "Tastes like melted mint chocolate chip."

"Yeah. I thought that the old flavors weren't really cutting it. Worked up a new formula. It takes a few more herbs and spices but it's much tastier. I was even able to make one that is close to hot sauce."

"Man, you know what I miss?"

"No, but I'm sure you'll tell me."

"Chicken wings—spicy honey, with a side of burn-your-mouth-off red beans and rice. Mmmm. Damn, I could go for some of that. Bit of cornbread. Oh, bacon—bacon, man! Bacon and grits!"

"Will you get focused? You're making me hungry, jackass."

"I wonder if we can get Jia Feng to try it out?"

Erik actually paused. "Well, if we could tell her the basics, I don't see why not. Like, we know how it goes, but you ever made chicken wings?"

"No, but I know how to make cornbread and red beans and rice. Would need to talk to the farmers about getting something similar and then testing that out."

"Hash browns, man. Oh, damn, I could go for some hash browns. You know, the—"

"Patties, not the jumbled-up, cut-up potatoes on the side. Yeah, I know." Rugrat nodded.

Erik looked outside and started to stand, wiping his face. "We've got to go. It's about time for the auction."

They settled up and moved through the city. They went through the recreational district. There were bars and spas mixed among different places selling Stamina potions and drinks. Food still took up too much precious space, but alcohol could be combined with different cultivation aids, increasing one's cultivation passively and helping them recover.

They went to a building that was a little away from the others. No one loitered outside its entrance; a guard simply stood there.

They nodded to him and he allowed them past.

Inside, there was a large bath house. People walked around the entrance wearing their bathrobes.

They walked up to the counter and a man smiled at them.

"A bath for two or separate baths?"

"Auction," Erik said in a low voice so others wouldn't be able to hear.

The man's eyes flashed in interest, looking at the duo. "Please, for the special, come with me." The man guided them back through bathing rooms that were separated by sliding doors. People were having meetings; others were having a bit more heady fun as the noises of men and women reached Erik and Rugrat.

They entered an empty room. The man closed the door and pressed a secret button on the wall between the two large baths in the room.

A set of illuminated stairs was revealed. The man bowed and waved them forward.

Erik and Rugrat went down the stairs, finding that they were in a bright and well-lit underground room. People moved about, coming down from other Ikazi bath houses dotted across the city.

Many wore masks or had cast spells on themselves, making it hard for one to see their appearance.

Erik and Rugrat hadn't changed their appearances since the auction earlier, so a few people looked at them, wondering whether they were the same two people who had stirred up the earlier auction, going up against the Agate Sword sect and the Divine Sunset sect.

Erik and Rugrat reached the counters at the entrance.

"Two entrance tickets," Erik said.

"Regular, or VIP seats?"

"Regular," Erik said. "As long as we can see the items."

"Two Earth-grade mana stones as deposit."

Erik waved his hand. Four appeared on the counter.

The man nodded and quickly took the stones, and then passed them each an entrance medallion.

They took them and walked past the guards into the large hall where people were gathering, reading the different information that was dotted around the room relating to the objects that were up for sale. There were also drinks on offer.

Erik and Rugrat moved to the boxes that had arts and techniques in them.

They scanned the boxes. They moved quickly, ignoring others and the looks that they were getting from people.

"Do you think that is the mysterious duo?" Auctioneer Yu Li asked his boss and the leader of the Ikazi baths, Wen Rong.

"Does it matter as long as they abide by the rules?" Wen Rong glanced over the two and then scanned the rest of the room.

"All of the sects have brought someone," Yu Li said.

"If they can get their hands on the Oleha fruit, then they can possibly split it and then start to create their own fruits and grow the strength of their beasts. All of them have to use beasts moving from place to place and they're invaluable guards that will have no fear, unlike human guards," Wen Rong said, seeing through these sects.

"I will be sure to bring us the highest price!" Yu Li promised.

"I expect no less."

Wen Rong's words seemed light but Yu Li's expression seemed to become a bit weaker.

"It's about time for the auction to start." Wen Rong turned and left Yu Li.

Erik and Rugrat went into the main auction hall as the doors were now open.

"Did you make a list?" Erik asked via sound transmission.

"Of course," Rugrat said.

They took their seats as the people filed into the auction hall.

As people finished seating themselves, a middle-aged man walked out on stage. He looked simple but there was a dangerous way he moved, as if assessing everyone in the room. This was an underground auction, after all, selling items that had been stolen or had dark pasts. Although they were kind on the surface, they had dark roots.

"Hello, everyone. Thank you for attending our auction today. My name is Yu Li and I will be the auctioneer tonight! First up, we have a rare enhancing material that can be used in smithing, the Goldencaste ore!"

The crowd's energy built up as different items were brought out. Their quality was much higher than the items that were held in the previous auction.

"I think that being a dark auction, they're only willing to put up items that are sure to get them a profit. Anything that will get them small grievances to sell it but aren't worth that much money aren't worth it," Rugrat said as they continued to sit there and wait.

"The formation technique is up next," Erik said.

"We have a formation technique up for auction next! To use it, one will need to create a formation that gains the approval of the technique and then they can get the information within. Thoroughly studying the technique, we believe that a high Expert-level formation technique is located inside."

"With risks comes opportunity," Rugrat said.

"How sure are you that the people in the formation workshop will be able to unlock this scroll?"

"I am not sure at all. Though I think that it will prove as a challenge for them—make them create more and more formations in order to open it, increase the power of their formations. Give them a goal to work toward and then promise resources to the person who opens it," Rugrat said.

"Sneaky," Erik said with approval, nodding underneath his doupeng.

"We will start the bidding at fifty Earth mana stones, increasing by a minimum of ten mana stones."

"One hundred and fifty." Rugrat's voice contained a challenge. He spoke as soon as Yu Li had stopped.

People were shocked.

"Why not increase the price slowly?"

"There are many who are interested, but how can one be so interested to increase the price by three times?"

"Maybe they have a key to open it?"

"A key to open it?" Another scoffed at the person's suggestion. "And I will just accidentally drink a potion that will allow me to ascend to the Seventh Realm in one shot!"

The rest of the auction hall looked at the two people. Once again, the scenes from earlier that morning played through everyone's heads.

"It must be those two from that earlier auction!"

"They only bid on the technique manuals and the arts there as well. Are they looking to buy them all up?"

"What does it matter? They're not the main attractions at the auction."

"Talk for yourself—the Vivid Art mid-Expert level painting art shall be mine!"

"Are there any more bids?" Lu Yi looked out at everyone, but the momentum had been lost. There was interest and curiosity that could be stoked, but hearing the price already reach such a stage, everyone felt as if cold water had been dumped on their spirits. They didn't want to compete for what might just be some unlockable scroll in the end!

"Sold to the gentleman in the floor area! Next, we have a Blood Ruby healing tool. It is sure to help one recover their lost vitality! It is a rare tool that is hard to find and harder to create, using monster cores and others' life force!"

"Nasty piece of kit," Rugrat said.

"Yeah, just sucking the power out of someone to be used by someone else. Though, it is the way of the Ten Realms."

The auction continued. As each technique manual came up, Erik or Rugrat would bid on it. When the bids went higher than they wanted, they would stop, not influenced by the atmosphere as the people who had been bidding found themselves paying a massive amount for the goods. Fewer people started to compete with them as it seemed as though they had an endless amount of mana stones, but didn't go above a certain amount.

"We have a bow art, the Dancing Archer, increasing one's speed and the strength of their attacks! Bidding will start at eighty mana stones!"

The price raced upward.

"One hundred and seventy," Rugrat said.

"Eighty!"

"Ninety!" Another looked around in challenge.

"Two hundred," Rugrat said simply.

"Two ten!" the first yelled out.

Rugrat sat back in his chair. The bidder seemed to be waiting for more of a reaction but there wasn't one coming.

"I wonder what we can have for dinner?" Rugrat asked.

"Fish or meat?"

"Could go for some catfish, or oysters," Rugrat said.

"You sure you don't want the bow art?"

"Well, I would be interested in the increased movement speed and it might be useful for some people, but we don't really need more strength with our weapons. We don't need to pull back on a string, after all."

"We have another locked artifact. This one is a compendium of smithing blueprints. One will need to complete a trial for the scroll in order to gain access to it. We believe that there are thirteen blueprints inside and none of them are below the Expert rank."

This created a stir. Most of the people who had come to the competition had a smithing background or smiths in their group. Smithing was one of the easier skills to get into as it could be completed in any realm without needing too many resources that were hard to attain.

"Bidding will start at one hundred Earth mana stones!"

"Three hundred!" Rugrat said.

"He did it again!"

"Three times the base price!"

The different people shied away from saying anything.

"Three ten!"

"Three hundred and fifty," Rugrat said.

The challenger was quiet, staring at Rugrat.

"Truly, the rich can step on any other! How much money do they have? Do they live on a mana stone mine?"

"Well, they aren't wrong." Rugrat laughed through his sound transmission as the scroll made its way over to them.

"This item needs no introduction as I am sure you know it—the Oleha fruit. An item that can raise the bloodline purity of beasts and increase their fighting prowess dramatically. They are rare to find in the wild as the groups that have them control their distribution tightly. I can tell you that this is not only a fruit, but it is a blossoming fruit!"

There was a stir in the crowd and Erik raised an eyebrow. *So this is why the sects are interested in it so much. They must have gotten information on this beforehand.*

If cultivated carefully, then it could turn into a tactical resource for the sect, allowing them to increase their strength. As no one knew one another's identities here, no one would be able to find out who the winner of the fruit was, so the sect or group could raise it in secret. Also, it allowed people from different sects that weren't as big as the main competitors to fight for it as they didn't have to worry about the larger sects finding out their identity at the auction.

"I can sense you're all eager to start the bidding! We will start at no base price and anyone can increase by any price, including mana stones and gold."

The room went quiet as people looked at one another, and then burned with a fiery passion.

It was a war of wealth. One could use everything at their disposal to go against one another. If they had just one more gold coin, then they could win!

The atmosphere only increased in intensity as people from across the room leaned forward.

"Let us begin the auction!" Yu Li smacked his hammer and there was a flurry of noise.

"Two hundred Mortal mana stones!"

"Two hundred and-twenty!"

He couldn't keep up with the bids being called out.

"Three hundred Earth, forty Mortal!"

The bidding started to cool down as there were less and less people able to compete with one another. Some people sent out their people to collect more mana stones so that they could bid higher.

"Three hundred and twenty Earth, four hundred Mortal!"

"Three hundred thirty!"

"Three forty-five."

"Three forty-seven."

"Three eighty-two!"

"Shall we bid?" Rugrat asked through sound transmission.

"No need to show off. We can find Alchemy formulas and work with our beasts on the healer side to increase their strength," Erik said.

"Well, how do they have so few mana stones?"

"So few? The sects might be powerful places, but most of their money is put toward increasing the strength of their people or in different ventures. They are powerful, yes, but that is due to their people's strength. They have to give out resources to these people. They have classes to run, people to pay. Their liquid funds are limited. We own Vuzgal, but as for our resources, we're just using the resources that we looted from Vuzgal or what the teams have collected from the dungeons we control. Our costs are much lower and people pay us to learn at our academies. We don't fork out resources to them unless we hire them and we can directly see their results and increase our strength. We also, literally, have mana stone mines and attract a ton of people to trade in the city with our low tax rates and high quality goods. Then throw in rent—the sects have that too, but then they're hosting most of their own people, instead of getting money from others."

"Ugh, just thinking about it all makes my head hurt," Rugrat complained.

"Yeah, I forget we're city lords and dungeon masters most of the time," Erik said.

"Looks like someone is about to win," Rugrat said as the bidding slowed.

"Four hundred and twelve Earth mana stones!"

"Four hundred and eighteen Earth, six hundred Mortal!" a woman who had been driven crazy with the bidding said, gripping onto the banister of her booth.

The others who had been bidding against her looked to the people in their booths, but they weren't able to come up with a higher bid.

All of this fell into Yu Li's eyes.

"Sold to the victorious lady in the booths!" Yu Li clapped.

Others clapped along with him. It was sure that the group that the woman was with would increase their standing in the future if they were able to raise the Oleha fruit properly.

"With that, our auction has come to an end. Please gather your purchases and I hope that you have a good competition!" The lights in the room became brighter.

Erik and Rugrat headed out before anyone could try to intercept them and strike up a conversation. They headed right to the rooms where they could get their goods.

They were allowed past with a flash of their medallion. They passed their mana stones over to someone wearing a mask.

They checked the amount and then waved them forward into a second room. They took their items and then left, leaving through a secret entrance so people wouldn't be able to follow them.

"Looks like the dark auction is considerate to its winners," Rugrat said as they appeared in the middle of a park, with no one around.

"It wouldn't do for people to have their goods snatched from them in the auction hall, but once they're out of the hall, then anything is free game," Erik said as they left the park.

Erik and Rugrat altered their outfits slightly, changing their cloaks and taking off their doupengs. They wrapped up their heads in a keffiyeh, hiding their features again but looking completely different.

They headed through the streets, reaching a simple inn and getting a room.

They took out all of their auction items. Erik looked at the information on all of them. There were four in total, showing the stats and information of the different techniques and arts that they were able to get.

"Not a bad haul," Erik said.

"How many mana stones do we have left?" Rugrat had finished checking the room and sat at the table next to the window, looking out to see whether anyone had followed them.

"We've got just about one Sky mana stone worth left." Erik pulled out a piece of paper that they had listed all of the auctions that were going on.

The list was extensive, with times and locations listed across it.

"Well then, we've got, what, two—maybe three—of the smaller auctions to go to?"

"Yeah. I thought that the items in the underground auction would be cheaper, but instead people were all excited and with being anonymous, they acted like big shots and put down more money." Erik sighed.

"Don't worry. We're sure to pick up a number of them." Rugrat pulled out one of the blacksmithing technique manuals, Forging Fist art, and started to read it.

"Bit eager?"

"I have to take every advantage that I can get over Taran. I might even be able to catch up with Tan Xue. Though shouldn't you be worrying about yourself—you know, the student catching up with the teacher?"

Erik let out a cough, trying to not think about how shameless Rugrat was, or admit how he was right. Delilah was running Alva and yet she was still able to increase her Alchemy skills to the point that they were close to his own. He had been able to reclaim his lead once again, but there was no telling how long it would last.

She was biting at his heels—and it only gave him more energy to compete.

His eyes rested on the healing technique. Alchemy was a powerful skill and it was the one that he used most of the time, but the healing arts couldn't be underestimated. They were one of the hardest skills to train as it needed to have wounded people. Seeing the darkness of the Ten Realms, Erik didn't think he wanted to imagine how the higher ranked healers had been able to get to their position.

So the two men started to read their technique manuals and new information filled their minds.

They started to exercise their skills in different ways, making noises of understanding as they seemed to be discovering a new path ahead of them.

Erik and Rugrat's horizons weren't the only ones growing as two new Experts agreed to join the Vuzgal Crafter's Association.

There were now only very few groups that had more Experts than Vuzgal and they were looking to buy more.

The Battle Arena also opened their doors to the first tournament they were hosting. The tickets were free—one only needed to make a bet, the minimum, one gold.

People flocked to the arena, with the seats quickly filling up in the one hundred arena second floor.

There were screens outside of the arena and there were screens in the Wayside Inns and the Sky Reaching Restaurants so people could see the fighting from across the city.

"Truly, Vuzgal is leading the way in other cities! They charge an extra fee but we can sit here in the Sky Reaching Restaurant, enjoying our food and watching the competition instead of being crammed into the arena!" Patrons would yell out in happiness.

People who had been unable to get a ticket now flooded these other venues in droves.

"It's as if they've forgotten that we control all of these businesses." Domonos stood beside Hiao Xen, reviewing what was happening in the city.

"People love a show," Chonglu said, sitting back and behind Hiao Xen.

Hiao Xen nodded. He had just come to know Chonglu but he was a smart man, loyal to his very core to Erik and Rugrat. Anything he was asked to do, he would carry out as soon as possible. He had tied his family to them completely, sending them to the academy.

Hiao Xen knew about his wife and could piece together some of what Erik and Rugrat had done. *I hope that it is worth falling out with the Stone Fist sect.*

Many of the Experts and the people from the academy had taken a break from their studies in order to come and see the match. It was the talk of the city and most of them had seating already. There had been a small competition within the academy for people to prove their skills and win seats to be there for the Battle Arena opening games.

Hiao Xen saw Tan Xue's hand at work here. The Vuzgal Academy had been stirred up with people competing with one another, but unlike other sects and large groups that had multiple skills involved, they were all considered students of the academy first and then their skill second.

People didn't look down on one another for working on different skills; instead, they worked together more often. The Alchemy and healing students were practically the same group; the smiths and the woodworkers were the same way, with the formation masters mixed in.

This kind of community, instead of a competitive mash of people, proved to create more results and reduce issues.

Those who were unable to put down their arrogance and tried to push their views on others or started to throw their weight around were quickly dismissed. This was a place for people to learn and to become stronger; there was no need to waste time on these people playing political games, trying to get some measure of sympathy or power from their displays. The only thing that mattered was one's results, not their background.

Hiao Xen looked at the other groups in attendance. There were members from the associations, the different sects and clans that had built up some influence in Vuzgal. Many of them had tried to insert people into the academy in one way or another, Hiao Xen had informed Tan Xue, to which she'd simply responded: "Well, if they're willing to pay for the classes then we're willing to teach them as long as they don't step out beyond what is written down in the school rules."

"She makes it seem so simple." Hiao Xen smiled to himself, impressed by the people Erik and Rugrat had been able to bring around themselves and allow to run their different responsibilities.

"Did you say something?" Chonglu asked.

"I was just thinking on when I was thinking about taking this job from Erik and Rugrat. I wondered just what would happen—I would have never thought that we would be here. There will be difficulties in the future, of that I am sure, but I think that it should be an interesting time in my life, seeing just what they do." Hiao Xen laughed.

"Have you heard the story of the two coppers?" Chonglu asked, sitting in his seat, his eyes looking out to the arena but not seeing it.

"Two coppers?"

"Erik and Rugrat were healing people. Whoever they were, whatever their station in life, they would take two coppers from the person who needed aid. No more, no less. If they needed complicated items or aids, then they needed to pay for that. But simple stuff—two coppers. My children were sick and I needed their help. I would have given anything to them, sworn my life to them if they were able to save my children. You know what Erik did when I asked what he wanted?" Chonglu locked his eyes with Hiao Xen, the corner of his mouth pulled up in a smile.

"What?"

Chonglu raised his four fingers. "Four coppers, two for each of my children," Chonglu said. "Erik and Rugrat don't really care about power. They just want to protect what they have. If someone does something in front of them that they can't take, they'll act on it. Thankfully, they've had the strength thus far that nothing too bad has happened and they've been able to get to this stage."

I just hope for their sakes and the sake of everyone here that they're always stronger than their opponents. They've come so far, but it will only take one large loss for it all to come down.

34 Seeing the Sights

Erik and Rugrat woke up the next day, eating their meals in their room as they started to look through the scrolls that they had gotten the previous day.

Rugrat looked out the window. People laughed and joked, talking about the people competing and going off to watch the game on for the day.

Rugrat looked over at Erik, who looked up from his studying.

"What?"

Rugrat sat back in his chair. It creaked underneath his weight. "How are you?"

"What kind of question is that?"

"Like, how are you feeling? We've been in the Ten Realms for a few years now, but we haven't even really stopped. We've run from one thing to another as fast as possible."

"Well, we slowed down after taking Vuzgal," Erik said.

They only needed to share a look before Erik sat back in his chair.

"Yeah, we really haven't taken that much time. There is always something to do. Having the screens and our stats is a blessing and a curse. We can see our progress but we're already competitive people, so when we have something that we can show our progress and ability with, then we just want to become as strong as possible as fast as possible, create our own ways to play the system. Which means that while it is fun, we don't take a break. We get caught up in getting the next thing so sleeping or anything else isn't as important."

"Then, if we increase our Stamina enough, we don't need to sleep." Rugrat snorted.

"Yeah, but it's so damn fun and rewarding to see those numbers, the prompts. Like getting these scrolls and then seeing their information, opening them. The things that we can do if we are able to learn them. Want to do everything and anything but we can't."

"We've both got two crafts that we're trying to work on, but we're prioritizing one over the other. You have the background knowledge for being a healer. Though you're focusing heavily on Alchemy," Rugrat said.

"And you're focusing heavily on smithing, with only a small focus on formations. Why don't you focus on formations more?" Erik asked.

"Well, I think that it's mostly because I see it and I understand it, but it's like computers to me. I know how to use them, and with a video I could put them together, but the parts inside it, what they do? The coding of the machine? That's not what I understand. Formations are the internal workings and I'm hoping that with advancing my smithing skills that I will be able to use that to understand formations. As I make more items, or see more smithed items, see other smiths at work, then I can learn enough with smithing that the formations stuff just clicks." Rugrat shrugged. "That's my hope. Will it work out? I'm not sure. I'm scared that without knowing about formations that the items that I make won't be as strong as they could be."

"Craving that perfection." Erik nodded as their conversation came full circle.

The two of them sat there in silence for some time.

"Why don't we go and check out the tournament? See others competing against one another, have some beers and hang out for the day?"

"I wonder if they have fried chicken." Rugrat grinned and stood. Rugrat pulled on his vest and jumped with it, settling everything down; he wrapped up his head with his keffiyeh and then put on his cloak. Erik followed suit.

"Do you know what is going on today?"

"Not really sure. I think that it might just be the first day of the competition, so it should be everyone fighting it out to advance. We can just ask someone what games are going on today."

Erik pulled his cloak on and made sure that it hid his weapons.

"Armed, armored, and ready to rock and roll!"

They checked the room, making sure they had everything before leaving. If they left a scroll behind, they'd definitely feel it the next day.

"With the whole Body Cultivation, you finding it hard to get drunk now?" Rugrat asked.

"Yeah. I guess with the body's ability to repair itself, it starts to sober you up quick."

"Damn, that sucks ass," Rugrat muttered.

"Though you can buy powerful alcohol that might also be a substitute for gasoline—or maybe your PBRs."

"Hey, what you hating on my PBRs for? They're a national treasure and a beloved drink for all college kids, broke-ass marines, and tailgaters," Rugrat said proudly as they reached the tavern and walked up to the tavern/inn owner.

"Anything I can help you with?" he asked, his voice as rough as his looks and demeanor. He was a man all too used to annoying drunk and angry patrons.

"What competitions are going on today?" Erik asked.

The man raised an eyebrow, checking whether they were trying to play some kind of joke on him.

He looked up at the ceiling. "Should be the formation masters and woodworkers today. Formations in the south side, woodworkers to the north."

"Thanks." Erik tossed the man a Mortal mana stone and turned around.

"You got anything that'll get a Body Cultivator drunk?" Rugrat asked.

The tavern owner cracked a smile and pulled out a bottle from under the bar. "This'll get someone with a Body Like Iron good and drunk. Just fifty Mortal mana stones."

"I'll take two of them." Rugrat pulled out a box of Mortal mana stones.

The tavern owner pulled out a second bottle and took the Mortal mana stones.

"Good doing business with you!" Rugrat said as he opened the bottle.

"Can we drink in the street here?" Erik asked.

"Yeah," the tavern owner said, as if the question were absurd.

"I'm liking this place more and more!" Rugrat said.

"Now we've got booze, but how in the hell are we going to drink it?" Erik pointed at his keffiyeh as Rugrat passed him the second bottle.

"Well." Rugrat stuck his fingers between the keffiyeh fold and his face, partly pulling it apart so his mouth showed.

"Heh, look," Rugrat said, proud of his handiwork.

"Now you just look insane," Erik muttered.

Rugrat laughed as he tapped his bottle against Erik's and tapped it on a nearby table before taking a big swig from the bottle.

To the fallen.

He let out a hiss and shook his head. "Damn! That's almost as good as my shine back home—pears and cinnamon or something like it, Ten Realms style!"

Erik, who had freed his mouth, tapped the bottle on the table and took a drink as well. He let out a whistle and he shook his head from side to side.

"Bit of the old day drinking! We should find some breakfast and we need to see about that fried chicken." Rugrat took out the other bottle and cracked it open.

"Formation master tourney?" Erik asked.

"Read my mind!" Rugrat walked forward before pausing and turning to face Erik. "Which way is south?"

Erik pressed his lips together and shrugged before taking another drink. "This keffiyeh is a pain to drink under."

Rugrat walked over to the nearest person, a girl who was trying to sell goods. "Hello, miss. I was wondering if you knew where the woodworker competition is happening?"

She looked him up and down: a big man in a bulky cloak, with only his eyes showing, and a bottle of drink in his hand with another behind him, messing with his scarf so that he could drink through it.

She looked from Erik back to Rugrat, her eyes thinning. "It's down that street. You just have to go straight," she said warily.

"Thank you!" Rugrat said, trying to be super friendly to cover over how weird he and Erik currently looked.

Maybe Erik was right about how dumb it looks while wearing a closed keffiyeh and drinking through it. Rugrat snorted and then took another swig as he and Erik wandered down the road.

"Shit, do you remember Doberman that one day when he got so sun fucked that the first sergeant thought he was drunk and wanted to call the MPs?"

"Yeah. I had to IV him. The idiot had only drank his canteen all day!"

"What an idiot." Rugrat shook his head and laughed.

"Didn't he marry a girl from back home? Wasn't everyone saying that it was his cousin?"

"Yeah, got married in Vegas," Rugrat said. "We nearly got arrested."

"Let's try and, you know, not get arrested this time?"

"I do like that plan, but come on, get to know new cultures, people, and places. Then get arrested and see what their jails are like. It's the full tour!"

"Rugrat, we are not getting arrested!"

"Never say never, my friend!"

"I…" Erik just looked at Rugrat and then drank through his keffiyeh. "Ugh, just filtered that a second time." Erik moved the keffiyeh, trying to suck the alcohol out of it.

"This looks like it," Rugrat said.

The two of them had gone through about half of their bottles. The city wasn't small and although the girl's directions were right, it was a two-hour walk to reach the stadium.

"Let's get tickets." Erik walked up to the stadium. Only a few people were outside; he could hear the sound of people talking from within the stadium.

"Two tickets for the formation tournament," Erik said.

"All of the games or just this one?" the woman asked.

"Just this one," Erik said.

"One hundred Mortal mana stones each," the woman said.

Erik passed her the stones and they got their magically scripted tickets, heading into the stadium.

They stored their drinks in their storage rings.

Even if it is open bottle policy, just rocking up to a stadium with a bottle of liquor feels weird.

They presented their tickets to the guards and passed through, waiting to be out of sight of the guards before they pulled out their bottles again and started drinking.

After getting lost a few times, they were able to find someone to help them find their seats. They walked out into the stands, looking around at the people there.

"There has to be what, like fifty thousand people here?" Rugrat said under his breath as they passed people and got into their seats, smiling and nodding to the people around them.

Erik used his sound transmission device to talk to Rugrat, not wanting to let anything slip. "The Fifth Realm is a big place. Don't forget, there are billions of people here still."

"I thought it was smaller than the lower realms because it is hard to get into. A lot of people die in the Fourth and the fighters are in the Fourth Realm."

"Yeah, but the population of the realms is really high. There are sects and clans because people only trust their families. They protect one another and have kids like crazy. With healers and alchemists, childbirth is rarely fatal and the children are already stronger than those on Earth as the mana and power of the Ten Realms is a part of them since they were created," Erik said. "What are they doing down there?"

Rugrat squinted, seeing across the stadium easily. There were stages set up, each of them partitioned by a line.

"They're making one offensive and defensive formation," Rugrat said, able to pick out some of the formation parts that they were working on.

"Okay, so they've got a battle or something?"

"I'm not sure. I just got here as well." Rugrat drank from his bottle and looked down, interested in what they were doing. "Hmm, that must be a technique." Rugrat's eyes fell on different people, seeing them use techniques.

One person lashed out with a sword. White lines of air appeared in front of him as he attacked the formation plate that he had stuck to a post.

The wind cleared and the man had a pleased look on his face, even if he looked paler from straining his abilities.

Rugrat took a closer look at the formation plate. The sword had cut into it but instead of shredding it up, it had cut out equal and exact lines into the metal.

"Impressive!" Rugrat said. "It's a quick method and flashy, but he must be a sword user already, with a few sword arts. For him, using a sword is much easier than having to learn how to work with special carving tools. Just takes one mess-up and then the whole formation is ruined, though."

"Look at that one over there. They're using their mana to refine the metal and change it into their formation," Erik said.

Rugrat looked over at the person who had a square formation plate hovering just above his hands that were moving as if he were one of those people who could solve a Rubik's Cube in just seconds. Rugrat used the Eagle Eyes spell, getting a closer look.

He could see that the man had lines of mana between his fingers that were going through the metal.

"If I'm right, then it takes a ton of mana to do that, but you can make really complex formations. Though they won't last for long," Rugrat said with a note of disapproval.

"Why is that such a bad thing?"

"Well, there is two parts to it. It takes a lot of energy to create. That's not so much of a problem, but it can make the formations really small. This is partly because of it using mana and partly because if it was much bigger then it would take more mana. Also, the material comes into play. He is working with wood as it naturally allows mana through it easier than metals. With a metal, it will take more mana to work on. Say the metal is stronger—more mana is needed or the formation needs to be smaller. It takes a lot of time to produce them as well."

"So it's limited in a lot of ways, so nearly every time, someone would make a small but complex one-use formation, a kind of trump card item?" Erik summarized, making sure he understood it.

"Yeah. Now, if you look at the lady three stages down, she is working with just a carver and then inlaying her formation. It's rough, yes, but with the larger grooves and the inlay, she can put *a lot* more power through it, and it'll last longer. It's not fancy but it works," Rugrat said.

They looked over the crowds. Others were talking like them, creating a low murmur over the stadium.

There were three hundred people on the stages competing against one another.

Some people had their formations fail at a critical point. Some were able to reset and start again. Others knew that they wouldn't be able to complete their formation in the allotted time and could only hang their heads in shame as they left their stages and the stadium.

The timer in the middle of them all looked like an hourglass with a blue liquid at the top, turning into a gas and then turning back into a drop as it went through the neck, filling up the bottom with more water, counting down the precious seconds that the competitors had remaining.

There was little time for them to mess up at this point. If they were unable to complete their formation, then this would be their last stage.

Erik's eyes passed over the different people, seeing the symbols that Elan had told him about. Although there were people from all of the sects there—they were in the majority; they did have the resources, after all, to get their people to this point—the others who had come from neutral cities or who had come up from the other realms were giving it their all, hoping to be black horses that made the sects pay attention to them. It was a sort of recruitment as well. If there were some good people among those who showed up, then the sects would fight among themselves to pull that person into their group.

Erik and Rugrat pulled out food and continued watching as people looked over at them, surprised by them having actual real food.

Crap, forgot about how most people here don't have food but they go for Stamina potions and concoctions instead.

Erik and Rugrat looked at each other and shrugged. Although it was abnormal, there were more people here who had access to food. In the Seventh Realm, it wasn't that abnormal to see cooks as people had the wealth that they could eat multiple times a day instead of just needing a few Stamina concoctions.

The gas in the top of the hourglass cleared and a gong was hit. People shook with the gong.

"Put your tools down and stop working!" a man said from his position as the officiator of the tournament. His voice carried across the arena.

"Damn, there must be a formation in that to make it loud as hell," Rugrat complained as he looked at the stage.

"Looks like some people weren't able to manage their time well enough." Erik looked at some people with pale or displeased faces.

Some people tried to cram in some more work but the referees walked over and immediately kicked them out, not caring where they came from or who they were or how close to completion they were.

"There were three hundred people who made it to this stage. Now there are only two hundred and thirteen left." The officiator looked out among the people. "All of your formations will now be tested against puppets to see how good their defense is and then against a testing circle to see how strong they are offensively. We will start the second round right away!"

The stages were cleared by one group. The stone ground where the stages had been changed and shifted to create the eight smaller testing arenas.

Puppets were thrown out into four of the arenas while pillars were put into other arenas.

Formations at the side of the arenas all displayed "0000," ready to calculate the scores of all of the different formations.

The competing formation masters were pushed forward. They went into the arenas and placed down their formation plates and any flags or other items that they had created.

Erik watched a man place down a formation with formation flags. He double-checked everything before he left the arena.

It was a defensive formation, so as soon as the gate had closed behind him, the puppet, a humanoid-looking creature with a sword and shield, stood.

"What is that?" Erik tilted his chin toward it.

"So, from what I've heard, puppets are kind of like robots. They have formations powering them. They can be made from bodies or materials like metals and woods. I thought that they were just gimmicks, not really fighters," Rugrat murmured, his vision focusing some as he looked at the puppets in closer detail.

It rushed toward the formation, slamming into the barrier that the formation created. Finding the barrier, the puppet lashed out with its sword in a powerful attack that stirred up the wind within the arena.

Other puppets had been activated and were throwing themselves at the barrier with no care for themselves as they rained down attacks.

The attack formations targeted the pillar, hitting them with different attacks. The numbers around the different arenas started to change as the attack formations ran out of power and the defense formations started to collapse.

The puppets, after destroying the formation, would be turned off by one of the referees. The next formation master would set up their defensive formation as the old one was cleared away. This kept people moving quickly. Erik saw all kinds of formations attacking pillars with flames, lightning, air blades, the ground itself.

"Look at that one," Rugrat said as the mana in the area was drawn into formation flags gathered around the formation plate. A whining noise built up as the formation started to shake with all of the power built up.

Suddenly, a pillar of multi-colored light tore out from the formation, burning through all of the energy that had been gathered, and striking the pillar.

People clapped as the numbers above the pillar shot up. Still, the pillar was unaffected by the blast.

"What? Where did the formation plate go?" Someone pointed at one of the arenas.

Erik and Rugrat looked over as the ground started to shake.

The stone lifted up and a golem rose from the ground.

"They made a puppet with a formation," Rugrat said, impressed. After seeing the other puppets, he had started to have all kinds of ideas. His mind felt as though it were expanding past its barriers once again, allowing him to see further than before.

The golem charged the pillar and slammed into it. The small mana barrier around it flashed into existence, dealing with the attack easily.

The golem rained down hits on the pillar. The damage continued to mount and the numbers started to change on the counter above.

"I thought that formations was all about hiding behind walls and providing support to others," Erik said, his realm-view changing as he saw these formations.

"Just how much can a high-level formation master change the flow of battle?" Erik muttered to himself.

"How much could they change it with an air carrier?" Rugrat laughed to himself but Erik could tell that there was something more going on in Rugrat's mind.

"Air carrier?" Erik asked.

"If we can use the puppets, they must have some kind of senses. But instead of using a formation, they use mortars or explosives, or rifles. If we could do that, then we could have them aiming out into the sky. Anything that comes close, then it shoots out at them. Like our own version of reactive armor. As long as we have enough power, then we can keep on going. If we could get a dungeon core in it, a small one, then we use that to recharge and power it. Though it would mean putting the dungeon cores in a vulnerable system. Though if we used it as a tactical system, only to be brought out when we absolutely need it, it could assist us if we need it. When dormant, then they just wait in Alva. We secure our power and our people's safety if anything happens."

Erik could only understand part of what Rugrat was saying.

He left him to it as he took another swig from the bottle, watching the formation masters challenging one another as he tried to guess what their scores would be.

It took a few more rounds for them to clear up all of the formations. The puppets had to be replaced if they ran out of power and the pillars against the offensive formations were charged while the arena was covered in damage just being in the blast area of the formations.

The results were all added together.

"It's smart. If someone made both just to make both, then their score wouldn't be all that high—good but not high. Though if someone made a powerful defensive or offensive formation and then a decent formation or no second formation, then they could do really well or poorly," Erik said.

"Defensive and offensive formations are the most used formations, so that way people have the chance to at least make one that they know. The problem is that everyone has different resources. If someone has better techniques, or better materials and formation blueprints, then they'll be able to beat the others," Rugrat said.

"The preliminary round of the formation masters is complete. These are the names of the fifty who will be heading to the second round!" the overseer announced. A formation in the middle of the arena activated and displayed fifty names in the middle of the arena.

The men and women who had competed against one another looked up at the screen. The audience started talking to one another, some cheering, others looking annoyed as the person they had wanted to do better had placed lower or not made it.

There were expressions of joy, helplessness, anger, and more among the competitors.

"Come on, I have plans to make!" Rugrat said.

"We're taking the day off, remember?" Erik looked at him and raised his bottle.

"Just some notes?" Rugrat asked.

"Fine," Erik said.

They tapped bottles and then tapped them on the armrests before taking a big drink.

35 Quest of Fried Chicken

Rugrat started to make notes, filling up several pages of information.

"Come on, this is supposed to be a day off, remember?"

"Just a few more notes." Rugrat didn't look up; he only wrote faster, as if Erik were going to take away his sheet of paper forcefully.

They walked through the city, Rugrat writing notes while Erik looked at the passing people and the different stalls.

"Ever since you said fried chicken, I haven't been able to get it off my mind," Erik muttered as he pulled out ingredients and started chewing on them.

There are no chickens in the Ten Realms that I have seen but there has to be something like them. How many things back home taste like chicken? Or gator?

Erik smiled and he took a deep breath in. His entire body had been enhanced, from his muscles and skin to his reaction time and his senses. He closed his eyes. With consuming so many ingredients, different kinds of drinks and food from across the realms, he cross-referenced the smells around him, finding out the kinds of meals that were being prepared.

I had plenty of chicken back on Earth; it's just a matter of finding it in my Alchemy skill book.

Erik saw the book in his mind. The pages blurred as information appeared. *Come on, everything can be turned into a concoction, so chicken should be an ingredient and in here.*

He felt as if the Ten Realms fought him on his thoughts, but it might have just been his mind playing tricks on him. He finally found what he was looking for. He understood the characteristics of chicken more than he had ever wanted to in his previous life.

Then, taking those characteristics, he started to search through the smells that he was getting from the area, searching out the similarities between the chicken and the other ingredients and meats that were around him.

Erik found something that interested him. He grabbed Rugrat, who was still working on his notepad, storing away information. The half-drunk, keffiyeh- and cloak-covered man with shining eyes followed behind as he laughed, nodded his head and worked on only what he knew.

They left the crowd behind and walked down a few streets as Erik continued to look for things that were similar to chicken.

There were herbs that smelled like it and then a blue and yellow fruit that smelled like it.

Erik bought the fruit and thanked the seller, spending twenty mana stones. The fruit apparently increased their mana circulation for a short period of time.

Erik took a bite of it, shivering. It was just odd. It tasted like raw chicken, but it had the texture of a plum and was slimy.

"That is just wrong, the texture and the taste. I can't help but think that I'm getting poisoning from a fruit." Erik checked his cultivation. It did speed up slightly, but it would take him eating the fruits constantly to try to get much of a benefit. It was a cheaper item to help those who didn't have that much funds.

Erik's search continued on.

He got to one stall, finding that it was actually selling items that could be used by tailors. There was a leather there that smelled like crispy chicken skin.

"What animal is this from?" Erik asked the stall owner.

"It's from the Skaiso beast," the man said.

Erik sniffed it, getting close enough to touch his nose to it. "Do you know if anyone cooks it around here?"

"There is a store down that way, three streets—take the left and then the first right." The man looked at Erik as if he were odd.

Erik started walking and he realized he had left Rugrat behind. He grabbed Rugrat, who was still writing down stuff in his notepad from in front of the stall and started walking.

Erik sniffed the air as he followed the man's directions. It wasn't long until they reached a small little place. There was a butcher shop in front and a tannery must've been out back from the smell of it. Even with isolating formations and spells, the smell of curing hides was potent.

"Done." Rugrat looked over the pages of the notebook and looked around to find where they were.

"Glad you could join me."

"Where are we? What are we doing here?"

"Chicken." Erik walked toward the butcher shop. There weren't many people there; most must have been driven off by the smell of the tannery. It wasn't the worst thing that Erik had smelled, so he could easily ignore it.

"Skaiso, do you have any?" Erik asked.

"Yeah." The butcher pulled out two lumps of yellow meat.

"I'll take it."

"Three hundred Mortal stones," the man said.

Erik looked at the other meat prices along the wall.

"If done in a soup, it can cure most ailments and when cooked up, then there are few people who don't like it and can increase the speed at which your body recovers Stamina and from injuries without needing a health or Stamina potion."

Maybe it was the drinking. Maybe it was the fact that he had now been thinking about this for nearly two hours. But he was getting that damn chicken/lizard.

"Okay." Erik put the money on the counter.

Rugrat looked at the lizard. "You want to eat that?"

"*We* want to eat that," Erik corrected.

"Why?"

"Chicken!" Erik said. As the man passed him the meat, he put it into his storage ring. "Where is the nearest park?" Erik asked the man.

He gave them a way point and they headed out of the butcher shop.

It didn't take them long to get to the park.

Erik pulled out a table from his storage ring and Rugrat looked at him.

"I'm not the Southern one—you prep the chicken. I'll heat the oil," Erik said as he put the meat on the table.

Rugrat shrugged and started to work as Erik got out his cauldron. He cleaned it out with some flames and then poured in oil, his Journeyman-level cauldron being turned into a deep fryer.

Rugrat finished off the Skaiso and then dropped it into the cauldron. "You sure that this is going to work?" Rugrat asked as the lizard was already cooking away.

"Nope, but I damn well hope that it does."

"Don't worry—I got as close as Momma makes as I could," Rugrat said proudly.

"You mean those hot as hell ones that have the spicy skin?"

"Yeah," Rugrat said.

"Well, hell yes," Erik said, "your mom could cook."

"That she could." Rugrat smiled.

"So what were you working on that was so important?"

"A reactive protection system. It should work against projectiles, but need to do more testing to see if it can defend against other threats like magical spells and the like," Rugrat replied with a sound transmission.

"How?"

"Those puppets, they must use some kind of system that allows them to find their target. Take that system, pair it with an effective formation to destroy other attacks, and then bingo. I don't know if people have thought about it already or not. It would take a lot of materials to make and would need to be affixed to something, but it would require less power than a shield, as it's only using power to disrupt the attack that is coming in. Cost less power that way," Rugrat said.

"Makes sense really." Erik sighed. "Do you think that the chicken is done yet?" Erik looked at the cauldron.

"Give it another minute or so," Rugrat said with another look, pulling out a spatula.

"Why do you have a spatula?"

"Hey man, I've got like a dozen storage devices and most of them are massive. Why don't you have a spatula?" Rugrat asked.

Erik waved him off as he went to go and find some more drinks.

"So spicy!" Rugrat let out a gasp as he looked at the meat in his hands, his eyes glowing. "And so tasty! Like spicy deep fried chicken!"

Erik grabbed water and threw some back as his eyes were watering and his nose was running. "Damn, we need to get this recipe to Jia Feng."

The two of them were silent other than the sounds of eating, devouring the spicy food.

Erik coughed a few times and the two of them had tears in their eyes, whether from the emotions or the park clearing spiciness that covered the area around them.

Erik patted his stomach. "Damn! I love good food!"

Rugrat stopped eating and put down the chicken piece.

"What is it?" Erik asked, looking at Rugrat.

"You know all of that stuff that we took from Vuzgal? How many books did we collect from all of the leaders, from the different clans that were in Vuzgal and the royal family?"

"I don't know. There must have been hundreds of books." Erik shrugged. "Why do you ask?"

"And out of them, how many did we look through?"

"Well, we were worrying more about the Blood Demon sect. Just say what you're trying to lead me to." Erik sighed.

"Those books, among them there should be crafting and fighting techniques, right? It was an empire that was able to control a vast amount of land and powerful dungeons. They must have had Masters and Elites who were able to go into the higher realms. Techniques are expensive but they had to have a few," Rugrat said.

The two of them looked at each other before they scrambled up to their feet and threw everything in their storage rings. They ran for the totem.

"How could we be so dumb?" Erik yelled.

"You said it! We were busy with other things and we didn't know what they were at the time!"

They ran through the city. People watched them as they tossed the guard an Earth mana stone before they reached the totem. Then Alva appeared in front of them.

People didn't have time to salute as they ran toward the academy, where all of the written works from Vuzgal were stored.

"So Erik and Rugrat came back from the Fifth Realm and went right to the library? What are they doing there?" Glosil asked, perplexed by their actions.

"They're going through the information collected in Vuzgal, collecting up all of the boxes of books and scrolls that we have. They're reviewing the items that have already been sorted out by the library staff." The messenger shrugged. He looked like a merchant and he was most days. His other role was that as an Alvan messenger, taking signed orders back and forth between the different members of the council who were spread over the realms.

"I bet Egbert is loving that." Glosil grinned.

The aide had to force their smile down as the corners of their mouth twitched.

"Did you get the latest report from Delilah?" Glosil asked.

"Yes, sir." The aide pulled out a letter and gave it to Glosil. He then pulled out several crates and stacked them up.

Here are the current concoctions that we have been able to finish. We should have another shipment completed in a day and sent to you via special courier.

Glosil moved to the boxes, opened one of the crates and looked inside to see several potion bottles that had been carefully packaged.

He picked one up and examined it. His appraisal ability was high enough that he could directly look through the potion's information.

Potion of Everlasting Flames
Highly flammable. Once ignited, the potion will not stop burning until all is consumed.

"Is that all of it?" Glosil looked at the twenty crates, with forty potion bottles in each of them.

"Yes, sir," the messenger said.

"Very well." Glosil nodded.

The messenger bowed slightly and retreated from the room as Glosil used his sound transmission device.

"Captain?" Han Wu answered the message.

"Report to my office. I have a job for you," Glosil said.

Glosil was studying the plans for the Earth floor when there was a knock at his door. "Come in."

Han Wu entered the office and saluted. "Specialist Han reporting, sir!"

"At ease." Glosil returned the salute before waving to the crates in the middle of his office. "Take a look."

Han Wu looked in the crates and examined the potions. His hands stilled and his face paled looking at all of the boxes stacked on top of one another.

"Will this work for the fuel air bombs that you planned?" Glosil asked.

"I'll need to do some testing but I think so, based on the description," Han Wu said.

"Carry out your tests. I expect a report on my desk by tonight," Glosil said.

"Understood." Han Wu collected all of the crates into his storage ring before saluting and leaving the room.

We've been working on this for a few weeks already. I can't help but feel like they should be back in Vuzgal, training people there. The barracks here has turned into a specialized training area for fighters, but we need people to fill those spots and Vuzgal's strength is still too reliant on the undead and the associations for my liking. Glosil was looking at the information on the Battle Arena. The staff who had remained in Vuzgal would finish their initial training at the barracks there. Then they would complete more advanced courses that would teach them different weapon systems or about different classes that people would use when fighting. Then people would enter the arena for friendly spars, or to go to different classes that were being hosted by combat freaks and masters who would hire out a space and then bring in people to fill the empty spots and make some gold.

These lessons were too expensive for regular people but the Alva military's budget was massive. Glosil wanted to bring more of these combat masters into the Alva military but few of them were willing to be tied down. Most of them already came from some kind of power. Being in the Alva military would expose them to the secrets of Alva. Training someone up from the ground, they would know more about them than someone who was coming in already at a high rank.

We are looking to follow the path of the Elite and increase our own power. As long as we can use these people to increase our strength, then it should be good. Glosil rubbed his face, feeling tired. He remembered the reports that Elan had compiled on the different militaries in the Fourth Realm. Although they were a fighting force, their systems were built on growing in power to increase their position. Whereas in the Alva Army it was based on their leadership abilities to increase their rank. And instead of vying for the highest contribution in a battle and trying to stand out, people worked together to complete their objective.

Competition is still good as long as it doesn't turn toxic, Glosil thought. Between Tiger and Dragon Platoons, there was a rivalry as the leadership of each of the platoons would talk up the other group, making everyone compete with one another to increase their strength.

Another purpose for the Battle Arena was to allow the troops to go toe-to-toe in a safe place and increase their combat strength. Glosil couldn't help but smile as he saw the path forward. He felt the blood rushing through his veins.

"Come on, Ten Realms—just wait until you meet my Alva Army." He felt goose bumps up his neck as he laughed. He saw a future of Experts who didn't care to dominate the spotlight, who would complete their mission and fade into the background, unknown by all.

He stood and grabbed his armor. Now that his tasks were dealt with, he wanted to get back to the Earth floor as soon as possible.

36
Quiet in the Library!

Tanya had been given an office in an isolated corner of the library, right in the middle of all the books that dealt with the magical side of the Ten Realms.

It was heaven for her. She had been jotting down notes and trying to connect the information in her game master book that she had brought through with her to the Ten Realms. She wrote out the points that she had made and started to look into the questions that had been burning in the back of her mind.

She noted down her findings and then wrote three signs that she put behind her desk, framing the window that looked out over Alva.

Mana. Instruction. Reaction.

Underneath all of these pages, there were notes and scribbles that had started to form the basis of her magical knowledge.

She had just added a second smaller note underneath it.

Spells: Mana+elemental attributes

She sipped on her tea as she scratched Tetsu's head. He had a space in the corner of the room and she had plenty of monster cores and monster meat to feed him now.

"People keep thinking of spells linearly, you follow the spell you get a reaction, what they're not thinking of is how that spell is created. If you combine elemental mana together in just the right combination then you create a spell. Without requiring the cast time, and for much less mana. Kind of like alchemy, mix together the different ingredients and it comes out with a final product."

Tanya was silent as she worked over her findings in her head pursing her lips together. She was silent for some time, Tetsu moved, making her return to reality.

"Never thought that I would be able to get paid to research magic." She chuckled to herself. Tetsu didn't seem to mind as he continued to accept her petting, pleased for the attention.

"All right, let's review what we know! Mana is a natural power that is in the Ten Realms. It permeates everything around us, another kind of energy that is outside the normal states of energy that were recorded back on Earth. Going with physics, energy cannot be destroyed, only altered, which seems like a good basic rule for mana. It cannot be destroyed but then it can be stored through mana cornerstones into mana stones. If it is used in a spell, or used by different plants and living creatures in the Ten Realms, then the mana is altered. Its polarization changes and it can gain a higher attribute. So kind of like if there were machines that would only work on one kind of energy—construction machines only work on green electricity, or they work better on it.

"Now, these attributes can be good, if well-suited with the item consuming the energy. A cycle of energy: Earth energy being consumed by Metal-attribute items, creating Metal energy, which then becomes Water energy. When you now insert people, they too are part of this cycle, but we have no mana originally. When we enter the Ten Realms, then the mana enters our bodies in all of its various forms. The different types of mana energy can make it easier for us to cast spells, but we aren't attribute creatures originally; we need to alter our bodies in order to operate better with different attribute manas.

"This is why there is a Mana Gathering system. The body has to get used to all of the mana inside it and then try to clean out the impurities. Humans are looking to store energy within their bodies, while the plants and items of the Ten Realms are storing up energy within themselves as a result of their actions. Humans are accelerating the process rapidly by controlling their bodies, where like ingredients become powerful over time, because more of the Ten Realms energy is refined into it, increasing its power. Mana is kind of like gasoline; there are many types that can be refined in different ways and used in different processes, but in the end it is a combustible fuel source."

Tanya looked at Tetsu, seeing that he was taking a nap instead of riveted by her talk.

"Spells, while they look exact on the outside, are more like cooking than chemistry. As spells become more advanced, then it goes further, getting closer to the chemical level than the cooking level."

Tanya stood and moved toward the signs.

"For mana, there are stages that people can change their body to hold more energy and purify it. For the instructions or the spells, there are levels that they go through in demonstrating their power. The higher the level that the spells get to, then the more power that they display and the less impurities they show. When someone has enough mana and has gained a deep enough understanding over how to control it, then they can create a domain. They go from affecting the different energies that are in the Ten Realms to affecting the Ten Realms themselves. This is the pinnacle of spells: being able to wield absolute control over the mana in the area. Which segues into reaction. The reaction of these spells can create impurities. The mana combines with the elements of the Ten Realms to create destructive attribute spells. Earth and Water attribute mana used together can make a healing spell, applied to the right place. Then dungeon cores are the only known thing right now that draw in impurities, consuming them and releasing pure mana."

Tanya tapped the instruction sheet and the latest note that was on a bright-green piece of paper that she had stabbed into the wall.

"But maybe we don't need to create spells—we just need to communicate better with mana. Instead of combining energies together to create spells, three parts of this attribute mana, two parts of that attribute mana, and one part of the other, what if we were to alter the environment, change the balance of the mana in the area? Use a Water spell to compress an area and then shoot out the concentrated mana in the area and turn it into static electricity that follows the path of least resistance, which is the water, and that hits the person? Boom—lightning spell but instead of needing to create the spell, we just made the spark.

"Instead of listing out instructions, we just give it a command." Her eyes shifted to another note.

"High power spells need a lot of instructions to pull the mana and the impurities in order to create the spells. In some areas, it will be easier to complete as the exact ratio of attribute mana is there. Others will take longer and be harder for the change in balance, though many people just cast spells with the mana that is inside their body. It's as if they're leaving behind all of the power that is around them. If you cast spells that were suited to the energy in the area, then your spells would be stronger, they would be faster and, damn..." Tanya couldn't help smiling as her eyes glowed with interest.

She let out a sigh as her excited expression dimmed and she looked back at Tetsu, who looked at her.

"Now, the problem is, we need to somehow find just what those commands and those instructions are. Also, I need to increase my Mana Gathering Cultivation faster. I have scheduled visits to the hospital to increase my Mana Gathering Cultivation, to open all of my mana gates. The more mana I can pull in, the closer I can come to being a person created from mana, then the greater control I will have over it naturally. Can't Rugrat already create a domain? But his spells are still very simple. He has only touched on the stage where his spells can draw in mana from the area to increase its strength, instead of relying on just that mana he can tap into.

"Guess that one's personal mana pool is like a water gun—pressurized and it can be used right away, but it is highly accurate as it is under control. Though mana is like being in the rain—there is much more volume but it is impossible to control. At least, it looks that way. The Russians fired artillery shells filled with stuff into clouds and caused it to rain before, manipulating the forces of the world around them. Much stronger than any fire trucks that would have taken months or years to pour out that kind of water in a short period of time. I just need to look for those artillery shells." She turned from her wall and back to her desks that were covered in books and notes.

She started to get in on the work, reading through her notes and questions that had come from yesterday's work. Then, drinking her tea, she started to look through the library records to see whether there might be books that could answer her questions or lead her in the right direction. After noting down a few names, she headed out of her office. Tetsu, seeing that she was leaving, hopped up and followed her into the library. She went to the help desk on the floor but there was no one there. Instead, she could hear people yelling in the back room, which were the offices for the library staff. They were usually quietly working.

There was a noise of something being tossed to the side before she heard a forced laugh from inside the office.

She frowned. It wasn't professional and they were making enough noise that the people studying on the floor looked over in annoyance.

There isn't anyone at the desk either! Tanya had the position of a researcher and was being paid by the library, so she felt responsible for it. And when the people who were working there weren't looking professional, then she felt that it reflected badly on her as well. She went around the desk and headed for the main doors that led into the offices.

She opened the door to see that the desks that were usually organized had been all moved to the side. There were books all over the place.

Someone ran in behind her and went to a pile of books and other scrolls and information. They weren't lined out at all, as there were two people going through them, sorting them out.

"Fighting art!" one yelled, holding up his hand and tossing it at a librarian, who had to react quickly. Their face paled as they juggled the scroll and then put it into a storage crate.

"Cooking! Woodworking, cat types, plants!" the other said. They picked up books, checking them and then tossing them back to different librarians, making them jump around as if they were part of a baseball team!

"What is going on here?" Tanya yelled, seeing the books being tossed around as if they were nothing but cabbages!

The two men looked up at her. They wore items that made it hard to see anything but their eyes.

They were wearing dirty body armor! Wait until I report this to Egbert!

"Ah, Tanya, I heard that Egbert personally hired you to look into mana," the one man said. His voice was muffled but she felt that he was familiar.

"Who are you?" she asked, confused.

"Don't you—"

"You're wearing a mask." The other man pulled off his helmet and his mask, revealing his blue eyes and brown hair.

She had never seen him before, but something she had heard about blue eyes made her frown in thought, trying to recall.

"Oh." The other man pulled off his helmet.

Egbert burst into the office and he waved his finger at the two men. "What do you think that you're doing, tossing around my books!"

The man with brown hair seemed to realize the state of the room as he looked around and let out an awkward laugh.

"They're our books and well, umm..." The other man had removed his helmet and mask, showing it was Rugrat.

Tanya had heard more about Rugrat and the special teams since she had arrived in Alva. She had heard of their abilities and their power. She had also heard about Erik, but she hadn't ever seen him. She wanted to jump into a hole.

I wanted to tell off Erik and Rugrat—they own the entire dungeon and everything in it!

"I'm waiting!" Egbert had his arms crossed and tapped his foot on the ground.

"So, when we were in the Fifth Realm, we were getting all of these." Rugrat pulled out a box of scrolls. Erik did the same.

"These are Expert-level techniques for the different skills and fighting arts. Then we were thinking about all of the books that we have from Vuzgal. They haven't all been sorted yet, but they had plenty of money and power. The other groups and sects in the Fourth Realm have to have fighting arts and technique manuals—else why would they have Elites and Masters who were willing to fight for them? Yes, their sect rules make it hard for them to leave, but they would find a way if it was to improve their strength. So the Edar Empire was able to take over a portion of the Fourth Realm, nearly a fifth of a continent—small one, mind you. So they must have some Expert-level stuff. So we rushed back here to look for those books and scrolls," Rugrat said.

It was now Egbert's turn to look awkward. Then the fire in his eyes seemed to burn brighter than ever. There seemed to be some madness contained within.

"What are you waiting for! Keep searching! Call in all of the librarians and the apprentices!" Egbert snapped out as he used a spell.

"I will assist! Time to show you my speed reading—fourteen romance novels at one time skills! Get ready!" Egbert yelled as the storage items that contained books and were piled up in crates flew over to him. Books started to fly out of them, appearing in front of him. As they flipped through pages, Egbert read them at hyper speed.

Books shot out from in front of him, sent toward the librarian "catchers"—who grabbed the books and put them into storage items. As the book shot out, a new one would replace it as he turned into a reading machine.

Erik and Rugrat went back to the piles in front of them, not looking back as they tossed books back, calling out what kind they were.

"Tanya, you're a person of the library! Help out the mana gathering catcher. They're a bit slower!" Egbert yelled out.

Tanya wanted to walk out, but seeing the pleading look on the person who was catching the books, she knew that she couldn't run away.

She jogged over to them.

"You take the right side. I've got the left!" they said.

"What kind of library sorts their books like this?" she complained.

"Ours!" the other person said with panic and fear in their eyes.

More librarians came in from across the dungeon as people learned that the librarians were fighting it out on the fourth floor. Medics were called as people emerged with bruises and cuts, being healed up and rushing back in as if soldiers facing their greatest battle.

"How can there be so much noise! This is a library!" one yelled out, complaining.

"Then use a sound isolation formation, Charles! 'Bout time you did something with that studying!" Egbert's voice cut through the library.

"Aren't you supposed to be looking up what kind of subset of the Klosa moss is supposed to be good for pain relief, Jasmine?"

"Yuan Jie! You still owe me two books. I want them by the end of the day or you can forget about coming back into my library!"

"Miss Jones, you better study hard for your upcoming cooking exam! You have been focusing on the same kind of food for too long. If you only bake food, then your path will be limited!"

The spectators quickly turned pale as they started to leave.

"I was looking for a book on the nature of birds in the mountain range?" a student worked up the courage to ask.

"Go and check the beast taming section. There is a compendium called *First Realms Beasts*. It was written by an Alvan beast tamer, has a great deal of information on the animals in the area!" Egbert yelled, still reading and sorting through tens of books as others asked for books and information, answering them easily.

"I had a question about Alchemy. I have been trying to make the water breathing concoction, Liquid Breath, but it keeps on turning into a flammable mass!"

"There are three sets of ingredients. Are you mixing the second set of ingredients in the preparation stage or combining them and adding them to the cauldron after the first set of ingredients are combined?" Erik asked.

"I am adding them ingredient by ingredient, like I did with the first set," the alchemist said.

"Read the damn instructions instead of glancing over them! What is your Alchemy rank? Spell scrolls!" Erik sent another book flying.

The librarian snatched it out of the air, lowering themselves to the ground as their eyes darted around for incoming literature.

"Low Journeyman?"

"Are you sure about that or are you asking me?" Erik yelled out. "Smithing, stone working tools!"

"I am?"

"Get some confidence there! Even if you are a Journeyman trying to make an Apprentice-level concoction, RTFM—read the freaking manual! If you did, then, while the first set of ingredients are combined inside the cauldron, the second set need to be combined separately and left for twenty minutes at least before they can be added to the concoction. Go and remake it!"

"Y-yes!" The alchemist ran off to deal with the issue. As others learned that Egbert, Erik, and Rugrat were in the library offering advice, more people appeared in front of the office and started asking their questions.

"I have been working on making a curved halberd but I am finding that the weapon's strength isn't that great."

Tanya felt as though the person was trying to hide their voice.

"Taran, are you still trying to make the blade as thin as possible?" Rugrat yelled out.

"Well, umm, wait, how did you know it was me?"

"Well, I know it is now!"

"Crap!"

"Make the blade thicker. A halberd mixes sword and pole arm together. The issue is that when stabbing and slicing, with greater momentum it needs higher strength. Use metals enhanced to increase the strength of the blade to deal with the forces that are at play. Also, is it a curved halberd? Are you making the blade a separate piece?"

"Yes and yes," Taran said.

"Does it look like a sword with a blade on the end?" Rugrat sighed.

"Yes."

"Dude! Take that blade and mount it right into the wood. Go and check out the book *Polearm Weapons* by Bradush Jokai. All kinds of designs in there that are stronger and easier to make," Rugrat said.

"Smarter not harder," Taran said.

"And it's learning! I always knew he would grow up to be a big strong smith," Rugrat said to Erik.

"Tell me that when I beat you to Expert!" Taran yelled.

"I look forward to it, short stuff!"

"Nudist!" Taran yelled back but Rugrat was grinning.

The day came to an end as the amount of books that they were going through slowed down to a crawl.

"Let's take a breather and take stock of the books that we have," Erik said.

Rugrat slowed down and Egbert nodded. His eyes looked dull from reading so many books so fast.

Some of the librarians dropped to the ground, looking dazed as they started eating and drinking from their storage rings.

"Okay, so we were able to get some books from the higher realms but then we figured that there must be some of them in those that we sent back here to be sorted," Erik said.

"And we found the formula to fried chicken!" Rugrat said.

"And that." Erik laughed.

"What is fried chicken? Is it a spell?" Egbert asked.

"It's magical, all right," Rugrat said.

Alva was turned on its head with Erik and Rugrat returning and the declaration that there were technique books and combat arts at the library that one could study. People who had been venturing to the other realms to deepen their understanding of their craft or skill now returned to Alva once again.

Erik and Rugrat, seeing the amount of people coming from all over to read the different manuals and gain a greater understanding, said that they would spend a month in the dungeon before they headed to Vuzgal once again with a selection of the books.

They sent a few of them up to the crafting academy. With them, Tan Xue and Hiao Xen could draw in more people to join the academy who were at the Expert level or waiting for that final impetus to enter the Expert level.

The library was busy with people heading to other buildings for quiet study. There were people lined up to read the books while more were uncovered from among the storage rings that Egbert and his librarians sorted through.

As they went through the books, they found other books that they added to the Alva library shelves. The copies were gathered to be sent up to the smaller Vuzgal Academy library.

Two more days passed. There was movement from the barracks as Han Wu and his helpers headed through the teleportation array.

Han Wu was greeted by the sounds of the Earth floor camp. There were those on watch; others were training in a small area that had been cleared for that purpose. Others gathered in the cafeteria, hanging out with one another.

"So, what have you got for us?" Niemm asked as Han Wu walked out of the teleportation array.

"I got fire and lots of it, Sarge." Han Wu grinned.

"Well, that scares the hell out of me, so the rest of the floor should be trembling in fear."

"Thanks, Sarge," Han Wu said, feeling a little touched.

"Come on, the higher-ups are waiting at the command post," Niemm said.

They walked across the camp to one of the bunkers that was buried half into the ground. Inside, there was Domonos and Glosil.

"Han Wu, what have you got for us?" Glosil asked.

"The last of the flammable materials was sent over from the Third Realm. Now the issue is with the delivery method. We want to get this all over the Earth floor and ignite it, burning everything to the ground. The ceiling is too short, so we can't use the mortars effectively. So…" Han Wu pulled out several spell scrolls.

"These are Wind Devil spell scrolls. Basically, we activate these, toss in the flammable material, and then the spell will spread it all over the floor, or at least as best as we can while being inside the camp. Then it only needs a spark." Han Wu pulled out a formation plate. "This is a timed formation plate. So we activate all of this together and it turns the whole floor into a big old flaming mess."

"You sure about this?" Glosil asked.

"Ran a smaller test in the dungeon and it went well, about a one-ten-thousandth as strong, though," Han Wu said.

"Okay. Pack up everyone and get them out of the camp. Special Team One will remain to protect the camp and keep an eye out as Han Wu and his people set up their devices. How long will you need?" Glosil asked.

"Should take, I'd say, twenty minutes. We've got most of it already organized and set up," Han Wu said.

"Good. Domonos, how long will it take for us to pack up and move?"

"Can start moving in forty and then be gone in twenty minutes?" Domonos said, looking at Yui, who nodded.

"Let's get to it. We might even control the Earth floor by the end of the day." Glosil tapped the table and stood.

Han Wu and his people moved around the camp, positioning different equipment as the rest of the camp gathered their personal items, the extra weapon systems, and valuable items that they didn't want destroyed.

Sections moved through the teleportation array, returning to the main floor.

Once they were all gone, the camp felt desolate as people could run across without running into people.

They made sure that there were no flames in the area, with Han Wu inspecting the entire camp.

Special Team One was on the teleportation array, their weapons out and ready.

"Place the barrels," Han Wu yelled. It carried across the empty camp.

Han Wu pulled out barrels that had holes all over them. The thick flammable liquid started to flow out of the sides and across the ground.

The barrels were on the walls and the concoction flowed out everywhere.

Han Wu and everyone else headed for the teleportation array.

Han Wu placed three of the timed formations and put them close to the teleportation array. He made sure that they were ready before he took out his dozens of spell scrolls.

Clouds appeared from above, turning into tornadoes that stirred up the Earth floor. They covered the entire floor, sucking up the concoction and throwing it out in every direction. The other tornadoes drew in the concoction, spreading it farther.

The floor disappeared and the Alva floor appeared.

"Well, beers?" Storbon stood up and put his rifle away.

"Everything go well?" Glosil asked, walking across the teleportation array to meet them.

"Seems so. We'll find out soon enough if our Experience starts to increase," Han Wu said. "The formations are set to go off in twenty minutes."

"I'll monitor in the dungeon headquarters. I hear that the academy has a few combat art manuals that you can check out now."

Blaze looked at the letter from the Willful Institute and the message from the First Realm. They had both arrived in the same day.

"Erik and Rugrat are back?" he asked the messenger.

A network of messengers had been set up from Alva, to the Adventurer's Guild locations, the Sky Reaching Restaurants, Vuzgal, and different key trading locations that the Trader's Guild was located in. They helped to pass information between different branches of Alva, keeping them all connected.

They also observed what people were doing and passed materials. They were the lifeline of Alva and Elan's spies and confidants.

"Very well. I have something I need to tell them as well."

Blaze stood and pulled on a bookcase that opened to reveal a set of stairs. He pulled a cloak on. The messenger frowned but followed Blaze out of his office and through the secret passage into Hersht's busy streets. They blended in with the seething, robe-wearing masses.

It didn't take them long to reach the totem.

I wonder what Erik and Rugrat will say. Blaze hadn't really seen them in a while.

He paid the fee of a Mortal mana stone and gained access to the totem. They disappeared with a flash of light.

Egbert stepped onto the Earth floor.

"Toasty." He stepped into the sky and flew across the floor. The heavy Earth mana in the floor now had a thread of Fire mana within it.

The floor had been burnt to a crisp, or cooked into oblivion. With burning all of the plants, the air was heavy with the Fire mana and lacked oxygen. The plant floor had grown stagnant, producing so much oxygen that the plants were suffocating. Now there were already shoots appearing in the soil, drawing in the liberated mana and carbon dioxide.

Egbert used his ability to talk through the dungeon, reporting directly to Glosil, who waited on the other side of the teleportation pad. "This floor is currently uninhabitable. I can't sense any life here. I'm going to lower the dungeon core," Egbert said.

"Okay, keep us updated," Glosil said.

Egbert flew across the floor. There were water features, pastures and plains; the different lands butted up against one another and connected in the middle to what had been a large forest but was now just a charred hill.

Egbert focused his attention on the dungeon core as he headed for the hill.

"First, change the power output from the dungeon core to the mana storing formation. Done. Now need to open up the tunnel." The mana storing formation allowed power out into Alva, powering the different magical systems.

Underneath the dungeon core, sections moved apart and revealed a dark hole. Other shutters opened in series.

"And then cut the formations holding the dungeon core in place." The dungeon core started to slowly fall down from its original position, passing the shutters. It went underneath the Alva floor, looking like a falling star as it entered the Metal floor. The Metal-attribute mana flooded toward it, being purified as it passed through the main command formation in the Metal floor and descended again.

It passed into the Earth floor. The impurities were so high here that a windstorm was stirred up. Egbert made sure that the doors between the levels were secured.

"Balancing out all of the floors again is going to be a pain in the thigh bone." Egbert sighed as he flew up and grabbed the dungeon core that was greedily drawing in the impurities of the floor.

Egbert stood on top of the main formation plate for the Earth floor. It had a fifty meter diameter, with all kinds of different inscriptions and shapes linked together. Beasts had torn it apart—out of boredom, in interest, or when they had fought to be the master of the floor.

Egbert took out a podium from his storage ring and put it down, resting the dungeon core on top.

The dungeon core drew in the impure mana from the surroundings, refined it and then used it to power the podium. Blue lines traced down the podium, reaching the floor, and began tracing out those complicated lines, restoring them to their former glory. It was a slow process and Egbert pulled out a recliner, patting it down.

"Well, nothing to do but wait," he said with a hint of excitement. He sat in the chair, curling his legs underneath him, as he pulled out his latest romance novel, holding it with one hand and his chin in the other. "Damn it, Daphne! Just stay with James! Come on!"

"Has the dungeon core been placed?" Glosil asked.

"Stop interrupting. It will take much time. I'm reading!" Egbert stopped listening to Glosil and he buried his head in the book, flipping the pages, not wanting it to end, but wanting to know what would happen!

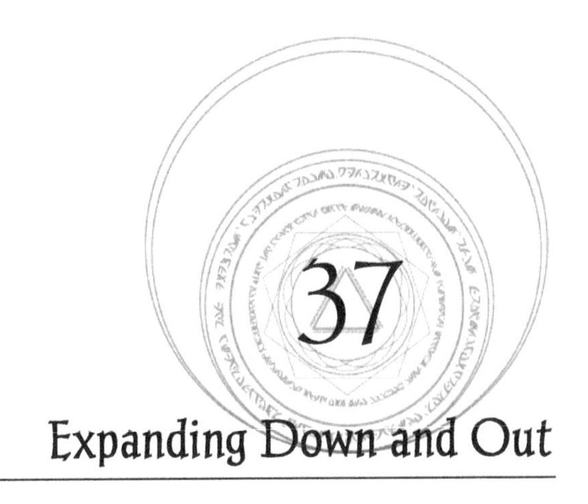

37 Expanding Down and Out

Everyone was there for the meeting: Elise, Blaze, Glosil, Jia Feng, Egbert.

"Three days ago, we began Operation Firestorm. Today, we sent Egbert down to the Earth floor in order to know the condition of the floor."

"Crispy, very crispy," Egbert said in affirmation. "Also, really needs some breathable air in there."

"The floor is clear but we can't inhabit it because there isn't any air inside," Glosil summarized. "Egbert is using the dungeon core and its area of influence to repair the formation on each floor, with the formations on the Earth floor rebuilt we will be able to change out the air and make it breathable for our people to head down."

"Might be an idea to work with the farmers, get some of their plants, throw some plant seed out there. With their speed of growth, the high, pure Earth mana concentration, they'll shoot up and produce air that we can breathe," Erik said.

Glosil wrote down a note quickly.

"The next floor we need to clear is the Fire floor. The Earth floor, we could burn out everything that was on it. The Fire floor, we could attack people with water, but then the floor would be damaged irrevocably and well, I think the flames would only make the floor stronger." Glosil took a breath.

"Our running plan is to send Egbert to check the environment. If it is safe, then we will send in the special teams; they survey the area. We have the plans of the Fire floor from Egbert but we don't know what the floor looks like now. We don't have any formations that are connected with the main dungeon core. Once we have an understanding of what's happening on the floor, we'll move forward."

"Sounds like I'm going to be real busy for someone who is supposed to be dead," Egbert said.

"You know, we didn't want you to get mothballed."

"Hah! Really funny!" Egbert said and turned to Jia Feng. "What is a mothball?"

Jia Feng shrugged, not sure herself.

"Well, you're undead, so you only need mana from the dungeon. And with the power of the dungeon, you're one of the strongest, if not the strongest member of Alva," Glosil said.

"Aw, you'll make me blush with all that flattery."

Glosil smiled but largely disregarded Egbert's words.

"Sounds like a solid plan to me," Erik said and looked over at Rugrat.

"Me too!" Rugrat then pulled out his book and started to jot down notes.

"We saw a competition. He got excited. He's been drawing things since then," Erik said by way of explanation. "How are things progressing with Vermire?"

Glosil stood and cleared his throat.

Erik and Rugrat looked at each other as Glosil finished the presentation.

"In conclusion, everything is in place. We have recruited and trained the main guard force. The secondary force has been, in turn, trained by them. Mister Silaz has been working the other outposts. We believe we have a good chance of roping a majority of them into this endeavor, or have them remain neutral."

Erik looked at Rugrat and shrugged. "It's a good plan, really good plan.

Let's see if it works, ladies and gents," Erik said.

The tension in the room seemed to bleed off.

"Erik and I can't make every decision. It's clear you didn't run into this. You used the systems and got approval from the necessary people. Good work," Rugrat said.

"How is everything else?" Erik looked around the table.

"The school continues to grow. All Alvans have a basic understanding of the skills and other practical knowledge. We are currently investing the excess funds we have gained so that when we increase the workshops to the fourth tier we hopefully won't need any funds from the treasury or very little. Since the Expert manuals have been offered at the library, the applicants to the teaching staff has increased. Junior teachers are heading to Vuzgal for training, with the more experienced teachers splitting their time between Vuzgal and Alva. This is in an effort for them to learn in Vuzgal and increase our strength there and then repeat the process here, keeping their minds active and giving them new stimulus constantly. I have factored this into the academy's budget.

"With the new manuals, I don't think that it will be long until we are ushering in new Experts to the academy. With the new Experts, I have started to brainstorm with the other department heads. For those who wish to remain in the academy, they will be able to take on teaching positions, to be paid back in higher priority for items, reduced cost on items, and a stipend from the school. They can also pay to use the workshops, but the students will have priority. Most of them, I believe, will look to increase their levels and then head to Vuzgal for employment. I know that a number of them have contacted the Adventurer's Guild about being power leveled." Jia Feng looked at Blaze, who nodded.

She settled back down as Erik spoke up.

"I would also be interested if the academy would create a competition program. It will have a few purposes—first, to organize and oversee competitions within the academy and Vuzgal. I am hoping to make a second arena there that will focus on competing crafters. Second, they will train up our own home crafting teams, whose goal will be to attend the competitions in Vuzgal, the Fourth, and the Fifth Realm. It is my hope that this program will incentivize the people in the academy to work harder, to learn more about the other realms and their different techniques. The Expert-level books are not just straight information like, say, spell or technique books that we've used in the past. Instead of giving a person an answer, it would be better to call them aids that are meant to help people create or find their own path. As people advance down their own path, they will need to experience others' paths, refining their own skills. If we just tell them what to learn and don't allow them to make their own path, then we'll stunt our own growth." Erik's eyes moved around the room before they fell on Glosil.

"Also, I hope that the army can participate in this trend as well. I want to turn the Battle Arena into a prime location for people all over the Fourth Realm to test their skills. I want to have our people up on those stages and training with the different combat artists in the training rooms."

"I know that there are plenty of people willing to join in." Glosil smiled. "I will only be holding back one platoon to remain in Alva. Every three months, the platoons will rotate between Alva and Vuzgal, training their own unit or training new units."

Erik smiled in approval. *Glosil has really stepped into his own element, commanding the military completely, understanding the people within it, looking to increase their power, protect our assets and looking at the big picture, planning ahead for the future and the higher realms.*

Erik looked over to Elise and Blaze. "It's been some time, though it looks like things have gone well." He laughed.

Blaze and Elise looked at each other and smiled.

Blaze cleared his throat as he sat up in his chair. "The Adventurer's Guild has continued expanding. We're still taking in applicants all the time. We're operating across the first three realms, and we have put out feelers to the Fighter's Association. One, to see if they're interested in taking on our best fighters who didn't pass vetting to become Alvans and two, to open up a new route to get training and personnel. Once we're connected to the Fighter's Association, then it will be harder for the other guilds to create issues."

"Issues?" Erik asked.

"We're becoming a force to be recognized. There are different sects that are fighters; they challenge our people...get into fights. There have been a few bad ones." Blaze's expression darkened.

"Such as?" Erik asked.

"There was a group from our association that had just finished running a convoy to their final destination. It was a long haul. Instead of earning gold or copper, they got resources; they worked it out with the merchants. The people from the sect, hearing about the resources exchanged, went after the fighters.

"They killed three of our people and wounded seven. The remaining ten escaped with the wounded and passed the word. It was in the Second Realm. We sent people over to talk to those in the sect. They gave us reimbursement and punished their students," Blaze said.

"What was the name of the sect?" Erik sounded calm but his eyes were locked onto Blaze.

"Willful Institute. I didn't want to push it too much. I blacklisted them. You told me to keep a low profile. I made a report and sent it to Delilah."

Erik looked at the ceiling, a rush of blood and adrenaline surging through his veins.

"Someone should really teach them a lesson," Rugrat said quietly.

Erik looked over to him.

"Elan looked into them, they have roots in the fourth realm and a small presence in the fifth realm. Though, there are a number of their sect members that gain the interest of more powerful sects, they head to the higher realms, joining the academies of the sixth and there are rumors that they have members that are in the seventh realm, possibly the eighth."

"So a sect reaching to the fourth realm, but really they can call on support from seventh realm experts, possibly the eighth realm," Rugrat said grimly.

"Exactly and we all know just how powerful someone from the higher realms could be, think of the power difference between someone from the first and second realm and then someone between the fourth and fifth realm. The gap is bigger with the higher level equipment, cultivation, techniques and any bonuses that people have, such as titles, add up quickly as people don't just have a handful of stat points anymore."

Aditya was studying a map in his office as there was a knock at the door. It opened to reveal Miss Evernight.

He waited as the door was closed and she activated a formation. She pulled out a bundle of papers and moved to the planning table next to the map. He moved around to be beside her as he looked over the documents.

"Training is complete with your primary unit and your reserve. Do you have any questions?" she asked after she had finished laying out the papers.

Aditya thought of the changes he had seen in his guards. It was as if they had been trimmed up and straightened into form. Now they were closer to one another than before. They had been all doing the same job and looking out for one another. Now they were willing to lay down their lives for one another, to leave their life on the line so that the other would survive. With them all thinking the same way, they were willing to take more risks for one another, exceeding their limits. A loss of honor, of not looking out for the person on their left and right, was more important than dying.

They had learned how to use their strength with greater effectiveness and coordinate with one another. Their levels hadn't increased but they had changed.

"I don't," Aditya said.

"Very well. These are the information reports on all of the outposts, from the basic information of their main imports, exports, the people who control the outpost, to the deeper layers of the thoughts and the back-door dealings that the outposts have, hidden alliances, motivations. The things that we can use to pressure or entice them into joining into the unification effort. Then we have plans for military coordination, as we have discussed. It will be your job to pull in these different outpost leaders and to move forward." Evernight looked at Aditya.

He felt a new weight rest on his shoulders as he looked at the information displayed in front of him.

"Your information network is impressive." Aditya then took a breath. "The first thing we need to do is create ties with these different outposts—invite them here for a meal, meetings, and trade. We can offer items for sale in the auction houses, use the cover of a newer, stronger Vermire wanting to connect to its fellow outposts. We do a bit of trade, strengthen ties on the outside; behind closed doors, we put into place the first alliances that we have with the different outpost leaders. We will probably need another meeting with them, less pressure in another outpost to confirm our plans and move forward."

"You will have the items needed to entice them," Evernight said with a sly smile.

Aditya nodded.

Just what standard have their crafters reached? Are Apprentice weapons and items that hard for them to manufacture?

38
Line in the Sand

Emmanuel stood in the guard tower, looking over the training area. He saw the men and women there, wearing their layered clothing as they fought with the small shields and curved swords of the Fayad family.

"Father." A woman's voice came from behind him as he heard Nasreen kneel on the tower floor.

Emmanuel continued to watch the men and women training and fighting with one another, the flash of blades and shields, the moving of fabric as they focused entirely on their attackers.

He pulled out a scroll from his robe and held it out.

Nasreen stood and took the scroll, reading it in silence as he continued to watch the fighters.

She closed the scroll and Emmanuel turned around.

He looked to be entering his later years, his features softening with time, but his eyes were still bright and there was a hidden energy in his bones and greater power waiting to be unleashed.

Nasreen might be the leader of the Shadowridge guards but she still wasn't able to defeat her father.

He looked at her, interested in her thoughts. She opened her mouth and then paused, thinking through the contents of the letter further.

It was a few more minutes before she started to talk.

"Do we know what their purpose is?"

"This is the only letter that we have received," Emmanuel said simply.

"Based on our reports, the Vermire Outpost has only grown in strength in the recent years. They have a group of healers who brought them more adventurers. Many high-powered merchants have moved over there, some of them even opening their headquarters within the outpost. It has doubled in size and there are more people looking to move there. They are so bold to raise crops outside of the outpost. They might not sell the best items of all the outposts, but they are more consistent. You might find rare items in the different outposts; you will always find them in Vermire.

"With being attacked by the former Zatan Confederation, they played nations like pieces on a board, and proved their strength. They became a neutral ground for many nations and powerful groups to mediate their issues within the city and trade. They have grown in power, which can make them arrogant. This letter can be a way of them exercising their power, though they have taken time to digest their gains, to stabilize their foundations. While they might be arrogant, they are also smart and showing us face by sending a letter and gifts to entice us into meeting with them."

Emmanuel waited for her to say anything else. "That is a good summary of Vermire, but what about this letter?"

"It is unclear what they want, if it is to show off their strength or if it is to become a powerful figure in the outposts. The wording makes it seem as if they feel that we're equals, even though Lord Aditya has only been doing this for a limited period of time. It makes me think that they want something from us?" Nasreen looked at her father.

"I think so too." A faint smile appeared at the corner of his mouth.

Nasreen smiled, seeing her father's acknowledgement before she frowned. "What do they want to work with us on? We're across the other side of the Beast Mountain Range. It will take us nearly a week to reach them. Although we know of one another, we aren't of much use to the other."

"Ah, Nasreen, what if I was to tell you that he has sent messengers to the Sea Breeze, Sea Castle, Hunter Frontier, and Sun Forge outposts?"

"All of our outposts are opposite one another across the Beast Mountain

Range. We're far away from one another, so we don't have issues with one another and we all have different beasts and items in our areas. Plenty of trade and no issues. Is he looking to set up a trading caravan between us all?"

"Would he ask us to meet to set up a trade caravan? What about our caravans? We send out caravans we have a stake in to trade in our stead," Emmanuel said.

"They could have just made a trade caravan themselves, so they need our help to do something? What would need the help of six powerful outposts?" Nasreen's eyebrows pinched together. "With that kind of strength—well, we would need others, but we could cut—"

Her eyes flashed and she looked up at Emmanuel. "They can't be thinking?"

"About cutting a road through the Beast Mountain Range? Well, we should go and find out. A total of twenty-five different outposts have been contacted, nearly all of the outposts that have not had a large conflict or are owned by a nation or outside group. We will leave in three days to make it for this dinner. You will take care of the arrangements. Your brother Majdi will be taking over command of the outpost while we are away."

"There is no need for you to go," Nasreen said.

"Thank you for your concern, but on a topic such as this, if it is as I believe, then I do not think sending a proxy will be in our best interests."

"These are the latest reports from the outposts?" Elan asked Miss Evernight, who was spearheading intelligence gathering activities in the area immediately around Alva Dungeon. With the recent expansion of the intelligence service, there was little that moved around Alva Dungeon without her knowledge.

"Yes, sir."

Elan made a noise of understanding as he read through the condensed reports. He took some ten minutes before putting the file down. "Thoughts?"

"It is as we believed it would be. There will be neutral parties, and those against. I believe that we can, with the right pressure and incentives, bring nineteen of the outposts to our side," Evernight said.

Elan looked over to Glosil, who was reading an identical report.

Glosil waited a few more minutes before closing the folder. “It looks good to me. For this operation, you will report directly to me and be Lord Aditya’s right hand. Make sure that you have support liaising with the military.”

39

Advancing on the Fire Floor

"How are things on the Earth floor?" Yui asked Glosil.

"Egbert is having a reading retreat. The main command formation is being repaired. He has sent up a list of materials that he will need to fill in and finish the formation with. The smiths and alchemists are working together to recreate the different enhanced metals. It'll take them a few days to complete it," Glosil said as he shifted his armor around.

"How are the troops?" Glosil asked.

"They're interested with the changes that will be happening. Got some names for the marines already," Domonos said.

"Either of you two want to try your hand at it?" Glosil asked, curious.

Domonos looked at Yui, who half laughed.

"I'm interested, but my people…you know," Yui said.

"You don't want them to think that you're leaving them behind." Glosil smiled, thankful that he had two unit officers who cared deeply for their people.

"Well, I need someone for it and if you want to, the marines are going to need a commander as well."

"Sir." Yui nodded.

Glosil checked his timepiece. "All right, get them formed up. We good to go, Roska?" Glosil looked over to the two special teams who were standing or sitting around, talking to one another. With his words, they got to their feet and readied their weapons.

"We're ready," Roska said.

Glosil looked at them. They were all fairly young. *Seems that everyone in the Alva Army is young, but that all of them have needed to grow up quickly,* Glosil thought, remembering what he had thought in the general meeting just two days ago.

"Let's go take that floor back," he said.

People moved to the teleportation formation. They were now veterans with training to set up defenses upon insertion into a new floor.

There was some muttering among the ranks. Glosil turned to see Erik and Rugrat walking beside George and Gilly. They both wore their full armor, releasing a powerful aura as Erik and Rugrat were wearing their battle rattle.

Glosil went up to them. "Sirs?"

"We're here if you need us," Erik said.

"Not that you will," Rugrat chimed in with a grin.

Glosil let out a smile. Seeing them both was reassuring. "A two-man reserve—the Fire floor should be scared shitless."

The trio laughed.

"All right, smartass. You must've been listening to Rugrat more in the lectures." Erik smirked. "Good luck."

"Thanks," Glosil said.

Rugrat held out his fist and Glosil tapped it.

"Bring them home safe."

Glosil nodded.

"Now go run the operation. I want to have a jacuzzi set up in the Fire floor by tonight!" Erik said in a mock growl.

Glosil chuckled and turned back to the formation. Some of the tension had been bled off through the simple jokes. "First group ready?"

"First group ready!" Yui called back.

"Teleport."

With Glosil's command, the man in charge of the teleportation formation activated it.

The group disappeared and the second group rushed forward and onto the empty formation.

Glosil was with them, sitting in the middle. Glosil looked around, seeing the thumbs up from the different sergeants.

"Second group ready!" Glosil called out.

The timer hit zero and they appeared on the Fire floor. Their breath caught with the heat but they were moving with what they had been trained to do.

The walls were coming up and creatures in the area didn't seem too pleased about the intrusion. The world was painted red and yellow, with an ash cloud that covered the roof of the floor. Black rocks had been twisted or created from the lava that ran through the ground and created burning seas across the floor. There was a group of volcanoes in the middle of the floor spewing out lava and smoke. Beasts could be heard fighting on the volcanoes and moving through the lava sea.

It was a land of war and chaos. Rivals fought one another for an extra inch, their tempers like the area that they resided in.

Creatures, sensing a new group with different mana, charged toward the camp.

"Grenadiers to the wall!" Yui ordered.

People put their rifles away and pulled out their grenade launchers, including Glosil.

The walls were being thrown up in record time. They cleared the formation and seconds later, the next group appeared, reinforcing and assisting as needed.

"Looks like they're really happy." Storbon adjusted his aim.

"Time to cool them off!" Deni replied.

Storbon sighed and rolled his eyes.

"Fire on targets of opportunity!" Niemm yelled.

The grenadiers opened fire. Their shells hit the approaching creatures and bloomed with ice energies as the gems within the shells cracked and released their energy into the formations covering the shell.

The dull *whoump, whoump* sounded along the wall and they took their time, not wasting shells as they put them among or on top of the beasts.

Reinforcements came through the teleportation formation. The front lines contained the beasts, firing in twos so that as one ran out of ammunition then another was firing.

The creatures were fighting one another as they pushed forward, creating chaos.

The camp was finished off as the creatures fled.

Storbon reloaded his grenade launcher and surveyed the area. The ice attacks were already being melted away in the oppressive heat. Premade formations were put together and beasts were sent out to survey the area.

Niemm came over after a few hours, the camp now fully established. "I've got to go talk to the big man. Make sure that everyone is good and ready to move out. We'll probably be heading to one of the command formations."

"Got it."

Niemm went off, talking with Glosil for a few minutes before he headed back to the wall, using the linked communication channel to the team. They had been tinkering and working with their communication devices to the point that Erik and Rugrat approved of them. They were the first thing to get upgraded if there was ever a new version. Communication was as important as a weapon to a soldier.

"Bring it in," Niemm said.

The team checked to make sure someone covered their position before rallying on Niemm, who had pulled out a table with an updating map on it.

"Okay, we're heading to this command formation. We're going to have two sections of scouts from Dragon Platoon with us for support." Niemm looked over to another group that was being briefed by Domonos.

"Plan is, we set up a camp there and hold it. We get images of the formations, send it back to the formation masters. Then either we'll have a few of them come down here, or we'll have some of the engineer types in the company assist us in repairing the formation."

"Support?" Storbon asked.

"We'll have the support from the main camp. We have three spell batteries right now," Niemm said.

Storbon looked over to the formations that had been placed down. One mage stood in them, ready to cast a spell that would be enhanced by the formation to support the wall if necessary.

With the ceiling, we can't use the mortars, but the mages are plenty powerful.

"Do we know average levels yet?" Setsuko asked.

"Beasts look like they're from level thirty to fifty—pretty powerful. Now, they might be a lower level than us, but we all know that depending on the animal, their innate traits can make them a hell of a lot stronger," Niemm said.

None of them relaxed, remaining focused as if they were going up against creatures three times their level.

"We will be moving by mounts, so make sure that they're good to go. We'll leave in two hours, give them time to acclimatize," Niemm said. "Anything else for me?"

"Quick reaction force?" Yuli asked.

"Special Team Two with Egbert, Erik, and Rugrat on call."

"Well shit, I'm getting all warm and fuzzy inside," Tian Cui said.

"Got the warm and fuzzies for Erik, huh?" Yawen joked, getting a punch to the shoulder from Tian Cui as the special team grinned.

"No fighting, kids," Niemm said. "Storbon, come on. Let's go say hi to the scouts."

"Rockstar row, have them seeing stars," Yuli said.

Storbon flipped her the bird as the others laughed and brought out their mounts. Their mounts moved around, uncomfortable in the atmosphere of the Fire floor. The special team tried to get them comfortable and ready for what was to come.

Storbon looked over the scouts.

"Play nice. With the expansion, we'll be growing to four special teams. Most of the new members will be coming from the engineers, scouts, and medics," Niemm reminded him.

"Yeah," Storbon said. He didn't miss the look in Niemm's eyes, or the way Yao Meng shook his finger in mock seriousness behind him.

It took all of Storbon's self-control to not laugh or smile.

He had packed on muscle, increased his strength and his mana. He was someone the rest of the military looked up to. He was unfazed with the looks that people gave him. In his mind, he was just repaying Erik and Rugrat for all that they had done for him.

Special Team One headed out of the camp with the scouts, riding on their mounts in a convoy. As the last person made it through the gates, they were locked and sealed once again.

Storbon looked over the Fire floor. He had thought that it would be desolate, nothing but flames and lava for miles.

There are plants and creatures here of all kinds. The heat and Fire-attribute mana here is impressive. If someone was to draw this mana into their body, they would be able to slowly increase their Body Cultivation. There are hotspots that naturally draw the Fire-attribute mana as well.

Storbon studied the floor, comparing what he saw with what he had learned, as they rode.

"Fliers!" someone called out. People scanned the sky, seeing the reddish winged creatures that were visible between the rock outcroppings and the Fire floor's sparse plant life.

"Explosive rounds, distance trigger!" Niemm said.

Everyone changed out their sockets on their rifles and reloaded their magazines with explosive rounds.

"Prepare to fire in half sections!"

Everyone got ready as the flying creatures' bodies were revealed more. They had the wings of a butterfly and the body of a salamander, and they seemed to sweat lava as it ran down their bodies.

"Yuli, use a wind-based Fire scroll. See if you can throw them off course," Niemm said.

"Yes, boss." Yuli pulled out a scroll and started to activate it. Mana increased around her as the spell scroll started to glow. A spell formation appeared above the spell scroll as it was burned away.

A replica spell formation appeared in the skies. The ash clouds that hung above were dragged together, creating flashes of lightning and flames as the clouds congealed together into a tornado that cut through the oncoming creatures' flying formation.

They had nowhere to hide or escape as the tornado dragged them in and threw them around, allowing the group to continue in peace.

They pushed on, and people altered their ammunition and sockets they were using on their rifle.

"Lava lake ahead and to the left!" Lucinda called out, acting as their lead scout.

They followed her out of the plant life and down along the shore of the lava lake. They had to follow it around a bay-like area and then cut in toward where the control formation was located.

"Contact!" someone yelled out as the lava lake moved. A reptile of some kind charged out of the lava, snapping his jaws at the nearest rider.

No one needed permission; they opened fire on the large beasts that were over ten meters long and half a meter tall.

They let out hisses as they were hit.

A pack of them emerged from the lava. Others moved into the lake again, circling around, moving faster through the lava than on land.

Storbon was still coming up on them. He stored his rifle and lowered himself so he was in line with his repeating ballista. He pressed the trigger. Bolts shot out, tracking across the beasts, striking them and turning into icicles. The beast cried out in agony as they were slaughtered on the lakeside.

Niemm guided them away from the water's edge. They had only been working together for a few hours but the scouts and the special team were adapting to one another rapidly, becoming a cohesive fighting unit.

Their reactions were amplified by their level and having been in life-or-death situations. Instead of panicking, they focused on their tasks, broke it down and pushed on.

Storbon stopped firing and he searched for targets. He started to reload one of the ballistas so the other remained ready to fire. *Impressive. We wouldn't have been able to have this coordination just a year ago.*

They left the lake behind. The beasts snapped at them, but they were too far away to do anything else.

"All right, the command formation is just up ahead. I want all-around defense as we discussed. Build up the forward operating base. Once we've secured our position, we will then check on the command formation!" Niemm said.

They climbed up the hill around the bay. Their panther mounts dug in their claws to find purchase as they climbed to the top of a knoll that was jutting out into the lava lake some, but still attached to the land. There was a tower located there. It showed signs of damage. Its once tall, clean lines were now scarred and pitted by fighting that had occurred in or around it. There were lines running up the tower and formations that had been long destroyed and now lay dormant.

"Special Team One, you're on point," Niemm said.

"On me." Storbon sped up, the special team breaking away from the rest of the group. Niemm would remain with them to maintain command and control.

The tower was about ten by ten and would have reached nearly one hundred and fifty meters in its prime.

"Anyone in there?" Storbon yelled to Lucinda.

"Nothing that my beasts can detect!"

"All right, as we discussed—Yawen, Deni, Setsuko, and Tian Cui in first. Setsuko will command. Yuli and Lucinda with me for support. We'll move through and clear the position. Once clear, Yawen, Tian Cui, and Setsuko, you're with me. We'll support actions on the ground. The remainder will take up overwatch position," Storbon said as they got closer.

"Understood!" they rang back as they closed with the tower.

Storbon pulled out his rifle. His mounted weapon systems couldn't elevate enough to give him full coverage of the tower.

Yawen, Deni, Setsuko Ket, and Tian Cui moved ahead. They dismounted and stored their beasts in a fluid motion, pulling together as they got to the wall.

Yawen moved up and pulled out a battering ram, activating the sockets on it. He slammed it into the door.

The main lock was punched out and a rippling wave of force threw the heavy stone doors open. The other three moved into the tower as Yawen stored his battering ram and pulled out his rifle, following them.

Storbon checked the sides, seeing the scouts and Niemm splitting in half and spreading out to watch the land around them.

The first people in position started to pull out the building blocks of the forward operating camp.

Storbon and the remainder of the special team headed into the tower.

The medallions that Egbert had given them flashed with a red light and then calmed down.

"Activate formation traps!" Storbon said. "Looks like the access passes Egbert gave us are working."

The interior of the tower was left largely untouched. The main floor was the command formation. The swirling shapes and scripts made it look like a piece of art.

Doesn't seem damaged. This main area looks fine.

A set of stairs started behind the formation, reaching the rear wall and then curving up the wall to either side.

The other team moved up the stairs toward the higher floors.

Storbon led his team up the first flight and headed to the left as the other team climbed the right stairs.

They moved upward. The medallion flashed amber as a click noise came from the door at the top of the stairs.

Storbon pushed the door open and the others moved through.

He followed them in. There was a transparent section in the floor, looking at the formation below. Then there were workshops, what looked like an eating area, a small library, and other rooms that seemed to be built for research or study.

They checked the rooms, finding nothing inside them. Another set of stairs against the wall led upward, this time much less grand than the set before.

"Keep your guard up," Storbon reminded them as they pushed on.

Yawen opened the next door as well. Setsuko went first. They moved through, finding the floor in a state of disrepair. The roof had been broken in places and the floor was filled with different trash and dust that had accrued over time.

They headed to the next floor. It was the first one that was open to the elements. There were parts of the wall that were open to the Fire floor.

There were signs of different creatures living on the floor and formations that had been activated, killing them.

They reached the next floor. The floor was destroyed, signs of fighting all over the place.

"Looks like there is nothing here. The top floors must have been broken apart and that's what's below," Deni said.

Her words were in line with what Storbon thought had happened.

"All right, get set up in overwatch." Storbon looked around, checking to see whether he could see any creatures or animals approaching the tower.

Those who were taking over moved over the roof and checked their arcs, making sure that they could cover every direction.

Lucinda released different beasts, most of them reptilian to deal with the heat.

Even the air was hot here.

Storbon let out a cough and he headed back down.

They went down to the command formation.

"It looks like it's fine," Setsuko said as they were passing.

"It does," Storbon said, stopping for half a step. He pulled out a Mortal mana stone and tossed it out.

It landed on the formation, glowing brilliantly. The mana from the mana stone was absorbed by the formation in a matter of seconds. The different lines of the formation lit up with power.

There was a slight humming as the formation went active.

"Damn," Storbon said.

"Hmm, Storbon, what happened?" Egbert asked.

"You can hear me?" Storbon asked.

"No, I can't," Egbert huffed.

"Well, there was this command formation and I tossed out a mana stone. It absorbed it and then, well, this is happening," Storbon said.

"Looks like the formation is actually okay. Problem was it wasn't getting power from the dungeon core, so it used up its reserve power and then nothing. This is good, though. All of the creatures within a one-hundred-meter radius of this command circle can be controlled by it and I have a complete picture of the floor. Yeah, that damage is extensive—nasty. The treasury is not going to enjoy that at all! Once the creatures come into the range of influence, then they'll fall under my control again. If you can bring the beasts to you, I can regain control over more of them!"

"How can you control them if they go outside of the formation's range?" Storbon said.

"Their ancestor's blood is stored in the control formations—they can't go against it. As soon as they get near the control formation, then it's like a contract is made with them and the dungeon core," Egbert said. "If you were able to get all of the beasts on the floor to come over to that control formation, you could take control over them. Though only as long as it is powered. To hook it up to the power, still need to take the main command formation in the middle of the floor and connect it into the formation network through the dungeons."

"So we need to keep on powering it with mana stones?"

"Looks like it. I'll have some stones sent down and I'll send a message to the formation people, see if they can do something to boost the range. In the meantime, if you get more creatures to come over to the area of influence, that would be good. I'll actually go and make the beasts now under our command go and piss off some of the beasts in the area and pull them in toward the command formation."

"I'll report this to Glosil." Storbon sighed.

"Have fun beast wrangling!"

"There's always more than one way to complete a dungeon."

"What is going on?" Davin opened his eyes, looking around the room. He got up off his bed. He stretched and yawned before scratching his butt as he stepped off the white-hot metal bed.

He stepped out of his cave and looked out over the red world. Lava pools could be seen everywhere among the black rock and the blood-red forests.

The Fire imp picked his long nose as he relieved his bladder into a stream of lava flowing down the mountain. His stream made the lava create steam.

He finished up and started to move his face, trying to stop the impending sneeze.

Beasts around his residence dove for cover before Davin *sneezed*.

He shot out a blast of flame that melted the rock that had been unaffected over the last few hundred years by lava and the immense heat of the floor.

Beasts were shaking in their homes as they cowered away from the true lord of the fire floor.

After several sneezes and smoking black craters Davin seemed to be done.

"Damn, had something hin my nose.

Davin stood there, looking over his domain, his hands on his hips and pushing out his bulbous stomach, leaving all bare.

"Same old, day after—wait, is there fighting over in the Baroush Forest?" Davin stomped his foot. It lifted a paltry amount of dust but the beasts in the caves underneath Davin all started to back into their homes.

The domain shook and then the volcano belched lava.

"It is Sunday! My day off and you're picking a fight in the forests! I like that forest! I had to replant it three times! By hand! If you want to fight, you can fight on the mountain!" Davin's tail moved around in irritation as his wings opened to either side.

His wings flapped angrily, straining before he lifted up, still in the same pose, glaring at the forest, his hands on his hips as he glided down the mountain.

Egbert was studying the control formation making noises when the volcano shook and rained down lava.

"Oh?" Egbert headed outside the tower. A full camp had formed around the tower. There were creatures of all kinds running around, all of them now friendly.

Egbert looked in the direction of the volcano and he saw a familiar pudgy figure. "No, it can't be!"

Egbert headed up into the air and he shot up behind the Fire imp.

"Davin?" Egbert tilted his head to the side as the angry Fire imp seemed to freeze, dropping a few feet before his wings flapped angrily, bringing him back up.

"Davin! That is you! I thought that you had died off!" Egbert said, flying on over.

"Egbert, you pile of bones! Where have you been!" Davin chastised, waving his finger at the skeleton as he rose up and faced him head on.

"Well, you know…running the dungeon and stuff?" Egbert said.

"Running the dungeon? I've been stuck down here for centuries!" Davin complained.

"You know, it's all in the past?" Egbert laughed dryly.

"All in the past! You know how much I hate having to organize anything! I remodeled the floor five times I was so bored. Well, one of the times, there was a war between the creatures, got a bit smart and thought that they owned the floor. Forgot about me 'cause I took a nap for seventy years. That is beside the point, though! I woke up and put them straight, only took ten or twenty year long naps after that!" Davin said proudly.

Egbert felt his mana flickering and the strength of his spirit wavering.

You're proud of napping for only one or two decades? You lazy Imp! I was running a whole dungeon competition for our masters and you were napping!

Egbert contained himself.

"Try this." Egbert quickly pulled out a spoon with food and put it into Davin's face.

Davin's eyes went as big as his stomach and tears appeared.

Egbert tried to pull the spoon back, but the emotional imp came with the spoon.

"Ish shouw gerd!"

Egbert let go of the spoon and pulled out a pie, wafting it toward Davin.

Davin released the spoon, his eyes totally on the pie. The part of the spoon that was in his mouth was half melted, forgotten as it dropped to the floor.

Egbert, seeing the look in Davin's eyes, quickly threw it.

Davin appeared next to the pie, he was so fast. He shuddered as he ate the pie. "You remembered!!" Tears fell down from Davin's eyes that actually caused the floor below to melt.

"Just how high of a level did you reach?" Egbert asked.

"Egbert!" Davin ran to Egbert, eating the pie and hitting him side on, wanting to hug him but the food was too good to let it go.

"There, there, Davin, don't worry. I have more pies for you, though you'll have to abide by the rules again."

"As long as I don't have to rule anything!"

"That's fine. You can sleep in the smithy furnaces if you want! Just have to supply the flames like before."

"Oh, the furnaces were the best. Too quiet here. Everyone's scared of me." Davin sighed in melancholy.

Egbert coughed but didn't say anything.

40

Fire Floor Secured?

Erik and Rugrat were silent as Glosil finished talking. Their eyes tracked over to the Fire imp that sat on top of the headquarters table, eating pie as Egbert stood beside him, like a proud parent.

"So you've ruled over the Fire floor since it got locked away?" Erik asked.

"Yup. Well, I didn't know what was going on. I was having a nap and then when I woke up, the floor was all sealed up. I told those beasts," the imp waved his spoon with an angry frown on his face, "no fighting anywhere but my volcano on Mondays, Tuesdays, and Sundays. Then the winner gives me a massage!"

"A massage?" Rugrat asked.

Egbert's hand smacked the back of the imp and he turned his hands to the side, karate-chopping his back.

Davin had a look of pure bliss on his face. "O-ooh-oohh, th-aa-ttss th-eee ri-iii-ggh-t sppp-oo-t!"

Erik put his fingers in his ears, swallowing as he saw Egbert karate-chopping Davin with enough force to shatter most trees.

Davin moved around to really allow Egbert to get in there as he ate his pie in bliss.

Erik and Rugrat looked to Glosil.

"This dungeon's weird."

Erik and Rugrat shot a glance at each other, agreeing.

"So, moving forward?" Erik asked.

"Well, Davin here has a great understanding of the power structure within the different floors. We just need to get an entrance to the Wood floor and we can take it; just let Davin bring everything under control.," Egbert said.

"He does formations too!"

"Fun games! Though magic creates more lights," Davin replied, his eyes shining.

"Lights, explosions?" Erik asked.

"My redneck senses are tingling."

"I'll take that as a yes." Erik ignored Rugrat and looked back to Glosil, who blinked, as if it were completely normal to have a pie-eating imp getting a massage from an undead while his bosses were talking about explosions.

"The Earth floor is still being cleared out. Should take no more than a week or two. Depends on the plants, really. The formations there are being rebuilt. It is our plan to move the formation core to the Fire floor and repeat the process on the floor above, the difference being that we remake the formations and the formation lines, instead of remodeling the floor," Glosil said.

"What is our next move?" Rugrat asked, looking to Glosil.

"We might as well try out Davin and Egbert's plan on the Wood floor and see if it works, and then look into the Water floor. If it works, then it will save us a lot of time. If not, then we can use the same tactics we used on the Fire floor," Glosil said. "Though we've still got training going on in Alva, Vuzgal, and with the soldiers from Vermire. It won't be long until they're trained up."

"If we need to, we can hold off on clearing the floors until we're sure we can take them," Erik said.

41 A Cultivation Plan

Erik studied the Earth floor plan. Egbert was still the only one who could go down there.

While he was there, he repaired formations and put down plants that drew in the impurities of the area and started to transform the environment.

"I'm not late, am I?" Rugrat burst into the room.

"Just in time," Erik said. "Egbert?"

"Come on, just one more chapter!"

"You can read once we're done. With the floor hooked up to the main formations, then we will be able to draw out the impurities faster and allow people down on the floor sooner."

"Just what I need, more people trying to ruin my peace and quiet!" Egbert complained. "It looks good on my side. Ready?"

"Good to go here," Erik said.

"Opening the passageway. Davin?"

"Why can't I leave the Fire floor! It's so *boring* down here!"

"Have you cleared everything off the command formation plate?" Egbert asked.

"Yes, yes, for the third time!" Davin sighed in deep suffering.

"You can go up to the higher floors once you have a greater control over your ambient Fire mana. We don't need you burning down people's homes or melting them," Erik said.

"Well, we could use him in the smithy," Rugrat said.

"Which is right next to the Alchemy building. What do you think the alchemists would do if he burned their ingredients?" Erik looked at Rugrat.

"Huh. Well, it'd be good for anyone making concoctions with Fire-attribute plants?"

"Are you two ready?" Erik sighed, looking away from the shrugging redneck. On the main interface, he could see the main channel from the Metal floor opening as the dungeon core dropped lower.

"Good to go," Egbert said.

"Same here," Davin replied.

Erik and Rugrat watched as the last door opened, connecting the Metal and the Earth floors together.

"Got an influx of mana being moved around. Closing the separation hatches. We'll have some bleed-through," Egbert said.

Sections along the main channel closed up and a wave rippled across the Earth floor, updating and changing it.

"Dungeon core added to the main formation. Damn, that is a lot of power! Starting to reconstruct some of the minor command formations. Repairing the command formation completely. This might take some time."

"Cards?" Rugrat pulled out a deck.

"Where did you get cards from?"

"Well, we have scribes. I talked to some of them and got them to make up a few packs of cards. Did a bit of poker—then euchre and solitaire got them interested."

"Solitaire then?" Erik asked.

"Simple but boring." Rugrat sat at the table and started to put the cards out.

They went through a few games.

"I'm *bored,*" Davin complained.

"Shh, I'm reading," Egbert muttered back.

"Couldn't you open the doors between the Earth and the Fire floors and then the Fire mana up there would come back down here?" Davin said in a half-thought.

"Actually, that would work pretty well. Opening the doors now."

Erik looked over to see the main channel opening as it started to descend another floor.

"So, what's the plan now?" Erik looked back to the game they had going.

Rugrat picked up a group of cards and moved them into line. "What do you mean?"

"The Willful Institute stepped on the Adventurer's Guild. We need to do something about that. Vuzgal is still developing, as is our military. We've been to the Fifth Realm. Vermire is looking to join hands with the other outpost trading towns to make a central outpost and bring the outposts under our command. We have Expert-level crafters for nearly every craft now. What are you going to do?" Erik glanced up.

Rugrat eyed the cards and then leaned back in his seat, looking at the ceiling.

"Learn Expert-level smithing techniques and my own path forward to increase my smithing skill level. At the same time, train up my Mana Gathering and Body Cultivation. I want to compete in the Battle Arena, increase my fighting skill. In the higher realms, armies don't clash so much. Most issues are settled in duels and matches."

"Makes sense. It costs a lot to train people up to that level. If they're just going all-out and killing one another, then the sects and powers would be losing a massive investment."

"Need a sparring partner? I think that I'm in the same boat," Erik said.

"Don't worry—I'd kick your ass every day of the week if you needed it!"

"Pretty confident, huh?"

"Well, just try to get close to me," Rugrat said.

George, who was resting around Rugrat's neck, let flames out of his nose.

Gilly opened one eye lazily and spat out a stream of water that doused George's flames and got on Rugrat, a gloating smile on her face. She closed her eyes, nestling into Erik's collar more.

George let out an angry bark as Rugrat wiped water off his face before using his Clean spell to get it all off.

"Also, we should teach some classes to the people here. See if there is anything that we can pass on to them that might be useful. Tips for going to other realms and so on." Erik didn't pay any attention to what had just happened, interrupting Rugrat before he could accuse Gilly of anything.

"Final shutter is open," Egbert said, breaking into their conversation as the Earth and Fire floors were reconnected. The dungeon core located in the Earth floor drew in a massive amount of mana, which was being split between the two floors. Mana flooded the formations that lined the main tunnel and was projected out as a single beam that connected with the Fire floor's command formation. The formation hadn't been damaged as it had been Davin's lair.

The power filled the circular formation and a wave pulsed out of the main formation, resolving the image of the Fire floor and revealing formations over and through the mountain. Lines descended and spread across the land as formations across the floor were powered up and activated. Subsequent waves rippled out from these formations, adding greater detail to the floor plans. The beasts of the floor couldn't do anything as they were brought under the beast control formation's power.

"The two floors are starting to balance one another out," Egbert said. "A large amount of Earth-attribute mana is rising to the Earth floor and Fire-attribute mana is descending."

"Looks like the plants like it. The Fire-attribute refining ones are getting weaker, though." Erik looked at the plots of plants that had been grown to change the atmosphere and mana attribute situation faster.

"How long do you think that it will be before we can start going to the Earth floor?" Rugrat asked.

"I think that in three weeks to a month it should be okay. Maybe the alchemists and the farmers can come up with more plants so that there is more breathable atmosphere down here."

"Can we open the Metal floor and Alva floor? Shouldn't that balance things out?" Erik asked.

"It could, if we were to close off the aeration tunnels that run to the surface. The beasts that have been living around the tunnels will be annoyed, though," Egbert said.

"What would that mean?" Erik asked.

"We use the crops and plants that are on the different floors to maintain a breathable situation within the dungeon. The housing floor has a lot of plants. If we can cover the Earth floor in those plants and create those growing slime dungeon monsters, then the Earth floor will produce enough air for the other floors," Egbert said.

"How were the floors getting air before?" Rugrat asked.

"Air vents that run through the Beast Mountain Range. They're small and cover a massive area. Used special boring creatures to make them all."

"Okay, let's open up the Metal floor, close off the housing floor from the outside, and then open up the main channel slightly. If the atmosphere starts to turn for the worse on the housing floor, then we'll close the shutters and try something else?" Erik looked at Rugrat.

"Is there anyone on the Metal floor?" Rugrat asked.

"There isn't anyone currently," Egbert said.

"I'm going to take a nap. Tell me when something happens," Davin said.

"He's always doing that—easily bored if there isn't some treat to be found." Egbert sighed.

"I think that we should open up the Metal floor, see what happens. Then we open up the housing floor just a little, for a few seconds. We see what happens and then we can anticipate what will happen in the future." Rugrat looked at Erik, who had stopped writing on his hand.

"Okay, that sounds fine to me. What do we have in the way to understand the air? I feel like we should have asked about this all earlier."

"Well, not all of us rely on air. And the place was nice and clean when you moved in. That said, the gnomes built in an air testing system into the formations. Guess they didn't want to suffocate from bad air or something," Egbert mused aloud.

Erik had a defeated look on his face as he sighed.

Rugrat just shrugged at him. "What do you expect? It's Egbert."

Erik nodded. "Yeah, yeah, I know."

"I can use those to keep things balanced."

"Then let's do it," Rugrat said.

"All right," Erik said.

Shutters opened from the Earth floor and the Metal floor, opening all the way.

"We've got mana and air moving between the floors. The unbreathable air is spreading out. Some of the animals might be affected, now that I think of it," Egbert muttered.

"Don't add that as an afterthought!" Erik barked.

"Well, there is only so much I can do with this big ole brain of mine!"

"There's a brain in there?" Rugrat asked.

"Of course there is!" Egbert said.

"Open the shutters between the Metal and housing floor—*slowly*," Erik emphasized.

The shutters between the two floors opened until there was only three shutters remaining; they opened only slightly. Erik could hear a whistling through the headquarters. He and Rugrat looked down beneath the table and into the hole extending below, illuminated by the formations that terminated in the light pillar that descended to the Metal floor, through to the Earth and Fire floors.

Brown, noxious-looking air passed around the command room and up through the top of the headquarters. It shot up and reached the roof of the housing floor.

"Close it," Erik ordered. The smoky brown clouds stopped passing through the headquarters.

The mana gathering formation absorbed some of the clouds while the rest of it spread over the housing area, being drawn into the alchemists' garden and the farmers' fields. The alchemists' garden organized the air and drew it in, while the plants in the farmers' fields consumed the noxious-looking gas clouds and drew in more, hungry for more.

"Egbert?" Erik asked.

"The gas isn't that concentrated—might make people cough some. Though it might be a better idea to run it through the sewage system and then feed it directly into the fields or the alchemist garden."

"Organize things. First we need to have a talk with Fehim and Waz the head of the farmers about pumping more of that air into their growing areas," Erik said.

Rugrat looked up through the ceiling to the mana gathering formation that, instead of growing, was now slowly being consumed. A small pillar of power dropped down and assisted in powering the dungeon. "How long can we keep up our current power burn?" Rugrat asked.

"Well, right now the housing floor is mainly sustained with the ambient mana in the area. With the amount of people and ingredients created in the area, the mana density is much higher and the mana gathering formations draw in a massive amount of mana from the surrounding area. Though a portion of that power and that from the mana gathering formation is passing down to the lower floors to repair and control them. We have focused on repairing the command and control formations instead of the mana gathering formations. The mana gathering formations increase the density of the different attribute mana on each floor and can be used as a power source for the formations.

"The aim of the gnomes was to have one main commanding dungeon core on the upper floors and then smaller subordinate dungeon cores on each floor. Each dungeon core would refine more mana, with people able to go to different mana-attribute floors for whatever they needed. Also, the housing floor being a holy land filled with only pure mana, which was found to rapidly enhance a person's body, made it easier for them to increase their Mana Gathering Cultivation and Body Cultivation," Egbert said matter-of-factly.

"Using pure mana to increase one's Mana Gathering Cultivation makes sense, but Body Cultivation?" Erik asked.

"Body Cultivation is tempering one's body, right? To damage it, you need to repair it. Pure mana makes it much easier to recover. It can be used in any spell and using pure mana instead of elemental mana has the ability to control attribute mana. It is the king when it comes to power that one can use."

Erik turned his head to the side.

"Something wrong?" Rugrat asked.

"With healing spells, we have been using Earth- and Wood-attribute spells. What if we were to use pure mana spells? Might that remove the Stamina issue?" Erik quickly pulled out a pen and wrote something on his hand as he kept talking. "So should we connect the floors or wait?"

Fehim and Waz agreed to having more of the air pumped into their gardens as the plants were flourishing faster than before. The clouds might be bad for humans, but they were great for the plants.

"Well, couldn't we make some kinds of masks? Your alchemists use them," Waz said.

"Yes, we have to use masks when working with different kinds of plants as they are hazardous to people's health. We can use either formation masks or Alchemy masks. The first have cleansing formations on them; the second have alchemical compounds soaked into the materials so that they counteract the effect of the different ingredients around the user."

"Where did you get that idea from?" Rugrat asked, thinking of gas masks.

"Well, working with livestock as I used to, sometimes you need a rag to try to cover the smell. If you put some herb that smells nice, then it counteracts the smell," Fehim said. "Why—is there something wrong with it?"

"Not at all. I'm just excited by your invention."

"Thank you." Fehim bowed his head to Rugrat, his serious expression broken by a radiant smile.

42 Strengthening

"How many do you think will come?" Pan Kun asked his lord as they sat within Lord Aditya's office.

"I'm not sure," Aditya said. There was an amused smile on his face, though, as he grabbed a fruit from the table and ate it happily.

"Are you nervous?"

"Nervous? A little. I don't want to shame our benefactors." Aditya's voice turned serious. "I am confident, though. It is hard to not be a little *too* excited, though, and overconfident." He seemed to realize how he had been acting as he leaned forward.

Pan Kun's sense had been sharpened and raised as he had been trained by the mysterious group in the woods. His eyes shook slightly as he could perceive the mana moving around Aditya according to his will. It didn't extend far, but Aditya had not been sitting back and relaxing. Pan Kun's eyes shot to Aditya's body, assessing him.

Is this an increase in Body and Mana Gathering Cultivation? I thought that there was something different about our teachers. Though I put that down to their higher levels that I couldn't see through. No wonder they didn't need to sleep and could train us at all hours.

"I'm not sure who will come from the outposts, to be honest. Though I have high hopes. I've reached out to many of them through different channels. How has the training gone with the second group?"

"It is going well. They have completed their training in the training camp. We fitted them with storage rings and communication devices. As you ordered, they are hunting in the Beast Mountain Range to increase their levels and strength while giving them cover to enter the different outposts—"

"Good. Then everything is going to plan. I have had messages from some of my people in the different outposts. They are performing well. They are new. This will be a test to see how well they operate," Miss Evernight said.

Pan Kun nearly jumped for the ceiling and Aditya let out a breath.

"Did I startle you?" Evernight smiled as she looked at the two big men.

"Just about," Aditya said. His relationship with the secretive guard had become more familiar in the past couple of weeks.

Miss Evernight seemed amused as she sat down at the table. "Everything is going according to plan so far. Still, we need to watch out for the outpost lords who are coming here with different goals."

"How will we know which ones are on our side or not?" Aditya asked.

"That will be up to you. I am just the person to assist," Miss Evernight said. "I brought some reading materials."

She placed down thick bundles of pages. "This is the condensed information I have been able to gather. I heard that you and Lady Sumi have something of a rivalry?" Evernight asked lightly.

"One could say that." Aditya's tone grew colder.

Pan Kun observed his lord. *In the past, he would go into a rage with that woman's name. She killed his remaining brother and mother over a set of armor when his group left. He was looking to sell it to support his family. He gave her the set of armor but she still killed them because he was too late. He had to grow his outpost in secret so she would not find out who he was.*

"Well, it is always good for the enemy to have a beacon. A clear dividing line between the two of you might make others group toward her. I don't doubt you would like to get rid of such an eyesore?" Evernight's smile had a vicious edge to it.

"What are my orders?" Aditya's eyes were glowing, locked onto Evernight.

Pan Kun knew that there was a power behind Aditya; he had seen the fighters against the Zatan Confederation. The trainers with their faces hidden behind masks. Now he realized something new.

We're not working for these people—we're part of them. Is that where the refugees and the people looking for work are going? He had felt confused about why they were sending people into the Beast Mountain Range without guards. Now he felt relieved. *They might have their plots and be ruthless, but I don't think that they're cold-blooded killers. Else they wouldn't have cared for us during our training.*

Pan Kun's emotions and thoughts were all over the place. All he did know was that he didn't completely understand everything that was happening.

"Remove the cancers around the Beast Mountain Range, create a headquarters for all of the outposts, and have the other lords bend the knee and come under our control."

"What if they don't wish to?"

"Then I will take action," Evernight said simply.

"I will do as commanded." Aditya bowed his head.

"Good. Now you have lots of reading to do and I have newly trained soldiers to herd across four dozen outposts." Evernight looked to Pan Kun and pulled out a bottle with a pill in it. "This is for you. This will allow you to temper your blood. The trainers have high hopes for you and your people."

Pan Kun knocked his chair over and kneeled, raising his hands. She dropped the pill bottle into his outstretched hands as he bowed his head.

"I will carry out my mission to completion." The pill bottle confirmed that the power behind the trainers and Vermire was possibly greater than what he imagined. He didn't know how he had the good fortune to reach their eyes but simply gifting him a pill to increase his temperings, seeing through his defects…he could feel that even if he ran, he wouldn't be able to escape their reach. Why should he run with the possible benefits offered?

Maybe only children of different royal families would be able to get this kind of resource.

"Don't worry, Lord Aditya. There are plans for you. Let's say good managers are looked upon favorably by my superiors." Miss Evernight stood and headed out of the room.

Pan Kun and Aditya recovered.

"Now you know what's at stake," Aditya said.

"You do not need to say any more, my lord." Pan Kun gave him a deep bow. He knew it was only through his trust that he was allowed to know these secrets and possibly gain this pill.

"Our paths have only started. Doesn't it fill your bones with fire?" Aditya stood. He no longer looked like the angered and wronged lord of the past. There was life in his eyes.

He's looking past Vermire, past the Beast Mountain Range. Pan Kun trembled and a grin appeared on his face. "Who doesn't dream of ascending to the higher realms?"

Aditya looked at Pan Kun and his smile turned into a laugh as the two of them couldn't hold themselves back anymore.

Glosil stood on the wall of the barracks, looking at the different groups training below.

"They're looking good," Glosil said as newly promoted Captain Domonos approached.

"Major Glosil." Domonos saluted.

Glosil returned the gesture and smiled. The two of them relaxed.

"It won't be long until we take another jump in rank with the way recruiting is looking in Vuzgal. It should slow down as we progress but learning how to manage so many people is a large undertaking. Have you sent up you Dragon Company's training staff?"

"I sent Sergeant—sorry, Lieutenant Choi up to Vuzgal already. He should be there now with the training cadre to train up the recruits and assist Tiger Company," Domonos said.

"Annoyed that they beat you in becoming a combat company first?" Glosil asked.

"A little, but my younger brother has always been determined." Domonos smirked.

Glosil snorted, a shadow of a smile on his face. "You will be heading up to Vuzgal to take their place in three months. At that time, we should have four combat companies' worth of strength. The first of the Vuzgal soldiers will have graduated their scout courses and be coming down here to complete their mage and engineer courses, or staying up there to complete their mortar and medic courses. Every month, we will add another combat company's worth of privates to the military."

Domonos looked out at the people in the barracks. There were all kinds of different courses being taught. Some groups were headed out to the academy for lessons. Others were sparring or listening to their leaders with rapt attention.

"So when will we make a move on the Willful Institute?"

Glosil let out a slow breath and his expression darkened. "There are two thoughts: leave them alone and they'll leave us alone, *or*, we make an example. If we make an example, the current Adventurer's Guild won't be enough. They'll need to be stronger in order to fight them. A long drawn out fight isn't to our benefit either."

Glosil didn't miss Domonos's cold look.

"They have tested us time and time again, we will tear them apart, but we will do it through the Adventurer's Guild, hit them where they're weakest, where they make their money. We'll weaken their powers economically, Elan is gathering constant information on them. We can insert our own people into the Adventurer's Guild and attack them, not drawing attention to us. Though there is a possibility that we will be found out. The best case, they find out that Vuzgal is behind the attacks, worst case, they could learn about Alva."

"What would happen if Alva is found out?" Domonos asked.

"We don't know, the fact we have a complete dungeon under our control, the resources we're able to raise there and items we can craft, it could be a minor issue, or it could lead to a fight we can't win," Glosil said.

"Being unknown is our greatest defense," Domonos said.

"You hit it on the head," Glosil nodded.

The silence stretched and Glosil rested his elbows on his desk, weaving his fingers together to hold his chin.

"I know that you have issue with the Willful Institute. I'll make a promise to you, if you make one to me."

Domonos turned to face Glosil, waiting on his words.

"Promise me that you will be the best commander possible, that you will carry out your orders to the best of your abilities and not let your emotions cloud your judgement and I will let you lead the campaign against the Willful Institute." Glosil held Domonos's eyes.

"I will uphold my position and follow my orders," Domonos said.

"Don't forget it." Glosil added a bit of steel into his voice.

"Yes, Major," Domonos said.

"Good." Glosil nodded and the atmosphere lightened. "You've done well with your people. I look forward to seeing how capable they are later on."

"No, if you just charge right in there, you'll kill them all. You've spent too much time on the Fire floor. You're spewing out flames from everywhere!" Egbert said.

"It looks cool, though!"

"It's wasteful. If you seal them up, then I can let you have some of that ice cream I talked about," Egbert said with a sinister smile.

There was a quick sucking noise and the flames around Davin disappeared in a second.

Egbert looked at him but Davin couldn't read the undead skeleton's expression. His long tongue hung out of his mouth and his too-wide eyes stared up at him.

"Fire imps," Egbert muttered to himself as he took out a small tub of ice cream. Egbert held it out.

"Here you are!" Davin had grabbed it. Using his tongue as a scoop, he pulled out all the ice cream. His jaw opened to take it all in and he closed it around the ice cream.

He closed his eyes in bliss but then he held his head, his eyes alternating between closed and open as he moved around on one foot to the other. "Urggh, my 'ead's 'urtin'!"

"Ah, I think that's what is called a brain freeze."

"'AIN 'EEZE! MY B'AIN WI' 'EEZE?"

"Your brain will not freeze, just be cold." Egbert let out a sigh, watching Davin alternate between loving the ice cream to undergoing a frozen hell that was affecting the interior of his skull.

It took him some time before he stopped. "More?"

Egbert studied the imp in front of him, blinking a few times.

"You okay?" Davin asked after some time.

"You just spent close to an hour with a frozen head and you want more?"

"It tastes really good, though."

"I don't get you flesh bags." Egbert shook his head. "Now, what is your plan to take over the Wood floor?" Egbert asked like a parent asking their kid how they were supposed to act in school. Davin was constantly forgetful. Now he was even stronger Egbert didn't want to repeat some of the mishaps that Davin had when he was younger.

"Well, I tell them that I control the floor or I burn it down," Davin said.

Egbert looked at Davin a bit longer before straightening and tapping his chin with a bony finger. "You know what, it's not your worst plan. They're all beasts…respect strength. Fire beats wood…you're enough beast and sentient to scare them silly. Worth a shot. Though it looks like the main formation is broken," Egbert said.

"Then I take someone with me to repair the formation," Davin said.

"If you use your flames, then you'll burn them too," Egbert said.

"What about someone in those heat things?"

"Those were the gnomes and people don't have those. Erik has a high resistance to heat but he's the lord of the dungeon. Can't put him in danger."

"What about you? You're resistant to fire," Davin said.

"I'm not resistant. You know how long it takes for me to get the burns off my bones." Egbert waved his finger at Davin. Who shrugged nonchalantly.

"I am not going down there with you! I hate repairing formations. It's so boring and dull!"

Davin continued to look at Egbert.

"Nothing you can say could convince me!"

Davin waited another five minutes, yawning.

"I just washed my bones three years ago!"

Davin laid down on the ground and started a nap.

"The stains took a special herbal remedy that was lost with the gnomes."

Rugrat slapped his legs, bringing all their attention on him. "Mana Gathering Cultivation is drawing mana into the body, compressing it and transforming the body to hold more mana! What is Mana Gathering Cultivation?"

"Mana Gathering Cultivation is drawing mana into the body, compressing it and transforming the body to hold more mana!" They started off slowly but pulled it together as they spoke.

"Good! Now, mana gates. So to start cultivating mana, you need to have at least one open mana gate. It is the path of mana to enter your body. If you don't have an open mana gate, then you can increase your mana attribute, but it won't change anything. To open mana gates, you need to blast them apart with mana. Think of them as debris in a dried-up river. You need to flush that river with water, bring it alive and then destroy that debris that has created a dam!

"When you open your mana gates, can you increase the density of the mana in your channels? Hell yes, you can. Why? Well, you have more mana entering your body. If you are filling a bucket, will putting it under one water tap or two water taps fill it faster?" He looked around and pointed at someone.

"The two taps?"

"Hell yeah, the two will be faster. So more mana gates mean it will be easier to increase your Mana Gathering Cultivation. When you compress your core, you can open another mana gate. If you open all of your mana gates, then it changes your mana channels, opening them wider—increases how in tune you are with mana. Gives you a big boost. If you only have one mana gate open but have compressed your core, does that mean you can't open your mana gates?

"You can still open your mana gates, but it's going to be harder than before."

A group of hands went up and Rugrat pointed to them.

"So it is better to open your mana gates before you compress your core?"

"With what we understand right now, yes, it will have the greatest benefit."

"I have reached the Mist stage of mana gathering but my spells aren't more powerful."

"Do you mean that with more power, the effect remains the same?" Rugrat frowned.

"The mana consumption to effect is still the same—shouldn't it cost me less mana?"

"Increasing the effect of a spell, or its power without increasing the mana you're supplying, you need to work on your spell casting. Mana is the fuel for your spells, but spell casting is directing it." Rugrat saw the person sink into thought as he looked at another person.

"I can't find the mana gates in my wrists. Might I only have twelve mana gates?"

"How many are listed in your quest?"

"Fourteen."

"I think you'll probably have fourteen then. I get asked this frequently—where are they?

"Your mana gates should be located in the arches of your feet, in your knee, in the base of your spine, your dantian. Where your back rounds at the top, at the base of your neck, base of your skull where your spine meets it, at the back of your head. Then, in the arms, you have one at your elbow and your wrist. Now, are all of these gates in these exact places?"

Rugrat looked around. "Nope! Go and see a medic. They can help you in locating your gates. They might be in your hands, upper arm, or something like that."

"What about mana gates and Mana Cultivation? Why are there fifteen gates? What about the fourteenth gate being your core?" one student asked.

Rugrat looked around, trying to find the right words. "Okay, so Mana Gathering Cultivation and mana gates are separate things, but they are linked to one another. So, I like to use the analogy of water when talking about mana. Mana gates are like little dams: you open more of the dams, then more water can enter. Mana Gathering Cultivation is the amount of water that you can hold within your body, how much you can compress it. One is the streams of mana through your body, the other the bucket of water you can hold. Okay, this is going to be a bit wordy but if you're interested pay attention!" Rugrat cleared his throat.

"Opening one's fourteenth mana gate and forming your mana core allows one to step onto a whole new stage.

It is also like resetting all of your previous mana cultivation.

People in the ten realms used all kinds of aids and supplies to draw mana into their dantian, many of don't even know it was where they could find their fourteenth mana gate, they just force the mana into that area and compressed it, drawing in more and compressing again and again, forcefully creating their mana core, some are lucky and open up their fourteenth mana gate, others just formed their mana core.

"If creating their mana core had been like filling a bucket of water with a spoon, filling their mana core was like filling a *pond* with a spoon.

"You have to draw mana in from their surroundings, in through your open mana gates to their mana core, it would automatically purify and cleanse the mana leaving only a small portion behind. Now, we know about the vapor, mist and Drop stages, I thought like you that they were their own stages, for mana cultivation, you need to have a mana core to truly start your cultivation. You see we used those stages to open our mana gates and form our mana core. Now to pass the mana core stage you need to compress your gathered mana into Vapor, then Mist and Drop stages again *inside* their mana core filling it up."

"What happens when you fill it up?" A student asked.

"Then your mana core becomes solid and you reach the Mana heart stage," Rugrat said.

"What are the pros and cons of opening our mana gate and taking the Alva route of mana gathering cultivation instead of forming our mana core right away and then opening our mana gates?" Another asked.

"Good question. You learn how to create vapor, mist and drops so it will be faster when you form your core. While you can open your mana gates after creating your mana core, it will be *much* harder than before and your capacity for your mana core will be smaller." Seeing that they were a little confused Rugrat paused.

"Okay, so I took the harder route, my foundation is stronger I opened all fifteen mana gates, going through mana rebirth that altered my body on a fundamental level, my mana channels transformed turning into veins that run throughout my body, they became more refined, able to hold more mana."

He drew in mana from the surrounding area a powerful suction force as power entered his mana gates, tracing through his veins and to his Mana core. The students muttered and talked to one another staring at him with wide eyes.

"My mana veins automatically compress the mana, my mana core is much larger than others, allowing me to store much more power, this will take longer to fill up, but my mana veins allow me to cast mana intensive spells easily, my mana channels would be strained and I couldn't use all my mana in one shot. I can utilize a mana domain, again something others who took the easier route wouldn't be able to do. Though the biggest advantage is that my mana core naturally draws in mana."

There was a collective gasp and some hastily raised hands.

"So if you're sleeping then your cultivation would naturally increase?" A student asked.

"Correct," Rugrat smiled, pointing at the speaker.

An older student raised her hand.

"So the stages are really mana core, Vapor, Mist, Drop, then solid mana core?"

"Yes, your mana gates will be your foundation to build your mana cultivation upon."

"It's a damn movement technique! That means it augments your attacks! Fight and move at the same time!" Erik barked as he walked around the barracks.

"Phillips, I swear, if you throw that fancy punching shit in here again I will put you through a wall!"

The man in question looked around, dumbfounded, as Erik wasn't even looking at him. "How did he?"

"You're pissing mana all over the place with your punch. It's wasteful and more than that, your body can't take that punishment. If your Body Cultivation was higher, it would be fine. Stop sneaking to the medics to get them to heal you up. They will have people who are seriously injured on the battlefield and don't have time to deal with your dumb cocky ass! What are the rest of you doing?"

Erik's voice dropped lower as people were slowing down their movements. They looked at their partners with equal parts apology and also determination as they fought harder, not wanting to draw his ire.

"There are many paths for combat techniques. No one of them is right. The fundamentals here are fluid for a reason. You can fight and listen at the same time, Tian Cui!

"As I was saying, the fundamentals give you a starting point. It opens you up to the field of study. As you grow, you will develop your own fighting style; fighting with one another will refine that fighting art. Reading and studying combat arts will inject new ideas and new inspiration to make up for the weaknesses that you have found. A combat art is not some holy sword that's going to allow you to Rampage Jackson across the realms and give the finger to some all-powerful being! You are the metal; your training, your knowledge, and your experiences will turn you into a weapon! This is why when you are fighting, you better damn well fight!"

Erik shot across the training grounds, one hand behind his back as he attacked Storbon.

Storbon ground his teeth together and fought back, taking hits but staying with it.

"Keep your feet behind you, not in front, to push forward and maintain your balance!" Erik swiped at Storbon's feet. As Storbon took the hit and rolled back to get distance, Erik was on top of him seconds later.

"Good use of the other's attack to gain distance. Training with a spear, you expect that reach—keep your arms closer to your body so you can pull back and defend!" Erik grabbed an outstretched arm, used his momentum and came behind Storbon, aiming a kick at his knee and his free fist for Storbon's kidney.

Storbon dropped, dislocating his shoulder but breaking Erik's grip as he used his strength to escape.

"Good!" Erik said, his eyes shining. "Pain is in your mind. You can use a concoction to recover, or your Body Cultivation," Erik said, lowering his defenses.

"Come here. Let's fix that." Erik popped the shoulder back into place and used a healing spell.

Storbon had his teeth clenched but as the pain flashed through his body, it dissipated with the healing.

"Good work," Erik said.

Storbon smiled, proud.

"The more you sweat and bleed here, the less you will on the battlefield! There are plenty of you trained to be medics. We can do a double course. You have one week and then we are heading to Vuzgal. I want to see you all qualifying in the Battle Arena! Get to work!"

Erik looked over them all as fists and legs flew, everyone getting into it; they fought harder, pushing their limits.

It went on for several hours before he let them rest and ask any questions they might have.

"So, like how do kids work in the higher realms?" An Alvan asked.

Erik stared at the man. *Well I guess we should include more sex-ed into the basic education.*

"So, when a man and a woman really love one another, they get together and have se—"

"I know that part! The leveling part!! Like how you have to be level ten, twenty, thirty etcetera to move up each realm, so everyone in the second realm is at least level ten to twenty and so on. What happens with the kids? I don't see people from the higher realms coming back to the first realm to raise them or are the born at level ten, same with beasts as they ascend as well. Like are people from the second realm that are born there start out at level ten?" The Alvan's face turning red as he coughed slightly.

"Oh that's much easier! I was thinking that our education system was failing for a second!" Erik cleared his throat.

"Everyone is born at level zero. Just in the higher realms the mana density it higher, which can have the effect of opening up more mana gates, or unlocking powerful constitutions. Some people need trauma in order to unlock these constitutions. Once they're born they need aid in order to survive in the harsh environments of the higher realms. What is a prize in the first realm is common in the second realm, you might have heard this before?" Erik saw heads nodding.

"Well people with their younger kids, if they feed them right they'll grow up just fine, stronger than people on the lower realms because they have a greater access to resources. If someone starts off in royalty instead of as a peasant, they'll have a better starting position higher level resources and higher-level beasts and better trainers mean that people in the higher realms gain levels much faster than those in lower levels. If someone leaves say the 5th realm, they must be level 40 to enter it again, There are no work arounds. There is a fear in people born in the higher realms about going to the lower realms, as if doing so will trap them there. They are warned to never go to the lower realms as children. As for leveling up quickly, we've done it here before, you wound a beast, get a lower leveled person to land the last hit, massive experience overload, teach them crafting, more experience, heck you can use monster cores as experience pots to power level your kids."

"What about the beasts?" Another asked

"If they reach a certain level they can be randomly transported to the higher realms by the ten realms. Beasts are nourished and gain levels different from humans, if they eat a stronger beast or powerful ingredients and concoctions or in mana dense areas they will increase in power. That is why most beasts take over places of power and high level resources. As long as their parents are in good health they'll be born pretty powerful, no stronger than their parents and probably a few levels weaker. They will need to consume more to increase their power. The stronger their parents the stronger their starting level."

"How did the class on fighting go?" Rugrat asked Erik as he dropped down into a seat opposite him in the pub.

"Few broken bones, lots of bruises. Trained the healers a bit and didn't need any healing concoctions—call that a win," Erik said.

"Ouch." Rugrat winced as two hot plates appeared.

They thanked and paid the waitress before they ate.

"How was teaching people about mana gates and Mana Gathering Cultivation?"

Rugrat held the fork up as he cleared his throat. "You know when someone asks you a question, you answer them and they're all like 'my mind is blown, dude!'"

"You know that sounds like a seventies stoner, but yes, I do. I *did* have three wives." Erik grinned.

"*Had*—guess it wasn't so mind-altering to stop them figuring out what a bad decision you were?"

"Nicely played," Erik said.

"Thank you." Rugrat smirked. "Though, yeah, I thought everyone knew about the mana gates. Like we wrote down those notes, but there's a big difference between notes, than seeing and talking to someone who has done it before. They took the positioning of the gates as being the same every time. They were trying to open up all of their mana gates and not increase their Mana Gathering Cultivation. That was a pitfall that we fell into but then we found out that you can do both; the two are related systems but increasing the one doesn't mean you close off the other. It was interesting to see."

Erik grunted as he kept eating. Rugrat joined in.

"Damn, that was good." Erik finished his meal and took a deep pull from his drink. "It was a good idea, teaching them how to make shine."

"Well, hard to go blind with it, and higher proof. Still need to get some newer drinks down here to get us drunk, though. Damn Body Cultivation keeping us all healthy," Rugrat complained before his expression changed. "Do you want to fight?"

"Huh?" Erik coughed on his drink.

"We've fought groups, but we haven't fought others one-on-one. You saw in those arenas in the Fifth. People fight one-on-one up there. If we want to win competitions, we'll need to do the same." Rugrat felt excited just thinking about the tournaments in the Fifth Realm. "We have rifles and weapons and tools, but fighting techniques—didn't you want to fight with your fists?"

"Yes, but—" Erik closed his mouth as he frowned and looked away.

A cold smile appeared on his face. "Don't tell me you don't want to fight."

Erik sighed and shook his head as he leaned on the table. The two of them looked at each other, the darkness, the dangerous part that lurked within seen in each other's eyes.

They could've stopped fighting after they left the military. Instead, they became private contractors. It was their skill, it was how they felt alive. When they were out there, it was scary as all hell, but they were *alive*. It was a drug, a straight hit to the vein of dopamine and adrenaline.

The danger honed them. It strengthened them. Seeing those competitions had ignited Rugrat's fighting spirit, his desire to be stronger, to triumph.

"All right, all right. Sure, I want to fight, but I know you want to increase your crafting as well," Erik said.

"We can do both—fight each other, grow stronger, train in our skills. When we can't advance anymore, what if we head to the higher realms, join those competitions?"

"What about Alva, and Vuzgal, about Vermire?" Erik asked.

"We helped them, but they got themselves to this point. Shouldn't we take a step back, let them prove to themselves what they can do? Didn't Delilah tell you to go to the higher realms, that they'll stand on their own feet? It's not like we'll be done training in just a few days. When we return, Vermire should be stronger than ever, Vuzgal will be stable, Alva will have digested the loot we got from Vuzgal and the people should have reached a new level of crafting."

Erik was silent for some time, working it over in his head. "Okay, okay, let's see what they can do."

43
A Different Auction

"How are the guests settling in?" Aditya asked his head of staff Armand as they walked through the castle.

"There have been no major issues so far," Armand muttered, looking tired and downtrodden, as much as he tried to hide it.

"The auction?"

"Everything is ready for tonight. The guards are checking on all of the people who have bought a ticket to go. No one will be allowed to buy the ticket on the night, to improve security." Armand glanced to Pan Kun, who cleared his throat.

"They've all been vetted by our doves," Pan Kun said.

Aditya nodded slightly.

Those in the castle and in Vermire, other than the military, still believed that Aditya was their ruler, not knowing about the secret hand behind him.

The doves were all unknowingly under the control of that hand.

In a few years, their information network had expanded rapidly, covering kingdoms and empires, small outposts and large cities. Just the funds needed to support a network that large is a heavy cost.

A messenger ran up to them, stopping and bowing as they caught their breath.

"Speak," Aditya said.

"Lady Sumi of the Twilight Outpost has appeared. She is camping out in the fields in war tents. Their gear looks like it was in storage rings. She brought a full fifty Twilight guards with her," the young boy said rapidly between breaths.

"Always the dramatic," Aditya sneered.

"My lord?" Pan Kun asked.

"Keep an eye on her. Do you think that fifty of her Twilight guards are enough to take on five of our Vermire guards?" Aditya looked at Pan Kun with a raised eyebrow.

"Not in a hundred years," Pan Kun said with genuine confidence.

"Make sure the guys and gals don't overreact," Aditya said.

"Yes, my lord." Pan Kun bowed and left, tapping the boy's arm and taking him away.

"She is obviously coming with bad intentions. She might not have known who you were in the past but there is no hiding it now," Armand said in a low voice, making sure that no one else could hear.

"Oh, but things have changed a lot in the last couple of years, have they not?" Aditya's voice dropped and there was a hidden darkness in his eyes.

Armand looked at him, his eyes tightening before relaxing. "I'm not able to see through your plans from beside you—how can they?"

Aditya reached out and patted Armand on the shoulder, taking care not to hit too hard and send him sprawling.

"With time, Armand, with time." Aditya had a soft look in his eyes. Armand had been one of the first people to help out a lost Aditya. It was with him and with his band of misfits that they had been able to build Vermire.

"How are preparations going for the feast?"

"Well, the food has been delivered and the layout has been altered in such a way that it will allow for hidden discussions. Those formations that were brought over to close off sound and to test people's truth have been laid down. This is the only copy of the new floor plan. No other person has more than a tenth of this plan." Armand passed Aditya a map.

He glanced at it and tucked it away into his storage ring.

"The stage is set. Now we just have to see who is willing to play the game," Aditya muttered to himself.

Lord Emmanuel Fayad stepped down from his carriage and looked at the Vermire auction house. He had seen many Blue Lotus auction houses in the First and Second Realm when he was younger.

The auction house was clean, presentable—even a bit opulent in such a place as an outpost on the border of the Beast Mountain Range.

He stepped down. Nasreen walked up beside him with three other guards; the remainder left with the carriage.

"Lord Emmanuel Fayad of the Fayad family and Shadowridge Outpost!" an announcer said as he stepped into the auction house.

Emmanuel smiled lightly as he looked at the other lords in the room. They had all gathered over the last couple of days, sending messages to one another, but only a few of them had interacted face-to-face.

Emmanuel saw some familiar faces and went over to greet them.

"Lord Emmanuel, may the sun shine down upon you and lengthen your shadows to reach new lands," Isobel Kilroy said in greeting.

"May your fires always be warm and the drink never stop flowing," Emmanuel said.

The two lords grinned to each other and shook hands.

"The two eccentrics have met now," Leo Adler said to Fang Ju, rounding out the rest of the group.

"It has been some time since we last saw one another," Emmanuel said.

"With plenty of trade and gold to make us rounder," Fang Ju said with a smile breaking through as the wrinkles at the corners of his eyes became more pronounced.

"A man needs to eat to train!" Leo patted his stomach.

"And a lady needs to drink to merry times," Isobel added, her eyes cutting to Leo with a smirk. "Isn't that right?"

Leo coughed and blushed slightly but there was a smile hidden in there somewhere as he looked down to Isobel. She might be shorter but she wasn't to be underestimated.

"All of you have looked at the items that are up for auction then?" Emmanuel said as the group walked over to a more secluded spot away from the other lords and their guards who were meeting and talking to one another or heading right into the auction hall.

The four lords' guards fanned out, blocking anyone from approaching.

"Low Journeyman-level weapons and high Apprentice-level formation plates. Seems like they're goods set out to make the different lords fight one another for them," Fang Ju said, the group turning serious.

"If they're willing to sell these items, what are they holding in reserve?" Leo asked.

"Are they pulling them out just to show their strength? They said that they wanted to have an auction unprecedented in the Beast Mountain Range. The goods are too valuable for us to miss, but there is something else going on here," Isobel said.

"Have you studied their guards?" Leo asked lightly.

The others' eyes shone.

"Don't take bribes. They were a bunch of broken but loyal dogs before. Now they're all healed up. That Alva Healing House is no small power." Isobel's jealousy wasn't hard for them to miss.

I wish I could bring them over to my side as well.

Emmanuel cleared his throat. "They are organized. They moved in groups. Did any of you notice how they reacted when Lady Sumi showed up with her war tents and a sixth of her military strength?"

The others all sunk into thought.

"They're confident against the Twilight guards, who are some of the strongest in the Beast Mountain Range. Their weapons and armor are a higher grade. It is conjecture, but I think that they must work well together. They weren't 'directly involved' but who were those mysterious people who infiltrated the Zatan Confederation and weakened it from the inside?" Emmanuel left his questions hanging in the air.

"Did you know that the Silaz boy, Wren, set up a new headquarters for his trading family?" Isobel said.

"The Silaz family who deals in the trade of monster cores? Who lived in Chonglu?" Leo confirmed.

"Yeah. They moved their base of operations here. I didn't know it, but they're selling mana stones here. Mortal grade mana stones. For gold." Isobel's voice was quiet and her eyes piercing as the others shook from her revelation.

"No wonder there are so many high-quality items for sale in Vermire. Most of the kingdoms and empires that I know hoard their mana stones to use them for their formations to defend their homes or to increase their Mana Gathering Cultivation when they hit a bottleneck. Still, they treat them with more care than they do their own children," Fang Ju said.

"Where are they getting these mana stones from?" Emmanuel asked.

"Well, his brothers, sister, and father seem to have disappeared. I'm guessing, and these are just my thoughts, but what if they went up?" Isobel said. She was rambunctious and impulsive on the outside, but she was sharp-witted and observant. All of them put a certain weight to her words.

"Why come to Vermire? There are nations that would be willing to name them as the official chamber of commerce," Emmanuel thought aloud.

"Then they are bound to that nation. Why didn't we become vassals for the nations, empires, and kingdoms that came knocking on our gates?" Leo smirked.

"As you said, Vermire is no longer some simple backwater. With the Zatan Confederation issue, they were able to display their strength, gain the attention of other groups that were affected by the issue. Vermire's hunting population and mercenary numbers have only increased, but the real new gold that's being injected into the city is their ability to become a neutral trading ground. Groups that should be fighting can trade in the darkness of a bar. Vermire's greatest trade is not the beasts and the items that come out from the Beast Mountain Range." Fang Ju captured their eyes and the corner of his mouth lifted up. "Have you looked at their smithing sector or the warehouse district?"

"It expanded when they increased the size of Vermire," Leo said.

"The smithies here never stop making simple weapons: spears, bows, helmets, and armors. Those goods aren't heading into the Beast Mountain Range but being sold to nations in massive amounts. Their warehouse district is nearly filled with food storage facilities. Have you seen the number of cats around?"

Emmanuel bowed his head slightly at Fang Ju's observations.

"Weapons and food, sure, things that people in Vermire might need, but not in those quantities." Isobel shook her head.

There was some noise from the front of the auction house as a woman walked into the venue with just two guards behind her.

"Sumi," Isobel said, her hands making her fingerless leather gloves creak.

"Lord of the Twilight Outpost," Fang Ju said, sounding intrigued.

Lady Sumi gave off an easy air. With her clothes matching the armor of her Twilight guards, she cut an imposing figure.

Her eyes moved over lazily to look at the four lords conversing in the corner. A smile spread across her face. It was anything but warm as she tilted her head to the side and gave them a small wave. She seemed to chuckle to herself and then turned to the lords who came up to greet her.

"Inviting the Twilight lord into his city—wasn't Lord Aditya humiliated by her?" Leo asked.

"He was, but look where he has come. He's no simple character," Emmanuel said, not thinking of his words but the others all agreed.

"We should head to our seats," Leo said as Lady Sumi was guided into the auction house by a group of other lords. There were those who didn't wish to annoy her, others who wanted to bring her to their side or wanted to have her. The games and power plays never stopped around the Beast Mountain Range.

There was another commotion as a man arrived unannounced. He walked through the hall with just a single guard.

"Is that Aditya?" Isobel hissed.

All three of the lords hid their frowns.

"Why do I feel like a tiger just walked into his lair?" Leo said darkly.

"That must be Pan Kun, his head guard and leader of the Vermire Guard. I heard that he was badly disfigured. He's fully healed, and the equipment they're wearing is high Apprentice grade."

Aditya seemed to sense their gazes. He gave them a friendly smile and nodded to them, not breaking his stride as he greeted those who walked up to him.

"This auction might be the least interesting thing going on," Isobel said with a laugh. "Good luck on the battlefield!" Isobel headed off into the auction hall.

The others nodded to one another and moved with their group of guards.

"Still think that Lord Aditya is simple?" Emmanuel asked Nasreen, who was beside him, without moving his mouth.

"What do you mean?" Nasreen asked.

His strength is concealed from others; it must be something that only us at higher levels can sense.

"We'll need to work on your senses again."

There were different booths around the auction hall. The lords of the outposts were in the third and highest ring. On the second level, there was the different powerful merchants, nobles, and people from other kingdoms and nations who had come to buy. There were less powerful people on the first floor who had come more for the entertainment than to bid. With powers such as these looking to bid, they only had a small chance to pick up anything worthwhile.

Emmanuel walked into his booth, finding several lords and Lord Aditya.

The atmosphere was light and enjoyable as people chatted freely.

Emmanuel smiled to a number of the lords and traded greetings. Most of them had done trade in the past and had a good impression of one another.

Lord Aditya wasn't imposing, standing at the rear of the booth as he drank from a glass, having an easy conversation with the different lords.

With their guards outside, the lords were free and the booth wasn't crowded.

A few minutes later, a young man walked out onto the auction house stage.

"Lords and ladies, valued guests, the auction is about to begin. My name is Xue Zan. Today, I have the pleasure of presenting this auction."

People settled into their seats, continuing their conversations in low tones.

"The first item up for auction tonight is a blueprint!" A woman brought out a box and placed it on a presentation pedestal next to the auctioneer.

The people in the auction hall seemed interested but only marginally so. Blueprints required crafters to work on them and crafters were expensive. Only a few of the lords were interested; they had the capital to not only get crafters but the necessary materials together to make blueprints worth their time.

"This is a carriage design. It requires a Novice blacksmith and woodworker to create it. It requires normal wood types and metals, but with its spring designs and new wheel designs, it can take on heavier loads across rougher terrain at higher speeds. Easily twenty percent faster than a normal trading carriage." The auctioneer spoke in an excited voice as information appeared on a stone table to the side of the auctioneer, detailing the blueprint's capabilities.

"There is no build restriction, so it can be made repeatedly," Aditya said out loud to the other lords. "For those lords who are in swamp lands or bog lands, its larger wheels allow riders to get through obstacles easily and the weight distribution makes it harder to sink on one corner. Perfect for long trade routes, or moving valuables. I do hate when carriages break their wheels because the suspension is too tight."

The other lords' eyes glowed and Aditya sipped from his drink. Clearly it was their good fortune to be close to him as he accidentally let slip information deeper than what was on the board.

"Though, if someone has pests around them, there are a number of useful items later, though their gains will be less in the long run." Aditya's eyes moved imperceptibly to Lord Caius Sidonius from Sea Breeze. To his east was Dryfall's Outpost, owned by Raphail Levas. For years, Raphail had been using the mercenaries within his walls to attack Sea Breeze. They had greater profits and being along a river and a small valley, they were able to cultivate a number of powerful medicinal herbs that attracted more beasts. With more beasts and more herbs came more money. While focusing on their front, their rear was being attacked to the point that traders were only willing to go to the outpost if Caius sent guards with them.

It stopped them for some time, but now even the guarded traders were being attacked by bolder and larger groups of mercenaries.

"The starting bid is ten silver, with a minimum of one silver each bid," Xue Zan said, drawing attention back to the stage. "Who is willing to open the bid?"

"Ten silver." One of the trader leaders on the second floor spoke up. Clearly they saw the use of the cart already.

"Twelve!" an outpost lord called out.

"Fourteen," a man from one of the kingdoms said.

Bidding heated up as the price increased drastically, clearing out those who had the spare funds and those who didn't.

"Eighty-seven silver."

"Eighty-eight!"

"Ninety!" a merchant called out.

The lords looked at one another.

We can take out fifteen gold freely without issue; more than fifty gold and we will need to shorten expenses within our own cities. Most leading traders only have twenty or thirty gold on hand.

The merchant took the carriage blueprint, with the praise of those around him.

"Congratulations on winning the first item of the auction!" Xue Zan hit his hammer on the table. The blueprint was removed and a new box was brought to the front and opened. There were three bottles inside of relatively clear glass.

"Three bottles of Rapid Clotting Powder, a true mid-Apprentice-level healing concoction that can heal and seal flesh wounds before your eyes, or can be mixed with water to heal internal wounds." Xue Zan's words fell on the ears of all those present.

Fayad looked at the concoctions, his hands tightening in agitation. *These bottles are a second life to many!*

"It's sad that the glass is of low quality and their efficacy will decrease with time unless one has a better way to store them or uses them rapidly,". Aditya said.

His words were quiet and didn't leave the booth, but the lords there all understood what he meant.

"The bidding will start at fifty silver, with no less than ten silver per bid," Xue Zan said.

"One and a half gold." A woman's voice covered the room with an invisible pressure that came with excessive funds. Everyone looked over to the lord of Twilight Outpost, Lady Sumi. Her blood-red lips pulled apart into a flattering smile filled with challenge as her eyes searched them for an opponent.

"Two gold," another lord called out.

They are bidding with gold instead of silver. For something that could save one's life, is there really a price one can place on it?

The room chilled some as her smile became more rigid.

"Three gold," Lady Sumi said, as if tasting the words.

The lord competing with her stared at her before he pursed his lips and sat back in his chair, pulling out a fan and fanning himself in irritation.

"The healing concoction goes to Lady Sumi." Xue Zan bowed to her.

"Ah, I do like it when the defeated know their place. Some people just keep on trying to appear after they've lost. The most annoying are those without familial ties." Lady Sumi's eyes fell on Lord Aditya, a mocking smile on her lips. "Don't you think, Lord Phillip Aditya?"

Aditya smiled simply and swirled his glass. "Ah, but a good challenge can make them rise stronger than ever. Isn't that the truth of cultivation, no? Seems some have a talent for it and others…remain the same?" His words hung in the air as Emmanuel and the other lords got his meaning.

Is he saying his cultivation has increased but hers hasn't? Only someone with a good eye of discernment or who is a higher level than the other person can see through them.

Lady Sumi's eyes narrowed slightly as Aditya drank from his glass and she looked away.

"Next we have a set of armor. It is called the Kuoni set. Apart, each piece increases one's Stamina Regeneration slightly. Together, one's Stamina Regeneration has a much higher speed and one's overall Agility increases as well. It has been evaluated as a half-step Journeyman set of armor."

The set of armor was revealed to everyone. It was a thin set of armor, covering a person's vital areas. Blades could be seen on the arms and legs that could double as weapons.

"Bidding will start at twenty silver, with a five silver increase each bid," Xue Zan said.

The room fell into heated bidding. A set of armor could directly increase one's ability, or the ability of their people.

The set of armor went to one of the minor nobles on the second floor.

Next was not only a set, but multiple sets of armor: ten sets of identical armor with two innate effects when assembled as a set. The first group went for eight gold, then there were two more sets, going for nine gold and eleven gold.

Beast mounts were brought out, in singles and in packs.

Then there were formations to create barriers. They went for sky-high prices, reaching twenty or thirty gold. This was something that the kingdom leaders of the second floor could afford based on their backing and only a few of the outpost lords could.

To finish it off, there were three Mortal mana stones up for sale. For those who had just bought the formations, these were invaluable treasures. There was a high demand for these mana stones but there was no supply. Some of the older outpost lords who had only been interested in concoctions now started to bid.

Each sold for no less than two thousand gold. Although they might cost fifteen hundred gold from the Silaz family, one needs a connection to be able to speak to them within the city. They only have five of them up for sale, one every weekday, and they have already sold the next four months' worth of mana stones.

"With that, I must thank you for attending our humble Vermire auction house." Xue Zan bowed deeply to the patrons and the lighting in the room increased in brightness.

The auction house broke out into excited chatter.

It is more humble than the Blue Lotus, but all of these items were aimed not at the people of the area, but those who are coming in from the other outposts, nations, and kingdoms. Those who missed the auction will quickly regret it.

Emmanuel had been able to get a few sets of armor and weapons. They all had innate effects that would work well with his fighters to increase their overall strength. With it, he could clear more of the Beast Mountain Range.

I wonder if there are more crafting tools that Aditya will be willing to sell. I should ask Fang Ju about what he saw in the crafting sector. With high-level crafters, one can truly prosper in the future.

Emmanuel's mind started to turn as the other lords congratulated and talked to Aditya, looking to become closer to him.

Emmanuel saw it and he glanced over to Lady Sumi. There was a sneer on her face, like a blemish. She turned around and stormed out of the auction booth.

She'll still have to head downstairs to collect her items. Makes one's anger seem weaker if they're just throwing a fit this way.

Emmanuel looked to Aditya, seeing a cold edge to his eyes as he looked away from Sumi's booth.

"As a thank-you for coming all this way, I'll be hosting a grand feast tonight. Please remember to attend. We are all traders here—of course everything has a price. Though, as friends, we should be able to drink and eat together freely." Aditya smiled.

The others laughed and agreed. Aditya handled a few talks with different people, making himself seem approachable.

This new lord has the makings of one who will do great things.

"My lord." Miss Evernight bowed as she opened the door to the carriage.

Aditya stepped up and into the carriage. She followed him up and Pan Kun sat up front. She closed the door behind him and activated the formation that would stop noise from being let out.

Aditya deflated in his seat. "Damn. All these negotiations, positioning and things is annoying. The items really did light a fire underneath the outpost leaders' asses, though. Should hopefully pull a few more of them to our side," Aditya said.

"Now we need you to work on the older lords, the pillars around the Beast Mountain Range. If we can get a few of them to our side, then we could bring in other middle lords and the newer ones," Evernight said.

"Who are we targeting?" Aditya leaned forward, alert.

Evernight smiled slightly and pulled out a list. "Lords Valk, Laas, Quan, and Hu." She looked up. "Do you need a refresher?"

"No, it's all in here." Aditya tapped his head and leaned back. "Quan will be harder. He has built up a mercenary company that works outside of the Beast Mountain Range. If we draw him in, then it might stop his contracts outside that give him a large revenue. He won't like that."

"He might not, but remind him about how people going through the Beast Mountain Range will need protection from the beasts."

"Yes, and we have a supply of Gire sorrel. He has pain in his joints. With its help, his joints should feel better and he can venture out to increase his level, hunting beasts in the depths of the Beast Mountain Range," Aditya murmured to himself.

Evernight smiled to herself. *He's grown a lot in just a few years. His strength lies in planning and maneuvering. His greed was an issue, but when he can see a higher goal, it focuses his mind.*

"Seems that this dinner will be an interesting one," Evernight said.

"You want to go in my place?" Aditya asked in an almost pleading tone.

"I'll leave that all to you." Evernight put the list away into her storage ring.

Emmanuel shared what he had seen in the booth with Aditya with Leo, Fang Ju, and Isobel. They had each been surprised by the items up for sale.

"Why do I feel like I'm balancing on a knife edge?" Isobel complained as they met up in the large open banquet hall inside Aditya's residence. Many of the lords had come exactly on time and found Aditya as soon as possible, heading off to some of the private rooms to discuss trades and future agreements.

"Well, on one side, we got powerful items to increase our strength. On the other hand, our rivals did as well," Leo said as he picked at some food on his plate.

"Just enjoy the wine," Fang Ju said.

Emmanuel saw Lord Quan and some of the other fighting-oriented lords coming out of a room with Lord Aditya. He laughed with Lord Quan, the two of them appearing to have a close relationship.

"What did I inhale, or is Old Lord Quan playing nice with someone? Ow!" Leo turned to Isobel.

"Just wanted to make sure you weren't seeing things."

"How can a pinch hurt that much?" Leo complained.

Isobel raised her fingers and pinched them together. "Years of training."

After some time, a waiter came over with food and drink. As they were passing them drinks, he passed them a piece of paper.

"Have a good night." The waiter disappeared into the crowd.

Emmanuel looked at his glass, reading the note. "Looks like Lord Aditya wishes to see us."

"We should go and talk to others," Fang Ju said.

Emmanuel nodded. The group slowly started to unravel as they saw different lords and did their rounds.

Emmanuel saw a waiter grabbing more drinks from a side room. He caught Emmanuel's eyes and indicated a door. Emmanuel would have missed it if not pointed out. It was just beyond the bathroom in what looked like an enclave.

He checked his surroundings and walked into the room. He found a number of lords inside the room.

Lord Aditya a circle of them around him.

"So what do you envision in the future?" Lord Caius Sidonius asked after a few more people had filed into the room. His question seemed flippant but Emmanuel could feel the eyes and ears in the room turn to Aditya, who chuckled.

"That is a good question." Aditya took a drink while looking thoughtful.

"I think in the future, to have a shared auction right between all of our outposts would even draw kings and emperors. I'm sure that my few trinkets are nothing compared to your own goods!" Aditya laughed. "It would be the king of auctions."

The other lords covered their shock with a laugh. Some seemed to have already received a few hints and didn't seem overly shocked.

Emmanuel wasn't stunned, just impressed. *This was only used as a cover for the outpost leaders to meet, to talk about Lord Aditya's plans to unite the outposts and create this King Outpost. Clearly his goals don't end there. This could lead to a much bigger stage. What is an outpost compared to an empire that controls Beast Mountain Range?*

Emmanuel's eyes flicked to the other lords. They were all evaluating one another.

"It would need to be a joint effort between us all, and should be split up in that way. There is too much bog land around Vermire, so maybe another outpost could lead the way, with our support." Aditya looked at Emmanuel as the others in the room seemed to be assessing the deeper ramifications of Aditya's words and separating thinly veiled truths from flowery words.

"It is not something that we need to decide on now," Aditya said.

"Would it be a Vermire Central Auction house?" Lord Quan asked.

"Vermire would only be another supporter, an equal partner," Aditya said. "It is better to have more friends."

Lord Ryan Mills thought on what he had heard from Lord Aditya. He was one of the newer outpost lords. With his limited funds, he had not been able to participate in the auction even as the items had attracted his vision.

He was jealous of Aditya. They had started their outposts at the same time. Now Lord Aditya talked to Old Lord Quan as if they were peers and the other lords listened to his words and placed weight with them.

Mills walked through his quarters, his mind working. Clearly there were plenty of riches in Vermire. Mills wanted them badly, but getting them would be difficult.

I will need outside help.

He thought of Lady Sumi. Her beautiful face had captured him and seeing her vocal attack on Lord Aditya, it was clear they were fire and water—they could not be mixed.

When we leave, I'll have a message sent to her. There have to be others who would be against a merger. Even if I only get a few leftovers, if it works out then we would become the new overlords of Beast Mountain Range.

44 Showdown

Gilly and George were at their full lengths, lazing around the outside of the sparring arena.

Inside it, Erik and Rugrat checked their gear.

Outside, there were people from the military and from the special teams watching them.

Erik stretched and got warmed up.

Rugrat checked his rifle, putting it together. He checked the magazine and loaded it.

"You sure these things will work?" Erik tapped the formation that was strapped to his back.

"I shot them a couple of times with rounds. Just adjusted them to our own defenses. Also, how did you become such a tank? Do you know how much I had to crank up your mana barrier to match your normal defense?" Rugrat complained.

Erik just shrugged. "You ready yet?"

"Sure." Rugrat stood and cocked his new semi-auto rifle.

Erik and Rugrat moved to opposite corners and Rugrat pulled out a coin. "When it hits the ground?"

"Works," Erik said.

Rugrat threw the coin up and changed his stance.

Erik looked at Rugrat, feeling the mana coursing through his body. He felt alive. It had been too long since he had fought.

The coin hit the ground. Erik raced forward. He shot mana bullets out of his hand and the world turned to liquid.

Rugrat fired his rifle, tracing out Erik's line of advance. He opened his left hand underneath the rifle, firing out two large mana blasts to either side of Erik that would force him forward. He launched his grenade round right between them.

Erik shot at the rounds and sped up. Each footstep broke the tiles beneath his feet. He fired out mana blasts, hitting those ahead of him, causing them to explode as he dove. He covered his head with his left arm that plowed through the floor, sending up tiles.

He felt the rush of air overhead and he threw his left arm down. His strength was such the force tossed him to the side. He got his feet underneath him and started to run.

Rugrat had already reloaded his rifle and was firing again.

Erik dodged between rounds as Rugrat used a movement technique, shooting across the square and changed formation sockets on his rifle on the fly.

As he ran, he dropped mana bolts on the ground but they didn't explode.

Erik fired at them, distracting and hurrying Rugrat.

Rugrat fired at Erik as he got within a few feet. Erik turned his body; his chest, shoulder, and arm were hit as Rugrat formed a blade of mana. It was as substantial as if made from mana stone. Erik grabbed Rugrat's armor.

The two of them stopped, rounds hitting behind Erik.

Rugrat was poised to slash or stab through Erik. Although Erik's arm shook, there was so much mana contained within to set off a mana detonation.

The two of them retracted their power.

"I thought that you were focusing on that finger thing?" Rugrat asked.

"Need more control for that. Don't have it yet. Mana bolt mines—that's pretty shitty to deal with," Erik said.

"Yeah, your speed is higher than I thought. Are you using a spell to enhance your speed?"

"Nope, just higher strength. Gives explosive speed when changing directions." Erik tapped his chest armor.

"Ugh, you need to stop getting the cool toys." Rugrat sighed.

"Again?" Erik asked.

"Sure. Want to do rifles, then mana techniques, then physical fighting, fighting on beasts, then everything together?" Rugrat asked.

"These things can handle it?" Erik tapped the formation plate on his back.

"Better than the fighting stage." Rugrat looked over Erik's shoulder at what was left of the stage.

"We'll just need to use stronger materials when rebuilding it." Erik turned to Rugrat.

They grinned at each other and laughed.

"Charge up with a Mortal mana stone—should be good for a few more bouts," Rugrat said.

Erik and Rugrat had the same rifles as they faced off against each other. They lined up, looking at each other. Erik threw the coin this time.

It hit the ground and Erik shot to the side. He shot his rifle one-handed, easily able to take the recoil. He fired out mana bolts with his left hand. Rounds struck his barrier as his hits struck Rugrat. Erik trapped Rugrat, who was just firing his rifle as a klaxon went off, declaring Rugrat as dead.

Erik stopped attacking.

"Your defense is too damn high," Rugrat complained.

"You put a lot of points into Agility, but not as many as me. With the extra strength, I could one-arm fire a fifty cal right now."

"These hit harder than fifty cals back on Earth." Rugrat held up his rifle.

"Mana technique time," Erik said.

They took corners and Rugrat tossed.

Mana bolts and bullets were slower than the rifle rounds. Rugrat's mana bullets were slower, but they were much more powerful and he increased their power by adding Explosive Shot and other spells layered on top.

Erik used his mana bullets and shots before using Mana Detonation. He let out a yell as he threw his fists. Mana shot out of his hands like shotguns, clearing the area in front of him as he rushed forward.

Rugrat went all-out, dodging and moving to get distance as he fired out mana bullets. He dropped mana bolts with his feet, making Erik have to travel around to get Rugrat. His mana pool was larger than it had been but it was nothing like the sea-like mana pool Rugrat controlled.

Erik's mana started to decline until he was swamped and the klaxon went off.

"I think that using the Mana Detonation was smarter than using the mana bullets and mana bolts," Rugrat said.

Erik looked up at him, about to fire a crude remark back before he saw that Rugrat was serious.

"You were using less power than mana bolts and bullets. It allowed you to advance. You're stronger when you're in close. Now, this simulation fight is good but in a fight you'll have healing concoctions and can heal, suck up the damage, get in there and land a hit."

"Yeah, I need to learn more close-quarters fighting techniques. I have a rifle—when will I need it?" Erik then realized what he had said and how dumb it sounded. "I should learn some more fighting techniques."

"You and me both. In close, I've got my mana bullets and bolts. If I use them, then the splash damage could kill or injure me."

"You're not that squishy yet," Erik said.

"In the higher realms, I might be. As you said, I have increased my mana, not my body. If I can increase my Body Cultivation, then my faster reactions will be a huge help," Rugrat said.

"Physical?" Erik asked.

"Sure," Rugrat said.

Erik tossed the coin this time.

They charged at each other. As Erik got closer, Rugrat grinned as mana formed around him, looking just like his mana blade.

Erik was already extending his body to attack and had to stomp his foot, breaking up his attack as Rugrat jumped forward. His fists were covered in mana blade spikes.

Erik dodged Rugrat's attacks, trying to get in a rhythm. The other's attacks were sure to damage him heavily if they connected.

Sneaky damn redneck!

Erik dropped back and sized up Rugrat, who was coming for him. Erik dodged to the side and threw a spin-kick. He focused his power into his foot as he did with the One Finger Beats Fist technique.

It struck and hit Rugrat. Erik took damage from hitting the mana blade but it wasn't as much damage as what he dealt on Rugrat.

Rugrat let the mana covering disappear. "Damn, it is hard to keep that up," Rugrat said, sweating.

"It's smart—though, on a battlefield, you'll become a massive target."

"You hit like a damn mule," Rugrat said.

"Another?" Erik asked.

They got onto George and Gilly and looked around.

"We'll have to expand the stage next time," Rugrat said.

"Or just go to the Battle Arena." Erik patted Gilly's neck and looked around the sparring area. They only had about twenty meters of distance between the two. On their mounts, it was a little cramped when thinking of how fast they could move.

"Now that would be pretty fun." Rugrat laughed. He leaned forward with his rifle across his legs as he absently scratched George's neck too.

"Shall we?" Erik asked.

"Fine. Whose toss is it anyway?"

"Yours, I think." Erik threw the coin over.

Rugrat caught it and tossed it into the air.

Erik got lower, his body ready, and Gilly leaned forward, her eyes locked on George, whose wings shot out to either side, ready as well.

Rugrat wrapped the sling of his rifle around his left forearm.

The coin touched the ground.

George's wings beat down against the ground, causing dust to rush out from the broken floor.

Erik threw out Mana Detonation punches as Rugrat's rounds shot forward.

Gilly let out a water jet in George's path, causing him to drop down as he breathed fire back. Gilly smacked the ground with her tail, creating a wall to take the rounds Rugrat was firing and stop George's breath. Erik jumped off her back and ran along the left side, hidden from Rugrat's view a half second later. Gilly ran forward, throwing up a plume of dust; the wall parted for her and she let out a blast of water.

George was already rising higher, his wings beating as he took the pause to gain altitude.

Erik was struck by a round and Rugrat smiled. *He saw through me? Gilly, I need steps.* Using his bond to Gilly, Erik jumped to the side and up into the air as she smacked the ground, sending rocks flying, blocking Rugrat's sight and George's breath. She smacked a rock with her tail, sending shrapnel at the duo in the sky.

Erik saw it all as he jumped up the rocks that shot up into the sky, using them as stepping-stones. The power he exerted on them sent them crashing into the ground as if meteors.

Keep them penned in.

Rugrat jumped off George and onto the rocks. George dropped and shot a blast of flame through the rocks, clearing a hole in them. The two had worked together perfectly. Rugrat fired through the opening, hitting Erik straight on.

He sent out mana bullets and bolts as fast as possible, panicking. *Come on, girl!*

Erik grinned as Gilly jumped up and bit at George; he clawed at her as the rocks around her turned into spears and shot at George.

George's klaxon went off and he reverted to his small form. Rugrat changed his point of aim to Gilly as he dropped to the ground with the falling rocks.

Erik used Mana Detonation on his feet, charging forward as Gilly shot a blast of water at Rugrat. He dodged it as she came back down to the ground and fired repeatedly. Erik hit the ground, rolling and sliding, with his legs pumping underneath him. Gilly hit the ground and created a quick wall, but Rugrat destroyed it and hit her barrier a few more times. Her klaxon went off. Erik grabbed the repeater on his back and fired at Rugrat, pinning him into the corner of the arena. He circled around, so Rugrat had a hard time pinning him down as his barrier was destroyed and the klaxon went off.

Erik stopped firing. Rugrat didn't hear it and shot Erik, and Erik's klaxon went off.

Rugrat grinned and then looked at the klaxons. "Dammit!" His grin turned into a frustrated noise before he walked toward Erik. "If we had more room, we'd show you a real fight."

"Good work," Erik said. The two of them bumped fists.

Gilly looked up at the ceiling with a proud expression as George prowled and growled, returning to his full size. The two of them started to squabble.

"You know, I hear that animals are much like their owners," Erik said, seeing the two beasts.

"Well, I know that George and I would love to have your help in increasing our cultivation and bloodline," Rugrat said.

The two headed off the stage as people who had come to watch talked with one another.

"I'm not the only alchemist out there, there are plenty of Alvans that have made pills that could help out you and George," Erik said.

"Huh, I keep on forgetting that. Also, what are we going to do about the stage?" Rugrat asked pitching his voice lower.

"Well, Matt helped to design the Battle Arena. Maybe he can do something here? Seems that we need some better materials," Erik said in an equally quiet voice as they picked up their pace keeping their heads together, so it looked like they had something important to talk about.

With a whistle and snap to Gilly and George, both returned to their smaller sizes and rested on their shoulders.

"We need to get clipboards, less people would ask what we're doing," Rugrat muttered.

"Works all the time," Erik agreed.

After escaping—uh, fleeing…hmm, leaving—the barracks in a much worse state than when they had first arrived, they headed to the manor to get cleaned up.

"I'm going to go and check out the library, see if they've pulled up any more of those Expert-level techniques. I've checked out the ones we got in the Fifth Realm and although they're interesting, I don't think that they're the ones that will help me progress," Rugrat said.

"I know what you're saying. They seem close, but not well-suited. I've got a storage ring full of ingredients from Vuzgal that I still need to test and understand. I'm going to test out a few of the techniques and see what they do. Maybe I can piece them together into something new. I've still got to craft that Age Rejuvenation potion for Elder Lu's wife," Erik said.

"Also, I think that we've kind of outgrown the mana bolts and bullets. They're effective as a sneak attack, but their power-to-attack ratio is too low," Rugrat said.

"They work pretty good," Erik said.

"Fighting at the higher levels is more about augmentation than it is about one thing. Is it the stats of the weapon? Or is it your strength and your techniques that bring out the greatest strength of the weapon?" Rugrat asked.

Erik didn't need to say anything; they both knew the answer to that question.

"That's why most weapons are crafted for the fighter in the higher realms. Most of the gear we sell out of the Battle Arena can be modified to suit the user, which is why it sells well. In a competitive or life-and-death fight, would you prefer the rifle you've fought with for ten years or the newest best rifle that came out yesterday?" Rugrat asked.

"Old, tried, and true—new one will probably jam after two rounds," Erik said.

Rugrat grinned. "True that. But you get what I mean."

"Yeah, using Mana Detonation with the force of my blow behind it increases the strength of both. Mana bolts and bullets need much more mana to power them up to have the same effect against someone in the First Realm and in the Fourth Realm."

"Yeah, so I think you use weapons to close with the enemy, then techniques to beat the shit out of them," Rugrat suggested helpfully.

"And you can remain in your perch in the sky, safe as can be," Erik said.

"Supporting fire." Rugrat clicked his tongue, closing his eye and raising the okay sign as if it were the scope of a rifle to his eye.

"Aren't Davin and Egbert heading to the Wood floor today?" Erik said suddenly, remembering.

"I guess so?"

"Now remember, no burning down everything that you see. Only burn and threaten the things that I tell you to burn and threaten," Egbert said.

Glosil and Yui looked at each other and then shrugged, looking back to the teleportation formation.

Davin was there, pouting and his arms crossed, looking like the cutest damn Fire imp you ever did see.

Egbert pinched his cheeks. As Davin tried to smack his hand away,

Egbert was already walking away.

"I told you to stop pinching my cheeks!" Davin complained, the air heating up around him.

"Now, now, Davin, with your baby face and your pouting, it's just too hilarious not to!"

"You!" Davin started to heat up more and the air around him distorted.

A spell formation appeared above him and dropped water on him, sizzling and turning the area around the teleportation formation humid.

"Okay, so shall we?" Egbert said.

Davin huffed but walked onto the formation next to Egbert.

Egbert smiled and waved to Glosil and Yui, looking like a proud parent taking his kid who was throwing a temper tantrum off to their first day of school.

The main floor disappeared and they were in a blacked-out wooded area.

The trees started to creak and turn, looking like something out of one of Egbert's horror romances.

"That was a great read, cute and fearful Anabeth running through the haunted woods to get away from her attackers when she runs into the valiant Charles!" Egbert raised his one hand, striking a pose and holding his stomach as his voice turned *deeper*.

"Oh, how he defeated those attackers with but a flash of his sword, showing off his valiant side to Anabeth." His voice returned to normal as he walked toward the forest, his hands behind his back.

"You see, Charles was stuck in the forest because he had been cursed by a witch. Seeing him and his looks, she wanted for him to become hers. When he denied her, she turned him into a half-man, half-swamp creature. At night, he would transform into a man and in the day he would be a swamp creature that would roam its depths, killing any that ventured inside.

"It is with Anabeth's love that he can overcome his curse and the swamp transforms into a grand castle, with poor Anabeth as Charles's queen." Egbert didn't seem to care in the slightest as he walked through the murky and humid air. The trees around him started to move as creatures with wrinkled, almost bark-like skin appeared. On the swampy ground, eyes started to appear and Davin moved closer to Egbert.

"Egbert," Davin said in a warning tone.

"Ah, damn, I got some mud on my robes. You know that these are Expert robes, though they're a pain to wash out?" Egbert still ignored his surroundings, stopping to clean it up some.

A beast jumped out of the water, opening its mouth wide to bite into Egbert.

Egbert raised one hand. A flash of light appeared at the end of his finger, slicing the creature into parts and cutting anything behind it for ten meters apart.

All the while, Egbert patted and scratched at the mud on his robe.

"Damn thing," Egbert complained. "Oh Davin, use your Fire domain, just this once."

Davin seemed relieved and his body started to glow red. He seemed more sinister and the beasts around him seemed to slink back, an innate fear toward Davin.

Davin grinned as he unleashed his power. A wave of fire burst from him. The floor rumbled as it shot across the swamp, vaporizing the water, ripping up the trees, and super-cooking the unfortunate beasts.

Egbert finished cleaning up his robe. He looked up at the destruction around him as the air around Davin was still burning.

"What is that—a one-hundred-meter radius? Is this your domain?" Egbert reached out.

"I can extend it farther but it's much harder." Davin sighed.

"So you can completely sense everything in this area and cast spells within it as if casting them from your body?" Egbert asked.

"Don't you have a domain?" Davin asked.

"I have a dungeon, not a domain. Everything within my area of influence is under my command." Egbert stepped into the air. "Come along. One Wood floor to tame. Will you put your flames out? Don't need another Earth floor situation."

Davin sighed and he flapped his wings. The skeleton and Fire imp headed toward a truly massive tree that dominated the floor. There were signs of buildings in and around the tree, and other plants and creatures lived within its branches.

"Really have to work with the lighting in here. I guess the sun formation must have gone out. Though the formations that simulate sunlight are still working. Became a swamp instead of a forest." Egbert talked to himself as they crossed the floor toward the tree.

Rugrat looked at the breastplate he had finished.

"High Journeyman level." He sighed to himself as he sat on the chair next to the workbench. He was covered in grime and he held his chin.

He looked over to the notes he had made from researching and using an Expert-level smithing technique. *I understand what I have to do, but what I have to do and how I get there are two different things.*

Rugrat moved to the bathroom attached to the workroom and washed his face, feeling a bit defeated.

"Okay, well, my smithing might have hit a wall. Although it sucks, if I keep on grinding at it, I might make *some* progress over time. There is still a lot for me to learn about formations. Formations and smithing are linked to one another. I'll take a look at formation techniques, make some notes, then work on formations. Maybe that will kickstart my brain." Rugrat cleaned up the workshop and he passed Taran, who was working on a blade.

Rugrat waved to him and he raised his hammer back in greeting and kept on working. He passed other smiths who were learning. Classrooms were filled with people learning about the different kinds of metals and enhancers that were in the Ten Realms. How they could be worked into one another, the effects that they would have.

The smithing department had grown with the rest of the academy, which was easily three times its original size. He exited the department into the halls, stairwells, and walkways that connected the academy. He stepped out of the buildings and into the green areas that lay between the different sections of the academy. There were people doing study groups, others having fun in the sun.

Rugrat's eyes were drawn to one of the main sights of Alva, the library. It had grown in size and height once again.

It remained in the center of the academy, with people from all departments within its halls.

It feels more like a college than those academies. I guess the fact of it is that people are all working in the same areas; no one person is more or less important than the others. There are people who are taking all kinds of combined classes and although the departments are in different areas, they're not segregated and people want to teach and share with one another. Sure, there are rivalries. Nothing is perfect. Though it's pretty damn good.

Rugrat walked into the doors of the library. He ignored the stares and the people talking to one another about him. He had dealt with it before when he was traveling from home to work, or his next station wearing his uniform.

He took the stairs and headed up to the top floor of the library. The Novice area now had three floors—same with the Apprentice and Journeyman—breaking up the levels of books from low, mid, to high.

There didn't used to be so many people up here, Rugrat thought, taking a stroll through the mid Journeyman-level floor. There were now two or three dozen people with the qualifications to be on the floor. Rugrat went higher, using his Alva medallion to enter the Expert-level floor.

It was still just one floor.

"Looks like Egbert has been working on security a bit." Rugrat saw undead from Vuzgal in the room. Each of them wore powerful weapons and armor of the Expert grade. Erik and Rugrat had shipped some down for study and to be used by Alva. Being undead, they could be stuffed into storage rings and transported, though they needed to be within a dungeon and animated by a dungeon core, or by a ritual in order to function.

Rugrat leafed through the books on smithing, checking his notes once again.

"Red sword dance—move the red-hot sword, maintaining temperature, as you use your movements to alter the shape of the weapon. These weapons will be best suited for those who walk down the path of high Agility, with their graceful moves dazzling and destroying." Rugrat sighed as he shook his head. "The descriptions sound like weird poetry."

He stopped looking at the smithing techniques and turned to the formation techniques.

"So what have we got here? The hidden formation—basically using threads of mana like someone knits together a blanket. They knit it into a formation, laying them upon one another in a design. Takes dense mana, and a lot of time. Using a hammer to smack a formation into creation. Need to have the entire formation in your mind and all of the working parts, then you put that onto your hammer and then just press it out as one. Very fast method but need to be exact, really high rate of failure and the metal can become corrupted and unusable. That sounds fun.

"Okay, so next we have the fine-tuned technique. It's a series of movements that one memorizes that can be used together to create a formation. This is a technique? It's more like an instruction manual." Rugrat read more. "Good pointers though, and smart." Rugrat listed down different information that was useful for him. Most of it was too complicated; he hadn't reached that stage yet.

After checking the information he had down and his head hurting, he headed out of the library and toward the totem that could take him to Vuzgal.

"Are you really going to follow me everywhere?" Rugrat asked Niemm as he walked toward the totem.

"Kind of our job, City-Dungeon Lord." Niemm smiled.

"Great, now I'm the one being babysat. This sucks," Rugrat said as he led the way. "I have to pay all of your teleportation fees as well!"

Erik sat across from Old Man Hei, chewing on some new ingredients.

"You've been chewing on that for a while," Old Hei said.

"Oh, can't taste anything anymore. I think it's good?" Erik put it into his storage ring. "So what do you think?"

"I think that you are trying to find a quick solution for a long problem," Old Hei said. "Go and create concoctions. Go and read about Alchemy. Chew on ingredients if you must. Information and time go a long way. Becoming an Expert isn't a quick thing. You must be in the right mindset and then it just kind of happens. Using other Alchemy techniques will bolster your strength, but they are someone else's path. You need to create your own technique. Maybe they will be similar to one that you learn from someone else. Maybe it is completely different. If you have blinders on and you charge down a set path, how will you know that there is a better road right beside you?"

"I feel like you're getting more riddles the longer I talk to you." Erik sighed.

Old Hei smiled. "The path toward higher crafting is not a simple one, nor is it easy. Books become closer to reference material than instructions. Maybe that is because an instruction manual has not been made yet. Maybe it is because we may always be searching to create that instruction manual but we will never make one that suits everyone, just the majority?" Old Hei shrugged lightly.

"So what should I do?"

"Train."

"Didn't you just say kind of with the blinders that I shouldn't focus on one thing?"

"Train in Alchemy, train in fighting, train in healing. How long ago was it that you spent time healing people? I know how much it means to you."

Erik saw a flashback of Chonglu and cleared his throat.

"Train your mana and your body."

"Well, for that I need supplies," Erik said.

"You have reached Body Like Iron, correct?"

"Yes. Now I need to temper my body with the Earth element. I can apply to get those concoctions but they will take weeks or months."

"And although you are my disciple, because you still wander the Ten Realms, you are an outer disciple, so you can only purchase the finished concoction instead of make it yourself. Bit paranoid about putting concoctions within your body?"

"A little." Erik smiled.

Old Hei pressed his lips together in an amused expression and pulled out a piece of paper. "There is an old recluse, an alchemist in the Fourth Realm. He has said that he is willing to give away a Mana or Body Cultivation formula in exchange for someone completing the low Expert-level Revitalization Tree Sap concoction. He will give you the formula, but you will need to sign a contract with the Ten Realms to attempt to make the concoction at least ten times. If you create it, then you will not need to make another concoction and you can use the formula freely as you wish."

When commissioning someone to make a concoction, they can pay for the alchemist's time, give them the ingredients and the formula. Giving the formula greatly decreases the cost. If they pass them the formula and make a contract for them to not use this version again, the cost rises. If the alchemist has the formula already, then the customer pays a higher price. Formula, compensation, and ingredients: these are the three parts that are the basis of a deal between an alchemist and their client.

With him supplying the formula, it is a high-grade formula and must have a powerful effect. If he distributes it to anyone but they must try to create the formula ten times, the cost of ingredients must be high or they are rare for him to not supply them. Though if he passes all of these formulas out, maybe there are six or seven people who create the concoction, he gets all of those, allowing him to resell them on.

"It's a gamble. How rare and expensive are the ingredients?" Erik asked.

Old Hei's smile grew deeper. "The ingredients are expensive but not all that rare. A set of them would cost around one hundred Earth mana stones."

Erik blinked a few times. "What does the formula do?"

"It is a formula that allows one to undo changes to their body. Powerful poison or curses, limited aging, adding in a beast bloodline to your own. Say your cultivation became chaotic. I thought about using it on your friend. It would have turned back the damage, but advancing is always better than reverting, I believe."

"Why would I be interested?"

"The one who completes the concoction first will be allowed to take one other Expert-level concoction. He made a list, but you might be interested in the Earth Soul pill. A foundational pill that will allow one to temper their body with the Earth attribute." Old Hei smiled and Erik felt his competitive side taking over.

"I will go and take a look. Maybe the formula will challenge my mind while the Age Rejuvenation challenges my techniques."

Old Hei was looking over papers; Erik had headed off somewhere to do as he needed.

He looked to a side door that opened, revealing Delilah. She had a confused look on her face.

"Grand Teacher, I have reached level seventy-four but I can't break through into the Expert levels."

These two—are they trying to beat me next? What would that be like, the grand student beating the grand teacher?

Old Hei coughed a little and there was another knock at the main door. "Come in," he said.

Captain Khasar walked in with a box and put it down on a table.

"What is this?" Old Hei asked.

"A present from Erik," Khasar said. "He gave it to me when I escorted him to the totem. Said it should help you both and even if Delilah beats him…" Khasar coughed before continuing. "That he'll beat you."

Old Hei stared at Khasar for a few seconds before he got to his feet. "That little rascal! It wasn't long ago he was just a Novice!" He moved over to the box and opened the lid. The next words on his lips died down.

"What is it, Grand Teacher?"

"Uh, technique books, Expert level, copies." His voice was stilted, looking at the items, and Delilah looked in as if they were nothing much.

"These should help me break through." She opened them and started to flick through.

Khasar and Old Hei shared a look before Khasar bowed and headed out of the room, leaving them alone.

It's not bad having a student who owns a city.

45 Recluse

Erik and his group of "merchants"—who were really half of Special Team One following him along and making sure that he didn't get into trouble—followed their guide and passed through the totem.

"Welcome to Elivas," the guide said.

Erik tossed him the payment as Yao Meng led the way and the others looked around.

The man waved good-bye to them as they passed through the custom gates. Erik checked the information that Old Hei had given him and they headed deeper into the city. Seeing a group in hoods wasn't that strange but with their powerful auras, people moved out of the way.

They went through the city. It looked ancient, with old carved walls covered in moss and hidden pictures of days past. The forest was close around them and a loamy smell of moss and humidity filled one's senses.

"Is that it?" Storbon asked.

"I think so." Erik looked at the long building with a tower that rose up into a disc at its peak. The trees around the buildings looked as if they were actively trying to reclaim the building, growing all around and over it. Vines crisscrossed around it.

A young man stormed out of the house, his face filled with rage as he met up with others. "That old man is too stubborn and cheap! We're leaving!"

He stormed off with his group as Erik and the others walked up.

"Seems like fun," Storbon said as he continued to scan the area.

"Thanks, Storbon. Great pep talk," Erik said dryly. The two of them looked at each other and smiled.

"All right, see you in a bit." Erik made to step forward.

A man yelled as he was propelled out of the tower's window, before he crashed down into a nearby field.

"Stop kicking people into other's fields! You've done it three times! If you hit my prized Roasi plums, I'll call the city guard!" an irate old lady yelled from the other field. "Stop rolling around! You're making it worse! Aren't you an alchemist? Don't you know how to act in a garden?"

The woman berated the poor alchemist, who was an easier target.

"Hopefully leaving through the front door." Erik headed up to the door and knocked on it. It took some time before it was opened and a butler appeared.

"Master is up on the highest floor." The man looked tired and worn out, barely keeping his appearance together as his master threw people out of his house.

"Thank you." Erik headed up the stairs and knocked on the door there.

It opened and he found himself in a large room. To the left side, it was closed off, with the sounds of Alchemy being carried out. In the main area, there were four guards.

They seemed to grow alert as Erik entered the room. He was different, not weak and fragile or a sheep in wolf's clothing.

He smiled to them simply, acknowledging other fighters. No one made it here on the Fourth Realm without killing a few people.

"I am here about the job for the completion of the Revitalization Tree Sap."

"What do you want in exchange for making the Revitalization Tree Sap?" A voice came from the other room.

Why does it sound like a child's voice?

Erik cleared his throat. "The Earth Soul pill."

"Are you looking to increase your cultivation or others?"

"Does it matter?"

"Hmm, you're an alchemist, but you also fight, interesting. Give him a contract."

A guard pulled out a contract. Erik checked it a few times. It was simple, requiring Erik to not share any information and agreeing to the terms that Old Hei had listed.

Erik dripped some blood on it and then passed it to the guard.

The door opened and a young man walked through from the Alchemy room. He looked young but he didn't feel it; his eyes were old and his brows were pulled together in a thunderous expression.

He pulled out a formula and held it in front of Erik. "I hope you are the fastest," the child-man said.

Erik took the formula, checked it and put it away. "I hope so too." Erik nodded to the man and headed out.

So that's what he wants help with—reversing the changes to his body. Going from an adult to a child must be annoying. Also, with the changes to the body's structure, I wonder if the mana flows smoothly or not?

Erik walked out of the house and toward the totem.

"Where to now?" Storbon asked.

"Vermire. Be easier to blend in there," Erik said.

Jen headed upstairs to her office, hearing that she had a new visitor. The Alva Healing House in Vermire had grown in size, nearly doubling. There were people looking to become healers all the time. It was a lucrative business, with people looking to cultivate their bodies. There were plenty of people looking for healers and the army would pay people a higher rate of pay if they were already medic qualified.

That's another thing—all of the medics! With the new healing houses up in Vuzgal, at least it is moving people around a bit more. Though I kind of like it here. I'll see.

She opened the door and found Erik sitting there, looking over books.

"Hey, Jen. So you must like Vermire—I heard that you got an offer to move to Vuzgal, or back to Alva," Erik said.

"Are you here to bend my arm?"

"Me? Nope, I'm here to put my hands to work." Erik smiled.

"You want to work in Vermire?"

"Well, in Vuzgal, I'm known as the city lord. That wouldn't be a good image if people found out I was working as a healer. I guess making things is one thing, but working for other people when you have a high position is weird." Erik shrugged. "Then in Alva, well, most people are just increasing their cultivation—interesting but it doesn't help out as much as your healing house. So, where do you want me?"

"Uh, well, how long are you here for? What can you do?"

"Well, I'm here for at least a couple of weeks unless something takes me away. I can shoot back between here and Alva easy. I'll work the nights on concoctions in Alva's Alchemy department. In the days, I'm here—all yours, wherever you need me. I can do triage, first aid, I guess kind of battlefield surgery. I haven't worked with all of the tools that you have here. You've been busy."

"Sanitation and prevention are the biggest things we focus on." Jen shrugged. "Well, there are always people looking for treatment. Even with the expansion, we have people coming from across the First Realm to be healed. Doesn't make the healing houses too pleased, but then they can't really compete. They're either too far away or the importance of Vermire to the people around us is higher than trying to pressure the healing house."

"I've heard that there have been threats?"

"Yeah, but what are they going to try to do? Attack us?" Jen snorted and raised her hand as a mana blade appeared in it. "They can try, but everyone is a medical professional here. We're the most upgraded Body and Mana Gathering cultivators in Alva—be hard to really attack us."

Erik grinned. "Good to know that you're safe. Have you made advancements in cultivation?"

"We have improved on your practices to open one's mana gates. Instead of using mana to punch through the mana gates, we use intraosseous infusion. With the new metals from Alva, we can easily get entry into the marrow or gate section that is blocked. Then we hook people up to a drip that is filled with a mana-concentrated concoction. It will take some time, but with the intraosseous infusion, that injection isn't going anywhere, so people can work with it. Then, over time…" Jen opened her hand. "The gate gives way and opens up. We are working with different concoctions to see what is better. It looks like the higher concentration of mana, the faster it works. If a person sits in a mana-rich environment and circulates their mana, then they will make a breakthrough much faster than someone who is passively circulating their mana."

"Which concoctions?" Erik asked.

Jen checked in her storage ring before she put down a folder in front of Erik. She sat down in the chair opposite and pulled out a still warm tea from the morning. She sipped it, closing her tired eyes as she let the smell of the tea and its heat relax her body.

She used a healing spell on herself to deal with the back aches and kinks that she could already feel.

"Experimented with different beast cores and mana stones. Seems that ingredients with a high mana concentration are the best for the basic ingredients to act as a catalyst for mana stones. I keep coming back to thinking that the mana gates are like plaque in one's arteries."

Jen looked at Erik as he flipped through the notes.

"It's thorough and the results are good. You have focused in on the issue, but I am thinking about the possible factors that led to it," Erik said.

Jen's eyebrows pinched together.

"We know that people who are born in the higher realms with greater mana density will naturally have more mana gates open than the people born in the lower realms. The mana gates become harder to open when someone has circulated high attribute mana through their body. These deposits, shall we say, of impure mana pass through the mana channels and then pile up in one's mana gates. If we were to create something that could purify the mana within one's channels, then the buildup wouldn't be so high, right?"

"It makes some sense, but resources cost. The concoctions we're injecting people with cost anywhere from three mana stones to an Earth mana stone. How much will a concoction cost to purify a person's mana? Wouldn't it just be cheaper for them to undertake the procedure in Alva?"

"Making a pill or concoction to do that would be hard as well," Erik said.

"Wouldn't a mana gathering formation with the right kind of Alchemy plants around it be better?" Jen sipped from her cup. "Use the formation to draw in higher mana; the plants suck up the different attributes and then you're good to go. A dungeon core would be perfect due to the high purity, but the plants might help. Though we don't really need all of this down here."

"Why?" Erik asked.

"People aren't that old. The older a person, the more impurities they've sucked up into their bodies. It takes them a lot longer and a lot more resources to open a mana gate." Jen sunk into thought. "I wonder if doing too much might have stunted them for later growth."

"Hmm?" Erik held his chin, playing with his beard.

"Well, with higher levels and stats, you can draw in more mana, right? Power grows through three ways: levels, cultivation, and resources. With Mana Gathering Cultivation, you can open your mana gates at any stage of your Mana Gathering Cultivation. There is a sort of paradox, though. The more mana you can circulate and use to break your mana gates open, the faster it'll open. At the same time, the more mana you can draw in, the more impurities that enter your body."

Erik snapped his fingers. "That makes much more sense now! Qin—she was never able to use mana due to her constitution. Then, with opening one of her mana gates, the surge of power was like a breeze through a dusty house—the dust or mana gate debris shot out of her mana gates. The effect was many times more effective."

Jen and Erik looked at each other, their minds opened to a new possibility. They both pulled out books and wrote down their findings and followed their line of thinking before they could forget it.

"No wonder people treat Vuzgal as a holy land. If someone was to draw in purer and highly concentrated mana while increasing the Mana Gathering Cultivation, then they would be able to open their mana gates with greater ease."

After their meeting and new theory, Jen took Erik around the healing house. Wearing their masks, it was hard for people to pick them out. Erik checked on a few people.

"Infections are everywhere and the most common thing we deal with.

Though, thankfully, after someone gets over the infection, they won't have further complications with it for the rest of their lives," Jen said. "We started to take out the infection from the infected, then infect others and heal them, temper them against ever getting the infection. We give it to babies and the elderly for free as they're at risk the most."

Erik's mouth twitched into a smile. "Good job. I forgot about that, to be honest. Guess I took it for granted."

"Huh?"

"Nothing. So where do you want me?"

"Need some help in emergency!" someone yelled. "Team coming in!"

Jen was moving and Erik followed after her.

There were people coming in—some unconscious, others screaming out in pain. It looked chaotic as other fighters were bringing them in on stretchers.

They were stopped and the patients given tags and sent to different areas of the emergency ward, which was broken up to triage people right away. There was a Red, Yellow, and Green section.

Erik and Jen moved to the Red section as there were people coming in already. A man came into the bay; a Clean spell was used on him as the team with him shifted him onto the bed.

He was groaning and turning, in pain. His face had been mauled.

"Cracked ribs, internal bleeding, possible punctured lung, obstructed airway." Erik read out the tag attached to the man as people cut his clothes off him.

"All right, I need an air tube." Erik used Simple Organic Scan on the man, picking out the different injuries.

"Tourniquets, numbing concoction on his missing limbs." Erik looked to see that tourniquets were already being applied and a drip was readied of a Stamina/healing mix.

Erik was passed the laryngoscope. He moved the guy's head, holding him steady. He held the man's tongue out of the way and fed the breathing tube down the man's throat, allowing him to breathe normally.

Erik checked the patient over. He used a minor healing spell on the man's brain as he had a slight brain bleed.

"Hook up the solution. Keep an eye on him. His shoulder is shattered and his ribs are in a bad way, but nothing life-threatening." Erik turned and looked at a new patient who had just entered.

He moved to them as he used a Clean spell on his clothes.

Another medic took over before he got there.

"Okay, we've got a collapsed side, ruptured organs, brain, heart and lungs—we work with those first. She's losing blood internally. We need to take her into surgery. We'll fuse her wounds internally. We can heal them later." The medic's words were clipped and professional as he checked the person.

"Her Stamina is looking good. All right, let's move her." They got her onto a bed and then headed for the operating rooms.

Another person came in. They were unconscious. Their arm was a mess and their head didn't look natural.

Erik checked their tag and used Simple Organic Scan on their head. "Stamina NOW!" Their nerves had been torn, their skull had been shattered, and there was a hole.

Erik started using healing spells on the man, healing the brain and the veins that had been badly damaged. He checked the man's body as he was cleaned and an IV was inserted; someone squeezed the bag to get it into the man faster.

Erik fused the nerves together, making sure to pay attention to the rest of the man's body so he didn't send him into a Stamina fatigue spiral.

Erik paused and he checked the man. "Arm is a mess. Skull is cracked. Need to drain excess blood there. Nerves are reattached. Immobilize his neck so he can't damage himself moving his head around. Spine is still shattered. Observe him. Stamina for now. Inform me if he wakes up. Don't give him healing solution yet—might need healing spells yet." Erik wanted him to have as much Stamina to work with in case he needed to do more work.

The team with the man carried out their work and Erik looked around.

It was two hours later that Erik stopped working on patients. He felt bone-tired and he used a Clean spell on himself again.

He checked the reports on the different people. He looked for the information on the man with the massive head trauma. He couldn't find it and he talked to an orderly. "Do you know where the man with the head trauma went?"

"The one with the shattered arm? He was stabilized and moved to a ward. He hasn't woken up though," the orderly said.

"Thanks." Erik knew he couldn't dwell on it. *He might come back okay, or he might be a vegetable, memory loss.* Erik shook his head, automatically going to the worst-case scenario as he flicked through the red clipboards. All of them looked stable so he looked at the yellows that hadn't been seen to yet.

He picked up a clipboard and headed into the Yellow bay, where there were several people with bad injuries.

Erik started to get to work with his patient who had been hit in the hip, cracking it. She'd hit a tree, dislocating her shoulder, and fallen unconscious for some time.

"Am I going to be able to walk again?" the woman asked with a broken voice, tears on her face.

"Of course you are. When was the last time you ate?" Erik put the clipboard down.

She seemed confused by the question.

"When was the last time you ate?" Erik repeated as a medic came over to assist. "Numbing cream."

"Uh, I think this morning," the woman in the bed said.

Erik checked the time. "Okay, that should be enough for the hip." Erik checked the woman's head, some minor bruising but it didn't look to have lasting damage.

The medic passed him the numbing cream.

"Good ole Wraith's Touch." Erik smiled, looking at the name on the tub. He took some of the cream and put it on the woman's hip.

Once her leg was numbed, Erik started healing the muscle and tendons, pushing the bones back into their original place.

Erik then used Bone Heal on the bones. He didn't heal the bruising and he took a look at the woman's shoulder. He used some more Wraith's Touch. He got her to sit up and moved her arm, popping it back into its socket.

He wrote down some notes.

"With a bit of healing on the muscle and tendons, it won't pop out easily later. The bruising on the hip will flare up in a few days and then go down.

No lasting damage and a good lesson to patients to not run into a beast lair," Erik said.

"Understood," the other medic said, listening attentively.

Erik filled out information on the yellow clipboard, put it on the end of the bed and he moved to the next one.

He checked the man's clipboard and used his Simple Organic Scan. They were stable and would be okay once they had some more Stamina and could be healed further.

Erik kept going, moving through the room.

46
Change Base of Operations

Glosil was in Vuzgal. The totem activated; the people had been cleared to the side. The gates were opened and in a dazzling flash, the empty area around the totem was filled with soldiers. They moved off the totem, riding their tell-tale armored panthers. They marched away from the totem.

Glosil felt pride looking at them. They had high levels when they had left but they didn't have the confidence or skills to go with it.

Now they were like a changed unit. With the new reorganization, the next level of training, the Dragon Combat Company was complete.

They marched out by squad and platoons.

The close protection details are missing still, but training for them will start next week.

People of Vuzgal turned to look at the passing military, who created a powerful display as they followed the roads to the training grounds.

Glosil put away his viewing orb that allowed him to look through other viewing orbs that had been given to the flying undead that roosted at the top of Vuzgal.

"Atten-shun!" Yui ordered.

Tiger Combat Company came to attention. Behind them, there were nearly eight hundred new recruits.

The massive doors to the military base opened, allowing Dragon Combat Company entry. They marched onto the training area and marched into position next to Tiger Combat Company.

"Dragon Combat Company, halt!"

The doors to the outside world closed and people looked at the ranks of soldiers that now rested inside the training square.

Glosil marched up in front of the two groups. Domonos and Yui dismounted, marched up to him and gave him a salute.

He saluted them back.

"Battalion, at ease!"

Twelve hundred feet and bodies moved as one as everyone relaxed.

"Feels good to say battalion. Hopefully I'll be saying regiment shortly," Glosil said to Yui and Domonos but his voice could be heard by those in the ranks.

"Captain Yui Silaz, you and your Tiger Company will head out for advanced training. Captain Domonos Silaz, your Dragon Company will begin the next rota of training here in Vuzgal. You will also take over the protection of Vuzgal and the city lord's interests. Do you understand your orders?"

"Yes sir!" They both responded, looking straight ahead.

"Very well. Turnover will take a week. Get each other up to speed and I best not hear about too much trouble." Glosil then let his eyes wander over the ranks.

"Atten-shun!"

Everyone responded as one.

"Dis-missed!"

They turned and walked off the parade square as the leadership started to pass orders and people were organized. The newly arriving Dragon Company needed to get moved in and the training needed to continue for the newest recruits.

Glosil greeted Yui and Domonos as they entered his office.

"So, how are things going?" he asked as they all sat down at the table in his room.

"We have the numbers, but we don't necessarily have all of the training. As we were told, we trained up people for one role at this time. So someone who took a medic course is now a medic, just to fill spots. Most of the people from Alva have all of their qualifications and are the backbone of the companies. We're teaching the newest members in our free time, but it will take time to train them up properly and get them all of their qualifications," Yui said.

"Our people have largely finished their training. We had the personnel to train them up in most areas. The new guys need an extra course or two still—just a time squeeze." Domonos spoke up.

"Training the new units? Thoughts?"

"We're going to have another seven, nearly eight hundred people joining us in just a few weeks. They will be basic, but I think we should hold to the training we've set out. Mix in our veterans with the newly qualified in the Dragon and Tiger units, overstaff them and then break off secondary units—half veteran, half new," Yui said.

"The training companies are a good idea. They each get taught in their own trade and then come together to see how all of the different parts work together. It will increase the training time, though," Domonos said.

"We need quality, not quantity. Some of the originals from Tiger Platoon will finish their training in all areas." Glosil's statement turned into a question as Yui smiled.

"That's correct. There will be thirty-eight who will have completed their basic, sharpshooter, medic, mortar, mage, and engineer next Friday."

"And Dragon Company should have another thirty-two to add to that," Glosil said. "We're about a course behind Tiger Company, but they only have one more course to go through to be fully qualified."

"I'm sure that you're all getting asked when selection for the CPD will be held. Three weeks from now, selection will be open. Up to thirty people from each of your companies are allowed to apply. There will also be an officer training course in Alva that your people can enter into—room for twenty from each of your companies. Once they complete their officer or

CPD training, they can complete the other course. Afterward, they can choose to remain at their rank, or become officers. For now, the CPD units will be teacher training pools, with one CPD squad active and the other training others in medical, artillery, mortars, and so on," Glosil said.

"How long is the CPD course?"

"One intensive month. It will be taught by Special Team Two and will have extensive time in the Battle Arena, fighting and training to increase their combat standards. They will learn directly from the special teams how to increase their effectiveness. They'll be placed under constant stress to perform. Once they're done, they'll be writing the manuals on how to use our different weapons systems."

"Still a lot to be done." Yui smiled.

"Yes, and then there is the issue of the Willful Institute. Cutting out that problem with minimal issued will be difficult."

Rugrat had returned to Vuzgal secretly and hid in the Vuzgal Crafting Academy. He had brought a number of Expert-level books with him but instead of diving into smithing, he had gone to the formation workshop, and started working there.

Rugrat spent his time reading books on formations and carving them out. He tried to make formations that were needed for Vuzgal. Although large areas had been reclaimed and rebuilt, most of them were missing the myriad formations that they required. Building was quick; crafting the different parts needed for the building was time intensive.

Rugrat's days passed quickly. In the mornings and afternoons, he would smith and create formations. At night, he would train with George. He and Erik had taken up learning combat techniques. Throughout, he would cultivate his mana.

Today, he was visiting the hospital.

"Okay, so I'll take this, then wake up in a few hours and I should have tempered my skin?" Rugrat asked, remembering the hell that Erik had needed to go through.

"That's it." The medic had a slightly nervous expression. His eyes turned to Storbon and the other members of the special team in the room.

"See you on the other side." Rugrat threw the pill back and swallowed. "Urgh, tastes like chalk," Rugrat muttered as he laid back and closed his eyes.

He opened them again, feeling a bit confused. *Where am I? Hospital...okay.* Rugrat looked around blearily. The special team looked a little paler but there was a new notification waiting for Rugrat.

"One more tempering complete. Just a few more to go and reach Body Like Stone." Rugrat rubbed the back of his head and he felt a breeze on his skin.

He looked down. "Well, who stole my clothes?" he asked, still looking down.

"You were, um, shedding," Storbon said.

"Oh." Rugrat stood. He could feel more on his skin—the temperature differences, the flow of air. He pulled on clothes. He could feel them more than before.

"Might need to change my shirts. Damn, these things chafe," Rugrat complained as he finished getting clothes on.

"Okay, time to go and hand Erik his ass." Rugrat headed out of the hospital, a smile on his face.

The special team and Rugrat got on their mounts and rode through the streets to the Battle Arena.

At the entrance, Erik and the other half of Special Team One were entering, drawing people's attention. Gilly's unique appearance and the levels of those around her drew people's interest.

They entered into the Battle Arena on their mounts. They were the only ones given the privilege.

"Ready?" Erik asked.

"Born ready. Bit busy in here." Rugrat looked around the busy floor.

"Good for business. Come on." Erik led them to a VIP elevator. They dismounted and their mounts went to their smaller forms but remained by their sides as the special team boarded the elevator.

They headed upward. The doors opened to reveal the largest Battle Arena. The stands were empty but the barrier around the stage was active.

"Well, looks like we invested well." Rugrat laughed.

The elevator behind them opened once again as the final member of their group arrived.

"So this is what it looks like when it is empty," the Fighter's Association Head Klaus said in interest.

He pulled on his gray and black beard. His fingers were covered in rings, each of them with inlaid formations. His beard was pulled back by metal ties and his hair was shaved short. He looked like a dwarf in appearance, but in height he was taller than Rugrat. He wasn't packed with muscle but there was a strength and presence in every movement.

"Looks like you two have the pleasure of being my trainees." He grinned as Erik looked at Rugrat.

"We need to learn how to fight up here—he's the best one for it," Rugrat said.

"Also, I'm bound to not tell anyone your skills or abilities, standard trainer contract. Not even the Fighter's Association will find out your abilities from me," Klaus said with a grin.

They went down to the training square, and the special teams stood to the side. Testing equipment lay around. Erik and Rugrat demonstrated their attacks, from their mana bullets to Erik's Mana Detonation.

The more they went on, the darker Klaus's expression became.

Erik and Rugrat stood in front of Klaus.

"Seems that you have been throwing things together. You are reliant on your firearms and you have not worked on your other fighting skills. It is as if you created these firearms before you could develop fighting in the Ten Realms. Erik, your footwork and movements show that you are somewhat on the right path. Your attacks are items added to one another. Although they can work together, it is more complicated than it needs to be. Rugrat, your entire fighting style is on fighting with your weapon. If you don't have one, then your power drops dramatically." Klaus took a deep breath. "That said, you seem adaptable, which means that this might not be a waste. So I will start from the beginning and we will go from there."

He stepped into the middle of the sparring area. "When one starts fighting, they learn that there are two major areas: melee"—he snapped out a fist, causing the air to shift—"and magic." He threw out his other hand and a thorn of wood stuck into a target.

"As it progresses, these two merge into a style that is suited to the fighter." He threw out a fist while creating a thorn at the exact same time. The thorn buried itself in the same target, nearly two times deeper.

"These are called techniques. Now, there are pure mage and pure melee techniques as well. They're both powerful in their own right, but pure mages are weak to close-in attack; pure melee types are weak to ranged attacks. There are few or no pure mages or melee types. Now, I'm not saying that everyone needs to wield a sword, a spear, or some kind of weapon. Think of techniques like shortcuts, combining multiple high-level concepts together: instead of having to recite all of the spell, you add in movements to simplify it. Instead of trying to follow the path of pure magic, you augment your fighting. It doesn't care who fights the prettiest or has the cleanest spells—it matters who wins. If you find a way to improve your spells, that will help you later," Klaus said.

"Erik, your fist thing—it's wasteful, shooting out mana like that. If you were to use a spell to make fire and lightning and then use just a part of your mana, then the attack power would increase greatly.

"Rugrat, if you could cast a spell on yourself to increase your defense and your speed, then you would be able to fight for longer and not have to fear for your life as much," Klaus said.

"Read these." Klaus pulled out two spell books and tossed them to Erik and Rugrat.

"Healing Dagger?" Erik asked.

"You create a dagger in your hand that you can throw out. The people it strikes it will heal instead of wound." Klaus looked to Rugrat. "Chains of the Darkness is a control spell. At its base, it can trap someone in a one-hundred-meter area. With your power, I would estimate that it would reach three hundred meters and you can capture multiple people. With this, you can control the battlefield more effectively. Learn them. We've got a lot to go through."

You have learned the spell: Healing Dagger. Your spell book has been updated.

Healing Dagger

Novice

Attack heals instead of harms.

Consumption of Mana based on effect and power.

Erik fell into a daze as he thought of the Healing Dagger.

Is there a way to combine this with my other healing spells and make it more effective? If it is just a general healing spell like Simplified Heal, then what if I was to add in Heal Bone, Heal Scars, Heal Muscle. Could I have a spell that uses Simple Organic Scan to search the body and heal the wounds as it goes? Could those then be combined with the Hallowed Ground spell? A Stamina recovery spell?

Erik felt information starting to click together in his mind.

You have learned the spell: Hallowed Healing Dagger. Your spell book has been updated.

Hallowed Healing Dagger

Master

Attack heals the target struck, creating an area of effect around them that will rapidly heal those wounded around them and harm their enemies. Increases Stamina Regeneration over time. The more enemies within the area of effect, the greater the Stamina and health recovery for allies.

Tier 1 Cast:

300 Mana, costs 50 mana every minute. Covers a 10-meter area.

Tier 2 Cast:

600 Mana, costs 100 mana every minute. Covers a 15-meter area.

For teaching yourself a Master ranked spell, you gain: 50,000,000 EXP

You have reached Level 58

When you sleep next, you will be able to increase your attributes by: 5 points.

39,048,136/70,000,000 EXP till you reach Level 59

Erik blinked. He felt drained, stumbling slightly.

"You okay?" Rugrat asked.

"Uh, yeah." Erik held his hand out. Golden power appeared within the shining blade. It looked to be made of glass. He stabbed it into Rugrat's arm.

"Hey!" Rugrat complained and frowned but he didn't feel any pain as the dagger stuck into his arm.

Hallowed Ground enveloped them both.

"Move around." Erik pushed his fatigue to the side.

Rugrat moved and the Hallowed Ground, a mix of light-green and golden flames, moved around with him at the center.

Erik stopped casting the spell and he started to laugh.

"What did you do?" Rugrat asked.

"Well, I thought of my other spells. Then I combined them together. I was thinking really fast and then with the spell book and my crafting book, they combined somehow," Erik said.

Rugrat waved his hands, a look of inspiration on his face. "If I was to create these chains, could I add in the different enhancements that I have for my rounds, focus on the ones that keep them in place? Then what about the power of the chains? If they are weak, couldn't I use my Simple Inorganic Scan to find the weaknesses and—" Rugrat's eyes moved back and forth and he stopped talking. A few seconds later, he was the one stumbling as golden power from the Ten Realms entered his body.

He raised his hand and chains wrapped around a mannequin on the training area. The mannequin showed the effects of the chains that were filled with the power of poison, lightning, and fire. They were incredibly strong and tightened around the mannequin.

"What do they do?" Erik asked.

"The chains can recover and increase their strength over time with enough mana fed to them. They have a paralysis spell to immobilize, with lightning and fire to passively harm over time. It is really wasteful in power, so I might create a spell that focuses on holding and another that looks at hurting over time. If I was to focus on increasing the strength, the paralysis, then silence…" Rugrat went silent for some time and he held his head.

"New spell—damn, that hurts," Rugrat said as more power entered his head.

"What if I was to combine the healing skills and the Stamina together, then not include the Hallowed Ground?" Erik felt all of the pieces being pulled together, joining information from his Journeyman crafting book and the spell book within his mind.

Divine Healing Dagger

Expert

Attack heals and increases Stamina Regeneration of the one struck.

Cast: 150 Mana

For teaching yourself an Expert-ranked spell, you gain: 5,000,000 EXP

44,048,136/70,000,000 EXP till you reach Level 59

Erik cast a new dagger and threw it at Rugrat, who didn't even notice as chains shot out of the ground and wrapped around a new mannequin. It clamped around it; lightning and flames danced around the mannequin. Rugrat closed his hand and the chains exploded, scarring the mannequin.

Klaus looked at the two freaks. One second he was teaching them Novice level spells and the next they were already starting to create their own advanced versions.

There is a reason that they are city lords of one of the strongest capitals in the Fourth Realm. Klaus couldn't help but shake his head.

He cleared his throat, regaining the two's attention. "Now that you have these spells, you have already formed techniques. By combining your insights with action, you created techniques."

"Techniques is merely the way one shows their knowledge in the physical world," Erik said, as if something clicked for him.

"Now, these are both supporting techniques. You still need something to increase your fighting power directly." Klaus looked through his bag, thinking on their fighting styles, looking at the different spell books and combat art styles.

"Scan." He tossed out those books at them both. "Aerial Mounted Beast Combat style. The Silver Falcons." Klaus looked at George and shrugged, tossing out two more books to Rugrat. "You'll need to both learn that one."

"Abnormal Beast Mount fighting techniques." He tossed out a book at Erik. "Your mount isn't normal. She is strong, great support—this manual will allow you to become closer and allow each of you to react to the other with greater fluidity.

"Erik, are you just going to use your fists?" Klaus looked in his bag.

"It's what I know best," Erik said.

"Movement technique, Cloud Footwork technique."

He threw another book at Rugrat. "Illusionary Fist spell, and then the Unhallowed Strike," Klaus said.

"Lastly, Shade's Covering for both of you and then, Bound Weapon and Aura of Swords for you, Rugrat." Klaus finished dispersing the books. He looked at the duo staring at the books. He nodded and then headed off.

"Make sure to study up. We'll meet here again next week. I hope that you don't take this lightly! I'll test you both personally. Only beaten up one other capital lord before." Klaus chuckled to himself, thinking of his younger and wilder days. He glanced back to see the two pass the books to their mounts and then started to devour spell books and the combat arts that he passed to them.

Their foundations are firm, stronger than some in the Fifth Realm, but their abilities are lacking. He continued on his way, interested to see just how far they would go.

I must be old, this interested in seeing what the younger generation will do.

Erik reviewed the books in his hands: Scan, Abnormal Beast Mount fighting techniques, Illusionary Fist spell, Unhallowed Strike, and Shade's Covering.

Erik took the Scan book.

Scan

Journeyman

Gain a deeper understanding of your opponent's weaknesses.

Cast: 50 Mana

Erik thought about his Simple Inorganic Scan and his information on the human body and other animals he had come to know.

Combat Scan

Journeyman

Gain a deeper understanding of your opponent's physical and technical weaknesses. More advanced information available on species you have studied.

Cast: 50 Mana

For teaching yourself a Journeyman-ranked spell, you gain: 500,000 EXP

He continued, pulling out the Illusionary Fist spell.

Illusionary Fist

Apprentice

Create an illusionary fist.

Cast: 50 Mana

He cast the spell, interested. A fist appeared from his shoulder as he imagined it.

Can I increase the realistic look of the fist? Erik altered the appearance of the fist and the arm so that they looked to be closer to the real version.

Erik fell into building it out; he started to trace out the muscles and the veins as well as the bones.

Semi-Illusionary Fist

Journeyman

Create a fist formed from mana. Hits for 25% of normal attack power.

Cast: 150 Mana

If I could combine the Illusionary, the Semi-Illusionary, and my own fists, then wouldn't it be hard or nearly impossible for someone to figure out where the attack is coming from?

Erik excitedly opened up the Unhallowed Strike.

Unhallowed Strike

Journeyman

Imbue your fist with necrotic damage. Can harm over time. Three second duration.

Cast: 100 Mana

Erik's head spun from all of the information that had been stuffed into it in the last few minutes.

"My damn head," Erik complained. "Feels like when I was consuming all of those books on Alchemy."

Rugrat had laid down at some point in time. "Ow, ow, ow." He was using his hand in the air as he reviewed information in his spell and skill books.

Erik sat down on the edge of the stage and pulled out the books for him and Gilga.

Her books turned into a ray of light and entered her brow. She frowned and found a comfortable plot of stage and laid down, closing her eyes and concentrating.

Erik read the book.

"There are just a few things that people need to take into account when fighting alongside their beast: their size, how they move and act with and without a rider, and how they attack with and without a rider. The rider and the mount must fight together and understand how the other moves and anticipate their attacks to overlap theirs, fluidly defending and attacking, sometimes doing both at the same time." Erik moved past the foreword. There were chapters listed out for different attacks that a beast might use and how the master should react, good positioning, and how to know when their beast was going to attack.

"Looks more like dancing than it looks like fighting, like learning the tango all over again. First I need to know what these new attacks do, so then I can try to figure out how to work Gilly's and my fighting style together."

Erik stood up, having recovered some. He headed to the closest mannequin and checked his mana. It had recovered completely.

"Still, my Mana Regeneration is much higher than my mana pool."

He threw out a semi-illusionary fist. He jabbed forward and it hooked. Both attacks registered.

Erik fired out a hook, and three illusionary fists jabbed in different directions, with one semi-permanent fist within and one semi-illusionary and an illusionary uppercut.

Five hundred mana drained out of him as the hits registered on the mannequin, causing it to rock back and forward.

Erik felt drained again but he was recovering quickly, an ecstatic look on his face.

He used Unhallowed Strike. His fist appeared darker as he struck out. The spell hit the mannequin, leaving a mark and passing over its body before disappearing.

Erik pulled out the last spell book.

Shade's Covering

Apprentice

Cover an area fifteen meters wide in darkness.

Cast: 125 Mana

Erik cast the spell and the area above the stage turned dark. He used his Night Vision to see through it.

"If I was to combine the spells for the different fists spells together, could I also add Night Vision and Shade's Covering—"

His head went off like an explosion.

47

Vuzgal's Land of Experts

Bai Ping walked back to the apartments that he lived in with the members of his family who had decided to stay. They had little after leaving their homes. With the military, the Vuzgal Academy, and the Vuzgal administration needing people, they had applied.

They had been accepted, even with their low levels. It was as if the people of Vuzgal didn't care about levels. Bai Ping's uncle, Bai Xuegang, had warned them to do their best. Some who had started to slack off were directly kicked out. Vuzgal did not suffer fools easily.

They hired and fired people constantly. Only those who worked hard and well with others remained. The Vuzgal administration was still small, but they were potent. Plans and action were quick to be drawn out and discussed and then applied instead of being held up.

Bai Ping had finished training as a regular recruit, only to be thrown into the next training group for the sharpshooters. He had thought he knew how to shoot before but the course was much more in-depth. He learned about sensing spells, how to defeat them, how to call in supporting fire from mages, from mortars. Scouting ahead of a path they were traveling, or scouting enemy positions and reporting on its conditions.

With it, he had killed beasts across the Fourth Realm, increasing his levels so he was no longer weaker than other people from the Fourth Realm.

He had given most of his money over to his uncle in order to grow a business. They had been a family of guards, banned from trading. Now that there were a number of them who were not guards anymore and they were not restricted from trading, many were working under Bai Xuegang to build up the Bai trading house.

Bai entered the apartment he lived in.

Bai Xuegang was there, working at a table. He looked up with an angry look, which relaxed as he saw Bai Ping.

"Sorry, I've been using your place to get away from the others when I need to do work, or else they start asking me how to solve all of their issues." Bai Xuegang was a thin man with a goatee and short hair. He was forty years old but he had a youthful streak within him.

"It's no worries, Uncle." Bai Ping smiled. "How is the business going?"

"Well, we finally got approved for those loans from the Vuzgal bank. With it, I have sent out three different groups to three different locations." Bai Xuegang pulled out a map that had green, red, and blue lines on it.

"The groups will head to the east. They will purchase mounts along the way and follow these trade routes. From the information we have been able to get on these locations, the blue trade route has a number of metal ore veins and mining operations along it, the green line has a number of rare ingredients that are harvested there, and the red line is supposed to have a large number of beasts in the area, so we should be able to purchase the animal products for resale here. We will build up a trade caravan that goes to these locations and farther. As our family members graduate from the academy, then we might be able to get higher quality goods that we can sell directly to these places, or here in Vuzgal," Bai Xuegang said with an excited look.

"So what are the others doing in the meantime? Have you paid for the tuition of those in the academy?"

"I have paid for the deposit and as much as I can, but we are using these loans all over the place. I found out that I can consolidate them so they are much more manageable. The family is working at any job they can find. All of them pay well compared to what we had before, but the cost of items is greater here."

"They're of a much higher quality," Bai Ping said.

"That is true." Xuegang sighed and then looked at Bai Ping. "Why are you back? Shouldn't you be training?"

"I have been given new orders. I will be heading off to do more in-depth training. I will be gone for three months at least."

"Have they told you what you will be doing?"

"Training to get qualified for artillery, magic, and mortars and then hopefully some more in-depth engineering and medic courses," Bai Ping said.

"Medic? Will that allow you to help us with our constitution?"

"It should. I have talked to the medics I know and have gone to the hospital. They say that through body tempering, it will take more to complete, but then we will all increase greatly in strength." Bai Ping was still falling behind the others in physical standards. He had pushed himself past his previous limits with his levels.

Bai Ping couldn't tell anyone else that they not only talked about Body Cultivation, but that if one had to pay for it, or reached a certain standard, then they would get an increase to their cultivation from the hospital.

If I can make it into the CPD, then they will advance my Body Cultivation all the way to Body Like Stone and they will help me in opening all of my mana gates. The special teams apparently have unlimited resources and the city lords personally assist them from time to time.

"Seems like Vuzgal has become our new home," Bai Xuegang said.

"Make sure that the family does their job first and assists their family second," Bai Ping said in warning.

"I know—the leaders of Vuzgal care about what people can do, not their backing. I have told the others this already. When do you leave?"

"I leave in four days."

Hiao Xen looked at the flourishing capital. There was a haze around the castle from the high purity of contained mana.

His eyes looked to the Vuzgal Academy. Students came from across the Fourth, Fifth, and Third Realms to enroll. Those who were willing to sign contracts to join Vuzgal afterward were given priority, but others who were associated with people working for Vuzgal came second and then those who were independent and able to pay for their way came afterward, with the sects' students following behind.

There was at least one Expert-level teacher for each subject now. With Rugrat's return, the library underwent an extensive renovation. It didn't take long with the power of magic, high strength manual labor, and the blueprint office. Now it had become a central building, resting between the inner castle and the outer wall in the middle of the campus that took over a third of the outer area.

Even the Expert-level teachers who hadn't had high expectations of the reading materials and only cared about the workshops and materials were shocked by the content of the library shelves.

His eyes moved across the landscape to the totem that worked all hours of the day, allowing people in and out of Vuzgal. Just from fees alone, they were able to make a heavy profit.

A bartering area had been set up and regulated by Vuzgal. This was great for adventuring teams and fighters. They could leave their items up for sale for a price and a stocking fee, and then others could bid and barter with them. Vuzgal contacted the teams with information; if they agreed, the item was sold and the money was held by Vuzgal for when the seller collected it.

One had to pay one Mortal mana stone to have their item listed and then one hundred gold a day every day it was listed and didn't sell. It was expensive, so that the bartering area wasn't flooded. Still, there were adventure teams that were happy to put up their items that were worth several Earth mana stones. Not only could they get money from the buyers, they could accept gear and items as well. These did not have a stocking fee and could be held for a month without charge, making it highly convenient.

It certainly worked in interesting adventure teams to come over and put their goods up for sale. As they were here, they checked the dungeons, the area around Vuzgal, the crafters for supplies, and then the Battle Arena.

Hiao Xen smiled. "The houses and plots of land should go for a high price."

Hiao Xen turned from the window and headed out through the offices. Things were still quick paced, but it wasn't the scene of chaos that it had been when he originally arrived.

He headed out of the castle, being met by a group of his personal guards mixed in with the guards from the Vuzgal military.

Their strength has increased again. These must be the people from Dragon Combat Company. Strong enough for the fourth realm. The more I hear about the higher realms and their combat standards, the more I understand why they do competitions instead of waging battles. The losses from a battle could cripple an organization. Fighters capable of using fighting techniques are a power onto themselves, but take a massive amount of resources to train.

Hiao Xen boarded his carriage and they headed out into the capital. People made way for the Vuzgal guards on their panther mounts.

The people got more packed in together the farther they went but people still moved to the side as they reached the day's most popular location.

Hiao Xen stepped out of the carriage and looked at the Vuzgal auction house. It was simply laid out. On the first floor, people could sell goods to the auction house or put them up to be bid on. Then they were sent to the different auction houses.

The building was wide and squat, with three auction houses on top of one another: the main auction house, the advanced, and the superior. The main was the largest, with the advanced and superior being smaller each time. They could all be opened up to one another, stacked upon one another, or left cut off.

The main auction house was used for the general auction that happened once every two days. The advanced auction hall required someone to have an auction house membership and pay a fixed rate of an Earth mana stone every two weeks to be able to access. This Earth mana stone could be counted with their bids if they appeared or was retained by the auction house if they didn't. An auction was carried out here once a week but it had items of much greater value, many being of the high Journeyman level and with a few reaching the Expert level.

The superior auction house was the Elite auction hall. It required one to have a superior auction house membership, which was one Earth mana cornerstone each month. Here, Expert-level items and the rare Master-level item would be sold off.

We might talk about Experts a lot but still, only Tan Xue is an Expert who is truly a person of the Vuzgal Academy. The other Experts are here on contracts and are not part of our reliable strength. Vuzgal trades in these items a lot but we are a capital. For the smaller crafters, these items are incredibly rare.

Hiao Xen smiled as people talked about him as he walked up to the auction house. He was escorted to a VIP booth, allowing him to look over the proceedings. The auction houses had been opened up, with the superior having the greatest view over the main stage.

With all of the building, our funds are starting to get low. Hopefully the auction brings good results.

People settled into their seats. The entire auction was packed, even with the lowest in the main auction hall having to have at least twenty Earth mana stones on them to attend.

Those on the main hall floor looked up at those in the higher booths with jealousy.

Even the superior booths were filled, a few powers buying out the different memberships to get a location.

Hiao Xen's smile grew wider as he saw the person on stage. *The famed Elise. Oh, this should be interesting.*

"Welcome, welcome!" Elise looked to the people in the auction house and, directing her eyes higher, she bowed to those in the highest seats.

"Today is the opening of Vuzgal's house and land auction. Don't worry—Vuzgal has plenty of locations open for sale! A reminder that for this auction we will only be using Mana stones as a form of currency. All other trades are off the table." Elise's blinding smile blunted the statement and people sat taller, looking at others who lowered their heads or started to grumble.

"With that, let us start!" She activated a formation and a drawing appeared above her. Those in the superior and advanced booths had formations within their booths that allowed them to scroll through the information.

"These apartments?" someone said.

"It must be like those large buildings that the people who work for Vuzgal live in."

"The first building here is an apartment building. Each residence has a kitchen and open space to entertain guests, with a mixed number of bathrooms and bedrooms. All locations will have illumination formations, heating and cooling formations for the rooms and for the water, with the power being supplied by the tenant. The space can be upgraded and the spare rooms turned into crafting or storage rooms. It is also possible to add in your own formations to your self-contained unit—mana gathering, mana purifying. Sound cancellation formations are included so you and your neighbors won't even know the others are there. Though the best part is the location!" She waved up and the image changed. A map appeared of Vuzgal.

"It lies in the inner city and is on a direct road between the growing marketplace, the auction hall on one side and the workspaces that are inside the inner city on the other. *With* a direct route to Associations' Circle!"

The crafters all leaned forward. They didn't need much in the way of accommodation. They spent most of their days working in the workshops, anyway. Something that was permanent that they could store their items in and was positioned well was perfect for them.

People wearing uniforms for the auction hall walked into the different halls and booths.

"My associates have floor plans with them that they will pass around. Please take a look. In five minutes, we will start the bidding! You will need to give your bid to them and then the formation above me will change," Elise said.

Ten blueprints appeared above her, showing it broken up into different sections with numbers on each for the different apartments.

The people from the auction hall distributed the reading materials and people looked through the apartment plans quickly.

The atmosphere was tense as people talked excitedly to one another as they found different plans that suited their needs.

Elise tapped her hammer lightly. "I hope you have enjoyed browsing the apartment plans. We will start the bidding now!"

In the superior and the advanced booths, there were more attendants, with one to each of the patrons in the superior booth and one for every three in the advanced. On the regular floor, there was one for every ten.

People called out bids to their attendants and numbers appeared underneath the apartment numbers, denoting the number of Earth stones people were willing to part with.

She did not give them a base number to start from—from the beginning, they are competing with one another. Not knowing who their opponents are, they can't be pressured externally to stop bidding due to the power behind them.

Hiao Xen studied it all. The lower floor apartments were smaller but had the basic necessities. As one went up floors, they gained more room. The tenth floor was broken into just four apartments, with the largest rooms and views that looked over the capital.

The bids climbed at an alarming rate in just a few minutes. Many people were knocked out of the competition as it went higher.

"Look at those prices! Two hundred and forty regular Earth stones for the lowest apartment!"

"That's nothing—those highest levels are selling for four and a half Sky stones!"

The numbers started to slow down and Elise brought her hammer down if the bids didn't move in ten seconds.

It built up the pressure as people kept up their bids, increasing their price instead of hesitating for fear of her selling it off.

Hiao Xen's eyes shone, feeling the energy that filled the room.

"Hah, it is a good thing that I sold that new Journeyman bow I just finished or else I wouldn't have had enough mana stones!"

The hammer continued to drop, quicker now. People were running out of funds as the numbers climbed.

The hammer started to slow down as the last bids were placed.

Hiao Xen scanned the information. *With just one building, we made nearly one hundred and thirty Sky mana stones.*

"Thank you for your patronage!" Elise said with a wide smile.

Crafters have most of their money tied up in their ingredients and equipment. There are still a number of plots that we can build more apartments on in the future.

"Up next, we have an apartment building located in the outer city between the Battle Arena and roads that lead out to the dungeon valley and to the eastern and northern gates, with easy access to the marketplace and Associations' Circle! A perfect location for any fighter or adventurer teams. The plans are the same as those listed in the first apartment building. We will start the bidding in five minutes!"

Adventurers had a lot more funds with them and Elise quickly collected more than one hundred and sixty Sky stones from the bidders.

Then she moved to land agreements. There were three properties that were up to be bid on. These properties didn't have anything on them and it was up to the buyer to build upon them. The first was located between Associations' Circle and the workshops; the other was located between the workshops and the auction hall. The third was positioned between the Associations' Circle and the Battle Arena.

The first went for 345 Sky mana stones; the second 521; the third 289.

Then there were the stores. These were not purchases but instead rental agreements. There were store locations around the Battle Arena, around the associations, around the workshops, the totem and auction hall and between these locations. There were only fifteen up for rent. People didn't dare to complain. Many gripped their seats in excitement, seeing the auction house explode as the merchants went to war with their assets.

For a three-year rental, the stores would pay 120 Sky mana stones on average. As a secondary benefit, they would receive a lower taxation rate on their sales, which alone made their eyes shine in excitement.

Hiao Xen was stunned by the numbers that he had seen displayed here.

"Elise is her own force." Hiao Xen chuckled to himself and stood as the auction came to an end and Elise bowed to those who had competed within the auction. People felt pleased with their purchases; others vowed to bring more money next time. Others simply enjoyed the display that had been put on.

With the extra funds, we can hire on some more people, speed up the rate that we expand the capital, and start building the secondary workshops in the outer city. We can offer higher loans and commission outside crafters to manufacture the supplies we need for the capital.

The metal in front of Tan Xue sang to her. Instead of her hand being numb with the vibrations, her body was in tune with the metal. It felt like an extension of herself. She injected mana into it, and drew out a pink fruit and put it on the blade. It sizzled and started to deform as she beat it into the metal.

Her hammer fell into a rhythm, shaping into a bracer. She quenched it and put it to the side. She wiped her forehead with the back of her hand and put the bracer down next to another.

The two shook slightly. A pink energy transferred between them both as they resonated with each other.

Tan Xue touched them both, comparing her analysis.

"They're about eighty-five percent similar, enough to create a resonance. With them both equipped, the effects will be stronger," Tan Xue assessed, opening her eyes and looking at them both.

She gathered them up and wiped her face with a rag as she exited the Expert workshop. She passed people, not caring about her appearance as she made it to the formation workshop.

Qin was there. Tan Xue slowed so as to not interrupt her.

There were two identical swords in front of her. Tan Xue had been the one to craft them.

Qin didn't even notice her. The carving tool in her hand flowed. It was more natural now. It looked as if she were a practiced calligrapher: each movement powerful, concise, and thought out; one flowed into the next without pause.

Qin worked on the left sword. To her right, there was a wispy image of her hand and the tool. One could see through it, watching the enchantment carved into the metal. The tool contained the enhancer and reactant required for the formation, leaving behind a fiery orange through the enchantments.

Tan Xue watched, entranced by what she was seeing.

Qin finished off the beautiful enchantments on each and then closed her eyes. Power from the Ten Realms was stirred up. A golden glow appeared around her body. Qin's eyes were closed in deep thought, as if she had realized something.

Did she make a breakthrough?

Tan Xue stood there as Qin's body glowed with the Experience that flooded her before it started to settle down. She opened her eyes, looking at the weapons in front of her.

"It is not just about the process but its purpose, like rivers that flow through the land, enriching one another. Like paper that is perfected by the calligraphy, bringing the blank page to life. Enchanting is combining the purpose, with function and the materials. Gaining greater strength across all.

Enchantments change so much as they need to adapt to different materials in order to draw out different effects." Qin pulled out paper and quickly started to write on it.

She didn't notice it but there were three hands on the page, each of them writing at the same time. They weren't repeating the first line, but each of them wrote a part of a whole that came together perfectly.

Qin turned to Tan Xue and saw the bracers in her hand.

She waved her hand. Using her mana she picked up the bracers and put them on her table. She stared at them, studying them.

She moved off to the side and pulled out a piece of paper and a brush. Several hands crowded around her hand as they worked together, each of them taking on a different section that formed together in a perfect and satisfactory way.

Even with the brush, her lines were clean, her circles perfect.

She pulled out another piece of paper, working faster than the first time. She repeated it three different times and made five different enchantments.

She looked at the final enchantment and then moved to the preparation station. She took out a clean carving tool and different reactants, combined them together to create an ink for the carving tool, and filled it up. Several other carving tools appeared in her hand and she poured ink into them all.

She moved back to the bracers. Four hands appeared around her own hand and several appeared over the other bracer.

Her carving tools worked on the metal, leaving behind black lines in the silver metal.

Tan Xue knew that state; she had been in it many times. Inside the academy and the workshops, it was easy for one to fall into a state of enlightenment.

Tan Xue moved to the twin swords, studying them. They were nearly identical. One was shorter than the other and was made to be mounted on a spear instead of being turned into a true sword.

Tan Xue studied them both. The enchantments were similar when looking at them, made in the same style, but their effects were different.

Flaming Silaz Spearhead

Attack: 130

Weight: 2.5 kg
Health: 100/100
Charge: 100/100
Innate Effect: Increase damage by 8%
Increase blunt by 9%
Enchantment:
Ember Edge—inflict burning damage for 5/s on target
Flame Giant's Strength—for two minutes, increase strength by 150%. Cooldown—three hours
Requirements:
Agility 65
Strength 72

Flaming Silaz Sword
Attack: 147
Weight: 5.7 kg
Health: 100/100
Charge: 100/100
Innate Effect: Increase damage by 8%
Increase speed by 9%
Enchantment:
Ember Edge—inflict burning damage for 5/s on target
Flaming Strike—Inflict 150% flame damage on targets within a 20m area in front of you. Cooldown—two hours
Requirements:
Agility 70
Strength 53

"They looked so similar and they are, but then the innate effects I was able to draw out with the enhancers and my skill have only been compounded on with the Ember Edge and the Flaming Strike and Flame Giant's Strength that draw on the power of the weapon to create a possible life-saving skill." Tan Xue looked at the blades. Each of them was a true Expert masterpiece, from the weapon to the enchantments.

Tan Xue looked over as Qin finished with the bracers.

She closed her eyes. A look of fatigue appeared on her face, but there was also another of searching as she threw out brushes and her several hands worked together, creating new notes.

Silence fell over the room as she worked.

Tan Xue stood there as Qin finished writing. Her other hands disappeared as she took a breath and opened her eyes.

"Unless I missed the mark, welcome to the Expert level," Tan Xue said.

Qin noticed her for the first time and she opened and closed her mouth, looking at the bracers and then Tan Xue before she hurriedly pulled up her notifications.

"I did it!" She seemed stunned and lost before her excitement met up with her understanding. "I did it! I'm an Expert formation master!" Qin laughed and hugged Tan Xue, who patted her on the back and laughed. "Julilah is going to be so jealous!"

"What is that technique you were using?" Tan Xue asked.

"It's the Many Hands technique. In the formation academy, I looked at combat and how people make formations. I had the idea of overlapping formations. So I added in a spell, Manipulate Object. I have been using it to copy out the same formation on different items—it works. Though when I was working on my brothers' weapons, I wanted the enchantments to align with the innate effects and with their fighting styles. I kind of sunk into thought and started to enchant them both at the same time, but with different enchantments. The information I had and then the spells, even my calligraphy lessons, all seemed to slam into one and I just followed what my instincts were telling me. Then, with the bracers, I wanted to check on what I had learned.

"I wasn't drawing out the best of the item, just looking to increase the enchantments before. I could use the hands to create one formation fluidly without breaks—that's what I was checking with the blueprints. Then I worked with the bracers. There are differences between them. Instead of that being a weakness, I created different formations in both that, when they work together, raise the effectiveness of them. They will increase a person's defense and create a mana barrier when they need it. Use them together and it will cover them all; apart and then it will only create a shield-sized barrier.

"Each of the hands is working on one section, but together they create a formation, tying the materials and purpose of the item through formations." Qin now looked around the room with hungry eyes.

"I'll work on making some more Expert-level weapons. I've got rather quick at it," Tan Xue said.

"Sweet! I'll see if I can get more items that are complete from the other crafters and enchant it. I could also work on the defensive enchantments on the walls. I need to increase my Mana Gathering Cultivation and my mental abilities to be able to create more hands and control them at the same time. What will this mean for my combat capabilities!"

Qin stumbled a bit, holding her head and groaning.

"First, take some time to rest. Write notes on what you feel and what you think for others who want to be Experts." Tan Xue pulled out a Stamina potion and pushed Qin to a seat.

She took the potion and drank it, still holding her head.

48 Revelation

Bai Ping checked his gear for the third time and moved in his armor.

"So where are we going, Sergeant?" he asked Sergeant Li.

Sergeant Li smiled mysteriously. "You'll see."

"Come on, Sarge. You're acting all mysterious. We haven't been able to get anything from anyone else," Private Mossa complained.

"Patience is its own reward."

Dragon Platoon left with just fifty people, but then they came back with a full combat company. Their corporals and sergeants haven't trained in as many areas as our leadership has, but their individual strength is much higher than ours.

"Why did we have to sign a new contract yesterday, Sarge?" Bai Ping asked.

"You'll see soon enough. And you must never forget your oaths." Sergeant Li's tone turned hard as he looked into Bai Ping's eyes.

"Yes, Sarge."

Sergeant Li looked to the others, who all came to attention and agreed.

"Trust me, you wouldn't believe me if I told you." Li shook his head and the corners of his mouth turned upward.

"Move into formation!" one of the officers yelled out.

The different squads moved into position, creating rifle platoons, artillery and support platoons. They stretched across the parade square.

Captain Yui marched out and stood in front of them.

"All right, we've got a path right to the totem cleared. We will march down through Associations' Circle, down the main road and take a left to the totem. We will go by platoon, First Rifle Platoon followed by Second Rifle Platoon, Third Artillery Platoon, and Fourth Support Platoon. Does this fuck anyone up?" Yui looked through the company, eyeing a few of the troublemakers.

"Nope? Good." Yui let out a slight grin and then it disappeared as soon as it appeared. "You are representing Tiger Company and the Vuzgal regiment! Do not forget that. Company!"

They snapped together, alert.

"To the right, right turn!"

The entire company snapped around to the right. There was something deeply satisfying about working as one complete body.

Yui marched out to the head of the formation. "Forward, march!"

They moved as one and headed toward the gates of the training ground.

Dragon Platoon watched them as they were leaving, opening the gates to the training area and pushing ahead with their mounts to clear a path for Tiger Company.

People stood in the streets and watched as the unit passed.

Bai Ping looked at the people out of the corner of his eye. He didn't know what to expect when he had joined the Vuzgal regiment. Training had changed the way he looked at the world and taught him how to be a soldier.

They marched through the roads. The gates to the totem were opened as Bai Ping's First Platoon moved around the totem.

Captain Yui accessed the command interface and they all disappeared in a flash of light.

They appeared around another totem.

"Forward, march! Clear the formation!" Yui ordered as they all double time marched off the totem and headed down a curving road.

There were people cheering and clapping as they headed off.

They cleared the formation and a few seconds later, the second platoon followed in a flash of light.

What is this place? The mana concentration is so high! There is a ceiling? There are glowing rocks on the ceiling.

No one gave answers but as he saw the veterans of the unit barely holding their grins, Bai Ping wanted to grill them. They were clearly enjoying the silent torture that their fellows were going through.

They reached a large barracks and marched inside. Even though he was filled with questions, Bai Ping didn't stop marching, nor did anyone else. They trusted one another with their lives.

Major Glosil was waiting for them inside the barracks. The last of the platoons stepped into formation and their commanding lieutenant turned with them to face him.

Captain Yui walked out and gave command over to Glosil.

"At ease!" Major Glosil said.

He was a quiet man but none had seen his strength. He was the leader of the military. They had only seen him a few times so he was still a mysterious figure.

"You are all members of the Alva Army and the Vuzgal regiment. It's about time you learned what Alva was. *This*"—he gestured to the barracks and the city beyond—"is Alva. A dungeon controlled by the city lords. You will be here for three months for training. Training to get your qualifications for promotion. Many of you are privates still. By the end of this, you will all be corporals at the very least. While you are here, you will be able to enroll in classes with the academy to learn different crafting skills. We don't want just trigger pullers here in the Alva Army—we need skilled soldiers. People who know how to make concoctions, know how to repair their bows and staffs, know how to make war weapons. Can see the weakness in a castle's construction. Here, we walk the path of Elite. You will get out as much as you put in. All lessons at the academy are paid for by the military." Glosil looked over them all. They stood tall as he seemed to weigh their worth.

"Very good, Captain Yui. Get your people settled. Classes will start in two days."

"Yes, sir." Yui saluted Glosil, who returned it and headed off into the barracks.

Yui turned to face them all. "I expect the very best from each and every one of you. You have all completed your basic training and some of you have had the fortune to complete your sharpshooter courses at the very least.

Training schedules will be posted. Your sergeants will pick out your training schedule. Any time that you have free between training, you will report here every morning. You will carry out fitness once a week. The rest of the time will be free. I would suggest that you head to the academy to learn there. Talk to the staff and older members of your unit. They are alive because of their training and what they learned here. Alva is your home now. Unless you are given permission from the city lords themselves, you will never reveal any information about Alva. Am I understood?"

They could feel Yui's protectiveness and determination. They could feel the same thing from the veterans within their units.

"Yes, sir!" they yelled out as one.

Bai Ping felt pride at being brought into such a big secret.

Erik awoke with two new notifications.

Illusionary Unhallowed Strike

Expert

You attack with three illusionary fists and a semi-illusionary fist imbued with necrotic damage that can harm over time.

Tier 1 Cast: 425 Mana

Tier 2 Cast: 850 Mana 5 Illusionary, 3 Semi-Illusionary

For teaching yourself an Expert-ranked spell, you gain: 5,000,000 EXP

Shade's Covering

Journeyman

Cover an area fifteen meters wide. In darkness, you see through it as clear as day.

Cast: 140 Mana

For teaching yourself a Journeyman-ranked spell, you gain: 500,000 EXP

51,048,136/70,000,000 EXP till you reach Level 59

Because I passed out, I wasn't able to pick what to put my points into.

With a groan, he looked around his room in Vuzgal. He checked the time and got up. He stretched and used his Clean spell.

He pushed up against the top of the bed and opened his character sheet.

Name: Erik West	
Level: 57 *Race: Human*	
Titles: *From the Grave II* *Mana Emperor* *Dungeon Master III* *Reverse Alchemist* *Poison Body* *Fire Body* *City Lord*	
Strength: (Base 36) +41	770
Agility: (Base 29) +72	555
Stamina: (Base 39) +23	930
Mana: (Base 8) +79	870
Mana Regeneration: (Base 13) +58	36.50/s
Stamina Regeneration: (Base 41) +59 21.00/s	

"Who would have thought I would have got to this stage? Faster than a damn car, as strong as a crane, and take hits like a tank," Erik said as he studied his stats.

My three weakest stats are Stamina, Mana Regeneration, and Strength. I can recover Stamina with concoctions, so I haven't cared about it much. I still need to develop my Mana Regeneration. Strength I can increase with gear and concoctions as well. Well, I can do that with Mana Regeneration but now I know how I have an increased control over Fire and Earth mana. Mana is now much more useful.

Still, that Stamina is really low at sixty-two overall and the next lowest being seventy-one.

"Three into Mana Regeneration and two into Stamina." Erik pulled out a sleeping concoction and poured it down his throat. He shook his head at the taste, but with the other ingredients he sampled, it wasn't the worst.

He was met with an old screen.

You have 5 attribute points to use.

He smiled and input the changes quickly.

Name: Erik West	
Level: 58	*Race: Human*
Titles: *From the Grave II* *Mana Emperor* *Dungeon Master III* *Reverse Alchemist* *Poison Body* *Fire Body* *City Lord*	
Strength: (Base 36) +41	770
Agility: (Base 29) +72	555
Stamina: (Base 39) +25	960
Mana: (Base 8) +79	870
Mana Regeneration: (Base 13) +61	38.00/s
Stamina Regeneration: (Base 41) +59 21.00/s	

He woke up a few minutes later. He could feel the higher amount of mana entering his body and felt more satiated than before. He stood and saw he had a number of messages on his sound transmission device.

"Qin has made a breakthrough to Expert formation master. I don't think that Julilah is far behind." Tan Xue's voice filled his ears as he got another message from Elise.

"We were able to rent out the next lot of buildings, total profit of thirty-two hundred and thirty-seven Sky mana stones—="

"What!" Erik yelled.

"And nine hundred and fifty-three Earth mana stones. We didn't get that many actual Sky mana stones. I have been looking at the different traders inside Vuzgal. Many of them are coming to trade here but there are very few of them who are looking to put their base of operations in Vuzgal. I want to see if we can get people to start more trade houses here. If they are coming from here originally, then they will come back more often and they will fall and rise with us. We could also hold a stake with them and offer them better loans. I am seeing the other merchants moving around and taking over, and I don't like having an external force owning our markets and a large portion of our power.

"Also, I wanted to talk to you about the agreements we have with the association and talked to Hiao Xen. We can get them to amend their terms. Right now the Alchemist Association and the Blue Lotus have agreements with you and Rugrat; with the new changes, they will have agreements with Vuzgal as a whole, which will make it so that they can't go back on their agreement in the future."

It was at this point that the special teams burst into his room, looking around for threats.

"Elise," Erik said, tapping his communication device as she kept talking.

"—Do you want me to proceed on this?"

Erik used the communication device and sent a message. "I agree to raising more merchants from within Vuzgal, having them tied to us. Also see if the Blue Lotus and the association will change their agreement, separating the different contracts from personal and those that they have with Vuzgal."

He looked at the special team. "All right, where is Rugrat?"

"He's still sleeping it off," Storbon reported.

"Okay." Erik pulled out his Journeyman-level Alchemy book. He checked the formula in there for the Revitalization Tree Sap. He checked the ingredients and then his notes.

"Okay, looks like we have some of these in the Alchemy department, and my shift at the healing house doesn't start for another three hours. I'll collect the ingredients and start preparing them, then work in the ward."

49 Selling Favors and Buying Allies

Emmanuel Fayad sat on the highest platform. Around the circular room, there were the different leaders of the Fayad family. They all sat on different platforms to denote their rank and the location of the different areas they managed: the outpost, trade, fighting forces, and internal family matters.

"A quarter of our fighting force, food and supplies for our forces, two hundred gold and we will be the base of operations for it all. That will make us the biggest target of the other outposts that don't want this to happen and we're still paying the same amount as the others!" The trading leader, Reema Fayad, shook her head.

"If we are able to make the path and the outpost, we will have one of the first roads through the Beast Mountain Range. Surely that will be worth more in the long run," Umar, the leader of the family, said.

"It might, but can we be sure that we will complete this road? If the others agree, then we will have a fighting force to do it. Are we strong enough to deal with everything that is in there? We are doing Aditya's work for him!" Reema's voice rose.

Emmanuel cleared his throat, calming the tensions in the room. "Reema, what scares you?"

"We are making ourselves a target for others. If we are the base of this road, then we are the main point to attack. We have one of the widest trading networks of any outpost. We are sure to lose some of those people as our caravans are cut off. We have no surety that this will even succeed. Even if it does, what happens to us?"

"We must take risks to earn rewards. Once this road is completed, then we will rent out our services to the other outpost leaders to connect them to King's Hill Outpost. We are not making anything off this first road, but then we can earn more helping out the others at a reduced cost." Emmanuel pulled out three different contracts and put them down.

"This contract is for the reduced taxation of all goods between the agreed outposts and allowing traders from other outposts access to theirs. It has been sent out and agreed to by several already. The next is an agreement for the council of King's Hill Outpost. There will be one main representative who will control the outpost for three years and then the leaders can vote to change them. They will make five percent more than the other outpost lords if we profit; otherwise, they will need to forfeit the pay they get for the year and can be voted for re-election. Major decisions will be decided by the council, which is made up of all the outpost leaders who join.

"The third is a mutual defense contract. The council in the previous document will assist one another. If one is attacked, then the others will attack the attacker and assist the attacked lord in defense. It also stipulates that the money that we have put forward will be put to expenses associated with building the first road, dealing with any major attacks and then building the King's Hill Outpost. The materials will be sources from the outpost leaders. We, the Fayad family, will be in charge of building the road. Once we site the outpost, then Aditya has supplied us with a blueprint for the outpost to rapidly increase our building time. I have studied it. There are places for people to stay, a small healing house, an auction hall, stables, inns, smithies, and a sparring area." With a wave of his hand, attendants took the contracts and passed them to the other leaders.

"With this, I am satisfied," Umar said.

"Reema?" Emmanuel asked.

"I still think we will become a target. I ask that we start pulling back caravans to make sure that they aren't used to retaliate against us," Reema said.

"Send them messages, but nothing overt." Emmanuel turned his head to Nasreen.

"What about afterward? Lord Aditya is not a simple man," she said.

A hint of a smile appeared on Emmanuel's face. "That is something that I have been debating. I feel that he has a number of cards to play. I feel like this young pup is really a wolf who is watching us dance in front of him. I don't know what will happen. From these contracts and our interactions, I don't think that he wants to wage war against us all. Though I think he does want to swallow us."

"He can try," Umar said darkly.

"I put this to you: if it comes to pass that he does want us to become part of his power, what do we do?"

"We fight." Umar shook his fist.

Emmanuel turned to Nasreen.

"We will need the help of all our allies and then more. It would be a hard fight. He is far away; we would need to loop around the Beast Mountain Range. With his people, I think he might be able to go right through it. If we siege his walls…" Nasreen shook her head. "I don't think we would be able to take Vermire easily. Yes, they used the power of other nations to defeat the Zatan Confederation, but their guards are well-trained, the people love Aditya, and he has a healing house, while we have weaker healing solutions. His people can get hurt and come back stronger; ours will need time to rest. They sold off war mounts, weapons, and armor. If they wanted, another kingdom or empire would happily swallow them and assist them in defeating us."

"We have two options," Emmanuel said, drawing eyes back to him. "We go all in from the start and we prove to Aditya and the others our strength. Otherwise we wait until the dust settles and make our move. Afterward, our rewards will be much smaller." Emmanuel opened his arms, leaving it to them.

"We go all in," Reema said with a sigh.

Emmanuel raised his brows and she gave a weak smile.

"Agreed." Nasreen followed.

"Now I feel like we are leaping into the tiger's mouth. What if he wants to take us over?" Umar asked.

"From the beginning, we have been traders. Our guards are strong but our tongues are faster." Emmanuel smiled. "If we prove our strength and our traders' abilities, we will step onto a new stage of trading across all of the Beast Mountain Range and beyond."

"Let us show them the strength of the Fayad family," Umar said.

Ryan Mills paced in his main hall. His captain guard entered, with a note in his hand. It was made of black paper.

Mills opened the paper and read the words inside.

You might have stepped over my head, but with Lady Sumi on my side, no matter your plans—you will fail.

"Secretly gather mercenaries who would be interested in making a little more coin. We will use them to bolster our own strength in attacking the other outpost leaders. We need to prove our strength to get better trading rights and more loot in the future," Mills told his guard.

"Yes, my lord." The guard nodded and left the hall.

Mills was not the only person to receive a letter. Evernight and Aditya were looking through the notes that were on the table. The contract in the middle of the table changed as a new signature was added.

"And that makes it twenty-three outpost lords." Aditya put down the last note.

"Twenty-one of which we can truly trust," Evernight said.

"Was it worth it, adding in the two spies?" Aditya asked.

"None of them know who is allied with you or not. With the different discussions and groups, the two spies will need to be careful. There are twenty-six other lords who might be interested in the news. If they learn of our plans ahead of time or as we are carrying them out, they have three options: attack, do nothing, or try to see if they can join. It is our job to stabilize the Beast Mountain Range. In the end, the aim is to have you as the leader of the Beast Mountain Range and those who are capable as helpers. Those who aren't will be relegated to a comfortable position, but without any power to shake our foundations."

"It's when you say things like that I remember just how much strength you wield. Makes me wonder why don't you just make them change."

"We do not want to expose our power if we don't have to. This way, we can know their true sentiments, know how they think before we move forward. How would you, or the others, grow if you didn't have some difficulties in your path?" Evernight smiled.

Aditya sighed. "All right, I will send out the orders. In two weeks, our forces will be at Shadowridge to break ground on the first road to King's Hill Outpost."

"Looks like you beat me fair and square." Domonos walked up to Yui, who was looking at the group of men and women headed out into the city to celebrate.

"First group fully qualified. Hard to believe that they will be the officers and CPD squads in a few weeks if they pass." Yui smiled as he looked to Domonos.

They fell silent as they looked over the barracks.

"It's completely different from what we were trained as kids to do. I thought that those with the best techniques were the best to lead," Domonos said.

"Now the pressure is to be stronger so that we can make sure that as many of our people make it back as possible. So that we don't need to sleep as much, so that they don't have to worry about losing us and so we can provide a greater impact in the fight ahead," Yui said.

"We don't need the strongest people leading us; we need the best people leading us. Erik and Rugrat gave command to Glosil, not because he is stronger, but he is better at leading and organizing people." Domonos snorted. "How hard you hit is not everything."

"You sure you're my brother? Doesn't seem like something you would say!" Yui laughed.

"We've changed since joining Alva. In more ways than just our fighting ability—our way of thinking is different too."

"People understand when we talk about increasing our strength, but not how we live with the possibility of dying and laying down our life for the others around us." Yui leaned on the railing again.

"I guess they just don't understand. Unless you've put your life in someone else's hands and they've put theirs in yours, you don't know what that bond is like, what this is all about," Domonos said. Yui grunted as the two scanned the barracks.

"I never felt like I belonged when I was training to be a trader, but as an officer, it feels *right.* It's shit at times—damn, it's shit." Yui's voice grew quieter and he looked at his hands. He saw the faces of those under his command and hadn't made it back.

"Though seeing them all working together, working for a singular goal, one order having the ability to change everything—it's a lot of responsibility, a lot of pressure to take them out, to complete the mission and bring them all back."

"But you wouldn't trust it to anyone else," Domonos said, filling in what Yui felt but didn't want to voice.

"Yeah." Yui nodded.

They stood there for a few minutes and turned as they heard someone approaching.

A formation master with a frantic expression ran up to them, pulling out two wrapped items. "Your sister sent me over with these. She says she's sorry but she had broken through to Expert. Oh, she said that you were lucky enough to get the first ones. And, uh…" The formation master looked awkward. "Don't break them." He coughed and bowed quickly, bobbing as he backed away. "Got to go—she promised me a class!"

Yui and Domonos shook their heads as the formation master fled the barracks.

"Looks like Qin'er is terrorizing the lower ranks of formation masters still."

"Either he is really looking forward to that lesson or terrified," Domonos said.

"Probably both. Have you looked in a mirror? You'd crack it."

Domonos opened the wrapped bundle and looked at the weapons inside.

Yui took the spear. He turned it in his hands, closing his eyes as it sung in the air. Domonos unsheathed the sword, giving a few practice swings.

"Balanced perfectly for me, focusing on increasing strength." Yui spun the spear behind his back and shot it out forward, the spear in perfect balance with his body. With his reactions, the two came together harmoniously.

Faint sparks floated off Yui's new spearhead with his thrust. He retracted his spear and studied it closer. He looked up, seeing Domonos move with his blade.

Domonos had trained with weapons since he was a young boy. Their father had not once denied his boy's tutors and teachers from the First Realm. With his connections, he was able to get his hands on trainers and manuals that kings wouldn't be able to acquire.

There was once a vast gulf between the two brothers but with joining Alva earlier on, he had been able to bridge that gap.

They had both continued to refine their fighting styles. The further Yui went, the less he felt he knew. There were so many paths that one could follow and none could be said to be right or wrong, a thought process that had started once he had become a soldier of Alva.

Still, although the gap is shorter, Domonos's skill with a sword is on another level. If we can create fighting techniques, then how powerful would we be? If I could make a technique before him, maybe I could beat him in a fight.

A still childlike desire to beat his older brother appeared in Yui's eyes as he watched Domonos. His attacks didn't have the flair from before. Now they were refined down into their simple moves, looking to injure, kill, defend, and alter the battle to his advantage.

"Looks like our sister is soon to leave us in the dust. Expert formation master…" Domonos laughed and Yui grinned, proud of Qin and the heights she had reached. Domonos cut his finger and put it on the blade. It shone, creating a link between them.

"Huh?" Yui said.

"It's an Expert-level weapon. You can bind your Expert-level gear to yourself. That way someone else can wield it but then they can't use any of the innate effects or enchantments," Domonos said.

"I knew that. I just haven't seen one before." Yui followed after Domonos, putting his blood on his spear.

"Talking about weapons, aren't we selling weapons to others on the

Fourth Realm?" Domonos asked.

"Yeah, I think Elise is meeting with them now. We will be selling repeaters, the first generation without the formations, to people in the Fourth Realm. As well as body armor and helmets," Yui said. "The repeaters are effective as a supporting weapon. We're selling exploding arrows with them as well and those who agree will have to sign an agreement saying that they will not attack us. They get weapons; we get an alliance, coins, and more people coming to Vuzgal to pick up gear and pay money to go through our totem."

"Your first order," Elise said.

Taran looked up from the smithy. "Did you run all the way down here from Vuzgal?" Taran asked as he turned around.

"Not quite." Elise put the notes down on the table.

Taran put down what he was working on and looked at the orders. "One thousand repeating crossbows, five hundred repeating ballistas with accompanying mounts," he summarized.

"Yes, as well as explosive arrows. How long do you think it will take?"

"Should be about four months for the crossbows, three for the ballistas. Arrows—you've got twenty thousand listed here. That will take…" Taran half closed one eye, thinking on it. "I'd say six weeks."

"Will that affect the production speed of the army's gear?"

"Shouldn't. Most of this stuff I can give to the students. The people working for military supply are working around the clock to make weapons and armor. We are already playing catch-up. We need more crafters and workers to keep up with the demand for clothing, weapons, and armor. The newest recruits, we can only supply enough clothing and armor for half a company. We don't have the weapons for them, so they'll be getting the latest generation of repeaters."

"I thought that production had increased?" Elise asked.

"Yes, it has, but we just had four hundred and fifty people to supply gear to. Now we have another four hundred and fifty who will finish training in just a few weeks, and another four hundred and fifty who will finish a few weeks after that. With an aim to train nine hundred people a month until we reach ten thousand men and women in uniform. That's ten thousand sets of body armor, helmets, and personal weapons. Now add in four sets of clothes and two sets of boots. Medical supplies, mortars, staffs used by the mages, grenade launchers, ammunition." Taran looked at Elise.

"Right. Not that easy to support."

"The armor and helmets are easy enough to make. The carriers for them take more time as the tailors are at capacity here. We should get some support from the tailors in Vuzgal chipping in. Just need more time to build up supplies and people to create the supporting backbone."

"Can we really do these deals then?" Elise asked.

"Making the repeaters is much easier than making rifles—won't take much time and people of lower skill can do it. Train them up. Also, it gets us allies and people who won't attack us. Can we not?" Taran asked.

"I guess not. All of them are asking for it. We need to take this time to establish Vuzgal in the middle of the Fourth Realm. Trade is the basis of all agreements. If we can benefit more from trading than we can fighting—" Elise let out a breath and straightened up.

"Everything good?" Taran asked.

"Yeah, crazy, but good. There is a lot going on up there. So much to be done. Vuzgal, if we build it up right..." Elise shook her head, thinking about the possibilities.

"I'll see what I can do on the side of the orders. See if I can give them smaller order sizes and then eke them out over a longer time."

"Remind me to have you on my side in a negotiation." Taran chuckled.

50 Frustrations

Rugrat let out a breath and he opened his eyes. He used a Clean spell to remove the sweat from his face.

"Mist Mana Core," A faint sliver of a smile appeared on his face. "I reinforced it a bit it shouldn't be long until I can reach Drop Mana Core. It's still slow though." He looked at his stomach, glaring at the mana core inside. "Who asked you to be so damn gluttonous?"

It didn't answer as Rugrat stretched out and fell back, getting out the kinks in his muscles from sitting so long.

He looked up at the ceiling, the lights of cornerstones and growing mana stones dancing above him.

Rugrat sighed to himself as he looked at the mana gathering formation around him. He looked over to the Vuzgal dungeon core that had been supplying him with the necessary mana.

Rugrat pushed himself up. Instead of feeling excited, he felt defeated. "Come on, dude. You're progressing quickly, after just a week of being here and concentrating on just increasing your cultivation." Rugrat's shoulders slumped as he headed for the exit.

Still, I can't lie to myself. I haven't made any progress in my smithing this entire time. My progress with formations is slow. I was never good with technology and figuring out how they work. I'm better dealing with things like nature. I can kill an animal, clean it, cook it, eat it. Teach someone to fire a rifle, scout a position. Physical stuff. Sure, shooting long distance is a lot of numbers—distance, drop, temperature—but it all makes sense. It just works *in my brain.*

Rugrat headed up just as Matt was heading down.

"Hey dude!" Matt said. He had been working in Vuzgal for a while now, commanding all of the building projects that were going on and establishing the blueprint office in Vuzgal. With so many crafters wanting to record down their items or to get blueprints the blue print office's grounds was one of the busiest in all of Vuzgal.

"Hey." Rugrat, not feeling like he wanted to talk, kept on walking.

"Do you want to grab a beer?" Matt asked.

"Not really feeling a bar," Rugrat said.

"Like up at the top," Matt said.

"The top?" Rugrat looked at Matt, who pointed upward.

Rugrat looked up through the pillar, seeing the changing sky.

"Sweet! I'll just put these into the dungeon—new plans for underground Battle Arena training rooms. They're expanding like mad over there. Also plans for the new defensive networks." Matt jumped down the stairs and put the blueprints into the dungeon core and then placed everything away and headed up to Rugrat.

Rugrat still felt defeated as he started to walk up the pillar.

"You okay, man?" Matt asked. The two of them walked up the spiraling steps inside the pillar toward the top.

"Just, you know, feel like I'm not going anywhere."

"Not going anywhere?"

"Like I started to work on formations, hoping that they would help increase my smithing skill. I have made progress with formations but it's just slow and I haven't figured out anything new for smithing."

"Maybe you're trying to focus on smithing too much?" Matt asked.

"It's my skill, though."

"It's *one* of your skills. Someone told me that you should only focus on one thing at a time, and put all your effort into that one thing."

"I am putting all of my effort into improving my smithing," Rugrat said, confused.

"That's it. When you're working on your formations, just work on formations. Else it's like trying to learn electrical wiring to figure out how to make a house's foundations. Every time you learn a little thing about electrical engineering, you'll go overboard trying to apply it to foundations. If you learn all of electrical engineering and about a house's foundations and compare notes afterward, it will be easier," Matt said.

"Just focus on formations." Rugrat felt a bit easier not having to worry about the formations and engineering. Though he really wanted to learn both at the same time. Smithing and formations went hand in hand with each other. *I want to make weapons from the ground up, from the base materials through the forging and the formations.*

"You seem really convinced." Matt smiled, seeing through Rugrat.

Rugrat wanted to rebut him and say that he understood it and would take the advice.

"What do you think is better: learning all about how to fight and then learning tactics, or learn tactics and then how to fight?"

"If I learned tactics and then how to fight, it would be harder. You need to build, learn your weapon, learn how to move, then learn how you slot into a plan. That way your foundational movements and attacks don't need to be figured out. Movement and fighting can be made instinctual. Tactics is a higher level," Rugrat said.

"So you would learn to fight and then tactics. So why not learn how to create formations. Then, once you have reached the peak of that, you try to see how you can adapt formations and smithing to each other."

"That makes some sense," Rugrat said. "Still, it feels as if I'm losing because I'm not progressing."

"Sometimes a change is better than a break and sometimes working on something laterally will increase your progress with both," Matt said.

"Sounds complicated." Rugrat grinned.

"Don't it?" Matt agreed with a self-deprecating smile as he nodded.

Rugrat let out a laugh.

"Look, I know I won't be the most powerful person in Alva, Vuzgal, or whatever. I know for you and Erik getting stronger, showing progress is like a drug to you. We each have our own path to follow. Has your life ever followed an exact plan? Or did it take twists and turns?"

Rugrat fell quiet.

"We each got a path to follow—sometimes there might be dead ends," Matt said.

"It's just, with smithing I can get it—you know, add in this, heat this up, form into a shape and then you have something." Rugrat moved his hands with his words before offering them to Matt.

"Yeah."

"Now, with these formations, it's like a computer. I know how to use a computer. Do I know how it works? Hell, no. I plug that thing in, switch it on, and then use a mouse and keyboard. I know that there are graphics cards, fans, a CPU and that in there, but how does it take electricity and turn it into music, video, words?" Rugrat grimaced and shook his head.

"So, mana is like electricity and then you're trying to figure out how to turn it into something useful?" Matt asked. "This is a long damn walk."

"Well, it is the tallest place in all of Vuzgal. Yeah, like knowing computers—it's all complicated and twisted."

"From what I know about formations, I think that you might be overthinking it," Matt said.

"What do you mean?" Rugrat asked.

"Mana is a power source, yes, but I think it's more alive than you give it credit for."

Rugrat clicked his tongue and paused before responding. He used his Mana Vision to look around him. He saw the mana drawn into the pillar by the mana gathering formations, the intermixed different attribute mana as it settled on the floor of the pillar and passed through it. He knew that the mana was purified and then turned into mana stones.

They continued walking, with the two of them not saying anything. They reached the top, looking over Vuzgal as the sun went down.

Matt opened a beer and passed it to Rugrat.

"Thanks," Rugrat said, his voice distant. "Maybe mana isn't just like electricity."

He felt as if he were on the precipice of something important. He looked at his hand, seeing the mana moving through it. The natural way it moved through his body.

"Maybe it's like water, like the creek on Jefferies Farm—just needs the right path to follow so it don't get blocked up."

"Jefferies Farm?" Matt asked as he drank his beer.

"A place close to where I grew up. They had this creek, would overflow every year. Was nasty as hell. It was all blocked up. We got the idea to stick one of those hydroelectric generators where the blockage was, then we opened up the creek; when it rained, then the generator would create power. You know, hydroelectric is like that."

"Like what? I feel like you're half thinking through what you're saying."

"Hydroelectric turns the power of nature into electricity."

"Yeah, don't have to tell me. I lived in Canada—water all around. Even turned Niagara Falls into a hydroelectric generator station."

"You ever see it?" Rugrat asked.

"See what? The generator station?"

"Nah, the falls—Niagara Falls."

"Yeah." Matt grinned. "You can feel the water turned mist from hundreds of meters away, just the roar of it. It looks so cool. The best is when it's winter. Everything gets covered in ice and then the lights play on it, lighting it up. You just need to take a moment, you know? Just look at it and you can feel that roar in your chest if you pay attention. Nature might not be the fastest thing, but it's the most powerful force in the world."

Matt sipped from his beer.

"You miss it?" Rugrat asked.

"Sure, I miss the people, miss video games and TV. Don't miss the taxes though, and being here comes with its benefits."

Matt summoned one of his beasts. A turtle-looking creature appeared. "This is Leonardo." Matt grinned.

Rugrat snorted as George padded over, tapping on Leonardo's shell, examining him.

"Do you?" Matt asked.

"What? Miss it? I miss my mom, my sister, but I feel like I belong here more than I did there."

"I can see that." Matt nodded.

They sat there quietly and Matt let out a snicker.

"It's strange. We're rushing around doing so much right now, but to butcher a good quote: it's not insane to think that with the medical professions and concoctions in the realms that we could live for two, even three hundred years!"

Rugrat let out a laugh and leaned back on his elbows. "Two or three hundred years—sounds like a long damn time."

"Ten lifetimes." Matt raised his beer in agreement.

Leonardo snapped at George, making him jump back, startled.

"Stop messing with Leonardo." Rugrat waved George over as the flames that had started to appear around him dimmed down.

Leonardo seemed pleased as he laid down, tucking his limbs in as he let Matt scratch his neck.

"Maybe it's like water, krill, and plankton as one. The attributes are the krill and plankton, in the water, or mana. The dungeon core and different items in the Ten Realms consume that plankton and krill, removing them from the water or changing them into a different byproduct. Like air back home and a dungeon core is the air filter."

"Or maybe you're overthinking it?" Matt said.

"Overthinking it?"

"When I use magic, I just use it and I get to know it more. Then it becomes like a secondary response. Talking and writing is something that we learned but now we use it every day. Maybe magic is just a different way to communicate?"

Erik sat in front of a cauldron as it started to shake and tremble.

Erik's forehead was covered in sweat as he watched the different ingredients reacting with one another, turning the inside into a chaotic mess.

Erik lost control and a thick, turbid, black smoke appeared in the workshop, filling his nostrils. He coughed and spluttered. He started up a formation that would draw the smoke out of the room. He leaned over the cauldron and took a deep breath. He coughed some more as he used his Reverse Alchemist ability to try to understand what had happened in the concoction.

"It's not a simple pill to make." Erik ran his hand through his hair.

"Everyone wants a pill or something to heal their ailments in one go. If you were wounded on Earth, then you would need to get treated for the wound. Then there might be follow-up operations, then they needed to rest up, and then there is rehab so if the change is big the person can adapt to it. There wasn't one pill but a series of medications, maybe a change to a person's diet and their routine."

Erik frowned as he pulled out his notes on the recluse.

"Making a pill might be too hard. But a treatment plan? I talked about using different parts to heal the body…can't I do that for him? I've been so focused on increasing my Alchemy, but what if I can get the same effects through different means?"

Erik studied the sheet without really seeing it.

"Could I use that to increase my cultivation? Not one pill or concoction to bust through, just slowly over time. I used a pill, a blade, and the floor to temper my body with flames. So what if it takes longer? If I can get the Earth attribute to permeate my entire body—wait a minute."

Erik turned his thoughts inward, to the power of Fire within his body. He opened his hands and flames appeared around his hand. He stood and closed his hand. His hand glowed with a red power as embers seemed to appear around it.

He struck out with his fist. Sparks scattered into the air. He did it a few more times before he shot a fireball from his fist.

"I'm such an idiot," Erik said as he executed Illusionary Unhallowed Strike.

Now his fists were imbued with the power of flames, increasing his striking power.

"I was so wrapped up with other things. I was following other people's paths and not mine. I wonder if I can use these flames instead of my spell flames? Can I use it in combination with the flame technique that Old Hei taught me?"

Erik's head hurt as two sets of knowledge, history, and abilities were forcefully merged into one.

Erik waved his hand. A Fire tiger appeared on his arm and walked up his shoulder.

A spurt of water came from the other side of the room, striking the tiger. Gilly gave an unimpressed look.

Erik laughed as a flaming turtle appeared in front of him. He seemed to be made of a red crystal with a blue flame that could be seen burning within him. Embers flowed together and spun into the form of a dragon that wove around Erik's shoulders and down his arm, charging the larger turtle. The turtle opened his mouth and the dragon passed through. It was formed of embers and fire, circling the turtle's blue flame.

"The mana drain is really high, but I can just maintain it with my Mana Regeneration. Though my control is much higher than it was. If I could have the two of them within the cauldron…"

Erik's mind was filled with more ideas.

"With the skill book, my spell book, and my arts combining together, I must be close to making my own technique. I feel like I am missing something still." Erik frowned before he dismissed the flames.

"Time to see if there is an Earth-attribute weapon for sale, or if I can get someone to make one."

"You want me to make you an Earth-attribute weapon so that you can stab yourself?" Taran asked.

"Pretty much." Erik nodded.

Taran opened and closed his mouth, then shrugged. "Okay. I can make the weapon. I'll talk to some of the people with the Formation Guild."

"I'm going to be at the library. I need to research Earth-based poisons. Egbert!" Erik yelled into the air as he was walking.

"What?" Egbert yelled back through the air.

"Is the Earth floor done yet?"

"It's filled with Fire-attribute mana still. Poisonous to others. The air is cleaner. Little Davin has secured the Wood floor. It is just taking us a lot of time to fix the formations. Stop eating rocks!" Egbert collected himself. "The roots went through the formation. It is a mess."

"Just has Fire-attribute toxins, right?" Erik looked down at his hand as it glowed with power.

"Yes. Why are you using Fire mana within your body? Do you know how? Oh yeah, you tempered your body."

"I'm going to the library and then I'll be down in a bit." Erik headed into the library. *I'll check out all of my options and then combine them together to temper my body and reach Body Like Sky Iron.*

Erik was filled with energy again as he saw a way forward.

51
Step by Step, Piece by Piece

"Something wrong?" Elise asked Blaze as she came out of their shared bedroom, seeing him working at his desk.

"I thought you were asleep," he said, looking over.

"Once I saw you weren't in bed and heard you out here working, I couldn't keep being lazy." Elise smiled as she draped her hands over his shoulder and leaned down.

Blaze gave her a kiss and she rested her head against his shoulder, looking at the papers on the table.

"So, what has got the Adventurer's Guild leader all worked up?"

Blaze's smile soured as he let out a haggard breath. "The guild isn't happy, though I have a meeting with some representatives from the Fighter's Association in a few weeks. Hopefully that will give them something to talk about. We all hate waiting. They killed our people and took their gear and rewards—now they're up in the Fourth Realm while their sect told us to stop being annoying."

"Well, what does the Willful Institute do to earn money?" Elise asked.

"They're a sect—people pay them money to join," Blaze said.

"An institution like that, they need to have people going out and earning them money."

"They go to tournaments, they have trade caravans, and they sell goods across the realms."

"Well, we have crafters and highly prized goods. If you could find the places for our traders to sell the goods, then compete with them?" Elise said.

"They're a massive sect," Blaze said.

"And we have our own Expert-level crafters now. Alva isn't just some small little village anymore."

"So we compete against them?"

"Anyone who is looking to compete against them, I think that Erik and Rugrat will agree with me that we can back them. Then you give them protection. We start cutting into the bottom line of the Willful Institute. They are a massive institution; they need to be constantly earning money to create a revenue. We have all of those items from Vuzgal that need to be sold as well." Elise had a cold look on her face.

Blaze laughed and kissed her as he pulled out his sound transmission device.

"What is it?" Jasper asked, answering as if he were still asleep.

"Elise just had an idea. I want to know every merchant and convoy across the Second and Third Realm that competes with the Willful Institute. Contact Elan and his people to get the information."

"I will have it shortly." Jasper sounded much more alert.

Elan sat in the Sky Reaching Restaurant, looking over Vuzgal. Someone knocked at the door.

He pressed a button on the formation and the door slid open. An aide, looking like a server from the restaurant, bowed before coming in. The door slid shut behind her.

"Head Blaze and Deputy Jasper request information on traders and groups competing against the Willful Institute." They opened their serving tray and Elan took the two letters on it.

He read the more detailed information.

"Send word to the Third and Second Realm intelligence heads to gather information on figures and groups that have issue with the Willful Institute."

He put the letters into a fire next to him as the server bowed and headed out of the room. The formation within the room wouldn't allow sound transmissions to enter or exit.

Elan smiled as the door closed.

Seems that Blaze has a new way to fight back against the Willful Institute. If they were to take direct action, then the sect might attack them head on. With aiding others, they reduce their footprint and do a greater amount of damage over a longer time. Elan looked at the reports around him.

He left the room. He went down a secret lift that went under Vuzgal into the dungeon floor underneath. Down here, the food for the Sky Reaching Restaurants was grown. It was also where the formations to supply power to the different bunkers that protected Vuzgal were hidden. As well as undead that patrolled the area and watched the city above.

He reached a complex. There were several houses that had been built up around a courtyard.

Elan knocked on one of the doors.

A lanky, pale-looking fellow answered the door.

"Head Elan." A scribe stepped out and greeted Elan with a bow.

"Scribe Dang." Elan nodded to the man. "How goes the recording process?"

"Please come in. I have sorted out information that I believe would be of interest to you. We have been recording different cultivation technique manuals and processes that people use. Still, our biggest advancements have been in spell scrolls, formations, and blueprints."

Elan smiled. "It was the right choice making you the overseer of the answering statue."

When I learned how underused it was and its capabilities...Rugrat might be a good smith and have great ideas, combining what he knew on Earth with the tools he has in the Ten Realms, but when executing some of them, he's not the strongest.

"It has been a wealth of knowledge. The different designs are creating an uproar in the Kanesh Academy." Dang smiled happily as he took off a medallion and then pressed it to a lockbox. It opened to reveal reports and papers inside.

"Anything that I should know?" Elan asked.

"There seems to be someone gathering information on us. Our military and our strength. I know a lot of people have been doing so, but this seems more direct, as if they're looking for tactical information and formulating a way to attack us." Dang's words were heavy before he continued in a lighter voice. "The associations are pleased with their positions. The Blue Lotus has lost some face and are looked down on by the other associations because they stepped on the feet of the city lords the most. They don't go overboard as there is someone from the Blue Lotus in charge. People are having more questions about the city lords. The military gained some attention. Minor matters, it seems." Dang shrugged.

Elan took the papers and nodded.

"Is there anything that I should pay attention to in the future?"

"With someone moving in the shadows and gathering information, it would seem they are local. We should look to the surrounding area and see who would benefit the most by taking Vuzgal. Also see what people think about the auction house and the arena," Elan said.

"I will do my best," Dang said.

The answering statues can give real-time information on what is happening, or when there is a blueprint within its area of influence, it can help people write it out. Still, it has to describe it line by line and can't show people. It is a great tool. With the scribes here, they can work faster, but we still lose information.

"I'll see you tomorrow unless there is an emergency," Elan said.

"'Til tomorrow."

"Are you sure this is a good idea?" Egbert asked as he and Erik stood on the teleportation formation.

Erik checked his storage ring. There were healing concoctions, Earth-attribute concoctions, and several needles with formations inlaid in them. *Formations have sure come a long way.*

"It's an idea. We'll test the environment around the teleportation pad. If I'm all okay, we can move deeper," Erik said as he finished checking his supplies.

"That sounds safe," Storbon said.

"And you've never done anything stupid?" Yao Meng quipped.

Storbon flipped him the bird as the rest of the special team grinned.

"Now don't kill one another while I'm gone. Egbert, kick it," Erik said.

"Kick it? What am I kicking? Is Rugrat around?"

Erik held his rifle at the ready as the formation flashed with light.

"I'm not in Kansas anymore," Erik said, looking at the floor.

He checked the area.

"There isn't anything alive on this floor other than you right now. Well, and some plants," Egbert said.

Erik lowered his rifle and checked the condition within his body. The Fire-attribute mana was thick in the air, more than the dungeon level he had been in. He breathed it in, coughing as Egbert gathered power in the formation.

Erik waved his hand at him and he kept coughing, taking a bit of time to clear his lungs. "Smoky," he wheezed out, grabbing a canteen of water and drinking it.

Erik checked on the condition of his body. Erik couldn't help but shake his head.

"Sometimes the thinking on Earth is useless here." He sat down and started to circulate his mana.

He could feel Egbert staring at him as if he were a peculiar specimen. "What's wrong?"

"You're okay? Why are you circulating your mana to temper your body?" Egbert's questions fell out of his jaw.

"People temper their bodies with the affinities, though most people aren't willing to waste the time tempering and suffering through a long period of time. Pills and Alchemy products are much easier to consume—they're powerful and fast-acting. People just use concoctions to increase the tempering of their body. Now, if we combine concoctions to increase the recovery, then I can temper my body faster, drawing in the power. I also found out something interesting when I gained my Fire Body.

"With my Fire Body, it will take a lot of Fire-attribute mana to affect me now. Fire attribute attacks are much weaker and my control over flames is higher. Though I was a bit of an idiot. When I saw Fire Body, I thought it was just a title to mean that I had passed my tempering. I only realized recently that it means a lot more." Erik raised his hand and the air shifted; the heat built up and a flame appeared within his hand as the Fire-attribute mana was gathered together.

"I didn't just temper my body with flames—I gained control over them. I treated it like another level that I needed to pass and didn't look at the benefits." Erik shook his head. "There is still a lot to be learned about the Ten Realms and although some of it can be explained by what I know from Earth, some of it just can't. As for why I'm circulating my mana, you need to break and remake one's body when body tempering, incorporating the power of the Ten Realms. Cultivation is looked at as increasing one's power. That is just a passive effect. It makes us closer to the Ten Realms—we can tap into more of its power. While I draw in the mana, my body has to grow accustomed to it. The Fire-attribute mana doesn't affect me anymore. The Fire attribute is turned into energy, restoring my Stamina. The remaining mana I can then compress into my mana core. The impurities temper my body.

"With my Poison Body, I can excrete poisons, using it in my attacks. They don't affect me as much and the impurities within my body are slowly resolved, turning from toxin to tonic.

"With the high amount of Earth attribute in the air, I draw it into my body and concentrate it around my bones."

Erik felt his bones itching and small cracks appeared. The Earth-attribute mana caused them to crack under the pressure. A small amount of the Earth mana entered the bones as they were reformed.

"This isn't high enough." Erik opened his eyes and stood. "Where is the Earth mana concentrated the most?"

"Under the mountain. It has built up for centuries, though," Egbert warned.

"If it is too much, then pull me out," Erik said. He pulled out Gilly from a beast storage item.

She looked out and snorted. She looked at Erik, an excited look appeared on her face as she took a deep breath. Threads of brown power were drawn in toward her. The flecks of brown in her eyes started to shine and her brown skin took on a deeper color as she gulped down the Earth mana in the area.

"I wish it was that easy for me," Erik muttered as he got on her back. They set off toward the mountain as Gilly drew in the Earth-attribute mana.

I wonder what changes it will have on her body. She was born in a Water and Earth attribute floor, but she lived in a Water room, so she hasn't been able to stay in an Earth type environment for long.

They reached the mountain and found a doorway into it. The doorway was untouched.

Erik got off Gilly and stepped toward the door. He felt a pressure falling on him as he stepped forward.

Erik frowned and moved farther forward.

"The Earth attribute increases with each step and so does the pressure on my body. I'm not even in the door yet." Erik reached the door and opened it. Air rushed out toward him, thick with Earth-attribute mana. The area past the door had a brown miasma that moved around, obscuring the interior.

Erik took a step forward; the pressure doubled in just one step. He took a moment to raise his head, stabilizing himself as he circulated the mana within his mana channels. Pain started to radiate from his bones as the pressure bore down on him.

Gilly walked in as well, pushing out ahead of Erik. She smirked at him as she took on the extra pressure. She went a full ten steps before she slowed down. Then she sat down, signs of strain on her face as she started to draw in the Earth mana.

Erik cleared his mind. Before moving anymore, he pulled out his supplies. He stuck an IV into his arm and taped it up. He hooked on an IV bag filled with Stamina and healing potion to a carabiner on his shoulder.

He put his rifle away, took off his drop pouch and Velcroed a set of prepared needles to his leg.

"Okay, bit by bit." Erik stepped forward. The itching deep in his bones turned into cracking pain. Erik gritted his teeth, drawing in more Earth mana, pausing and pushing ahead.

He reached seven steps and sat down. He could feel the cracking in his body. He adjusted the IV drip and opened it slightly. His bones cracked, absorbing Earth mana and regrew, stronger than before.

After twenty minutes, Erik got up slowly, forcing himself to breathe through his gritted teeth. He pushed one foot across the ground, without the strength to lift it. He was panting by the time he moved his first foot. He forced his other foot forward.

His bones twisted and cracked, then came back together.

Erik waited until his body got used to the destruction happening internally. He pushed onward, crawling now, his eyes closed as he groaned at the pain. It was no longer just the bone sheathing cracking; they cracked internally, the marrow becoming exposed under the pressure.

When he couldn't crawl anymore, he dragged himself forward.

Erik cried out as his body let out a series of sickening cracks and pops. Gilly hissed in pain but breathed in more Earth mana.

Erik ran out of the healing solution.

He used Healing Dagger, stabbing it into himself, and relief filled him. He pulled out a new IV bag and hooked it up.

He kept going, running out of healing concoctions. His fingers were breaking so he had to use his wrists to point a needle at his leg and used his body weight to press down on it, injecting it into his leg.

The pain was too much to keep crawling. Erik gathered himself. The Earth mana had drilled deep into his bones, but he could take more.

The greater the pain, the greater the gain! Pain tells you you're alive!

He threw his body over in a Herculean effort.

He breathed into the dirt. His eyes flashed with viciousness as he let out a yell and threw himself forward again, rolling onto his back again.

Egbert watched beast and master advance into the brown fog. He couldn't see them anymore with his own eyes, but nothing was beyond a floor that he controlled.

Erik laid on the ground, using healing spells to repair his body. Noises like dry branches cracking could be heard from the depths of the room.

Brown threads of mana passed through his mana channels and gates. His veins stuck out like worms against his skin and showed up as brown instead of blue.

Instead of advancing, Erik pushed back into the weaker regions of the Earth mana. He stopped moving after about five minutes. His body was still being tempered but it was easier to deal with. He stuck a needle into himself and used his weight to inject himself.

Egbert read his books, keeping an eye on Erik as he controlled the dungeon core as it remodeled the Fire floor and made sure that Davin wasn't slacking off when he should be repairing the Wood floor's control formation.

Days passed in quick succession. As people asked where Erik was, Egbert would answer them.

He had new supplies delivered and would then create an Earth golem to drop them off with Erik.

Erik would advance as far as he could safely, taking as much pain as possible, then move away, recovering and then advance again: three steps forward, then one step back, repeated.

Gilly moved at a slow pace, no longer looking to compete with Erik. She had grown in size and her brown markings were more pronounced. The blue and the brown mixed together instead of one dominating the other.

Her features were a deeper brown, while dark and light blue highlighted her features and ran down her face, along her neck and down her body.

Deep within the Beast Mountain Range, a man and his mount were undergoing massive changes, as changes happened above it.

Emmanuel looked at the groups of traders arriving from across the Beast Mountain Range. All of them wore simple clothes, looking like mercenaries. Most of them had only just left the mercenary path behind.

It wasn't abnormal for mercenaries to move from one outpost to another in search of better hunting grounds and for larger profits.

"How are our preparations?" Emmanuel asked Nasreen at his elbow.

"We can't be sure that information won't get out, but it should take time to reach the other outpost leaders. All of our support from the other outposts should be here by tonight. I have dispersed them throughout the outpost, so it is hard to find where they are. Pan Kun is waiting to meet with you," Nasreen said.

"Aditya sent his guard captain?" Emmanuel was a little surprised.

"Yes. I didn't know until they were inside the outpost either."

"He is a powerful force. Sending him over here shows how much importance Aditya places on this plan." Emmanuel stroked his chin. "Meet with all of the guard leaders tonight. You will remain in command but we need to organize them and the crafters who came with them. Have Pan Kun as your second-in-command. His strength is high and we can possibly learn more about his lord."

"Yes, Father."

Pan Kun and most of the other guards all left the outpost at different times the next day, meeting up in a secluded spot.

They were organized into different groups.

Pan Kun had received a new weapon from his benefactors, a war axe of mid Journeyman quality.

"We have a lot of work ahead of us. The sooner we start, the sooner we finish," Nasreen said.

The guards weren't all united but they had their orders. They pushed forward.

"I hate scouting," Pan Kun muttered as he looked through the forest, a small bow in hand.

"It's kind of peaceful, no?" Nasreen asked, scanning the forest.

A tree crashed behind them. Behind them, the road was being formed.

"Don't know about that," Pan Kun muttered as he kept looking around. He waved to the two guards on either side of him.

They nodded and pushed up.

"You and your people have good coordination," Nasreen said.

"Time together," Pan Kun said.

"You know that this might take months?" Nasreen said.

"Hopefully not."

"Why, better things to do?" Nasreen asked.

"More questions to ask?"

"What else am I going to do? Sulk in the silence like you?" Nasreen raised her eyebrow.

Pan Kun shrugged as if it wasn't his issue.

"What do you think will happen if the other outposts find out what we're doing?"

"Attack or wait," Pan Kun said bluntly.

"Well, that was *riveting,"* Nasreen said.

"Don't worry about that. We have a job to take care of already," Pan Kun said.

"Escorting mages and crafters—you do pick out the most boring items," Nasreen said.

"You might think it boring. I think it's interesting. All of us working together for one goal. We clear the path; they make the road. We will be going deeper than anyone else has. Then we're building an outpost in the middle of it all." Pan Kun smiled a little as he looked over to Nasreen.

"Are you a guard or a builder?"

Pan Kun saw movement. He stopped moving and readied his bow. A whistle came from the front. Pan Kun headed up to where the noise came from and Nasreen tagged along with him like an unwanted shadow. He saw the scout and slowed down as they gestured to him. Pan Kun took his time reaching them.

What the—?

He looked through the trees at a shipwreck. It lay on its side, covered in moss, with trees that had grown around it.

The scout pointed at the bottom of the ship.

Pan Kun looked at the collection of loot. There were parts of wagons, weapons, bags, treasures and random items piled together. He looked from it to the scout, who gestured to the loot again.

Pan Kun studied it for a few more minutes. *It is moving, as if it's breathing.*

A tentacle appeared from underneath the loot.

The pile of loot moved and a multi-limbed beast moved, revealing its three teeth that opened and closed as it slept it didn't have lips to cover the massive fangs.

Each of those teeth are as big as my breastplate.

Pan Kun signaled to the scout, giving them orders as he and Nasreen backed up.

They moved back out of earshot.

"Loot squid," Nasreen said.

"What?"

"They're scavengers. Anything that they don't own, they will steal from others. They love to kill. Good for us that they never stay in groups. They claim a territory and will fight any others that come into it."

"And it is right in our path. Weaknesses, strengths?"

"When in its own territory, it can create illusions. It has the ability to create a dark area around it in a ten-meter-wide area. We can't see it but it can see us. They are weak to lightning and fire, high resistance to poison. Limited regeneration. Also, if we're in their range, they not only hit hard, they have a lot of limbs so need more fighters to pin them down."

"So pin it down and hit them from range?"

"Yes, but they have a spell attack that will cause one to go into a rage and attack their fellow, saying that they stole their items," Nasreen said.

"Uh huh." Pan Kun pulled out a spell scroll. "I'll need the ranged fighters."

Nasreen looked at him as if he had gone stupid. "We should bring up the rest of the guards to deal with it."

"We should be good," Pan Kun assured her.

Nasreen watched as Pan Kun organized the guards. They didn't look pleased, getting orders as they moved up around the loot squid.

He took all of the ranged guards with him and positioned the melee types back a bit so that they could fall back on them.

They were getting into position and the loot squid seemed to sense something. It stood up on its tentacles and looked around with its two large eyes above its mouth that looked like an owl's eyes.

Someone fired at it and it let out a clicking hiss as it spat acid at the attacker.

Pan Kun was lit up as he activated the spell scroll in his hands.

Two people were hit with the black acid. They screamed out and others fired at the loot squid. It turned, using the loot on its back to create a shield as it ran toward them backward.

The spell scroll activated. The ground underneath the loot squid was changed; the loot squid lost its footing as the ground beneath it started to draw it down.

It let out an angry hiss as the ground had been turned into quicksand.

"Move around to get a good hit on it!" Pan Kun yelled.

The guards moved around to get a better position. They fired arrows and spells at the loot squid, dyeing the ground pink with its blood.

The quicksand spell wore off and the ground solidified once again. The loot squid moved around, trying to push itself up. It had dropped most of its loot and was bleeding from multiple wounds.

It got up, giving the ranged attackers more to shoot at that wasn't protected by loot.

The loot squid couldn't take all of the hits and dropped to the ground, releasing the loot around it in a pile. A tombstone appeared above it and golden tendrils of Experience spread out from the creature, entering the guards' bodies.

"Well, that was effective, and costly," Nasreen said. Spell scrolls were rarities in the First Realm.

"Should have plenty of loot off the squid. I'll leave that up to you. Shall I continue scouting and tell the crafters to keep moving forward?" Pan Kun asked.

"Uh, yeah, sure," Nasreen said. It was clear that Pan Kun's spell scroll and his scout finding the creature had made the battle easier. Most groups would want to fight over getting more loot. Instead, Pan Kun was wholly focused on completing the road as soon as possible. Personal gains seemed to come secondary.

The builders were put into action once again and people returned to their duties. Nasreen headed down to the loot squid and the shipwreck.

The loot squid's body had powerful poison and its skin could be used to make light armor and bindings, while its teeth were stronger than iron and could be used for weapons or armor.

There was an odd assortment of loot that the creature had been carrying. The ship in the trees was old and decrepit, but it had a large amount of loot within it as well. She ordered the trees cut down.

The ship crashed to the ground, sending up dust as the wood at the bottom of the ship broke.

"A ship in the middle of the Beast Mountain Range," Pan Kun said. The other guards had elected him as their representative to make sure that Nasreen didn't screw them out of loot.

"There was once a large lake that ran through the Beast Mountain Range. It reached out to the Eastern Sea and down to the South Western Rolling Sea. Legends say that the water is still here in the Beast Mountain Range, but it runs underground."

"Hmm," Pan Kun grunted.

"So how should we divide up the loot?" Nasreen asked.

"Five percent to the guards, those with us and those back in camp. The rest we leave to the lords, break it up according to contribution," Pan Kun said.

Nasreen took a few moments before agreeing. "We are all part of the King's Hill Outpost Alliance—we should start acting like it from the beginning."

Pan Kun gave another grunt. "We are getting supplies tonight. We should send this back with a group of the guards with us. They'll make sure nothing happens to it. Use the guards sent out here to replace them. Should put a group of mixed guards to protect it all. Have a few of the guard leaders who are wary of one another sort the loot and prepare it to be moved and to watch one another."

"Think we'll find any more loot along the way?"

"Maybe not loot, but beasts and useful materials? Probably," Pan Kun said.

With this load of loot, the outpost lords will have already started to make back some of their investment. Should make them all the more supportive.

Lady Sumi looked at the information that had been gathered in the last couple of weeks. Since she had received the message from Ryan Mills, she had been planning.

A man walked into the room and bowed. "There are reports of a caravan heading out into the forest around Shadowridge Outpost. The guards were different coming back and they were carrying a lot of loot, apparently."

"Very good. So it looks like the Fayad family is where they will make the first road to King's Hill." Lady Sumi tapped her chin.

"With twenty-five percent to forty percent of different outposts' guards missing, they're practically begging to have a new outpost lord." She smiled to herself.

She pulled out a piece of paper and handed it to a guard who looked like a statue; he took the paper with a bow.

"Reach out to the people on this letter. Tell them about what this new alliance is doing. At the same time, contact the different large mercenary groups we know. I will hire their mercenary bands in two weeks for double the price. They will need to write Ten Realms contracts, though."

"It looks like she has taken the bait," Evernight said as she walked into Aditya's office.

He looked up from his communication device.

"Something important?" she asked.

"Not really. The road is progressing well. Pan Kun was giving me an update. He has sent forces ahead to scout the path and is working into the night to make things faster. The builders are faster than we had feared. Seems that the other outpost lords are putting their best efforts in. They found a loot squid and a ship that was stuck in the trees."

"A ship in the trees?"

"Apparently there is some history to the Beast Mountain Range I don't know, something about a lake that ran through the range and now runs under it."

"That is very interesting. I'll have to look into that more," Evernight said seriously. *Does this have something to do with the Water floor?*

"What was the news you wanted to share?"

"Oh, Lady Sumi has sent out messages to some different people, alerting them to our alliance and she is starting to make plans. It looks like they are aiming to attack different outposts."

"Our people are already in place within their outposts."

"I have looked into them. Some of them, the ones that are usually held by a kingdom, have the interfaces. Most don't. With an interface in Vermire, then you will be able to have things like access to trading. You can purchase building designs and gain bonuses for the outpost, upgrading it through village to town, city and so on. Another can be transplanted into King's Hill

Outpost as it will have access to the same interface. As long as its population and size grow, then the buffs will mount with it."

Lord Aditya sat upright, his eyes glowing as he thought about those bonuses.

Rugrat sat underneath the dungeon core. Since talking to Matt, he had been taking his time. Erik had disappeared into the Earth floor a week ago.

Rugrat spent his nights working on his Mana Gathering Cultivation and during the days he just studied formations. He would tinker with smithing ideas and designs, and had come up with complete designs for a workshop. Once the machines were created in Alva, people found that they didn't need to be trained as a smith to use the machines.

Ammunition production speed had increased by nearly two times. Weapon manufacture was up twenty percent. Formation plates, bows, shields, armor—all basic materials and components could now be made in a matter of minutes instead of taking a crafter days.

There is art and beauty in functionality.

Although simple items could be mass-produced, the higher level items needed to be made on a person-by-person basis to get the greatest power from them.

He had watched Domonos and Yui sparring.

Yui had to use his reach to overcome Domonos's speed. Their weapons snaked out at each other and there was no awkwardness to their movements; the weapons had turned into extensions of themselves. They weren't perfectly balanced and weighted, but they were perfect for them and their fighting style.

Rugrat felt a disturbance in the mana around him. As he had been cultivating mana, he became more sensitive to it. He had to close off his senses last time or else he would have been overwhelmed.

"Elan, do you walk in the capital anymore?" Rugrat asked.

"Well, it's faster in the dungeon." Elan walked out into the dungeon core room.

It was filled with mana stones now. The mana gathering formation had been working hard since they took the city. Even with the increased mana purity and density in the capital, it kept on growing.

"I have a request to make from the First Realm. You know about the operation that is happening down there with Vermire and the King's Hill Outpost?"

"Yeah, connect the other outposts, control King's Hill Outpost, take over the Beast Mountain Range?"

"That's it. Well, there are people who are looking to attack Vermire and its allies while their guards are clearing the road. We have people positioned in these other outposts. Some of them have interfaces, so we can declare war on the outpost and then take control. We kill off the defenders and we have another outpost. Once we have control, then all of the buffs come under our control or anything connected to the outpost."

"Won't the kingdoms and such react badly if we take their interfaces?"

"Probably. They would need time to prepare a counterattack. Which, by that time, we should have at least the road to Shadowridge completed. The road from Vermire is already under construction in secret. King's Hill Outpost should be complete and other outposts will be looking to connect to it. If we make the captured outposts under the control of all the members of the King's Hill Outpost Alliance…" Elan paused, as Rugrat thought.

"They will work together to fight off the kingdom, bring them closer together, fighting external enemies. Use it as a way to tie our forces and people together more," Rugrat said aloud. "So what else do you need from me?"

"Well, we can capture another outpost and then move the interface, for use in Vermire and King's Hill Outpost, or if we can give them interfaces from the beginning, they will get buffs that could aid them."

Rugrat tapped the interface on the ground and went through the menus. "Looks like we've got a few." Rugrat looked at the interfaces. They were all ranked the same.

Outpost—Basic

This interface can be used to create an outpost. Requires 100 people to be upgraded to a village.

Costs: 50 Gold

10 Low Mortal Grade Monster cores

Rugrat had a limit of twenty-five. He clicked on two of them. There was a stream of light as Rugrat lost one hundred gold and some cores and two square-looking bricks were created on the floor.

"Well, that should do it," Rugrat said, looking at them and then Elan. "Kind of anti-climactic, y'know?"

"A little." Elan grabbed the interfaces.

52
Embrace the Flow, Dude

Rugrat stood in the sparring square. Niemm and his people were also training in their different fighting styles. After Rugrat had learned from Klaus how to combine spell knowledge and combat arts, they had been combining their different techniques together.

Their combat power had increased in leaps and bounds as they became more specialized.

Rugrat faced a mannequin. There was a sharpness in his eyes as he looked at the mannequin. Blades appeared within the air around Rugrat stabbing and slicing into the mannequin with different effects, coloring it with fire, poison while tearing it apart under the weapon's onslaught.

The blades disappeared and Rugrat fell into thought.

There was a noise and everyone stopped practicing. A few minutes later, Klaus appeared at the entrance to the Battle Arena.

"No Erik again?" Klaus asked.

"He is busy," Rugrat said.

Klaus nodded but didn't say anything. "How has your progress been?"

"Interesting. It is fun seeing how the different spells, effects, and knowledge combine together," Rugrat said. *I've made it the furthest in fighting techniques. Smithing still eludes me and formations are slow for me to get but I am progressing.*

"Show me what you've learned." Klaus held his hands behind his back.

"Chains of Restraint." Black spell circles appeared around a mannequin; chains shot out of them and wrapped around the mannequin.

A wave of his hand dismissed the spell.

"Then there are Chains of Stun." The black spell circles had silver running through them as they grew in complexity. The chains bound the mannequin as lightning flashed across the chains and the mannequin's body.

"Chains of Adverse Effects—it binds for a longer period of time and damages over time. If they break free, then for ten seconds they will still take damage, poison, stun, and fire. Also, they are silenced. I combined the Aura of Swords into the chains; increases the damage and it hurts others who are not bound but in the area of effect. Chains of Silence silences people in the area as well; those in the area are silenced for ten seconds after leaving. Those bound will be silenced for thirty seconds once they leave." Rugrat didn't show the last two; their mana requirement was on his upper limit and they were trump cards.

Klaus had an unnatural color to his face.

"You okay?" Rugrat asked.

Klaus coughed. "It's nothing. So, anything else?"

"I am still working on the Aerial Mounted Beast combat style. It will take me some more practice. The Cloud Footwork technique is useful when dodging. It created thin sheets of mana around my body to act as sails to increase my speed and allow me to dodge attacks. Although it is good for defense and moving in the sky, it is bad for increasing my speed on the ground.

"I used Night Vision with Shade's Covering so that I don't have any negative effects on myself. I can combine it with the chains to annoy my attackers but most people should have something that allows them to see through the night easily.

"Bound Weapon is useful. I can use it on things like explosives and then pull them toward me, hitting my enemy in the back. Though I have been working with the Aura of Swords extensively. I found that it was too weak, so I kind of combined the control from the Aura of Swords with a few of my spells and well, the results are pretty sweet." Rugrat smiled.

"Could you show me?" Klaus asked, indicating to a mannequin.

Rugrat created mana blades from raw mana of the five elements, imbuing them with his Silence spell. With his control over the surrounding mana, he didn't need to look at the target to hit its weak spots accurately.

He looked over to Klaus as his attacks rained down on the mannequin. He stopped after a few seconds. The mana drain was hefty.

"A domain," Klaus said in a serious voice.

"Domain?" Rugrat asked.

Klaus raised an eyebrow before he frowned, seemingly thinking and picking his words with care. "Domains, as you might know, are areas around you that you can sense the slightest change in and exert your control over. It is beyond the realm of what humans can do normally. People need to have a special constitution, a deep understanding of magic, their body, or a high body or mana tempering. It is rare, even with people in the higher realms. Someone can have much more powerful techniques and be at the same level as their opponent, but if their opponent is weaker and has a domain, they will win."

"Why?" Rugrat asked.

"If you know everything that is happening around you, it is easier for you to anticipate attacks. You know the terrain that you are fighting on and can immediately adapt to the area around you, using it to your advantage. With your opponent in range, you can see through their openings. They have to focus on just you, but you are seeing it all and apply your power nearly instantaneously within your domain. The base of your domain must be off your Mana Gathering Cultivation. You can instantly cast spells around you and contort the mana into weapons for your use. You use external mana at the same time, greatly reducing the cost of creating the spell."

Rugrat felt a bit unnerved having Klaus see through him like that.

"I won't and can't tell anyone. Damn, you're a monster. Would you be interested in joining my Fighter's Association?"

"Um, can I?" Rugrat asked, a little alarmed.

Klaus laughed a bit awkwardly. "Well, sure. There aren't any rules against city lords being a member of the association. You would get these lessons for cheap."

"What about fighting competitions?" Rugrat asked.

"Well, we do host a number of them. Although I am offering you a position, you would need to prove to others that you deserve the position. I cannot recruit people in my area; you have to go through qualifications to make sure that I'm impartial."

"Right now, I don't have the time to go into any competitions. I will think about it in the future, though."

Klaus didn't seem to be expecting Rugrat's answer and brightened visibly before he became serious again. "I would warn you against showing off your ability with your domain. Using the Aura of Swords, and combining it with the mana blades, yes. But having the blades appear in your domain at will? It will make more people look at you closely."

"I am a city lord, but there are stronger people who would be interested in finding out my secrets."

"It is a smart idea to have some protection in place," Klaus said, looking at the special team.

"So what now?" Rugrat asked.

"Now, we see just what bad habits you've picked up." Klaus walked onto the stage and stood in the corner opposite. "Use everything at your disposal."

"Are you sure?" Rugrat asked.

Klaus gave a smile. "I am not like those Blood Demon sect wimps who only competed a few times and only cared about levels as a measure of strength."

Rugrat took Klaus seriously and pulled out his rifle.

"Begin!" Klaus said.

Rugrat fired his rifle. Klaus walked forward and seemed to step to the side, after-images pulling together. Rugrat adjusted and fired; Klaus shifted again and Rugrat continued firing. It seemed neither fast nor slow to Rugrat but his rounds hit the barrier around the stage instead of striking Klaus, who looked as though he were walking in the park.

Rugrat's rifle fired as fast as a machine gun but it still wasn't fast enough. He dropped and changed the magazine.

He cast Chains of Darkness on the ground. Klaus dodged them as well. Rugrat jumped and used his Cloud Footwork technique, gaining a new angle and distance as Klaus kept coming after him. Rugrat sent out more of his chains. Klaus dodged one that had just been cast.

Rugrat sent out several but Klaus somehow walked through them all. Rugrat smiled as he fired into the air beside Klaus and used his Aura of

Swords to send out mana blades while he detonated the newly formed chains.

It all happened at the same time.

Klaus dodged the chain explosions and waved his hand. Sharp blades of wind struck the mana blades, destroying them. He advanced, flitting across the ground. Rugrat fired at him; as he got closer, he had to move his rifle more.

Klaus closed with him. Rugrat smiled; he had been using his domain to hide his Aura of Swords as it lashed out at Klaus.

Rugrat's smile halted as he felt a blade on his neck. His spell froze and he looked at Klaus, who was outside his domain. He held out his hand; from it, Rugrat couldn't see anything but he could sense the condensed air mana.

"If you were to dispel my air weapon forcefully, then the energies would go rampant and at least severely wound you," Klaus said as he dissipated the weapon safely.

"Did you use an illusion?"

"When you thought I was inside your domain? Yes. It allowed me to focus on my spell. Domains are powerful but if I can draw you into focusing on one thing, then you have as many holes as someone without a domain. Using a domain to its full effects is not easy. It takes incredible control and while resting it is easy to comprehend and use, when in a fight or active, not so much. You adapted quickly, trying to close off my movements. Made me have to use air attacks to destroy your blades. When you didn't move as I was getting close, I knew that you had prepared something for me within your domain. Let us start again." Klaus moved back over to his corner as Rugrat reloaded and changed the formations on his rifle.

"How are you feeling?" Matt asked Rugrat, who was lying down in one of the Sky Reaching Restaurant's upper rooms.

Rugrat let out a complaining grunt from the ground.

Matt looked to Niemm and the others. They looked away and closed the door.

Rugrat recounted what he'd gone through. "Damn guy is a ghost. Some *Matrix*-ass shit, dodging bullets like that. I even increased the speed. At the highest speed I can shoot, he would just destroy the rounds with his little air tricks." Rugrat dug into some sauce-covered meat slices. He closed his eyes, savoring the taste.

"Damn, that's good." He sighed.

Matt checked his communication device as he got a message. Matt let out an annoyed noise.

"Go deal with it," Rugrat said. "We can meet up later."

"Thanks. It's the new renovations and building for the apartments. Someone messed up and put a wall in the wrong place," Matt said.

"Well, good luck," Rugrat said.

Matt headed off and Rugrat sat there. He ate his food and looked out of the room, thinking on fighting Klaus. Rugrat hadn't been able to draw out any more abilities, beyond his movement technique, his formed air weapons, and him sending out air blades.

His twin axes had remained on his hips.

Rugrat had been confident in his power, but fighting Klaus, he could feel that he was riddled with flaws. Rugrat wanted to get back in the ring and fight again. Even if he was beaten up and his mana was left drained, the feeling of progress, increasing his strength was powerful.

The best part is that I don't need to increase my level, or my cultivation; it is just using what I already have in different ways to have a greater effect.

Rugrat ate his food absently as he looked at Vuzgal through the windows. From where he sat, he could see into the dungeon valley, the paths that led to the three different dungeons.

Damn, I want to go adventuring again.

He smiled to himself and looked at the gardens that the Alchemist Association controlled. The lake where Fred and his people had stayed.

"Even with no formation, that valley naturally draws in and contains mana. Nature is incredible."

Rugrat looked at Vuzgal, seeing the people move through the city, flowing through the streets, bringing it to life. His eyes went north, seeing the roads in search of other cities. The forests that had laid untouched.

Rugrat felt something pulling at his mind, as he tried to focus on unravelling what he was thinking about.

"Nature's power…us imposing our will upon it…nature taking over?" He looked at one of the streams that weaved down the mountains and into the valley. "Nature's path controls the flow of power, even without humans imposing their will on it." Rugrat felt relaxed with that thought. He let out a deep breath through his nose, thinking of the incredible sights he had seen in nature, from waterfalls to oceans, to deserts and mountains. Forests that stretched to the horizon and trees that towered above. How Earth worked in harmony and the planets of the realms did as well.

"Nature shapes the power of mana. They coexist together. They are part of one another. Humans are part of nature as well. All things created from the realms are part of the realms. Formations are just a way to communicate our control over mana. What if it doesn't need to be controlled? What if it just needs to be allowed out naturally? Instead of beating out a sword through smithing, you are merely guiding the material into a balanced state—not just the weapon's balance, but a balance between the user and the Ten Realms. Items are a way to communicate with the Ten Realms, to gather its power and use it in different ways. Humans are always looking to impose our rule upon nature, but what if we let it flow into us?"

Rugrat pulled out an Earth-grade iron ingot and used Scan on it, combining his domain with his Simple Inorganic Scan and the Scan spell that Klaus had given him.

Rugrat looked through the ingot. He didn't just look at the purity and the grade; he saw the makeup of the ingot; he saw how the mana flowed through it. How it had been pressed into a shape filled with weaknesses.

"Just because it is solid, I have been treating it like a brick. That would be true on Earth, but here, everything is a part of the Ten Realms. Everything is part of everything else through mana. If I look at it like alchemists look at ingredients, then it changes everything. I said from the beginning I wanted to build a weapon that from the base up made it the strongest it could be. I started to focus on how to hammer, how to shape the metal, but I forgot that original goal. Damn, this is a dumb idea, but I need to see if it works."

Rugrat sat there and pulled out a notepad. "I need to check with Tanya about pure magic, talk to the alchemists and refiners about how they prepare their irons and their ingredients, delve into the external use of mana, formations and specifically, natural formations. I should return to the dungeon to see the different floors. Study how different mana attributes move."

Rugrat was filled with energy as he put down notes.

53 Halfway Point

Lady Sumi read through the letters that covered her desk.

A man wearing armor and a red band on his arm stepped into the room and dropped to his knee in front of her.

She finished working on the letter in front of her. "How are the preparations, Valter?" she asked, looking down at him.

"Our forces are ready to move at a moment's notice. I have scouts who are already watching Vermire. Nothing will move in or out of the outpost without our knowledge."

"Good. Once they reach the halfway mark, they should start to relax some. They should reach that point in a day or two," Sumi said. "Head out. I want Aditya's head on a plate."

Valter hesitated for a second.

"Is there an issue?" she asked.

"Lady Sumi, leaving you with such a small guard—I think that it is wrong. My instincts tell me to leave more guards with you."

"Are you sure that you can take Vermire with a smaller force?" Sumi asked.

"No, I am not," Valter said.

"We have the walls and I am not without a few tricks. They have been planning this for some time and they're still keeping everything hidden. If they had something to deal with the rest of the outposts, don't you think they would have done it already?"

"Lord Aditya has powerful means," Valter said.

"Lord?" Lady Sumi stood and her chair fell to the floor. "That worthless creature had my treasure and I had to find his family members to make him appear. Now that spineless coward has crawled his way up to his current position. He is nothing more than that worthless mercenary from before, looking to go over my head. This time I will not leave him alive."

The room chilled and Valter bowed deeply, not wanting to gain his lady's ire.

She took some time to calm down before she shook her head. "The other lords are all attacking different outposts. All of the outpost lords taking part in the alliance will be demanding reinforcements, placing pressure on Aditya. Each of the people we have contacted will be sending half of their force to take their rival's outpost, and most of them have an outpost interface that give their military forces a bonus when claiming another's land. Although Vermire does not have an outpost interface, we do. We also have a high population. The only reason I let so many live within my walls is to increase the buffs that we receive. We have surprise, we have strength, we have numbers, and you have spell scrolls to use. If you fail, you shouldn't come back alive."

Valter pressed his forehead to the ground. "I will win or I will die in the attempt!"

"Then go and get me another outpost," Sumi said.

Valter got up and bowed again, rushing out of her office.

"Send out the letters to the other outpost leaders. It's time we did something about this King's Hill Outpost Alliance," Lady Sumi spat.

"These..." Aditya looked stunned at the two plates in front of him.

"Are these not what you were looking for? One is to be used for Vermire. The second should be sent out to Pan Kun. I can have some of my people do it, but I wanted to make sure that you knew of it beforehand," Evernight said, clearly pleased with his shocked look.

I was only talking about these and in just a few days you have two spare outpost interfaces?

Once again, he could only shake his head. Instead of trying to figure out how Evernight had been able to get the interfaces, he cleared his throat and put them down with some reluctance. "We will have to explain this to the other leaders."

"Tell them that you were able to get them through some shady deals. With this, the more people who are in King's Hill Outpost, the greater the buffs. If they base their troops there, then they will all get a buff as well."

"If we reveal the interface now, as a halfway to completion prize and enjoying it with the others, then when the other outposts attack, we offer for them to base their people in King's Hill Outpost, to gain a buff, allowing them to hold off the enemy easier," Aditya said.

"I didn't think of that but that would be a good idea," Evernight agreed.

"Our scouts have reported that several outposts have started to send their people out of the city. The outpost lords have started to lock down the outpost to make sure that no information leaks. My people tell me that people are talking about how rich Vermire is recently." Aditya looked to Evernight.

"Well, a few good words here and there can sway the people. If they look at Vermire in a good light, it might make things easier later on."

"It will be a day or two until the attacks start," Aditya said.

"Well, I hope that the road is going well," Evernight said.

Emmanuel Fayad read the latest letter from Aditya. They had celebrated reaching the halfway mark yesterday.

Aditya sent a private message to several other outpost lords, revealing one of his cards that he had kept close to his chest.

"An outpost interface." Emmanuel shook his head. "This will make defending and upgrading the outpost much easier. The more people we have within the walls, the greater buffs that we can receive. Most of the outpost leaders don't have one of these interfaces. He has even volunteered for us to base our forces there in name and then they would gain passive bonuses to increase their strength."

Emmanuel put down his letter. "It is a smart move to bring us all closer together, show that he is with us by revealing something so powerful. Also sharing that power with the others. Though he makes it clear that he didn't share it with everyone and he thinks that someone has leaked information on our operation to others."

He mentions who he has sent the letters to, which means he trusts all of us, creating an iron-like alliance within the alliance. He only misses out on two lords who are part of the agreement.

Emmanuel tapped his hand on the table and wrote up a message to be passed to Nasreen.

Pan Kun scouted deep into the forest as there was a bird call from one of the trees. He looked over as a man walked out. He wore the same armor and weapons as the people who had trained the guards of Vermire.

Pan Kun tilted his head to them as they pulled out a covered square.

"You know what this is?" the man asked.

"Interface," Pan Kun said.

"Make sure that you protect it," the man said.

"I will." Pan Kun glanced at the markings on the man's arm. "Sergeant."

The man nodded and passed the interface over. "This is on you guys. We won't assist—though, we did pick up tracks of a bator."

"A bator?" Pan Kun asked.

"Flying beast. Able to carry off large beasts. Lives on top of a hill near King's Hill. It isn't strong enough to reach into the mountain range. It is, however, more than enough to kill a number of people on your trip." The sergeant pulled out a spell scroll and passed it to Pan Kun. "This will restrict their ability to fly for a few minutes. This will tame a beast."

"Thank you, Sergeant," Pan Kun said.

"Don't worry, I don't think it will be long until you're one of us." The sergeant smiled and waved his hand. A panther appeared and he headed off.

Pan Kun heard others moving in the distance but he couldn't see them.

Pan Kun put the scroll away and put the interface under his armor. *Although we have to move carefully through the Beast Mountain Range, it isn't much of a threat to them.*

Pan Kun grinned, excited at the thought that he might become one of them in the future. He turned and headed back to where the caravan was stopped for the night.

54 Strength Reserved, Strength Displayed

Rugrat finished his lecture on Mana Gathering as the class came to an end and the bell sounded, telling people to head to their next class.

Rugrat left with them but was surrounded by Storbon and his half section.

"Erik still on the Earth floor?"

"Yup, he's been down there for three weeks now," Storbon said.

"Don't worry. He's a hard bastard to kill, and a determined one." Rugrat grinned. There was pride in his voice. They didn't give up easily.

People looked over at Rugrat, feeling the unconscious pressure he released with his domain. He retracted his power.

I want to see how strong he is the next time he comes out.

"Davin should have the formations complete today," Rugrat said.

"The Fire floor?" Setsuko said.

"Well, at least it should be warm," Rugrat joked.

They opened up the other floors for training for the military, to passively temper their bodies and make it faster for people to adapt to different environments.

"You going to complete your Earth tempering to get Body Like Sky Iron?"

"I'm not like Major West—I don't have that high of a pain tolerance!"

Old Hei and Delilah watched as an Expert from one of the sects was presented with a box. It was opened to reveal a brown-looking pill that looked like dirt that had been turned into a packed ball. An earthy smell like that of freshly made mud pervaded the room, making it feel damp.

The young man held the pill. He calmed himself, focusing on his breathing. He took the pill and swallowed it.

He lay back as brown lines traced through his body. Popping noises came from within his body. He let out a hiss of pain as alchemists waited, ready with healing potions.

The boy cried out as his bones started to snap and then reform. It went on for a few minutes before the man collapsed from the pain. His bones stopped cracking. A golden power surrounded him, signaling his body tempering had reached the Body Like Sky Iron stage.

"His bones were tempered a total of ten times! Pill Head Zen Hei is unparalleled in the Third Realm!" The sect head bowed to Old Hei.

"It is not much." Old Hei waved his hand and stood, leaving the room.

It wasn't until they reached Old Hei's rooms that Delilah opened her mouth.

"Why did you not tell Erik that you had a formula to reach Body Like Sky Iron?"

"I could see you wanting to ask that the entire time." Old Hei smiled. "There are two reasons. One, he hasn't been spending that much time working on his Alchemy recently. Giving him a challenge is the fastest way to get him to dive into Alchemy completely. Second, the concoction I know allows one to increase their Body Cultivation, but there are stages of Body Cultivation. One can reach the next level of cultivation and they will be fine but they will only have a small amount of Earth mana in their bones; they have not infused their body with Earth mana, tempering themselves throughout. Tempering is torture. The more you subject yourself to it, the stronger you will become afterward. Your teacher has the strongest foundation I have seen in a long time. He not only tempered his body with poison, he gained Poison Body. He didn't just temper his body with Fire mana, he gained Fire Body." Old Hei's words hung in the room.

"So you were doing it to motivate him and devote himself to his task more." Delilah nodded, falling into deeper thought.

Old Hei had come to admire the young woman. She was a worthy student and hardworking. He knew that there was a lot on her shoulders, not only her Alchemy. Still, when she was working on Alchemy, she put everything into it.

"So when are you going to tell him that his student is just a half step away from reaching Expert?" Old Hei asked after a few minutes.

Delilah coughed a little, hiding her smile behind her hand.

"Make sure that you take the time to practice in between work." Old Hei waved his finger at her with a severe expression, even as his eyes shone with pride.

"Yes, Grand Teacher." Delilah smiled and bowed to Old Hei.

"You rascal," Old Hei said, hearing the teasing tone of Delilah. He let out a hearty laugh, shaking his head.

"Do you know where you will be staying in the Sixth Realm?" Delilah asked.

"Seems that you figured it out," Old Hei said.

"Watching you perform Alchemy… and talking to some of the people in the headquarters helped," She admitted with a smile.

She might be young but she is wise beyond her years, with the meetings she is constantly attending Erik has laid a heavy burden on her shoulders.

"What level are you, Grand Teacher?"

"I am a few levels away from Master. Expert is combining knowledge together to perform the necessary actions of your craft; Master is using those combined techniques to prove your theories of Alchemy. Levels and Experience are different when advancing at the Master level." Old Hei looked over to Delilah, seeing her rapt attention. He felt his own excitement build. There were not many he could share his passion with.

"At Master, levels are called concepts. You can make a concoction that is a level-one concept. This then advances to a level-ten concept and then the Star system. Every Master-level concoction gives a massive amount of Experience. One gains a higher level based on the higher level concept they have interpreted. Some stop at a certain point and cannot advance, so one needs to go back, correct their theory, and push forward again, hoping to have a higher level concept the next time.

"As you know, it is possible for an Apprentice to make a Journeyman-level concoction and higher level concoctions. The Star system concoctions are concoctions that touch upon the theories that govern the Ten Realms and one's body. The difference between Master and the Star level is a Master-level concoction is much weaker than the Star level. A Star level changes a truth of the Ten Realms. Gives people a complete beast bloodline. Can turn beasts into complete humans. Temper the body completely, opening the seventy-two acupoints to make one as strong as Divine Iron. It is breaking not only the normal limits upon the body, but the limits that one has within the Ten Realms. With these concoctions, the Ten Realms are affected."

Delilah was lost in imagination, picturing it.

"Those who are able to reach the Star system are rare. One in ten, maybe twenty billion becomes a person who even touches upon making an item of the Star system level—in *any* skill. So there are only a few hundred people in the Ten Realms who are capable of making even the first Star system level concoction."

Delilah let out a sigh. "The path ahead is not simple nor clear."

"No, but its challenges are their own joy to overcome." Old Hei smiled. "I will be heading to the Sixth Realm in two weeks to take up a teaching position there. If I am able to break through to Master, then the Alchemist Association might even take me to the Eighth Realm."

"What are the Sixth and Eighth Realm like?" Delilah asked.

"Well, I have never been there, but from what I was able to learn, the Sixth Realm is largely tame. There are a lot of schools and academies, and competitions are held all the time. Dungeons are operated by the dungeon clans that control the higher realms. That way, everyone can access the dungeons as long as they pay a fee instead of fighting over them as they do in the Fourth Realm."

"Dungeon clans?" Delilah asked.

"As there are city lords, there are dungeon lords—people who can create, modify, and destroy dungeons. They are one of the greatest powers in the Ten Realms. Not even the associations would want to anger them. They control the dungeons in the Sixth Realm and some in the Seventh."

"Why not at the higher levels?" Delilah asked.

"In the Seventh and higher, dungeons undergo a qualitative change. Well, that's not completely true. They are called holy lands in the higher realms. They are places of high mana concentration. They draw in the surrounding mana, purify it, and make rare and powerful items and materials from the gathered mana. Dungeons can have their own races living inside them—orcs and goblins—that are creatures unable to speak human tongue and they're able to use magics, weapons and armor.

"People go to the dungeons in large organized parties like down here. They gather a massive amount of materials and increase their strength. If they can get to the core of the dungeon, then they can absorb the purified mana, increasing one's Mana Gathering Cultivation, healing hidden wounds, and increasing the strength of their bodies. Also, dungeons can have restrictions, like it might only open once every few years and then allow only twenty people inside. They can be halls that were created by ancient Masters looking for people to inherit their power, or increase the strength of the younger generations. Some sects have been able to remain in their positions just due to holding onto one of these locations."

Delilah made some quick notes and Old Hei sat down on a couch.

"Fights are rare there. Everyone who has reached that stage is a powerful Expert. There are many competitions, sects actively looking for the most powerful stars to grow their strength. In the lower realms, one's birth is enough to secure them a position, then one's overall level. In the Eighth, one needs to prove themselves against others to draw the sect's interest. Even the associations get in on the competition. People sell lessons there. Ingredients and mana stones are used to increase one's Strength. Bartering is more normal to the people in these realms."

"People use the competitions in order to fight over resources and power in the higher realms—why doesn't that happen in the Fourth Realm?" Delilah asked.

"Life is cheap in the ten realms, it makes more sense to have people fight it out and increase their level in the fourth realm, prove themselves before powers are willing to invest more resources into them. Having someone who knows how to kill is a powerful asset. Although people here might be able to change the fate of a small battle, the power of people in the Seventh and higher realms have much greater effects. Melee types who disappear as they move, mages who can cause the ground to shake and destroy mountains."

"If they only know how to compete against one another, they'll lose that killing edge that they could need in a real fight."

She doesn't shy away from the realities of the Ten Realms. It is a battlefield where the strong use or prey on the weak. Thinking we live in a world of peace is for the ignorant or arrogant. Old Hei privately praised his grand-student for not being blind from the realities around here even if she had grown up rather sheltered.

"Correct, strength gains you power, and enemies," Old Hei warned.

"I have heard that people from the Seventh Realm don't descend, that the mana down here is too thin?" Delilah asked.

"Yes, in the Sky realms that start at the Seventh Realm, people are usually very sensitive to the ambient mana. If they are not in a highly concentrated area of mana, then their Mana Gathering Cultivation starts to decrease. Think of it like a cup of tea: if it is surrounded by water, then it will remain full, even if upside down. Now you take that cup of tea and turn it, the water, or mana, comes out, but the power left only decreases. The power of that water or mana within the cup can change continents but once it is gone, then a person only has the peak power of the Sixth Realm. It will take them a lot of time in the lower realms to recover their power, or a lot of resources to increase their Strength."

"If someone was able to fill an area with a lot of mana, then would that prevent the person's power from decreasing?"

Old Hei scratched his face. "I don't see why not, if the ambient mana is at the same density as what is found in the Sky realm. That would be a ton of mana and you would need powerful formation masters to do it."

The two of them fell into silence, each with their own thoughts.

"Thank you, Grand Teacher, for all you have shared with me." Delilah bowed to Old Hei.

Old Hei stood up and patted her shoulder. "I'm just happy that my student was able to find you. Remember, if you ever have trouble, I will be there," Old Hei said seriously.

Erik and Delilah gave his life some color and seeing them driven to improve, lit his own competitive fire. He had laughed more, been more motivated with them around than he had in his life before. *Having people to share in your happiness is a powerful thing.*

Delilah hugged Old Hei, shocking him a bit before he laughed and hugged her back.

"Now, don't think that you are getting out of your afternoon lessons that easily! We'll be going over the core theories of Alchemy."

Deep in the earth, a man lay on his back, his body making painful noises. He let out a hoarse noise, his throat dry and raw from screaming and groaning in pain.

The air around him was thick with a brown haze that he drew in with every breath.

The man opened his eyes, looking ahead. Just a few feet ahead was the center of the formation. He pulled himself forward, inch by painful inch, his eyes filled with determination. He collapsed within the center of the formation.

The surrounding Earth mana was pulled in through his nose and mouth, through his mana gates.

Erik didn't know how much time had passed as he waited for his body to get used to the new changes happening within.

The Earth mana entered his lungs, entering his blood, staining it brown as it moved through his body, reaching his bones. The powerful vitality of his body fought to repair him as the Earth mana worked to break him.

Earth mana traveled through his mana channels, coating the inside of his body and flowing into his bones. The power was too much to deal with the demands of the Earth mana.

His bones continued to crack and reform. It must've happened hundreds of times in the past. A black sludge covered him. His Poison Body removed the poisons from his body. The Fire mana within his body purified the Earth mana as the Earth mana broke his bones. The Fire mana refined his bones, fusing the Earth mana completely into his body.

As his bones started to crack less, Erik pulled out enchanted needles and stuck them into his leg.

His bones continued to break less. Runes started to form upon his bones. Runes from the Poison Body and Fire Body appeared across his body. They weren't part of any known language but contained the power of his temperings.

Erik used more needles, then he used the dagger. Days passed as his bones settled down again, the Earth mana fusing into his entire body.

Erik studied the power of poison, Fire, and Earth within his body, watching them working together and acting in ways he didn't think possible.

Unknowingly, Erik sunk into thought, studying the human body and the mana system, and contemplating Mana Gathering and Body Cultivation.

Egbert looked up from what he was reading and then looked back down.

Gilly seemed to have gone to sleep, drawing in Earth-attribute mana. She was undergoing a massive change as well, transforming her body.

Both of them are monsters. They've been in there for three, almost four weeks.

Qin looked up as she felt the power shifting around her. She frowned; it felt familiar. "Is someone making a breakthrough to Expert?" Qin's head cleared a bit. "Julilah!"

She put down what she was working on and headed to the workshop at a run. The door was closed and she waited there impatiently.

She had waited ten minutes and was thinking of knocking down the door when it opened.

Julilah stood there, looking tired, but there was a triumphant look on her face. "Hah! Did it!" Julilah grinned.

"You—" Qin held what she was going to say next and shook her head before laughing.

"Couldn't let you get that much of a head start. I will become the department head!" Julilah said, looking even more sleep-deprived with her announcement.

"What technique were you able to create?"

"I call it the Pressed Formation technique!" Julilah yelled.

More people were coming over, having heard Julilah yelling or felt the amount of Experience that was flooding the area.

Qin took Julilah back into the workshop and closed the door, sealing it.

"See, what I do is I create a print in the air with my mana. Then I press it into the metal, stamping a formation upon it. It takes more time to prepare and a lot of mana to strengthen until it is completely impressed into the material, but with the prep time I can make much more complex and intricate formations, also smaller formations as I am using mana to shape it. What I need to do is create a tool that I can create the mana imprint on, then it will save it and then I can print that into the metal. I could make the prints so that they could be used without my mana. I could make much stronger formations, just need to draw them out on that tool if I could. Take like a day to prepare it, then support it with mana from a stone and then bam, formation in a few minutes."

Hearing Julilah talking, Qin was shocked.

"You could mass-produce formations with that kind of tool," Qin finally said.

"I guess that you could." Julilah yawned, not getting the complete implications that Qin had fallen upon.

Qin wanted to shake her as Julilah fell into a chair, her eyes half-closed as she kept on yawning.

"It was strange. You know, as a kid, I thought that smiths just hit the metal once and formed it into a shape. I thought it was pure magic. When I watched smiths, they were just hammering metal together. When I watched Tan Xue, then I saw all the preparation. She took time organizing everything, then she would work the metal as if it were a system. I liked the order of it all. Sure, she hammered out the metal, but it was methodical, with steps, you know. So I took that with my formations: lay out everything ahead of time and then carry it out. I thought it would be funny if I could create a small formation with my mana, a mana blade that was in the shape of a formation. I was going to use it on the formation plate, but then I stopped. I knew how much work Tan Xue put into it—shouldn't I?"

Julilah shifted in her chair, turning it from side to side as she let her head hang back, resting her eyes.

"So I studied the metal, methodically, took the time to understand it. I looked at how it had been formed. Then I created a formation that added to the materials and shape. You know, like how some people paint—they have the finest papers and brushes with them and they can bring out the greatest beauty. Sometimes formations do not need to look pretty—sometimes, they just need to do the job."

Qin looked at the formation that was on the workstation. She pulled over a formation-enhanced glass on an arm. It looked rough and not elegant at all, but as Qin studied it and the formation plate, she found that they were in harmony with each other.

"Harmonizing the workmanship of the smith and altering one's formation to it." Qin held onto her chin. "I looked to draw out the power of the metals and the weapon, but I didn't think of the smith's workmanship—I just thought of the overall stats.

"This formation has only been carved out, but it is of the Expert grade already. Looks like you are a half-step…" Qin turned to face Julilah and her words trailed off.

Julilah's head was over the back of the chair; her arms and legs hung down limply.

Qin cringed seeing the way that Julilah was sleeping. She poked Julilah but she was already out.

Qin used a weightlessness spell on Julilah, reduced her weight and then put her over her shoulder. She cleared up her friend's supplies with a wave of her storage ring and walked out of the Expert-level workshop.

People had gathered there, seeing Qin, one of the three Expert-level formation masters, carrying a passed-out Julilah. The two of them were the leaders of the formation department.

"Don't you have formations to work on?" Qin asked, trying to sound serious as her friend shifted and snorted in her sleep.

The different formation masters had awkward expressions as they quickly disappeared and Qin stood there with a red face.

"Couldn't you be more lady-like!" she yelled at her friend, who lazily hit her. But with where her hand was, it just smacked her in the backside.

Qin stared at Julilah, her gaze filled with accusation. *Aren't you a great Expert-level formation master now!!*

Qin shook her head, her image of Expert-level crafters ruined as she carried Julilah off, heading to their quarters.

People saw her walking through the school grounds with her friend passed out on her shoulder.

"The things we do for friends," Qin lamented.

"George, watch where you play with the lava!" Rugrat said as he used his sword domain to strike the lava that was coming for him out of the way.

George pouted and lowered his head into the lava, his breathing making bubbles in it.

"Go play in the deep end with your friends," Rugrat said.

George raised his head with a pleased smile and doggy-paddled deeper into the lava. The group of fire lizards he was playing with followed.

"Aw, look at the puppies, so well-trained and they listen." Rugrat closed his eyes, extending his senses out to the section of rock in front of him. *Well, sometimes.*

Rugrat cracked half an eye open and he saw George playing in the lava and on the different rock islands.

Erik probably finds this floor easy to be on. Damn, I'm sweating my balls off! My ass is burning through my pants!

Rugrat pulled out a shield, put it on the ground, and sat on it. "Better. Right—rock research." Rugrat cleared his throat.

Since he had his idea at the top of the Sky Reaching Restaurant, he had started heading to the lower floors of the dungeon instead of smithing.

He reached out and touched the ground, his senses moving to the stone in front of him. He had needed to get Davin to go to the bottom of the lava lake and get the rock.

Just standing there, the surrounding area was heated up by the rock. There were different layers to it, some compressed to the point that they had been turned into gems. Decades had been turned into thin lines.

It created a record of the floor and of Fire mana.

Rugrat looked through the different layers of the stone.

He pulled out his spell, smithing, and formation crafting books, checking the information within.

"The cycle of stone and metals is much like the system of water, with more sediment thrown in and more processes. Water evaporates, rain clouds, comes all back down as rain. The planet's surface is always moving, pushing things up or down. As that gets lower, it heats up and starts to rise through any opening they can, like steam through a steam cooker. The heat, the pressure, the compounds included, change the composition of the heated materials. This way, we get different deposits of different metals."

Rugrat's Simple Inorganic Scan had grown in leaps and bounds, using it while he was smithing and most of the time without even realizing it. Combining it with his heightened sense and control of mana, when he looked at the stone now, it told him a story.

He could see the flow of power that moved through the rock and its different layers.

"Mana isn't sentient, but it follows a path, like how creatures might move around an area throughout the year, a place to give birth, different feeding grounds, so on. How animals know how to build a nest, how they know how to walk at first. Mana is just like water; it flows through its own path, following its own rules. It doesn't mean to shape its environment; it just does."

Rugrat sank into thought, thinking on the Fire mana, thinking on the Metal mana, the Wood mana, pure mana. Each of them were connected, just different states of the same item—one water, one solid, one gas—all the same, but having greatly different effects.

The difference between mana and water is that in their different states, mana acts much more wildly than steam, or ice. Rugrat halted his line of thinking. "Is water that tame?"

Rugrat thought of the times he had been aboard ships, looking over seas and oceans that stretched to the horizon. Heard as ships were torn apart by those forces, the high possibility of being injured if one was boarding or dismounting from one ship and a smaller craft. How the waters could swell and crush a person. It wasn't tame in the slightest, it was a raging beast fueled by the power of nature, able to turn on those that relied on it in a moment.

"Maybe to tame it, I just need to get used to it like I got used to water?" Rugrat continued to study as George and the newly tamed lizard beasts of the Fire floor swam in the lava lake.

Bai Ping sat down in the cafeteria in the barracks.

Peng Yi sat down with him and pulled out a book. He started to read as he was eating.

"Where did you get that from?" Bai Ping asked.

"I rented it out from the library. You can take some books out from them," Peng Yi said, not looking up as he ate his noodles. His eyes followed the words on the page.

"Are you that addicted to reading now?" Bai Ping asked.

"The more you read, the more you will know," Peng Yi said.

"What's the book on?"

"It's on animal husbandry," Peng Yi said.

"So on how to raise animals? It doesn't sound that useful to fighting," Bai Ping said as he ate his food.

"It might not sound like it, but a beast master can tame all kinds of beasts—those that fly through the sky, or go through the ground. Both can gather information for their master without being detected. Also, it teaches how creatures can have their strength increased through training, through consuming different resources. If they get sick, different ways you can test what they're sick with and how to treat them."

Bai Ping fell into thought as Peng Yi kept reading.

Once I'm done training with mortars, I should take a look. Next is learning higher level magic, though; that's going to be hard to learn by itself.

Bai Ping snorted. *I once thought that being a soldier was just learning how to fight with others. It might be how other groups operate. Here, the Alva Army works together, different parts all working as one to win. Using everything that they can. Who knows, maybe if the beasts are sick, then Peng Yi can help heal them, allowing us to ride them and go forth to defeat the enemy.*

"Don't you have mortar training starting today?" Peng Yi asked.

"Yeah, starts this afternoon. Moving my stuff over and then training for three weeks." Bai Ping checked the time. "Which is in ten minutes! Got to run!" He got up and ran out of the hall. He dropped off his cutlery and tray before he ran through the barracks.

He saw others running to the parade square.

They were all in position as a sergeant marched out to them. He stood in front of them all.

"Some of you might know me. My name is First Sergeant Sun Li. I am in charge of you all for this training period. You will create first and second mortar squads of Third Artillery Training Company. You will understand how to call in artillery in a fluid manner. You remember the basics from your sharpshooter courses?" He looked around at the general nodding of heads.

"Good. We're going to take that basic knowledge and go into it more. You will know not only how to call in artillery—you will know what the mortar team is thinking. You will be surprised with how effective mortars can be with the right spotter. You all know how the army was able to bleed the Blood Demon sect with the special teams observing the enemy and then our own Tiger Platoon dropped mortar round after mortar round onto them. We didn't need to see the enemy, but we destroyed the enemy's morale and we killed thousands of their members. The Tiger Combat Company will not have weak mortar squads, or else you will have to answer to me, as I will need to answer to Captain Yui!"

Sun Li looked them over. "Am I going to need to answer to Captain Yui?"

"No, First Sergeant!"

"Good! You will learn how to set up, tear down, fire, reload, clean, and love the mortar. You will also learn how to aim it without an observer and create mortar range cards, similar to your fire position range cards that you learned with the defensive portion of your basic training. You will become experts of this weapon system, to the point that you will be able to teach others how to use it easily. We are an expanding military and we need to train up people faster than ever." Sun Li looked them over. "Sergeant Williams!"

"First Sergeant!" A voice came from behind.

"Take them to their training racks," Sun Li said. "Follow Sergeant Williams. We are not here to screw around with you. You learned how to be a soldier in basic training. We will treat you like an adult here. You will attend class from morning until night for six days, with one day off. We will have some people on staff for you to ask them questions and go over training. You are here to learn how to hone your abilities. If you don't know something, speak up. Others won't know it either. We want to teach you as much as possible."

Sun Li braced himself as Bai Ping and everyone else straightened up. "Dis-missed!"

They turned to the right and marched off, heading over to Sergeant Williams, who waited for them.

"Follow me," Williams said.

They gaggled together and talked to one another as they followed Sergeant Williams. Some of them had trained together; others were in the same squad. They were all fresh to this, so they started to talk to one another and figure out who was who.

"Wilky," one girl with her hair cut short said, pointing to her name tag, *Wilkinson*.

"Bai," he replied with a head tilt. "You from Alva?"

"Nah, Vuzgal. You?"

"Same. You have any idea that they were hiding something like this?"

"No idea. I thought that Vuzgal was already hard to believe. Imagine if we told anyone up there about this massive dungeon that they control that has more mana and an even larger academy?" Wilky chuckled.

"I don't think anyone would think we're telling the truth." Bai shook his head. "What brought you to Vuzgal?"

"From the east, Chaotic lands, wanted to be a crafter. Headed to Vuzgal—heard it was somewhere safe and had crafting. I showed up, but the academy wasn't up at that time so I joined the military—food, free classes on crafting and a service term. I just thought that the crafting was a lie but I checked the service term, figured that if I worked in the military for some time, got stronger, then I could get some decent money together to start learning how to craft. You?"

"Town got raided. We were in the middle of the war. Fled with my family. I used to be a guard. I knew only how to fight and I saw how strong the Vuzgal army was. I wanted to be as strong as them so I joined them."

"I keep waiting for the catch, you know?" Wilky said.

"Yeah, I'm used to being screwed over, but it seems that the contracts were true."

"I don't know about that. Did you read that if you die then your family will get what's worth a year of your wages and that the army will do what they can to take care of them?"

"I did. Did you see how specific the terms are?" Bai Ping asked.

"It looked like a lot of words, so I skipped it." Wilky shrugged.

"If you are wounded in any way in the line of duty, from getting the fear shakes and seizing up, to losing a limb, you will get healed. The army will give you wages until you are fully healed, then you will be returned to duty. Or if you don't want to, you can move to one of the support units, join the policing or guard forces—just need retraining. If you get out of the military after finishing your contract, you get a bonus for your service. You get free schooling for the rest of your life—you just have to pay for supplies. If you die, then your family gets a year of your wages and assistance if they require it, have someone talk to them. Also heard that the city leaders and dungeon leaders, Major Erik and Rugrat, they're true soldiers, like they came up from the bottom. With that, I think that they're looking out for the people at the bottom of the ranks," Bai Ping said.

"Damn, I didn't think it was all that."

"Then why did you sign it?"

"Easier than reading it all!" Wilky grinned.

55 Forming King's Hill Outpost

Nasreen looked at the road. It stretched behind them, going all the way to Shadowridge Outpost. It was still hidden and none of the mercenaries had found it yet. Linking the road to the outpost would be the last thing to happen.

Working together for a week, the guards had gotten closer to one another. Working in close quarters for a long time would do that. Their rotation was six days on and two days back in the outpost. They had all taken the time off, except the group from Vermire; they stayed on, working as hard as anyone else, if not harder.

The crafters had been nervous this far into the Beast Mountain Range. Now they stopped caring about the beasts and focused on their tasks, speeding up the process.

The guards scouted ahead and cleared the area well before they reached it.

Something seemed to have gotten into the Vermire people the last couple of days as they pushed harder than before, even using their weapons to clear the path. They had nearly doubled the distance they did in the previous three days. They had passed the halfway mark four days ago; they would reach King's Hill early tomorrow morning.

They pressed on well into the night so they would have less work in the morning. The people from Vermire, instead of taking a break, continued to clear the forest. Each tree took them only a few blows to clear. It would make things easier for the mages and casters to create the road behind them tomorrow.

Pan Kun finally finished up and joined the guards in the camp.

"Get out your lumberjack on the trees?"

"They'll be useful in building the convoy. The trees in here are much older and stronger than the ones at the fringe of the Beast Mountain Range," Pan Kun said.

"You Vermire guards ever rest?" another guard asked.

"Only when the job is done," Pan Kun said.

"Then you need to have one of McVoy's meads and his wife Maria's stew," one of the Vermire guards said.

Pan Kun grinned and the others agreed.

"Nothing like our Mister Xia's pizza!"

The groups went on, boasting about their outpost's food and entertainment. Nasreen and her guards were no different.

"Ugh, why is it morning already," Nasreen said as she got out of her bedroll and dressed.

She saw the Vermire guards, looking as fresh as anything and hacking at the trees once again.

Pan Kun saw her and waved her over to the pot of tea that brewed all night long to give the night watch something to keep them warm during the night.

"The night has to end at some point." Pan Kun grabbed a cup, filling it with some tea and passing it to her.

"Well, it doesn't seem like you Vermire guards seem to understand the concept of sleep," Nasreen muttered.

Pan Kun chuckled and sat back. "We will be heading out in a few hours to scout King's Hill. We've encountered a few beasts but it seems like their numbers are dwindling."

"With our high levels and our numbers, we're able to wear them down faster than mercenaries who are just thrown together for money," Nasreen said.

"We need to remember that there are powerful creatures to be found in the Beast Mountain Range. We can't be complacent." Pan Kun sipped from his tea.

Nasreen nodded. "All right, we'll be laying the foundations of King's Hill Outpost tonight."

"The sooner we start, the sooner we can have walls around us."

"With the new products coming from the Edo empire, they need a greater supply of monster cores and ingredients that are found in the Beast Mountain Range."

"So if we put up a bounty on the ingredients, then we should pull in a lot and make a nice little profit. Have you been able to find a new supplier of grain? The Rama kingdom is starting to increase their prices and Wilson County's crops were hit with an early frost, which will drive up their prices—if they have anything spare to sell." Leo looked to Peter, his direct subordinate and second-in-command. "Check with the ingredient gardens, see what we can grow. Let's see what the other outposts might need. It seems that trading with outside powers is more complicated," Leo said.

Peter nodded with a knowing smile. "Yes, my lord. I will look into more trading contracts with other outpost lords."

Leo looked at the merchants in the room, seeing ideas appear in their mind as they started changing their perspective. At this time, only Peter and the captain of his guards knew about the King's Hill Outpost.

"Well, what about Vermire?" one of the merchants said.

Leo indicated for them to continue.

"They have been trading with most people in terms of grain. It seems that some people are trying to pressure them with an increased price in foodstuffs. They have created a trading agreement with multiple partners, some that are months' travel away. If we can contact them, they can possibly act as an intermediary. The prices wouldn't be as cheap as that from Wilson County, but they would be much cheaper than what we could get from the Rama kingdom if we buy in bulk."

The door burst open and Leo had a small crossbow in his hand. Seeing it was Nicolaas, the captain of his guards, he relaxed.

"There is an army of other outpost lords heading toward us. They will arrive tonight or tomorrow morning," Nicolaas reported.

The merchants looked shaken and Leo looked to Peter.

He put the crossbow back into his jacket. "Excuse me. It looks like we have some unwelcome guests." Leo strode out of the room.

"Who are they?" Leo asked.

"Looks like it's from the Goldgrip, Brownspine, and Embergrove Outposts," Nicolaas said.

"How many?"

"About six hundred. They brought mercenaries with them as well."

"Did they leave anyone to defend their outposts?" Leo hissed. He had one hundred and twenty guards. With thirty of them working on the road, there was just ninety remaining in his Sea Castle Outpost.

"Send a message to Aditya and the other outpost lords in the area. Notify them that we are under attack and request aid."

"Kingdoms sure are powerful," Lady Sumi remarked as she read the latest letter. "With the units from their armies, we should keep all of the outposts occupied, pinning them all down. Then we start picking them off one by one. Bring all of our strength to bear on one outpost after another, grinding them into nothing." Sumi ate some fruits as she glanced at the map on the wall.

"Tomorrow the Beast Mountain Range will be consumed in the flames of war. I should really thank you, Aditya, for creating this opportunity."

She grabbed a glass and toasted the map, before letting out a laugh that filled the empty hall.

Aditya looked at the reports as he stood in his office. "Well, today we will establish King's Hill Outpost and fight our first battles. Tonight, I will order our people to act."

"Nervous?" Evernight asked.

"Terribly so!" Aditya said.

"We've rolled the dice and prepared our cards. It's time to see if we get the rolls we need and our cards are strong enough to win," Evernight said.

"Well, this is shitty," one of the scouts said as they moved with Pan Kun, looking at King's Hill.

"Huh." Pan Kun frowned as he looked out in the field. "Looks like a cow, a deer—a very big deer—and a hairy ox got it on."

Pan Kun looked to the scout. "Well, you can't say that it doesn't." He shrugged.

"Let's scout around," Pan Kun said.

The group broke up and moved around the one hundred strong big beasts that were grazing atop King's Hill. Each of them were powerful beasts; they had to be to survive in these lands.

The forest curled around King's Hill, which was a large hilly area that surveyed the area. There were few trees on the hill and it was flat at the top, perfect for an outpost, and for the grazing beasts.

Pan Kun kept his eyes out as he looked around. He climbed a tree to take a look around. He couldn't find signs of the bator.

He kept on looking but didn't see any signs. The scouts grouped up again and shared what they had seen.

"There is a creek to the east. Nothing much of note. Rocks there, making it harder to get up the hill," the first scout reported.

"The hill to the west is fine. Big trees. We climbed up, saw that the ox-deer cover the entire top of the hill."

"To the north, there is a second hill. It is rockier, and it stands taller. There is a cave in it. There was a winged beast standing in the entrance. It's a mean-looking creature, has a beak on it, and it was eating what looked like to be part of a mountain wolf."

The others looked to the scout, seeing the slight fear in his eyes.

"Well, looks like we can use one to solve the other," Pan Kun said.

"What do you mean?" Nasreen asked.

"If we can draw out that beast in the hills, we have it attack the herd that is on the hill, have them weaken one another and then we can swoop in and kill whatever remains."

"Well, how are we going to get it on the ground?"

Pan Kun pulled out one of the two spell scrolls that he had been given.

"Trap Beast?" someone asked as he showed it to them.

"It will hold a beast within five feet of a binding location, so it will be stuck on the ground. The creatures in the herd are nearly seven feet tall, so they can easily hit it at that kind of range."

"What if it kills them all? It doesn't look weak," the scout who had seen the beast said.

"Then it'll be more tired out and we can get in there and kill it," Pan Kun said.

I doubt that it can take that much punishment. With herds, if I can find out which one is the leader and I tame it, then the rest of the herd should follow. If the beast survives, then I use the binding scroll on it and capture it. Whichever group is strongest, I'll be able to reap the rewards.

The others seemed to agree.

"So how do we get them to fight one another?"

"Easy. We piss off the flying beast," Pan Kun said.

"Kite it into the herd, have it attack the herd," Nasreen said.

"Rollo is our best runner."

"Hey, I didn't volunteer for anything!" one of the Vermire guards complained.

"You didn't need to—you just got voluntold." Pan Kun smiled, using one of the terms that the training staff had used and stuck with the guards.

"Damn," Rollo muttered.

"Go and piss it off and draw it over to the herd. If it's angry enough, then it'll attack. So do your best," Pan Kun said.

"I fucking hate this plan, just so you know," Rollo said.

"Don't worry. I'll be here and ready to use the scroll the moment it's within the herd," Pan Kun said.

Rollo shook his head as his friends gave him commiserating pats on the backs. "Thanks, you assholes. Just going to go and piss off a big bat—make it feel like a funeral."

"Let's get all of the guards in position. Once we are, Rollo, do your thing."

Pan Kun waited. The guards were set, the herd was still munching, and Rollo had been sent off.

He heard a cry out in the distance. Pan Kun moved, feeling the scroll tucked into his armor and the other that was in his hands.

The herd looked up from their grazing as Rollo appeared. He turned and fired an arrow through the trees he had come through.

There was another screech of anger as Rollo ran and threw himself forward. There was a rush of wind. As the bator appeared, it let out a yell, a wave of force contorting the air as it struck the herd beyond Rollo.

The herd let out groans and snorts as they pawed the ground. The bator cut its descent and flapped its wings to gain altitude and pass over the herd.

Pan Kun activated the spell scroll, watching the bator get away and higher. "Come on, come on!"

The bator let out another screech at the herd below. The large beasts raised their front legs with deep bellows, before landing on the ground, one challenging the other.

The scroll activated and spell circles appeared around and attached to the bator. It was dragged from the sky. A chain appeared from the ground and a square formation there. The bator hit the ground, letting out an alarmed noise.

The herd beasts rushed in, charging with their horns now that their enemy was on their level.

Rollo quickly escaped into the trees, forgotten by the beasts.

The bator used her screech, stunning the beasts rushing her as she used her beak and talons to attack them. They tossed their heads, hitting her with their horns. She let out a yell as she was thrown to the side, the chain holding her in place.

A beast lowered his head to pierce her with his horns. She sliced at him with her talons, opening his face and neck. The beast let out a pained cry, half blind and in pain. She tried to escape but the chain stopped her from getting far.

The beasts passed through the chain to attack her.

She fell under one; they raised their hooves to stop and her beak shot forward, piercing their chest and neck as she backed up.

She was hit in the back but she screeched at them and dug her claws in, savagely hitting them with her beak.

The beasts were hitting one another with their bulk and horns.

She stunned, clawed, and attacked. Her beak and talons were vicious tools.

Three of the herd lay dead at her feet; half a dozen others were wounded.

She tore open a beast and swallowed their beast core whole, covered in their blood.

A larger member of the herd let out a roar. The others parted for the older and larger beast.

There you are. Pan Kun looked at the leader of the herd.

His bulk was impressive and there were a number of scars on his body. He raised his front, smashing on the ground.

The bator let out a yell that struck the king head on. His eyes were rolling but he stayed on his feet. She jumped over and stuck her talons into his side, at the limit of her chain, and she pecked at the beast relentlessly. The king roared out in pain. Foam appeared from his mouth and his eyes were still focusing as he tossed his head back and forth but wasn't able to get her.

She left ragged wounds on him and he finally turned and ran. The herd, seeing their king leaving, ran after him. They ran across the hill and into the forest, fleeing the flying demon.

The winged beast opened her wings, one of them not opening fully. It was clearly broken. Its scales had been torn off in places and it was heavily wounded.

It pecked at the chain around its neck and strained, but it was too tired. It looked around and made to eat the fallen beasts.

Pan Kun pulled out the second scroll. He activated the beast taming scroll. A spell circle fell around the beast. Stunned and tired by the change, she tried to escape once again. Red runes appeared on her body. Her actions became weaker as she calmed down.

Pan Kun looked at the other members of the Vermire guards. He had told them about his complete plan and the second part to try to tame either the bator or the herd king.

They moved out of the tree line, ready to attack as a second spell formation appeared opposite the bator.

Pan Kun grabbed his war axe, the other hand holding onto the spell scroll.

"Pan Kun," Nasreen hissed.

"One second." Pan Kun walked up toward the beast and stepped into the second spell formation.

He waited and runes appeared on his body.

Do you wish to bind this creature to you?
YES/NO

"Yes," Pan Kun said.

The beast looked at Pan Kun. Her eyes started to clear and a power flashed around them both. Pan Kun felt a connection to the bator.

Bond formed

The spell formation disappeared. The bator's eyes cleared fully and it looked at Pan Kun and tilted her head, waiting for a command.

Pan Kun looked at the bator, a little stunned. "That seemed easier than I thought it would be." Pan Kun said, "Come here."

She waddled over on her talons and looked up at him.

"Get me the monster cores," Pan Kun said.

She turned and hopped over to the beasts, using her half broken wing. She rooted around in the beasts and pulled out one beast core and handed it to him. She pulled out the other and passed it to him as well.

Pan Kun held his axe tighter as she stared at him for new orders.

He cancelled the first spell scroll. It dissipated into motes of light and the chain disappeared from around her.

She stretched out fully. She was nearly a meter tall and had a four-meter wingspan.

"Eat your fill." Pan Kun indicated to the beasts.

She happily went over and started to eat.

He picked up the monster cores, shaking his head as he looked at her.

He took the monster cores to Nasreen. "We should start to build the outpost," he said.

"Next time, tell me when you're going to do something like that," Nasreen said.

The corner of Pan Kun's mouth lifted. "Maybe." He pulled out the interface and blueprint for the outpost. "Want to do the honors?"

Nasreen seemed to think about it for a moment. "Sure." She grinned and took them both. She went to the top of the flattened hill. Here they could just see over the large trees in the Beast Mountain Range. To the north, there was a pass between the two mountain ranges that curled down to the south like wings. King's Hill was nearly in the middle of the pass between the mountains, giving it the most central and easiest path to the surrounding outposts.

Nasreen put the interface on the ground. Pan Kun and the other guards watched as the interface activated. It was already linked to the different outposts so she couldn't make it just Shadowridge's outpost.

The interface sunk into the ground, flush with the grass. She accessed it once again and the blueprint was added to the interface. She altered and moved it around before placing it.

A skeleton blueprint flashed into existence atop King's Hill.

"Welcome to King's Hill Outpost," Nasreen said with a laugh.

The other guards let out cheers and laughed. It had been a long week and a half, fighting across the Beast Mountain Range.

"Let's get that road finished and start laying down the foundations," Pan Kun said.

"Team one, you protect the outpost location. Team two, construction. Team three, help with the road. We've got a lot of work to be done." Nasreen quickly organized them and they got to work.

Nasreen wiped her face as she looked at the tree that she had cut into shape. A pit marked the border of the outpost. With everyone's strength, it hadn't taken them long to create the wall's foundations. They moved to creating the outpost's headquarters' foundations.

They dropped off their food supplies and building materials inside the walls, tents creating their current shelter from the elements. The carts and beasts were used to gather the trees that they had felled along the path to use them.

"Looks like you're about done with that log," Pan Kun said, offering her a canteen of water.

"This blueprint makes things easier, but building still isn't easy." Nasreen gulped down the water.

"That doesn't sound confusing, and the blueprint only makes it easier to see where everything should go and speed up putting it together. Hopefully we can get some more crafters to help with shaping the wood, working with the stone. Earth mages are great at this kind of thing." Pan Kun looked over to Kai, who had fallen asleep on a cot. She had been using her magic to pull stone from the earth, bonding it together to create foundations in the dug holes. She had passed out from mana fatigue.

"With the stone that we've collected from down the side of the hill, we should be able to make the walls. Wish we could make the doors with them," Nasreen said, staring at the planks she had created.

"At least someone had the foresight to send us smithed hinges or else we wouldn't have anything to hold them up with." Pan Kun snorted. "Once Kai is awake, it should be easier for her to just fuse the stone together into the walls we need. We'll still need to make the wooden roof for the village headquarters." Pan Kun looked at the simple hall in the middle of the outpost that had been dug out.

"How does being a bator dad feel?"

"Umm…" Pan Kun gave her an odd look before he shrugged. "Well, she's hurt pretty bad. She needs plenty of food and rest to recover. Hoping that the Alva Healing House can heal her up properly."

"Everything takes time," Nasreen said. She heard hooves approaching and she looked down toward where the road would be. *We need to grade out the ground still so that carts aren't just shooting down there.*

Two guards from Shadowridge climbed the hill, looking at the outline of King's Hill Outpost. Nasreen waved them over.

They arrived in front of her. "The alliance is under attack. A number of outposts that weren't part of the alliance found out about it and are attacking different outposts or locking them down so that people can't enter or leave."

"Crap," Nasreen said. *We just broke ground on King's Hill Outpost. With their outposts being attacked, would the outpost lords care about an outpost in the middle of the Beast Mountain Range, or about trying to keep their own outpost?*

"Vermire?" Pan Kun asked.

"Lady Sumi's people arrived yesterday. She has sent out nearly all of her Twilight guards and mercenary bands. It looks like most of them have the backing of different kingdoms and empires. They have siege weapons."

Pan Kun snorted but didn't seem worried.

"This is from your father." One of the riders passed Nasreen a message.

She scanned through it quickly.

The alliance is on the precipice of falling apart. With everyone pinned down, they cannot support one another. They are employing a lot of mercenaries and have numbers as well as weapons on their side. Outposts are demanding their guards to return. Others are asking for us to retaliate. It has created chaos. Notify me immediately as soon as the outpost interface is completed. We can send out word to the other outposts and bind their troops to it to increase their strength with passive bonuses. With the force that is located at King's Hill Outpost, remain there and send the other guards back. You will work on the outpost, then we will send out the guards with our own to reinforce and support our allies.

"Did you come with the supplies?" Pan Kun asked.

"We have brought crafters and people to assist in building the road," the guard said.

"Okay, well then, time we got to work." Pan Kun headed down the hill.

"Aren't you afraid?" Nasreen asked.

Pan Kun looked to her. A smile spread across his face that didn't reach his eyes. "My lord won't fall with a few mercenaries and war weapons pointed his way."

Nasreen felt that he was hiding his true thoughts, but he just turned and kept walking down the hill toward the supplies to organize them.

Nasreen whistled and drew the attention of the other guards. They all came over in high spirits.

"A group of outpost lords have attacked outposts of the alliance. The Shadowridge guards will hold this position and continue to work on King's Hill Outpost. The rest of you will return to Shadowridge to meet up with our guards to support the members of the alliance," Nasreen said.

The atmosphere plummeted.

Their outposts were their homes, where their families lived. If they fell, then their families would be in the midst of it all.

"Collect your gear and move to the road. You'll ride back in the supply carts," Nasreen said.

They started to disperse, quickly gathering their weapons, armor, and gear.

56 War in Beast Mountain Range

Leo looked at the small army gathered outside his gates. Their camp lay out of arrow range and his strongest mages could only send spells that would be mildly annoying to the attackers.

They had been waiting for three days. Neither of the two sides sent messages or communicated with one another. They prepared their weapons, readying for war.

Leo looked at the enemy with a dark expression.

"Well, at least my cousin's army came prepared. Looks like they allied themselves with the Dapan empire and hired out every mercenary in their outpost," Leo muttered.

They're well prepared and ready for a fight. We have supplies for a fight if we need it, but that is an empire's army. Although the outpost guards are good at dealing with powerful mercenaries and beasts that cause trouble, they aren't trained to siege.

An empire's army is completely different. They are trained to siege. Just looking at their formations and their weapons, it's clear that they are well prepared to take down my Sea Castle Outpost.

Leo gritted his teeth and his hand tightened around his sword.

"Lord!" a woman said, running up.

The guards around Leo all tensed, holding their weapons.

Leo waved for them to calm down, recognizing the messenger. "What is it?" he asked in a clipped tone, at odds with his normal easy smile and relaxed manners.

"A letter has arrived from Vermire," she said.

A guard took the letter and opened it. They checked inside and pulled out a bracelet as well as papers with magical runes on them. He checked it and then passed it to Leo.

Leo looked them over. "This is one of those communication devices and sound transmission talismans." Leo checked the device and put it on his wrist.

The bracelet glowed slightly. A few seconds later, a voice came from the bracelet.

"Ah, Outpost Lord Leo, it's Aditya. I know you're not one for small talk. King's Hill Outpost has been established. I am informed that the forces there are moving to reinforce the outposts closest and band together with guards from those outposts to sweep around the Beast Mountain Range to assist our allies. Now, this might take some time. My forces have remained at King's Hill Outpost. They are defending the crafters and have planted a true outpost interface there. I wanted it to be a surprise, and I guess now it is." Aditya laughed.

"How does that help?" Leo asked in a terse voice, feeling he was being played with.

Aditya let out a dark laugh. "Well, it is simple, really. The outpost's leadership will be the alliance leadership. Which makes you a leader of the outpost, which makes your population part of the outpost's numbers. Have you heard of the passives that an army defending their home can gain if they are recognized as a village, or a city?"

Leo's eyes shook.

With all of the outpost lords as the alliance leaders, that means that all of the people sworn to us will become the outpost's citizens, boosting the population of the outpost interface, upgrading it to village or city grade, increasing the passives placed on the army. It should bolster our strength considerably, increasing the chance that we can defend against the other outpost lords' attacks.

"When will it take effect?" Leo asked.

"Tonight. By that time, I should have reached out to all of the outpost lords and contacted them. The papers are sound transmission talismans. Inside the letter, I also gave you information on how to contact the other lords. With it, we can create a network, knowing where to strike and where to reserve our strength."

"That is a good plan. Communication is a powerful tool," Leo said, hidden meanings within his words.

"That it is, and information can be like a knife or a shield. Once this is resolved, I am planning to host another dinner to our victory and discuss King's Hill Outpost," Aditya said, as if the current predicament wasn't anything to worry about.

"Once this is all done, I hope that we can share a beer as allies," Leo said.

"I would like that, too—to the King's Hill Outpost Alliance." Aditya sounded amused before the bracelet dimmed.

"Well, Lord Aditya doesn't fail to surprise still." Leo looked at the gathering forces, his mind turning over.

Who is the real threat? Who is the one that is a greater problem? Does Aditya mean us good or are we simply jumping out of the fire into the tiger's mouth?

The attackers started to move, pushing their rolling siege towers, catapults, and wheeled trebuchets.

"Ballistas?" Leo asked, not looking away from the enemy.

"Ready, my lord!" a sub-commander said, standing nearby.

Leo waited as the trebuchets got into place. He looked as the catapults paused. They had coverings on their front to protect their crews.

The other groups halted, their shields ready as they waited for the order to charge, standing in their formations or hiding behind the siege towers.

Still, they were outside of effective bow range.

"Light the ballistas," Leo commanded.

A bagpipe sounded off and the ballistas heads were lit.

"They are all lit, my lord," the sub-commander reported.

"Fire!"

The bagpipe sounded out, followed by the whoosh of released arrows and the deep wooden noises of the ballista arms' tension being released.

They shot out their nearly meter-long loads. They were tilted upward, creating a fiery rain that struck the catapults and the trebuchets. Some missed, hitting the ground, while others cut through the formations. It didn't kill many but it sent the groups into disarray and they had to reform.

The catapults were hit with multiple ballista arrows that stuck into their hides, trying to reach the wood and set it on fire.

A few who were caught outside of the defenses were killed and a few started to smoke as the wood was catching on fire.

The trebuchet crews were safer, due to their range. Ballista hit the ground around them, saturating the area around a trebuchet to kill the operators and strike the siege weapon.

It only took out a fraction of the enemy's ranged attack power.

The trebuchets creaked as they released their payloads and the catapults joined in.

Rocks struck the ground ahead of the wall, walking their fire up to the wall and landing beyond.

The wall was rocked in places. The battlements exploded when hit straight on. A few unlucky people were killed in the attack. The defenders hid in stone-constructed huts along the wall while the ballista crews in their own stone towers rapidly reloaded and fired again.

Leo watched this from his own tower, looking at the shield warriors and those around the siege towers.

They really think highly of us. There must be close to two and a half thousand out there, while our normal guard force is reduced to four hundred and fifty. They're confident that they have the time to wear us down as well. Their commander doesn't seem impatient, ready to wear down our walls and our morale with constant bombardment.

Valter stood outside of his command tent, looking at Vermire. The outpost stood there, its new walls standing uniform across the two rises it rested on.

Ballistas rested on the walls. Soldiers could be seen moving between positions on the wall—their armor well cared for, their actions orderly.

Their training is no less than ours. Their weapons and armor are on par. Though it didn't feel as though they were pressured when we were attacking them.

Valter's eyes looked at the marks on the walls where the siege weaponry had hit. They were scuff marks; nothing showed signs of destabilizing.

The dead had been moved from the battlefield, but the bloody spots where they had stood remained.

Although we can't do much for the wounded, Vermire has healers who can get even the severely wounded back on the front lines in just a few hours or days.

He was disturbed, looking at the outpost.

"Just how was he able to amass so much power without our mistress knowing? He was just a small figure a few years ago. She was thinking of dominating him and using his outpost as her own in the future, but then we lost our spies within his walls and then there was the reversal with the Zatan Confederation. Now, when I look at Vermire, it doesn't look like a simple outpost anymore. It looks more like a capital. Well-trained forces, strong construction, and with hidden means."

He looked down at the weapon on his hip. It had been purchased for him from Vermire. It was the strongest sword in the Twilight guard's arsenal. Though Vermire had sold it like a simple cabbage.

"Tomorrow, we will fight once again. I refuse to think that our force of ten thousand can't defeat them. No matter the losses."

If we don't defeat them now, then they could grow to be the lord of the Beast Mountain Range. We need to destroy them now.

Aditya stood on the wall in his armor, his eyes looking across the battlefield. He watched as Valter returned to his tent.

"The Twilight guards…I always wanted to pay them back for what they did." Aditya's voice was cold, filled with fury he had hidden when meeting the other outpost lords.

"Well, I am told that they will no longer be a problem shortly," a familiar man's voice said a short distance down the wall. Aditya was startled and Miss Evernight cupped her hands and bowed to Elan as he walked up.

"Please, Miss Evernight, we don't want to give anything away. I am but a simple merchant," Elan said.

Aditya's thoughts were washed away as he studied Elan. There was a new depth to him. He realized that he couldn't see through the other man's cultivation. When he had left, Aditya felt that they were on the same level, but in such a short period of time he had been left behind.

"Elan," Aditya said, tilting his head to the other man.

Elan seemed to read his thoughts as he looked over the wall at the enemy. "Don't worry. I feel that Vermire and the Beast Mountain Range will soon enter into a new period of prosperity. As the one to do so, I don't think that the rewards will be small."

Aditya smiled, feeling a bit awkward.

"Something on your mind?" Elan seemed more perceptive than ever.

"Seems you really have taken over the information networks. I can't keep anything from you," Aditya said with a self-deprecating laugh.

"Ah, I don't know everything, but that is something I am looking to rectify," Elan said mysteriously and glanced to Aditya. "What is on your mind?"

Aditya debated for a second but he knew that it would be useless to try to hide his thoughts.

"I, well…well, when I started this, I was simply looking for the rewards. I wanted more power, wanted to grow Vermire. You and your people have dealt with me in good faith. I didn't deserve it—what I did when meeting Mister Jasper… You gave me a chance. I took it and I didn't like it at first—I won't lie. Now, well, Vermire is my greatest achievement, and although I care for it, I am your instrument. I want to prove myself to your leaders. Show that I can be trusted. That I can take on more responsibility. I want to use my strengths to grow something bigger than myself."

Elan and Evernight looked at each other. Both of them turned their gaze on Aditya.

"Maybe one day you'll learn the truth. I know that my leaders are interested in you. I can raise the subject with them, but there must always be someone controlling Vermire and the King's Hill Outpost under our command. It will take time to get to that point."

"I'm not in a rush. I have plenty of years ahead of me now." Aditya smiled.

"It looks like the outposts going against you have used all of their contacts to wage this war," Elan said.

"They've certainly got a lot of strength right now," Aditya said.

"The situation in the other outposts varies. With all of the armies needing to prepare their siege weaponry, it has bought us a few days," Evernight said.

"Your forces are in place?" Elan asked.

What he didn't know was that Elan's orders weren't his own, but came from Glosil, who was watching the battle above Alva closely.

"Thank you." Glosil lowered his sound transmission device.

"Something important?" Roska sat in the chair opposite.

"Aditya's second army is mobilizing to take out the other outposts," Glosil said.

"We could have dealt with the issue easily," Roska said.

"There were enough questions when you dealt with the Zatan Confederation leadership. Thankfully, each of the other groups thought it was the other that carried out the attack. This is a chance for Vermire to prove their strength."

"Are we going to add them to Alva?" Roska asked suddenly.

"We might. We still have a lot of people who are willing to join from the Fourth Realm and it takes less resources to train them. Talking of training, shall we get back to the main subject at hand?"

"Your close protection details?" Roska smiled.

Glosil nodded.

"For the first three days, we pushed them to the limit. We all gave them medallions that made them the same strength. The majority held up through it all. Then we moved them into specific training, testing them on shooting, scouting, engineering, spell casting, mortars, medical support, close combat, and ranged combat skills. The basics were already there; we gave them the tips and tricks that will turn them from a good operator to one who can jump from one task to the other without issue. Next, they will be participating in the tournament held in Vuzgal. While there, they will be matched against people from across the realms. This is to temper their fighting styles."

"Unlike before, they were trained as soldiers first and warriors second. They'll be able to reintegrate quickly into units. Bringing that higher combat capability with them," Glosil said.

"Good to know that those annoying reports are of some use." Roska smiled.

Glosil snorted as she continued.

"Once they have completed their combat training, then they will be organized into CPD or close protection detail squads and assigned to different combat companies."

"Have you organized the group that will take over advanced training for roles beyond sharpshooter? The staff teaching right now are the best we have and I would prefer to keep their skills honed by allowing them to train with their units."

"I wanted to clarify that with you. The CPD squads will be on a rotating basis. They will train and be active with their units, but every combat company will effectively have three, not two, CPD squads. One attached to the artillery platoon, the other to the support platoon and the third on a three-month rota giving advanced training to the new privates and overseeing the recruit training?"

"Correct. They're our best fighting force. The more information that they can give our basic soldiers, the stronger they will be."

"Is this competition within Alva thing going to happen as well?" Roska asked.

"The competition will be for school-related subjects. While the military is in Vuzgal, they can go to the Battle Arena to train, but unless given permission they are not allowed to enter the tournament events," Glosil said.

"Okay," Roska said, curious.

"Competition is good, but I don't want the units fighting one another over something stupid. Now, how is the training program going for the special teams?"

"After completing their CPD training, then they will need to wait a month until they can go on and apply to join the special teams. If they want to become an officer, they can begin their officer training right away."

Glosil nodded in confirmation, following along.

"Training for the special teams will come in three parts. One, test of training. They will go out with a special team training cadre, to clear dungeons, to traverse different terrain. Instead of checking what they have learned, they will have to demonstrate it in every environment. The second part is that they will run missions to scout, gather information and plan out an attack on different groups in the Fourth Realm. They must do so without being detected and complete these faux missions to a high standard. This will also aid us in knowing just what kind of strength our neighbors have.

"Finally, they will be bid on. They must not only be the best person at the tasks set out for them; they need to be part of a team. The special teams and their leaders will pick out the ones they want, bidding upon them. They will remain within the special teams on a three-month probationary timetable. If they are a good fit with the rest of the special team, they will remain. If they aren't, then they will be up for bid once again. They can be bid on three times before they will be returned to their unit, with an invitation to attempt the course again in six months."

"Sounds rigorous," Glosil said.

"Our job is to be able to operate on our own under any condition in any realm. I aim to make sure that the new special teams are all capable of this task."

Glosil could see the determination in her eyes. The special teams were a ragtag group, but they were one hell of a fighting force.

"I'll leave it to you," Glosil said.

"Do you want us to be ready to act if something unsuspected happens in the Beast Mountain Range?"

"If the Alva Healing House is targeted, then I will send you in."

"Understood." Roska nodded.

57
Vermire's Second Army

Lukas moved forward through the alleyways, his cloak hiding the dagger in his hand. From three other alleyways, a total of eight others appeared.

"Where's Donner?" he said in a low voice.

"Watching a noble who came from one of the kingdoms. He'll give us a signal if they are on their way to reinforce the outpost lord," Simone said.

"All right." Lukas nodded. "Ready?"

The rest of the squad all nodded as they opened up their cloaks to reveal their armor. They all wore dark armor to not reflect the moonlight. On it was the Vermire coat of arms.

"Let's go and earn our pay."

Lukas kept his shield on his back, half hidden in his cloak.

They moved through the alleys and then stole across the streets, edging closer to the lord's manor.

Lukas was from the old guard, the ones who had trained with the unknown trainers. Simone and Donner were the only other veterans. The rest were the new guard, trained in secret and unknown to the other outpost lords.

A screen appeared in front of them all as they held back.

Your position has changed. You are now an Outpost Level Guard.

Your position has changed. You are now a Village Level Guard.

Your position has changed. You are now a Small City Level Guard.

Your position has changed. You are now a Medium City Level Guard.

When attacking another outpost, city, village, or location with an interface, a war status is applied. You gain a 5% bonus to your stats. When you are defending your lands, you gain a 13% increase to stats.

Strength filled Lukas's body.

A title—never thought I would get one of those!

He looked at the others who had shocked, excited, and pleased looks on their faces.

"All right, for the city of Vermire," he said in a low whisper.

It focused all of them as they pushed on. He sheathed his sword and checked his boots that had a sharpened spike on them, and the two hooked climbing picks.

They reached the road around the outpost lord's manor.

The dark castle stood higher above the village. The gate was closed and there were guards on the walls, looking out.

"Archers, get a vantage point to support as needed."

The archers helped one another, climbing up the walls and houses quickly, hiding in the shadows of the chimney stacks or on balconies, anywhere that gave them a clear line of sight to the wall. Everything was lower than the manor walls, but it was better than nothing.

Lukas saw another cloaked group appear down to his right, then another to his left. He made eye contact with the leaders and nodded to them.

We need to attack while they're not watching but not take so long that they start to get suspicious.

Lukas laughed and staggered; the group laughed and chuckled, looking as if they had just been out drinking.

"You got any more of that brandy, Vax?" Lukas asked as they kept walking, taking a shortcut around the castle.

The guards, bored and jealous, looked away and kept on their routes.

"Now," Lukas hissed.

He turned and ran with Simone. They jumped the moat around the walls. Lukas got a pick in, hitting the wall. He nearly lost his grip and stabbed his spiked shoe into the wall. He stuck his other spike in.

There wasn't a noise as faint spell lines could be seen on his gear.

The Silence spell won't last long.

He looked to Simone. Groups disappeared into the alleys again. Others with the climbing gear stuck to the wall, starting to climb up.

Someone fell into the moat with a splash.

The team started to laugh as they looked to fish out their fellow, another drunk who had fallen down. The Twilight guards all looked over, something to draw their attention.

Lukas got to the battlements. Simone had beaten him there. They looked at each other and nodded.

They got over the crenellations and onto the wall. A door opened to their right. Simone rushed the door, Lukas behind. The guard was laughing as Simone used her pick, hitting him in the throat. He had a surprised look on his face as she pulled him out of the way with her pick and threw the second, hitting someone inside the defensive tower on the wall.

A guard ran at Simone, tackling her. The two of them fought on the ground.

Lukas took a lesson from Simone. He saw a guard moving around the brazier that was inside the tower and he threw his pickaxe. It made a dull noise, piercing their armor and sticking in their chest. The last of the Silence spell wore off as they dropped to the ground.

Lukas used his other pick, hitting the man who was fighting with Simone in the head.

She rolled him off and spat to the side.

Lukas was about to talk when there was a yell down the wall.

"Guess it's time we went with Plan B." Simone threw off her blood-stained cloak, revealing her armor as she pulled out her mage's staff.

"I liked Plan B more from the beginning." Lukas's cloak dropped to the ground as he drew his sword and grabbed his shield. "Time to kill this bitch."

They went down the winding stairs to the gates.

Lukas kept an eye out as Simone started to cast a spell.

Another two groups met them there.

"Sounds like the fighting is coming from the northwest."

"Hopefully they can keep them distracted," Lukas said.

Simone finished casting her spell. The inner metal gate started to rise quickly; the second door opened outward and the bridge started to lower.

People jumped up onto the bridge before it had come down all the way. They rushed in. Other groups had circled around through the alleys to the three main gates.

They headed into the manor, using the maps and detailed blueprints on the manor. They didn't head for the main castle, but a secondary tower that looked out over the city.

Alarms were being sounded out and guards were woken from their rest; torches were lit and the castle started to come alive as the outpost looked at the manor in shock.

Teams broke off to their different goals: groups to ambush the forces coming out from the barracks, others to force their way into the secondary tower.

Lukas touched the spell scroll he had been given and passed it to Simone. "Channel this when we get near the gates—don't have time to slow down."

"Got it," Simone said.

Lady Sumi woke up to the alarms, frowning as she got up. "Whoever dares to wake me up will not live for long," she hissed.

She got her clothes on and her shoes, moving to the tower's window to look down at the castle. She saw her guards running out from their barracks with their torches. Suddenly, archers' fire and magical attacks landed among them, stopping the torches from advancing.

She looked at her second courtyard. Her guards were on the walls. There were only a few of them. The others were running across the ground, getting ready.

Suddenly, a golden spell formation appeared in front of the gate.

A spell scroll? Sumi felt shock for the first time as a blast of power hit the gate. The gate exploded and a section of the wall fell apart.

As the dust settled, armed and armored men and women passed through the gate, attacking the Twilight guards.

Your outpost is under attack by a city's army!

They're on the same standard as my Twilight guards? Who are these people? Is it Baron Jermei's people? Are they looking to support me on the outside and stab me in the back? We have been monitoring the other outposts—they couldn't have sent people over this fast!

Fighting raged underneath her feet and the door burst open.

"My lady, we have to leave," the guard said, a pale expression coloring his face.

"Help me get my armor on," Sumi said, dismissing them. She was an outpost lord. She had needed to carve out her position in life. She would meet these people without fear.

"What do you think?" one trader asked the other as they sipped drinks from a window, looking out over Twilight Outpost.

"Haven't the leaders supported them? Of course the alliance will win. I wonder if we will see some of the special teams?" The second laughed.

The two of them continued to drink even as Twilight Outpost turned into a chaotic battlefield within the outpost lady's manor.

"Did you give them that thing?" the second trader asked after a few seconds.

"It will give them an edge if they need it," the first said.

"It is up to them now."

"To lower taxes and proper roads!" The first raised his glass.

"Don't you want to head to the higher realms?"

"Ah, with time. Why is there a rush? I want to make sure that my family is safe. Helping the intelligence department is the easiest way. Looks good for promotion," the first said, as if a sage who had seen the rise and fall of nations.

"You and your promotion." The second rolled his eyes.

Suddenly there were a series of spells launched from the sieged tower and the manor lit up with destructive light.

"Looks like the lady has woken up."

Lukas worked his jaw, trying to get back his hearing. The lightning bolt that had come from the sky had left him partly blind and deaf.

The Twilight guards had protected their eyes at the last moment and were attacking with gusto. A woman appeared behind them, wearing black armor and cloak with red accents. Guards surrounded her.

Lukas got to his feet, looking around for his squad. He found Simone. Her neck was at an odd angle, her eyes glassy as she looked off into the dirt.

Lukas hissed as he grabbed the bottle on his hip.

A flare shot up from within the castle.

King's Hill City has taken control over Twilight Outpost!

The Twilight guards all looked around, screens filling their vision, and the Vermire soldiers attacked.

Lukas pulled out the potion and drank it.

Power filled his body.

You have consumed: Berserker's Rage Increase your Strength and Agility by 30% for three minutes. Fall into a weakened state for one hour.

He wasn't the only one as others poured the potions down their throats.

Lukas let out a yell but he could only hear humming as he raised his shield and moved forward with the rest of his squad.

They clashed with the Twilight guards directly, losing their outpost defender buff and now dealing with the organized berserker Vermire guards working together. They were quickly being pushed back.

"For Vermire!" Lukas yelled.

The guards repeated his yell, pushing on. If they didn't kill the guards and Lady Sumi, then they would die.

Mages had taken a different potion and were buffing the Vermire forces, going all-out, not looking to conserve their mana as they fired curses and attacks at Lady Sumi. Her guard were defending her with their lives, but she had walked out too far; there was no escape backward.

Lady Sumi pulled out spell scrolls, using them to throw the Vermire forces back.

The wounded used healing solutions from Alva Healing House to recover. Even if they weren't in the best state, they were able to rejoin the fight.

They broke through the guards in the courtyard and hit the guards around Lady Sumi.

She was yelling out and casting her magic, her face a picture of rage.

Lukas blocked a Twilight guard's attack while Vax stabbed forward with his spear. The two of them worked together to take him down as the guards were whittled down. There were too many of the Vermire guards for the Twilight guards to work together.

Suddenly, mana filled the area.

An explosion went off and Lukas found he was sent flying again. He hit a rock and tumbled, finding his feet, his body battered and bruised.

Lady Sumi was chanting and casting spells. She had pulled out a spell scroll that was stronger than the spell scroll Simone had used to break open the gate.

Lukas's sword had been lost in the fight. He grabbed the climbing pick and threw it with all his strength. It hit Lady Sumi and the power of her spells backlashed at her all at once. Lukas had a bloody grin on his face as the Silence spell on his second pick ran out of charge.

Lady Sumi coughed blood, the mana in her body tearing her apart. She dropped to the ground, collapsing in a heap.

The other Twilight guards collapsed as well. Tombstones filled the courtyard.

"What the hell?" Vax asked.

Lukas helped him to his feet, holding his shield ready.

The Vermire guards stood up, confused.

Valter was looking over his maps as he felt a pain coming from his mana channels.

He grunted, fighting to stand. He heard people collapsing outside of his tent. The pain ran into his head and a tombstone appeared above his head.

"No wonder they were willing to do anything for her." Aditya looked out of his manor and at the camp. It was the dark of night but things weren't calm over at the attacking camp.

"She was a ruthless ruler. Her guards would follow her into the afterlife, making them fight for her. Many of the Twilight guards were family members, so they would die in order to protect their family members and her life." Evernight snorted and shook her head.

"Now, it means that her forces have been cut from within." Aditya got another message through his sound transmission device and turned to the map nearby, putting a cross through another outpost.

"Well, it looks like the Beast Mountain Range will be undergoing a number of changes tonight."

Deep within Alva Dungeon on the Earth floor, Erik opened his eyes. A flame flashed in the depths as his blue eyes now had hints of brown and red in them.

Erik turned his vision inward. Earth mana was being dissolved in his mana channels. His gaunt body started to fill out, the Earth mana increasing his recovery rate, acting as a tonic to him. Instead of having to tirelessly draw the pure mana from the Earth attribute, the two separated out naturally, the pure mana blasting through his nearly clotted mana channels. It followed his cultivation path without Erik applying conscious thought, becoming thicker and denser as it reached his dantian. The mist within gathered slowly before combining into a single pure drop of mana.

Erik cleared his throat and coughed for a few minutes, recovering quickly.

"You okay in there?" Egbert asked.

Erik made to stand but he felt a stabbing pain in his stomach. He quickly looked into his body.

Five drops of mana were trembling, fighting against one another.

If I don't deal with them, then they could break free. The pressure of the Earth-affinity mana is forcing them to remain in my dantian. If I leave, then they could run free and destroy my Mana Gathering Cultivation.

Erik grit his teeth as he sat down, connecting his mana gates in his hands and his legs.

His mana gates opened, glowing a swirling red and brown as streams of mana were drawn into Erik's body.

If I was to alter one of the drops like the Earth mana, attract the others, could that work?

Erik focused on one of the drops. It shivered and then started to slowly turn from a slight bluish hue to a brown coloration. He circulated his mana, drawing it inward.

The outside pressure and the attraction force—Erik felt a greater control over both.

A drop was drawn forward. It resisted as it hovered just out of reach of the brown Earth-affinity drop.

Erik lost track of time as he focused on the two drops.

It lost the fight and it was drawn in. The first drop grew larger, its light-brown color turning a deeper brown.

Erik pulled in another drop. It took less time than before.

The mana that was being drawn in held hints of other affinity mana. There was no such thing as pure Earth mana; even the dungeon cores only processed the mana that passed through them. They didn't revert them to some true pure state.

Erik started to use his control over Fire. His mana gates turned red as it refined out more of the impurities as it was drawn in.

Erik concentrated, compressing and drawing in the next drop. It combined easier than the first and the second. He looked at the last mana drop.

He took a breath, calming himself. The power contained within his body was much higher than before. His body had been refined with Fire mana, then compressed, broken down and reformed with the Earth mana. His control over mana had reached another level. Pain was easily ignored and his life force was stronger than ever before. Erik felt removed from the situation, as if he were looking at someone else's body.

His entire body had changed, nourished by the power of Earth.

The last mana drop was combined.

Mana rushed in toward Erik's body. He hungrily drew it in, circulating it through his mana channels, refining it with his Fire Body as his Earth Soul drew it in, compressing it easily.

Within his dantian, the brown cleared from his core. A clear core remained; a sphere of brown and a blue flame appeared within it, orbiting within his core.

Threads of other affinities created ribbons through the clear area of his core.

A mana drop condensed within Erik's core. It dropped off the inside of the core and dropped into the middle of the sphere.

Erik felt as if an explosion went off within his body. He let out a cry. It felt like molten metal was pouring out of his dantian. Erik collapsed backward. Cracks seemed to spread from his mana gates. His mana channels stretched out like roots of a tree growing through the ground, threading through his muscles, transforming from channels into veins.

Erik glowed from within as mana was fused into the very cells of his body, transforming him inside and out.

The mana veins reached up to his skull and Erik lost his battle with consciousness.

The Earth floor shook as Erik was undergoing massive changes within his body. It felt as if a monster were being born at the center of the floor.

Erik slowly opened his eyes. His blue eyes shone, with flecks of brown and blue deep within. He felt that he had changed completely.

"Damn that Rugrat," Erik muttered, feeling that he had kept something hidden.

Erik felt that his control over mana had reached an unfathomable level. The area around him came under his domain. Even passively, he was drawing the mana in, bending it to his will without conscious thought. His mana channels had transformed into mana veins. His entire body thirsted for mana. He could exercise his will anywhere within his domain, increasing the speed of his casting. He looked to his side, where Gilly rested.

Even without touching her, he could scan her body with his Simple Organic Scan. He could see the changes happening within her body. Feeling his gaze upon her, she opened her eyes. There was an intelligence and pride within those eyes.

"You've worked hard." He smiled and patted her nose.

She let out a pleased snort, preening with the attention.

Erik felt her share an emotion and image with him.

"Is food the only treats you like?" Erik muttered.

She cooed slightly.

"I'm working on something to unlock your bloodline. I need time, though," Erik said.

She huffed and laid her head down away from him.

"Fine, fine! Food it is," Erik said, complaining.

Gilly brightened and nudged him before she put her head in his lap.

He sighed and patted her and gave her scratches. Her hide was much stronger than before. If Erik hadn't undergone his latest Body Cultivation, then her hide would have stripped off a layer of skin just petting her.

Erik pulled up the angry notifications that were waiting for him. They streamed down in front of him.

"Well, damn."

Quest Completed: Body Cultivation 3

The path cultivating one's body is not easy. To stand at the top, one must forge their own path forward.

Requirements:

Reach Body Like Sky Iron Level

Rewards:

+12 to Strength

+12 to Agility

+12 to Stamina

+20 to Stamina Regeneration

+10,000,000 EXP

Your personal efforts have increased your base stats!

Stamina +6

Strength +6

Agility +6

Stamina Regeneration +6
Mana Pool +4

Title: Earth Soul
You have tempered your body with Earth. Earth has become a part of you, making your body take on some of its characteristics. You have gained:
Legendary Earth resistance.
Legendary Recovery Ability.
Increased control over Earth Mana.
Physical attacks contain Earth attribute.
Can completely purify the Earth attribute in Mana.

Quest: Body Cultivation 4
The path cultivating one's body is not easy. To stand at the top, one must forge their own path forward.
Requirements:
Reach Body like Diamond Level
Rewards:
+24 to Strength
+24 to Agility
+24 to Stamina
+40 to Stamina Regeneration
+100,000,000 EXP

Quest: Body Cultivation 5
The path cultivating one's body is not easy. To stand at the top, one must forge their own path forward.
Requirements:
Unlock your Bloodline
Rewards:
+48 to Strength
+48 to Agility
+48 to Stamina
+80 to Stamina Regeneration
+100,000,000 EXP

"Two Body Cultivation quests, what the heck is that for?"

You have opened another Mana gate!
+1 to Mana Regeneration

Quest Updated: Opening the Fourteen Gates
Congratulations! You have opened your fourteenth Mana gate.
Requirements:
Clear all of your fourteen gates (14/14)
Rewards:
+1 to Mana Regeneration base stat
Undergo Mana Body Rebirth
1,400,000 EXP

Title: Blessed by Mana
You have become closer to Mana, exerting a greater control over it.
The strength of your spells has increased by 60%. Your Mana Regeneration has increased by 60%.
Can create a Mana domain.
(Replaces Mana Emperor)

Title: Mana Reborn
Your body has undergone a deep transformation, bringing you closer to Mana, reborn with greater power and control over its forces.
Mana channels are transformed into mana veins. Your mana sense and control increases greatly.
You can now convert Stamina into mana and vice versa.

Quest Completed: Mana Cultivation 1
The path cultivating one's mana is not easy. To stand at the top, one must forge their own path forward.
Requirements:
Compress your Mana Core
Rewards:

+15 to Mana
+15 to Mana Regeneration
+10% mana capacity
+10,000,000 EXP

Quest: Mana Cultivation 2

The path cultivating one's mana is not easy. To stand at the top, one must forge their own path forward.

Requirements:

Reach Vapor Mana Core

Rewards:

+20 to Mana
+20 to Mana Regeneration
+50,000,000 EXP

Name: Erik West

Level: 59 *Race: Human*

Titles:

From the Grave II
Blessed By Mana
Dungeon Master III
Reverse Alchemist
Poison Body
Fire Body
City Lord
Earth Soul
Mana Reborn

Strength: (Base 54) +41	950
Agility: (Base 47) +72	654
Stamina: (Base 57) +25	1230
Mana: (Base 27) +79	1166
Mana Regeneration: (Base 30) +61	73.80/s
Stamina Regeneration: (Base 67) +59	26.20/s

You have reached Level 59

When you sleep next, you will be able to increase your attributes by: 5 points.

2,448,136/86,100,000 EXP till you reach Level 60

"So I got the title Earth Soul for Body Cultivation, Mana Blessed for Mana Gathering Cultivation. Then, with compressing my core, I unlocked the requirements to get the Mana Gathering Cultivation quests. What the hell is with this mana core?"

Erik felt a little lost. Some of his stats had nearly doubled. Though unlike when he put stat points into his character sheet from leveling up, there was no disassociation with the power he felt in his body. He looked into his body. There was now two circulator systems within his body: mana and blood flowed through his body, the two systems complementing one another. His dual cultivation changes had transformed his body. Erik reached out with his hand and the mana in the area stopped, unable to move, the area around him under his complete control.

"Damn, this is a lot of power." Erik was a little scared of the power in his hands now. *If I have this power, then who else does?* That thought sent a shiver through his body.

"You done in there yet?" Egbert asked.

Erik looked back to see Egbert in a flower pattern shirt in a wooden reclined chair, reading a book.

"I have so many questions," Erik said.

"Oh, about your cultivation?" Egbert asked in an excited tone, leaning forward.

"Mostly about the shirt," Erik said with a raised eyebrow.

"Hey, Rugrat talked about these Hawaiian shirts and someone made up a print. People really started to enjoy them. Even got a pair of shorts and sunglasses!" Egbert pulled out a pair of sunglasses and put them on his face. He had to tilt his head back so they wouldn't fall off his head due to the lack of nose and ears.

Erik cleared his throat. Gilly moved and the two of them headed out of the Earth cave. As Erik walked out, he had to adjust the amount of strength he used, getting accustomed to the changes within his body.

Erik remembered his mana core and looked at it once again.

Still there were the ribbons of colors that moved through it, appearing and disappearing, weaving their way through, the blue flame and the dirt sphere that orbited where his mana drops rested. The dirt sphere drew in the mana and the flame refined it as two mana drops rested at the center of Erik's mana core.

Erik explained what he was seeing in his core.

"That must be because of your cultivation," Egbert said excitedly.

"How?"

"So it looks like your body cultivation because it has been tempered by flames, it refines that affinity out of your mana, increasing its purity without concious thought. Its like what Old Hei told you. You can use the affinity mana to temper your body, but you've tempered your body to such a degree it has taken on the attributes of the affinity. Increased resistances, greater control over the affinity. Which means that as you increase your cultivation, your body will automaticlaly refine the mana you are gathering, the two systems working together to become stronger. People who have an innate constitutions have greater control over one or another type of attribute mana, which allows them to gather and refine it easier. So an ice type consitution, if in a cold place with only ice attribue mana their body will refine the ice attribute, increasing their body's power and the mana will be much more refined as they use it in their mana gathering practices. I never thought of it, but based on what you're saying and what I've read on innate constiutions is makes sense!"

Egbert pulled out a notepad from somewhere and wrote down his learnings.

"Seems that I am walking the right path then," Erik said. "What happened while I've been cultivating?"

"Well, you started four weeks ago. A lot has happened."

58 Redesigned Beast Mountain Range

Glosil left the battle in the hands of Aditya and his trained guards, but it had to do with the future of Aditya and their security. He had been watching what was going on and getting regular updates from Miss Evernight and their intelligence officers across the Beast Mountain Range.

He watched a shimmering mirror in the middle of the room.

A mage sat off to the side, controlling the divination spell that allowed Glosil to see the overall battlefield.

In the higher realms, the more rampant mana that people contained within their bodies and spells that armies used to stop others from spying on them made divination a hard task. In the First Realm, there were few people with the amount of mana that would make it hard to use a divination spell and they didn't have spells to distort the spells. Only the powerful armies of different kingdoms had those kinds of abilities.

"Since they have been able to free up their allies, they've turned the tide on the enemy," Yui said, watching with him.

"Taking out the leadership of the opposing alliance has thrown the others into chaos. Knowing that their homes are being attacked while they're trying to attack another outpost—one hell of a blow to the attacker's morale. It has bolstered the allied outposts as well."

Aditya's second army had done two major things. They had attacked and taken down a number of outpost lords and ladies, and they had hit the rears of the enemy alliance that were attacking the outposts that supported King's Hill Outpost. Miss Evernight's people had done their job well. The people in the outposts had long heard about Lord Aditya. Knowing his people were occupying their outposts and were going through and restoring order, it went a long way. When hitting the rear of the outpost armies, the Vermire army called for their enemies' surrender. Not many were willing to lose their lives and most were mercenaries there to earn coin, not lose their lives.

The Vermire army linked up with forces from the King's Hill Outpost Alliance. Then, driving the mercenaries and surrendered forces ahead of them, they pushed into other outposts. Even if the lord ordered it, many of the guards on the wall weren't willing to shoot their friends and family who had been sent out to take another outpost and were now charging their walls. So the army grew.

"Using those binding contracts, the guards and mercenaries can't do anything but follow the army's orders," Yui said. "Feels dirty."

"It works," Glosil said, not disagreeing with him.

"What will happen with the mercenaries and the guards afterward?"

"Not sure. Some might remain as guards, retrained. Others will be released back to their old lives. Miss Evernight's people will figure it out," Glosil said.

He looked from the divination. "You can go rest," Glosil said.

The mage opened her eyes and the spell disappeared.

"Thank you." She got up and stretched lightly before leaving the room.

"How are things on your side?" Glosil asked.

"Training is almost complete. A lot of people have at least two or three courses under their belt now. They're taking the time to go to the academy, try learning a new skill. They can take more courses when we're rotated back to Vuzgal. I know a lot of them are interested in going CPD and testing out for the special teams. Do we have any news on operations?"

"Train, rest up and get ready. We still need to build our numbers up to defend Vuzgal and Alva properly. There might be something coming down the pipe soon."

"Sounds good. You hear about Erik and Rugrat?" Yui stood.

"How they're teaching in the academy, Erik is working in the healing house, Rugrat is taking formation lessons and both of them are creating Alchemy and smithing items like madmen?"

"Yeah. Do those two ever stop?" Yui snorted and shook his head.

"I don't think it's in them to," Glosil said, his voice becoming distant. *With the weight on our shoulders, how can we give everything less than our all?*

"I heard that Erik got stronger, a lot stronger," Yui said.

Glosil remembered standing in front of Erik. It didn't feel as though he were standing in front of a man, but a beast that was ready to pounce at any moment, that could tear him apart with casual ease.

"Yeah, should be enough to terrify the hell out of some people."

Nasreen looked at the outpost ahead. The flags of the lord had been removed and now they were bare as she and the rest of the King's Hill Outpost Army rode into the outpost.

The people hid away from them, but there were guards from Vermire waiting within the walls.

Just how did they do it?

"Report," Veli, a high-ranking Vermire guard, asked the group waiting within the walls off to the side.

"We took the outpost without issue. Once the lord was killed, we allowed the guards to surrender and they did. Didn't like their lord much but he used the threat of spell scrolls to keep them managed. With him gone, they were happy for a change of guard," the woman guard said.

Veli snorted and nodded. "Very well. We're going to rest here for the night and then head onto Dundeep. They are still being attacked by the enemy."

"We got word ahead of time. We have got barracks prepared, hot water for cleaning as well as food. We checked it already," the woman said.

Nasreen was impressed and a little scared. *Communication devices are rare but all of these groups have to have at least one in order to coordinate their attacks.*

"Good work," Veli said.

The woman guard bowed, a pleased smile on her face. The others with her grinned.

Nasreen and Veli moved away from them.

"How long have you been planning this for?" Nasreen asked.

"I'm not sure. The lord might know that." Veli shrugged. He wasn't as brooding or quiet as Pan Kun.

"Though getting all of these people into place into the outposts to strike out at the outpost lords and ladies… Eight outposts fell in the first night. Seven had fighting break out in the streets. Twelve of the neutral outposts pledged to the alliance right away, forming up and supporting the other outposts of the alliance. Now there are just five more outposts that remain standing. The people within are not sure who is an ally or a spy." Nasreen felt that Vermire was an enigma.

"Interesting, isn't it," Veli said with a smile. "Our lord is not a simple man."

He let out a laugh and Nasreen moved with him. Her thoughts moved to King's Hill Outpost.

Aditya looked at the changing map.

Once the forces of the outposts were freed, with those attacking them being driven back, the outpost lords had sent out their guards to join the KOA, or King's Hill Outpost Army, sending support to their fellow outpost leaders and clearing the armies attacking them faster than before. Now there were three different KOAs that were moving between outposts, with a fourth nearly formed.

Aditya's communication device lit up.

"Lord, the basic structure of the outpost is complete. We have wooden walls in places and there is a village headquarters made from stone. We should have the barracks created tomorrow. We spent most of our time sourcing the materials from the surrounding area. Now it should be a lot faster to build."

"How long do you think that it will be until the second phase is complete?"

"Should be three weeks," Pan Kun said.

"I'll send crafters and laborers ahead of the road team from Vermire. I want the second phase completed in no more than a week and a half."

"Yes, my lord." Pan Kun paused.

"Wondering how the fight is going?"

"A little, my lord," Pan Kun said awkwardly.

Aditya chuckled and looked at the map.

"There are still some lords holding out on us. Some have started to pull back their forces, looking to defend what they have instead of taking more. Some are suing for peace. With the head of the enemy alliance gone and with three armies of three thousand strong, the pressure upon them isn't small. With our eyes and ears, we have been able to disrupt the outposts from within and create openings for our armies to exploit. To be honest, even I didn't expect these results."

Aditya's eyes moved to Miss Evernight, who was reading over a report on the kingdoms that were backing different outposts.

"Seems that the second army has done better than I hoped." Pan Kun laughed in relief, though Aditya could sense the pride as well.

"Don't let anything stop the construction of the outpost. We'll need it soon."

"A week and a half with our crafters, sir."

"They're on their way." Aditya closed the connection and then sent a sound transmission to his guards, ordering them to escort crafters, builders, and laborers to King's Hill Outpost. With the new building that Vermire had recently undergone, there were plenty of skilled builders in the outpost.

"Should be about time to send a message to the other outpost lords," Evernight said, standing.

"Already? We haven't cleared the remaining outposts."

"Yes, sending them a message now shows your confidence and your arrogance. Being arrogant is something they're used to. Being cautious and analytical, it will be harder for them to control," Evernight said.

Emmanuel got the message from Aditya, requesting a new meeting of the alliance. This time, it would be held at the King's Hill Outpost.

He is sure confident that we can win this war, and he has set the date for us to meet in just a week.

Emmanuel was not expecting so many changes in such a short while. When he and the other outposts had been just reacting, Aditya had been executing a well-thought-out plan. He had been able to take down eight outposts with his people, using them as supply points for the KOA's (Kings Own Army) as they pushed to attack the enemy outposts and support their allies.

The reversal had been too quick for the enemy alliance to have time to react, with Aditya's people focusing on breaking up the chain of allied outposts, putting a thorn in the middle of their support and supply lines.

"I wonder for how long he has been planning this," Reema Fayad said.

"He is young and bold, but he has the ability to back it up." Umar sighed.

"What are our actions now? Do we continue to support him? Look to take the outpost for ourselves?" Reema asked.

"Right now, we are more vulnerable than ever. There are many eyes gathered on us from outside. Kingdoms and empires are moving. We must show that we are working together, not fighting amongst ourselves. Some are looking to take over; others are guarding against any actions we might take. We need support, or else those wolves might take a bite of us," Emmanuel said.

"So we support the King's Hill Outpost Alliance." Umar snorted softly and looked to the others. "Very well. If we stick together, we must make sure that it is all the way and that none can get out of the agreement."

Emmanuel nodded. He wasn't as headstrong to think that his own outpost could challenge a kingdom or an empire.

59 Work for It

Erik jogged into the Battle Arena, waving to the others. Behind him, Niemm and half of Special Team One were following behind.

"You're not normally late," Rugrat said as Erik jumped from the top of the arena and landed in the sparring area with a thud.

"Show-off," Rugrat muttered.

"Sorry. I was dealing with a patient," Erik said.

Gilly was on his back in her smaller form, looking excited, as if she wanted Erik to do it all over again.

After he had finished his body tempering, Erik had headed to the Alva Healing House to help out with the patients there. He had come to be known as the Godly doctor. He'd needed to tone down his abilities with the increases to his mana control, mana pool, regeneration, effect; healing people became easier as he was more exact with his efforts. With the laser-like focus of his healing, the people under his care didn't need to expend so much Stamina in order to recover.

When he wasn't working on patients, he was working on concoctions. Instead of trying the high Expert-level concoction formula he had received, he was working on lower-grade concoctions and increasing their overall efficacy.

He had been able to make Apprentice-grade Inscribed pills. These were at least fifty percent more powerful than the original pill and unlike the original pill, Inscribed pills would not lose their efficacy over time.

Through further research, Erik had learned about all the levels of pills.

There was the Newborn pill. This was a pill with no additional effect; this was a minimal kind of pill, just being formed.

Then there was the Condensed pill, which would display a twenty percent greater effect than the Newborn pill. Then there was the Concentrated pill that showed thirty percent greater effect. Inscribed had a fifty percent higher effect and wouldn't lose its strength with time. The last was an Enlightened level pill. This was a hundred percent stronger than a Newborn pill; it would not lose its efficacy and over time it would passively increase in strength. Creating a High Apprentice-level Enlightened pill would be harder than even a mid Journeyman level Concentrated pill. For low-level pills, it wasn't worth the alchemist's time to go past the Concentrated level as a higher level pill formula would be much easier to learn and create a stronger pill.

Upon reaching the high Journeyman and Expert level of Alchemy, people would focus on their efficacy more as the distance between grades was vast.

A high-level Journeyman Inscribed pill was on the same level as a low Expert pill.

Erik was churning out high Journeyman Condensed pills with ease and Concentrated pills one in three batches, but Inscribed were still out of his reach.

"Ready to lose?" Erik asked.

"You said that you were going to help me out with tempering my body," Rugrat complained.

"Give me like two weeks. Then I'll reach Body Like Stone. You didn't tell me about all of the damn Mana Gathering Cultivation quests!"

"Whoops?" Rugrat shrugged with a smirk on his face

"Whoops?" Erik's eyes thinned as his own face split into a cold smirk. "Do you want to spar? I'm not sure how strong I am and should be easy enough to put you back together."

Rugrat laughed awkwardly not saying anything before he sighed, seeing the look in Erik's eyes.

"Fine," He sighed, preparing himself mentally as he headed over to the fighting stage.

The two of them went to opposite sides of the stage. Those from Special Team One couldn't look away as they stepped up. It had been some time since the two had stepped on the stage.

They had all started to learn their techniques and were interested how Erik and Rugrat had adjusted and adapted to theirs.

They stood on either side, with Rugrat pulling out a repeater.

"You sure?" Erik asked.

"Ammunition is cheaper and the effects are weaker. Don't want to be cleaning you off the floor," Rugrat said.

Erik shrugged and got ready.

"Coin toss?" Rugrat said.

"I've got it." Erik pulled out a coin and threw it up.

Rugrat lowered himself, set in his stance. He smiled as he let out all of his power, not trying to contain it. Erik grinned in reply as he also exerted his domain. The mana shifted between them, causing the air to ripple with power.

"Why do I get the feeling like there are two mountain beasts about to fight?" Storbon asked.

"Well, 'cause I feel like a damn shepherd who can only watch them," Yao Meng muttered.

The coin landed between the two of them.

Rugrat fired his bolts as the air underneath his feet glowed and he stepped up into the sky as he insta-cast Chains of Silence.

Chains tore out of the ground where Erik charged forward. Flames appeared under his feet as he avoided the chains. Rock formed over Erik, creating a second armor over his body. He still entered the silence area of the spell and couldn't cast a spell. His body accelerated faster as he dodged the arrows.

Rugrat got serious as he imbued the Aura of Swords on his bolts, attaching them to a solid thing. The arrows shot out, turning into three arrows: an arrow with the power of silence, another with the power of flames, and the last with increased hardness.

Erik's body was covered in a stone armor as he threw his fist forward. He met the arrow head-on. A blue flame appeared on his fist and tore through the arrows.

Erik avoided those that he could and hit those that he couldn't with his fists covered in stones and blue flames.

Rugrat had dodged over Erik and was circling but he was quickly catching up.

Rugrat used Explosive Shot. Erik's reactions were faster than before, finding impossible ways to dodge the attacks.

"Looks like you've found your domain too!" Rugrat laughed as he drew out a grenade launcher.

"So much for budget cuts!" Erik said.

Rugrat fired out the grenade launcher as Erik smirked.

He executed One Finger Beats Fist but he had modified it. A rock shard formed in his hands, with red magma veins running through it and black smoke that rose from it.

It shot out like a bullet but Erik fired a small but focused blast of mana into its base. It *screamed* through the air, creating an explosion as it passed through the sound barrier and hit a grenade. The first was destroyed, and the others were tossed to the side. They hit the ground and bounced, without the time to properly arm themselves.

Erik ran forward, hoping to catch Rugrat unawares as he went through the smoke and debris.

Chains snapped up around him. Black smoke appeared around the chains as they withered; flames appeared around where they wrapped his body.

"I used Chains of Silence!" Rugrat yelled, firing his rifle. The round struck Erik. Chains sprouted from it in different colors and tied him to the ground. Rugrat fired two more rounds. Erik hit the ground and a dome of stone appeared around him.

Inside, Erik fought the chains with his flames.

Rugrat switched back to his grenade launcher, emptying and reloading it in fluid movements. He used Piercing Shot on the rounds. They shot deep into the stone dome and broke it apart.

Erik was blown backward and he rolled up to his feet. The chains had scratched him but he was largely unaffected.

Erik let out a yell as red magma-like veins traced through his stone-like skin. His skin let off a toxic-looking smoke.

"Looks like you've changed a bit," Rugrat said.

Erik shot forward and Rugrat fired his grenade launcher. Erik shot out the molten core spikes, hitting the rounds in the sky as Rugrat switched to his rifle.

Erik reached Rugrat's domain. Four mana blades of different attributes appeared around Rugrat as he executed his sword domain. Around Erik, flames appeared in mid-air as well as stone, clashing with the swords. Erik cast Shade's Covering but there was no getting closer to Rugrat, who adapted almost immediately as he had the same technique.

Erik fired his fists forward, sending out blasts of stone and fire that intercepted the incoming rounds and destroyed them as his conjured flames and stone intercepted the swords that were circling him.

Erik and Rugrat settled into a rhythm, looking for the other's weaknesses and using this as an opportunity to refine their control and their techniques. Finding an opponent who was able to stand up to them was a chance that they wouldn't be able to have often.

To the others, it looked as if there were explosions happening between the two of them even as they were attacking one another. Erik and Rugrat didn't rely on their eyes but their newfound senses through mana to know where the attacks were coming from and where to strike.

Erik used his Illusionary Fist but Rugrat saw through it easily, and Erik took a hit. He followed it up with another and a third; the fists were all around Rugrat but he was able to see through the illusions and find his real fist.

Erik hit with a Semi-Illusionary Fist. This threw Rugrat off and he frowned at the secondary fist that carried real power with it instead of being empty like the fist before.

Rugrat sent a sword at both. His eyebrows rose in shock as the illusionary fist took the impact. It was formed from stone, from fire, from poison.

It exploded in flames and poison. Rugrat used a flame to burn and purify the poison, but he had let Erik get closer and he sent multiple fake fists at him, throwing in his magma core spike and accelerating it with a beam of mana from behind.

Rugrat was pushed to his limits and Erik exceeded his previous abilities. He stomped forward and unleashed all of his strength, holding nothing back. The two men met attack with attack. Rugrat pulled out two rifles and fired them with each hand as his mana blades were half formed, going from just three to five in a second.

Spherical walls met one another; waves of force tore at the ground, tearing it apart, as they clashed their bodies, their minds, their domains.

Rugrat could no longer use his rifle. He threw it to the side as they clashed, fist against fist. Mana formed into gauntlets appeared around his fist as they clashed. Erik was forced back a few steps; he ran forward, his magma-covered hands meeting Rugrat's forged mana.

The two of them had smiles on their faces. Their eyes were alight with joy, excited as they unleashed and learned more about their bodies, their abilities. They lived on the edge of winning and failure.

Erik went for a cross. Rugrat pushed Erik's arm, moving him to the side and opening his back. Erik ducked and used the momentum to kick at Rugrat.

Rugrat, seeing his opening disappear, jumped backward in an explosion of rocks, using Explosive Shot under his feet. He fell backward; he had never used it before and he stumbled.

Erik faced him side-on. With a blast of fire under his feet, Erik shot forward, his fist shooting toward Rugrat as he had a magma spike appear.

Erik stopped and the dust cleared around them. Erik had several stone plates around him, mana blades focused on the plates. His own spike pointed at a shield forged and formed from Rugrat's armor.

Erik coughed with all of the dust and then he dismissed his constructs and lowered his hand to Rugrat.

"Well, that was fun." Rugrat laughed as he took the hand and stood.

Erik used his domain. The dust settled back down and he fused the stage back together in parts, allowing them to see out.

"Well, it seems that you two have been taking my lessons seriously," Klaus said. The two of them didn't know when he had arrived.

"Looks like you got a domain as well. You're lucky we have that contract in place—two of you, both with domains, that makes you quite the threat." He walked down toward the fighting stage.

Erik and Rugrat both looked at Klaus.

"With this, I wouldn't reveal it to outside sources, even without the contract." Klaus smiled. "After all, you two are pretty reasonable city lords, unlike the others who might take over. Now, once you've rested, go again. Erik is the stronger one but Rugrat, your control is much higher. This is a good opportunity for you to temper your fighting abilities."

Old Hei smiled as he looked at Delilah, her fingers moving independent of one another. Thin lines of thread appeared from her fingertips. Only if one had acute senses would they notice that the threads were not threads at all but flames that had been woven together.

When she was a child, she had been taught how to sew and look after the clothing of her family. She had a good eye for detail and with her work, the clothes and shoes of her family members could last longer. Even as the leader of Alva, she had repaired her own clothes and spent time going to the tailors, designing her own clothes and dabbling in the craft. She had quietly raised her crafting skill to the low Journeyman level with her tinkering and creating of simple clothes.

Now, she combined her knowledge and passion for Alchemy with her skill with sewing. Each of those threads weaved their way into the cauldron. To the outside eye, the interior of the cauldron looked like movements that followed a set but unknown rhythm.

Old Hei found his eye drawn to the process. It seemed to be almost like sorcery as the different ingredients were weaved together: the flames, the needles; the ingredients, the thread and patches.

To do so, the pressure and the heat within the cauldron had to be perfectly regulated. One had to know the exact limits of the cauldron and the characteristics of the different ingredients. When she wasn't working on Alva, she was learning. Erik's lessons and Old Hei's guidance had made her more reserved, taking her time, planning out what she was going to do, researching every variable. She was ready for the unknown, planned to change on the fly, and it meant that her execution flowed together. The slightest discrepancy she was able to adapt and overcome.

She had fallen into a trance-like state, forgetting where she was and what she was doing, focusing on the pill that she was making.

Old Hei recognized it for what it was. She had reached a deep state of enlightenment; her ideas and information came together with her movements and actions, melding into one.

Will she create her own technique?

Old Hei waited as she continued to work. Hours went by but it was nothing to Old Hei as he watched. There were some close calls but Delilah handled them well.

Her cauldron started to shake as power started to leak out.

It settled down and Delilah let out a sigh, looking pale and overdrawn.

Golden power of the Ten Realms flooded in through the walls of the Alchemy workshop, flooding into Delilah's body.

Old Hei could feel as the power surged through her previous bottlenecks, clearing a number of levels before calming down.

She took a breath, opened the lid of the cauldron, and tapped the side. She caught the pill in a container and looked at it. The pill was a deep red color, with white veins tracing through it.

She frowned, looking at it.

"Something wrong?" Old Hei asked.

Delilah let out a little shriek as she jumped up but protected the pill. Seeing her grand teacher there, her cheeks rivaled the color of the pill.

Old Hei coughed, hiding his smile.

"I—uh…"

"When one is making a concoction, it is easy to forget where they are. May I?" Old Hei said with a kind smile, holding out his hand.

Delilah smiled sheepishly and passed it over.

He took it out and studied it for some time. "Low Expert *Condensed* pill," Old Hei said with praise, sealing the pill bottle again and passing it back.

Seeing her expression, Old Hei laughed.

A Condensed pill of the Apprentice or Journeyman level might not be that impressive, but at the Expert level, even getting a normal pill was difficult. With a Condensed pill, one wasn't at a half-step mid-Expert level, but maybe a quarter-step mid-Expert level. Which was more than some people who had lived for centuries had achieved.

Seeing her, Old Hei couldn't help but smile. As a man without attachments or children, Erik and Delilah were the two he cared about the most.

The many around him always wanted something, while Erik and Delilah strived to follow the path of the alchemist.

Working with them, he had regained his passions and his younger side, challenging barriers he wouldn't have pushed against before.

He got up and sent mana through his body, revitalizing it.

Delilah ran up to him and gave him a hug.

He was a bit stunned, looking at the grinning young girl.

"I did it! I made Expert! Wait till I tell Teacher about this!" She laughed, her eyes shining as Old Hei joined in before tapping her arms in a mock serious way.

She giggled at Pill Head Hei trying to fend off her hug weakly. She squeezed him once more and stepped back. She looked revitalized after all of the long months and years of effort.

"So, the Heartflame Transformation pill—your teacher has already tempered his body with flames, so who might that be for?" Old Hei asked.

"Rugrat. The two of them are always in some kind of trouble. With this pill, Rugrat can temper his body as well. It is a high-tier transformation pill, drawing out a great amount of power within his body. I would estimate about seventy percent. With a few more aids, as well as Teacher's and my help, then he can complete a full tempering."

Old Hei led the way out of the workshop, opening the door to the blinding light outside as they stepped into his office. It was mid-morning.

"Ah, following your teacher's footsteps of combining different concoctions and techniques together to achieve a result," Old Hei said.

"If I could make things of the high Expert grade, then I could make the Essence of Fire Transformation pill, which could temper one's body completely and even has a chance to unlock the rare Fire Body title."

"Looks like you have been doing some research." Another voice came from the room. Delilah looked up to see Erik sitting there.

Her smile lit up again, seeing her teacher. Her eyes thinned. "You got stronger again," Delilah said, looking at her teacher. An Expert alchemist had acute senses, allowing them to see what others missed and gain a greater sense of their surroundings and environment with their mana.

"How so?" Old Hei asked, turning it into a learning opportunity.

"The area around him is distorted. It makes it hard for me to see through, but I can sense a powerful force of Fire and Earth within him. A sense of destruction, but that of vitality. The surrounding mana is drawn to him. It doesn't fight him; it is hotter, as if he is the cauldron, the mana are the ingredients and the flame his tool of refining and controlling it all."

Erik raised his eyebrow. "I didn't think of it that way." Erik tilted his head and looked to the floor, thinking. "Well, that might be a useful way of looking at it."

"Grand Teacher?" Delilah looked to Old Hei.

"I don't know much more than you," Old Hei admitted. "It seems that he has completely tempered his body with Fire and Earth, though he hasn't completed the quest that I learned about. He has also done something else. I think that all around him might be a domain or a technique he has learned. Though I do not wish to pry more. I am a member of the Alchemist Association and even I am asked about the reclusive City Lord Erik from time to time."

Delilah closed her mouth and Erik nodded.

Old Hei could only smile. This was the divide between them. He knew that they had their secrets and although he could tell they wanted to share them with him, he didn't want to learn them lest he be asked about them later on. He could only give the truth to his superiors if they enacted his contract binding him to the Alchemist Association.

"Well, it looks like the student has beaten the teacher." Erik stood, breaking the serious air. "You did well!"

Delilah, who looked nervous, seemed to relax. "Though I've missed a lot of work while doing it." Delilah sighed.

"I get reports from Egbert frequently. You're as hardworking as they come. I was wondering if you would like to work under Hiao Xen in Vuzgal, learn the ropes from him—be close to the academy, work on your Alchemy skills," Erik said.

"Vuzgal?"

"You don't have to make a decision now. It's something that came to me. It won't be immediate, but something in the future. Still have some work to do before then."

"Talking about running a city in the Fourth Realm like it's cabbage," Old Hei muttered.

"I heard that someone might be moving to a higher realm soon?" Erik asked.

"In a week, I'm heading to the Sixth Realm to teach. Will I be seeing the two of you?"

"I still need to gain a few levels," Delilah said.

"I'm thinking of wandering a bit more. Being tied down in one place can wear a bit." Erik smiled.

Erik, Delilah, and Old Hei shared a meal. Delilah retired early. The strain of making the Expert-level pill left her drained.

Erik had talked to Old Hei privately, talking about how he was going backward, looking to increase the efficacy of his concoctions, take his time to master each stage, moving on to the other slowly instead of jumping ahead.

Old Hei agreed with his methodology.

Erik headed out with Storbon and the half of the Special Team One waiting for him. They went to the city where the odd alchemist who had reversed his age was.

Erik went to the door and knocked on it, being greeted by the butler, who didn't allow any of the guards once again.

He went to the top of the house, where the boyish-looking alchemist waited.

"Have you completed it?" The man jumped up in agitation.

"I haven't," Erik said.

"Then why are you here? Come to plead with me to give you the formula you seek?" The man sneered.

"Instead of a pill, I created a treatment plan." Erik pulled out a box and put it to the side. "The pill is hard to make, time consuming and expensive. After thinking of your condition, studying the different concoction smells that came from your workshop, I believe that this treatment plan will remove the effects of the pill you consumed from your body. It will take longer but it will be no less effective," Erik said.

The boy started to shake as he stood there. "Do you take me for some kind of simpleton! You think that just because I am in this—this *form,* I am a doddering fool! I am no idiot, man, and I will not be taken as one! Guards!"

Erik frowned. It seemed that he had touched on a nerve. He opened his mouth to speak and a guard rushed him.

Erik and Rugrat had been fighting each other for five days, every day for five hours. They'd quickly fallen into a rhythm and cleared any cobwebs that might have been remaining.

Erik threw out his fist, creating two semi-illusionary fists.

The man countered one, but the second and Erik's true fist struck the man, sending him flying through the wall and out into the city beyond.

The guards in the room stopped and Erik pulled his aura back in. For a second, they had felt as if they were staring at some kind of beast king. The alchemist was stunned but he had not fought as much as the guards, so he recovered the quickest.

"I will never give you that formula!" he hissed.

Erik shook his head and turned, leaving the room.

"Y-you think you can leave?" the boy yelled, regaining his voice as he pointed at Erik.

Erik looked back at him. "Keep your formula. I don't need it anymore. Maybe this form fits you better, after all. Boys don't think about what consequences their actions might have."

Erik departed the room.

The guards shuddered and the alchemist boy lowered his finger.

Erik found the special team in the stairwell. They'd subdued the butler and the staff.

I'm not the only one who's improved.

"Time we were leaving," Erik said.

They headed out of the building, pulling on their cloaks. Erik took a trip down a side street, finding a man who had crashed into the neighbor's garden.

Erik quickly healed the man. He opened his eyes, unable to see into the darkness of Erik's cloak.

"Don't fight for idiots or else they'll get you killed." Erik used a stronger version of Wraith's Touch and the man's eyes rolled back into his head.

The group departed, leaving the city behind.

60
Upon a Firm Foundation

Aditya put down his sound transmission device, a wide smile on his face.

"The outpost has completed its second phase of construction. The lords are creating roads through the forest as quickly as possible. For now, the Yearin and the Tairith kingdoms are gathering their strength. Something that the other outpost lords are acutely aware of."

"It is said that a foundation needs to be properly tapped down. Pressure increases how strong it is bonded together. With the exterior threat, the lords and ladies don't have anyone to turn to but one another."

"It also happens that with the King's Hill Outpost between us all, if we can move troops through it, then we can support any of the outposts easily, defend the exterior and protect the interior."

"You're getting it now, Lord Aditya. Are you ready for the meeting?"

"As best as I can be. In two days, all of the remaining lords and ladies who control an outpost in the Beast Mountain Range will gather in King's Hill Outpost for the first time. It's a momentous occasion!"

Hiao Xen looked at the people within the room. It was a rare time when all of the managers of Vuzgal were in one location. There was Elise, who managed the trading; Chonglu, who controlled the arena; Tan Xue, the leader of the academy; as well as Mallory, the leader of the police force, and Domonos Silaz, the current commander of the Vuzgal military. Glosil was the overall commander of the military but he was part of the Alva Council. Yui or Domonos ran the military when their units were stationed there, becoming the VDF. Then there was Matt, the host of today's meeting, grand architect of Vuzgal and manager of the Sky Reaching Restaurants, Wayside Inns and all building that was going on in Vuzgal. They were in the main Sky Reaching Restaurant, looking out over all of Vuzgal, only shorter than the mana barrier pillars.

"All right, well, we've got a lot to discuss, so shall we start?" Hiao Xen looked to Elise. The group didn't stand on many traditions, other than having their meetings at dinner shared with the others. They said it went back to their founding days when the only spare time they had was over meals.

"Sales are stronger than ever in Vuzgal. There are more people coming through on a daily basis. Our biggest issue is with housing. I have a number of merchants and people who are interested in when more land will be available for purchase. Many are even willing to build their own buildings. We are trying to grow our own traders with loans, but we have a number of powerful merchant houses that are coming in. It makes us more revenues but it is stifling our own traders. I am wary that if we are not careful then these merchants who don't have ties to Vuzgal will control the markets."

Elise then looked to the next person.

"The arena has grown in leaps and bounds. The private training areas are a hot commodity. We have introduced a membership option. Every two weeks, people can reserve two time slots in the tier-one private training areas and one in the tier-two private training areas. Those with a membership can get four slots in the tier-one training area, two in the tier-two and one slot in the tier-three. For the VIP membership, people get two free time slots in the tier-one training areas and can book one slot in the tier-four training rooms. These memberships are rewarded to those that place high in the championships as well. So far, we have been running weekly tournaments. In two weeks, we will have the first official tournament.

"We have coordinated with the auction house." Chonglu looked to Elise. "There will be items up for sale that will interest fighters and those who come to view the tournament. The entire Battle Arena will be open for a week. The first three days will slim down the tournament to just one hundred people. These one hundred people will be broken into ten groups. They will need to compete in these groups. The top three will go on to fight in the final tournament. With the last competitions, from the quarterfinals and semifinals, we will host them in the main arena. Those who are knocked out will go to the lower levels, fighting it out there to get our rankings. The top thirty will all gain rewards of some kind. We hope to run a tournament every three months."

Tan Xue sipped her tea and cleared her throat. "The academy is progressing smoothly. We have nearly tripled the number of crafters who have signed exclusive contracts with us and there are plenty of people willing to pay for the schooling. We have even turned a slight profit to cover the expenses of the academy. Among our staff, we have thirteen Expert-level teachers. Among our own people, there are five who are on the border of becoming Expert. I hope they will cross that barrier soon." She took another sip of her tea, done talking.

"Crime is low within Vuzgal. Many of the people within the city are incredibly powerful, meaning that few people are willing to try thievery. We do have people fighting in the streets. We fine them and send them in the direction of the arena if they want to fight. Some people like to throw their weight around, using their position to try to get us to pressure others. My officers have kept their oaths and dealt with situations freely. It has got us some ire from powerful people." Mallory, the head of the Vuzgal police force, shrugged.

"To the people of Vuzgal, it means they can rely on you and can come to you if they are in need or have important information, even if it is against someone powerful," Domonos said.

"Thank you."

"The military's training is going well. We are stronger than before and we are recruiting more people than before. We are now able to fully support the wall and have active patrols around Vuzgal. There might be a possible threat to the north, but we are looking into it."

Tight-lipped as ever. Hiao Xen knew that there were secrets he was not privy to; one was the training and overall strength of the military.

He looked to Matt, who was struggling with his noodles and chopsticks. Seeing the eyes on him, he quickly slurped the noodles back, coughing slightly.

Domonos passed him a water; he nodded in thanks and used the water to calm his coughing.

"Wrong tube. Okay, umm, well, we've got building projects across the city. We have reclaimed the remainder of Vuzgal. The streets have been cleared; the defenses and water treatment systems are all in place. Areas have been designated as park land, or left empty for future development. In the other areas, we just need the buildings. Staffing for the restaurants is still low, but we have more people arriving all the time willing to learn and a number of the cooks are going to the academy on their time off to increase their skill."

"What is our plan with the new space?" Hiao Xen looked to Elise.

"Sell it off in lots like we have done before. We take our time to plan out the city, build the different buildings and auction them off. Again, if we grow too fast, then we lose control over the people," Elise said.

"Okay, I'll leave it to you. In the meantime, administration has started to get easier. Instead of needing to hire more people, the different managers and workers have a good grip of their job and are able to take on more. The academy healers offering cheap services to the people in Vuzgal has made more people apply to become Vuzgal citizens and increased the people's sentiment toward Vuzgal. Schooling opportunities, loans, security and areas that you have all affected has impacted their lives greatly, leaving us with a rush of people applying to be citizens."

"We will need to hold back some of the residences for the people of Vuzgal, give them loan options in order to buy homes," Elise said.

Hiao Xen felt the minds and gears of the different people moving around him. This was one of the powerful and great things of working in Vuzgal: there were no roundtables and committees to carry out an action; an order created action and reaction, increasing the effect dramatically.

Olivia knelt in front of Nadia.

"Don't you think that by now you can greet me without kneeling?" Nadia muttered.

"I am trying to be more humble." Olivia smiled.

"Working well for you?"

"Some days…" Olivia's words trailed off.

"The moves of Vuzgal, what do you think of them?"

"Opening the academy to all, heavily recruiting military forces? The missing combat company, or how strong the Dragon Combat Company has become once they returned? Building up their traders, investing in their defenses, selling weapons and arms to other cities and creating trading alliances with cities to the east?"

"When you put it that way, there are quite a lot of changes," Nadia said. "What I am asking is about how they have scouts heading to the north."

"We can confirm this?"

"Not totally. They are good at hiding their tracks."

"Seems that someone in the north is not pleased with them. They have gained quite a lot of strength here. Why do you ask?"

"You know how the Blue Lotus looks at battles," Nadia said.

"As long as we are not targeted, we are informed, move our people out of the way and compensated with damages and a new contract is agreed to at the same stipulations or higher than before, we won't care. Remaining neutral in these conflicts allows us to grow. Are you saying that the north has offered terms?"

"Not yet, but they might. They just took the northern territories and Aberdeen. They need funds and strength. If they can take Vuzgal, they should get it," Nadia said.

"If you think that, then Erik and Rugrat will have taken that into consideration."

"Do you think that they could win?" Nadia asked seriously.

Olivia had seen how Erik and Rugrat fought, their strange but highly effective tactics.

"I'm not sure. I don't know what the other side looks like. Though they slowed a force numbering fifty thousand with planning, positioning, their strange weapons and one hundred men and women. Now there is a complete combat company of nearly four hundred people, training eight hundred people every three months. Each of them are an Elite, have at least some degree of body tempering and have made progress toward compressing their cores. Each of the mages have compressed their cores and all of the sharpshooters have reached Body Like Stone."

Nadia was silent, her thoughts unknown. "What of the merchants? Their power is growing and they can't be fought through conventional means."

"They didn't hesitate to ban Experts from Vuzgal and they have not regretted it for a moment. Now they have nearly twenty Experts, a number that increases by the week as more of their people have breakthroughs." Olivia let out a self-deprecating laugh.

"I feel more and more that Vuzgal is only the tip of an iceberg. There is plenty happening underneath the water."

"If you only knew," Elan Silaz said from his office underneath Vuzgal as he read the transcript of Olivia and Nadia's meeting. He turned his eyes to three piles of information: one on the merchants of Vuzgal, the kingdom to the north, and the last a copy of a report he had sent to Blaze, simply titled *Willful Institute.*

Roska looked over the men and women who would become the future of the Alva Army: the leaders commanding people in battle, Experts who would train the later generations and would be called to be Alva's spear in times of need.

Sixty people stood in front of her. Each of them radiated a dangerous air. Even then she could tell that their auras were heavily restrained.

If there is one core rule within the Alva military, it is to leave your strength hidden to the last moment. Then strike with everything. Let the enemy come in, confident and cocky, then show them the error of their ways with strength.

The people in front of her had become soldiers, trained as sharpshooters, learned the secrets of artillery and the magical arts. They'd undergone extensive medical and Alchemy training to become medics. They'd learned how to work with metal and wood as engineers, learning tens of spells. The nervous excitement when they had joined on the first day had turned into hardened determination.

"You are all here to complete your training to become a close protection detail member. Each of you is qualified as a sergeant. Upon completion, you will retain your previous ranks, but be paid as specialized staff sergeants and will be able to take up staff sergeant positions. Others will continue on to become officers and the leadership of the Alva Army. The rest of you will rise to the challenge to join the special teams."

To her right and left were the members of Special Team Two. Their eyes scanned those in the ranks ahead, finding them lacking.

"We will not treat you like children here, unless you have somehow found bad habits through your training! We are here to make you the strongest you can be to defeat our enemy and defend our strongholds: Vuzgal, Alchemy Association Division Headquarters, Hersht, Alva, and the Beast Mountain Range. You will all be participating in the competition starting in three weeks in Vuzgal. Till then, we will be training in fighting techniques in the tier-four facilities day in and day out. Once you have proved your strength to us and in the competitions, we will head out into the field for a month. Each group will have different missions. These are not mock missions; these are real missions with consequences. These are missions that the special teams would undertake but we're stretched thin. Questions?"

A man raised his hand. Roska pointed at him.

"As part of the CPD, do we operate with our units or with the special teams?"

"When your combat company is on operations, you will be there to support them as needed, tasked with missions that couldn't be left to any other group. In a battle, your primary concern is to protect medics, engineers, mages, and artillery—people who are focused on other tasks. The CPD is meant to be mobile. You can carry out any task you are set and act as a tactical reserve and quick reaction force. If there is an issue, you're the first group that is called on. The special teams usually work in isolation, behind enemy lines, a small group making a large impact. You might have missions to this effect but it is not your primary concern."

She looked at them again. "All right, those with ten mana gates or more open on my right side. Those with less on my left side in a line."

61
Down to the Roots

Erik and Rugrat were having a beer in Alva. They sat outside of the bar. People pointed to them as they passed.

Alva's population had only increased. Now, with recruiting happening across four realms, the reach of Alva was spreading farther.

Seeing the two city lords drinking beer outside on the patio was strange to them.

Erik and Rugrat nodded and raised their beers to the familiar faces they saw. The older residents of Alva didn't mind, used to their eccentric lords.

"Want to go wandering again?" Rugrat asked.

"Didn't you want to become an Expert smith?" Erik asked.

"Been grinding at it for weeks. Had an inspiration the other day, or whatever you want to call it." Rugrat fell silent. "Smithing is bending materials into new shapes, but what if it fit with the path of nature?" Rugrat raised his arm, looking at the Norse-style tattoo sleeve that ran down his left arm to just before his wrist. He looked at the different Norse symbols within. On his right arm, there was a black ink-only American flag. As one looked up his arm, his shoulder had the Marine Corps emblem, while underneath it there were poppies slowly progressing down his upper arm.

"I think I know what you mean. Why don't we head to the higher realms, check out a few academies, see if we can't join a few fighting competitions and search for some new dungeons. You can smith as we go and I can heal people. Alva Healing House is good to work at, but they don't need me. They're more than capable of healing all the injured who come through their doors. Time we got back to what we're good at, a sniper and a medic," Erik said.

"Damn fucking right." Rugrat raised his beer and Erik tapped his bottle against it. The two of them grinned as they drank. There was risk, there was the possibility of failure, but that was what they lived for. If not, then they wouldn't have become private contractors after leaving the military, following that buzz and sense of purpose.

Aditya looked at King's Hill Outpost. It stood high above the forest, taking a commanding view of the surrounding area. There were crafters swarming over the location still. A large stone wall surrounded the outpost. The ground was being flattened out beyond the wall, for the next expansion. Trees had been cut down and sharpened, sticking out to defend the workers against any creatures that might try to rush out from the forest.

There were guards on the walls, looking outward.

Aditya went up the winding road. The inner outpost only had one entrance, while the outer outpost that was under construction would have four entrances.

Inside the outpost, the main roads had been laid down. There were outlines for the different buildings to be created. The lords and ladies all had a plot of land within the inner outpost. There was also a crafting sector and a region that would be sold off to traders, a place for an auction house, stables, and all of the things an outpost needed.

The buildings were going up rapidly. The outpost headquarters had been completed first. It stood back from the entrance to the inner outpost. It was a hexagonal structure, its walls as thick as the inner outposts. Towers were at every corner and the actual building within was just a few meters back from the walls and rose five stories up. Making it one of the taller buildings outside of capital cities.

As Aditya entered on his mount, the guards saluted.

Aditya continued on, finding Pan Kun waiting for him. The man looked tired but pleased.

"Well, to me it looks like you're even ahead of schedule," Aditya said.

"Just a few days or so," Pan Kun said.

"The other outpost leaders?"

"Most have arrived or are expected to by nightfall."

"Very well. Send them word through the messengers that I wish to have a meeting tonight and a feast. Best we get things started instead of waiting around."

"Yes, my lord."

"And well done, Pan Kun."

"Thank you, my lord."

Emmanuel and the other lords and ladies from the different outposts filed into the big hall within the headquarters. They were allowed to bring their guards. Everyone was on edge, so most were thankful to have some kind of strength with them.

They all filed in, talking and greeting one another. They admired the outpost and talked about small matters. With how things had changed so rapidly recently, it was hard for them to talk of future plans or much of anything that wasn't related to what had happened.

The table in the feast hall was round, making everyone equal and allowing them to converse easily with their partners.

Aditya was all smiles and had the biggest group around him. He dealt with the lords and ladies with ease.

The master of ceremonies, the auctioneer from Vermire, hit a small gong, signaling people to take their seats.

As the conversation quieted, the tension that was hiding beneath the surface rose up once again.

Aditya cleared his throat and raised his glass. "Well, we did it! We took King's Hill and established an outpost while weathering a war aimed to cut us down from behind. Here is to the King's Hill Outpost Alliance."

The others raised their glasses in salute and drank.

"Also, to clear the tension, I wanted to bring up a few things before we eat."

That tension returned in full force as some sent discreet looks to the guards nearby.

"I propose that we collaborate together, using the mercenaries and the guards who were captured to assist in clearing and creating roads to link all of our outposts to King's Hill Outpost in order to improve our internal support of one another. Also, the cheap labor is pretty nice." Aditya laughed as the other lords joined in.

Smart, Emmanuel thought, his eyes flashing at Aditya's words.

Creating those roads would connect all of the leaders together. They would be able to move their guards in order to support one another. It would bind their defenses and their trade together tighter than before. On the surface, it was to protect their interests, but deeper, it would make them one group, the headquarters located in King's Hill Outpost and the other outposts its subordinate.

"What of the outposts that we have captured?" Old Lord Quan asked.

"This was an effort that we all underwent. I do not know the minds of the other outpost lords, but I only wish to govern Vermire." Aditya chuckled, getting compulsory smiles from the others. "All of the outposts under my control, bar Vermire, I say will be governed by the King's Hill Outpost Alliance. I also wish to place a stipulation upon the alliance and the management of it."

People were shocked into mumblings as they talked to their partners, but quickly grew silent, feeling that the second part was Aditya's knife to the alliance's heart. He had proved himself to be a capable and ruthless schemer, brilliantly turning the war against the other outposts into a windfall.

"The leadership of the King's Hill Outpost will be made up of four people and one leader. The four people will coordinate with the crafters, the farmers, the traders, and the mercenaries. They will be elected by the people. The overall leader will be elected by us. The overall leader's wealth will be placed upon the line. Fifty percent of the gold made will be split up evenly between all of us here. A further ten percent will go to the alliance leader. Thirty percent will be given over to the treasury to be used to create new roads, hand out loans to different groups, improve the conditions of the outpost, and help to raise our own crafters. The remaining ten percent will be devoted to the military, to take people from all of our outposts and train them into a true army to protect the alliance and not just our interests. They will be given the best gear, weapons, and training we can afford them. My major condition is that if the outposts do not make a profit but incur a loss, then the leader will not make anything and instead must pay for those losses out of his or her own pocket."

The lords and ladies fell into discussion again.

With this, in one shot he makes the leadership position look unstable; he then amalgamates the guards into one fighting force. If one outpost leader goes against the alliance—well, we saw it with the other outpost guards. They weren't willing to kill their own people just for their lord or lady. It ties us all closer together, while offering greater rewards and benefits for those who don't wish to rule King's Hill Outpost. If we want to see any return, then we need to pick the best person for the job, or else we'll earn nothing extra, won't see any new crafters and the army's strength will fall.

Emmanuel felt his scalp tingling with Aditya's declarations.

"You are too right, Lord Aditya. I will give up the captured Starfall Outpost to be managed by the King's Hill Outpost Alliance," Old Lord Quan said with a smile, stroking his beard.

It made it awkward in the hall as people looked over to the lords and ladies who had captured outposts from the enemy.

One by one, they turned control over to the alliance.

Emmanuel couldn't help but smile. *Giving it up, they lose the outpost's direct control, but then the potential earnings of everyone increases. They might be bitter but they want to remain inside the alliance so that they might rise to power and control it all once again.*

"I am humbled by your contributions. With this, our foundations couldn't be firmer." Aditya smiled to them all. "Now that is all done with, I will vacate my position and wait for the next alliance leader to be elected."

This created an even bigger stir within the room. With Aditya leaving the position, it took away a large portion of his platform and it opened it up for everyone to compete, bringing him back down to their level.

He sat back down in his chair at the round table.

"In these turbulent times, I think it would be in everyone's best interests if we elect a leader as soon as possible," Leo said.

"First, let us vote on the changes that Lord Aditya has proposed," another lord said. "Those in favor of using the mercenaries and guards from the enemy alliance to create the roads needed between our outposts to King's Hill Outpost, raise your hand."

Nearly all of the outpost leaders' hands went up and someone noted down the number of hands raised.

"Those against?"

Hands went up and the number was noted down.

"The motion is passed and will be carried out as soon as possible." The lord cleared his throat again. "Now, those in favor of enacting the new budget of the alliance and making the leader responsible for the shortfalls, raise your hand."

There were less hands in agreement this time.

"Those against?"

Hands went up and the number was noted down.

The lord checked the numbers and a few other lords did as well.

"The motion is passed as well."

"We need a new leader soon. I say that we should have voted one in by the end of the next three days, before we return to our outposts," Leo said.

"Those who agree?"

All of the hands in the room went up.

"Well, then it is passed. In three days, we will choose the new leader of King's Hill Outpost."

Before, if he remained in his position, then he would have been domineering. Now, if he is elected, then he is their choice, not the one who was forced upon them!

Emmanuel wanted to laugh but held it in as he looked around the room. There had been too many announcements and information. Although all of the agreements bound them closer together, after what they had faced, having allies they could rely on didn't sound too bad.

Although the outposts had been left alone, they had attacked a number of outposts backed by different kingdoms and large powers.

These places had left them alone for the most part but the recent changes in the Beast Mountain Range could change all of that.

Author's Note

Thank you for your support and taking the time to read **The Fifth Realm**.

The Ten Realms will continue in the **Sixth Realm.**

As a self-published author I live for reviews! If you've enjoyed Th Fifth Realm, please leave a **review**! (https://amzn.to/38D2Bum)

Do you want to join a community of fans that love talking about Michael's books?

We've created this Facebook group for you to discuss the books, hear from Michael, participate in contests and enjoy the worlds that Michael has created. You can join using the QR code below.

Thank you for your continued support. You can check out my other books, what I'm working on, and upcoming releases with the QR code below.

Don't forget to leave a review if you enjoyed the book.

Thanks again for reading ☺